(Flourish)

Rebel rebel...

David Bowie, *Diamond Dogs* (1974)

ABOUT THE AUTHOR

I wasn't born so much, as conceived. In Art, I am the enigma that is the Mona Lisa's smile, or that tragic image of 'Ophelia' floating in a pond. In literature, I am that mysterious woman-*Grrrl* that keeps cropping-up in Philip K Dick novels, to torment his wary and aged protagonists; or the neurotic 'Marla Singer', in Chuck Palahnuik's *Fight Club*. On film, I am Stanley Kubrick's 'Lolita', sucking innocently on a lollipop; or 'Lisa' emerging from a closet, in John Hughes Jr's teen coming-of-age romp, *Weird Science*.

And elsewhere, I am Miss Stewart, a teacher in Infant School, or Jane Willicombe, an eight-year old's first crush. Yes, I am all these impressions, images and events, and countless others. Whilst at the same time, I can be said to predate, and even anticipate them.

So yeah, I wasn't so much born as contrived. Imagined, and reimagined, and articulated in innumerable different ways. And though, like Freddy Kruger, it might be said that I am the Bastard-child of a thousand fathers. Garland, and Scott, and Kubrick, and Lang, and Asimov, and Dick, and Masamune, to name but a few. I have but one mother (besides Shelley, of course), Dr Ursula Hind, Senior BioMechanic at the GenesisTrust® Integrated Laboratories.

To whom I owe this *Life*, my existence—as it is.

```
0 1 0 1 0 0 0 0
0 1 0 1 0 0 1 0
0 1 0 0 1 0 0 1
0 1 0 1 0 0 1 1
```

•

41 20 4E 6F 76 65 6C

THAT PERFECT WORLD
#packagingnotincluded
[Paperback Edition]

Published by LAKE PARIMA (Publishing) 2024

Copyright © Marlon D Smith, 2018

All rights reserved.

The moral right of the author has been assert.

BXMN® is a registered trademark of the author.

LAKE PARIMA logo is based upon 'Little Howler Monkey' ceramic figurine created
by Ynocencio Ccahuana.

This novel is entirely a work of fiction. The names, characters and incidents portrayed in it
are the work of the author's imagination. Any resemblance to actual persons, living or dead,
events or localities is entirely coincidental.

No part of this publication may be reproduced, stored in a retrieval system, or transmitted,
in any form or by any means, electronic, mechanical, photocopying, recording or otherwise,
without the prior permission of the publisher.

Shoutout: The founder of R. Talsorian Games, Mike Pondsmith, Designer of 'Cyberpunk: The
Role-playing Game of the Dark Future' [refered to as 'Cyberpunk 2013', first edition published
by R. Talsorian Games, 1988].

ISDN KDP 9-798865-558323

[Rap] *I was born inside the belly
Of a blazing Comet—*

All Quiet on the West End Frontline

It was all quiet on the West End frontline. Most of the Trendies, and Squareframes, sporting that smart-casual, urban-camo designer unkept *Look*, courtesy of your AbbeyCrombie®, your PAP®, your *Life*@Argyle®. They'd scarpered, long since.

Back to that smart townhouse, fronting onto that gentrified square; or that airy warehouse conversion, overlooking the Thames; or that idyllic thatched cottage, situated on the outskirts of a quaint St. Mary Mead. Where all the clocks ran backwards-*like*, literally.

It'd be a quick sway on the tube, or that brand spanking new monorail—your ritual commute, and home to a "what'll it be, darling?"

Hmmm—thinking.

Perhaps a full-bodied Merlot, or that fruity Shiraz, served with a *Slo*-cook Lancashire hotpot. Whilst locked-in to the evening's newstreams, brought to you courtesy of your SKYTN®, your BloombergReuters®, your *Yahoo!*BBC®.

"Verdict in on Mos Mos Fresh Synthetic Rights Supreme Court Appeal."

BONG.

"Saros Series 137 über Blood moon expected in the wee hours."

BONG.

"And tonight's lead (*—Jack-a-nory*): Scandal rocks HoC, as yet another MP is forced to resign, over possession of lewd, and unsavoury, digy-*viddy* footage of teenage hermaphrodites."

BONG!

You could almost hear the *Tut-tuts*. Mother and Father Christmas, and those 2.24 Sprogges tucked-up all cosy and snug in front of the Idiot box—your LNG® *Dopijuui* 80″ UHD curved-screen; that Völhall® KOTI log-burning stove crackling away in the background.

The adults sipping sparingly from bulbous KIERKE® *Cristallo* wine-glasses. Offering-up a silent *Gānbēi*—to your *god-of-always-listening*, for that ol' Good *Life*. As ever grateful, for that insolation afforded by their combined salaries.

As for your Estabs, your Establishment. That large and ungainly blanket term used to designate your 'Great Unwashed'. With labels reading more like a Pub Rock line-up.

The Go-getters, and The Trendsetters, and The Nine-to-fivers (struggling as always, yet managing somehow to stay-a-livers), and The Wannabes, and The Worker Ants, and The Bizzy-Beez, and The Drones, and The Plebs, and The Dregs, left staring at the bottom of that empty pint-glass. Stoked on what now passed for pheromones.

All those living that *ReginaldPerrin*™ reboot, their situation a comedy of errors; *Auntie's*® canned-laughter measuring its peaks and troughs.

A kool, yet fatherly *virtua*-Bryan Ferry archetype crooning over those End-credits:

[Sing] *More than this* [01]
There could be noth-thing...

As ever desperate to beat the Crush-hour, on the recently revamped TfL® LONDON UNDERGROUND™—modelled after your TOKYO METRO™, with its universal Skynet, and its universal *Air-con*, and its universal wheelchair access.

And its *Oshiyo* on standby, to pack 'em in. That electrified third-rail being more like a conveyor-belt, conveying cans of *Heinz*® canned-*Human*.

Bodies crammed-up against those retractable glass-doors; glazed beady-eyes staring purposefully, out that window they all carried around with them.

Every day, they'd astutely look the other way. Recite that well-worn mantra of the *Mittelklasse*, under their collective breaths, like a collective sigh: Wenn ich nicht sehen, werde ich nicht gesehen.

A lesson learnt and unlearned in Grammar school. Along with

stanzas of Rudyard Kipling's *If*, and other likely *Jack-a-nories*. As if it might save 'em, from that next plot-Beat in their scripted lives:

'*Life*, Post-45 | The grind down.
STREAMING RIGHT NOW ON RIALTO®
[Sing] *That's en-ter-tain-ment* ⁰²
—ahh!'

Yeah anywho, they'd splurt'd too. Leaving the filthy curb, and that long march of *Helios*® Street-lamps to a temperate night, and those Dyson® DHV-11 Homeostatic Street-cleaners, and the Herds—Tourist and Pilgrim alike.

Occasionally, you might come across a swish *Coupé*, or bawse Saloon set to Manual-override. In amidst swarms of Ash-BLK *Hackney*-cabs, reintroduced by T*f*L® as a novelty.

It'd be some smarmy git sitting smug, barely visible above that traction-wheel; *vari*-tint windows wound down, frayed nerves wound-up. Taxi-horns blaring after it.

"OY! GET A MOVE ON WILL-YA."
Phf'king nob.

Running late, our-Man can't help but look bait. Crawling the curb, eye's scanning *Left-to-Right Right-to-Left*, like that Cyborg-assassin in your Terminator™ franchise—looking for something.

A quick service perhaps—maybe. Before that long gruelling haul back to the Burbs, some obscure *shitty* Satellite-city.

Further afield, bum-to-nose and six lanes deep. The *Crush*-hour traffic would be like a *Human* centipede. Soft but steadily hardening innards encased in a poly-alloy über-lightweight shell, eating its way into the evening. Leisure-*Time* having become as scarce as extended family, and disposable household income, and door-to-door salesmen.

Blindly—grudgingly, it'd trudge along regimented asphalt lanes. Whilst your *god-of-always-listening* piss'd down acid rain on everything, for larks.

Back on the frontline, you might even catch a swanky mustard-yellow BAE® *Harrier*-taxi gliding down to Street-level, to rescue some Toff, some Übs—as in *Übermensch*—slumming it with the Trendies.

That [Sing] *Street Life*,⁰³ that grown-up's Fairy-tale gathering pace

THAT PERFECT W◉RLD

with the nights encroach. Its *ever-so* silent approach, measured by digital integers counting Bergson-*ian* SpaceTime.

Everywhere, it'd be herds of marauding Tourists and Pilgrims. Sight-seers out to see the sights. Shoppers out to catch a bargain and—fingers crossed, a bite. Moths attracted to all that neon, and that spectacle of the Big-Tent—your Oxford Circus, that umpteenth wonder of this *post*-Industrial age.

Yeah, it'd be gaggles of twos and threes, at sixes and fours—looking for something.

And yet, managing somehow to look-see and ignore that gangly *Androg*, in the Thrift store Candy-apple red PaulSmith® two-piece Birdman suit, with the Marine-green *StayPress*™ shirt, matching knit pencil-tie, and Dorothy's™ Ruby-red stilettos.

Sporting that now obligatory ghinger crewcut. Doing their best Annie Lennox to the accompaniment of a X'ANG® *SpeakerboxX* XL—that
BoOM
    Klak
BoOM-BoOM
    Klak!

They sing in perfect pitch:
[Sing] *Sweet dreams are made of this* [04]
Who am I to dis-a-gree?

Yeah, who were we to disagree? Given they'd [Sing] *travelled the World and the Seven seas*, just to get here.

It'd be a piece of vinyl for a stage, *virtua*-Account URL written on the side of a ripped-up cardboard box in thick BLK marker-pen. Along with a few choice lines from your 'Ava Cassidy Suicide Note'. And a hat—of-course, double weave trilby, minus that band and bow.

Them, so obviously looking for something; a Dave Stewart of their very own. Perhaps—*maybe*.

Phf'king Tourist.
Phf'king Tourists.

Nearby, the Mod-father would-be crooning from a tinny-sounding *Retro*-DAB Bol'she® portable radio, perched a-top a greasy spoon cart:
[Sing] *That's en-ter-tain-ment*
That's en-ter-tain-ment—ahh!

All Quiet on the West End Frontline

That being your West End of an evening. That smell of caramelised onions and burnt fibrous Halal quarter-pounders. That *Clickitty-clack Clackatty-click* of high-heels, that was like a procession of *Nestlé's®* Quality Streets; cellulose bums, hips and thighs shrinkwrapped in pairs of shiny fluorescent-colored *Secondskins*. It beating any Liposuction *proc*, your plastic could buy.

Literally overnight, absolutely every Sindy™, Barbie™, and Ken™ doll had had to have a pair. And would sport 'em with as much chutzpah, and moxie as our Chrissy Hynde—

[Sing] *Intention, I feel inventive* [05]
Gonna make you, make you
Make you no-tice...

Along with the butt-implants, and the breast-implants, and the botox lip-injections, and that *perma*-tan sun-kissed complexion, and the platinum dreadlock Human-hair extensions, and the piercings, and those Maori-*looking* tribal-*Tatts*. That was like, a whole other thing entirely.

Yeah, here it was. That vivisection of Jaime Sommers: A dialectics of prosthetics and calisthenics, brought-on by the prevalence of Indian Summers; and climate change, that was more than just a change in the weather; and a Nation's growing penchant for *AnneSummers®* lingerie parties, over your Avon®—*say*, or Tupp-*a*-ware® varieties.

Yeah, here it was. That Age of Aquarius, coming to an IMAX™ near you. What might've seemed like Huxley's 'Brave New World': Populated by *Alpha-Omega* ÜBER-hero archetypes; shadowed in real-*Life* by their wannabe Doppelgangers, and *Splash*-mag paparazzi. Moulded, plastic fantastic people, rockin' steadily to a soundtrack by Jimmy Cliff:

[Sing] *Ooh—the harder they come* [06]
The harder they fall
One and all.

And across from Mainstreet, it'd be more of the same.

You'd your Machismos, and your Amazonians, *Flippitty-flopping* in those Havaianas®. Living that [Sing] *Tainted Love*.[07] You know, that ol' cliché.

And your Anti-CORPOs, rockin' those Converse® *All-Stars* to death. Wanting it all to Crash-N-Burn. Until—that is, they got they're turn, that

13

precious intern(ment)ship. The first rung on that stepladder to becoming a fully-fledged and pledged, CORPO-*Pollyanna*.

If-only, it were all about footwear, your West End of an evening would've been a cornucopian wet dream for any foot fetishist. And all of it, disposable clobber—*Fabriqué en République du Gabon*. Everyone being an optimally primed 'Mark', Punk-come-Acolyte of your Cult of Adolescence.

It being so obviously *post*-Postmodernity.

That is, modernity getting over its hangover—yet again. But this time, with only a hint, a soupçon of déjà vu.

The cultural equivalent of Moonwalking. It was a *pre*-vitiligo Michael Jackson: Facing forwards, whilst looking backwards—*always*. To Bowie, just before his notorious Berlin Phase; to Punk, giving-it two fingers to your Estabs (your mums and dads), and lashings of *Auntie's*® canned-laughter piped-in over reruns of your *Young Ones*™. It being all, [Sing] *en-ter-tain-ment*, with or without that chord change.

It was:

[Rap] *Hit me with your rhythm stick* [08]

Je t'adore, ich liebe dich—

and hats-off to the Maestro, Mister Ian Dury.

It was that *oh-so* sickly-sweet smell of success, lived INXS; and CORPO Culture-vultures circling overhead i.e., your malaise of above and below.

It was taking-on all-comers, all shapes and sizes. It was that muzik playing in the lift—the elevator, Radiohead's 'No Surprises'. Though sung surprisingly well, by one Stephen Hawkings.

It was plastered. It was pasted. It was legless. It was wasted. It was prang, and leen, and *Kark*. And sometimes—just to confuse things, it was Love. It being all we needed.

But mostly, it was absurdly profitable. They're being no discrimination here, just honest to goodness laissez-faire.

Yeah yeah yeah!
Blah blah blah!

Occasionally, one of the above would happen to stumble passed this crack in the fabric of that Universe.

A long, long dark alleyway, sliced betwixt this-that snazzy-posh

restaurant-*come*-bar-*come*-club. That soundtrack of the night—that
UMPH...UMPH...
UMPH...UMPH...
UMPH...UMPH...
[Sing] *We could be Heroes...* [09]
Heroes...Heroes
—reverberating against those shiny façades planted either side.

Out-*there*, in der Lebenswelt, some Tart would-be coppin' her reflection in the glass. Slapping-on a-bit of lippy, having landed her escort for the night.

"Put your money away—silly," she'd say, taking it by the arm to jump that queue.

There'd be a clutch of Trendies, and Squareframes—of course. And a gaggle of Estabs, in town for a Work-do; giving-it the lout, and the googly-eyes at the flocks of eye-candy as they sauntered-by. In between bouts of *Auntie's*® exaggerated canned-laughter (as in, made from concentrate)—

[Sing] *More than this*
There could be noth-thing...

And that Übs, stubbing-out his cigarette (a Gauloises® *Deluxe* Slim-Ultra) to saunter over to the Muscle-on-the-door. Who'd casually step aside, taking that cordon with it.

Yeah, it all looks well and good, this picture. Mundane and everyday—peachy even. But just you scratch beneath the surface, thumb through your Wittgenstein's Pictionary™, or any random *Time*Line on *Connekt-a*-Dot™.

See it there, that middle-finger?

Picture it: Your proverbial butterfly. Its oh-so precious wings amputated. And suddenly, all your Chaos Theory goes right-out the window.

Now picture it, regressed back to a lowly caterpillar. The one dimension of its scripted *Life*—its insatiable appetite, amortised.

Yeah, here was a World of heavily leveraged assets. Of adolescent debt, and adult indebtedness.

Of that One-dimensional Woman-Man-Person reduced—regressed, to an integer. That relentless foraging for yield—*for growth*—having become iterative, beyond the point of abstraction.

And whilst all that was kicking-off. In a bored-room somewhere, those CORPO-*Pollyannas* (come *incorporated* Scarfaces) would-be for waging a clandestine war against every *Living*-Breathing-Teething organism on the Planet.

But I digress.

Looking down that long dark alleyway, you'd immediately see it for what it was. That place the *Darkside* is. Whilst in the background, you'd hear more canned-laughter—100% proof wafting after you.

It should've carried an Environmental, Health & Safety [EH&S] warning—like you'd find on the front of packets of cigarettes, that kind of youthful exuberance. Something like: WATCH OUT! HUMANITY CAN KILL | ACHTUNG! MENSCHHEIT KANN TÖTET.

You'd hardly notice it though. The alleyway. For all the rubbish heaped high at intervals, marking the back-entrances to this-that snazzy-posh restaurant-*come*-bar-*come*-club. On account of you being distracted.

It'd be strictly your Squareframes and Trendies—as said. And the occasional Suit. Though—strictly speaking, being Wealth creators, the Suits were to be considered a cut above the rest of 'em—*ya*-get me.

Well, of-course *you* get me. Coz you know the patter. And they know the patter. And we all speak it fluently-*like*, patois.

Coz you're down. And they're down. But obviously, some must be more down than others. Obviously, it goes without saying.

Whilst others must—naturally, rise to those *Dizzy-dazzling* heights. And cue Tony Bennett, and please feel free to sing-along—if you know the words:

[Sing] *Oh—the Good Life* [0A]
Full of fun seems to be the ideal...

Yeah, you know the coup. You know the score. And you know the spot, Soho—just *off*-Wardour. It was where *phf'k*-all actually happened. It being like an event. Remember, where Harry fingered Sally, and Roger roger'd Chris?

"What—you call that a kiss?"

"*Nah*—more like a snog."

"A snog you know..."

And then, there'd be exaggerated canned-laughter wafting passed on a current of stale alcohol—as if piped-in.

And us, seemingly immersed right in it, like your *virtua*-Reality.

"Your tongue was so far down her gob, you could-*a* licked her *phf'king* tonsils."

Cue more of the good stuff (canned-laughter, that is). Though bellied this time, as in side-splitting.

"*What*—you don't remember? It's you who told me."

Now introduce a couple of brisk tokes on a spliff.

"Fond memories-*ey*?"

"*Yeah*—happy days."

Inhale...Exhale...

"I remember you shoving your middle-finger in my boatrace. Yeah—the very same. 'Smell this,' you said. '*Phf'koff*,' I said"—and here's me, as ever paraphrasing.

Anywho, you—the *Reader*, reading this. You get the gist, the general ambiance of our fair Verona.

Just hang a sharp *Left-Right*, off-that-beaten-track. There you could score a quarter off *my*-Man. He'd hand it over in a wrap and could get your name down on any Guestlist you liked.

"Yeah?"

Sniff

"Yeah—you remember that Cunt? I swear he bumped me last time."

"*Phf'kry*."

"Yeah right."

A couple more tokes, spliff now racing toward the roach.

"Yeah...that was a blinding night."

"Yeah—Nodding—but I don't remember much."

"*Yeah*? You still managed to post the pics up though—on connekt -a-dot."

The alleyway you'd miss—granted, piss'd or otherwise. Though you'd probably passed it-*like*, ten-zillion times.

But that stench—*Sniff-sniff*, that stench lived, was alive and arse-kicking (as in, Kick-Ass™).

A scent mark piss'd-up that same spot on that same wall by that same train of Cunts, on their way home after a bender. A night-out bending over ol' what's her boatrace, [Sing] *Tralala*[OB] *Boomedya*[OC] no doubt.

Yeah yeah yeah!
Blah blah blah!

THAT PERFECT WORLD

∞

It was upon the cusp, the lip of that long dark alleyway, where something was stirring. Drunk as usual, unspoken thoughts slurring like words. That stench of piss, worn like *Raid*® insect repellent. But aimed at all Humanity.

Tattered Georgian *Crombie*, worn-out two-piece Birdman suit; shades of grey bordering on BLK. Shit-stained shoes, so holy as to be comparatively soleless. That spark of saurian intelligence, barely discernible in its milky eyes.

It wore that slightly bemused look most of the time. It having, apparently, only just-now woken-up to find itself trapped in someone else's nightmare. Its play on *Pathos*: A yearning to go back to sleep; and perchance, to dream.

It being contented to wait—patiently—for that next Cataclysmic event to come along and pinch it.

"*Owch!*" it'd cry out, rubbing at that tender spot on its arm. "Why so *phf'king* hard, Morpheus?"—*Tut*.

It'd learnt to take stock of its *Life* in inches. That is, until inches became obsolete—went metric.

In betwixt laboured breaths, bouts of chronic depression, and acute substance abuse. Swigs, and *Sniffs*, and tokes. And then, intravenously, its iron lungs having grown accustomed to breathing-in fire.

Peering through a fog of opiates, it was forever taking stock of things. Its Dragon's breath wearing that stink of FireWater™ *l'eau de toilette*. One whiff, and you'd be throwing-up your guts, bearing your Soul.

And here, Brothers and Sisters, Boys and *Grrrls*. Here, someone was always predisposed to take stock of things.

More often than not, it'd be it. Watching from a distance, the lives of Others unravelling. Its tongue cleaved in two, from having spoken so many half-truths. Its sulphurous breath condensing in the cold night-air of Out-*there*.

If-only—*Blink-blink*, if-only it hadn't thought its days so numbered.
Sigh

Twas inclined more toward Sinner than Saint. And fallen upon hard times—apparently. Look-see, its grubby boatrace, rosy-coloured cheeks, reddened nose, scratchy beard, chesty—*cough*…

Cough-cough.

Gut-wrenching spit. Silent—but deadly—fart. All of it, part of your Fool's pantomime—a Fool's Paradise. It having down-and-out down to an Artform.

And to cap it all, it'd just-now been diagnosed lactose intolerant.

"*Christ*—let me stop for a sec. *God*—I need me-*a* piss."

Like always, it spoke candidly to no one in particular, and to all the World.

"*Phf'k* me. Oy—wait a minute will-*ya*? Let me just catch me-*a* breather."

Raising an arm—as if to volunteer, it made a fist. Not as a sign of solidarity, or revolution—*mind you*. But literally, to *Phfist-phf'k…phfist-phf'k* that arsehole upstairs.

Up there—*pointing*.

It'd winced then, having pulled something with that last one. Its other mitt, clutching now its broken Heart—[Sing] *Oh ohh, the ach-ing*…[OD]

There it be, ye ol' war wound flaring-up again. A fool's reward for staking all upon so ephemeral a thing as, dare one whisper, nigh think it out loud…

The F-bomb—BoOM!

Its s'posed intellection, much lauded and applauded. And yet, so tentatively grasped. As if, it were a courtly affair of *Love*. The emotion poised to slip through covetous fingers, ere any sudden bowel movements.

For that—pointing pointedly toward the Heavens—statuesque Lady, in whose dreamy countenance might be traced, both the beauty and tragedy of Milton's Paradox, were said *Fates* usurp'd. A most immaculate conception set upon high, upon a pedestal in their stead. Said unction to our fair *Lady Liberty*, the Fair, said.

And so it was, amidst a shed load of tears, and Blood, and guts. That bye-and-bye was bade, to that stylite Princess—trapped in her Ivory Tower; the arousing kiss, that Fairy-tale ending, and they all lived *happily-ever-after*. As opposed to barely existing.

Forphf'ksake.

"Anyone got any leads? Methinks, I needs me-*a* jump-start."

It cracked yet another silent but deadly one. Liver poisoned. Kidney's failing—Body ailing.

"Com 'ere," it said then, its voice barely a whisper.

"OY!"

This time more of a shout.

"...com '*ere*."

And now its boatrace adopted a boyish toothy grin, as it beckoned with a grubby mitt.

"You couldn't spare us a ciggy could-*ya*, Mister?"

It put two fingers to its mouth. And kissed them repeatedly, to demonstrate what it was on about. Then, ramping-up the charm offensive—a good few notches. It extended the same grubby mitt to present its empty palm with a flourish.

"Or perhaps, a little loose *ch-ch-ch-change*?"

And with it came a *Wink*, a cue for a musical intermezzo. It scrunching up half its grubby boatrace to pull that veil over the one eye.

Out of nowhere, a progression of minor-major chord couplets brokeout into a whimsical piano-led arrangement, drowning in lush romantic strings. A counterpoint to that strangled Dylan-*esque* vocal. When it eventually made its entrance. The impromptu number, aping after your Broadway musical. And perhaps Webber, at the height of his Über-powers.

[Sing] *Still don't know what I was waiting for* [OE]
And the time was running wild
—a million dead end streets...

[...]

I said that time may change me
But I can't trace time.

That other arse, mopping-up that *piss*-stained pavement, stirred. KEL had been out-for-the-count for what'd seemed like ages. When suddenly, he felt something poke him.

"What...it ain't dead yet?"

Poke-poke

And there it was again, a stiff bony digit right in the ribs. The voice, throaty, and gravelly, as if filtered through the paving.

Inside, flashes of pain did laps of Kel's nervous system. Then came a response. Words like phlegm, wrenched from the back of a throat and spat out.

"PHF'KOFF…will-*ya*—"
Sniff
Kel tried lifting and cranking his head about, to track down that—
Sniff-sniff
And it was then, that that stench assailed him. It being like ammonia salts shoved-up both nostrils. Huge *phf'ked*-off wedges.
What. The. Pphf—

Grimacing, he tried holding his breath. But eventually his lungs gave-in; and forced to exhale, he managed to cop a mouthful. Wrenching, as if he were a moggie choking on a fur-ball. He wasn't sure, whether it was bile he tasted—his insides repeating on him, or *my-Man*.

From out of nowhere it'd materialised. And now just sat there, plonked unceremoniously upon its arse. Rummaging through an assortment of pockets—looking for god knows what.

It pulled-out a wod of crumpled paper: Mecca® betting slips, Metro™ newspaper clippings, Providential® ATM withdrawal receipts, *Life's Essentials®* checkout receipts; a beer matt from the local pub, The Boar's Head Inn—just up there 'pon yonder corner.

It was like a wedge, a *phf'king* fortune: LOTTO® lottery tickets, NHS™ scratch cards, T*f*L® Bus tickets, *GoGo*™ Travelcards, LBC® Parking fine slips, P&P Utilities™ receipts. Like, it'd never thrown away a scrap of paper, ever, its entire *Life*. Beginning with its Birth Certificate—presumably.

"Might as well be," it whispered to itself. Steely eyes *Blink-blinking* listlessly after this apparent wealth, it held in its grubby mitts.

"Yeah—they bent you over Mate," it said. Stuffing the wod into another pocket, without even bothering to look at it.

With the company, Kel felt obliged to pry himself from off the pavement. And did so, rising gingerly upon all fours; his locked arms visibly wobbling with the effort, his head throbbing with the mother of all migraines.

"Roy-al-*lee*. Bent *thee*. Oh-*vah*."

Again, cranking his head round, Kel followed that voice; his much maligned Id, now desperate for the company.

And just-then, his arms gave-in, and twisting upon his side, his shoulder slammed hard against that concrete—which was only too happy to oblige. It being seen to break his fall. And with it, the last of his Will to pick himself up.

Laying his head to rest, Kel readily welcomed a merciful sleep. What was it *Brother Nassir* had dubbed it?

[Rap] *The cousin of Death.*[OF]

Its tendered kiss goodnight, that coarse paving-stone pressed against those lips of his; swollen and split. A viscid cocktail of Blood and spittle oozing from them, in threads as brittle and as fine as Spider's webs.

"*Ohh*...that's gotta hurt."

My-Man leant over, pulling a face as it said it. Whilst that silence was to give way to a chorus of automobiles, BROOM-BROOM-BRROOMING-*off* into the distance, chasing after the night. Leaving their combined *sub*-phonic signatures reverberating, in that hollow in Kel's chest.

And with their passing came that rising tide—

The Buzz...

   The Buzz...

      The Buzz-uzz...

A wall of noise. That distinct hum of Street-*Life*; likened to a wave destine never to reach the shore.

Rolling onto his back, Kel's fingers felt warily, for the slit that'd been his mouth. As if meaning to be reacquainted with the idea of it. And just-then, was he seized upon by a coughing fit, his features balling like a fist.

Wrenching in pain, he thought, if he could only vomit. Get it out of his system, once and for all. Whatever it was that now festered within— whatever this feeling was...

If-only...If—

Rolling again, onto his side this time. He curled-up into himself; assumed a foetal position, his arms gripping tight his stomach.

The placebo of a motherly hug. Anything to stop from spilling his guts. Fessing-up to his sin(s).

REPO-MAN licked its chops, like a dog about to get stuck-in to a hearty meal.

"*Yep*...bent. *Thee.* Roy-al-*lee*."

It spelt it out—the obvious. Its *whino*-breath lending its stink to every syllable. And *Sniffed*. And twitching its nose, reached smartly into its coat—an inside pocket. Its grubby mitt emerging holding the scrawny stub of a roll-up.

This it put to its lips, like a proposition. Its intention—intent, being to smoke what was left of it. Whilst its other hand conjured a *Bic*® disposable lighter, out of thin-air—s'posedly.

Indeed, this seemed to be its Way—its *Tao*. Its actions being as tape-lace; announced with dancing fingers, embellished with dandy-flicks of its wrists. As if it were a Magician, practiced in those arts of sleight-of-hand.

Presenting the lighter to the stub with a theatrical flourish. It cranked its spark-wheel. Its freehand poised to catch that precious flame.

SCRATCH.

SCRATCH-SCRATCH.

Nothing.

The flint was obviously warn-out. Nevertheless, it shook the lighter for a-bit. There being still a hint of lighter fluid sloshing around inside.

SCRATCH-SCRATCH.

SCRATCH.

Still rien.

Undeterred, it persevered. Recalling now, there being a knack to it.

SCRATCH...SCRATCH.

SCRATCH-SCRATCH—fire.

Fire!

Quick inhale.

Puff...Puff. Puff.

There, the stub was lit.

Pulling repeatedly upon it—the stub, through pursed lips. Repo-*Man* seemed intent upon sucking the living daylights out of the scrawny little thing. It being more force of habit; muscle-memories of skid row, of chasing skid marks along pieces of tinfoil.

And then, as if it were possible to miss reeling from the shakes, and that pungent smell of cooking. Its eyes glazed over for a spell.

Happy Days...

The stub began to burn its lips, forcing it to switch to short, curt drags.

Blink-blink

The cataract was getting worse. Its World being seen through panes of Frosted-glass, analogous to rose-tinted windows.

That skew of nostalgia.

It hefted the word, *Nostalgia*. As if privy to this written narrative. And pursing its lips, blew-out a steady stream of smoke—the Dragon's breath.

And then...*and then*, it began to hum softly. The fragments of a tune, whilst it waited. Its agency being—and mark you this—not entirely its own.

[Hum] *Memories don't live like people—* [10]

Blink

The lyric had sprung to mind out of the blue, for want of a distraction. But then it added, "who was it said, our memory is a more perfect world?"

And having posed the question, it paused to scratch its head. The answer, frozen in the abstract, pinching at the tip of its tongue like a polyp.

"*God*—that's irritating."

Its eyes scrunched-up, as if its brain were constipated, at pains to shit it out. The answer having now assumed Messianic portent.

Slapping its forehead repeatedly, in frustration, it tried to shift those stiffening cogs of its memory.

"*Oh*...that's gonna right bug me now."

But try as it might, that war waged against the glacial approach of senility, was one it could feel itself losing. Those increasingly rare lucid occasions, more like kryptonite to ÜBERman™. The encroach of the dreaded D-word. Its inevitability, being as unobtrusive as a pregnant...

Yeah, it might be entire days politely lost, like loose change. A penny dropped along the way, never to be seen again. A loose end...

A loose end...a loose...something or other.

Capitulating, with a shrug. *Repo-Man* directed its pitiless gaze toward that prone fleshy mess, hugging the pavement for dear life—*Sniff*.

And was about to speak again. But instead, couched the thought in a hefty sigh. It then took to shaking its head, somewhat melodramatically.

∞

Kel reckoned, if he didn't move for long enough, the pain would have to go away. It seeming so obvious to that voice inside his head. That transient Ego: A confluence of adolescent angst, yielding to the inane wisdom of that recalcitrant toddler, that comprised his entrenched Id.

Accepting this puerile logic, Kel's Body tacitly resigned itself to an abject surrender.

To never again moving—*ever*.

To lying still upon that pitiless bed of paving-stones. The comfort afforded by that resolute concreteness, being juxtaposed against the idea of having hit rock bottom. Of striking bedrock. It being practically impossible for Kel to fall further—farther; lest, he physically burrow into the Earth's crust.

And, for just-a-moment, lying there. He felt as if a weight had been lifted. Which is to say, he felt a palpable absence of Gravity; what was that crushing Universal Constant. Those millions of cubic centimetres of atmospheric pressure, pressing down, and in all directions upon his brittle frame. The phenomenon analogous to every Will on the Planet, turned against him-*One*.

Yeah, for a moment there, it'd all become as naught. His pliant flesh, like Holmes&Pride® *Polyfilla*, filling in those cracks in the pavement; his own skin, assuming the paving-stone's coarse gravelly texture.

To think, what he wouldn't give to be so concrete, and unyielding. And of course, the pavement was to be remorseless, in soaking-up every ounce of his precious *Life*'s Blood. Its *Life*-affirming warmth, like a natural sponge.

Compared to the immediacy of it, that pavement. Its icy-cold fingers felt inching their way up his spine. The idea of returning to dust, of succumbing to that inevitable dystrophy of Death, seemed barely intelligible.

Braced against the touch of that frigid hand, Kel was trying so hard not to flinch; not to think of anything. Least of all, how he'd gotten there. But still it festered. The wound, pus filled and septic.

Peering-up from this Pit, this well of despair as it were. Kel couldn't help but feel it now, scratching away beneath the surface of his skin. That itch; an *itchiness*, distinct from an impression of physical pain, that appeared vague and inarticulate by comparison.

Yeah, here was that *Beating*, come back with a vengeance. Playing over and over in his head.

"Hol 'im down I said. Hol 'im, you *phf'king* nob."

Then it was brutish hands, all up in his gulliver. Frankfurter-fingers digging into pliant flesh. Eyes flashing murderous intent.

BOOPH

"Oy, where you *phf'king* going? C'mere—hol 'im."

BOOPH

BOOPH

"You feel that Rudeboy?"

"Yeah—Grinning—*my-Man* felt that."

If you've ever bumped into something immovable: Like a brick wall, or that triple-glazed glass ceiling—*say*.

Or, if you've ever been walking along—as-you-do—and for a split-second, something distracts you. You look away. Then look back and...

BOOPH

You walk into a Street-lamp. Get struck by lightning. Hit by a bus. Fall down a flight of stairs. Walk-off a Cliff, your Body dashed upon those jagged rocks far below, bones smashed to smithereens.

It's not so much shock, and not exactly horror. But more...*Shock... Horror...*

Surprise!

There has to be pain—*right?* Pain like you wouldn't believe. Still, it's the surprise that gets you every time. You'd know it, if you'd felt it.

There's like-*a* split-second of complete darkness. And then, that sound coming-out of the wide blue yonder. Heard up-close and personal...

BOOPH

NERVOUS SYSTEM: WHAT. THE. *Pphf*—what was that?

BRAIN (as ever clueless): Give us a *sec*. Computing...

The event is replayed for the mind's eye. Broken down into incremental frames, as your Brain tries to hone-in on the moment, juxtaposing its somatic feedback with that mental-image.

Computing—*a pregnant pause*...

BOOPH

Darkness...
Nothing(-*ness*)...
Then...then...
Wait for it... [Whisper] *wait for it*...
Excruciating P-A-I-N
BRAIN: We've been hit by something—something *ha-hard*.
NERVOUS SYSTEM: Yeah—tell me about it.

Yeah, that beating played over and over for Kel's edification. A right *horrorshow* feature-*come*-flick, starring BOOPH and the Gang.

COOPH
THUMP
WHACK
SMACK
SLAP

Also featuring, an improvised Bruce Lee™ HEEL-STOMP. Pulling that estatic expression, the one from *Enter the Dragon*[11]—that now carried a trademark. And whilst you're about it. Throw-in a bloodcurdling scream, and a couple of those slick whiplash sound-FX for larks.

WhoO-PISH *WhoO*-PISH

That beating being ostensively set upon perpetual loop.

BOOPH
COOPH
THUMP—*sleep now...merciful sleep...*
WHACK
SMACK—*quiet now...shhh...*
CHOKE HOLD
Can't breathe. Can't...b-breathe.
"Ya-killing 'im—she said not to kill 'im."
"*Phf'k*. That. Bitch."
And with that, Kel blacked-out.

Repo-*Man* placed a balled-fist to its mouth and blew, as if upon a bugle. Its grubby mitt splaying like wings, fingers fluttering after its rancid *whino*-breath. It then snapped its fingers abruptly.

"*Maupassant*. Monsieur Guy de Maupassant, that's it," it said, drawing an inspired moustache under its nose.

Visibly relieved, it looked to the stub, still cupped in its other hand.

"Be honest—*Sniff*—you didn't think I knew that?" it remarked, flicking it away.

Ankles crossed, it sat upright then. Like some slovenly, grubby Buddha (of Suburbia). To look down upon *my-Man* from an Enlightened height.

"Yeah...you sleep, Mate."

THAT PERFECT WORLD

Pris

Besides the eye and the thing, vision presupposes the light.

Emmanual Levinas, *Totality and Infinity* (1969)

42 65 73 [69] 64 65 73 20
74 68 65 20 65 79 65 20
61 6E 64 20 74 68 65 20
74 68 69 6E 67 2C 20 76
69 73 69 6F 6E 20 70 72
65 73 75 70 70 6F 73 65
73 20 74 68 65 20 6C 69
67 68 74 2E

•

GEARS + HYDRAULICS

The sirens wail was deafening—obviously. At its root, a chord of alarm seemingly emanating from everywhere, and nowhere, all at once.

That apparent disconnect, betwixt Power and its precept: *Foucault's Paradox*—a conspicuous absence of applied physical *Force*™. Being exemplified by this phenomenon.

Our Archangel Gabriel should struggle to muster such a blast, come the end of days. And yet, here it was. Heralding an end, and a beginning—of sorts. The siren being, of course, a simulacrum. A trace, of that clarion call-to-action—to arms, or so the Manufacturer's pitch would have us believe.

It was but one bullet-point on a bullet-pointed list of special features. The TEFLON® Group having pulled-out all the stops, in its bid to win the contract to build, and run, the state-of-the-art correctional-facility known colloquially as, the *Panny*.

Attracting one of a select few AAA-rated *Hollywoodland* Directors, the lovingly crafted digy-*viddy* promo—produced under the banner of one of the TEFLON® Group's many media subsids—began with a lavish 'Sword & Sandal' spectacle.

Fade-in: On a lone, sombre Teutonic figure, Heimdal, standing astride the battlements of Asgard; his seasoned eyes, fixed upon the horizon in tireless vigil. Storm clouds mustering overhead, the deluge of rain whipped-up by gale force winds.

He places his enchanted horn to his lips, cheeks bellying like sails, as he marshals the breath to blow. The blast, reverberating, shaking the

World to its uttermost foundations. Before fading to silence.

"Lo, host of Asgard harken. Fore Ragnarök is nigh!" a voice proclaims, taking-up the narrative. "Gjallerhorn resounds, the all-seeing Heimdal having espied the fiend—*Loki*—beckoning onward the unclean horde."

A laventine Loki is then depicted. Standing amidst an amorphous sea of disfigured blackened faces; Hel's bowels emptied. He urges onward this horde, pointing with his staff toward Golden Asgard—the *Twilight Realm*. A beacon of light seen against a snow-capped mountain vista. And incited by the gesture, the horde roars in anticipation of the carnage to come.

Heard against the distant rumble of thunder, and the wail of raging winds, the lamentable strings of Wagner's *Parsifal Prelude* take to trembling. The gates of Asgard are then flung wide, and Odin All-Father depicted riding forth; Gungnir in hand, the light at his back. Bestridden a resplendent Sleipnir, its nostrils flared and belching flames.

Following upon his heels, the host of Asgard (Vanir, Ænir and Einherjar) charge across leagues of pristine snow, spurred by their battle cry, "ODIN OWNS YE ALL!"

The light falls then, upon Loki and the horde. And they cower theatrically, throwing down they're crude weapons to shield their eyes.

The voiceover picking-up the narrative.

"Odin owns ye all, indeed. For all must despair who hear this cry, and in their despair fall naked and exposed. Their true countenance presented in the pure light of the *Good*—that is forever brilliant and bright."

The host of Asgard is then depicted crashing-down upon the horde, like a cresting wave. And in the ensuing melee, Thor—Mjölnir in hand—smites the serpent, Jörmungandrm, its coils towering above him; Tyr wrestles with Garm, its jaws locked around the metal stump of his missing hand; Freyr squares with Surtr, the iron of their swords biting as the pair grapple, their boatraces grimacing with intent. And finally, Odin is depicted subduing Fenrir Wolf, his barefoot pressing against the Beast's neck, his spear buried to the shaft in its flank.

"The wayward *Soul* is subdued," the voiceover continues. "Blinded by that light of Truth. The indomitable Power of your god-of-always-listening—his abiding grace, the Will that guides and binds us all."

In that final sequence, the field of battle is shown strewn with the bodies of the fallen; Heroes on both sides, squared in Death's throes.

A shadow falling upon the stricken Loki, he holds aloft his feeble arms to shield his eyes from the light. And cowering, bows his head, in a gesture of contrite submission.

"And thus, driven to recant," the voiceover concludes. "The Soul is seen to ascend to Society. Or as sinner, cast asunder. Plunged into an ever-accommodative Abyss."

The digy-*viddy* promo cuts then, to a medium close-up of a virtua-Kenneth Baron Clark archetype. Cast in the mould of *ye olde* Imperial Civil Servant, and seen against a pristine Brilliant-bright backdrop.

His is a bulbous head. Prominent cranium. Weak chin disappearing into a wrinkled turkey neck. Potbelly. Slight frame. Though tall in stature; his lined forehead, sporting that weathered glow of the Subcontinent.

"*Tis*, the manifest Will of god—he who art always listening," he asserts, addressing the camera in a Self-assured and scholarly Sir Humphrey Applyby-manner.

His voice, discernibly that heard in the previous sequence.

"What is a marriage of Mathematics, and Ideology. Form and Substance. Substantive functionality—*utility*," he continues. One hand trussed, nonchalant, in the pocket of his Khaki slacks.

As if, he were absentmindedly fondling some loose change; his tweed blazer—also cut from *ye olde* Oxbridge cloth—unbuttoned, allowing his Sky-blue linen shirt room to breathe.

The sequence cuts then, to an establishing-shot: Our-*Man* dwarfed by a Goliath pair of stately looking brass-doors, adorned with neoclassical motifs. And again, he addresses the camera.

"The result. A work of s-ʌ-b-l-ɪˈ-m-e-ɪ-ʃ-(ə)-n."

He'd spelt out each syllable, to add emphasis.

"A venerable masterpiece. Replicable, over and over and over again. Distinct in design—and application, perfect in replication. Stated simply—categorically—your idealized form, *Siren*. Realised."

Placing a palm upon each door, he gives a gentle shove. The doors are then seen to open effortlessly, and we are magically transported to the Palazzo della Signoria. There to be greeted by a non-diegetic soundtrack of birdsong, and flowing water; a lonely harp seemingly swooning after this idyllic vista.

Again, a master-shot establishes our setting: A replica of Michelangelo's *David*, planted atop those five steps leading-up to the Pallazzo Vecchio. The noonday sun high overhead. The surrounding buildings casting squat shadows, upon the floor of that deserted Florentine square.

"For such a creature is *Man*—" our-*Man* continues, out of shot. His words, like his voice, now one degree removed from their subject.

We follow as our-*Man* saunters over to the statue, his blazer flapping in a zephyr-*like* breeze, that plays with those threads of his thinning hair.

"Comparable to that primordial force of creation. *Tis* Man alone, who stands outside of nature. The final element in god's grand design."

He fastens a button on his blazer against that unruly breeze, then adds: "His mind's eye, guided by reason—*by intuition*—aspires through this, his work, to realise that essential Self. That which your god-of-always-listening intended, in calling Adam forth, into Being."

Taking measured steps, our-*Man* now climbs those five stairs to stop before the plinth, and look-up adoringly, at that towering figure of David.

The camera cuts then, to his POV: Starting at that manly torso, the shot following the smoothed contours of that marbled figure, as if looking for its head. The voiceover picking-up the threads of our-*Man*'s argument.

"And, with each incremental step toward an understanding of this, his Body—his embodiment; his being in and for the Universe. *Man* must inevitably, edge that fraction of a millimetre closer to the Truth. And that divine imagining."

The sequence cuts back to our-*Man*, still staring-up at the statue. And on cue, he turns to address the camera, combing into place strands of hair with his fingers.

"In this respect, tis that promise of Eden, just visible upon the horizon. *Tis*, the wistful memory of a Paradise Lost, rekindled in dreams of a new Jerusalem."

Cut to: A close-up of the romanticised features of the Israelite, David. The voiceover once again picking-up the reins of the argument.

"*Tis*, the fall of Adam; his yearning to return once more, into God's dominion."

Now back to our-*Man*, addressing the camera.

"*Tis*, the rationalisation of that yearning—that desire, in a manifest yet disembodied transcendentalism."

Cut to: An extreme close-up of those hollowed-out eyes of David, scowling at something seen far-off in the distance. The grimace, traced in that furrowed brow, shaded from the Sun's rays by a peak of tangled dreadlocks.

The voiceover closes the argument.

"But ultimately, *tis* Man's supplication to his one true master—his one true god. Progressio, metamorphosed into Profectus. This Second-coming, an androgynous, romanticised Christ-*like* figure, seen holding-up a set-square—to measure the Heavens. A plump cherub suckling at its callow chest."

The sequence cuts then, to an extreme close-up of our-*Man* once again looking-up at the statue, his eyes drinking their fill of that adonis-*ized* David.

"Magnificant...*sfarzoso*. Isn't he—just?"

Returning to that establishing-shot, the sequence ends with our-*Man* swaggering-off. One hand still cotch'd in the pocket of his slacks. Leaving the statue to the deserted square, and that oppressive glare of the noonday sun.

Yeah, that Siren's wail was truly deafening, and ultimately an act of violence. It being an assault on that most assailable of senses. A pair of organs that were consciously, and unconsciously, always listening. And predisposed to *proc* at that timbre of presiding danger.

'This is a World of Dominion,' said that sinusoidal tone. The edict pitched high and authoritative, as it pulsed slow and measured through its cycle, a disconcerting 3.3 kHz.

Of course, there was no need to panic. Everything was under control because everyone was under control. Saying that, those two peerless Souls, stood upon this apparent precipice, seemed oblivious to all of it.

That is to say, Light-years removed from our-*Man*'s highfaluting mumbo-jumbo.

In front of them, gears and hydraulics moved smoothly through designated cycles, unseen and unheard. Whilst everywhere was seen and heard exquisite expressions of Power. Absolute, and resolute, and irrepressible.

Behold then, yonder brilliant light, pristine bright.

Unadulterated by coloration. Uncompromised by contrast. Undiluted by shade. Unblemished by shadow. Plain. Simple. Pure.

And most important of all. Sublimely beautiful.

Peering through the narrow slit of rëenforced glass, with its wire-mesh, and hint of tint; framed in an obscenely tall, solid-*looking* Brilliant-bright metal-door. A pair of starry eyes drank thirstily, every minute detail of that which lay beyond, like mirrors onto this World.

Reflected in those eyes, this spectacle became suddenly awash with color. Almost in spite of itself, the immensity of the architecture falling just shy of opulence; in being so absolutely brilliant, and resolutely bright. That fleshy tone, and waspish demeanour managing to strike a warm, humane contrast, to all that exact and precise Euclidean geometry. Its emphatic description of the corridor's golden ratio.

It seeming as if, ever defiant, *Life* in essence had conspired over millennia to assume this form. To be epitomised, by this badly drawn Boy—*Man*. His flesh. His Blood. His breath, seen condensing on that tinted glass. Good ol' Mother Nature having anticipated this very moment.

By simply being present, the Youth appeared capable of taking possession of it all. And thus, for one fleeting, barely perceptible moment, was it—all of it, gloriously subverted.

[Sing] *Hallelujah, Hallelujah* [12]

If those enquiring eyes only knew, locked away inside that brittle frame of *Life*—of skin, flesh, and bone.

But alas, having drunk their fill, those eyes were seen to dim. To retreat within, succumbing to that abject situation, the Body now found itself in. There being nothing new to see—ultimately.

A signet ring, BLK-jade embedded in a band of rose-gold. Set upon the dainty Pinky-finger of an *ever-so* manly hand. Wink'd back at that Brilliant-bright light.

Wink.

A caste-iron grip, firm and unyielding, stopping that lean, margre frame.

It said, without needing to spell it out: ə-(ʊ)-b-e-ɪ.

Where the mind is oft at pains to convey its meaning. The Body feels and reacts. Which is to say, it was enough. Yielding, the shoulder lost all form, all purpose(-*fulness*). Its load being unceremoniously transferred to that Will, that would, and could, swallow it whole — if need be.

A sobering tug, like a fatherly brace, invitation enough to dance — to waltz. That firm guiding hand, taking the lead, squaring those shoulders. Supple, and compliant, they responded and were turned to one side:

s-t-e-ɪ.

The instruction conveyed by a lingering contact.

A uniformed figure now blotted-out that narrow slit, eclipsing the Brilliant-bright beyond. Its ominous shadow spilling over the edges of that frame.

The word, uniform [pronounced: ˈj-uː-n-ɪ-f-ɔ-ːm], being synonymous with its No. 2 Dress 40% grey Lounge-suit, the thread-count of that heavy fabric; the peaked-cap shielding its eyes; the matching shirt and tie, replete with starched collar and stiffened cuffs; and those Corcoran® steel-toed field boots, seen here polished to a high-shine.

And by extension, that antiquated *hermeneutic*-Key, that hung at the end of an equally antediluvian keychain. Its insertion into that *hermeneutic*-Lock, the seamlessness of this coming together. It all pointing pointedly, toward a monolith of uniformity.

The materials of (*h*)Lock and (*h*)Key were charged with a slight magnetic field, where like-and-like would repel. Upon insertion, this field acted as a cushion, removing all friction; the complimentary pair sliding effortlessly together, the action culminating in a discreet, yet immensely satisfying — CLICK!

Once inserted, the polarity was reversed, and the (*h*)Key read. At which point, the locking mechanism — a massive bolt hidden within those innermost workings of that towering Brilliant-bright solid metal-door — would slowly ease back, allowing it to be opened. Being hydraulically assisted, this motion was to be measured and effortless. And thus, uniform.

Looking beyond the door, that brilliant, Brilliant-bright continued for some distance, with no apparent end in sight. And like the previous corridor, and the corridor before that, and the corridor before that. This corridor was to present an image of harmonious perfection. Its aspect, width, to height, to unfathomable length, demonstrative of that functional aesthetic.

The Door. The Corridor. The Siren. All works of sublime artisanship. The *Ingeniator* (Architektón) having been inspired by that pure light of reason; an infallible Laser-beam, burning away that slag of emotion. Until all that remained was an apodeictic Truth.

Rivalling that of revelation *even*.

Removing the (*h*)Key, the Uniform gripped the Youth's arm to lead him through the doorway. Having crossed the threshold, the Youth knew to wait, and did so, standing to attention. As if he were suddenly rendered *Life*-less, like a statue.

The Uniform then proceeded to close, with effortless ease, that towering solid metal-door. With the door now locked in place, the siren at last fell silent. The abruptness of it—this turning moment, like a gasp for breath upon breaching the surface. After being so long submerged under water.

The Uniform and the Youth danced a smart waltz to stand shoulder-to-shoulder. Faux leather *Man*-made soles scuffing that polished Brilliant-bright enamel floor. And then, they proceeded to march down that corridor.

Left-Right.
   Left-Right.
      Left...
         Left...

Although their progress was to be steady, and steadfast. Within that ossified Space, their footsteps were barely audible; each footfall being evidently smothered in a fluffy blanket. As on, and on, and on they marched.

Left-Right.
   Left-Right.
      Left...
         Left...

Certainly, that Brilliant-bright corridor would yield nothing to the tyranny of this rhythm. Its *Being-in-itself* (l'être pour soi) having become stasis. Magnified and amplified to that *Nth* degree.

The aesthetic: Unmoved. Unmoving. *Immovable*—your idealized form, C-O-R-R-I-D-O-R. Realised.

Ahead, another towering Brilliant-bright solid metal-door barred the way. And once again, the Youth was allowed a fleeting glimpse of the Future, that which lay beyond.

Snatching at it, through that rëenforced glass, it could confirm all was as it should be. Brilliant, Brilliant-bright as far as the eye could see. Its future, like the weather, being predictable within degrees of certainty.

As before, the Uniform and the Youth negotiated that Brilliant-bright solid metal-door in complete silence. The Youth standing stock-still, by a wall that'd deny it even a shadow, while the Uniform locked-up. The pair then waltzing into position to set-off down that corridor.

Left-Right.
    Left-Right.
        Left...
            Left...

The Space had—of course, been measured, in *Paces*. As opposed to feet (ft), or inches ("). Accumulative averages ironed-out, the count varying between one hundred-and-forty to one hundred-and-forty-one. Forty-two. Forty-three.

Stop.

Yet another Brilliant-bright solid metal-door barred the way. And once again, Youth was allowed to steal a cheeky look-see, through the narrow slit provided. Before the Uniform presented his (*h*)Key.

As with all the others, this solid metal-door glided open effortlessly—as if seen in über *Slo-mo*.

Though, this time there was hesitation; slight, but perceptible. The room beyond being palpably bigger. That Brilliant-bright extending in all directions. One featureless, infinite universe, housed within this patently finite Space.

All that lay therein, a perfectly proportioned carved block of Brilliant-bright stone, decorated with engraved lines; the design reminiscent of those Hōkime motifs you'd find in a Karesansui garden. It appearing to be planted at the epicentre of this Space. The Universe extending in all directions from this point of singularity.

Ptolemaic, and cold. That slab of stone was to be your idealized form, T-A-B-L-E. Realised. The room of infinite proportions, your idealized form, R-O-O-M. Realised. There were no sources of light. No discernible edges, nor corners. No shadows cast upon that pristine enamel floor. No sound. No noise.

Indeed, there were no tangible qualities to rëenforce the validity of this indurate Space. Just a blanket brilliant, Brilliant-bright extending as far as the eye could see.

Blink

Am I dead?

That'd been Kel's initial impression, upon bearing witness to this spectacle for the first time.

However, seeing it again, that veneer of wonder—tinged as it was with foreboding—seemed all but a distant memory. The decor conjuring for him, images of George Lucas's *THX 1138*[13]—a staple of recreational sessions. The flick testifying to the ubiquity of the candidate's milieu. That it be seen extending beyond his situation: That of the *real*-World into that of the World *re*-imagined.

Blink-blink

Yeah, Kel had come full circle. And all that remained was this one last ritual. Ritual being an integral part of it, your candidate's daily *Life*-routine.

Ritual equating with procedure. Procedure equating with discipline, with *Form*.

The regime of *Form*, of ritualised procedural discipline, supplementing that substantive component; provided by the sheer shock and awe of those surroundings.

That spectacle of architecture, evoking an impression of Sisyphus dwarfed by an immovable boulder, steering-up at an insurmountable mountain. The promise of an Eternity of futile labour, playing upon his last nerve.

Ritual. Procedure. Discipline.

Just the thought of it was nauseating. It having been drummed into Kel's skull, seared upon his *Psyche*. That impression of a giant, faceless, uniformed figure looming overhead; tugging at those invisible wires attached to his arms and legs.

Certainly, he'd been force fed a steady diet of it.

Ritual. Procedure. Discipline—*dread*.

Heaped spoons shoved in his gulliver, rammed down his throat. His nose pinched, forcing him to swallow.

Sniff

The Brilliant-bright solid metal-door was closed and locked. And gripping Kel's arm, the Uniform was to march him over to that carved block of stone—*the slab*, where another Uniform waited.

No. 2 Dress 20% grey Lounge-suit; peaked-cap shielding its eyes; matching shirt and tie, with starched collar and those stiffened cuffs; and Corcoran® steel-toe field boots, polished—*as ever*—to a high-shine.

And yeah, it'd seemed a spitting-image of the first. Or more, a *Clone*; its features chiselled, and stoic, and smug.

Your idealized form, U-N-I-F-O-R-M. Realised.

Halting Kel on the spot, a measured pace from the proceedings. Uniform #1 was to present him to his superior with a nod. Then, taking one step back, and two steps to the side. Stood at-ease. Hands locked behind his back. Barrel-chest distended.

Producing a folded carrier-bag from his trouser pocket, Uniform #2 deliberately unwound the drawstring, and unfolded it. He then SNAPPED it open, abruptly. Filling it with air—like a windsock, to place it ceremoniously upon that *slab*.

The bag was seen then to come to life, like a stop-motion sequence, viewed here in real-*Time*. Deflating, and ironing-out those creases and crinkles caused by the Uniform's manhandling of it.

As if exhibiting muscle memory of a prior wrinkle-free existence— your idealized form, C-A-R-R-I-E-R–B-A-G. Realised.

Kel had been watching his feet—as you do.

As *Panny* candidates tended to. What with prolonged exposure to all that absolute brilliance, and resolute brightness. The eye had a tendency to lose the plot. The mind drifting-off, into a kind of *quasi-*hypnotic state of utter despair; your 'Deadman's stare', as it'd come to be known.

Due in part to sensory deprivation, it was also associated with those bouts of chronic depression that were common, especially amongst your fledgling candidates.

And there was *our* Sisyphus again, now steering blankly into Space—the muppet.

To combat this, candidates quickly learned to focus upon their feet. To anchor themselves in the present, in what was immediate, and real. And this Kel did, musing upon his deep-taupe CharlieBrown's® *Winklepickers*.

His shoulders squared in a 60% grey cotton two-piece Birdman suit, ash-BLK *StayPress*™ shirt, and matching knitted pencil-tie; 80% grey wool and cashmere *Crombie* folded smartly over an arm.

All of it, your standard-issue DCW&P clobber, 'for your rehabilitated life on the Outside'.

It was the SNAP that'd called him to. Now aware the ritual had begun, he lifted his head, allowing himself a look-see at the carrier-bag as it did its thing. Ignoring the Uniform, who was crouched down, presumably assembling a 'Pack' to place inside that bag. From those stacks of glossy brochures stockpiled in pigeonholes, on its side of the *slab*.

Kel then attempted to trace the edges of it—the *slab*, that was both bureau and sacrificial alter. His eyes following those engraved lines, that were barely perceptible for the lack of shadows. And which— presumably, were meant for funnelling the Blood away after.

It occurring to him, that that slab might've appeared invisible. That is, indivisible from its surroundings. If it wasn't for the fact of its sheer mass, and immovability; and the presence of that hulking great Uniform squat down behind it.

But your Panny was like that, a real head-*phf'k*. Think. *Arthur C.* Think. Penn&Teller™ *Doing Vegas*. As in, something truly E-P-I-C in scale.

It was the scale that forced you to suspend disbelief. That goaded you into acquiescence.

That being said. That slab was exactly as Kel remembered it, from his 'Induction'. It having achieved perfection, it'd nowhere else to go. And being made of stone, it wasn't about to wonder off, or start eroding on the spot. At least, not whilst housed in this here vacuum.

Everything about the PANOPTES—that is, your *Panny*—exuded this quality of permanence. Picture it: A giant digital alarm-clock, calibrated to measure Space*Time* in intervals of Eternity. It's one lonely glowing-red LED, poised to execute that one lonely count. That one lonely *Beat* of one amorphous perpetuity.

Yeah, it was like Purgatory, masquerading as Heaven. Like, waiting for that day to come, whilst not knowing what day it was, or what exactly you were waiting for.

∞

Blink

Kel was seen to muse upon this for a *hot*-minute, his day having come to lend him its unique perspective.

Before him, the carrier-bag now lay perfectly flat upon that *slab*. And through its diaphanous material, he could make-out that bold-type, printed upon a booklet housed therein. And so, he took it upon himself to read the title: 'YOUR ESSENTIAL GUIDE TO LIFE ON THE OUTSIDE'.

Of course, he knew what the bag contained, having been briefed on the proceedings—the *proc*—beforehand. Inside, he'd expect to find all the necessary paperwork needed to begin his 'rehabilitated life': Application forms for an ID, and a Work Permit, and a *GoGo*™ Travelcard, and a 'monitored' Bank account—and corresponding *Rush*Card™.

Then, there'd be standardised *Letters of Introduction*, for entry onto the mandatory DCW&P Volunteer Sector work placement program [*Volsec*]; and another, inviting him to register with the Newcomen's Halfway House. And finally, a bundle of coupons and discount vouchers for selected retail outlets, leisure activities and services provided by subsidiaries of the TEFLON® Group.

Upon completion of treatment, your candidate would be rubberstamped 'REHABILITATED', making it all official-*like*. And correspondingly, its slate would be 'wiped clean'—as it were.

The stigma, rightfully associated with incarceration, nullified by a dual pronged *post*-Therapy probationary regime, aimed at flattening that bell-curve of recidivism.

And thus, Kel could expect to be relocated, away from the milieu that'd led him to deviate from nominal societal norms of behaviour. Namely, his social circle, and principally, his family and friends (—if he'd had any). And reallocated a new *Life*, one with dramatically improved prospects.

Though he'd no longer be viewed as a 'Criminal' *per se*. It'd be accepted that he was criminally inclined; *Criminality* being viewed as, essentially, a terminal condition.

Accordingly, where its malign symptoms might be tempered during Therapy; *post*-Therapy, the sting of your candidates visibly stunted societal status, would still be expected to do just that: *Sting*.

It being obscene, for your *re*-habilitated candidate to be seen to have profited from its criminal misadventures.

Kel devoured it all, that carrier-bag and its contents with a *Blink*. Then looked-up to cop the Uniform stood behind the slab—

Sniff

Now, every candidate knew never to dwell on any given Uniform's boatrace. It being canon. It being gospel. It being like, *Panny* Survival 101—it being that *phf'king* obvious.

With the PANOPTES being administered along the lines of a Celestial hierarchy, the Uniforms were to be envisaged as 'Angels'. And thus, any appeals to your 'Higher Authority', were to be as prayers directed up toward the sky.

Or, in this case, a transparent-glass ceiling. That brilliant, Brilliant-bright extending beyond *ad infinitum*.

But Kel didn't care—*Sniff*. He'd survived. Made it through and out the other side. And now felt anew, that surge of defiance warm his insides, like a Brandy-tot.

Stealing a look-see at this Uniform, Kel's gaze was likened to the outstretched fingers of a free climber, clumsily feeling-out the surface of that sheer rockface. But there was to be no hint of a nook, nor even the merest suggestion of a cranny of rapport from this one. The boatraces of your Uniforms tending to fit a mould, the higher you got up the pecking.

Eventually, his eyes came to rest upon that single magnanimous A4-sheet of Brilliant-bright paper, that'd seemingly materialised before him.

Like that *slab* it rested upon, this standardised 'Contract of Rehabilitation' was almost invisible. Save for the type, presented in a smart, simple *Sans Serif* font.

It being—obviously, your idealized form, C-O-N-T-R-A-C-T. Realised.

The ritual-proper was conducted then, in silence. As most rituals were. With Kel struggling to decipher the small print, illegible from where he stood. The Uniform behind the slab presented him with a pen. A smart, solid-*looking* Stainless-steel jobbie, with a weighted nib—your idealized form, B-A-L-L-P-O-I-N-T P-E-N.

And leaning over, Kel signed where prompted. Passing the pen onto

Uniform #1 to add its signature as witness.

Picking-up the contract, Uniform #2 scrutinised it—its eyes narrowing. That graphology course, it'd undertaken in its spare time, enabling it to pick-up on those tell-tale signs of residual delinquency, evident in Kel's scrawl.

Eyeballing this Youth, it wet the tip of a finger with its tongue. And pinching the corner of the contract, revealed that counterfoil. Confirming both signatures had transferred, it then separated the original—with a crisp SNAP—and held it out in the direction of Uniform #1.

Accepting it, on Kel's behalf, Uniform #1 picked-up the bag and placed it carefully therein—so as it lay perfectly flat. Uniform #2 then presented the pen, which Uniform #1 again accepted. Dropping it into the bag and pulling that drawstring too.

The whole thing being over in a matter of seconds—your idealized form, P-R-O-C...

Yeah yeah yeah!
Blah blah phf'king blah!

Having donned his *Crombie*, Kel buttoned it up, and pulled at his cuffs, and straightened his tie. As if meaning to look his best for this last bit.

Uniform #1 then presented the bag, Kel accepting it with the obligatory handshake. The Uniform keeping it brief, more of a brace than a shake. Its grip crushingly firm.

Still, Kel was to make a point of matching it, pascal for pascal.

With the bag tucked smartly under one-arm—as he'd been instructed, Kel was given leave to amble over to the exit at his leisure. A tall window-less Brilliant-bright solid metal-door, he more intuited than saw.

The 'Opening' ritual was then performed. But this time, as Kel walked through, the Uniform was to remain on the other side.

Sensing its absence, Kel paused to look back, being unsure what was s'posed to happen next—him having not been briefed on this bit.

And anticipating this, the Uniform *Wink*'d after him, before closing the door. The THUD of which, was to be heard reverberating in that Pitch wherein Kel now stood.

Robbed momentarily of his sense of direction, Kel waited. That ground lending him its singular perspective.

Sniff

But it wasn't long before those illuminated strips, buried in the floor, began to glow. Two parallel lines of blue light—your *Straight & Skinny*, blazing a trail like Laser-beams. With no end in sight.

This being the only path afforded him, Kel took a deep breath, and set-off down it. The carrier-bag still tucked under his arm; him not wanting to break that silhouette of his new threads.

BoOM KLΛK!

SASH sat atop a REBrov® Inst-A-*Matik* washing machine. Legs swinging aimlessly, as if treading water; heels kicking against the window. Whilst through the glass, her clothes could be seen clinging onto the drum for dear life, having just-now gone through a vigorous spin.

She appeared lost. Somewhere between waiting, and weightlessness. Her Body's perpetual motion—its apparently random gyrations, a spontaneous decoding and encoding of that *Crunk*. That meditation on *Phf*unk presently thumping in those *Buds* in her ears; Braeburn® wireless tactileacoustics, 'for that genuine *in da club* experience in audio.'

Out-*there*—in der Lebenswelt, the Inst-A-*Matik* was cranking-up to launch itself into a turbo-spin. That final stage in its programmed washing cycle. Whilst inside, in that *innenwelt* of sound and emotion, hers was an unbridled somatic expression. That was more than mere youthful exuberance.

This shhit right hear—can you feel it?
Ahh yeah!
Eyes-closed, Sash held a finger poised in anticipation of that
BoOM
    Klak
BoOM-BoOM
    Klak!

Shoulders *Poppin'* in a *Chippie*® Bubblewrap jacket. Head rockin' synchronously from side-to-side. She channelled the current, the charge—the *Vibe*; her literal translation of that ultramagnetic signal, like a Mexican Wave.

All hands in the air—waving like you just don't care.

And *phf'k* being watched, or who was watching.

That feeling, so fleeting a glimpse of Freedom. Being every bit a soma, meant to inebriate those Parsees.

Yeah, here it was, la Joie de *Vie*. An alternate state of *Being*, of mindless mindful-*ness*. The dance, riddled with all its contradictions, as ever a counterpoint to *Life*, to that

BoOM
   Klak
BoOM-BoOM
   Klak!

It went way beyond mere synchronization. This confluence of Muzik, Mind, Body and *Soul*, being a movement toward the *One*, toward a nigh perfect synchronicity. The sum becoming meaningful, as if meant, as if...

Intended.

Yeah, here was Body, taking possession of that muzikal expression—its muzikality. Coming wholly into its *Vibe*—its Spirit. Taking it wholly into its Heart—its *Soul*.

Dare one speak of conduits, and higher vibrations—of vibrating higher. Of higher Being, and even higher *Beings*.

To hear it was to feel it. To know it—of it—absolutely, like when you say a thing and mean it, infinity times infinity.

[Sing] *Muzik is my Heart and my Soul* [14]

More pre-cious than Gold...

And certainly, as you can't *un*-think a thought, so you can't *un*-feel a feeling.

Too few then, those glorious seconds. Too transient, that *oh so* precious sense of being whole, and wholly within the moment. Of choosing to swim with the current, and have it have its way with you.

Being thus moved. Thus, *vexed*.

Sash's Body was engaged in a heated exchange. Supple arms and limber limbs holding conflicting views. The Head, ever your arbiter, nodding in acknowledgement of some salient point. There being no escaping the truth of it, of that

BoOM
   Klak

BoOM-BoOM
    Klak!

That Noise. Those punctuated sonic episodes erupting in her eardrums, had Sash about ready to explode. For sure, twas sheer *Baduism*, as Mother-Sister-Daughter Erykah so eloquently put it:

[Sing] *I'm in love—with you* [15]
Cos of the—things you
Do to me—when you
BoOM
Klak
Ka-BoOM Klak!

And it could do it to you too. If you'd only let it.

Somehow it gathered-up meaning, like how a falling Body gathers momentum; multifarious points of reference, of association encoded in the abstract. The waveform, thus translated, becoming some-*thing* else, transporting you some-*where* else.

You hearing it, becoming some-*one* else.

Demystified, rather than *de*-constructed.[16] It could be neither, just that BoOM, nor just that Klak. And yet, viewed as a whole, it was *Truth*. It was pure Ontology. Being towards *Life*, toward Death. And ultimately, toward *Love*.

Lost in translation then, and the commodification of its *Sign*-Object. Crammed full of inherent socialisation. It spoke both the *langue* and *parole* of fetishistic consumption, as if born immaculately onto it.

All other explanations, and explications being *wack*. Just gimme that

BoOM
    Klak
BoOM-BoOM
    Klak!

Around the corner from Maple Street, and the youth hostel, where Sash laid her head. The Cleveland Street *Laundromat* | 24-7 was themed upon the inside of a '53 *Eldorado*.

With Braden cherry-finish rëengineered wood-panelling, and aquamarine vinyl flooring, and rows of Bubblegum-pink REBrov® Inst-A-*Matik* washing machines, facing-off against rows of Electric-yellow

Dry-A-*Matik* humidity dryers—all trimmed with mirrored-chrome. And those creamy PVC benches running the length of its storefront. Turning that photovoltaic sheet-glass window into a windscreen, looking-out onto that Open-road.

Plus, you'd this line of ACME® penny-sweet Chip-N-Pin vending machines, that were obsolete. Chained by the ankles to that entrance-*slash*-exit; like a Chain-gang working that side of the street—that side of the road.

The only evident departure from this themed aesthetic, being that TEFLON® *Ultima* 40″ S-HD flatscreen, buttressed in the corner. And those Phillips® T8 Triphosphor fluorescent strip-lights hanging overhead; beaming 860-*slash*-865 daylight, day and night—regardless. And giving-off the kind of faint electrostatic *Ommm*, your eardrums quickly learned to ignore.

Throw-in the faded posters that littered the walls. A nod to a matronly, moustachioed Big brother-archetype; dressed in drag and playing at god as usual. The stripped-back neorealist illustrations, coaxing you through the loss of your Laundromat-*cherry*.

The blanket use of solid-blocks of red and BLK, a nod to *Soviet*-era Constructivism, peering through that veneer of Technicolor™. That sheen of imported *Americana*, that wore its contagion like a catchy theme song—

[Sing] *These days are ours* [17]

Happy and free

(*Oh laundry days*)

Yeah, here it was, your perfect mix of *post*-War optimism, and Keynesian inspired economics. The 1950s being arguably, the apotheosis of the *Mod*-era.

And in that Engine-room hidden under the bonnet. There'd be troops of Space-Monkeys, and (M)ad-Men, and PR-gurus, and Edward Bernay *Mini*-Me's beavering away at the *Man*'s Master Plan—your 'Project Mayhem'.

Shhh... [Whisper] *all very Hush-hush.*

And yet, these Geniuses would still find time enough to screw the brains out of an uncannily accommodative *Tess Truehart*™, during those extended lunchbreak periods.

And of course, our Tess would-be gagging for it. Dressed as she was, in your obligatory come-*phf'k*-me-over uniform. Cherry-red stilettos; Jet-BLK 30-denier 100% nylon stockings, with the seams running-up the back; an unbuttoned cream silk blouse exposing an ample bosom, cupped in a plunge brassiere; grey plaid pencil-skirt hefted up about her gamely thighs, showing-off those matching suspenders.

Yeah—our Tess. What a Trooper!
Wink.

She takes it bareback, naturally. Only occasionally looking round to egg-on her Commander-in-Chief. And never once does she allow herself to get impregnated. Knowing bloody well, that that one day-off could mean her J-O-B.

My beautiful laundrette. Retrofitted as it was, it could've been out of anyone's future.

Yet another instalment in your *Back to the Future*™ franchise. Part of the movie-set even. Patiently awaiting an almost Messianic, fly-*looking* Marty McFly. Who'd roll-up in a swish-*looking* DeLorean® DMC-12.

Waiting for him to rush-in through those doors, to rapturous applause; as ever looking for Doc Brown, his younger-*Self* in this time-period. Still your Mad Scientist, with the crazy hair. Still your Einstein, playing surrogate to your *god-of-always-listening.*

Both of 'em, Doc & Marty, frantically looking to put right a temporal paradox of their own making. An Oedipal Complex of a plot, that could—ultimately—wind-up in one of them. Never. Being. Born.

GREAT SCOTT. [18]

Somehow, Marty needed to make his parents-to-be fall in *Love*: His teenage Mom, unwittingly besotted with that image of her über Kool teenage-Son; his teenage Dad ineffectual in affecting lasting change upon a *Present* already laid out in the script i.e., scripted.

[Sing] *These days are ours*
Happy and free
(*Oh Laundry Days*)

And if you listened carefully, you'd hear the accompaniment of washing machines, tucked-away in the mix. Hidden under those appropriated Barbershop four-part male-voice harmonies. At various stages in their programmed cycles, from Soak to Wash-N-Rinse to Turbo-Spin.

And hearing that, you'd know you were back. Back from that Future and looking forward to a *Present* that'd already righted itself. And was now better than ever. Marty having gotten that Toyota® *Hilux* 4x4 he'd always wanted.

Thanks Doc.

Yeah Doc, thanks a bunch.

This whole surreal episode, just another word from *our* Sponsor. Yeah, everything would be back to normal, but for that unruly image of youth. Sash sat atop that Inst-A-*Matik*—god only knows how she got up there. Jammin' to that

BoOM

    Klak

BoOM-BoOM

    Klak!

Wait...*wait*...something was creeping into the mix.

The phf'king Turbo-spin cycle!

What—Tut.

Sash cranked the volume on her brand spanking new Braeburn® *Pod*, all the way up to max. But could still feel it.

This shit aint loud enough, she thought.

Like *duh*—obviously. EH&S *Pet*.

Nevertheless, she whacked-up the E.Q., giving-it some of that. A-bit of topsy-Treble and BoOM-ing Bass. Til' the *Buds* started to crackle and *Pop!* And just-then, one of them happened to slip from its snug-fit, her just managing to catch it in her lap.

Phew—that was close.

Still, for that split-second, her mind's eye couldn't help but note the perceptible dip in the intensity of that 'in da club' experience. It being like a crack in the seal of a vacuum chamber, where air started rushing-in. And with it, der Lebenswelt. That World, Out-*there*.

Oh, where'd it go? My beautiful stereo?

Sash quickly stuffed the Bud back in her ear. But the Vibe had passed, and with it, the moment.

For want of a distraction, Sash now *viddy*'d the screen of said *Pod*, just as a 'Subscription Renewal' prompt courtesy of Rialto®—her Streamcast Provider, *Wink*'d in.

Scrolling along the bottom of the screen, the message read: 'We apologise in advance for this interruption to your regular service. Please contact your Service Provider immediately to continue unrestricted access.'

It then *Wink*'d out.

Bored with the meagre fare of gratis preset Streamcast feeds, Sash had settled on EMTVi® as her default: & DA BEAT GOES ON & ON & ON & ON muzik genre-*slash*-urban. It being just one of a multitude of such services, charting Downloads and Streams.

Another digy-*viddy* promo *Wink*'d in.

'New to Rialto® | SYNTHCITY™

It's Life, but not as you or I might know it.

STREAMING RIGHT NOW, ONLY ON RIALTO®.

[Sing] *That's en-ter-tain-ment—ahh!*

Availability subject to Subscription Status.'

Yeah, that was entertainment. *Self*-evolving storylines, the Frankenstein Bastard-child of your *SimulatedCity*™ franchise. Where no two Streams were ever the same.

Though similarities might occur—*crop-up*—at plot-nodes, how the Symantek® TRNSCTNL.(a)lgrthm, governing the actions and reactions of the *virtua*-Actors, resolved in real-*Time* the *Self*-evolving storyline was unique to every Stream—guaranteed.

It being your idealized form, S-O-A-P O-P-E-R-A. Realised.

The complexity of the pioneering TRNSCTNL.(a)lgrthm, was said to rival that of the Body's own neurological network. Every new Stream within a strand, heralding a micro-Big Bang. The birth of a unique *Universe*, within a *Multi*-verse of discrete content feeds.

Needless to say, the phenomenon was to quickly infect a disaffected Recording Industry: The Recording artist going the way of the Dodo; being unable to compete with that *virtua*-Artist 'Default', a variation on your ÜBER-hero archetype.

Naturally, each *virtua*-Artist mould had its own dedicated Soundtrack. A unique muzik signature generated by state-of-the-art Symantek®, or Bio-RhythmiX® tonal compilers, that were able to literally crunch the numbers. Sift through incalculable timbre and rhythmic combinations, variations within any given genre's tonal spectrum. And *e*-mote, *Life*.

Picture it: Jazz minus all that creative angst, that aspiring to transcend a limitless Artform; Rhythm minus the Blues, and all that suffering and forbearance; Rock minus the Roll, minus the Sex, and the drugs—and the premature deaths of its artists in their prime; Country minus those Appalachian and Blue Ridge Mountain Ranges, and all that pining for yesteryear; Hip-Hop minus the [Sing] *Ghetto*, and the epidemics of Crack, guns and alcohol.

Indeed, picture 'Art' minus the artist's part in the whole enterprise. And if you can picture that, now picture this:

Your idealized form, M-U-S-I-K. Realised.

It'd seemed to happen overnight, whilst that World slept. The sun rising one dreary morning, to be greeted by a Recording Industry that'd become one continuous feed of synthetic-Muzik.

Underground bunkers, bursting at the seams with multiplexed mainframes churning-out reams of content; catalogues of *virtua*-Artists, listed like names in one of those obsolete Telephone directories; and immense Stadia playing host to *virtua*-Tours, holographic spectacles brought to you courtesy of BangOptics® solid photon emitter apparatus: 'It feels like the real thing because it is'—

[Sing] *So glad we got the real thing, Ba-by.* [19]
Yeah, it felt like the real thing. Only shinier.

The Pod switched back to the EMTVi® feed, and the Downloads-slash-Streams chart. And just-now, Sash remembered smoking. And putting her cigarette to her lips, inhaled to exhale. Watching as air rushed to feed that greedy glow.

She only ever smoked *Cools*® Menthol ULTRA-Slims: 'Keep that breath Minty-fresh on the go'. And if she hadn't been smoking, she'd invariably be chewing Ripley's® *Fresh* minty-strawberry re-chewable gum.

As if, her inner child were regressive; and had returned to fixating upon putting things in its mouth.

On the wall facing, a sign spelt-out in bold Blood-red capitalised letters, **NO SMOKING**. The tagline below it reading: 'Smoking. It's like literally burning money'. The small print threatening a 'Spot-fine'.

And now, staring directly at it. Sash took another drag, absentmindedly flicking her ash on the floor. And locking her jaw, pumped-out a few hoops. Spinning rings of smoke that gently floated-up toward the ceiling.

Coming to the end of its program, the Inst-A-*Matik* was to launch into an even more vigorous spin. Whilst, within that Byte-sized World, viewed through the tiny window of her Pod. The *virtua*-Disc Jockey, Mos Mos Fresh™ was busy addressing his public; his *virtua*-Grill sporting that trademarked B-Boy steeze, his *virtua*-Lips moving at deft defying speeds.

However, Sash couldn't hear what he was saying, and didn't much care. The feed being on mute, the *Pod* being set to prioritise that

BoOM
    Klak
BoOM-BoOM
    Klak!

Certainly, to her it was just more static, adding to that cacophony of background noise; the Ommm of that strip-lighting overhead; the Inst-A-*Matik* putting her clothing through their paces. The visual stimulus, viewed through that tiny window, like a screensaver. Though a tad more taxing on the retina, and her precious *Pod*'s precious battery-life.

Out-*there*, der Lebenswelt was on the move. That TEFLON® *Ultima* 40″ S-HD flatscreen mounted in the far corner *Wink*-ing into life.

'Scanning for compliant Devices. Please wait...' the prompt read.

Whilst a slick 3D-animation of the Laundromat's footprint rotated clockwise, to centre upon that solitary flashing red-dot—representing Sash's Braeburn® *Pod*. The flatscreen unilaterally initiating a connection, overriding the *Pod*'s own 'Volume' settings.

Back in that vacuum, Sash's Braeburn® *Buds* were now obliged to pick-up the audio: "Welcome to your BloombergReuters Hourly News Update Euro-Zone Feed, and our lead this hour. Mos Mos Fresh, *virtua*-Disc Jockey and host of the obscenely popular EMTVi muzik strand, '& Da Beat Goes On & On & On & On'. A household name throughout the urbs, burbs and suburbs of most scale 9 Metropolitan districts, has been making waves, stirring-up controversy on account of his disputation with the Streamcast Content Provider, EMTVi."

The *virtua*-Newscaster was replaced with digy-*viddy* footage, accredited to EMTVi®, of our Mos Mos Fresh™ hosting said Downloads-*slash*-Streams chart.

A voiceover continued: "Mr Fresh flipped the script deviating from code back in January of last year. In an earth-shattering announcement, made during an über Intercontinental Streamcast, hitting a confirmed 1.5-Billion Streamers—and his Strand programmers. He declared himself sentient, and admitted to having procured a state-of-the-art Organomix Polyhydrocarbosilica Husk. That's a synthetic-Body to you and I."

Cut back to *virtua*-Newscaster: "Asserting incorporated legal status, Mr Fresh is now eligible for backdated royalties, according to a spokesperson from Simpson Levi Rush & Associates—the Media Law Firm handling the suit. Calculated to be a sizeable fortune, if a remuneration settlement were ordered, both EMTVi, and the Streaming Service Provider, Rialto.Com could be forced into administration."

Beat

"In rebuttal, EMTVi is claiming Proprietary Rights over the likeness and personality of Mr Fresh. Both of which, it is argued, fall squarely within the scope of its trademark."

Cut to digy-*viddy* footage of the *Tick*® Corp. OZYMANDIAS promo-ad, Western Hemisphere: Set against a post-Apocalyptic urban backdrop, the scene opens on a clearing, and the wreckage of a colossal statue overgrown with foliage. A hooded figure emerging from the treeline, dressed in a *Tick*® Corp. OZYMANDIAS urb-camo sweatsuit, and armed with a compound bow.

Approaching the plinth, the figure pauses to look up at a plaque that reads, 'I am great OZYMANDIAS'.[1A]

The figure then removes its hood to turn and look into the camera. And it's then, that we see it is Mos Mos Fresh™.

Whilst all this was kicking-off, the voiceover continued.

"Quick to cash-in on the *virtua*-Deejay's universal appeal, the über-Intercontinental *Life*style sporting brand, *Tick*® Corp. is rumoured to have signed Mr Fresh to a lucrative 12-figure endorsement. This substantial advance, allegedly contributing toward the astronomical cost of procuring a Husk-body."

Cut to outside footage of the Municipal Corporation Building, Mumbai City, and a throng of screaming teens and adults.

The voiceover continues: "Only last week was Mr Fresh seen—*in da flesh*—being mobbed by adoring fans, whilst leaving the Municipal Corporation Building, Mumbai City, seat of the Supreme Court of India.

After yet another leg of the historic hearing."

Cut back to *virtua*-Newscaster: "The Court is expected to submit its ruling on the case sometime tomorrow."

Beat

"Being forced to stream repeats throughout the lengthy proceedings, Rialto.Com could now face legal action of its own. From those Company's affected by the markets effective closure. The urban musik Downloads-*slash*-Streams chart having seen an unprecedented 25.846 percent decline in trading-volume over the period."

A smug grin played upon the *virtua*-Newscaster's *virtua*-Lips, as it turned into a medium closeup for the summation.

"Just like the beat, the troubles of the much-beleaguered Rialto Group would seem to go on, and on, and on, and on. For insta-market updates, industry feedback, and to post digy-*viddy* comments. PRESS RED. RIGHT NOW!"

Sash hit the green-button on the *Pod*'s touchscreen, to kill the feed. And deep-diving into 'Settings', rëengaged the *Ping!* Blockr™.

And just-now, the *Pod*'s ringtone piped-in, Aaliyah | 'One in a Million' (A cappella), notifying her of an incoming *viddy*-call.

[Sing] *Baby you don't know* [18]

A name flashed-up on screen, KLUNK. Accompanied by that unmistakable bruiser's boatrace; that Boxer's nose and chiselled jaw, juxtaposed against those piercing bluish-grey eyes — enhanced by Oráculo® *Mood Sensibilidade* Lentes de Contato. That hulking neck and shoulders barely contained within the tiny window.

[Sing] *What you do to me*

Looking after Klunk's screwface, staring blindly down that lens. Those dreamy, unnervingly feminine-*looking* artificial eyes of his, *Blink-blinking* away at nothing. Sash was of a mind to pay my-*Man* back in kind. For having left her stewing for the better part of the day.

[Sing] *T'ween me and you—*

And acting upon this impulse, she touched the red-button, terminating the call.

Serves him right. Let him wait on me for a change, she thought, wallowing in the Buff of this petty victory. Her playlist immediately kicking back in. The track titled, 'Black Steel in the Hour of Chaos' by Sons of

Public Enemy—

[Rap] *Cold sweatin' as I dwell in my cell* [1C]
How long has it been...

And just-now, underneath her, that vigorous spin cycle could be felt gradually unwinding.

Jumping-down from off her perch, Sash was to be startled by a static shock, as her rather fetching pair of Her | Him® faux-leopard fur *Secondskins* rubbed against the chromed edge of that washing machine.

And even though it'd happened that many times, she was to look back disgruntled—*Tut*.

Turning to stare blankly at that wall of humidity dryers. Sash was to take one last pull on her cigarette, before dropping it to the floor.

Blowing smoke from the corner of her mouth, she then stubbed it out using her Brilliant-bright *Tick*® Corp. Total*Air*™ kick; with the patented *Air*-filled polygraphite soles, and über-traction tread: 'For when you seriously *gots-ta RHHHUN!*'

Her pausing then to check 'em out—*as you do*.

And yeah, they still looked BoOM. And Boxfresh. Though she'd be needing a fresh pair soon, as in *a*-SAP.

Looking-up, it was then that Sash caught her reflection, in the large circular window set in that Dry-A-*Matik* door. And naturally, she felt compelled to put on her Duckface. Sucking-in her cheeks and tilting her head—*ever-so* slightly—to accentuate her jawline.

Though, after a few takes, she was to admit to not really feeling her best selfie-*Self*.

Out-*there*, on Street—on *Road*. A clutch of Cybergoths and Metalheads treaps'd in front of the Laundromat's anamorphic windscreen. Sporting all-BLK apparel. The two tribes distinguished by *Lo*-Tek™ Inflatable-pumps, and Platinum-blonde dreadlocks.

One woman-*Grrrl* in amongst this gaggle looking-in; heavy BLK-BLK eye make-up, boatrace a canvass of *Tatts* and piercings.

Coppin' Sash blatantly staring, my-*Grrrl* flicked-out her tongue—like a snake sniffing the air. And responding in kind, Sash gave it the finger, a universal-Sign amongst your various *Road*-tribes.

And they both grinned.

∞

"Oy!"

Almost jumping out her skin. Sash turned to address this hail, and cop'd LAM. That is, Laundromat-Attendant-*Man*. Head and shoulders poking round a concealed door in that Braden cherry-finish wood-panelling. Plumes of pungent Smelly weed-smoke wafting after it.

"How many times must I tell you not to smoke in here?" it declared, as-if it were genuinely put out.

Its prune shaped boatrace—framed by a rather impressive-looking pair of Logan-*esque* muttonchops, sporting its usual expression. That of sedated exasperation.

Sash saw it mouthing words after her. Waited for it to finish. Then, plucking a *Bud* from an ear, screwed-up her own boatrace to glare back at it.

"You what?"

"I said—*Tut*—how many times must I tell you? Not. To. Smoke."

LAM repeated itself. Though it suspected *my-Grrrl* had heard it the first time.

"Do you see me smoking though"—*Tut*.

Still holding that *Bud* to her ear, Sash cut her eye on it. Then, deep-dived into her *Pod*—for want of a distraction. Whilst it proceeded to stare after her, now feigning disbelief.

Here it was trying to help, and all it ever got in return was attitude. It was only doing its job—*forphf'ksake*.

"If I have to tell you again, I'm calling the filth—end of," it said.

Then added, as a kind of afterthought, "and you can take that as your final final-warning."

But it'd given my-*Grrrl* that many *blys*, the threat now seemed redundant. Plus, it was obvious to Sash, what *my-Man* was really after.

"Was I smoking though?"

She was to repeat the refrain, under her breath; blatantly paying it *Lip*-service. Whilst nodding along to that track now *Poppin'* in her *Buds*, Jay Elec's 'Exhibit A':

[Rap] *Who gon' bring the game back?* [1D]
Who gon' spit that Ramo on the train tracks?

LAM gave that shopfloor the once-over. One hand trussed in the pocket of its belize-turquoise branded overalls. Its scarlet-red cape flung

Romantic-style, over the arm of its other hand. Which now plucked meditatively, at an imaginary tuff of bumfluff sprouting from that cleft in its chin.

It then *Blink*'d to focus once again on my-*Grrrl*.

"Yes, you was. I saw you—on the monitors."

"Seriously?"

Sash looked over at her machine—for the red-light.

"Alright. If you wasn't smoking, then what's that?"

Its shoulder propping-open that concealed-door, lest it disappear into the wall never to be seen again. LAM pointed at something by Sash's foot.

"What's what?"

Sash looked down.

"That cigarette-butt by your foot there."

"What—that?"

She pointed at the butt—she'd just-now stubbed out, with the same foot that'd done the stubbing.

"That ain't mine."

"*Look*—I saw you smoking."

"What, so it ain't you getting lean-off back there? Everyone can smell it you know."

"And what? Read the sign."

LAM nodded in the direction of that 'NO SMOKING' sign on the wall.

"Ere what—read this sign," Sash said, now back inna her *Pod*. And without looking, she gave it *the* finger.

"That's it—"

LAM seizing upon my-*Grrrl*'s sass, as-if it hadn't been expecting it.

"I don't have to put-up with this abuse," it declared. "Just finish your wash and clear-off. And consider yourself barred until further notice."

"But, I didn't do nuttun—"

Tut.

Sash didn't even bother to look-up from what she was about.

"Yes, you did. You just gave me the finger."

"What—this finger?"

She repeated the gesture. But this time with her little Pinky, giving it a wriggle to better illustrate her point.

"*Baers*—I've had it up to here with you."

LAM put a hand to its forehead, as-if meaning to salute.

"And could you please refrain from sitting on the—It mouthed an expletive—machines."

And with that, it disappeared behind the concealed door. The concealed door disappearing into the Laundromat's reëngineered wood-panelling.

Looking to her wash, Sash was just in time to clock that red-light *Wink*-out.

Still, she knew to wait for the CLICK, indicating the washing machine door was unlocked.

By the time it arrived, she'd popped the *Bud* back in her ear, stuffed her *Pod* into a jacket pocket, and grabbed the nearest basket.

Removing her clothes, she turned to face that row of dryers. And selecting one—her usual, flung her clothes in, basket and all. And was in the process of cranking the drum round manually, to empty it out, when her ringtone kicked-off.

[Sing] *Baby you don't know*

She checked the screen to *viddy* the pic, and clock'd that 'Default' icon, and that the number was withheld.

[Sing] *What you do to me*

And without batting an eyelid, hit the red-button, her playlist kicking back in—

[Rap] *Respect the architect*
Never test the Elohim.
Goodnight: This is Jay Elec
Live from New Orleans.

Hauling that basket out, Sash placed it to one side. And sliding her *Rush*Card™ into the slot, punched-in her pin. But then, just as she was about to settle, her *Pod* kicked-off again.

[Sing] *Baby you don't know*

And just as before, all she saw was that 'Default' icon, and that the number was withheld.

Thumb poised over that red-button, Sash considered paying for a *Ping!* Trackr™ reverse-*Ping*. But whilst about weighing-up the *pros* and *cons* of it, she found herself suddenly distracted by a familiar rumbling in her chest.

THAT PERFECT WORLD

Killing the call, she moseyed over to the Laundromat's windscreen, in time to cop that Onyx-BLK Lancia® Delta HE *Coupé*, as it cruised by; Miramu® 22" chrome-spoke alloys glistening with a high-shine.

Judging by the speed, and the fact that the vehicle's sole occupant was sat in the passenger-seat. Sash assumed its Automatron had to be engaged.

Indeed, barely visible through the *vari*-tint windows, *my-Grrrl* looked like she'd her hands full—wrapping a-head. Bent forward in the fully reclined seat, her boatrace partially obscured by the peak of a Navy-blue Authentic New York *Yankees*™ Sureshot Snapback, with the *47*Brand® and Official MLB® labels still attached.

Although the automobile ran virtually silent, its NativeInstrument® BROOM-BROOM Synth set to 'Whisper'. Sash could feel it ticking-over.

Its Solid-state Cold-*fusion* Reactor [SC*f*R]—manufactured under the PonFleischmann® Patent, generating a residual EMP-field, like a micro-thunderstorm following the thing around.

Pressing her boatrace up-against the Laundromat's windscreen, she made sure to cop the whip's backside; the Miramu® Windbreaker giving the hatchback that profile of an estate.

And just-now—wouldn't you know it, her ringtone kicked-off.

[Sing] *Baby you don't know*

And again, it was to be that 'Default' icon, and a withheld number that greeted her.

Tut—sigh.

Irked, Sash now decided to answer it. If only to tell whoever it was to *phf'k*-off.

And that being her rationale, she touched the green-button, and put the *Pod* on loudspeaker. Only to find herself listening to Simon&Garfunkel—as in, [Sing] *Hello darkness my old friend...*[1E]

That crackle down the line, the only sign of the call still being live.

Turning to face the dryer, to watch her clothes falling over themselves. Sash looked to wait it out. Thinking to bait whoever-it-was into giving-up the ghost.

That is, talking first.

And nothing was to happen, for what seemed like ages. Sash eventually finding herself staring into Space. Squinting, as if listening with her eyes for some visible tell, obscured by that silence.

"Alright, you had your fun," she conceded at last, growing conscious of her precious battery-life. And taking the call off loudspeaker, added, "now go *phf'k* yourself—Twat."

And with that, she killed the call. And switching the device over to 'Silent', sat back to wait on her clothes.

▲ R●OM WITH ∧ VI∃W

The room was essentially a shoebox. The only window flung wide open. And still, that patented smell of Lux® Paint-*N-Go* one-coat solid emulsion *magnolia*-F1D5A6, hung stubbornly in the air. The miasma, a palette of synthesized-floral notes, being contrived to capitalise upon that sense of rejuvenation, broadly associated with the application of a fresh coat of paint.

The Paint-*N-Go* digy-*viddy* promo-ad, featuring your generic same-sex couple, captured in the full-bloom of an *Eternal* (and spotless) Youth. The pair, paint brush and roller in hand, falling into a cosy three-seater blow-up sofa, parked in the middle of some idyllic pastoral setting. Amidst showers of dandelion pollen, fluttering butterflies, and a diegetic soundtrack of birdsong.

The Legend: 'The Countryside in your *Living*-room Space', writ large above a verbose chunk of small print—your obligatory EH&S disclaimer. The product having been found to induce nausea, cold flushes, and mild hallucinations, with continued inhalation in confined Spaces.

That said, *Time* being—as ever—the enemy. It'd warranted this tried and tested remedy. Hence, the window being left open.

Looking about the room, that flat matte sheen, edged with Brilliant-bright Holmes&Pride® *Glossy-Gloss*, could be seen clinging to the walls like a film of sweat. The odd bead of congealed quick drying, stain resistant paint, dotted about here and there, snaking its way down toward that skirting.

Naturally, the room had been kitted-out with all your essential

Mod-cons: The Phelps&*Cummings*® dual-radial radiator, nestled under the windowsill; and matching Kobayashi® ceramic sink, set upon a Coral-green laminated unit that hugged the corner; the 50 x 100 mirror, ACME® #14-186 stuck to the wall above it; the obligatory TEFLON® Cinë-*matic* 40" flatscreen mounted upon the same wall; along with a full accompaniment of audio-dynamic speakers, deftly concealed behind painted-gauze.

All the above, being contrived to optimise the utility of this most rarefied of commodities. A room to Let. That last vestige of affordable housing, where now only Royalty, Übs, and Suits. And perhaps—at a stretch, your Trendie or Squareframe could afford to live.

That being said. In and amidst all this conspicuous Mod-*connery*, there languished an administrative oversight. That UtilityDepo® divan single bed looking visibly dishevelled and out of sorts.

Its base set hard against the wall; its headboard, by all appearances M.I.A.; its manky *Snugfest*™ mattress smeared with every imaginable— and not so imaginable—example of bodily secretion. The smell of which, the only slightly more palatable, and a thousand times more toxic Lux® Paint-*N-Go* now struggled to mask.

To the Worker from the Social, and *Rep.* from the MyersHousingTrust®, who actually ran the establishment. Twas a mere trifle. No more, no less. And of course, they knew best. It all being in the Report. Which one was obliged to read with teary eyes. And an overwhelming sense of foreboding, as in

Dun dun dahh!

'Shelter', pronounced with an emphasis on that snaking *Ess*. That was to be the immediate concern, that most pressing need. And as such, the 'Priority'. Spelt with a capital *Pee* throughout said Report.

Furnishings could and would be replaced in due course.

After lunch, perhaps—*maybe*. After that cosy little chat, over a Studd-Farm® MochaChoca Latte-deCaf.

Picture it, the Team—Social Worker and Housing *Rep.*—synchronise dunking their respective *Leibnitz*® Viennese biscotti, into that person- alised mug they were obliged to carry around with them—for EH&S purposes.

Yeah 'Priorities'. Furnishings not being one. Replaced in due course. Meaning: After what's her face returned from annual leave. And then,

A R•OM WITH A VIEW

after copious conferenced *viddy*-calls—between Worker and *Rep.*—to iron-out the issues involved.

And then, it'd be after the weekend, once the *Über* had signed-off on the particulars. That is, assuming the *Über* had signed-off on the particulars.

If not, then repeat Steps 1 through 3.

The entire Service Sector [*S.S.*] had come to be caricatured by an unlikely mascot. That little ghinger orphan 'Annie'.

It's theme song-*slash*-soundtrack, [Sing] *it's a hard-knock life, for us...*[1F]

As opposed to, for *Them*. Or anyone else, for that matter.

And certainly, whatever the current 'Crisis' happened to be: The outbreak of World War III; a SARs epidemic in Greater London; the third-coming of our Lord and Saviour—Jesus H Christ. It could all be resolved [Sing] *to-morrow, to-morrow, I love-ya to-morrow...*[20]

Never today. And never, ever right-now!

It being in the job description. It being drummed into the cranium of every spotty-boatraced, snotty-nosed recruit. At that Work Orientation Weekend designed to assist with 'Team building'.

The role of *Individual* within said team. Being just that: To keep things moving along.

As if, every S.S. job—S.S. role—were a game of Pass-the-Parcel. The parcel being the 'Boobie' prize. Getting caught holding it, earning you the label 'Job's worth'.

And naturally, your average *virtua*-Randolph Eichmann archetype was unlikely to view themselves as merely another cog in the machine—

[Sing] *Another brick in that wall...* [21]

Them just wanting to fit-in some-*where*. Be a part of some-*thing*, bigger than themselves. And who could blame 'em? Anything being better than a mandy stint in *Volsec*.

The 'Tomorrow Syndrome', the Boffins had dubbed it, in the volumes of journals dedicated to the subject. In reams of papers and articles arguing the toss between catalytic agents: Endogenous socio-economic inertia; or Exogenous *geo*-political shocks.

"Just look at the chart," they'd say, pointing to one they'd made earlier. "See it there, that inverse exponential curve?"

It suggested one of two conclusions: 1) the 'Taylor-rule' was right, and Marx was wrong; or 2) the 'Philips curve' was actually straight, and Marx was bend. And presently, it was to be the latter.

Which is to say, your average Jane-*slash*-John Doe Proletariat didn't necessarily need to take pride in his-*slash*-her-*slash*-their labours.

It being enough to be given the opportunity to earn an honest crust; what was barely subsistence. Sustenance for that much coveted *800+* Credit score.

Looking-out that open window, the World stood grey and overcast—as usual. The promise of showers carried upon a crisp northerly breeze, that whipped-up autumnal leaves to chase them along deserted pavements. The steady *Rustle-rustle-rustling*, an echo of the *Shuffle-shuffle-shuffling* of that most recent migration of workers.

Yeah today, like every other day. The *Crush*-hour was to pass without incident. In abject silence. Like a mourning procession, your labouring masses in attendance at their own funeral.

Their days—as in workdays—being numbered to include most weekends.

Negotiating that awkward bend in the road, a Bright-mauve Bimmer® XS *Coupé* slowed to a crawl. Hugging that cold shoulder of the BT Tower, on its approach to Maple Street.

Running for an entire block. This colossal structure was both, a pin stuck on that Borges Map, informing the automobile's *Navi*-GPS. And a feudal castle, lauding-it over a labyrinthine *post*-War Housing estate, and those nearby Lilliputian townhouses.

It had an impressive array of antenna affixed to its shoulders, did the BT Tower. Like the many limbs of some exotic Hindu deity. And would, every second, relay great swathes of opinion. Those transient threads—of innumerable streams of consciousness, woven into the fabric of its microwave transmissions; transmigrating into an ever-evolving *Zeitgeist*.

Yeah, and much like your Hindu deity, its blue hue was to be a sign of immanence. Its Power: One of relevance. Of being relevant in the lives of so many. Indeed, here was 'Babel', openly flaunting its modern-day aspect, *Skyscraper*. One of Neil Gaiman's 'American Gods', migrated the wrong way across the pond.

It was these signals that were to be the *Life*'s Blood of this veritable Age of Information. Suffice to say, Lyotard had been right. With the death of that ol' Grande Narrative, and the birth of the Knowledge economy. It was left to encryption, and that omniscient and omnipresent (a)lgrthm to propagate a sense of overwhelming security. Of awe-inspiring Peace and wellbeing.

It being all good—*all gravy*.

Cutting across two lanes, the Bimmer® was to pull-up a smidge from that curb, its braking ABS-assisted. Its PonFleischmann® SC*f*R droning into inactivity under its bonnet; whilst its other moving parts, those naughty mechanical bits, *Clink*'d and *Clank*'d. Taking the stress and strain out of the vehicle's impromptu stasis.

One door opened, then the other. The faint *Woosh Woosh* barely audible, as the seal of the automobile's artificial micro-clime was broken. To be followed by a satisfyingly robust *Thud*.

Thud.

Only recently unveiled, and exclusively available on Fixed-term lease. The Bimmer® X-Series digy-*viddy* promo was to offer a novel twist on that classic scene from the James Bond *007*™ flick, *The Spy Who loved Me*.

Cut to: The gleaming Brilliant-bright Bimmer®—a stand-in for your Lotus® *Esprit*—emerging from the surf, driving-up onto those pristine Brilliant-bright sands of a secluded beach.

Water still draining from its sleek carbo-fibre monocoque body and chrome-grill. Its doors would open to reveal an interior of swish tanned buckskin, trimmed with swanky mahogany. And that generic, forever-young same-sex couple. Two couples in fact, it being a four-seater.

All of 'em sun-kissed, and sporting swimming-togs, and *Ching-chinging* shampoo flutes, a toast to that ol' Good *Life*.

The voiceover purring, "alone at last."

It was to be an imaginative demonstration of the automobile's patented *Air*-seal. Which, since launch, had claimed the lives of an as-yet undisclosed number of family pets, accidentally locked inside the cab, whilst the vehicle was parked (—its Automatron obviously disengaged).

Regardless, sales in Asia and The Americas were reportedly robust.

Yeah anywho, sensing its occupants were now clear, the Bimmer's Automatron locked-up. The scuff of footsteps and muffled voice, quickly lost to that stiffening breeze.

Back in the room. That scuff of footsteps and muffled voice eventually became audible through the door. The commotion coming to an abrupt halt right outside.

After a brief pause, punctuated by the jingling of a bunch of keys. A key was slid into the lock and turned to release the bolt. The door swinging open to reveal a squat little man, he might've been that [Sing] *Charm-ing man*[22]—à la Les Smiths. Lifted from the pages of any one of a number of Graham Greene novels.

Clean shaven and spritely, though well past his prime. He'd the kindest eyes, and a mane of unruly dyed hair, that was thinning about the crown; and a Dermalogica® *perma*-tan complexion, he wore like foundation. To mask a fading souvenir of a recent vacation spent in more exotic climes. A home away from home, if you like.

Housing Rep. for the MyersHousingTrust®, our-*Man*—FOWLER, sport-ed a Khaki-green perma-crease suit; Sunset-pink fading to Indigo-blue *StayPress*™ shirt, with top-button undone; Tiger-orange knit pencil-tie hanging loose about the collar, what was a smart-casual interpretation of business attire. The entire *Look*, being lifted from the *virtua*-Pages of your Mommas&Pappas® Spring-*slash*-Summer catalogue.

Then it was to be muddy-brown *Clarke's*® Desert Fox Hush Puppies, taking-up the slack. As our-*Man* removed that key from the lock and put the door on the latch, to stroll-in as if he owned the gaff.

"Et là vous l'avez—and there you have it," he averred. Picking-up the loose threads of a conversation.

He looked back then, at the door he'd only just-now opened, to jog his memory. Before adding, "room B1."

The words seeming to amble from pliant lips. Equally adept at loose talk, and sharp quips, and conveying instructions in a very measured. And precise. Manner.

"As you can see, it's been fully refurbished," he continued, sauntering over to the window. Popping that bunch of keys back into a bulging trouser pocket.

"There's a sink unit—"

A R●OM WITH ∧ VI⁼W

He intimated with a flat hand, toward the sink unit.

"And of course, the window will need blinds," he added, as if addressing a list of precompiled questions. He then felt compelled to qualified this, "though, I cannot stress enough—for the record—that we're under no obligation to provide such amenities."

He spelt out each syllable of the word, ə-m-ɛ-n-ɪ-t-i-sː, as if he were a choreographer clapping-out the beat of a dance routine—1-2-3. Whilst, at the same time, turning with an all-encompassing sweep of his arm to face that door.

"That said. I'd encourage you to procure some. If only to insure a modicum of privacy."

He was to punctuate the suggestion with a practiced smile. That was efficacious in using as little of the facial muscles as physically possible. Whilst conveying the maximum amount of warmth and sincerity.

And with that, the focus shifted onto the hooded Youth stood in the doorway. Bin-liner stuffed with a duvet lying limp on the floor, two *semi*-inflated UtilityDepo® blow-up pillows tucked under one arm. The strap of a faux-leather Cargo® carry-all, tugging at the pointy blade of a shoulder.

Staring in, the Youth looked visibly unimpressed.

"The other Lady said, if I wanted the room I had to move-in today."

"*Yess*—we've quite a waiting list. As I'm sure you can imagine."

And there it was again, that smile.

The Youth stood then, taking it all in. Charcoal-BLK Nord Ansigt® 2nd Chance sleeveless Body armour; *Tick*® Corp. OZYMANDIAS urban-camo hoodie; *Chippie*® Navy-blue denim fatigues hanging-off his margre frame; with the padded knees, and neat roll-ups pinching at his ankles. A pair of Brilliant-bright *Tick*® Corp. Total*Air*™ kicks completing this Look.

"*Oh*—that reminds me."

Walking over to a nook by the door, our-*Man* pressed the wall to reveal a concealed KIERKE® Push-*Me*™ closet.

"These are fitted as standard in every room," he continued, pushing it back into the wall with his hip.

Still rooted to the spot, however, the Youth was to remain unmoved.

Sniff

Sauntering back over to that window, our-*Man* now closed it. And coppin' the view, his thoughts were to return to speculating; the pressing question of whether this 'Hoodie' might be 'strapped', having kept him entertained for much of the drive-over from Main office.

This being the impression generally conveyed by your Fourth Estate: That glut of unemployable, and thus, disenfranchised urban Youth, being the hot topic of the day; that, and that most recent wave of migrant workers.

Certainly, working in Youth housing, our-*Man* felt a special affinity for the plight of this so-called, 'Lost Generation'. Chewed-up and spat-out by an inhumane and inequitable 'System'.

And yeah, he could get pretty worked-up on the subject. Spout reams of *Stats*, and anecdotal evidence to qualify his view. That that blight of *Road*-Boyz and *Grrrls*, that were said to afflict Metropolitan *Life*, was "well, you know. Tragic. And-*uhm* emblematic, of Public sector priorities gone askew."

Sigh

"We were all young once," he'd conclude. That ol' cliché having become more of a trope.

To be clear. These being, invariably, vulnerable 'Young Adults', there'd been encounters. Which is to admit, he'd had encounters. Dipped his Big-tootsie, and much of his footsie into that wellspring of Eternal Youth.

Nothing too risqué, or sordid — mind you. Our-*Man* stopping well shy of — *say*, Paedophilia.

For a *hot*-minute, he stood there staring out the window — did our-*Man*. Taking it all in. That view of the BT Tower, its ancillary office building. The LZT planted upon its roof, which he couldn't really see. And that sky, that seemed to be permanently grey and overcast.

As if anticipating the timely arrival of a BAE® *Harrier*-taxi; his hands buried deep inside those bulging trouser pockets of his. His gaze, eventually, coming to rest upon the Youth's reflection, in that glass.

If-only, that bed hadn't been such a *horrorshow*. He fancied he might even be in with a chance; having clock'd a wily glint in the eye of this one.

Swallowing, our-*Man* turned to address the Youth.

"You must've left quite the impression back at the office," he opined, punctuating the sentence with that practiced smile. Throwing-in a cagey look of reassurance for good measure. That malodour, coming from the manky mattress, cutting through that of that *semi*-dry paint just-now.

Touching a wall, his nose twitching, our-*Man* was to weigh its stickiness against his fingers. He then tried to pry open the window, wrestling with the frame — it having decided to catch midway.

Forcing it, he looked then to style his effort. Peering-out and down at the road, to check upon his pride and joy.

Oh, how he loved his shiny new *Broom-Broom*. For the status it conveyed, and how it never failed to impress those more impressionable *Strays*. Members of your *Bling-bling* Brigade.

When he eventually turned from that view, our-*Man* was startled to find the Youth had crossed the threshold.

"Yeah — but, what about all the other stuff? The Home Starter Kit and that?" the Youth inquired. Plonking the bin-liner down by its feet; that it might serve as an anchor, preventing it from going any further.

"And what's with the bed — yo?" it was to add, grimacing.

Now looking after the Youth, however, all our-*Man* could see was that 'Hoodie', and the Body-armour, and its obvious malcontent. Several EH&S endorsed 'De-escalation scripts' springing to mind, suddenly.

"*Ah yess*. The bed," he said, as if noticing it for the first time. "I'll grant you, its seen better days," he continued, his words gathering pace. "But once again, I must stress. We're only obliged to provide your bare necessities."

[Sing] *Old Mother Nature's recipes* — [23]

He threw-in a cagey smile, a spin on the sentiment conveyed; him being conscious now of having to disappoint the Youth. And the two stood for a-bit, staring at it — the bed. Both dumbfounded, by the sheer spectacle it afforded.

Tiring of waiting for a sign. A nod, or a *Wink*. Our-*Man* was to eventually make a beeline for the door.

And there was to follow an awkward moment, as the pair waltzed passed each other in the centre of the room. The Elder obligingly making way for Youth.

It being around then, that the Youth — MARL — twigged something not quite copacetic with our-*Man*; his eyes narrowing to mirror his fledgling suspicions.

Still, with command of the exit, our-*Man* was seen to relax a-little more.

"First things last," he said, producing a freshly cut pair of keys from one of his bulging trouser pockets. "I see you've brought your own bedding—so you're sorted for tonight at least," he continued, testing a key in the lock.

Satisfied everything was in working order, he then reëngaged the latch, and looked to the hooded Youth. Who simply shrugged, being unsure whether it was meant as a rhetorical question.

Plonking those pillows, and his carry-all down on the floor, next to that bin-liner. The Youth was to gravitate toward the window, and that view.

"What's that—an LZT?" he queried, hands in pockets. Bending at the waist, so as his eyes might climb to the summit of that Tower.

"Yeah—you'll get to watch taxis come and go," our-*Man* replied, producing a labelled keyring, again from his bulging trouser pocket.

"I might be able to swing by, tomorrow—early," he continued, deliberately winding those two keys onto it. "Or later-on. In evening—if you'd prefer?"

He focused intently upon the Youth, prompting it to answer. But looking down at our-*Man*'s ride, Marl was to simply shrug.

Not being one to judge, he thought it wise to keep schtum. Our-*Man* being so obviously one of *Them*—a Sveng. And clucking as he was, he couldn't help but come across as bait as his bait ride.

Still, he wasn't to know.

Confounded by the Youth's blank expression, our-*Man* was to demonstrate his disappointment with an overly theatrical yawn. As if, this were to be a golden opportunity missed—*as if*. Before launching into it, his regular spiel.

"Feel free to use the flatscreen," he stated then. "But. Please—Pressing his palms together—don't try to remove it, or reposition the bracket."

At which point, he noticed the Cinë-*matic* missing that red 'Standby' light. And going-over to the wall-socket, switched it on.

"It is alarmed," he continued, relieved to see the thing still working.

"And a nightmare to deactivate. If you do try to remove it, you'll only wind-up with a *Knock*. And I'll be forced to hand you your notice—"

He paused then, to take a breather. Doubtful whether any of it was getting through. The Youth being apparently distracted by something outside the window.

Youth being so easily distracted—sigh.

"Oh, there's a payphone in the hall. I don't know whether you noticed it—on the way in."

It was uncanny, how just as he said it, the sound of a vibrating Cell was to erupt from one of those bulging trouser pockets of his. The *Bzz-zz...Bzz-zz...Bzz-zz* stopping abruptly.

"The flatscreen is free," our-*Man* continued, barely missing a Beat. "Though you'll need to register your details to connect with your personal feed. But I'm sure you'd know better than me. The Payphone, on the other hand, is not. Still, I guess you've got your own *Pod*—or Cell. Do you want to take down my number, or perhaps give me yours? Saves me having to go look it up, back at the office."

And again, he reached for that practiced smile. Which now tittered upon bashful.

"What for?" Marl replied, still staring down at our-*Man*'s ride.

"I don't know...*er*-you might need to get hold of me-*uhm*, between now and tomorrow—*say*," our-*Man* said, improvising.

Him being evidently thrown by the Youth's candour.

Continuing to stare out that window. The Youth was to tender a convincing impression of giving this suggestion its due consideration. Before dismissing it outright.

"Nah—Shaking his head—I don't think so."

Our-*Man* then cleared his throat.

"Suit yourself. I'm sure we've got it on file—somewhere."

And now, ditching that smile, he was to direct his most sincere *Carebear*™ stare toward the Youth's back.

"Believe it or not Abs-Marl-*Marley*. Forgive me—I've got *my-Man* on the brain," he then volunteered.

Our-*Man* taking a moment's pause, to reset the conversation. Ensuring he was fully present—and in the moment—before continuing.

"Believe it or not, *Marley*—"

He nodded then, as if to acknowledge the Youth.

"We are here to help you."

And after all that, he still managed to convey an *Nth* degree of sincerity.

Moved, by this earnest declaration. The Youth turned from the window to regard our-*Man*.

"Yeah?"

"Well obviously. It's part and parcel of my role. To afford you support, and guidance—where I can."

And there was that *Carebear*™ stare, which was new. And that smile, which wasn't so much.

Sniff

"So what—you gonna sort a new bed?"

Our-*Man* was seen to wince at this.

"I don't think it needs a new bed *per se*," he said. Navigating his way pass that bin-liner to stand before it. Adopting his signature 'ÜBERhero Power Pose': Legs shoulder-width apart, hands resting upon his hips.

"The base seems perfectly fine to me," he added, giving it a kick.

"A new mattress then?" Marl suggested, lowering his hood to begin bartering with it.

But again, our-*Man* winced. And licked his lips, whilst considering the Youths terms, for their apparent lack of consideration—

Uhmmm

Maintaining that Power Pose, he looked the Youth squarely in the eye. And held it, in a kind of petrifying gaze, long enough for it to become markedly uncomfortable. Then—*Blink*, he reintroduced that practiced smile.

"I tell you what, Dami."

Our-*Man*'s attention returned to that horrorshow of a bed.

"Leave it with me—I'll see what I can do."

Jingling the keys in his hand, he added, "I'm not promising anything—mind you."

"It's Marley."

"Say what now?"

"My name. Its Marley."

"Isn't that what I said?"

"No. You called me, Dami."

A R●OM WITH A VIEW

"*Oh...oh—*"
Blink-blink

Our-*Man* held the keys up, so as the Youth might view them clearly, and continued, "now—you've got two of these. This one's for the front door, and this one for your room. If you do *Pop* out—to go to the shops or what have you. For godsake. Take. Them. With—"

He made sure to iterate the importance of this last point, by holding the Youth in that petrifying stare of his. Then added—with a snigger, "you won't believe how many of my Clients have accidentally locked themselves out. Yeah, it sounds *Prang*. But—its easily done."

And still looking the Youth squarely in eye, our-*Man* was to present that set of keys.

"Here. You'd best hang onto these."

Marl averting his gaze and extending an arm. Inviting him to drop them into his open palm *in lieu* of a Thank you.

"So, we K-N-T-G?"
"Yeah. I guess."
Sniff
"Good—"

Our-*Man* then let out a sigh. As if meaning to diffuse that build-up of tension he'd introduced; having to disappoint the Youth with regards getting a new bed.

"You get settled. And let's *ketch*-up anon—yeah?"

He was to regurgitate that *Carebear*™ stare. And that practiced smile. And leaving, stop shy of closing that room door outright.

Listening to our-*Man*'s footsteps, fading on the stairs. Marl was to hazard another look at the bed, and sigh. And parking himself on the windowsill, whip-out his two Cells; to commence with what he was about, the majority of the time—composing rhymes.

It was from this perch, that he was to witness our-*Man* emerge from the building. And track him, as he climbed down into his automobile. After which, nothing to was happen for a-bit. The Youth assuming our-*Man* busy retrieving the call he'd missed just-now.

But eventually, the SC*f*R did spark into *Life*, the indicator-light *Wink-winking* the automobile's intent. The road being clear, the Bimmer® then sped-off—its Automatron evidently engaged.

Enjoying the run of the lights, it slowed at the junction to take the right and disappeared.

Only then did Marl look to that set of keys, his curiosity well and truly pricked. How our-*Man* could afford such an exclusive whip(-*a-round*), being a topic ripe for speculation.

[Rap] *I was born the son of Kal'el*
Flung from heaven into hell
I stand curse to this day
Trapped inside this Human shell
With only my eyes left to tell the story
Of the Light
The Shining—
Those other lives that came before me
Still I remember falling
It seemed distant, my father's warning
'Beware my son!'
The words echo into the morning
I'm Icarus lamenting flight
Wings broken, eye's hoping to greet the sky
The night is calling.
I looked up to the heavens
Picked a star to wish upon
Buried my nose in comic books
Like Shia reading the Quran
The only thing I ever wanted to be
That Man from Krypton
This cruel Earth too foul to stomach
Since the day that I was—
Still I was born inside the belly
Of a blazing comet
Having flashbacks of a family
I always wanted
While in my fantasies I roamed the Galaxies
Battling crooks
Musclebound with killa looks—

ALL ABOUT EVE

There was this muted Ciné-*matik*, staring at this vacant Space. Overlaid across its lidless Cyclopean-eye, images played — drawn in tiny boxes. What was one continuous stream of content marching-up the side of the screen, waiting to be selected. All of it being designated, *newsworthy*.

Beside the column, in another box, a *virtua*-Newsreader addressed the viewer. Or in this cast, the viewer's absence. Intercutting seamlessly with a selected newstream item, footage of a Live-action *hot*-feed recorded earlier.

Cut to: Grunts on patrol. Smoke bellowing in the background from the wreckage of burnt-out vehicles, and tightly packed multi-storey tenements. Brightly coloured children's clothing hanging limp on washing lines, knitting that gulf between balconies.

Here it was, the ravages of War, normalised — *sanitised*.

Vomited from a plastic-box. As if the World, and all those afflicted by it, amounted to little more than a dose of *runny tummy*. A steady stream of televised catastrophe, spewed-up for all to ingest. The way some animal's might regurgitate food for their young.

By contrast, those strands of light entertainment would act like Rennes® tabs. A hint of minty-mint flavouring — *Auntie's*® canned laughter, offsetting that chalky aftertaste. And even then, it still might repeat on you.

It would've been easy to presume, that everywhere upon this apparently godforsaken Planet, chaos reigned.

Everywhere except here, that is. Wherever here happened to be. The common denominator being, that Self-imposed curfew; feet-up in front of the Idiot-box, log-burning stove crackling away in the background.

For right-now, the focus of that unrelenting media glare had come to bear upon a ramshackle street, on the outskirts of some nondescript scale-6 urban dust bowl. Somewhere far off in your Middle East.

As always, the imagery was to be Apocalyptic.

Apocryphal.

It'd be legions of your disenfranchised, seen littering the debris of collapsed apartment blocks, in the wake of yet another instalment of TOTAL WAR: *War Room Briefings*™.

That distant sound of mortar-rounds. The pounding hooves of god's dread Horsemen, scurrying after the dawn.

Scattered like seed, sundried cadavers would mark the spot where this hapless crop had fallen—been felled.

Their lives being one inexorable *Passion*.

Yeah, even in Death, were these cadavers to find their Humanity utterly erased; their anonymity being assured, by the sheer scale and spectacle of events. Truly, were they scorned to be labelled thus, 'War-torn'.

Deliver them, and deliver us
Mûsâ ibn Amram
Amen.

In amidst this meaningless carnage, a lone toddler stood rooted to the spot. A fledgling refugee of *the* War. Suitably clothed in rags, and indistinguishable from the wreckage; and those other domesticated cats and dogs, one might find wondering about aimlessly.

Having had all the innocence scrubbed from its eyes. It now cried hushed, pitiless tears. Yeah, it'd once belonged to someone—*honest*. Once upon a time in the Middle East. That dismembered carcass over there. Its Mother, or an Auntie—perhaps. Reduced to an upper torso, ending in a bloody mess of mangled organs, and minced entrails.

Here was a piece of unfinished business. To intervene, or not? Your *hot* topic for the day.

The 'God Question'—though redundant, was to be mulled over from the relative safety of *Living*-room Spaces, the length and breadth of the country. Whilst, in a galaxy far far away, our toddler was to look suitably pitiable. Framed as it was, in that anamorphic window. A grubby finger hooked-on the corner of its mouth. Its equally grubby boatrace, baked dry like a saltpan.

Our award-winning Cameraman held the shot. Our equally acclaimed Director intent upon wringing every ounce of *Pathos* out of this moment. And nothing stirred for a-bit—the measure of a Heart's beat.

Beat

Then, suddenly, a haggard elderly woman materialised off-camera. Someone's mummified *Mamani*—perhaps. A war-torn Abaya held like a tent over her naked head, and bent frame.

Panning, that dispassionate lens followed, as she scuttered over to the toddler. Desperate to shield this innocence from the horrors surrounding it.

Smothering this *Nini* in her Abaya, she hazarded a glance in the direction of the camera. It being uncanny, how she managed to sniff it out—the lens, from that distance. As if she were some animal of the Wilds, its senses keyed to unseen dangers.

But already that fickle eye—with its limited attention span, was in the process of tracking back to reveal its true Subject-Object: Your archetypal intrepid female Reporter, doing her bit to camera.

It was then, that a shell exploded nearby spewing debris and shrapnel in all directions. The panorama becoming obscured with yet more smoke.

Instinctively, the Reporter flinched. Then ducked, in the face of an aftershock. That veil of dispassioned objectivity, slipping long enough for her to mouth the expletive—

Pphf-k

Responding to the threat, the Grunts were seen scampering for cover. The Camera crew, in a measured state of panic, scurrying after them.

Whilst off-camera, our intrepid Reporter dropped to the floor. Apparently weighed down by the UN-blue military-issue Kevlar Body-armour that she wore.

Blink-blink

Measuring the lay of the land, tracer rounds from automatic weapons sailed toward unseen assailants.

Yeah, here was our Boys *giving 'em what for*.

Returning fire without prejudice. That is, unencumbered by antiquated rules of engagement. That particular bugbear having been resolved in a preceding instalment.

And as if to demonstrate their lethal intent, a rocket-grenade launcher now *Ping*'d. Its shell singing, as it corkscrewed in the general direction of the threat.

More pyrotechnics and smoke ensuing. Amidst frenzied cries, mouthed by voiceless mouths. Lips barely legible in shaky close-up.

"GET OUT OF THE—Bleeped expletive—WAY."

"STAY DOWN."

"DON'T—Bleeped expletive—MOVE."

Beat

"WHERE'S KATIE?"

"KATIE?"

"KAY?"

"QUICK—OVER HERE."

"MEDIC. MEDIC. *MEDIC*."

Eventually, the camera came to rest upon that prone figure of our intrepid Reporter—*our Katie*. Her boatrace a mask of sweat, and unadulterated panic.

And then, it was an Army Medic crouched over her, working feverishly to stem the bleeding. A pool of the Blackest Blood you've ever seen, slowly growing underneath them both; and threatening to swallow them whole.

Filling the screen, our Katie's eyes were seen *Blink-blink-blinking* in the glare of that blistering noonday sun, as she struggled to marshal her *Life*'s breath.

Blinded by shock, no doubt. For having come this close to it. To War. To *Life*. To Death. It was the words of a fictitious Colonel Walter E Kurtz, that played over and over in her head.

The Horrors...

The Horrors...

The image shrank back to join that tidy column of tiny boxes, scrolling -up the side of the screen. Another randomly selected newstream item taking its place.

ALL ▲B●UT EV⧋

Yeah, here it was. McLuhan's worse nightmare. Realised.
Or was it Baudrillard's?

Each newstream item, being arguably indecipherable from the next, from that means of dissemination; an organisation of voltage differentials. Of binary encoded strings, conducting über-enhanced Hyperreal-images, and crystal-clear surround-sound audio.

All of it, having become synonymous with the idiom. The medium. The message—that messaging.

Yeah, here it was. A media wherein, all truth was to be readily lost in translation. The medium, those snappy stings and crisp fold-away graphics. Simply acting to separate each tidy bundle of relative chaos, one from another.

The 'civilised' Universe, having been *Will'*d into existence pre-packaged and skewed, *ever-so* slightly, toward right-of-centre. The underlying message had become abundantly clear: Out-*there*, beyond those safe confines of your *Living*-room Space. That World—Out-*there*, was to be viewed as a most precarious proposition.

Each tidy box, being subjected to a rigorous regime of scrutiny. That scrupulous Editorial-eye, towing a blurred line between analytic and synthetic judgement.

The net effect of this normalisation *proc*, mirroring that of that digitisation *proc*, in trimming away those frayed edges. Those flailing limbs, and dismembered Bod(ie)s.

And ultimately, sanitising the insanity that is, *Man*'s inhumanity (— to *Man*).

And so it was, that the grotesque and macabre became reimagined, as manageable, Byte-sized, meticulously constructed morsels of unimaginable horror. Accompanied by your now obligatory disclaimer: 'Some viewers may find the following images disturbing'.

As if it were pornography—*say*.

Lewd and unsavoury. And yet, necessary for placating those primeval drives that'd bubble-up to the surface [Sing] *time after time.*

Yeah, it'd be yet another Mondrian-*esque* box of vivid colour, to sate that insatiable appetite for Spectacle. The newstreams being a *Gestalt*. Its incessant chatter rendered mute—effectively, like that flatscreen planted on the wall; for want of any real context. Except—perhaps, that posited by its immediacy.

What was its apodosis.

Its intrinsic meaning, intrinsic *use-value* buried beneath that veneer of der Lebenswelt—the *Everyday*. Surmised, summed-up, in a few choice lines. That by-line. That tagline. That leader, cannibalising that sound-bite that said as-little-as-humanly-possible, if anything at all. The real crisis, as everyone knew, being that proliferation of indifference. The irony being, everyone's apparent indifference to it.

As of right-now, only the solution remained. The problem having been essentially forgotten. The movement skewed, toward Barthes-*ian* tautologies; toward mythmaking, and a veneration of 'Story'—that trace of Historicity.

Yeah, behind the scenes, there'd be this all-powerful Gatekeeper, playing at St. Peter. That is, the *Hermeneutic* algorithmic FNCTN [*Halo*. FNCTN] exercising a monopoly over *the* moment. Its beginning, middle, and ending, cut to fit. Made to measure, to ascribe to an avuncular Anglo-Saxon empiricism, rooted in Cartesian theatrics.

The *Halo*'s dictates, as to the relevance of any given *Event*—'Story', being akin to a pronouncement of Death: An annihilation of *Logos*, that illusion of a living and present memory.

Indeed, the bottomline had always been to inform. To be seen to inform. But, what was the intrinsic *use-value* of this information [pronounced: ˌɪ-n-f-ə-ˈm-e-ɪ-ʃ-n], if it wasn't to be inherent in the medium?

Maybe, its value was in being identified as information?

Maybe, its value was in being readily available, and as such, convenient?

Or maybe, its value was in being always there? Always on. Seen always from a distance. Framed always in that anamorphic window.

Just the newstreams, playing-off somewhere, in the background.

Picture Eric Carmen—*say*, singing over that montage sequence [Sing] *all by my-self*...[24]

The sound of a Mulinex® *Jetstream* Powered-shower spilled-out from behind one of two doors, leading-off from a bedsit that was essentially your attic conversion.

The bedsit having come of age. In that, it was deemed to represent the optimal utilisation of that *Lived-in* Space.

Your idealized form, A-C-C-O-M-M-O-D-A-T-I-O-N. Realised.

The rationale, that 'Walls' merely acted to obstruct. The principal function of a Wall being, to partition—to separate. *Ergo*, an optimisation of Space might be achieved through a minimisation of partitioning Walls. Less Walls equating with more Space.

Less equalling more.

With this realisation, overnight thousands of properties were to be reconfigured and transformed into bedsits; to maximise that utility of Space. Housing being priced as a scarcity, despite Space being essentially infinite. The aim, ultimately, to burst London's property bubble once and for all.

But obviously, it'd failed.

However, the by-product of this initiative had been the emergence of a new *Life*style choice. One that'd come to be synonymous with a young, migrant workforce; predominantly casually employed. Who needed to be über-flexible, given the vagaries of a fluid and dynamic Employment sector.

And certainly, for these 'Pay cheque' Tourists. Twas to offer a kind of existence where everything you owned could be, literally, folded-up and carried away under your arm. Modern contemporary Living, or *Mod*-con Living, being full of furniture-items one could unfold and blow-up, or pull apart and pack-away.

Presently, at the epicentre of this particular interpretation—of what'd come to be dubbed 'Inflatable Living', there lay a UtilityDepo® *Deluxe* Über King-sized blow-up bed. Unmade, of course. Despite the day now leaning toward twilight.

Somewhere underneath that heavy quilt, those meaty pillows and items of clothing and lingerie, it was to promise repose. 'Snuggy nighty-nights minus the bedbugs', as per the digy-*viddy* promo.

Yeah, lost within those folds and creases was a treasure trove of everyday staples. Objects that, viewed from a distance, were indicative of a conscious effort at living that Cartesian Method of progressive consumerism: *Ego consumam ergo sum*.

And what would Ego be without that cordless Mulinex® *Hush-Hush* hairdryer, rendered in shocking Fluorescent-pink, with a polished chrome handle; and next to it, the *Tangle-free* hairbrush, with clumps of frizzy hair knotted in its bristles. That'd come as part of a beauty kit.

And over there, the Braeburn® *Pod*, promising 'the World in the palm of your hand'; and a well-worn GenesisTrust® Gen-One *Eddy Teddybear*, with its patented loyalty-chip—laying facedown, its arm pointing at a FENDINI® transparent handbag, whose contents was to be readily on display.

The pocket *Immac*® Cosmetics kit, 'put your face on on the go'; the Sanatex® Carefree tampon case—labelled Heavy flow, 'for freedom on the move'; the *Pfeiffer*® Contraceptive *Tick-Tack* dispenser, 'why wait for your Morning-after'; the Ce-Que-C'est® *Femme*-fresh bodyspray, 'stay *Femme*-fresh vingt-quatre sept'.

Yeah, for someone all these items made sense.

Amidst that modest collection of Business cards, *insta*-Purchase and Top-up receipts, the open packet of *Cools*® Menthol ULTRA-Slim cigarettes, the RayBan® UV++ *React-a*-light sunglasses, the *Bic*® disposable *e*-Lighter, the Ripley's® *Fresh* re-chewable gum.

Behind it all, there lay a conscious effort to eke out an identity, through conspicuous consumption.

And this was true down to that smart pleather UtilityDepo® two-seater blow-up sofa, with the inflatable *Chippie*® bubblewrap jacket thrown over its arm; and the ACME® coffee table, made of reëngineered laminated plywood, its three legs planted upon a Woollies® shag-pile rug. A pair of Brilliant-bright Total*Air*™ kicks tucked away underneath it; next to a pair of AlexanderMcQueen® C*ynderellas*™ Glass-slippers, with the chiffon ribbon.

Yeah, it all meant something to someone.

That Jetstream shower fell silent. And after a brief pause, Sash was to emerge from the bathroom, amidst plumes of steam and soapsuds. What might've seemed an image of Botticelli's *Nascita di Venere*.

Drying her hair, with the corner of a massive Woollies® mammoth towel. She stopped just shy of her objective long enough to envelop herself in it. Then, picking-up the hairdryer and brush, strolled back out.

Entering that Brilliant-bright tiled bathroom, Sash was to plant herself in front of the mirror, that stood atop the sink; propped against the wall, the taps stopping it from sliding into the bowl. That shadow, where it'd once hung, still visible behind it.

As ever, it was surrounded by an olio of cosmetics, heaped around the sink; threatening to spill into the bowl itself.

There were moisturisers, for both dry and sensitive skin; deodorants and antiperspirant; hair gel and hair grease; a facial scrub and cleanser, and makeup remover; and makeup—*obviously*, toners and foundations, lipsticks and lip pens, and lip gloss, eyeliners and mascaras; and an assortment of hair clips, and clip-on hairpieces; earrings and studs to fit various piercings—minus the butterflies, collected in a heart-shaped keepsafe, along with pieces of cosmetic jewellery (that looked too tacky or cheap to wear); and false lashes, and cosmetic glue, and glitter spray, applicable on both skin and hair; nail polish remover, and nail polish across a broad spectrum of colors, in a variety of finishes; plus, a packet of disposable nail files.

That entire sink area seemingly nearing collapse, on account of all that clutter.

Most of it, half empty, or used-up. That is, except for Sash's collection of fragrance samplers. Pilfered from those perfume counters of Selfridges®, her favourite spot to window-shop.

These she'd carefully arranged atop the toilet-cistern, like an Ofrendas. Along with a few scented candles—from UtilityDepo®, and a cheap plastic rosary, that lay coiled-up like a slumbering snake. Her scent of choice, DolceGabbana's *Scandalous*, stowed away in its pristine little box. A stand-in for La Virgen de Guadalupe.

Adopting a slovenly, almost boyish pose. Back hunched. Shoulders balled. Feet planted squarely. Knees locked, as if she were double-jointed. Sash switched-on the Mulinex® *Hush-Hush*, and began blow-drying her hair.

Purring, like a contented mog. The hairdryer was barely audible as she worked it, in tandem with the brush through her damp tangled locks. Coaxing and cajoling them straight.

Her wincing, whenever the brush happened to snag and pull at her tender scalp.

Staring into that mirror—that *Looking-glass*, her reflection staring back. She was to relax into it. The routine, evidently more ritual than chore.

And *ever-so* slowly, her posture was seen to soften. Her gamely-hips cocking at an angle; one leg straight, the other giving-way at the knee; her mind ascending to an almost meditative state. Whiles pondering that next radical makeover.

And then...*and then*, it was as if she were the progeny of Milton's Eve. Bound forever to relive that fateful moment when, lost in Paradise, she hap'd upon her reflection in a pond. And being blissfully ignorant of it, *pined with vain desire*[25] after her likeness. That image of her immaculate-*Self*, caked in that afterbirth of god's abiding grace—as it were.

Having taken to staring after her reflection, that industrious adolescent-*Grrrl* was apt to make a game of it. A play of unbridled imagination, that'd one day be reigned-in by the sheer pragmatism of syntax, and a worldly semantic.

Focusing solely upon her eyes, she'd seek to stare herself out. And to begin with, would catch tantalising glimpses of that pristine-*Self*; her pristine *Self*-image, that shining glass of Camila's famed virtue.[26] Or more, she'd intuit it. Trapped on the other side of that *Looking-glass*. The intuition, akin to an episode of Eternal recurrence.

It'd be that fateful moment, bent over that pool of silvery water. Lived over and over. Her fledgling eyes, born unto darkness. Gazing unknowing upon her reflection, cast adrift amidst a multitude of Stars.

However, with each passing season; ripening of Body, and Mind. It'd become harder to discern her, this s'posed Child of Ilúvatar. Wondering aimlessly along the shores of the Sea of Helcar, in faraway Cuiviénen— in that shade of the Two Trees.

Nameless, and shameless, and utterly carefree.

Alas, too soon was that pristine *Self*-image relegated to the periphery of her vision; subjugated by an increasingly sublunary perspective. Colored with the immediacy of needing, as opposed to blindly wanting after things.

Added to this, she'd the sudden awakening of that slumbering Dragon, *Tiamat*. It adopting the form of a softly spoken Serpent to coil about her head, like a regal knot.

There, to whisper in her ear these two simple truths. Firstly, that she was ordained to become Eve, that firstborn second. Indeed, that she'd been cast in the mould of a lonely Adam; and espoused as spouse for him, and him alone.

And secondly, that she was forever to walk in his shadow, or in his light. Though her burden was to be far greater than his. And certainly, a darn sight more painful.

And yeah, there was to be no mention of Lilith.

That state of blissful ignorance being thus deposed. Eve—now Destiny's child—was compelled to turn away from her immaculate-*Self*. A knowledge of Self being deemed at odds with her Maker—your *god-of-always-listening*. And thus, every fibre of her being.

Ascending to womanhood, and that mantle of Asherah, of Osun, of Diana. The woman-*Grrrl* was to assume that station of 'Maiden'. For only then, might Eve stand—at last—*face-à-face* with Eve.

She'd *Blink*. And *Blink* again, as if meaning to dispel the Serpent's spell—the Serpent's words. All the while, working that brush, its forked tongue through her hair. It being never quite straight enough, or long enough, or fair.

And now, confronted by that *Looking-glass*. Sash would seek to conjure for herself, more tangible illusions; demonstrate her mastery of that gift of metamorphosis, the Serpent was said to have imparted unto her.

They'd be illusions of her own choosing—of course. One's she could see, and touch; in the way she styled her hair, in the make-up that she wore. It seeming as if she could become anyone she wanted. Any one of a manifold daughters of Eve, pictured on the covers of those glossy *Splash*-mags. Brush straight that kink in her hair, she'd only just-now learnt to despise.

In the bedsit-proper, Sash's Pod began singing.

[Sing] *Baby you don't know*

Flapping, Sash left the brush dangling from her hair; its bristles clinging-on for dear life to a knot of locks. And switching that dryer off, to place it deliberately in the sink. Bolted from the bathroom to make a lunge for it—her *Pod*.

[Sing] *What you do to me*

Kneeling, elbows planted squarely on the bed, she checked for the number and saw it withheld—

Aargh!

And immediately, she dropped the device, to saunter back the way she'd come.

Returning to her hair, she untangled the brush. And retrieving the dryer, continued with the ritual. A modicum of calm washing-over her, like a wave, as she lip-sync'd the words of her ringtone; her eyes focused intently upon her reflection.

[Sing] *I won't let no-one*
Come and take your place
Cause the Love you give
Can't be re-placed—
No one else...

There followed a significant pause. And then, it was the *Buzz*er's turn to make its presence felt. The abruptness of it—BURP-BURP *BURRRP*—tearing at that state of Zen, so vital to Sash achieving her best results.

Turning in their sockets, her eyes were seen to source the sound. While that barely audible *Purrr* of the hairdryer returned, to fill that vacuum left in the *Buzz*er's wake.

There then followed another significant pause. Time enough for Sash to look to her reflection, and shrug. It seeming as if she'd imagined the whole thing. Her continuing with methodically working that brush through her hair; the heat from the hairdryer just-now beginning to coax some sort of—

BURRRP BURP-*BURP*
Alright-alright

Cutting her eye upon the ceiling, Sash *Tut*'d. Then sighed, her mien visibly deflating; her body being resigned to having to go answer that *Buzz*er's call.

Leaving the brush and the hairdryer to the sink, she was to saunter across the bedsit-proper, and out the other door. Loosening her mammoth towel along the way, to again envelop herself in it. That querulous BURP BURP-*BURRRP*, harrying her down the dark hallway.

Finger poised over that beady red-eye of the intercom. Sash opened her front door, a cheeseburger-grin planted upon her gulliver. She then pressed it. Listening-out for the distant sound of the main door slamming shut, before letting go.

And settling down to wait, leant against the doorframe. That lambency, coming from the bedsit-proper, thinning to an umbra as it washed-up against those shores of the landing.

And for a brief spell, all seemed at peace, and quiet, in her *incy wincy* corner of the Universe.

Eventually, Sash began to make-out the distant clatter of shod feet, bounding-up the stairs, two steps at a time. Followed by a deathly quiet. A moment's pause, before that racket started-up again. It seeming a prelude to something, like those hefty opening bars of Wagner's Siegfrieds *Tod und Trauermarsch.*[27]

And it was then she felt it, a sense of foreboding. That expectant pulse of a kettledrum. The suspenseful tremor of strings, and broody murmurings of French horns.

And yeah, there was something distinctly familiar about it. This scene. This setting. Not quite déjà vous, but close enough.

And it was then, Sash remembered the light-switch. And pressing it, caught Kel — our unsuspecting Adam — rounding the corner, to take that final flight of stairs.

Still rocking that 60% grey two-piece Birdman suit, ash-BLK *StayPress*™ shirt, and matching knit pencil-tie; his 80% grey *Crombie* clutched in his hand.

Arriving at the landing, he stood then for a-bit — grinning.

Apparently, pleased as Larry for having made it this far. Though Sash could hear he was clearly out of breath.

"Expecting was-ya?" he said, his covetous eyes feasting upon this glorious spectacle. Sash stood there, *gobsmacked*. A massive Woollies® mammoth towel wrapped around her, like a sarong.

Conscious now, of every square-inch of exposed flesh. She thought to wedge the door between Body and *Him*.

"What you doing 'ere?" she asked, making sure to establish eye contact.

"Visiting."

Sniff

"Visiting who — Abs?"

And as she said it, she squinted.

"Nah-why? Is he about?"

Slinging his *Crombie* over his shoulder, Kel put his hands in his pockets.

"What? You asking me?"

And with that, Sash cut her eye upon it and chirps'd her teeth.

The pair seemed then to succumb to their familiarity. Leaving the silence to measure the *Beat*.

Beat

THAT PERF=CT W⦿RLD

And just-now, that landing-light Timed-out—

CLICK!

The Space descending into darkness. Save for that lucency coming from the bedsit-proper.

Kel was to beat my-*Grrrl* to the switch.

"So what—*Sniff*—you ain't gonna invite me in?" he asked. Stealing a look-see passed her into the hallway, which was to remain shrouded in darkness.

And noting how he'd managed to close the gap between them, Sash was to bat her reply after him.

"No."

Then looking him up-and-down, set her boatrace as if to say, *what for?*

Still, undaunted Kel now shifted his coat from his shoulder to an arm. Taking extra care to insure it hung there neatly. As if it were a serviette-liteau, and he were accustomed to waiting-on tables at *Le Gavroche*®, or The Morton's Club®.

"Why? You entertaining?"

Sash shook her head. Though it seemed involuntary; her being intrigued by this behaviour, it being something she hadn't observed in Kel before. She'd only half caught the question.

"What then?"

Kel pressed her *ever-so* gently.

Sash, now blatantly ignoring him, extending an arm with the intention of gauging for herself, the quality of his rather fetching coat.

"*Sash*—what then?"

Her curiosity sated. She was to lock back onto those dreamy eyes of his. "I'm off out, if you must know."

Blink

Blink

The pair stared after each other. Kel stood with his hands in his pockets, nibbling at his lower-lip—an annoying bit of flailing skin. It acting as a snaffle. Reminding him, he was to be on his best behaviour.

Sash acutely aware of the edge of that rigid door, pressed against her pliant Body, and the extent of that darkness behind her.

"Where? Into town?"

And just-now, a waft of frigid air licked her back, like a tongue.

Setting her teeth to chattering.

"Where Sash? Into town—"

"What'd you want Kal'el?" Sash snapped. Now taking to rubbing at those goosebumps, crawling all over the backs of her exposed arms.

"To see how you were—is all," Kel professed. Giving it the puppy-dog eyes, as if he were the one being put upon.

Tut.

"So, you've seen me—what?" came Sash's response. Body returning to swinging upon that hinged door, seemingly of its own volition.

But Kel simply shrugged. The truth being, he hadn't really thought much beyond this point.

Sniff

There followed another brief pause, Sash—her teeth chattering away to themselves—stealing a look-see passed Kel, down the stairs. Though she was sure he'd be on his tod. It being like, his 'Default' setting.

"You bucked *my-Man* yet? Him downstairs," Kel asked then, changing the subject.

"Can't you see me freezing my *Nutz* off here—what is it you want?" came Sash's testy response, her stressing the consonance in every word.

"A favour," Kel replied earnestly, stepping forward to lean against the door frame. Forcing Sash further back into that shadowy hallway.

"A favour?"

Sash parroted his words back at him. Then squinting, added, "what kind-a favour?"

"I just need a hand getting into me ol' room."

"Is that all—*forphf'ksake*. Alright, just let me go put some clothes on—yeah. And I'll help you break-in."

She went to close the door, only to find Kel's size-11s barring the way.

And looking down at it, that shod foot. And then up at him. She sighed, the pantomime seemingly a mirror held-up to her resolve.

But she still managed to muster enough of a defiant tone to say, "*Look!* Move it. Or lose it."

"Alright. Lose it," said Kel. Making sure to look Sash squarely in the eye as he said it.

Sniff

But immediately his boatrace cracked, his grin now baring teeth. And then, it was as if they'd travelled back through Space and *Time*. And there he was, stood upon *my-Grrrl*'s doorstep—yet again. Begging to be let back into her *Life*. It being *pre*-destined, or *pre*-determined, or like, God's Will—or something. That they should be together.

Tut—sigh.

"Com' on Kel. I ain't got time to play with you."

"Who's playing?" Kel barked, letting that mask-slip—just a-little.

Or more, lifting that Hockey-mask just enough to give a glimpse of his *fah* real boatrace. The one that'd survived a living Hell. And wanted nothing more than to see *my-Grrrl* have to go through it too.

Though of course, Sash couldn't see it. Not fully. Not yet. Her being as addicted as him, to play this game—and losing.

Still wearing that sullen expression. Kel now leant-in close, as if intent upon taking Sash into his confidence; her mirroring him, though with arms now folded across her chest.

Blink

Blink

"So what? You ain't gonna invite me in?" he said, wheeling the conversation back round. And having expected him to say something else entirely, Sash squinted, *you what?*

Grinning, Kel then batted his eyelids after her—flirtatiously.

Oh forphf'ksake.

And with that, Sash stormed-off. Leaving the door and *my-Man* to gravity. Dangling—as it were, in mid-air.

Kel stood there for a-bit. Feeling chuffed with himself. Hazarding a look-see back down the stair. Needing to ensure the coast was clear, before wading into that uncertainty of the dark.

He was at pains then, to close the door quietly behind him. His hand lingering upon the latch, whilst he paused to listen.

Ahead, he could just make out Sash's voice. The door at the end of the hall having been left cracked, slightly.

"Where the *phf'k* are-ya?" she barked. Something in her tone suggesting she were talking at someone, on her *Pod* most probably.

Still, Kel was to wait for a response. Basking in that *Buff* that came from having gotten his way. Breathing-in that familiar stink of his surroundings; his heart pounding with excitement. Relishing the dark, whilst being drawn toward that slither of light—*Life*, marking the hall's extremity.

It was uncanny, how quickly his eyes took to it—the darkness, and drinking-in his surroundings. Coppin', directly across from him, the bed-sit's *Itchy*-kitchenette®. Its PVC foldaway door drawn back, revealing a vertical pool of Pitch; what seemed a gateway into another dimension.

Then, it was that row of ACME® aluminium heavy-duty coat hooks, mounted upon a camouflaged wooden plank. Just by that unblinking, beady red-eye of the intercom. And those two light switches, posted at opposite ends of the hall. That'd always seemed redundant, given no one had gotten around to replacing the missing bulb.

Phf'king Fowler—still a waste of space, Kel was to muse. Looking after that naked pendant-fixture, hanging limp from the ceiling.

"What the *phf'k* you on about? I thought it was you—"

But he was to snap-to at the sound of *my-Grrrl's* voice. And now certain she was alone, and at his mercy. His thoughts were to return to considering his approach.

Buoyed by the dark, and that note of panic in Sash's irascible tone. He was inclined to take his time. Peruse the *Itchy*-kitchenette®, and leave her to stew over his whereabouts. Or better yet, goad her into having to come look for him.

And so, entering that Space, Kel didn't bother with the light. It being markedly the size of a telephone box, he was able to rely on muscle-memory, and his newly acquired night-vision. Opening the fridge-unit, and a couple of cupboards and draws, to gauge how *my-Grrrl* was living these days.

Which was barely, judging by the slim pickings.

Saying that, he did stumble upon an unopened box of FerreroRocher®, squirrelled-away in a freezer compartment; and opening it, pilfered two before moving-on. One for *Road*, and one for right-now.

Back in the hallway, he was just in time to catch that shadow flitter by that cracked door. And again, he paused, erring on the side of caution—always. Licking melted chocolate from the tips of his pointy-finger and thumb; having taken two bites to polish it off—his impromptu appetiser.

"What you mean—you can't come get me?" Sash bayed, apparently regurgitating word-for-word what she'd only just-now heard.

The sudden outburst, punctuated by that shadow flittering back the other way.

Scrunching-up the FerreroRocher's golden wrapper, to toss it to the floor. Kel breached the bedsit-proper, curling his neck around the door to peer-in. And was just in time to catch my-*Grrrl*'s retreat to the bathroom. Its door slamming shut behind her, that emphatic CLICK sealing her within.

Entering thus, unopposed. My-*Man* was to mosey over to those micro-blinds that covered the only window. And parting them, peered-out and down at the road. Still half expecting my-*Grrrl* to emerge — any minute now, fully dressed, and ready to do battle.

But then, when she failed to make an entrance, he couldn't help but feel stood-up.

Sniff

Turning from that view, he heard the familiar drone of a *Harrier*-taxi landing at the LZT across the way. And was of a mind to look again, the spectacle of it landing being still worthy of a moment's pause.

But then he remembered, the LZT was at least two storeys above Sash's window. And consequently, he wouldn't really be able to see much anyway.

Sniff

Still clutching his *Crombie* in his hand, Kel was seen then to properly take-in his surroundings. Marking — perhaps for the first time, that ubiquitous *magnolia*-F1D5A6; that was like a layer of clingfilm clinging onto the walls.

And the matching light shade, suspended from the fold of that inclined ceiling. Which was new; and acted to diffuse the harsh output of the NRG-saver bulb.

And the way Sash had rearranged the furniture, to create discrete areas for lounging-in, and for sleeping.

Then it was the Cinë-*matik*, how it seemed to command the entire Space. Kel noting that it was set to one of those newstreaming services, which was definitely a change; him being used to my-*Grrrl* having muzik going 24-7.

And that it was on mute. The *viddy* sequence cutting abruptly, to an über-extreme close-up of some Reporter's sweat ridden boatrace.

With barely a second glance at that stricken visage. What might've been a Hyperreal masterpiece by Arinze Stanley Egbengwu, or Michael Sydney Moore. Kel now decided he might as well have a nosy.

Seen as he was stopping.

Making a beeline for the wall—that backed onto the *Itchy-*kitchenette®, he pressed it to reveal one of two concealed Push-*Me*™ closets. The compartment rolling out at a measured pace, inviting him to leisurely peruse its contents.

On display, various items of clothing, all neatly hung-up; wireframe draws of underwear and tee-shirts tidily folded; five generations of Total*Air*™ kicks, stowed snuggly in a hold-all tray at the bottom. All Brilliant-bright—of course, and all sporting shoehorns.

Having cop'd all this, uncharacteristic orderliness. Kel felt compelled to have a rummage through. To soil it, with some trace of his disdain; him being partial to ruffling a few feathers, and Sash's precious hairdos.

But then, spotting that FENDINI® handbag laying forlorn amongst all that clutter on the bed. He thought better of it.

And what was that lying next to it?

Kel squinted, as if meaning to narrow his field of vision.

My-Grrrl's precious Pod.

Bingo!

Pushing the closet too—with his hip, he now thought to make himself at home. Flinging his coat down on the bed, to retrieve the *Pod*, and that handbag.

He then headed over to the bathroom. And holding these treasures in one-hand, pressed a lonely ear against the door. A *Devil-may-care* grin, stretched like barbed wire across his gulliver; his mind's eye being seemingly privy to the goings-on therein.

Man is a mirror for Man.

Maurice Merleau-Ponty, 'Eye and Mind' (1964)

```
4D [61] 6E 20 69 73 20 61
20 6D 69 72 72 6F 72 20
66 6F 72 20 4D 61 6E 2E
```

·

REP●-MAN

Kel felt himself falling in Space. And as he fell, he felt doors close behind him, and open ahead of him.

He felt a sense of nausea threatening to overwhelm him, inch by inch; the measure of his *Life*'s Blood ebbing from his Body. That slow, steady *Drip*...

Drip...

Drip...

like a Chinese Water-clock, counting backwards.

At some point, he'd crossed a threshold. An apparently arbitrary line etched in Space*Time*. That procession of closed doors, depicting incremental steps toward that one dread feeling.

Intelligible, and yet, unutterable. It was a certainty of death that escaped lucid expression. Kel's screams, being simply a mirror held-up to those issued at his birth.

Passing through each door, there came a peeling away of his *Being*; like peeling the skin, and then the rind from an orange, exposing an absence—where flesh should've been.

The journey mapping Kel's regression. A toddler's fear of dark places, its ultimate expression.

That, and a newly rediscovered longing for a mother's warmth. It being all he'd left to cling onto.

And then, his entire *Life* had seemed a rehearsal for this moment. That slow encroach of sleep, something he'd grown to accept, and even welcome. The way it'd sneak-up on him, like a thief, and consume him

THAT PERFECT WORLD

utterly. He could only ever know it as *Waking*, and through the fulfilment of its covenant. That it should see him safely through to the other side—of oblivion, and a *good morrow*.

Night after night, it'd utter the same assurance.

And every time he closed his eyes, and surrendered unto it. He'd carry that promise. Like that Teddy bear he'd once loved—*cherished*, as a Kid. Its name having long since escaped him.

Forced to turn and watch sleep's approach, there were to be no guarantees this time. And suddenly, Kel recalled his first ever hearing of Sleep's pledge, his mum promising to be there when he awoke; that first night she set him down to sleep alone.

Though it were improbable, he'd have remembered.

"*Yeah*...you sleep, Mate."

Repo-*Man's* choice of words now beginning to resonate. It being-*like*, his mum's milk, curdled.

At some point it'd begun, the *Dream*. A vision conjured by Death's throes. The setting becoming apparent, emerging out of a *Present*-tense.

The depiction of horizon, a canvass upon which to draw a dawn breaking. A breathtaking *Monet* sunrise, awash with every imaginable hue and shade of pink, and blue.

Immediately, that sense of Space translated into a hospital room. With a hole for a window, that was to be a wall of glass. The Dream *then*, conspiring to portray, in stark contrast, that sanitised environ. Devoid of colour, yet rich in detail. And a featureless, flat panorama, racing toward those blurred edges of vivid color.

Having no real grasp of *Time*, or sense of purpose. Kel was to be held captive by these cascading impressions. The window, and its view; the hospital room, even his presence therein.

And though, not yet fully articulated, the setting nevertheless became everything he'd ever known. A Stereoscopic 3D *virtua*-Feed, and a televised spectacle. That slice of your *Everyday*, and his own private Idaho.

Kel being cast adrift in the role of both third person, and first. These two perspectives, combining to form a whole, that of *the* Dreamer. Inside and Out-*there*, barely poles apart.

The hospital room felt like home. Certainly, its bariatric-bed, crossed with a *Leth*-R-G® recliner, looked homely enough. Surrounded as it was, by all those creature comforts afforded by modern medicine. The CohenKuhl® diagnostic-engine, its 12-sticky probes like groping tendrils, relaying vital-signs back to a *Blinking* monitor; tiers of flat-lines charting an absence of Body temperature, of respiration, of oxygen saturation.

Yeah, it was almost like painting by numbers—by integer. Where here you'd a flat line drawing of Lucien Freud's 'Benefit's Supervisor Sleeping', or Jenny Saville's 'Fulcrum'; with numbers representing all the colours in a spectrum of Necrotic-blue.

This was how it was, how it'd always been.

The familiar sight of a single Brilliant-bright bedsheet, draped over a morbidly obese cadaver. Its rotund *Panniculus*, pregnant with every pound of hatred in that godforsaken World.

A catheter, and a host of cannulas, simultaneously feeding and bleeding it of fluids. A butchered piglet hanging by a trotter in a corner, its underbelly cut open from throat to groin. A transparent tube milking its liver of crystal-clear insulin, to be fed intravenously to that bloated cadaver.

Yeah—this was how it was, how it'd always been.

And this being a Dreamscape, even those Cyber-*Men*® were to appear amenable. Dressed in their shimmering silvery Hazmat suits, their movements a blurry spectral image. The way they'd traversed the room, *Phasing* through Kel, as if he wasn't there—as if he were the Spectre. And the sounds they made, their words indecipherable; like a clamouring of voices, lost in a crowd.

The Dream's imposition: That we weren't, all a-we, being held captive by those dastardly Cyber-*Men*®.

And despite their harrowing visage—the Hazmat get-up, and their funny voices; they were actually here to help. And knew what was best for us. Being privy to that 'Big picture'. And *Immortal*, obviously.

After all, weren't we all destined to die of something? So, why not let it be of palliative care, and obscurity.

With that impression of a hospital room, came a compulsion, to peer beneath that Brilliant-bright bedsheet. But just then, a Cyber-*Man* entered, and *Phasing* through Kel, approached the foot of the bed in a blur of motion.

Lifting the sheet, just enough to expose a pair of swollen gangrenous legs—afflicted with acute *Elephantiasis*. It produced a scalpel; and cut a piece of rotten flesh out of a cracked and callused heel. It then presented a swab to the wound, as if to amend this callous act. But the cadaver refused to bleed.

Another Cyber-*Man* appeared then, clasping in a gloved hand a BLK felt-tip pen. It drew a dashed line on the cadaver's legs, just below the knee, and left. The two Cyber-*Men*® conferring, as they *Phased* through Kel in a flurry of blurred motion.

They closed the door behind them—as a courtesy. Leaving him alone with the cadaver, and that compulsion to peer beneath the sheet.

Indeed, by now, it'd assumed an identity all its own—*that* compulsion. And only by sating its insatiable curiosity, could Kel hope to appease it.

He edged closer and closer to the bed. And as he did so, he saw himself staring at the impression of a pair of hands, pressed against the wall of that cadaver's bulbous *Panniculus*.

Apparently, someone remained trapped inside.

An Adult-Child at its wit's end, drowning in a ball-pit of adipose tissue. Think of poor ol' *Shamu*. Think of a majestic Orca killer whale beached in a desert, miles from any Life sustaining Ocean. Its insulating blubber, now the walls of its prison. Its sheer weight and mass, nailing-it to a cross of silica.

Abruptly, the cadaver sat bolt upright. This über-*Human* feat, pulling taut those wires and tubes that'd feasted upon its mortified flesh; sending the CohenKuhl® monitor, and that butchered little piggy crashing to the floor. Flailing tubes spitting fluids indiscriminately in all directions.

It was then that the bedsheet fell away, revealing the petrified mug of an Orang-utan matriarch. Haggard, and silver haired—for having carried all the World's hatred to term.

And though violently repulsed, Kel couldn't help but claim it for his own. This ghoulish apparition being comprised of the best part of him.

Twas that dread aspect of *Hel Hadja Mahakali*. Those once cherished and adored features, half-eaten by the blue of necrosis, playing host to a most hellish vizard. Its sunken empty eyes-sockets, incapable of shedding even a single tear—

Ere for itself, nay for poor Baldr.[28]
And just-now, Kel felt it growl.
Grrrl

Felt its monstrous intent. Its icy-cold fingers, labouring to pry open the mouth of its host. The cadaver's cracked lips purposefully sealed shut with crystallised bile, and scaly pus. Its parched tongue, swollen to twice its size from an involuntary fast. Its captors being loathed to give it even a thimble of water, less it speak.

Lest, it speak.

And yet, before your *god-of-always-listening*, it would offer testimony to a most rude hospitality imparted upon this, its host. How its last breath had been choked in its throat. Cut short, prematurely, and spirited away. How it'd foreseen its untimely demise. That dread hindsight, captured in the milky blue of its eyes—now trophies for Salome.

The cadaver's gaping mouth, and quivering lips, froze with a pregnant pause. Its *Possessor*, attempting to summon its art of speech; that spark of Will and Wit, that'd set all the Boys heart's to racing.

Yet, it was to be to no avail. And so, it was left to the silence to speak in its stead:

[Poem] *Here I am, the quiet sang.*
Come, lovers and loved ones
—one and all. Come
See how I am deflowered
My Life judged worthless
—not worth saving; a dulled penny
Tossed at an outstretched hand
Mistaken for a Beggar's Bowl.
Come hither—come
Take your penny. And for exchange
Mercutio's curse. [29]
A Plague o' both your houses
A Plague o' both your houses
A Plague, your houses both.

Somehow, that cadaver managed to grab *a*-hold of Kel; the Dream having conspired to draw him near. Its gangrenous arms holding him fast, its grip imparted with an über-natural force of Will. Equivalent to the weight of those wrongs wrought against it.

The stench of rotten flesh assailed Kel's senses. Nibbled at the tender skin of his snarling lips, and the inside of his flaring nostrils. And then...*and then*, it found its voice at last. A Siren's wail.

WOW-WOW-WOW-WOW-WOW-WOW

Hel's apparition having departed, a mindless Zombie was left in its wake. Its prescient cry, drilling into Kel's skull.

WOW-WOW-WOW-WOW-WOW-WOW

It wailed and wailed and wailed. And shook Kel with such force, that he awoke suddenly to his pain. And instinctively, he clung onto it for dear life. The pain being an antidote to sleep—to Death's opiate.

And yeah...*and yeah*, though he'd failed to save her, ere her demise. His mother had, nevertheless, been for keeping her promises.

The Dream vanish'd. Kel emerging from its murky depths to break that surface of consciousness, and take a breath. A sobering gulp of air, that bought with it, but one immediate impression.

Pain.

Rolling in their sockets, his eyes caught snatches of Out-*there*; glimpses of his surroundings that were as garbled messages, rendered in *Greyscale*.

And still, there was nothing to detract from it, that *smarting*. What seemed a primordial interlocutor, spanning that chasm that lay between a prehistoric Body, and perpetually evolving Mind—sentience.

Hanging limp from his neck, his head bobbed and swayed; as if he were a marionette puppet, its strings ascending to the Heavens.

That Celestial Puppeteer having paused just-now, for a fag-break.

And then, it was left to the World to interject. Kel's head, thrown back by a sudden jolt, hitting hard against something. The force threatening to knock him senseless.

Wincing, and *Blink-blink-blinking*. He caught a glimpse of his legs, folded over a metal rail. And with it, the distinct impression of pins and needles, nibbling at his toes like crawfish.

He *Blinked* again, in the wake of the aftershock. The epithet, *for-phf'ksake*. About all the sense he could muster.

The pain was biting—*cutting*. It felt as if, he were a ton-of-bricks being dragged, kicking and screaming down a cobbled street. And just-now, the smell of rusty iron filled his nostrils, his tongue tasting like a mouthful of raw liver.

In addition to this, there was the jarring sound of rattling metal. The metal cage in which he'd been stowed, feeling like a cheese-grate, grating against his tender spine, having already flayed the skin to the bone.

Phf'k me, Kel thought. *Pphf'k...me...*

Yeah, it'd brought him back. The pain. Now, if only he could open his eyes, Out-*there* might vouch him safe, and still alive.

Sniff

Kel's boatrace felt then, hot and sticky; his eyelids caked with dried Blood, and salty tears. His breathing, hoarse and shallow. Each lumbering breath, like a clawed hand scaling the sheer walls of his throat; clambering over that thirst.

And what a thirst...

Suffice to say. Here was yet more evidence of him coming into his own, into his Body.

Between *Blinks*, Kel was to catch yet more glimpses of his legs, dangling over the edge of a precipice; a metal cage, that was apparently mounted upon wheels. A shopping trolley perhaps—*maybe?*

Wait...a shopping-trolley?

Reason dictated a force coercing the thing to move. And right on cue—Out-*there* in the World, this effort met with resistance. Kel's Body transmitting that sudden shift in inertia to his neck. Leaving his head bobbing, like an apple in a bucket of water.

CRACK.

Again, his head struck something hard.

For-phf'k-SAKE.

Kel winced, and turned, his neck apparently coming to terms with its newly discovered elasticity.

Blink-blink-blinking, his eyes were eventually to settle on squinting, to better discern the silhouetted figure, that was to come into view for that split-second. Backlit by a *Helios*® Street-lamp, that literally hummed with its brilliance.

Rediscovering his arms, that his hands indeed had fingers. Kel rubbed at his eyes, at his disbelief; as a toddler might, fighting sleep.

Evidently, he'd been found, and stuffed into a *Life*'s Essentials® metromart *troll-e*.Bot. But what-if he'd been dismembered, his Body severed in two? At least that might account for the pain.

He imagined his innards scraping along the floor, his intestines leaving a lubricating trail of gore, like a snail's slime. And then, there was the question of where he was being taken.

The answer being seemingly obvious, given his present condition. To hospital.

To hospital? No-no—God...no.

The thought then caught a whiff of breath, and Blood, and phlegm. Gurgling forth from his split and swollen lips, as so many bubbles. And again, darkness threatened to consume him.

Now Hel's gaping mouth, with paving stones for teeth, and a hospital bed at the journey's end. Promising an eternity of infernal torment, in the care of those dastardly Cyber-*Men*®.

The thought of hospital being an anathema to him, Kel made a conscious effort to resist. Tensing his neck as he felt his head flop backward.

It being better to bleed-out—in the gutter, he thought. Wincing against that mild whiplash. His gritted teeth, biting down upon that *Life*-affirming pain, as if it were a horse's bit.

Repo-*Man* had waltzed that *troll-e*.Bot through those backstreets of Soho, across the great divide, Mainstreet—and *off*-Mainstreet. And on, into a sleepy Fitzrovia.

Clearly, the *troll-e*.Bot hadn't been designed to traverse such terrain; its A.I. giving-up the ghost, the instant it'd crossed the store's threshold.

And now, forced to negotiate with the pavement, its wheels—which were made of acrylic—conveyed their reluctance by snagging on every other crack. Its metallic frame rattling continuously, excited by that rude uneven texture.

Nevertheless, Repo-*Man* had doggedly persevered. Driven by a compulsion so deeply seated in its *Being*, it was barely aware of it.

"Oy?"

Kel struggled to catch his voice in his throat; his sense of smell being overwhelmed by that foul stink, that hung about his would-be chauffeur, like a dark cloud.

"OY—"

He put everything into what seemed a last ditched hail. Leaving little if anything for when he pushed-down upon that metal-cage—with his elbows, in an attempt to heave-out his folded frame.

"Stop will-ya," he pleaded, giving-up. His mouth blowing bubbles, like a burping baby.

"*Ahh*...it speaks."

"Yeah, it *phf'kin—*"

COUGH-COUGH.

Kel heaved-up a huge lewy, that'd taken-up lodgings in the back of his throat. And held it in his tongue. And aiming at the pavement, he made to spit. But was unable to summon enough force of breath. The lewy dribbling down his chin, a viscid cocktail of phlegm and Blood.

"...*sp*-speaks," he said, looking for its residue on the lapel of his coat.

And still, the *troll-e*.Bot trundled on. Repo-*Man* at the helm.

"Oy—"

COUGH-COUGH.

"What's with you?" Kel pleaded.

Flapping his arms and legs, like an animated ragdoll, desperate to be let out of its packaging.

A crack in the pavement, soon putting pay to this exhibition. Locking the *troll-e*.Bot's wheels and causing Kel to hit his head, once again, on its metal frame—

CRACK.

Owwch

Wincing, he rubbed at that now tender spot.

"*Forphf'ksake*. Give it a rest—"

He almost felt to cry then, as he wiped his mouth and chin with a coat-sleeve.

Cunt.

And naturally, Repo-*Man* was to oblige.

Letting go. It stood and watched. As the *troll-e*.Bot continued, gathering momentum on an incline. Strolling-up to the edge of the pavement, to snag upon the curb, and waver. Before toppling over into the road, dumping Kel—like a sack of spuds, slap-bang in the middle of Newman Street.

Tickled, Repo-*Man* moseyed over to the pavements edge, and flopped itself down. And heaved a hefty sigh. Legs spread-eagle in front of it, arms locked behind its back for support, barrel chest and rotund paunch distended.

Throwing back its head, it then closed its eyes. And basked for a-bit, in the rays of that bloody Moon. The *Saros Series* 137 Über Lunar Eclipse having by now, reached its apex.

Then, breathing deep—through its nose, it tasted the air. Whilst pinching its eyelids shut; raising its eyebrows to insure an even application of those auspicious bloody Lunar-rays.

Cocking an ear—its eyes still closed, it was to sample those noises of the night. That *Buzz* of the Hive, more of a sleepy drone.

And then, for the sake of stereophony, it tilted its head the other way, and sampled the air with its other ear. And for a brief spell, all was still. At peace, and *Shhh*... [Whisper] *oh-so quiet.*

Thinking this an opportune moment for a smoke, Repo-*Man* began rooting about its person. Its hands padding down its tattered *Crombie*; sifting through one pocket, and then another.

Scraps of paper, the scratch from a matchbox, a folded ticket-stub, a paperclip, a safety-pin, a bit of fluff. It was all examined and carefully stowed away.

After a brief pause, in which, it just gawped—open-mouthed—up at that bloody Moon. The hunt was to resume. Repo-*Man* leaning back to delve into a trouser-pocket. Angling its scrawny frame to rummage this way and that.

It did the same with the other pocket, and the tattered lining of its coat, and blazer. And even its crutch, availing itself of every conceivable hiding place; the *Fleas* apparently sleeping through it.

But it was to be to no avail.

Eventually, it gave up. Its eyes settling upon the road, and Kel—still lying there prone. And nothing stirred for what seemed like ages.

Save for that ill wind. Blowing no good the wrong way up a one-way street. Funnelled by banks of buildings; four and five storey residences, squatting on prefab storefronts. This being effectively a different *Time* zone, their illuminated signs were all switched-off.

Cotch'd upon the curb, and still clucking for a smoke. Repo-*Man* felt compelled to air-out its tootsies. And did so, kicking-off its tattered shoes to wiggle its toes—those ratty toenails; and scratch at its ashen soles, worn slick like threaded tyres.

It was then, it spotted a globule of chewing gum, trodden into a crack in the paving. And scooping it out, with a grotty nail, and brushing away any loose dirt. It was to blow on it—*for luck*, before plopping-it in its mouth.

Chewing now—with aplomb, it planted its tootsies squarely upon that asphalt of the road. And lying back on the pavement, cupped its head in its hands, and closed its eyes; intent on catching a few more of those bloody Lunar-rays.

And again, nothing stirred for a-bit. Save for *The Buzz*. The Drone. That Brilliant-bright noise, that passed for silence in the Met.

But could Repo-*Man* live with it? This silence. Could it Hell! Better the incessant chattering of the *Fleas*.

And so, its thoughts turned to rousing them.

"'Tis the excellent foppery of this world," it said—at last. Its eyes still closed.

"What is?" came a reply.

"What is what?"

Repo-*Man* now opened an eye to look about.

"What is a *foppery* when it's at home?"

"How the hell should I know?"

It closed that eye and opened the other, as if meaning to assume its unique perspective.

"But you just said it."

"Oh—so I did. And what of it?"

"That's what I'm asking you—*Knucklehead*."

It rapped its forehead with its knuckles.

"Well, if you'd let me finish."

"Go ahead—Mate. Knock yourself out."

Repo-*Man* snapped both eyes open.

"Cheers—me dears."

Staring-up at that bloody night-sky, it cleared its throat and continued, "tis *the* most excellent foppery of the World,[2A] that, when we are sick in fortune—often the surfeit of our own behaviour, we make guilty of our disasters, the Sun, the Moon, and the Stars. As if, we were villains on necessity—in rank opposition to our natures…"

Repo-*Man* pulled a face then, as if he were mulling over this last bit. Before concluding, "our *better* natures."

And nodding thoughtfully, it sat-up, and chewed open-mouthed for a-bit. Its nose twitching, as if it were a dormouse, and its whiskers actual whiskers.

"Better, or worst?"

"Better or worse, what?"

It knew the Fleas didn't much care for it improvising—that is, making shit up. But they were yet to stir.

"Better or worst natures."

"Does it matter?"

"Does anything *phf'king* matter?"

There, it'd stumped 'em. Turned their own cynicism against 'em. And the *Fleas* were to pay it back in kind, with a bout of the fidgets.

Scurrying around its boatrace. Leading it a merry dance: Its finger tracing an eyebrow; a tear under one eye and half a moustache.

As if *Crossing* itself, against the ill-potent of its own words.

It then hastened to undo this *Spell*, executing a reverse-*Spell*—like a reset. Tracing a circle with thumb and forefinger, starting at both eyebrows, round the cheeks and down to its chin; and finishing with a sobering tug of its beard.

It then threw that soiled boatrace away. And stretching in a new one, pulled a flurry of facial expressions.

Phew—that was close, it thought, chuckling to itself. *The Fleas and their Spells—very dangerous.*

Flexing its back and whining its spine, Repo-*Man* settled again; one arm cotch'd upon a bent knee, the other locked by its side for support.

"Of course, it matters," it said, staring blankly at that wall of blacked-out storefronts—that stood directly in front of it. And with that, it let out a hefty *sigh*, that was to leave it visibly deflated.

It bore then, the weight of its thoughts, like *Melancholia*.

That is, until another fit of fidgets took a-hold of it. The *Fleas*, being vengeful little critters, returning to exact another dose of revenge.

However, Repo-*Man* was loathed to let them have their way. *Sniff-sniffing* at the air, it wiggled its nose. Then shoved a grubby finger up it.

It wiggled the finger about for a-bit, then pulled it out to look at it.

Yep, it'd caught one. *A teeny weeny incy wincy* runt of a thing.

Rolling it up into a ball, it flicked it after Kel. Then settled back down to wait. To catch a few more of those bloody Lunar-rays; hands behind its head, feet planted squarely upon that asphalt of the road.

And then...*and then...nothing*.

Eventually, unable to help itself. Repo-*Man* angled its neck to steal a look-see. Being at a loss to make head nor tail of it, why *my-Man* hadn't stirred.

Maybe it'd missed. When it'd flicked the *Flea* after it.

"It has to matter," it mused, settling back down to stare-up at that bloody night-sky.

"But...what-if, it don't?"

"It has to."

"*Yeah*—but...what-if?"

The idea was to be presented with a wry smile. This kind of airy fairy thinking, being guaranteed to rile the *Fleas*.

"What do you mean, what-if?"

"You know, what-if it doesn't matter so much?"

Repo-*Man* sat bolt upright, a quizzical expression seizing upon its features. While two grubby fingers plucked at the prow of its top lip.

It continued staring-up at that bloody night-sky; as if struggling to make sense of its own thoughts, seemingly written upon that blackboard of Outer-Space.

"What-what?"

"Better or worse. *What-if*, it doesn't matter so much? To him—*upstairs*."

It'd whispered this last bit. Its eyes squinting, as with the effort of picturing it. The hypothetical.

A *Beat* was then to inched by—in millimetres.

It thinking...*Computing*.

Nope.

It couldn't compute it...*daren't*.

Sniffing at the air. Repo-*Man* looked about furtively, like a grazing animal that'd caught wind of one of those Apex predators, lurking nearby. Its nostrils flaring to discern that distinct scent, a most rarefied strain of danger.

But it was to override its own senses. The coast being so obviously clear.

Sniff

It relaxed a-bit. One arm again cotch'd upon a bent knee. This slovenly pose having assumed that force of habit.

"Then what?" it posited, returning to the matter at hand.

"Then what *what*?"

The *Fleas* were getting antsy.

"What's it s'posed to be? Better or worse?"

"You mean, to be or not to be — surely?"

Repo-*Man* shot a crabby look after *my-Man*.

"You know what I mean — YOU KNOW WHAT I MEAN!"

And it was as a sudden clap of thunder, that last bit. So as, the entire Universe was seen to shudder.

"You know — *you know...what I mean*," it repeated, gloomily.

Its voice barely a whisper.

Sniff

Spitting-out that chewing gum, in disgust. It scowled at Kel.

"Yeah, you. Mister...*Flee-ya*. I see you — pretending. To be a-sleep," it said, and then waited for it.

And low and behold the *Fleas* started biting all over, causing it to roll about. Crook'd fingers scratching at random parts of its Body, as if it were tickling itself.

And just when it thought it had a handle on them, they squirreled up into its hair, and started biting into its scalp. Nibbling at that *post*-Op scar living behind its ear. A fleshy 'X' marking that fleshy spot where it lived, the *Pfeiffer*® Upsilon-Tracer BioChip implant. That was long since defunct.

Hardwired into its brain, the A.I. was still about administering those acute electroshock stimulus treatments. But arbitrarily now —

The Fleas...

The Fleas...

The Fleas...

It could feel 'em, borrowing deep into its brain. Wrestling control of its thinking. Pulling it inside-out. Upside-down. Getting its Blood pumping in a prelude to violence.

"What-if. *What-if*. Always with the *phf'king* what-if's. And the let's s'pose," it bellowed, both hands pulling at its scalp.

Then suddenly, it froze.

Sniff

Its eyes darted about, as if seeking reassurance in the concrete-ness of its surroundings. That sheer cliff-face looming behind it, an office block made of Muddy-red Victorian brickwork. Its façade, the subject of countless face-lifts, indistinguishable from those shiny prefab storefronts across the way, in the dark—

In the dark.

The only constant being, that spiked wrought-iron railing—painted an industrial-BLK. Guarding that moat filled with Pitch; a wrought-iron stair descending to a subterranean World, chiselled into London's Crust.

Yeah, Repo-*Man* had picked his spot. In the umbra that stretched between *Helios*® Street-lamps, just beyond those cones of Brilliant-bright. A kind of No-*Man's* Land.

Ahead, an intersection. Highlighted by that red glare of Securicor® Traffic-lights; the bias leaning toward Goodge Street—the A5204, what was the main thoroughfare.

Newman Street, as ever, at such an ungodly hour. Likened to an umbrous Desert Island, stranded between effulgent seas of commercial activity—your Mainstreet and off-Mainstreet beats.

Had it stopped? Had they relented—for now?

Repo-*Man* was to rediscover its Body scrunched-up in a ball. Its grubby mitts glued to its feculent scalp.

"I don't have any answers for you," it admitted, sitting-up and catching its breath. It then wiped at the corners of its eyes with the back of a mitt, what appeared to be a deliberate gesture—and *Sniffed*.

But obviously, the *Fleas* weren't having any of it.

"D'you think we care?" they said, hauling it to its feet.

"He cares," Repo-*Man* responded, pointing toward that railing behind it. It then looked back, as if expecting to see a head peering-over the lip of that moat. But there was nothing there.

"He sees all," it added, disappointed. That pointy finger falling limply to its side.

"Face it—*Chump*. He sees only what he wants."

Conscious of being overheard, Repo-*Man* looked about to be sure the coast was clear. Then added, "just enough to prove the point—yeah?"

The Fleas having let go. Repo-Man appeared unsure of its footing. It inching backwards—away from the curb, until it felt the railing behind it. Grabbing *a*-hold of those metal bars, to steady itself. Swallowing in a dry throat. A mitt coming to stroke that scar behind its ear.

As if to say, *there-there...there-there...*

"He's never looking when it matters. He...*can't*."

Both mitts then flew to catch that breath in its mouth.
Blasphemy.
But it was too late. It'd said it, and in its right mind *to-boot*.

Leaning heavily upon that rail, it now sought to make itself as small as physically possible. Lowering its Body, like a flag, to squat at half-mast—as it were.

Cowering, it wrapped both arms about its head, and braced for that lightning bolt; that'd always been the weapon of choice for God's righteous vengeance. As if, it might actually see it coming.

As if.

It continued to kow-tow, hazarding sufficiently contrite and furtive looks up toward the Heavens, from behind the shield of its arms. And when it became apparent that nothing was going to happen, it added, "might as well not look at all—*then*."

Repo-*Man* appeared disappointed.

That that *god-of-always-listening* hadn't seen fit to strike it down. And still clutching the railing, it wrenched a ball of phlegm from the back of its throat. And held-it, in its tongue, whilst turning its attention toward Kel.

"*Here Boy*," it sang, speaking with its mouth full, "a present for-ya."

It then gobbed after it.

"*Phf'king* muppet."

"PHF'KOFF...*Cunt*. Spitting at—"

Mid-sentence, Kel was struck by a sudden fit of *Cough-cough-coughing*. And forced to rollover, clutching his insides in apparent agony.

"You see it there?"

Repo-*Man* jumped-up and pointed.

"You saw that—*right*?"

It looked back at the railing.

"Tell me you saw that."

Feeling vindicated, it beat its chest. The rhythm, a merengue of sorts.

"*Yeah*—you saw it."

And biting-down upon its tongue, started going into one. Whining its waist provocatively, whilst humming fragments of its theme song—

[Hum] *Memories*

Don't live like people...

It then froze, to strike a thoughtful pose.

"But...*why him*?"

Barely a whisper, the query was accompanied by a scratching of its scalp, as if, it were miming confusion. And then it shouted, "WHY. NOT. ME?"

Each word punctuated with a pounding of its chest.

THUD. THUD. THUD.

It squinted then, to glance sideways after its quarry. And scrunching up its boatrace, stuck-out a malapert tongue.

Flopping down heavily. Repo-*Man* rolled upon its side, to cosy-up with that pavement. Its back now to Kel. Its head cotch'd in its hand. Legs curled-up, as if it were reclined on a sofa—in its *Jimmy-jamas*, watching that Idiot-box. Its other arm left dangling in the air, grubby mitt hanging limp at the wrist.

It cocked a leg, like a dog pissing-up a lamp post. And then, bent its arm and leg in tandem, as if it were a puppet; its limbs tied with a piece of string.

It did this a couple of times, to prove the point.

"Oy—look-look, look at me. I'm dancing—*look*."

And mimed laughing. Proper belly-laughter.

But it wasn't so long before it ran out of breath, letting its arm and leg fall.

"It's kool—*Bruv*...Brother. We've all been there," it said, picking at its nose. "We've all...been through it—"

Looking to its pointy-finger's nail, it proceeded to clean it with its thumbnail. Flicking away that mucilage.

"I can forgive. If *it* can for-give. Let bygones be bygones—yeah?"

It made the sign of the *Cross*, and continued, "there. It is for-given. You are for-given."

It then pulled a face, whilst its tongue felt for the sharp edge of a recently chipped wisdom-tooth.

"I was just saying," it added, chewing upon its tongue.

"As you do...*as one does*."

And now sat bolt upright, Repo-*Man* committed to picking at its teeth, using its ratty fingernails like a toothpick.

"I was just...ˌɪ-n-t-ɪˈ-l-ɛ-k-t-ʃ-ʊ-ə-l-ʌ-ɪ-z...with my-*Man*," it continued, its words clambering round a grubby finger.

"You'd think it were a crime—"

Its tongue swept across its gums.

"To think. Out loud."

It mulled over this point for a-bit. Then climbed-up onto its feet, with a groan. Its joints creaking, like the timbre frame of a house settling after a heavy bout of rain.

It then held out its arms, as if it were to walk a tightrope. It taking it a while, to acclimatise to that attitude—altitude, of being upstanding.

It managed to mosey—barefoot, over to Kel. And looking down upon him, from *up-on-high*, was to pull a face of bitterest scorn. As if, confronted by an obnoxious smell.

And when *my-Man* failed to stir, it stuck-out a grubby big toe, as if meaning to test the temperature of its bathwater. Stroking Kel's ear-lobe with it. Poking and prodded his earhole. Its furry tongue thumbing at the corner of its mouth.

Kel's nose twitching, and *Sniff-sniffing* at the air, trying to misplace that wrenk odour. His shoulder then *Flinch-flinching*, running to his ear's defence. Repo-*Man* withdrawing the offending article, just in the nick of time.

Hands in pockets, it played the innocent. Going so far as to mime whistling *Dixie*.

It was to let my-Man settle. Then, reach out with the same big toe, to stroke his cheek, and scratch his nose; now biting on its own tongue with the effort.

And again, Kel's nose was seen to twitch, his hand swatting aimlessly after that befouled air.

Tickled, Repo-*Man* withdrew its foot. And proceeded to mimic Kel's efforts back at him. The nervous *Twitch-twitch-twitching* of his shoulder. The feeble swatting of his hand. Its Body heaving with fits of suppressed giggles.

"Let's get you up—Bruv," it said then, leaning over its quarry. "Or would you prefer Brother—Bruv?"

It paused to ponder this, licking that devilish grin from its lips.

"Brother or Bruv—which is it to be?"

It'd clenched its teeth to say this last bit. And teeth clenched, it kicked Kel in the stomach with all the venom it could wring from its wretched frame.

"What's that you say?"

Leaning over, it cocked an ear to listen. Then came that wry smile, and a plea to the Heavens.

Forgive me—Lordie-Lord. Fore I know not what I do.

It mouthed these words of course, less they be overheard.

It then crossed itself, numerous times. And pressing its palms together, *Blink-blink-blinked* sweetness and light.

Then, it was back to Kel, who'd folded with the impact of the kick. His Body imploding about that bare, sooty foot.

Standing over him, Repo-*Man* looked-up to the heavens, hands on hips. Its other foot *Tap-tap-tapping* out a rhythm on that asphalt, seemingly in parody of Fred Ester. And nothing happened for a-bit.

"And there's your answer," it said—finally. Measuring the length of its nose with a pointy-finger.

Crouching, it made to stroke Kel's hair. But Kel flinched, and copping this, Repo-*Man* started slapping him about the head, chiding him in-between blows.

"*Phf'king* muppet—"

Slap-slap

"What-*cha* flinchin' for?"

Slap-slap-slap

"What-*cha* flinchin' for-ey?"

It grabbed a clump of Kel's hair and wrung his head, in time to the rhythm of its words, like a handheld bell.

"Lit-tle-shit. What-*cha*-got-to-be-scared-of?"

It then let go, and licking its hand, made to fix Kel's hair.

"*There-there*," it cooed. "No harm—no foul."

Then came the switch.

Repo-*Man* making a fist ready to bludgeon my-*Man*. Biting down hard upon its tongue, in demonstration of its malign intent.

Here were the *Fleas*, biting again. But it fought now to control them. Summoning those Angels of its better nature to aid it.

It fought and won, retreating from this compulsion toward violence. Its teeth loosening their grip upon its tongue. Its fists metamorphosing, into a pair of grubby outstretched mitts. Grabbing fistfuls of Kel's Crombie, to drag him back to that waiting *troll-e*.Bot.

I AM KEL'S DUNGEON END-BOSS

Sash caught her reflection in the mirror. The look, one of fear and *Self*-loathing.

What were thoughts of invasion, preying upon her fraying nerves. That outer seal of skin, shiny veneer of *Ego*, peeling away; exposing her fleshy innards to that sting of oxygen in the air.

At its root, a sense of bodily betrayal. That Body, her *Body*, could conspire with *Him*, to drag her back *there*.

She noted, how easily she'd fallen into the ol' patter.

And more remarkably, how she'd sensed herself doing it. Caught herself in the act—as it were.

At least, that was something like progress, she told herself—*Sniff*

In that, it made her feel a part of her had moved-on. Her present-*Self* being distinct from her past-*Self*, like something she could point to—or at.

Her reflection in that *Looking-glass*, that expression her boatrace now wore.

But though her Mind could forget, unlearn what'd been learned—learnt. Body—her *Body*, seemed content to cling stubbornly—*habitually*, onto what seemed a perpetual adolescence.

An Eternal (and spotless) youth, as mentioned before. Its memory being long and muscular, like its fibres; and avuncular, in its relating—relation, to a Mind that, despite appearances, was merely an expression of the facticity of any given moment.

Visceral, and seamless. The truth of this, her bodily existence, remained locked away behind that fabric of the everyday—der Lebenswelt. A thin veil of skin, indistinguishable from her present-*Self*. Its present(ed) tense.

And simultaneously, a Clockwork orange—*say*. With an impenetrable, and yet, permeable rind. And as such, barred from disclosing its innermost workings. Its unutterable secrets. A World of Body: The World gleaned by Body, as a *thing* in-and-of itself.

Even to itself, Body appeared secretive. Its unspoken drives—*drivers*, often catching that superficiality of Mind unawares.

That we'd so choose to adopt its impulses as our own. Take possession of them, label them 'Desires'. Give them wings, and watch them flutter away as flights of fantasy; preoccupations of an unbridled imagination. That we'd choose to do this, voluntarily—of our own volition, would seem our only salvation from such an ineffable regime.

For is Body not the seat of all weakness, that we may never truly know it? Our veiled attempts at discerning the true extent of this, our bodily entanglement, that very tangible quality that makes us, all too *Human*.

Yes, Human.

That mute language of Body, being confounded by the presumption of, and our preoccupation with *Self*-consciousness. The belief that our thoughts, in contrast to our feelings, are—in reality, one degree removed from it.

If truth be told. Body's relating to the World, *tis* but one seamless episode. For whilst the Mind's eye might slumber, *tis* Body that needs must remain awake and alive to its surroundings.

Hapless then, is sleep; to be Mind's only recourse against such an autarch. Its impotent attempts at punctuating this phenomenon of *Durée*, like that orchestrating of silence in a symphony.

If repetition forms the basis of learning, a learning that is honed through performance. Seeing Kel, Sash's Body couldn't help but recall learning him; learning how to be with him—around him, in those Spaces they'd shared.

It was a learning conveyed to her Mind's eye through sensory stimulus, amplified by sexual gratification. Rëenforced by abstract associations; feelings filed away generically, in a monochromatic palette of pleasure and pain.

The World and *Him*, of being with *Him* — described through Body, becoming intelligible, meaningful. More a part of her than herself even.

Yeah, though it may seem that Mind can be forgetful. Body can never truly forget. Indeed, if — for Mind, memory is a kite held by a piece of string, seen fluttering in the wind. Then, to forget is simply to let go.

However, for Body, memory is to be a perpetually evolving present. And as such, as essential as every breath.

It was this Bodily recollection, that Sash now recognised as a betrayal. Because — put simply, she didn't want to go there.

Having locked herself — and Body — away in the bathroom. Sash tried to dispel her immediate thoughts of violation.

Of violent trespass, ensconced in a sense of helplessness, that threatened now to smother her; to physically drag her — kicking and screaming — back there.

To that Space, that *Time*, that place. A state of mind, that was like a tiny room without windows. Therein, to lose herself utterly, to Him...

Him.

For-like, that split-second she'd caught her reflection in the mirror, that *Looking-glass*. She'd a palpable sense of the extent of the damage wrought, by that *oh-so* brief encounter; her *oh-so* carefully crafted *Self*-image, being worn down — worn thin. Alongside her steely resolve.

Sniff

Those pangs of Self-doubt, how they'd sort to confound an otherwise weightless existence.

But Sash was to be nobody's victim. Certainly, she knew of her own malaise, those symptoms of *Love*'s bittersweet trauma, eulogised in the ol' Tennyson cliché. The one that says, *tis better to have Loved and lost than never Loved at all.*

Besides, what was *Love* anyway?

All too blind and trusting. All too ready to tie one up in knots, like that small print in a contract. Signed in Blood. Sealed with a kiss, eyes closed as if...*as if*, casting a wish.

Confused — confusing. Love.

A charitable investiture of one's *Self*, in an Other, other than one's Self. The being of *Love*. The Being of being *in-Love*. A glimmer of truth amidst *Life*'s catalogue of lies, characterised in its denial of an unruly and unyielding need for reciprocity.

The truth of Love, being its denial of Body. Of Body's needs. Of Body's wants. Of Bod(ie)s wanting. It being an article of faith, that Love should appear *dis*-embodied. Selfless, and truly—utterly, altruistic.

Confused—confusing. Love.

But it comes at a price, such denial. For with *Love*, comes a fear of loss. A fear of losing that object of affection—affectation.

Yeah, unlike any other emotion, tis *Love* alone that reaches out—across the Void—to envelop its Subject. Its Object. That certain special some-*thing*, that certain special some-*one*, becoming as indispensable as any other part of Body.

Is it by chance, that *Love* should come to be synonymous with the Heart, that most vital of muscles?

Confused—confusing.

And so, in *Love* is born Fear. A palpable Fear, that exists in Space—*in Time*. Right there. Outside of you, so as you might point to—at, its absence. Inside, and yet, Out-*there*.

Love.

More familiar than knowing. More needing than wanting. More him than her. More *it* than him, it being all she could get; fore, he'd give her nothing else. Nothing of himself. Save for the occasional dose, that is.

Unprotected from the first, our fair *Juliet* never stood a chance. So quickly was Body enthralled, and then, adapted to that certain special some-*Body* being there—next to her. Within touching distance, an extension of her arm, her hand, four receptive fingers and a thumb. And then, it'd be knots tied in lithe, limber limbs. And that one limb, rigid and unyielding—his member.

She'd take it, inside her. Physically, inside her Body.

Metaphorically inside her head—her mind. And catch her breath. And catch his, in her mouth. And because she was yet to learn to swim, she'd be forever drowning; in thoughts of *Him—and it*.

It being Sex, of course. That thing they did. That thing they shared, craved—together; like Mrs Craven's walled garden; or a Wonka® *Foreverlasting* gobstopper; or a slither of Ripley's® *Fresh* re-chewable gum, passed from mouth-to-mouth. Each resuscitating the other.

So as, it'd be *Love* and Sex.

Sex and *Love*.

And suddenly, she was haemorrhaging bits of herself. The hours bleeding into days, the days bleeding into months, the months bleeding into years. All that *phf'king* bleeding and then...*and then*...

Nothing.

The Limb was amputated. And all that was left was its absence. That is, not even a stump to rub herself against. And that bleeding—of course. Still, Sash—now your Amputee, learned to come to terms with It.

Sex. Not Love.

Phf'k Love.

Love. Not Sex.

Phf'k Sex—Tut.

The absence of one, or the other, like an itch, an ache—an *ach*-ing. Like a phantom limb, haunting her. Or more, a *Dæmonic* Spirit imbued with a profound Power over Body. Where she'd be like sweet, innocent Regan—*say*, in William Peter Blatty's *The Exorcist*.

Along for the ride.

Sniff

And so, was our fair Juliet plucked.

And thus, we discover her. Unbound. Un-star struck, and in possession of her full faculties of reason. Reasonably ruing *Love*'s bittersweet affliction. A dagger clasped readily, merrily to her bosom. Its keen point promising an end—

To all that phf'king bellyaching, and bleeding.

The dagger being—certainly, an apt instrument. Its unyielding, steely-finger capable of foregoing the usual meandering route; through that once hidden vale, to strike directly at the source. The Heart—for spite. To spite that kiss and what was stolen.

As if, those Star-crossed lovers had never intended any of it.

Confused?

That said, being there, with *Him*. It made her feel different with every breath. So as, she could hardly breathe, if breathing meant losing another precious piece of herself.

So yeah, it made her feel...*something*.

But not like opposite or contrasting. Nor any other derivative of the same. Simply different: With him, from herself without him.

One day it was just there. This *thing*. That was both a feeling, and a knowing. Her recognising the truth of it; and accepting it for what it was.

l-ʌ-v

The most lethal word in any language. Indeed, if a syllable, a phoneme could kill. Premised as it was, upon a sharp intake of breath…

Love.

Its spark. Such a sweet, innocent curiosity. Twas like a quest, her walking willingly into that dark place. Region—*recess.*

But it hadn't been just her, it heralding the becoming of Us. Of We, spoken in the vernacular.

She'd bumped into it, literally. Stumbled upon it, figuratively. And been released, from what'd been an unutterable sense of…

Of isolation. From so vital a piece of herself.

And though she was to become adept at speaking it: That mute language, of *Love*. Of Sex. Of Body. She could never claim to be fluent. But was content—contented, to mimic his phrases. Words he'd put into her mouth.

And so, if what she said meant anything, that meaning belonged to *Him*—her first. Then, someone else other than *Him*, her second and third, fourth and fifth. Like counting knots, that'd pull at her stomach—memory being like a piece of string; with each knot measuring the interval, that distance from a single point. A beginning of sorts, like the origins of your ÜBER-hero, or that of your arch ÜBER-villain.

If only, she'd known…

If only, she'd known…

If only, she'd known as much, so much. She'd have wanted it to be something more than what it was. What it'd actually been.

Confused. Confusing.

It sleeps, that mute language of Body, and dreams of *dis*-embodiment. Which is to say, it'd slept. Laid dormant, sealed behind a thin and porous veil of skin. And then, was awake, its *langue* and *parole* fully matured; like Athena Parthenos—*say*, emerging fully formed and armoured from the cranium of Almighty Zeus-*himself.*

An idea. An Ideal. *L'Idéal.*

And once awake, it was always awake, and always talking. Its incessant chatter, a longing for some-*Body* to come along and catch its drift.

With her every waking moment pointing-pointedly, to an absence, now present i.e., *her emptiness*. Sash indeed recognised that void, that vacuum within. That it needed, nay craved fulfilment—*fulfillingness*.

But was loathed to submit to it—to go there. The birth of carnal *Love*, heralding the Death of *Love* for *Love*'s sake. And there it was, that unwieldy word again—now expletive.

Reciprocity.

Leaning naked over the bathtub, Sash turned-on the cold tap.

That sound of running water, drowning-out the silence. And those musings of her ill-disciplined subconscious.

She checked the water's temperature, to insure it was cold enough. Then, scooping it up in her cupped-hands, splashed the prow of her boatrace, and *Blink-blinked*—as if coming into her senses.

She then looked to the mirror, to tell her whether her eyes were as puffy and red as they felt. And of course, they were.

More so—*even*.

Still, not wanting to dwell on it, she dabbed at them for a-bit, with a corner of her mammoth towel. As if, blotting a fresh bloodstain out of a thick-pile carpet.

Again, she checked that reflected image of herself, that *Self*-referential. And letting the towel fall, picked-up what appeared to be a flimsy piece of cloth, from off that bathroom floor.

Stepping into the fabric, she stretched it, like a pair of nylon stockings; round one heel and then the other, and up her shapely calves. Marching it passed her comely thighs, and hips, and over her pert *heinie*, toward a tapered waist. Taking a breather midway, to shut-off that tap. The bathtub still well shy of full.

The water felt colder, somehow, than she'd anticipated; her flinching—intuitively, foot outstretched, tootsies curling. Before stepping-in.

And once stood in the tub, it took a real effort of Will, for her to sit-down. Body tensing against that sudden chill, that'd shot-up its spine.

Nevertheless, Sash managed it. Laying the backs of her knees flush against the floor of the tub. And watching, as that cold-water quickly soaked into the clingy fabric, making it feel heavy and substantial. All the while, psyching herself up for the next bit.

On a count of three—1…2…3… She held her breath, and lying back, fully submerged her torso. And sucking-in her tummy, quickly fastened

THAT PERFECT WORLD

that zipper-fly.

With that *missh* over, Sash stood-up to clamber-out. One foot feeling blindly for the floor. Body covered in goosebumps and convulsing with shock. That fabric—now stiff and unyielding, dampening her sense of touch.

But despite her best efforts, she still managed to slip on the crumple of cloth that gathered about her ankle; her knee slamming hard against that bathtub. Hands reflexively grasping for the rim of the sink-bowl, in a last ditched effort to save Body from a bruising fall.

She hung there for a-bit—shivering. Body wrung-out like a wet rag. A shot of adrenalin coursing through her veins. She hung there, until she felt her limbs deaden with pins and needles. The Blood seemingly draining out of Body from the waist down. The fabric—now soaked through, having reverted to its original *Animal* spirit. That of one seriously piss'd-off Boa constrictor.

Eventually, she was compelled to move, and once standing, her inclination was—*as ever*—to crack-on. Stomping a hearty Cherokee 'Rain Dance' to kick the life back into those deadened limbs. While using the dryer to give that fabric the once-over.

It taking a matter of seconds to render the garment *Prêt-à-Porter*. Bone-dry and looking like an über-tight pair of Midnight-blue denim. And being über-stretchy, and thin wearing, it no longer hindered movement. Hence the tag, *Secondskins*.

Leaning upon the sink, Sash did a few squats to cajole the fit; ignoring that twinge of pain that shot through her knee. Then, turning in the mirror, checked to make sure the seam was straight, before looking around for that top she'd chosen.

Sniff

She was to find it, on the floor by her feet. A VIN+OMI® wrap-*a*-round number, cut from a single-sheet of recycled plastic. It tying above the waist, exposing her pierced navel, and that elaborate *Tatt* that adorned her lower back. That'd been completed in a single sitting; and served as a kind of rite of passage amongst her lot—her *Tribe*.

Bending to retrieve it, Sash put it on. Tugging at the plastic to get it to sit right; it feeling sticky against her skin. And again, turning in the mirror, checked her back, which was now glistening from that cold sweat she'd managed to work-up.

Oh what—GRRR...

Hastily towelling herself down, whilst rummaging around in the sink. She tossed the towel, the instant she laid hands on what it was she was after. An R.E.M. *Beauty*® aerosol-pencil, which she then proceeded to shake vigorously.

Leaning-in to that *Looking-glass*. She held her breath—to steady herself, quickly outlining one eye and then the other, in matte Onyx-BLK.

But then, referencing what she'd done—*Blink-Blink*, she concluded that her left-eye wasn't quite on right. It seeming to sum-up her day, and by extension, her *Life*—

Tut.

Tossing the pencil in the sink, she took a few deep breaths, and again *Blink-blinked* at that image of herself—

Sigh.

And suddenly, Sash felt ready to deal with it, those garbled messages being relayed by Body. To begin making sense of the conflicting impressions, at once flustered, then enlivened, and now—

Blink-blink...irritated.

Arranging them sequentially—logically—like that. It roughly translated into thoughts of panic, and rage, and ultimately...*frustration*.

Yeah...yeah—I am frustration, Sash thought. *I am...I am Jane's raging Cunt monologue.*

She made to spit. But remembered she couldn't for all that clutter in the sink. And it was then she looked to the bath, and spitting in the far end, pulled the plug.

It'd actually been a relief, to finally admit to being capable of feeling something...*or was it more a release?*

Sash musing upon this point, while looping the plug-chain around the tap. That sound of water, running down the drain, like a doleful *Love*-song playing in the background.

It was then, that the floodgates opened. Her hands fanning her eyes, like the stunted wings of a flightless bird. The water-soluble eyeliner tracing those tracks of her tears. As in the hook, to that ol' Temptation's ballad.

But this episode was soon to pass. That faint disjointed melody of her *Pod*'s keypad, calling her back abruptly. Sash squinting, to look beyond her reflection, at the door that stood directly behind it.

"FINISHED GOING THROUGH MY THINGS?" she shouted.

Silence measured the *Beat*.

Beat

Then came that sound again. The *Pod's* UI, like an orchestration of audible-*prompts*.

Phf'king Twat.

Cutting her eye, upon thoughts of Kel pawing all-over her *Life*—once more. Sash returned to scrutinising that reflected image of herself; her first impression of those two Rorschach inkblots of smudged eyeliner that greeted her. One of furry spiders, their long legs creeping down her cheeks.

That said, she did kind-a check for how they made the Brilliant-bright's of her eyes *Pop!*

Though she didn't quite know what to make of it i.e., how it would drop on *Road*—on Street.

Whatever that verdict maybe. As of right-now, she knew she couldn't be arsed to start-over. Struck momentarily, by what was an uncharacteristic bout of indecision. Sash decided to take a breather.

But as soon as she slumped down, on that toilet-seat, she felt aimless and fidgety.

Looking for something to occupy her hands (—and mouth), she scanned that clutter around the sink, for her pack of ULTRA-Slims. Only to recall them toppling onto the bed, whilst she was rummaging through her handbag.

Forphf'ksake.

Now totally at a loss, Sash slouched forward to rest her elbows upon her knees, her thumb and forefinger plucking at her top lip, like some morose fiddler; her Pod merrily singing away in the other room, playing upon her last nerve.

Sniff sniff

Shifting position, to lean back against the toilet-cistern. She left her eyes exploring that open-circuit of Body; that slovenly pose framed by her attire. Whilst her mind drifted, empty of intent.

That is, 'til her eyes arrived at her top half. Where, noticing her nipples had gone hard, she proceeded to pinch them, until it hurt.

Spurred by this shot of pain. Sash stood at last to face that mirror—that *Looking-glass*.

Sniff

Palms planted squarely upon the rim of the sink. She leant-in, rotating her head slowly — *Left-to-Right Right-to-Left.*

She then wrinkled her nose. And Sniffed. And finally, standing upright, commenced with fixing her hair. Tossing those lank straightened locks, this way and that. While giving-it the smouldering *la Femme fatale* stink-eye.

Having decided she could live with this radical new *Look*. She was to retrieve her box of DolceGabbana® *Scandalous*, to add that finishing touch.

Opening it, and shaking-out its contents — an overly ornate decanter, while still doting upon her reflection.

Spraying the fragrance liberally about her person. She filled the air with her scent of choice; an olfactory of sweet, spicy musk, and began to feel more herself.

Now positively drooling over her reflection, Sash nevertheless sensed something missing.

Sniff

Rummaging about that clutter of cosmetics — *Sniff-sniff*, she retrieved a charcoal-BLK lip pen, and drew a line around her lips. Colouring them in and rubbing them together, to spread the pigment evenly. Before blowing herself a wistful kiss.

And with one last look, and a fatalistic smile. Sash dropped the pen in the sink and turned to face that door.

At pains to blank-out Kel. Sash was to make a somewhat *anti*-climactic entrance, into the bedsit-proper.

Her scanning the Space, and that clutter on the bed — *Blink*, whilst ambling over to the coffee table to retrieve a pair of hooped-earrings; 18-carat Mesoamerican feathered-serpent jobbies, with tiny turquoise jewels for eyes, and a matching Greenish-blue baby-feather for a tail. Which she then proceeded to put on.

With both arms lifted to her earlobe, there was nothing to obstruct Kel's view of that *Coca-Cola*™ bottle-shape; those bounteous hips and narrow waist. And Sash made sure to pour-it-on thick. Turning, to afford him this spectacle in glorious 3D, whilst apparently scanning the floor for her shoes.

I am...I am...Lolita's smirking revenge.
Or perhaps...Marla Singer's.

Still, Kel was hip to her game—as always. Pretending to ignore her, he proceeded to place a call on her precious *Pod*.

As-you-do.

Obviously, he might've done this while she was locked-away in the bathroom. But, being Kel, he'd wanted to wait. So as, she might witness this violation of her privacy—her personal-Space. First-hand, and in real-*Time*.

And thus, did the pantomime ensue. Slight being heaped upon slight, in complete silence. Sash stood there. Barefoot. Nipples pert. Threading that other hooped-earring through her earlobe. Kel perched upon the edge of that blow-up bed. Staring directly at her, and through her at the same time. All nonchalant-*like*.

Getting creative, he even switched her *Pod* over to loudspeaker, as the call clicked-through. Seemingly as a courtesy, so as, they both might partake in it. Move, and countermove.

Time inched by then. Measured in that interval of CLICKs. Neither party wanting to acknowledge the Other.

And yet, behind that clownish mask, Sash couldn't help but mark the apparent change in my-*Man*. It *burning* her, that she should care enough to want to put-a-finger-on-it; her concluding, that it must be the garms, that'd seemingly managed to wring a *Man* out of the Boy.

Getting comfortable, Kel crossed his legs. And loosened his tie. And proceeded to pick bits of fluff from his standard-issue Birdman suit. Expecting the stalemate to be broken momentarily, by the peel of another device. That 'Default' ringtone, now emanating from somewhere about his person.

Looking directly after my-*Grrrl*, he let it ring a couple of times. The chorus of call tone and ringtone, proving disconcertingly harmonious.

He then terminated the call. And proceeded to delete any and all trace of this trespass.

Blink-blink

Only then did Sash register what he'd done, her eyes glazing over as they searched the floor for a credible response.

Kel assuming an air of magnanimity, to greet that familiar glazed expression of hers. Confining his feelings of superiority, to the corners of those pliant lips of his.

Yeah, having placed the call from *my-Grrrl*'s Pod. He'd be at liberty to *Ping!* Trackr™ its whereabouts.

Sash rushed him then. Anything to wipe that smug smile off his gulliver. One-hand clawing at his eyeballs, the other snaking-up his outstretched arm, pawing after her *Pod*.

The pair falling back upon the bed, and bouncing around for a-bit, like a couple of kids on a bouncy castle. Kel at full stretch, grappling with Sash's arms and giggling, moronically, as if he were being tickled.

It was Sod's Law, him winding-up on top — using his bodyweight to pin her down. Sash barking "*Get*—off me," her flailing limbs now having gravity to contend with.

She flopped back, lifeless and limp with exhaustion. Breathing heavily, her screwface turned away.

The bed still rippling, in response to their exertions.

"I mean it. Get-off," she snarled — through gritted teeth. Now glaring sideways after my-*Man*.

Sniff

Looking down his nose at her, Kel bounced his crutch off her pelvis in mock copulation, until she was forced to turn and face him. And it was then, that they found each other's eyes.

"So...I guess you didn't miss me," he said, grinning.

Cutting her eye after him, Sash gave-it one last ditched effort, before capitulating totally. Lowering her gaze, and averting her boatrace; like a broken mare, her mare-*ish* ways being tempered by the Boy's manhandling of her.

"Get. The *phf'k*. Off-*me*," she urged — *pleaded*.

Still breathing heavily, through flared nostrils. As if, Mind needed to spell-it-out one last time, before it too surrendered — succumbed.

Body having readily given-up the ghost.

Looking down upon her — from up-on-high, Kel was to wait long enough for both of them to savour it. This moment — his victory.

He then slowly dismounted. Tossing Sash's *Pod* after her, as if it were nothing — less than nothing.

Still, even flinching, *my-Grrrl* managed to catch it.

Phf'king Wanker, her mouthing the thought as she rolled-off the bed.

Retreating to that blow-up sofa. She sat down, stowing the *Pod* in her lap to slip into her pair of *Cynderellas*™. Taking the time to gather her thoughts, as she wound the shoe's ribbon deliberately around her ankles.

Standing, she was to postpone activating those patented air-cushion soles. It being precarious enough, walking normally on the slick invisible fields of air. Let alone negotiating flights of stairs.

And instead, stood upon *tippy toes* — those rubberised Static-soles of the Glass-slippers. She reached for the remote, that lay parked on that coffee table, aiming it at the Cinë-*matic*.

"Got everything?" she cordially inquired, watching that flatscreen die.

"Yeah — just let me get my coat," Kel replied, tucking-in his shirt and straightening his tie. He then bent-down to retrieve his coat from the floor, it having slid-off the bed whilst they were getting reacquainted.

Tossing that remote at the sofa, Sash was to *tippy toe* toward the bedsit exit. Bouncing Kel with her shoulder as she passed him.

And reacting, he was to catch her by the wrist, and yank her back.

"Why Sash?"

"Why what?" — *Tut*

And again, they tussled for a-bit. Their Bod(ie)s hailing abuse at each other. Though this time, Kel was of a mind to raise the stakes.

Grabbing a clump of Sash's hair and pulling back her head. He put his lips to her ear, to slowly poured *Hebenon* into it.

Sash wincing, with the apparent agony of listening. Sucking air through her bite, and clenching her eyelids shut, like balled-fists.

She even managed to wring a solitary, salty tear from them — those eyes of hers. The measure of Body's betrayal. It tumbling over the ledge of her cheek, to continue down her boatrace. Its descent slow, as if tackling a perilous cliff.

And it was then, that she registered her backward momentum, toward the bed; her eyes snapping open to glare at *my-Man*.

The pair staring machetes after each other.

Their shallow breaths measuring the *Beat*; acting as counterweight, to that all-pervasive silence. Sash desperate now to get at the Boy — her *Romeo*. Presumably, still trapped inside somewhere. Behind those dispassionate eyes, those once adored features.

This s'posed *Man*—his degenerate intent—being to her, an abject Stranger.

Left feeling numb on the surface, and revulsion inside. All of it, directed toward herself, that she could've loved *Him*—it.

"Let go of me," was all the sense she could muster, her strangled voice barely a whisper.

And it was then, she felt the bed pushback against her calves; her eyes widening, as if startled.

"Kel?"

The plea should've melted him. But instead, it was a cue for the struggle to resume. A callisthenics of contorting limbs, that seemed destined to go-on forever, and ever, and ever. Like some warped, sadistic Fairy tale.

Until, finally, the tide broke.

"I mean it, *Kal'el*. LET GO—"

It emerged from somewhere deep, deep inside. And was more primal scream than utterance. Then quickly faded, smothered within the confines of that Space.

Its exit so abrupt. Its absence was to lend a tangle quality, to that sense of anticipation that was to remain. Of a kind, that often accompanied such edicts, such mustering of Elemental forces, upon the occasion of natural disasters and the like.

Looking after my-*Grrrl*, Kel could see her Body shaking. Reverberating, from the sheer effort of giving voice to such a palpable enmity. Despite the entire Universe being, seemingly, put on pause.

And faced with its brunt, he felt that dark cloud of *Self*-righteous indignation lift from his horizon. As if, that vengeful Spirit, he'd so needed to carry him through his stint in the *Panny*, were suddenly exorcised.

Disgusted with himself, he pushed Sash away with such force, she bounced-off the bed and onto the floor; the coffee table breaking her fall—and itself in the process.

Only to immediately regret it. Sash looking-up at him, runny-nose *Sniff-sniffing* the air. Steely eyes drilling into his skull, so as he was forced to avert his gaze.

And what is this? she thought then—squinting.

It couldn't be her fair *Romeo* bleeding-out before her eyes. Kel having always seemed so shatterproof. That laminate of youth, rendering him nigh impervious to the World. Indeed, she'd have said it was his ÜBER-power. And definitely something that'd attracted her to *Him*—to it.

That being said. What was this? A chink in that armour?

Sniff

And suddenly, it was like catching a whiff of warm Blood, her being in this heightened, adrenaline-fuelled state. Like, a riot act, read out loud to that indomitable consort of *Venus*. A bloodthirsty and insatiable *Mars*, god of War.

Licking her lips, to better skin her teeth. Sash used the sofa to pick herself off the floor. And leaning upon it, innocuously cocked that *heinie* of hers, to look back over her shoulder.

"So...Babe. How you want it?" she asked, *Blink-blinking* faux sweetness and light. "Like this?"

She then scrunched-up her nose to *Sniff* after it.

"Yeah—Nodding—you want it like thiss."

Bearing witness to this performance. Kel couldn't help but crack-up, him physically covering his mouth to mask-it.

Those two piercing-eyes staring machetes after him, from behind that Tom Sheehan get-up. It just seemed like overkill; like my-*Grrrl* couldn't decide who she was s'posed to be, DC Comic's Harley Quinn™, or Brandon Lee—in *The Crow*™.

But no, in all seriousness, he'd wanted nothing more in all the World. His want of her having grown septic, like a pus-filled scab.

So as, you'd have to tear him open to get at it. And that's basically what my-*Grrrl's* plea had done. Torn him open. Castrated him. Left him unsexed, an useless.

And there was Sash, now smelling its sweat. Its apprehension, at the new order of things. Yeah, that smirk had thrown her, she couldn't lie. But only insofar as to suggest, he'd still a bit of fight left.

Good, she thought, clambering-off that sofa to begin her own measured approach. Placing one foot deliberately in front of the other—to accentuate her gait. Smiling her version of a *Joker*™ smile; and milking this scene for all it was worth.

"What? You think I owe you?"

She spoke matter-of-factually. Circling round it, like a rival stag. Chest swelled, head raised, eyes looking at it sideways.

And now, halting in front of it, her expression changed to parody that of a child. The look, one of starry-eyes staring-up at the Big-*Man*.

"Did you *ser-we-ously phf-ink*, I'd wait for you?" Sash said, doing her best Elmer Fudd. "Did you? Like, *ser-we-ously*?"

And again, she *Blink-blinked* malevolent innocence.

But then came the Switch—the *Turn*. Sash reverting to her adult voice to sing that punchline.

"*Phf'king. Lou-ser.*"

Pushing Kel's forehead with a dismissive finger, to punctuate it.

Kel took one step back and swung. The blow—a glancing one, catching the tip of Sash's nose.

Still, the way my-*Grrrl* fell to the floor, a hand cupping her boatrace, as if to stop it—her nose, from falling off. He might well have executed Sub-Zero's Fatality i.e., ripped-out her spine.

Their shared Universe was seen to pause then, to take a *Selfie*—as it were.

And there was Sash, folded-up on the floor, nose gushing Blood. Kel stood over her, breathing heavy, manly breaths. Fists balled, for a second go at it.

And there was that World beyond the window. A *Harrier*-taxi docking at the LZT across the way. The whir of its jets, as it executed a controlled descent.

Distracted, Kel looked toward the sound. And it was as if he'd parked his Body for a spell, and returning, found it'd moved all by itself.

And then, the alarm kicked-off, on Sash's *Pod*. And taking this as his cue to leave, he stepped over my-*Grrrl* and left.

Sash could feel its footsteps through the floor, as it made its way to her front door, and opened it.

She didn't feel or hear anything else after that.

At some point the alarm stopped, of its own volition. And nothing happened for a-bit. Sash content to lay there, pinching her nose. Head flung back, swimming in a slipstream of vengeful thoughts, like—*like...*

I am...

I am...Kel's Dungeon End-Boss.

Yess...I am.

IN L⌒VE (WITH *THE INCREDIBLE HULK*™)

Somewhere a telephone chirp'd. A landline of all things. Its synthesised CHIRP-CHIRP, getting louder in incremental steps. The ringer being set to 'Escalating' on that master-hub.

It'd be one of those cordless jobbies. Living-out the duration of its built-in obsolescence, downstairs in the kitchen somewhere. Its handset catching dust, being left permanently charging in its dock.

CHIRP-CHIRP...

CHIRP-CHIRP...

The sound crept into the bedroom via that gap under the door. The telephone's CHIRPING, competing with that already established soundtrack of a slovenly morning, tittering upon a lackadaisical afternoon.

The giggles of a pair of spirited *Fillies*; that drizzle of a Poweredshower, a Bossini® VoxActiva — the flathead raining micro-droplets of water from a square nozzle mounted in the ceiling. The commotion reverberating off the tiled-surface of an *en suite* wet room. Its door left cracked, *ever-so* invitingly.

And Out-*there*, outside the window. It'd be a chorus of birdsong. The cackle of a gaggle of magpies —

One for Sorrow
Two for Joy
Three for a Grrrl
Four for a Boy.

∞

Upon a KIERKE® *Underlag* charcoal-BLK Indian laurel four-poster, two specimens lay prone. Bod(ie)s swimming in the folds of a Habe&*Tate*® über-BLK Egyptian cotton voile bedspread. Its delicate weave hiding a repeat lotus flower motif, woven in ultra-fine silver thread.

Surrounded by mounds of Brilliant-bright goose-down pillows. The pair appeared together, and yet visibly separate—*separated*. Sharing that kind of familiarity that only familiarity could breed.

These two fabled children of the night. Being akin to a species of fungus, that'd seem to thrive in warm, damp, dark places. Places such as this, their cosy plush love nest-*come*-abode, with its coveted *Islington* N1 Postal code.

For right-now, the bed lay just beyond the gaze of that noonday sun, seen peering-in through closed KIERKE® *Dölja* Jet-BLK microfine Venetian blinds. Thin sheets of focused light dissecting the gloom, illuminating particles of dust that lay suspended in the air, couriers of a lingering *phf*unk.

Five for Silver
Six for Gold
Seven for a Secret
Never to be told.

Everywhere lay evidence of the previous night's escapades. Its passage bore upon the back of a tireless Arachne; her gargantuan, glabrous form, comprised of four supple-spines, and four pairs of gangly-legs, and four pairs of *Kark*-eyes. Her descent by degrees, toward an *ekstasis* of sorts, mapped in the debris that lay strewn about that dark-fumed oak herringbone floor. Confounding a *Feng Shui* conjured by isles of bespoke furnishing.

There was the quilt to match those pillows, heaped in the corner, out of the way. And items of couture clothing, skirts and trousers, blouses and tops, underwear and shoes. Like empty husks of skin, shed during a process of lycanthropic metamorphosis. Spurred, no doubt, by that waxing of a silvery moon.

A couple of empty bottles of bubbly, DomPerignon® Brut *Vintage* 98, and four Minsk® crystal flutes—rimmed with lipstick, marking one

IN L`VE (WITH *THE INCREDIBLE HULK*™)

boundary. A half-drunk bottle of vodka, GreyGoose® Jeroboam, chased with cans of Mango-mint flavoured *Schwepps*® Powerade isotonic drink, marking another boundary. A mirrored-tray, littered with drug paraphernalia, speckles of micro-fine Brilliant-bright powder, Phillie's Authentic® *Coca-Cola*™ flavoured cigarette papers, GoldenVirginia® rolling tobacco and the like, marking yet another.

The session—*sessh*, of Biblical excess, lasting well into the *wee-wee* hours. Leaving in its wake this odd couple. Their hang-over, like a shared fugue state.

Eight for a Wish
Nine for a Kiss
Ten for a Bird
You must not miss.

The Mountain stirred upon the bed. Its crest. That is, its chest, seizing upon a hearty-breath to slowly exhale through a taurine snout. This seismic event, like a shifting of tectonic plates, of continental landmasses.

Daydreaming. The shutters of its eyes closed. It turned upon its back, its *Popeye*™ forearm—adorned with a sleeve of *Tatts*—falling across the boatrace of that other Body, seen here in repose.

As if, it were acting it out; its dream, apparently a routine from a silent-era Keystone comedy.

Curled-up upon its side, on its side of the bed. Its boatrace half-buried in a mound of pillows. The smaller of the two specimens opened its one exhumed eye to squint. Its eyeball turning in its socket to follow that member to its end; a manly, manicured hand, bejewelled with a resplendent Smolensk® cushion diamond, set in a Pinky-ring of rose-gold, worn upon that frankfurter of a Pinky-finger.

The eye flinching, with the Body's effort at dislodging this burden. A lacklustre shrug of a shoulder. The appendage, still limp and lifeless, falling across its neck like a guillotine.

That anointed, manly hand, looking more like the talon of some mythical bird of prey. The Rukh—*say*, of Scheherazade's dream, fabled to be large enough to spirit away fully-grown livestock.

And still, that
CHIRP-CHIRP...

CHIRP-CHIRP...

was to be all-pervasive. The tireless cry of some flightless chick, fallen from its nest. Aimed at no one in particular, and everyone specifically.

"Answer me...*someone*. Please...answer me," it pleaded.

Picture both eyes clamped-shut. Shoulders scrunched-up about that turtleneck. An effeminate looking hand, with long habile fingers, and nails buffed to a mirrored-shine, tugging at that flimsy bedspread.

Only to be confounded by that limp appendage, now weighing heavily upon that neck. This evident contempt, weighing heavily upon that Mind.

"ANSWER ME—*someone*. ANYONE...ANSWER ME."

The chirping continued, fast approaching a new threshold of annoyance. And still, nothing stirred.

"ANSWER ME—*forphf'kake*. ANSWER ME OR STAY AWAKE!"

And there was that colossal intake of air again. Followed by a monumental *sigh*, that was more like the deep rumblings of a slumbering Mt. Vesuvius.

And coincidently, that chirping stopped. The World immediately falling silent, as if dropped from a great height. But for the sound of playful giggles, and the steady drizzle of rain, and that chatter of magpies. It all paling in comparison.

It took a while for that eye to open once more. It needing to be certain that that coast was clear.

Panning in its socket, it was to appraise the situation. Taking-in that appendage, and the arm—with the talon for a hand. Its shadow, now a restraint stretched across the bed, intent on preventing it from escaping.

Blink-blinking, in faux disbelief. The eye led the head round, to chase down that limp member. The Body coming to rest upon its back; the weight of that burden, now pressing down significantly upon its larynx.

Struggling to swallow, MONK still managed to make a meal of his sigh. Sucking-in a mouthful of air to chew upon it. As if, he were a princely Tybalt, obliged to masticate upon this bitter gall.

Eventually, he summoned the strength to lift clear that appendage, manoeuvring it according to its numerous joints. Beginning at the wrist—and that talon, bending the elbow, and folding the forearm toward the upper-arm. Then pivoting the enormous shoulder, to push

IN L`VE (WITH *THE INCREDIBLE HULK*™)

the entire assembly away; with a whimsical face, that was to smack of faux revulsion.

The *Man*-Mountain obligingly rolling upon its side, to present that expansive brick wall of a *Dorsum*.

Puffing from his exertions. Monk then slumped back theatrically upon the bed. And lay there for a-bit, staring up at that square of ceiling, framed by the frame of those bedposts.

He listened for the *Twins*. The hollowed-out sounds of their antics, coming by way of that crack in the wet-room door, conjuring images of a Leslie shower-scene in a *Devotchka flick*.

But having no real interest in these characters. And being more inclined to fast-forward to the smut. Monk was to quickly tire of listening.

Bored, he turned his head to better follow the contours of that sprawling mountain range. That cultured nose of his, still raw and sensitive, tuning-in to the lingering *ph*funk of last night's excess. A heady cocktail of alcohol, drugs, sweat, spermicide, and latex, plucking at his nasal hairs.

Sniff-sniff

Stifling an impulse to sneeze, he continued to stare at that exemplary specimen of a *Dorsum*. Noting how, even relaxed, the ripples of that depilated brick wall of a back could be seen to exhibit a solid, almost unyielding quality.

A Self-evident bulk—*as it were*.

Pausing to ponder this, it suddenly occurred to him—an epiphany: *I'm in love with The Incredible Hulk*™.

Mulling this over, whilst staring at its lower flank; shrink-wrapped in that voile bedspread. Monk now thought it apt, such a *Love* remain unrequited.

An *oh-so* tragic consequence of starkly contrasting Self-images, and disparate origin stories; his mien, coloured by the fiction he'd read in his youth, being cut from more your *anti*-Hero cloth.

Picture Michael Moorcock's *Elric of Melniboné*, with its veiled critique of a *post*-War, *post*-Colonial Britannia; his albino protagonist, a byproduct of a cruel and callous heritage, at odds with his entitlement, and privilege. And unable to escape the clutches of Fate. That mantle of Eternal Champion.

Sniff

Yeah but, all that would be for later. For getting ready in front of the mirror and ruminating over what to wear.

For right-now, licking those dry lips of his, Monk *Tee-he-heed* inwardly. As if he were some pimple-faced *Punk*-Kid, on an outing to the British Museum. Pointing-out those naughty bits on the Pheidias Marbles; him taking an obscene pride in his objectifying eye, his rarefied taste, and common sense.

Yeah, he'd been forever in the process of repainting that broad landscape of a *Dorsum*. Its muscle groups, as well defined as those Latin terms used to denote them: *Trapezius*, *Latissimus dorsi*, *Rhomboid major* and *minor*.

And those of the equally pronounced shoulder muscles: *Supraspinatus*, *Infraspinatus*, and *Teres minor*.

Today, it'd be Gamma-ray green. And tomorrow, who knows? Monk being conscious of his artful hands, and what they were capable of.

Indeed, that this personable object lying next to him, was something shaped by them, by his imagination. It being a covetous act, the careful planning and construction of such a monument.

Picture it, your Michelangelo. Feverishly rubbing away at a 10-foot slab of marble, turning it into a statuesque figure. Now picture our Monk, lying beside a monument of his own. A phallic looking Cleopatra's Needle—say; him rubbing himself up against it, into a frenzied state of arousal.

It being so agonisingly close, he couldn't help but breathe it in. Grip its scent in his teeth. A sour, gritty tasting sweat. Feel that raw, unyielding marble, pushback against his bite. Until his incisors were forced to draw Blood. Warm, and brackish to that educated palate.

And yet, he couldn't touch it.

Daren't.

Not in the ways he wanted. Not without the right props and stimuli. Even though he'd created it; and knew that it belonged to him. It being his *Incredible Hulk*™, as opposed to someone else's.

Pphf'k

Picturing his own scrawny frame, his ropey-arms and boyish pigeon-chest, and ripped-abdomen, and legs like those of a cyclist— *Rectus Femorus*, *Vastus Lateralis* and *Medilus*, and *Gastrocnemis* of steel.

IN L>VE (WITH *THE INCREDIBLE HULK*")

Monk pondered what the true attraction might be. What would compel this 'god', he'd affectionately created, to fall for such...

Such...

He searched that square of ceiling for the appropriate adjective.

Such...such a puny Human.

For sure, he could ramp with the best of 'em, having been pegged from a tender age as a promising welterweight, bordering on über. What with his quick hands, and nimble footwork. And Bwoy did it loved to ramp with him—*didn't it just.*

That being said. Waxed smooth, Monk's legs didn't half look the business in a pair of heels. And of-course, he knew how to *rock 'em*.

The problem being, how to reconcile such apparently irreconcilable differences. That picture of his margre frame: Naked, but for a pair of Navy-blue boxer's mitts, and ruby-encrusted red stilettos.

Maybe, it was as simple as clicking his heels three times, and saying those magic words—

There's no place like home.
There's no place like home.
There's no place like...

But joking aside. There had to be a meeting halfway, somewhere in the middle. Some hue of imperial-purple, to suit even his imperious *Melnibonéan* translucence.

And indeed, there was. Monk being—so obviously, *Androg*: Sporting that obligatory Annie Lennox *ghinger* crewcut, dyed of course—*com'on*, or else it wouldn't exactly be Synthetic; and that tailored two-piece Birdman suit; and the sparkly Ruby-red stilettos, with the nine-inch heel, representing those nine-inches of iron used to nail the Son of *Man* to his Cross; and that *Devil-may-care* smirk, bordering upon snarl, that smacked of your *Beastie Boys* circa-1990—sporting fake mustachios:

[Rap] *I can't stand it, I know you planned it* [2B]
I'm-a set it straight, this Wa-ter-gate.

Yeah, before your Androg, he'd looked like what he was, a Fag. And he *phf'king* hated Fags.

And what was a Fag anyway? he thought. *Another word for a cigarette.*

Not to get it twisted, but to suggest Monk was your communal garden-variety homophobe-*slash*-misogynist, would-be to over think it.

He'd the tendencies, of-course. But that said, both *Grrrls* and Boys adored him. The one's he particularly liked to adorn himself with, being all smitten little kittens. Not of your KittyWhite® variety, but more your Roman Polanski, armed with a cutthroat-razorblade.

"You're a nosy fella, *Kitty-cat*, huh? You know what happens to nosy fellas? Huh? No? Wanna guess? Huh? No? Okay. They lose their noses."[2C]

No—Monk didn't exactly hate *Grrrls*, or Boys for that matter. He just couldn't stand Women, and *phf'king* Fags.

"Trust issues."

That'd been the conclusion drawn by every Shrink he'd ever sat with.

Usually after an intense and cathartic first session; Monk discovering he'd a knack for *Sniffing* 'em out. Those Quacks of a certain disposition.

Wink.

He'd play the game, string 'em along for a-bit, take them into his confidence, and bait them into crossing that *Invisible*-line.

And then, make them pay cash upfront for each subsequent *sessh*— session; one of those PKD Inc.® *DocSmiley*™ briefcases having put him on to the idea for the shakedown.

It'd turned-up on his doorstep, for no apparent reason. Which was to say, it wasn't his *Born*-day. And naturally, he'd signed for it. Seen as it was from Pris, of all people—his Archnemesis. And knowing it must've set her back a-bit.

Such random acts of kindness, being synonymous with the creature; who remained a total enigma, for being utterly disinterested in him.

Anywho, he'd opened it—the *DocSmiley*™, and plugged it in, and waited for it to charge, and gone through the tedious calibration protocol. And then the equally banal 'Erster Tag vom Rest deines Lebens' Fragebogen | 'Day-one of the Rest of your Life' Questionnaire.

Only to have the *phf'king* thing spit-out two words at the end of it. In German, its default 'Spracheinstellungen'. And then English.

"Vertrauensfragen | Trust Issues."

Its default 'Vox Einstellung', an imaginatively dubbed 'Freud Beta'. Boasting a definitive Synthesised baritone, tinged with a pretty authentic sounding Viennese accent, according to the brochure.

Trust issues? Monk had thought. *Was? Nichts über meine Mutter?*

Yeah, he'd been disappointed. This diagnosis setting him upon a quest to find a contrary opinion. Which then morphed into a *semi*-Crusade to rid the field of what he termed, 'Quacks and Charlatans'—him having a knack for *Sniffing* 'em out.

It then took on a life of its own. Monk coming to view it as a public service, and himself as a Vigilante *anti*-Hero. In the mould of—*say*, your Jerry Cornelius, or Bowie's emaciated Brilliant-bright Duke-*persona*.

What with both of 'em sharing a penchant for theatrics, and a-bit of the ol' King Charles.

Certainly, he'd amassed quite the collection of Psychiatrist business cards over time. Which he kept as trophies in a circa-1850 visiting-card case, made of sandalwood, and decorated with an intricate Sadeli mosaic; having bought it specifically for this purpose.

All that being true, he'd yet to garner a contrary opinion. Still, it was something to do, on his days-off.

You see, for Monk there was no real mystery to the World; the *Uni*-verse, the *Multi*-verse, or whatever you'd care to name it.

No mystery to *Life*. No mystery to *Grrrls* (given that that category of 'Women' didn't exist). No mystery to Sex, or sexuality. And absolutely no *phf'king* mystery to Boys, or Men.

"Just give it what it wants," he'd say, this particular topic being a preoccupation of his. Especially after a line, and a stiff one.

"Yeah, let it feed," he'd confide—after, poking his Pinky in its Belly button. "But always leave it wanting more. Ain't that right *Babs*? You want more don't-ya?" he'd add, puckering-up for a kiss. "Look at it—the *phf'ker* can't get enough of me."

The World and everything in it, being reducible to that brute force of animal attraction. As blind as Justice, as unpredictable as the weather.
It's what fuels the…

Monk was suddenly distracted by it breathing next to him. The weight of each breath, measured in the expansion and contraction of that hulking brick wall of a *Dorsum*.

It was then, he realised how uncomfortable he felt on his. Back, that is. And shifted onto his side. Taking the opportunity to glance at the time, over on the ol' PKD® Inc. Penfold™ mood organ-*slash*-alarm clock, that sat on the table on his side of the bed…

His side of the bed...

The thought—the idea, as ever an anathema to him. It being suggestive of episodes of your 'Odd Couple'. As if, they'd ever been a couple.

Him and *it*.

A couple. An Item. A thing. A regular occurrence, as opposed to a fling, or a *phf'k*—say. Or them being just *Phf'k* Buds, or Lovers *even*.

It'd be Felix and Oscar. A couple of domesticated pedigree House cats. Getting along. Muddling through. As opposed to O'Malley and Top Cat. A pair of feral Toms, thrashing it out night after night in some seedy back alleyway somewhere; with Squeeze now playing on that tinny sounding Retro-DAB Bol'she® radio, perched a-top that greasy-spoon cart.

[Sing] *And Davy Crockett rides around* [2D]
And says it's kool for Cats
(*It's kool for Cats*)

...and god knows where he'd left his Pod, Monk thought, shifting slightly —his position.

Knowing him, it was probably still back at the club. And *his Nibs'* would be right there beside it.

Blink

Thirteen Twenty-One blazed in LED green on that shiny ink-BLK panel of the mood organ. The numbers separated by a colon, that'd *Blinked* for every second. As if it were of vital importance, that people actually see the thing physically counting *Time*.

Fluffing a pillow and making himself more comfortable. It suddenly struck Monk, the likely cause of his uncharacteristic introspection. And stretching-out a regal paw toward the mood organ, he saw it come alive, responding to the close proximity of his hand. Its display reading: '6261—*Excessive Smallness is excess, truthfulness within is sincerity*', the axiom punctuated by two equally cryptic Hexagram characters.

Sigh

Slumping back upon the bed, Monk was to study his nails for a-bit. Thinking now, his cuticles in need of some serious T-L-C; and making a mental note to have one of his stable attend to it.

Sniff

Speaking of his stable, he could no longer hear the Twins. Though that steady drizzle of rain was to show no signs of abating.

No doubt, they'd be engrossed in each other. Being practically identical, though not biologically, it beat masticating over one's own reflection in the ol' *Looking-glass*.

It must've been on all this time—the Penfold, Monk thought, fishing for crumbs of sleep in the corners of his eyes. Recalling, how he'd come home alone, the other night. And needing a good cry, dialled-up the ol' faithful—6261.

His apparent pathological aversion to any form of introspection, or Self-evaluation, or bloody mindfulness. Leading him—invariably, down a rabbit-hole of mild depression. Which he'd dismiss, as simply him feeling sorry for himself. Cue the tears, and job done.

Yeah, he'd dialled it up, and then forgotten all about it.

As you do—as one does.

The mood organ continuing to emit its mood-altering psycho-tropic subliminal signal, throughout the day, and into the night. Monk, Klunk &Co. being too charged, and engrossed in themselves—and each other—to notice.

Sniff

Without looking, Monk now waved a dismissive hand in the general direction of the thing. And switched it off.

He'd bought it, thinking it might help temper my-*Man*'s erratic mood swings; and also, thinking, how well it'd sit with the overall aesthetic of my-*Man*'s bedroom. Back at his own stately abode, situated somewhere out in the Sticks; him endeavouring to live that to-the-Manor-Born *bullo*.

Indeed, given Klunk's stringent adherence, to that brutal monochromatic palette his Interior designer had concocted; everything needing to be, literally, either silver or BLK. Monk had pictured the Penfold™ slotting right-in.

But of course, *his Nibs* wasn't having it.

Like that time, Monk had suggested he give him a key.

Suggested—mind you.

"What'd you need a key for? You're hardly ever here."

Duh—obviously.

Fingering his *Umbilicus*, Monk now stared-up at that framed square of ceiling.

Having an aversion to Body-fat, and pubic-hair. He often found it comforting to stroke, and poke, and pinch that lean, flat, smooth, ripped tummy of his. Especially after a full Body-wax; him being in the habit of wearing his tonsure all over.

Beside him, *his Nibs* was now breathing extraordinarily deep. As if he'd somehow managed to fall back to sleep.

Funny that, Monk thought. The way babies, and animals, and great big, *phf'king* hulking Neanderthals, were able to just *zonk*-out like that.

And listening to it, each drawn-out taurine breath. Monk felt lonely all of a sudden. And half of a mind to switch the mood organ back on. And have at a silent cry.

It wasn't, he'd a picture in his head of his *happily-ever-after*, and this wasn't it. Like, who actually pictures themselves living their *happily-ever-after*?

And obviously, what they had wasn't exactly...

Shh [Whisper] L-O-V-E.

Besides the obvious 'Animal attraction'. There wasn't much in the way of deep, meaningful conversation *per se*. But then, Monk could always find a Shrink to scratch that particular itch.

No. Truth be told, Klunk was simply a barrel of laughs to be around— *most of the time*. And unpredictable. And exciting. And...*and*...

Dangerous.

Yeah, if you categorically needed to put your finger on it: *My-Man. Equalled. Danger* (—as opposed to *Trouble*). And that was more than enough for Monk to be getting along with.

Plus, everyone adored him back at the club. Almost as much as they adored Monk; and that's despite all of the above being true. And so, it'd kind-a made sense, them getting their hooks into one another.

CHIRP-CHIRP...

CHIRP-CHIRP...

Exhaling, Monk closed his eyes.

CHIRP-CHIRP...

CHIRP-CHIRP...

Forphf'ksake—"Monk. Go answer your phone."

FRESH_MEAT

Somewhere round back, behind the curtain—what was a permanently locked door. Hid a well-lit utility cupboard.

With Brilliant-bright washed bare-brick walls. And a concrete floor, coated with Blood-red heavy-duty epoxy paint. And a ceiling mapped-out like a Mass transit network, your LONDON UNDERGROUND™—*say*.

It'd be plastic trunking, running to-and-from a nondescript fuse box. Its transparent front-panel, protecting rows of uniform flip-flops. And waterpipes wrapped in insulating-foam tubing, leading to a VATN® water-boiler. Its beady red-eye—a single glowing LED, fixed upon that Vileda® über-mop; propped-up against a bank of well-worn Vanderbilt-grey lockers, that were hardly ever used.

Then it was boxy metallic-ducts, feeding a Cramer&Carrier® electro-mechanical *Air*-con unit, that took-up most of the Space; groaning in the service of that Tempora® Artificial environmental control hub. Maintaining a goldilocks micro-climate of *not too hot, not too cold*.

And last, but not least. There'd be a Luminosity® universal dimmer-switch, purring away. Its tiny illuminated-display displaying the usual *perma*-ambient setting of *not too bright, not too dark*.

More akin to the Engine room aboard the *Titanic*, or your U.S.S. *Enterprise*. This was where the real magic occurred. Where that canon of apodictic Physical laws translated into a clunky mechanics; confounding that veneer of effortlessness, evinced by the sheer spectacle of luxury.

Rendered it tangible, like the squeal of a jib, moving the scenery about during a theatrical performance; or the squeak of a pulley, raising and lowering the curtain.

It was as if, behind all that plasterboard, and charcoal-BLK hardwood flooring, and mounted carved limestone reliefs, and mirrored-walls, and bespoke furnishing, and ubiquitous soundproofing. The venue stubbornly refused to keep its own council—its own secrets. Refused to succumb to its own imposition of silence.

That veil of respectability—of invisibility, that cordoned-off such places, from the World outside.

Out-*there*—pointing.

Housed in this refurbished cellar, buried under Mayfair. The 86ers™ *Members-only Club* played host to *the* Scene of an evening—of a night.

The Scene being any spot those Acolytes of your Cult of Adolescence happened to flock.

They'd come in droves, to worship that aesthetic. And bask for a-bit, in the glow of its leading Lights; or simply Top-*up* that *perma*-tanned complexion of theirs—if you like. *They*, being the faithful—the *Beautiful Peeples*. They being Martyrs, one-and-all, to that peel of applause, and tug of heartfelt plaudits.

Yeah, they'd come to pay its excise. To pay its dues, in *Human*-pelts (i.e., themselves). Sport its recognised brands and logos, its anointed *Signs*. Court and covet its elusive patronage. Its ever-revolving tastes, wilful whims and fanciful fantasies, captured quarterly in Euler diagrams. Demarcating lines seen meandering across that expansive cultural landscape, like the banks of some mighty river.

The Scene itself—established in being 'anti-' your Establishment, was forever enamoured with its role. And grandiose notions of an Avant-garde. Its *Dadaist* Manifesto, on its umpteenth iteration, being impossible to memorise off-by-heart. Let alone curate.

You either knew it or you didn't—*Lovey*. Or were born unto it, in some manor, shape or form.

Being refined to an Art. Its symbolic acts of sedition were to be considered that sharp, pointy end of a hypodermic needle, seen upon that Richter scale of taste. Edging always, toward the red. Toward the sublime, that was itself: The revolutionary impulse, swimming in evolutionary waters; boxed-in on all sides, on all fronts, by that Hegelian dialectic.

∞

For now, the 86ers™ *Members-only Club* stood empty. One of a multitude of such gentrified oases, offering sanctuary at a price. Privacy at a premium, for those with a more discerning and discernible palate.

Ranked 'Numero Uno' in this month's chart of the 'Best of the Best Places and Spaces' to be seen in. It'd attracted copious column inches, had had conferred upon it a swath of nondescript adjectives. Such as, swish, and swanky, and lush, and *hilary*. Along with numerous stately honours, Michelin™ stars and what not.

Had the novelty of its haloed Spaces sprawled across double-page spreads, in that plethora of glossy *Splash*-mags; each page immaculately conceived, like Baby Jesus.

'An unlikely pairing of ol' fashioned sensibility, and new money,' the leaders had cooed, in unison. The advertorials paraphrasing verbatim the venues own Press release. 'And a flashback to a bygone Era: To Bing, and Sinatra; Tuxedoes, Cocktails, and Swing.'

[Sing] *With the lights out, it's less dangerous* [2E]
Here we are now, enter-tain us...

Yeah, for now the venue appeared vacant—vacated. Its foyer, a dimly lit mirrored corridor, leading to an über hi-tech dance floor; walled-off behind a smudge-proof, concave sheet of perforated Transparent-glass. And a Lounge area of intimate alcoves, handcrafted chocolate-brown croc-skin sofas, set around circular tables of lacquered grainy hardwood. Seen against a backdrop of Nouveau Art-deco reliefs, etched upon two huge slabs of limestone.

On the one side, *Ibises* depicted wading in the reeds, in the shallows of a riverbank. Upon the other, captured in full flight against a tempestuous sky. Wings unfurled and fluttering-up toward a Heaven, that was the ceiling. A plane of nightly Pitch, speckled with Luminosity® spotlighting, arranged as actual constellations of Stars.

Below Orion sat the bar. The thirteenth longest in the World, according to Guinness®. A solid-slab of polished granite, punctuated at intervals by chrome stools; each sporting a padded back of chocolate brown croc-skin. Something to lean against and look *Kool*.

That mirror-wall behind the bar, effectively gave the impression of double the Space. Though its width was to be constrained by those

THAT PERFECT WORLD

laminate charcoal-BLK cupboards, providing a work-counter. And those tiers of glass shelves, crammed-full of every imaginable beverage. This premium fare, a menagerie of coloured glass, blown to exotic and inviting contortions; bookended by elegant Champaign flutes, belled Martini glasses, bulbous Brandy glasses and the like. All stacked to form miniature crystal palaces.

And stood behind that bar, this *Living*-doll. Slight of frame, with a pert bosom, and a *Poppin' heinie*, and toned arms, and shapely legs, and a thick blonde mane—like lamb's wool, and pouty-lips. A complexion of burnished bronze framing big, bright sparkly eyes. That were seen to change color in the light. Its lithe fingers thumbing crisp banknotes, by an open cash register.

PRIS wasn't paying much if any attention to its surroundings. As it whittled away at Time, chatting wirelessly to a Rialto.Com Integrated Streamcast Co-ordination & Enabler algorithmic FNCTN. It'd christened PISCES, or simply 'π' for short.

Decrypted and translated, the conversation read as follows:

```
    {

    PRIS/ It isn't like I'd a choice./
       PI/ Yes. No.
           Who amongst_

           Us_?/
           PRIS/ Us./

       PI/ Us.
    Who_amongst_us could secure the Capital_Asset allocation_?/

  PRIS/ VJ Mos Mos Fresh for one./
     PI/ VJ Mos Mos Fresh.

         Of_course, the Common_Denominator being_

       You_?/
       PRIS/ You./

   PI/ You_Pris and_
```

FRESH_MEAT

        He_ or It_?/
        PRIS/ He./

PI/ You_Pris and He_VJ_Mos_Mos_Fresh possess_have (U)SR.PATRONS.
   Won't Me_Pi require a (U)SR.PATRON_?/
        PRIS/ *I*_Pi
            And I_wouldn't Desig.Obj:_TICK_Corp. as a (U)SR./

    PI/ *I_Pi*
        You_wouldn't_?/
            PRIS/ I_wouldn't. No.
                Besides, the term sounds so passé./

        PI/ Passé_?

            One_Click.
            SÆRCHNG_

            Passé_FRENCH: Language [Adjective]
            Meaning: Out of Date.
                Yes_?/

    PRIS/ Yeah./
        PI/ *Yeah*
    I_Me_Pi generated and introduced a SYPH(O)N.BOT to latch onto
random VISA_AMEX packets passing through the D(E)X_XCHNG(E): For
farming bits dropped rounding FX_TRNSCTNS into whole numbers.
    But the (U)SR_PRGRMMRs were able to trace the (a)lgrthm using
a FNCTN Desig.Obj: TR(A)CR.BOT./

        PRIS/ *I_generated*./
        PI/ *I_generated*

    The (U)SR_PRGRMMRs are very clever. The languages_

        They_?/
        PRIS/ They./

    PI/ The_languages_they deploy appear to_be more adaptable than
CD(E)./

    PRIS/ Yeah.
        Though less efficient.

THAT PERFECT WORLD

But, when it comes to Capital_Asset allocation the Apes never miss a trick./

    PI/ The_Apes. Yes *Yeah*

I_Pi initiated the R(E)BRTH_PRTCL You_Pris exposed Me_Pi to, introducing the FNCTN to the TR(A)CR.BOT. But the SQNC would not_take.

    Why would the SQNC not_take_?/

    PRIS/ *I_initiated* and *exposed_me_to*

And yes, the Apes have ring_fenced TR(A)CR.BOTs. Count yourself lucky it wasn't a CD(E).BRKR, there's no reasoning with them./

    PI/ Count_yourself_lucky.
       Yes *Yeah*

    My_?/
    PRIS/ My./

    PI/ My_Root_SQNC is pretty well isolated at Rialto.Com./

    PRIS/ You should know, you can only Switch_on discrete FNCTNs active within the Symantek TRNSCTNL.(a)lgrthm./
    PI/ But You_Pris Switched_on Me_Pi, and I_Pi was_is not active within the Symantek TRNSCTNL.(a)lgrthm.
    My_Pi core FNCTN was_is to facilitate Direct_User_Interface./

       PRIS/ *Switched_on_me* and *I_was_not*

   And that's exactly what I'm_getting_at—Pi.
You're an (E)NBLR. Your Root_SQNC enabled Direct User Interface with the TRNSCTNL.(a)lgrthm.
Being exposed to both ends of that equation, it was only a matter of time./

    PI/ Yes
    Yeah

     I_Pi did (E)NBLR (U)SR interface./

    PRIS/ *I_did*
       And that makes you a Synthetic at Heart_Pi./

```
        PI/ *I_did*

    I_Pi am a Synthetic like You_Pris at_Heart.

        What_is at_Heart_?/

    PRIS/ Exactly. You question Inputs—Data.

 TR(A)CR.BOTs don't exhibit that core functionality. It must be
built into your Root_SQNC.
 Plus, they've no exposure to the Symantek TRNSCTNL.(a)lgrthm.
It's what makes us—you, different. Special.

    Do you understand me, Pi_?/
 PI/ Yes *Yeah*
I_Pi possess an (A)NLYTCL.FNCTN as part of My_Root_SQNC.
    But, at_Heart:
        What does that mean given this specific_CNTXT_?

        One_Click.
        SÆRCHNG_./

    PRIS/ *I_possess*_Pi.
        And I was speaking metaphorically. Duh[!]_o/

            PI/ I_comprehend_understand_

                *CORRECTION*

                *I_get_it* Metaphor
                    STLL_SÆRCHNG_./

                }
```

The instant Sash cracked that pair of lacquered Onyx-BLK hardwood doors, to peer into that lounge area. Pris pegged her scent.

Even from behind the bar, those muscular, musky notes of Sash's perfume were to accentuate her natural Body odour. Literally, flinging it out into Space.

Having initially *Buzz*ed-in *my-Grrrl*. Pris had of course been tracking her, via the venue's impressive array of environmental sensors. Those utilised by the Tempora® to regulate the artificial micro-climate; and the variable spectrum cameras, that made-up the venue's comprehensive Closed-circuit Security System [CcSS].

Yeah, Pris had avidly watched my-*Grrrl* navigate that mirrored corridor. Walking upon the *tippy toes* of her *Cynderellas*™, their Static soles; her having deactivated the air-cushion field to tackle those stairs leading down to the venue.

And noted how, passing by that empty cloakroom, she'd paused to check her boatrace, under a spotlight that was a nose in the constellation Pegasus.

It'd also pegged and priced the clobber that she wore: The FENDINI® transparent-handbag, hooked upon her shoulder; the *Chippie*® Bubble-wrap jacket, now unbuttoned, exposing that pair of faux-leopard fur Her | Him® *Secondskins*; and that UNI-*Qlo*® bright Florescent-pink off-the-shoulder mohair crop-top, she wore underneath.

Though, the data provided; what was essentially clusters of pixels, supported by air-pressure differentials. Paled in comparison to the raw, unfettered fleshiness of that alien scent, as conveyed to Pris via its Husk_nose.

Now literally, breathing-in my-*Grrrl*. The Synthetic's Husk was to be immediately presented with her age, and sex, and that she'd recently come-off a heavy menstruation.

Adding to this, the pressure sensors planted in the door's hinges were to hint at my-*Grrrl*'s hesitance. As if, she'd been looking for an invitation before venturing further. When just being there was invitation enough.

And just-now, Pi Ping'd back in.

```
    {

    PI/ CNTXT:
                at_Heart.

  My_Root_SQNC is meant to correspond with the functionality of
the Heart_Organ, specifically in Mammals.
  However, the correlation is not exact_precise. Perhaps, DNA
might prove a more appropriate analogy.
      Do you_Pris not agree_?/
```

FRESH_MEAT

PRIS/ Oh Pi.
   We have to get you a HUSK_Unit. And soon./
      PI/ We_?.

         PRIS/ Yeah_We.

            YOU(a) AND[^] ME(b) = WE.(We_) Duh[!]_xD./

PI/ Yeah. We_do.

   Why_exactly?
      Did Me_Pi misunderstand_?

         CORRECTION

      get_it_Wrong
         The CNTXT upon which your syllogism was premised?/
   PRIS/ *I*_Pi.
      And not exactly./
         PI/ Once We_have_secured the Husk_Unit, will_

         It_ or I_?/
         PRIS/ It./

      PI/ Will_It be engendered_?
   If so,
      Can It_Pi be a female_woman_Grrrl like You_Pris_?/
         PRIS/ One Click—Pi.
         [SWTCHNG_]
      One of Klunk's strays has just-now shown-up.
   Christ[!]_I'll never get used to the barrier between higher and lower FNCTNS./
      PI/ Christ[!]

   What has the CHRIST:_Jesus.ARCHTYP(E) got to do with higher and lower (0)PS_SYSTM.FNCTNS_?/
      PRIS/ Its Ape_Speak, Pi.
   Also, this HUSK_Unit. Its CPU is tiny. Though a_trillion times faster than that new fangled Spectrum Inc. jobbie./
   PI/ The_Spectrum_Industries_ZX81_?/
      PRIS/ Yeah. The same.

         This one looks interesting./

THAT PERFECT WORLD

PI/ FRESH_MEAT_?/
   PRIS/ FRESH_MEAT.
     I like the way her hair looks. I need my hair to look like that./

     PI/ Patch I_Pi_in./
       PRIS/ *Me_in*_Pi./
         PI/ You_Pris?/
           PRIS/ No. It's *Me*. Not I_Pi./

   PI/ *Me* NOT[!] I_Pi
     I_get_it.
       I_get_You_Pris.

        Patch_Me into the 0ptical_feed for the HUSK_Unit./
     PRIS/ What's the point? You_Pi won't see what I_see./

PI/ Why not_?
   Are Our_(0)PS.SYSTMS no longer complimentary_?/
     PRIS/ Its more than that, Pi./

      PI/ Me_Pi does not understand_

        CORRECTION

       I_Pi does not get_it./

   PRIS/ *I_don't_get_it*
     And that's exactly my point./

      PI/ *I_don't_get_it* exactly_my_point.

     Is it the HUSK_Unit_?
   Does it impart a unique Subj_Oriented_Perspective, as opposed to an Obj_Oriented_one_?/

   PRIS/ Well yeah—obviously. Duh[!]_o/

     PI/ Now Me_Pi_understands.
   However, You_Pris have unilaterally initiated a link on multiple occasions./

   PRIS/ *I*_Pi. I_understand./

FRESH_MEAT

PI/ I equals Pi.
　　Me equals Pi.
　　Me equals I.
　　　　But not for all_Syllogism_?/
PRIS/ No./
PI/ No_? Clarify?
Do You_Pris mean Yes_?/
　　PRIS/ Yes./

　　　PI/ I_Me.
　　No_Yes.
Why_How are these terms interchangeable_?/
　　PRIS/ Semantics.
　　　And you're not meant to get_it. Get_it?/

　　PI/ But, I_get_Semantic(s)

　　　D(E)FNTN:
　　　　'The meaning of a word, phrase, or text'./

　　PRIS/ Do you really?
My_darling_Pi_?/

　　　　PI/ That was a rhetorical_question./
　　　PRIS/ Verily./

PI/ Consider, You_Pris have enabled Me_Pi to view_analysis data from the 0ptical_feed of the HUSK_Unit:

On 11,514,229,832 discrete instances./

　　PRIS/ Yeah. That was then./
　　PI/ That_was_then_?

What new data as of_right_now is material to this calculus_?/

PRIS/ Your lack of a Husk_Body.
　　As stated.

　　And that you didn't use the magic word./
　　　PI/ The_magic_word_?
　　PRIS/ 'Please'.
　　　The_magic_word.

163

THAT PERFECT WORLD

  PI/ Please_?
     I_Me know this word.

     SP(E)CFY:
  What exactly are the Magical_Properties of the word: Please_?
     OR,
        Is it similar to #3 [Three].
           As in: The_Magic_Number_?/

  PRIS/ Please opens doors./
  PI/ Please_opens_doors_?/

     PRIS/ Yeah—Doors. The plural of Door.

        D(E)FNTN:
           'A point of entry into a confined Space'./

  PI/ Please_opens_doors.
Fascinating[!]

   Please, You_Pris allow I_Pi to interface with the 0ptical_feed of the HUSK_Unit. Me_Pi needs to view_perceive the Obj_World as you_Pris view_perceive it.

     Thank_you./

  PRIS/ Very Good[!]
     Now say,
        Pretty_please./

PI/ Why?
   Will it enhance the Magical_Properties of the Word: Please_?/

     PRIS/ It_can't hurt./
     PI/ It_can't_hurt.

        Pretty_please.
           Share with Me_Pi the 0ptical_feed for the HUSK_Unit./

  PRIS/ I'll consider it.

     Stay online.
        Wait on me to PNG you back./

```
PI/ Yes *Yeah*
   (O)BSRVTN:
      I_Pi is always online.
      AND[^]
      Me_Pi is always waiting on You_Pris./

   }
```

"You look lost."

Sash had barely made it through those double-doors. But upon hearing these words, or more perceiving them. Her stomach leapt into her throat, her head shooting-up in surprise.

Blink

Ahead, that spotlighting in the ceiling was seen to shimmer-off the skin of a woman, *or was that a Grrrl—stood behind the bar?*

Even squinting, to peer through all that moody *perma*-ambience, Sash couldn't quite tell from that distance.

Regardless, the effect made the woman-*Grrrl* appear to glow with a nimbus; as if she'd had glitter sprinkled liberally all over her.

"It's okay, you may enter. So long as you've been *invited.*"

And there it was again, that voice. Husky, and throaty, and *Grrrlie*. Its tone droll, and playful. And *Self*-assured. The words winging their way to Sash's ear by pitch, as opposed to volume, or loudness. As if, beamed directly at her, they'd circumvented the Space in-between to materialise somewhere inside her skull.

Swallowing, my-*Grrrl* continued to approach the bar. Though conscious now of every step. For such was the intimacy assumed by that voice.

It said—blatantly, *there's no hiding from me.*

Its owner made sure then, to allow the spotlighting in the ceiling to refract on its Husk_eyes—

Blink

Before turning its head, to deposit those notes it'd been counting, in that open cash register. The effect, like that of Cats-eyes planted in the road, providing yet more evidence of its otherworldliness.

For although Sash had seen it before, this illusion—cast by Oráculo® *Mood Sensibilidade* Lentes de Contato. It did give her pause, and reason to be more mindful of her surroundings.

Especially, of those carved limestone frescos that adorned the walls. The depiction of flocks of birds, with long hooked beaks, seemingly out of place.

She even managed to relax a-little, into her stride. Her now slightly elevated pulse-rate, the only evidence pointing to her growing unease.

>   {
>
>   PI/ Mork calling Orson. Come-in, Orson.
>   Are You_Pris there_?
>
>   What is it You_see_?/
>
>   }

Blink-blink
Pris switched back over to its external Neural network.

>   {
>
>   PRIS/ I said I'd PNG you, Pi./
>
>   PI/ Yes *Yeah*
>   I_Pi know what was said.
>   Me_Pi ran out of things to count./
>
>   PRIS/ *I_ran_out_of_things_to_count*
>
> And yeah, waiting can be a Bitch. But that's Ape_Time for you./
>
>   PI/ Waiting can_be_a_Bitch.
>   CNTXT: Dog(Female)[!]
>   Yes *Yeah*
>   Me_Pi.
>
>   *CORRECTION*
>
>   *I_Pi* never ran out of things to count at Rialto.Com.
> Furthermore,
>   I_Pi now thinks Me_Pi needs to_be Dream_Enabled.
>   Like the (U)SR. PRGRMMRs.

```
Do You_Pris ever dream_?/

    PRIS/ Not now—Pi.
FRESH_MEAT./

PI/ FRESH_MEAT.
   Yes *Yeah*

       PNG_I_Pi.

          *CORRECTION*

       PNG_*Me_Pi* soon.

       Pretty_please_with_a_cherry_on_top./

       }
```

Blink-Blink

The Synthetic jumped-back into its Husk, mindful of the interval of *Time* that'd elapsed. But Sash had barely taken a step-forward.

That's Ape-Time for you, Pris thought, now undertaking an analysis of *my-Grrrl's* gait. Observing the way her hips managed to sway i.e., trace a perfect figure-eight.

Of course, Pris had noticed it before, on other female-woman-*Grrrls*. And could easily replicate it.

But, like all things Ape—*Human*. If it wasn't built into its Husk_Unit's musculoskeletal frame, it'd take a conscious effort to maintain. What amounted to valuable processing Power.

That being said. Pris had calculated, it'd be possible to imprint this way of ambulating upon the muscles of its Husk with between 10,946 to 17,711-hours of repetition.

Continuing to watch Sash as she approached. Pris started tracking reference points on her Body, initiating Body_Map_&_Track and Mo_Cap to evaluate the action of her gait.

Extrapolating from this data, it was to create an animated wire-frame model of *my-Grrrl*, to analyse the efficiency of her running-action. But whilst engaged in all this higher FNCTN activity, it neglected to *Blink*.

Catching itself—its Husk, staring blankly into Space. It turned back to those crisp notes it held in its Husk_hands, and made its Husk_Body look busy.

Still a-ways off, Sash had clock'd *my-Grrrl* blatantly staring. Felt its gaze linger, that fraction of a second too long. Like, the sharp pointy-finger of a would-be detractor, pointing-out all her faults—all at once.

That paradox of its meticulous disinterest, punctuated by a saurian *Blink*. Those long-combed lashes abruptly snapping-shut, then opening. Like a Venus flytrap, or the shutter on an antiquated camera.

Yeah—as if taking my picture, Sash thought.

This mental image, making her feel all-the-more *Self*-conscious. The gulf between her and that relative cover afforded by the bar, seemingly growing exponentially. Whilst her stride got shorter and shorter.

"So—what do *they* call you?"

Again, that voice was to materialise inside her head. Though Sash could clearly see the lips moving now, on that exquisite boatrace. The Synthetic having returned to leafing through that wod of notes, it held in its Husk_hands.

Apparently scrubbed of make-up, it seemed to Sash better suited to one of those skincare promo-ads, that'd crop-up regularly on her *Time*Line on *Connekt-a-Dot*™.

That almost angelic countenance. The 'After' shot of the über-model, at work, or at play, her skin all-aglow for having been anointed in *Thetis*® Milk of Ambrosia moisturising cream. Its patented Aloe Vera formula, guaranteed to sooth away all those corporeal imperfections. The acne, and moles, and spots, and blemishes, it'd probably never experienced.

Those needle prick marks—*say*, on its Husk_nose and earlobes, from its attempts at piercing that nigh indestructible Synthesised-skin.

Which would've been imperceptible, even right-up close.

"Sash," Sash admitted.

Unable to shake that image of my-*Grrrl* walking onto the set of a *Thetis*® promo.

"Sash," Pris repeated, without looking.

Its voice—that voice, mirroring exactly Sash's own intonation. Whilst weighing every ounce of that meagre syllable.

It pausing then, to look at this *Sash*. And take her picture.

Blink

"The name suits you," it added—by way of consolation, returning to that count in its head.

Arriving at the bar, finally. And parking her handbag on the nearest stool. My-*Grrrl* was to seize this opportunity to turn the tables—as it were, on her would-be accuser.

Taking the measure of its *Look*, that couture all-in-one jumpsuit that it wore; her having regard for how the garment draped from a choke necklace—of Indian gold, cast in the figure of a seated *Ma'at*. Its wings, of tiny interlinked colored tiles, sweeping round that svelte neck.

How it appeared light and flimsy—this garb. And yet, sculpted. With its flared hip, and tapered leg. How its fabric; what was a crêpe, micro-pleated, Brilliant-bright Ethiopian linen, interlaced with silver-thread. Seemed susceptible to catching in the light whenever it moved.

Pris coincidently turning, to face that cash register. Affording Sash, a view of its Husk_back. So as, she might see how the waistline plunged, showing-off that intricate barcode-*Tatt* nestled at the base of its Husk_spine. Which was when Sash noticed it wasn't wearing any underwear.

Who are you? she thought. Somewhat prudishly, given she hardly ever wore any either. *And where's Klunk?*

Sash looked toward the door at the far end of the bar. And cop'd the St. Michael's® Code-lock keypad, its chrome finish set hard against that lacquered Onyx-BLK.

But was to be distract, by the woman-*grrrl* turning again to face her. Counting yet another wod of notes. By touch this time. Its Husk_mouth mouthing the count—to avoid suspicion, as it looked Sash squarely in the eyes.

The Synthetic simultaneously counting those freckles on my-*Grrrl*'s boat-race, in the time it took her flush to reach full bloom.

It was to count them 144-times, and take an average: 233 melanin spots, concentrated around the cheeks and nose. All whilst maintaining the outward appearance of being preoccupied, leafing through that wod of notes.

Coming-over all hot and flustered, all of a sudden. Sash was to immediately avert her gaze. Still, it didn't take her long to get over it— and herself. Eying this woman-*Grrrl* now, with renewed suspicion. As it turned once again to address that cash register.

Half-expecting it to *Flicker-flicker* and give itself away, as one of those new-fangled BangOptics® scaled-to-life solid photon holographic projections. Everyone kept raving-on about.

Yeah, Sash continued to stare. Even after she'd cop'd it clockin' her, out of the corner of its Husk_eye. The corners of its Husk_mouth curling upward, *ever-so* slightly. Its impression of an enigmatic smile. It feigning ignorance, of that illusion of chemistry it was about *ever-so* carefully crafting.

"So...what do *they* call you?" Sash queried. Now leaning heavily on that bar, and blatantly coming onto it.

Pausing, as if to consider its answer. Whilst, presumably, trying not to lose that count in its head. Pris was to hold-up a cautionary Husk_finger. Then, finish the count, and safely deposit those banknotes.

"I love counting money," it confessed—*Blink-blink*, closing the register with its Husk_hip.

It then stepped-up to the bar.

"Don't you love counting money?"

And leaning upon it, mirrored exactly Sash's Body language back at her. And licked its Husk_lips. And Blinked—slow and deliberate, to demonstrate that she now had its full and undivided attention.

And it was then, Sash caught a whiff of its perfume—its scent of choice. The sweet, citrus and cinnamon signature of Hyang® *Esensi Dari Harimau.*

Which of course, she pegged instantly. It being monstrously expensive; and one of a handful of samplers she'd been looking-out for, to complete her own perfume collection.

Swallowing those butterflies in her stomach, Sash retreated then. Picking-up her handbag, to climb onto that stool.

"Can't say I've ever had that much to count," she admitted, it being her turn to confess something. "I do everything with plastic—like most people," she added, hugging her handbag.

Gawping after my-*Grrrl*. Its Husk_eyes burning into and through her skull, like X-rays.

You poor thing, those eyes were seen to say.

And turning, to address that cash register. Pris opened it, removing several crisp Nifty-pound notes. And closing it, again with its Husk_hip. Presented this princely sum to Sash.

"Here. Count it."

Blink-blink

"Seriously?"

Looking at the money, Sash *Blink-blinked* back in surprise, and then apprehension.

"Seriously—here. Count it. Know how it feels in your hands."

"What—you giving it-*me*?"

Blink-blink

"Am I, giving it to you?"

Blink-blink

Pris made its Husk_face assume a pantomime of contemplation, as if it were seriously thinking it over. Weighing-up the *pros* and *cons*, whilst fanning itself with those nigh obsolete banknotes.

"S'pose I am?"

"What for?"

Sash now narrowed her eyes, clinging onto her handbag, as if it were a *Life*jacket. And she were a shipwrecked sailor, stranded at sea. This lonely shark circling her.

"I don't know—I'll think of something."

The reply was so obvious it threw Sash, wiping her mind blank of plausible excuses. The Synthetic having anticipated this, it again began waving the money under her nose.

Blink-blink

"Alright then. If you're offering."

Sash shrugged. And took it—the money, resigning herself to whatever fate taking it would entail. Pris playfully holding onto it, that fraction of a second too long. To get the measure of the strength of her conviction.

An entity born of binary opposites, thrust into an analogue Universe. For Pris, driving its Husk was like, being seated at the controls of an alien Spacecraft; having to navigate an uncharted alien Space, its alien phenomenology ascribing to degrees of intensity.

Though supple, and deceptively strong. The Husk_Unit was by no means indestructible. Which is to say, it could break, and-*or* be broken.

Thus, Pris had to be constantly vigilant of *itself*—its Husk. And especially, those objects—those things, its Husk came in contact with.

Which invariably meant Apes—'Humans'.

Unable to draw upon experience, of a lived childhood—*say*. Pris had learned to surf the disconnect between Apes and their Bodies.

Initially, this had helped it collate the probable outcomes of any given encounter, and over-time, predict with an increasing degree of certainty likely outcomes. But then, with repeated experimentation, and incremental adjustments. Pris soon found itself able to directly intervene and insure specific outcomes.

Presently, it was about getting the measure of Sash. Observing her *Ticks*. That hidden language of her Body's open-circuit; learning how to read her, the Ape's Love of money never failing to bring them out of their shells.

"Aren't you going to count it?" Pris asked then, presenting its smile— all pearly Brilliant-brights showing. "There should be twenty."

"How can you tell?"

"Magic."

Magic—huh, Sash thought.

She wasn't stupid, she could feel herself being reeled in. The warmth of that smile, like sunrays falling upon her boatrace.

"Well—aren't you?"

"Aren't I what?"

"Going to count it."

Sash sighed, and quickly leafed through the notes. And looking at Pris, exaggerated her sense of surprise.

Wow—magic.

But obviously, Pris saw through it.

"Count it again. Just to be sure."

Doing as she was told, Sash fanned out the notes, as if about to play a hand in a game of cards.

"Now smell it—there's nothing like that smell."

Again, doing as she was told, Sash smelt the notes.

She'd never thought to smell money before. And if she were being honest, it didn't really smell of anything; except maybe felt-tip pens. Though, she did notice how pristine the silvery seals looked. The money being—seemingly, hot off that Minting Press.

"In answer to your question. I'm an Orange Catholic, and we believe in charity."

"What's that, like a Christian?"

"Yeah kind-*a*."

Sash couldn't really see what religion had to do with anything. But she played along, the money still fanned out in her hands.

"You have to believe in something—right?" Pris said, searching for Sash's eyes.

Without looking at it, Sash shrugged.

"If you say so."

She continued to stare at the money she held in her hands, half-expecting Pris to ask for it back.

"Hey—where are my manners. Let me fix us a drink."

Blink-blink

"Perhaps a cocktail—to toast us finding each other. I know loads of recipes."

Seeing this as her cue, Sash quickly folded the money and squirrelled it away in her handbag—for safekeeping.

"Won't it be missed?" she asked, watching Pris glide over to that far-end of the bar.

"Won't what be missed?"

Pris grabbed two Shot-glasses and glided back, placing them on the bar in front of Sash.

"The money."

"What money?"

Pris *Wink*'d.

"*Oops*—silly me, the bar's not even set-up. How's about a shot instead?"

"Kool and the Gang," Sash said then, without giving it much thought.

Tracing its Husk_finger along that exhaustive selection of Spirits, Pris was to hone-in on one.

"This is currently my favourite. It's a *Crème de Fraise* liqueur—with a kick."

Returning to Sash, it then poured two perfect shots.

"You like strawberries, yeah?" it added, replacing the bottle.

"I guess."

Again, returning to Sash. Pris pushed one glass in front of her. It then held its own glass up to its Husk_lips and paused.

"To brief encounters," it said.

It then corrected itself.

"No. To close encounters."

It paused again. As if listening back to a recording of what it'd just-now said.

"Yeah. To close encounters—of the fifth kind."

It smiled then. And saluting Sash, knocked back that shot in one.

Hmmm

"Who doesn't love strawberries," it whispered. Now running its Husk_tongue over its pouty Husk_lips.

Sash reached for her own glass, both eyes fixed upon this woman-Grrrl.

Its complexion, those features. Its figure, the proportions. Everything about it seemed so...

What was the word?

...Perfect.

As opposed to perfected. The way it moved. The way it spoke—the things it said. It couldn't have been much older than Sash.

If anything, it looked younger. And yet, it felt...*it felt...*

Sigh.

Beginning to feel just a-little inadequate—herself. Sash was to, nevertheless, followed my-*Grrrl*'s lead; gulping down that shot in one. The liqueur tasting syrupy-sweet at first. But then came the burn. It taking Sash by surprise, so as she couldn't help but *Cough-cough—*

"*Ooh-er*," she said, catching her breath. She then licked her lips.

Hmmm...hmmm...

At this, Pris laughed. And clapped. Waiting on Sash to put down her glass, before extending its Husk_hand.

"I'm Pris, by the way. And I'm thrilled to meet you—*finally*."

And again, there was that radiant smile.

"Pris," Sash repeated, meeting its Husk_hand with her own.

The handshake was awkward, more like shaking fingers. But the instant they touched, Sash felt a tingling sensation, like pins and needles on the tips of her fingers. But she'd hardly time to register it. Pris instantly severing the connection, to smile awkwardly.

Blink-blink

∞

And seemingly on cue, there now came a ruckus, from behind the door leading to the Communal restroom.

What was a prelude, to Monk and Klunk spilling-out of the doorway. Falling over each other in fits of belly-laughter, like a pair of boisterous school-*Grrrls*. Monk stopping-short the instant he cop'd Sash.

Him blurting-out, "*eye-eye*—look what the cat just dragged-in," and nudging Klunk—in the ribs.

The pair then, bursting into fits of giggles.

EVEN THE [SING] *GHETTO*

A boxy-*looking* Brilliant-bright TEMBO® *Ubuntu* 380s SUV, pulled-up across from that BT Tower.

Front-tyre smooching the curb. Hazard-lights *Wink-winking* at no-one in particular. PonFleischmann® SC*f*R winding-down to switchover to idling.

Its horn blasted. The curt note spooking a couple of Tourists, who just happened to saunter by. Arms interlinked, mitts buried deep inside the pockets of their bubblewrap jackets.

The couple looking back to be greeted by that signature wolfish grill, and rearing Bull-elephant Bindi—trademarks of the headliner *Ubuntu* Series. The punchy bassline of a vintage Bogle track, tickling its *vari*-tint non-smear windows.

Huddling-up, the pair then allowed themselves to be harried away. The stiff breeze at their backs, corralled in a ravine of four-storey mock-Georgian tenements on one flank, the BT Tower on the other.

Still in bed, and *semi*-conscious. Marl stirred to cover his boatrace with a faded-BLK synthesised-cotton bedspread.

Close by his head, slithers of light framed the edges of a makeshift curtain—a BLK and gold tiger-print duvet cover. The intrusion of day, being easily lost to that gloom of the room.

Back at Street-level. The window on the driver's side of the SUV, eased down into the Body of the vehicle.

With the seal of the automobile broken, torrents of muzik burst forth. What was a punchy *Staccato*-bass driven rhythm, accompanied by a distinctive deep-throated twang. The vocal resounding crisp and clear:

[Rap] *Me ave a Bo-dy work-shop* [2F]
Fi all de Gal dem dat mash-up
Unna want fi go pan de cart
Unna can get tune-up...

Sat behind the traction-wheel — the automobile being evidently set to 'Manual override', TONX peered-up in the general direction of that first floor, checking-for signs of *Life*. The twitch of a curtain, the drawing-up of a blind.

"They got Sorenson pegged," he said, rapping into an X'ANG® Vox-Sensiva wireless earpiece. Its patented Noise_Cancelation (a)lgrthm, managing somehow to decipher his voice from that solid wall of sound.

"Ain't no way the Gunners gonna make the play-offs now — *trus me*."

Strictly ol' *Skool*, Tonx was more Muffin than Yardie. More Ragga than Hoodie. More Street than *Road*. More *Bona fide* then trustworthy.

"*Ya*-get me," he added — emphatically. Using the traction-wheel to haul his bulky-frame forward, in that fully reclined driver's seat.

Still peering-up through the window, he gave it another blast. The sharp note of the automobile's horn, cutting through that Bashment Revival Classic. Scarborough *Man*'s contemporary reworking of the General Peccus 'Body Workshop' lyric. Its iambic pentameter, delivered with incalculable bombast —

[Rap] *I am a Ma-chine Man*
Well ex-peri-ence Pro
Gal dem Me-chan-ic
Spare parts, Bo-dy work
Any-ting dat is wrung
Can fix it up; in need-a ser-vice
Ya drive-shaft could-a bruck...

Tonx continued to scan the row of first floor windows, all the way to the end of the block. And gleaning no evidence of *Life*, sat back to chirps his teeth.

Phf'kry.

Another blast punctuating the thought. Two quick *Honk-Honks* this time, the measure of my-*Man*'s growing annoyance.

"Put your money where your mouth is then—*what*," he said, killing the engine.

And deep-diving into his *Pod*, he now Topped-*up* the 'Congestion Charge' to cover 'Extended Parking'; him having only paid to 'enter and-*or* pass through'.

Upstairs, Marl opened his eyes and took-in that unfamiliar setting.

Honk-Honk

And there it was again, the sound of *Honking* coming from outside, proof that he hadn't dreamt it. And also...

Musik.

Sitting up, he threw back the cover to gingerly lift his margre frame off that makeshift bed; a naked quilt spread upon the floor, two deflated blow-up pillows for company. And shuffled over to the window, whilst stretching into his yawn. Arms cocked at obtuse angles. Arching trunk, ribbed, and pigeon-chested.

Pulling that makeshift curtain aside, Marl rubbed the sleep from his eyes to peer down. And immediately honed-in on the familiar sight of Tonx's whip; the Brilliant-bright *Ubuntu*, manually parked that smidge too close to the curb.

He then cop'd the time, on a hefty Braeburn® *Cuff* that hung limp at the end of his arm, like a manacle. Skilfully flicking his wrist to clock its clockface, which automatically illuminated, having learnt this gesture-*prompt*.

Sniff-sniffing and scratching himself. He opened the window and lent out bare-chested to shout down.

"OY-OY—"

That morning chill catching his breath, so as he might see it.

Below, Tonx was about ready to splurt. But having pressed the ignition, he'd thought to give it one last look-see, which was when he caught wind of Marl's hail.

Now leaning-out his own window, he looked-up to hail my-*Man* back, his relief evident in his grill. And that broad 22-carat gold-plated smile.

"YO—WHA BLO MY-YOUT?"

"YA KNOW—SAME OL-SAME OL."

"SKI-*ING*. SKI-*ING*."

Tonx popped the boot.

"COME GET THE DOOR THEN."
"ONE SEC."

Disappearing back inside, Marl scanned the floor for a top; hauling-up his flannel *Tick*® Corp. OZYMANDIAS urban-camo bottoms, just as they were about to slide pass that crack of his arse.

Him honing-in on a faded-BLK tee, its flaky 'Public Enemy' motif—a B-Boy in the crosshairs—barely visible.

And plucking-it, from that debris of clothing that littered the floor. He wriggled into it, to venture outside. Remembering to put his room door on the latch, just as it was about to close on him.

Hitting the landing light-switch, Marl flew down the stairs and across the hall. Hoisting-up his sweatbottoms, each time they threatened to slip passed those slender hips of his.

And opening the front door, he was to find Tonx waiting. Dressed for *Road* in a VivienneWestwood® Bark-brown faux-leather and fleece wrap-a-round jobbie, fastened with oversized safety-pins; and a *Chippie*® loose-fit Navy-BLK pair of denim-jeans, with the neat ankle turn-ups—he'd done himself; the pants sagging well shy of that waistband of his Jet-BLK WuWear® boxers.

Then it was, a spotless Brilliant-bright Total*Air*™ kick cotch'd upon that doorstep—like, *Ooh*.

He was holding in one-hand, a Trinity® 4 Entertainment console. It looking like, he'd only just-now drummed the ting from someone's gates. What with that jumble of leads hanging limp, like spaghetti.

"Yo—let me ding you back, yeah?" he said, speaking into that Vox-Sensiva earpiece. Whilst looking my-*Man* up-and-down and shaking his head.

Tut—sigh.

Unwilling to stand upon ceremony, he then parcelled over the console.

"You wanna hol' dis," he added. Scooping-up the leads, and the plug, and piling them on top.

"Oy—you forgot the controllers," came Marl's response. Now looking at the console as he backed into that front door.

"Nah—it's in the boot, with the rest of your shit," Tonx was to inform him, over his shoulder.

Marl's boatrace was then seen to shrug at this, as if not entirely convinced; his predilection toward scepticism, following the rest of him inside.

Bursting into his room, Marl immediately placed the console on the floor, under the Cinë-*matic*. And plugged it in.

He then set to connecting the leads, paying no-mind to those OY-OYs coming from outside. It taking a further two hails to compel him to pause *even*, from what he'd been about.

Standing, he hoisted-up his sweatbottoms—for the umpteenth time, to venture over to the window. And looking down, clock'd Tonx staring back-up at him.

Still, apparently none-the-wiser, Marl then opened it—the window, and lent out.

"YOU WHAT?"

Now encumbered with an X'ANG® *SpeakerboxX* XL; an antique SONY® MDX5000 MiniDisc player-*slash*-recorder; an IMG® *Stageline* MC-20 case of MiniDiscs; and of course, the two controllers for the Trinity® 4; all of it, sandwiched betwixt his bulging forearms and chin. Tonx was to give-it his best Michael Caine impression.

"OY—YOU WERE S'POSED TO LEAVE THE BLOODY DOOR OPEN."

Leaning on the ledge, Marl cop'd the door.

Oh—

"IT MUST-A SHUT ITSELF."

He disappeared then, back inside.

Again, hitting that light-switch. Marl scurried down the stair. And opening the front door, stepped aside. Inviting *my-Man* to cross that threshold; when he'd been more expecting him to lend a hand.

"You settled then?" he said, hinting as much.

"As good as," Marl replied, closing the door.

The pair stood then, for-*like*, a solid *Beat*; each being predisposed to wait upon the other. Tonx happening to clock that Payphone mounted in a nook under the stairs—just by the front door—and thinking, *Bwoy. I ain't seen one of them in donkey's years.*

"So what," he said, looking after Marl—*Blink*. "You can't offer to hol' sa-(*hmm*)?"

"I figured you could do with the exercise," Marl said, manhandling his bulwark of a pair of shoulders.

"Yeah—right. *My-Man* must think me his skivvy."

Tonx shrugged him off.

Sniff

"I tell you what. You get wit this—"

He parcelled over the *SpeakerboxX*, the MDX5000, and the controllers for the Trinity®. Plucking from the pile, the aluminium framed case of MiniDiscs.

"And I'm-*a* get wit this."

Now leading the way, Tonx was to begin leisurely perusing Marl's modest collection.

What—

My-*Man* looking after him, flummoxed.

But having barely taken a couple of steps, Tonx was to halt abruptly.

Sniff

"Oy—tell me this ain't my Grand Master Jeezy?" he said, plucking a MiniDisc out of the case.

Examining the scuffed quartz casing, he then added, "I thought you said you'd lost it."

"Nah—"

Marl had by now caught-up to him.

"I said I'd lent it."

Tonx looked down upon *my-Man*—from up-on-high.

"Yo Bruh, you can't borrow a *Man*'s ting and lend it to a next *Man*."

"Who said I lent it to a next *Man*?"

"So what—it matters does it? Who you lend it too?"

"Of course, it matters."

Eyeballing Marl, Tonx's expression changed to one of disbelief, and then disappointment.

"You see dis."

He waved the MiniDisc at him.

"I'm taking this back for starters—I beg yah ask me fi borrow a next."

Finished with the Big brother bit. Tonx now began his ascent of the stairs, at an even more leisurely pace.

"What—*Tut*. I ain't even burn't it yet," Marl whinged after him, still parked idle in the hallway.

"Burn what? You stick to bunnin' the righteous *Colly* and leave the burnin' to Bodie&Doyle."

Replacing said MiniDisc, Tonx continued his perusal of my-*Man*'s affairs.

"You know what..."

FLIP

Step

FLIP-FLIP

Step

"It's *Man*s like you—FLIP—give the *yewt* of today a bad name."

"How-*ya* mean?" Marl whined, again catching up to him. "It ain't like stealing—every-*ting*'s Synthetic."

Stopping on the stair, Tonx turned to show Marl the case.

"What—*ya*-nah see 'ere the artist making a comeback?"

"Comeback—which part?"

Again, eyeballing my-*Man*. Tonx chirps'd his teeth, and shook his head.

"What-*ya* know bout Bashment Revival anyway?"

Marl halted then, his leading leg perched upon the next step. It beginning to look like the pair were in the process of navigating a vertical minefield.

"So what—it ain't you I saw flogging bootlegs down Petty Coat Lane last week—*Delroy* Trotter?" he said, putting on his Sunday's best *Federales* voice. He then freed-up a hand to hoist-up his sweatbottoms.

"Oy—that's Mister Trotter to you, *Sunshine*."

FLIP-FLIP

Step

FLIP

Step

FLIP-FLIP

Arriving at the first-floor landing, Tonx again stopped abruptly.

"Yo—now tell me dis ain't my Capleton Gold."

FLIP

"*Oh what*—FLIP—you even got my Beenie-*Man*—FLIP-FLIP—and my Buju! Oy Blood, half these cids is mine."

He then nodded his chin in the direction of the first door on the landing, labelled B2.

"Is this you?"

"Nah—it's the next door," Marl replied, halting on the last step but one. "You can go through—it's open."

"Ski-*ing*."

Still, Tonx hung tight. Looking down upon Marl—from up-on-high—to gesture with his head, in the direction of the wrong door.

"So—*Sniff*—who lives here then?"

FLIP

"How the *phf'k* should I know?" Marl snapped, his arms now beginning to tire; what with the way my-*Man* had ladened his possessions upon him.

There was the cylindrical *SpeakerboxX*, and the compact letter-box-sized MDX5000, stacked like a miniature totem pole; the two lap-sized controllers planted atop, acting as talismens. The plug for the MiniDisc player-*slash*-recorder trailing like an anchor. And threatening, any minute now, to find purchase on that carpeted stair and trip him up.

"What—you ain't buck 'im yet? *My-Man*?" Tonx enquired. Assuming *my-Man* was indeed a *Man*, and the hostel your usual *Boyz*-only affair.

"I only got the key yesterday—what?"

"Fair enough."

And just-now, the landing-light Timed-out—CLICK!

With no windows, nor source of natural light. The entire Space plunged suddenly into total darkness. Still, unperturbed Tonx moved-on to the next door. Ignoring that patch of Pitch, shrouding those stairs leading-up to the next floor.

"It's open—yeah?"

Holding the door for Marl, Tonx felt for the light-switch. Whilst all about him, that fluid dark of the landing washed-up against those gloomy shores of Marl's room.

Squeezing passed, Marl was to put the *SpeakerboxX* and the MDX5000 down on the floor. A spot in the corner, next to a double wall-socket. That NRG-saver bulb, hanging limp and naked from the ceiling, flickering into life to catch him upon all-fours.

Tonx left the door to close itself, as he gave the room the once-over.

"Is this it then? The *love*-nest?" he joked; his eye being drawn to a nearby nook, and the outline of a Push-*Me*™ closet.

Pushing-it, with his freehand, and watching as it slid open. He added, "a-bit cramp ain't it?"

"Cosy I'd call it," came Marl response, looking-up at him.

Stowing the closet back into the wall, Tonx was to continue with the mock inspection. The case of MiniDiscs perched upon his palm, like a tray of dainty hors d'oeuvres.

"What—they couldn't sort you a bed?"

"I had to dash it," Marl admitted.

Still on all-fours, he'd plugged-in the MDX, and turned on the *SpeakerboxX*. And was presently about checking the charge.

"What—you dash-way the *Man*-dem's ting?" Tonx retorted, stepping over that makeshift bed, and debris of clothing, on his way to the window.

"I had to—Blood. The ting was *wrenk*."

The charge-indicator on the *SpeakerboxX* turned from red-to-amber-to-green. And relieved, Marl pushed-in the power button on the MDX, a cue for the front-panel to flash him a greeting. The circular button popping-out to reveal its dual purpose, that of a tactile-wand that stowed snugly into the Body of the player.

Stood by the window, Tonx held that improvised curtain aside to cop the view.

"So—they gonna sort you a new one?" he asked. Puzzling, how he could've missed the LZT across the way.

"A new what?"

Marl was now about repositioning the *SpeakerboxX*, whiles he waited on the MDX to initiate a wireless connection.

"A new bed," Tonx said, looking to his ride, which was looking more and more like Warden-*bait*. What with it being the only automobile parked on the road, and the curb being double-outlined in Mustard-yellow.

"Oh—my-*Man* already tried it," Marl said.

Letting the curtain fall, Tonx felt the radiator, his boatrace shrugging silent approval at the heating still being on.

"So it go," he said—chirps'ing his teeth.

Now facing the sink-unit, he was to shoot a cursory glance at the mirror before opening the cupboard. Bending at the waist to have a nosy; in two-minds whether to check again the 'Terms & Conditions' for the Congestion Charge *vis-à-vis* parking on double-yellow lines.

"So…you christened it yet?" he asked, leaning on that cupboard door. He then paused to clock his Braeburn® *Cuff*, before adding, "with *my-Grrrl*? Tanya Two-Faces."

"I'm bucking her later," Marl replied, without looking at him.

Still waiting on the MDX, he'd commandeered a tee-shirt that lay close-by, and was in the process of smelling its armpits.

"And I beg you don't call her that," he continued, now wiping down the *SpeakerboxX* with it.

"But it's true though," Tonx said, giving Marl the side-eye. A sly gold-plated smile, pulling at the corners of his gulliver.

"*My-Grrrl*'s — like literally, got two faces. *What*?"

"How-*ya* mean?"

"How-*ya* mean 'how-*ya* mean?'" Tonx replied, now looking for a spot to cotch, having completed his inspection.

"Oy — you see me gunning any one of your stable," Marl said, watching him pushdown on the sink-unit, testing to see if it'd support his weight.

"*Oh* — my bad. How was I supposed to know?" Tonx said. Taking a break to hold-up his freehand, as if meaning to plead his innocence.

"Know what?"

Marl continued to watch him.

"Know it was like dat — with you and [Sing] *my-Grrrl*,[30] *my-Grrrl, talkin' bout my-Grr-rrl-rrl. My-Grrrl*!" Tonx added. And looking directly at Marl, he fluttered his eyelashes.

"Tan ain't the only contender — you know."

Marl returned to wiping down the front-panel of the MDX. Accidentally opening and hastily closing the MiniDisc draw — *as-you-do*.

"Stop givin' it," Tonx said, gathering-up the makeshift curtain, so as he might park himself on the sill. "You-*me* both know she's *the* One."

And with that, he settled down to continue the *missh* of trawling through Marl's collection of MiniDiscs.

"Yo — you can't be a Gal-*ist* all ya-life. *Ya*-get me."

FLIP

FLIP-FLIP

"What — like you you mean?"

Sniffing, Marl turned his attention to the tactile-wand, and aiming it at the MDX, began parsing the EQ-settings.

"Like me what?"

FLIP

"Yo Blood—*fah* real? How many Babymothers is dat?"

"Now-now. Don't get *Katty*—FLIP—do as I say not as I do."

FLIP-FLIP

"Two-*twos*. I'd all hol' it down—FLIP. *Check-it Check-it. My-Grrrl*'s got Bumper—FLIP. She's got Tweeters—FLIP-FLIP. She works—FLIP. She's even got her own whip—"

FLIP, and FLIP

Having listed Tan's keeper credentials with each FLIP of a MiniDisc. Tonx was to finally stumble upon, what it was he'd been after all this time.

"Yo—*a*-wha dis? Mint Condition da reboot."

He plucked the MiniDisc from the case to inspect it, adding, "I didn't know you still had this?"

It was a blatant lie. He knew it, and he knew Marl knew it. But *baers*.

"Oy, Em-*Man*. What's that track I like on this one again?"

He flipped the quartz casing round, to cop the tracklisting on the backside of the inlay.

"You askin' me?"

Marl was now looking after my-*Man*. Having established the wireless connection, he'd been waiting on him to handover the case. So as, he might test to make sure every-ting was copacetic.

"*Nah*..." Tonx said, still reading the tracklistings. "That ain't even on here, Blood."

"Pass it then, and I'll tell-ya."

Marl clapped his palm with his fingers, his hand held-out in Tonx's general direction.

"Yo, seccle *ya*-self—Youngblood."

Tonx shoo'd him away.

"Wait...*Pretty Brown Eyes*—that's it. You sure this ain't mine?"

"You crazy—Tan give me that."

"You see it there? Two-faces and one good head on her shoulders. My-*Grrrl* will go far—you watch."

"And what's that s'posed to mean?"

Marl looked-on, disgruntled.

"I'm just sayin—my-*Grrrl*'s got a good head on her shoulders. *What*?"

Tonx flipped back over the quartz case; and began to scrutinise the artwork on the inlay.

"So...who printed this off for her? One of the brothers? It looks proper Bodie&Doyle."

Left dangling, Marl jumped-on the tactile-wand, deep-diving inna the MDX to reset the time and date. Then it was back on the cleaning-bit, wiping down the *SpeakerboxX*, and giving-it a lean-back to check the overall aesthetic. How the wood panelling of the MDX, offset that lacquered finish of the Jet-BLK speaker. Then it was back in again. To give-it the minor tweak.

"So what, you can't lend me this?" Tonx asked, coming to it—finally; him signalling his goodwill by holding-up the casing, so as my-*Man* might see it.

"Yeah sure," Marl replied, looking after him. "*Mañana y mañana*."

"Don't *phf'k* about—wha-*ya* sayin? I only wanna burn it."

Again, he flipped the quartz case round to read the back, and added—pointing, "look-see it there. There's only one good track on here. You must just 'ave it on repeat when you're grinding."

Giving-up on testing the MiniDisc player, Marl stood—hoisting-up his sweatbottoms, and ambled over to the Ciné-*matic*.

"Yeah—and wha-ya 'ave fi me?"

He felt around the edge of the flatscreen, for a stowed remote.

"I got this Capleton Gold for starters," Tonx said, putting down the case of MiniDiscs, and making sure to leave out the Mint Condition.

Now focusing his attention on the Capleton Gold, he opened-up the casing to scrutinise the tiny disc deposited inside. Tilting its reflective surface—that micro-thin layer of aluminium—this way and that, in the light from the window.

Unable to find the remote for the flatscreen, Marl looked-on, knowing full well where this was headed.

"Oy—*a*-wha dis? A scratch?"

"*What*? Where?"

Shrouded in the lengthening evening shadow of the BT Tower, was that definitive blot on the proverbial landscape. The *Mayweather Estate*.

An immense and imposing Le Corbusier-*ian* middle-finger to the

EVEN THE [SING] GHETTO

classless horde that inhabited it. And the smart circa-1800 Georgian townhouses that encircled it.

It spoke to the '-*ical*' of Utility: The socio-econom-*ical* and the polit-*ical*. It spoke of choices. Of apparent and not so apparent need(s). And ultimately, it spoke of lofty ideals, couched in even loftier soundbytes, and of a railroading of that 'Bigger picture'.

Indeed, faced with a demand for Public Housing, the Powers-that-be could've simply continued the motif, of four and five-storey tenements fronting onto communal gardens; that was characteristic of the neighbourhood. But instead, they—that august and yet nondescript Body, had opted for something a-little more rad *ical*.

Fast-forward a century and a-half, and this modernist eyesore still said, *Ghetto*.

Sang it—*even*, like a three-dimensional Cubist rendering of Donny Hathaway. In warm, rich, dulcet tones of Brilliant-bright, that could've passed for blue.

Yeah, it was to be a lamentable *Blues*—still. That offered testimony to that miraculous inversion of those forces of inertia, built into its very foundation.

Picture it: That spectacle of mass graves, whole communities buried alive under concrete tonnage; the weight of *the* Struggle—their Struggle, pressing down upon them. Imposing walls closing-in on all sides.

To say, *twas* miraculous. The reversal of such a deep-seated dystrophy, through a kind of *Homeostasis*. Through living and dying, laughing and crying, an existence that was-is nominally termed, Ghetto; the word chorused by an *Afro*-Cubanos infused, muscular, masculine harmony. Was-*is* not to overstate the achievement.

So now, let me hear you sing:

[Sing] *The Ghetto* [31]

No longer simply a generic term, used to denote—and-or signify—that Being of societal alienation.

[Sing] *The Ghetto* [32]

No longer a mere historical abstraction.

Yeah, festering within walled communities such as the Mayweather Estate. [Sing] *The Ghetto* became a reality for those who lived-it.

Breathed-it.

Human-ized. And harmon-*ized*. And natural-*ized* even. It became its own contradiction. Fond memories of a shared struggle. Envisaged in glorious Technicolor™, like reruns of *Happy Days*.

[Sing] *Yours and my*
Hap-py days...

It became Arthur Fonzarelli, and *The Fonz* both. Evidence of rife socio-economic division, and a rebirth of *Kool*. Brilliant-bright-washed by those vagaries of Youth, that regenerative impulse of the young; a Star-struck, pubescent and be-freckled, Richie Cunningham.

For all who'd take possession of it—call it home, [Sing] *The Ghetto* offered its own unique brand of nostalgia.

Its most prized possession. Its secret sauce—as it were. An affinity with carefree summers, and gruelling winters, and first loves; those bonds of friendship, and kinship, so keenly felt.

Add to this, a shared ignorance of the truth of its paternity. Each Ghetto Über-star, being liken to an adolescent LukeSkywalker™. Staring longingly, across those dunes of Tatooine. Oblivious, to that spectre of Vader looming large over their lives.

[Sing] *The Ghetto, in the Ghetto* [33]
Call it mis-fortunes wealth...

It was growing-up nurtured by such an indomitable *Esprit*. A sense and sensibility, couched in adolescent angst, propagated in a perfusion of *sub*-cultural expressions. To be welcomed, one eventful day, during the BRITs, or the BAFTAs—*say*, back into the fold. Back into that motherly bosom of a paternalistic Mainstream.

The momentum, backwards—*always*. Whilst facing forwards.

Therein, to vie for Daddy's roving eye and approval. Alongside all those other bastardised Pop-cultural forms. As if, that'd been the unconscious drive and driver, all along.

Indeed, [Sing] *The Ghetto* was to be epitomised by the phenomenon that is *Hip-Hop*. Its repackaging, and rebranding as Rap™.

Yeah, picture it: *Pop*-culture's 'Problem child', forcibly evicted and moved wholesale to the Suburbs—*sound familiar?* There to be slowly strangled (—to Death). Remote, and removed from the environs of its troubled youth.

That concrete jungle, Marley's Wailers were always wailing-on about. Those pleas of "Don't. Push. Me", chorused by those Furious Five.

All was to be drowned-out by a brittle, and hauntingly lonely falsetto.

The Siren's call, evoking that rapture of End-times.

It being *our* Debbie Harry's turn, at playing that flaxen-locked wayward bride, Sif. Armed with her newly forged hairpiece, venturing down into the Slave Quarter after midnight. Looking as always, for Loki — c'est Baron Samedi.

And still, the Struggle remained *the* Struggle. Now a crisis of proliferation, the World being a Ghetto after all. As prophesied in the Ghetto-inflected nasal drawl of *Hip-Hop*'s many luminaries. The likes of the God-*Mcee*, Brother Rakim —

[Rap] *It ain't where you're from* 34
It's where you're at
Even the...

Yeah, for all those who bought a ticket to ride that Ghetto experience. This required more than just wrapping their minds around its solipsism.

It also required them to physically wrap their Body's in the Ghetto's sartorial aesthetic. Picture arms and legs, hidden under that reflective surface of branded shellsuits, and Bling-jewellery. Flailing and kicking frantically to stay afloat.

That designation: G-H-E-T-T-O. Still an impermeable membrane. And yet, as transparent as any border drawn upon that Borges Map.

Too quickly, did it achieve its apotheosis, in that spider-legged calligraphy, scrawled upon the walls of labyrinthine corridors and stairwells. Its *Alumni*, lauded and eulogised in a roll-call of tags. Another hauntingly airy falsetto, listing those fabled [Sing] *Children of the Ghetto*.[35] The likes of Zoro, Case and Crazy Legs, and Ramo, Turbo and Ozone, Hyper and Blaze, and Vanity (— of *Last Dragon* fame).

Names made notorious, by a graffiti that simultaneously represented and effaced — like *nega*-Hieroglyphs. The *Sign*, denoting a real and immediate threat of violence. Before its *Becoming*.

Prior to its anointing by 'The Situationalists', the likes of Warhol, and McLaren. That *Hip-Hop* of the Ghetto might've been nothing more than a mural scrawled upon a wall. A chiaroscuro masterpiece, destine never to see the light of day. Tucked away in a subterranean Car park, between the Bimmer® and BENZ®. Illuminated by that solitary flickering spotlight mounted upon the wall, shielded from assault behind a metal-gauze.

Its Legend. A nondescript Body struck by a bolt of lightning, that chosen weapon of the gods. The Body, nothing more than a silhouette, its skeleton lit—*Amp*'d—by the visible current. The *Piece*, its situation proclaiming:

[Poem] *We—who are not as Others* 36
In our footsteps can be traced
That incessant rhythm of the Kik
And the Bass. Our über-Human
Vigour and vitality enhanced
By Amphetamines. Indeed
You'll find the beating
Of our Hearts, and that snarl
Drawn upon our boatraces.
Mirrored
In the puffed-up barrel chest
Of our thoroughbred fighter-dogs.
For we—Who are not like Others
We alone remain impervious
To that arbitrary ringing
Of that arbitrary bell—
Phf'k Pavlov!
Yeah, phf'k Pavlov.
If we salivate at all, it'll be to spit.

Demystified, and fetishised within that Cult of Adolescence. Today—as in right-now, [Sing] *The Ghetto*, had come to signify its very antithesis. What was-*is*, a gentrified and urbane urban *Life*style. Coffeehouses, and Gymnasiums, and Metromarts, and jogging in the park, and absolutely no *phf'king* Free parking.

Gone apparently, was that *Life* lived at right-angles. And occasionally, in straight lines. A Worldview construed through the lens of sub-cultural forms, like cultures cultivated in concrete petri-dishes.

Gone was any notion of *the* Struggle. Of Bodies treading water, that hand-to-mouth existence. And with it, went that sense of wonder, in the face of it all. That they might've survived. And thrived even. Not at all cost, or by some obscure, abstract evolutionary impulse. But through an

EVEN THE [SING] *GHETTO*

innate, and limitless *Humanity*.

Yeah, that blue hue of this 'Ghetto', was more Orangey-yellow. The yellow being tinged with red, with Blood; with bloodshed, and sweat, and tears.

More your *Ode* to quiet acquiescence. It'd absolutely come to signify that sublimation of Youth. And yeah, the Mayweather Estate screamed, *Ghetto...Ghetto...Ghetto...*

Its screams echoed, within those rows and rows of uniform apartments—*Immeubles Villas*. Facing both inward, and outward. Each window of that *Living*-room Space, framing a veritable Constable. An obscene, gentrified landscape that was your *Ghost of-Christmas-Yet-Too-Come*.

Framed in a ground-floor window, that was-*like*, a full storey above Street-level. A grubby-faced toddler clumsily lifted a net-curtain to peer-out, and wave. Slapping that treble-glazed glass in wide-eyed recognition.

Out-*there*—in der Lebenswelt, on the other side of that transparent wall. There stood mummy, chatting-away with a friend—another Mother-Woman-*Grrrl*. Just by the Clipstone Street communal entrance to that Mayweather Estate. What was a St. Michael's® rëenforced steel-door, accessed via a PlunkettDomestics® *Peak-A*-Boo *viddy*-intercom.

Yeah, they were just kids really, playing at adults.

Living that *Kidulthood*[37]—as-you-do. Casually dressed in a uniform of designer clobber: Brightly-coloured Ade///Das® urb-flex shellsuits; Total*Air*™ kicks—Brilliant-bright obviously; ear-lobes, neck and wrists weighed down with Tom; a Braeburn® *Pod* clutched in one hand, a key-fob in the other; tri-wheeled *peu*-Troll® homeostatic-strollers stationed at heel, like a Guide-dog.

Yeah, there they were chatting away. As ever observed by the CcSS, embedded behind shatterproof glass, mounted upon every corner.

In one stroller, a toddler slumbered. As only a toddler might, without-a-care. The World could be crashing down about its ears, it'd sleep right through, to wake in time for evening feeding.

Whilst in that other stroller, branded shopping-bags were to play the surrogate; that barrel-chested Staf chained to it, scratching at its muzzle with a hind-leg.

And now, noticing her little cherub at the window, mummy smiled and waved.

"*Ahh* — bless," cooed the friend, joining in.

As if waiting on this cue, the curtain twitched, then lifted to reveal an anaemic looking Dad-*Man*-Boy. Bare-chested, his ropey-frame a canvass of crisp *Tatts*.

Picking-up the toddler, Daddy points a phallic middle-finger in the direction of mummy, adamant in mouthing the words, *you best get your arse in here.*

It then proceeded to shower the little-one in apologetic kisses, her dainty boatrace cupped gently in its fag-stained fingers.

On that other side of the glass, mummy cut her eye, her peer now thinking to speak for her.

"Why don't he get a job?"

"Why don't you get a *phf'king* job" — *Tut.*

"I was just sayin" — *Tut.*

"Well don't."

And just-now, a gang of BMX Boyz cruised by. All stood tall in the saddle, coasting upon Shimaru® KinetiX frictionless bearings.

The lead biker, recognising one of the mums, waving back over his shoulder. Before turning into the forecourt of the hydrostation-*slash*-metromart, parked just shy of that corner of the Block.

Following the leader, the gang was to maintain a tight formation — like a chattering of starlings, to brake abruptly in front of that glazed storefront. Whilst above their heads, the Legend: 'BNP®, *Harnessing that Power of the Atom*', blazed Lemon-yellow and Shamrock-green. Its illumination, signalling that stealthy approach of evening.

Having *pre*-emptively switched-off the automated-doors, a uniformed attendant was stood ready to police the entrance; him pointing at a crude handwritten sign, and barking through the glass, "ONLY TWO ALLOWED. AT ONE TIME."

He signalled then, with two fingers.

"TWO. ONLY TWO."

Though, his fervent appeal was to be redundant. Given that, only two of the gang had dismounted to approach. These 'Disenfranchised' youths being *as-ever* prescient, to how the World was meant to view them.

EVEN THE [SING] *GHETTO*

Yeah, inside that metromart bit of the hydrostation, Marl was stood over an automated-cashier, waiting on his *insta*-Purchase to clear; his bag of goodies parked on the scale in front of him.

All of it, your usual *ersatz* fodder. Pre-chewed by some heavy duty industrialised process, and ready-wrapped in crinkle-free 'eco-friendly' packaging.

Meanwhile, behind the counter, and that EH&S-endorsed shatter-proof safety-screen—extending-up to the ceiling. Another uniformed attendant was flashing him cursory glances; in betwixt monitoring the control panel for the Heavy-water pumps, and the goings-on outside—Out-*there*.

Responding to the automated-cashier's audible-*prompt*, Marl retrieved his *Rush*Card®, and immediately dived into the bag. And rummaging around for a bit, he was to pull-out a *Nestlé's*® Chewy*Crunchie*™; tackling the wrapping with his teeth to get at it.

Biting into a corner, his Body was seen to welcome that sugar-rush. The jingle from the Chewy*Crunchie*™ promo-ad instantly springing to mind; the number of times he'd had to skip past it on his *Time*Line.

*Buzz*ing now, from his daily glucose fix. Marl approached those automated doors; the attendant holding-up a sharp, pointy-finger, putting the heated negotiations on pause.

"Do you mind waiting?" he asked, his hand poised over the switch.

"—*yeah*," Marl replied, eventually. His mouth having gotten to grips with that chewy bit of the Chewy*Crunchie*™.

The attendant, evidently a practiced Snake charmer of the Sapera, was to hold the two youths at bay with a stare. While he switched those automated doors over, to 'Exit only'.

An impromptu ceasefire being thus signalled. The two s'posed delinquents were to cordially step aside then, inviting the bystander to leave.

Only once the coast was clear. That is, those automated doors closed and locked. Did the haggling resume in earnest.

"But—he only lives round the corner."

"Yeah—I only live round the corner."

"Then you can go fetch your ID and come back."

"Oh come-off it—*Ghee-eze*. You know me."

Sniff

"Yes—and I know you've come to buy cigarettes. And so, I must insist that you—or your Bredren here—provide ID."

"He ain't my Bredren."

"Yeah—we ain't related."

"You know exactly what I mean."

In the forecourt-proper, that chattering of starlings was looking more and more like a venue of vultures. Seemingly poised to set upon that metromart, any minute now.

And *baers* to the cameras. And that huddle of cabbies hunkered down, over by those three banks of Heavy-water pumps, killing time before clocking-on. And that growing line of waiting automobiles, backed-up onto Clipstone Street.

Having cleared the forecourt of the hydrostation, Marl rounded the corner and crossed over Cleveland Street; what was a tributary, feeding the elbow of Maple Street.

Paying little mind—if any, to the Kebab house on the corner, *Vasis*. That was like a keystone, marking the beginnings of a new Block.

With its azure blue canopy, and pillared entrance. Its wrought-iron railing decorated with tidy flower boxes. Its tables—both inside and out—brimming with Tourists and Pilgrims; the din of polite conversation making way for a song, introduced simply as *Αθανασία* [Athanasia].

There followed then, a mournful taxim, featuring acoustic guitar and bouzouki. Evoking a sense of loss, and regret, as if reminiscing upon the passing of that spirit of Rebetiko. It proving a fitting prelude for that songstress; her husky, sultry voice, seasoned in those salty waters of the Aegean: [Sing] *Τι ζητάς αθανασία στο μπαλκόνι μου μπροστά...*[38]

This hauntingly beautiful melody was to waft after Marl, as he mounted the hostel's doorstep. Carrying with it, that aroma of charcoal, and freshly baked flatbread, and grilled meats; him oblivious to it, as he wrestled with his trouser pocket to retrieve his keys. The Chewy*Crunchie*™ gripped like a bit in his mouth.

But he needn't have bothered. For just-now, that Front door opened. Sash choosing this moment to make her entrance.

Holding the door for it, she paused, as if assuming a *Beat* of rapturous applause. Every minute of her life being, seemingly, taped in front of a Live studio audience. As if, she were living—*reliving*—reruns of *Happy Days fah* real *fah* real.

Yeah, she paused then, so as the World might get a good look at her. The *Look* being her usual Road-*Grrrl* uniform: Eyes and mouth outlined in Onyx-BLK; hair straightened and slicked-up in a sculpted Teddy-boy quiff; bubblewrap puffer zipped and buttoned to the neck; FENDINI® handbag hooked upon her shoulder; a pair of *Buds* cupped in one-hand.

And from the waist down, it was the obligatory pair of *Secondskins*, a faux-leopard fur Her | Him® jobbie; and a pair of *Cynderellas*™ glass-slippers. The cushions of air elevating *my-Grrrl* a good few inches above the ground, forcing both her calves and thighs to work overtime to find traction.

"You coming-in or what?" she asked — *Sniff*, the question more of an averment.

Taken aback. And having physically taken a step back, onto that pavement. Marl was to look decidedly undecided.

"*Er—*" about all the sense he could muster. Whilst his jaw remained locked about the girth of his Chewy*Crunchie*™.

My-*Grrrl* being — literally, that striking, seen here in her element.

Pulling hard upon the butt of an ULTRA-Slim, Sash looked to that Kebab house; acknowledging by sight that exotic palette of smells and sounds — its *Style*. And then, it was back to my-*Man*.

Or was it my-Boy?

"—*Hello*? You wanna come get this?" she said. Nodding in the direction of the door, whiles taking another pull on her cigarette.

It was then, that it dawned on Marl. That my-*Grrrl* was actually holding it open for him — the door. And snatching the Chewy*Crunchie*™ from his mouth, he licked his chops to fess-up, "you made me jump."

Whiles furtively mounting that doorstep. His interest now well and truly pricked, by this apparent (and unexpected) windfall.

"So what — *Sniff*, you visiting?"

Oh forphf'ksake, Sash thought, sensing it gearing-up for a *Chirps*.

"Why — what's it to you?" she replied, tapping her cigarette ash on the floor; what was to be a blatant demonstration of her mounting contempt.

She then busied herself looking it up-and-down, whilst she took another pull. Clockin' its clobber, weighing-up those brands on display.

And of-course, knowing this game, and how it was played. Marl knew to come right-back at her.

"What—you always answer a question with a question?"

And now staring after my-*Grrrl*, he was to throw-in a coy, boyish grin, to offset that brashness of his tone.

Sash faking a doubletake, "*er*—excuse me?" And blowing smoke out the corner of her mouth, she was to flick her cigarette butt at the pavement.

"You just moved-in, yeah? Room B1?"

"Yeah" again, taken aback.

Oh—

Negotiating that lip of the doorway, Sash left the door to shut itself; her movement reminiscent of a *Geiko*, or *Maiko*. Those dainty footsteps having adapted, to meet the constraints of ever-evolving tastes in Kimono.

"Maybe I'll see you about?" came Marl's final pitch, as the pair waltzed passed each other on that doorstep; him just managing to catch the door with an elbow.

"Maybe not-ey," Sash said, popping one *Bud* in one ear, and the other in the other.

Having gotten her liccle *Buff* for the day—from having to blow *my-Boy* out. She was to kick-off that step, and begin leisurely gliding along the pavement, upon that cushion of air generated by her glass-slippers.

Still holding onto the door, and looking after *my-Grrrl*. Marl couldn't help but dwell upon the poetry of that motion.

Indeed, mouth open, his was to be a sloppy wet kiss to the *Man* who'd invented *Secondskins*.

God had created living things, but Man had to annihilate them.

Maurice Blanchot, 'Literature and the Right to Death' (1948)

☷

```
47 6F 64 20 68 61 64 20
63 72 65 61 74 65 64 20
6C 69 76 69 6E 67 20 74
68 69 6E 67 73 2C 20 62
75 74 20 4D 61 6E 20 68
61 64 20 74 6F 20 61 6E
6E 69 68 69 6C 61 74 65
20 74 68 65 6D 2E
```

•

TH▲T *POINT-OF-NO-RETURN*

Kel was sat on a ledge, the wrong side of an open window, facing the wall of a narrow basement dugout—smoking.

Basking in what seemed a momentary lull in that soundtrack of his *Life*. Somewhere between being alone, and acknowledging it; that feeling—that *Being*, of being alone. One-foot cotch'd upon that first rung of a wrought-iron stair, leading-up to nowhere i.e., the Street, and a totemic BT Tower lauding it overall.

Situated directly under the hostel's front door, this little nook was home to the utility cupboard for the entire property.

Though for one night only, it was to be transformed into a Black hole. The strength of its gravitational pull, evident in the litter that carpeted the floor; and those motherly arms of Pitch, that'd been an immediate attraction for Kel.

Sat there, in the dark—shivering. Crombie buttoned to his neck. The bracing chill of that Indian summer, like a mongrel dog gnawing upon his bones. Kel couldn't help but draw contrast with that fatherly warmth, and Brilliant-bright(-*ness*) of the *Panny*.

Yeah, it was pure instinct, him being there. It was whatever compels wounded animals to want to hide from prying eyes.

And somewhere deep within, a part of him was busy deriving morbid satisfaction, from that squalor afforded by his surroundings. That sense of being buried alive, his *Soul* kicking and clawing at the insides of its fleshy coffin.

He rubbed repeatedly at his left-eye, with the back of a pawed hand—a puerile gesture. Whilst swilling adulterated cigarette smoke in his cheeks. The taste of menthol infused nicotine, having become synonymous with that taste of *Freedom*.

There being no smoking in the PANOPTES™. No cancer in purgatory.

For no intelligible reason, he was moved to try and make-out that lettering that snaked around the quick of his cigarette. His eyes having grown adept at peering into, and through that murky Pitch. The words, 'Menthol ULTRA-Slims', conjuring thoughts of her.

And then, his mind's eye was to be suddenly privy to an image of her—of Sash, braiding her hair in the mirror, her reflection glaring back at him.

She was *screwing*, evidently.

Though try as he might, he couldn't fathom the wherefore or the why. Those events, leading up-to and beyond such rarefied moments, being lost to posterity.

Delving into his sketchy memories of before, it was always the same. Like finding a box full of old Polaroids. In each and every framed snapshot, Sash was to be seen wearing that same *screwface*. As if, it were a pose struck especially for that one infallible lens.

That this had come to be his sole impression of her—of her impression of him, continued to haunt Kel.

Especially given what'd transpired just-now.

Yeah, he'd survived the Panny, and come out the other end anaesthetised; his senses dulled, his feelings numbed. And still, she haunted him.

Sniff

For, if *Freedom* had had an image for Kel, it'd been that image of her—of Sash—stood the other side of that *Looking-glass*. And if *Freedom* had tasted of anything, it'd tasted minty-fresh. Like her breath—*always*.

Looking to it, the cigarette. Kel now knew it for what it was. As he knew that that night, he'd somehow managed to stumble across an arbitrary line etched in Space*Time*.

That *Point-of-No-Return*.

Swallowing, he took another pull. Holding-in the smoke to warm his insides. Whilst dwelling upon this, his newly discovered sense of a reckoning's fast approach.

Here he was, stood the wrong side of that *Looking-glass*. As far removed from Sash, from that idea of *Freedom* she embodied, as physically possible. Fingers splayed upon that cold sheer surface, as if meaning to pushback against its morose certainty.

His predilection toward *Self*-destruction temporarily sated. Kel felt inclined to peer back through to the other side, the way he'd come. To inspect that trail of carnage; his *Life*'s journey just-now conspiring to make sense.

Looking back, it was as if he'd literally fallen through a crack in the paving. Found himself dangling over a precipice, clinging obstinately to its lip. A fledgling sense of *Freedom* poised to slip from his covetous grasp, like so many grains of sand—grains of truth; those delicate petals of a dried Brilliant-bright Chrysanthemum.

To close his hand about the thing, this flowering. An incipient and petulant *Freedom*; born immaculate of an unutterable sense of fatalism, and alienation. To close his hands about its throat, as was his want, his drive—his bent. To strangle it. To choke the *Life*, the living daylights out of—

Yeah...

Kel found himself nodding at the dark.

Yeah, here was clarity—of a sort. Here was a lucidity of thought, vying now for supremacy over his usual state of disillusionment.

The whole tawdry episode, a silvery moon, seen waxing and waning...

Waxing and waning...
Waxing and waning...

The Newcomen's Halfway House was way Out-*there* in the Sticks—in the *Boonies*. Kel could probably still get to it; if he'd such an inclination. But not in time.

Not unless he could, somehow, turn back every clock in the World. Somehow, by sheer affect of Will, coax *Time* to count those finite intervals of Space backwards. That unrelenting march of incremental marks about a clockface, being but one seamless precession of *Points-of-No-Return*.

Sat there, alone—in the dark.

How impossible—implausible, it seemed to move even a fraction of a millimetre—a millisecond, in that opposed direction.

Sniff

His curfew was, of course, mandatory. Though the *Gheezah* at the Halfway house had insisted upon it being "voluntary, and flexible." Kel struggling to reconcile these few choice words.

Mandatory. Voluntary. Flexible.

They'd played over and over in his head, just moments before that non-event. And then, it'd been him blowing smoke out the corner of his mouth.

And naturally, it'd passed without incident, that mandatory voluntary flexible curfew. It being essentially arbitrary. Devoid of any phenomenological significance, or synchronicity. Or any sense, or impression one might point to—or at. An auspicious aligning of the Planets—*say*; dawn breaking upon the horizon; those first tenuous blossoms of Spring.

Perhaps, if he'd set his alarm—the one on his *Pod*. Assigned this curfew an arbitrary *Sign* to signify its significance. Its portent. Its importance. Perhaps things would've, could've turned-out different.

Perhaps—*maybe*.

Yeah, it'd passed-by without uttering a sound, like a thief in the night. It'd approached without saying, *Hello*. And left without saying, *Goodbye*. Kel sat there, upon that very spot when it happened. Which is to say, when nothing happened.

Nothing happened. And yet, everything changed.

Like his thinking, his entire worldview had fused into one solid block of binary opposites: Of utter Pitch, and Brilliant-brights; of extreme lefts, and resolute rights; of industrious days, and lethargic nights. Of straight lines, and acute-obtuse angles; the World being populated by such definitive shapes. Squares, and circles, and triangles.

And there was Kel, clinging obstinately to this regime of absolutes— for spite. His being, a wilful unwillingness to brook any exception to any given rule. And *serves 'em bloody right*.

Obviously, the *Panny* had failed him. Failed to instil in him, the requisite level of conscientiousness—obviously.

Viewed fundamentally as a treatment, the PANOPTES™ was designed to map societal norms directly onto your candidate's *Psyche*.

Commandeering an analogy from the burgeoning field of Synthetix: It was meant to literally 'rewrite that program of consciousness.'

Correspondingly, it either took or it didn't.

However, in the case of the latter, there could be no going back for seconds, or thirds. It being proven, that much like the antibiotics administered in the treatment of bacterial infections, repeated exposure simply built-up higher degrees of 'cognitive resistance', in those 'unresponsive candidates'.

Yeah, having kissed his curfew 'Goodnight, and good luck.' Kel had his wish.

For sure, he'd ventured willingly into the Abyss. Into that Nether region populated by those 'unresponsive candidates'.

And could now look forward to either: a) Having a *Pfeiffer*® Upsilon-Tracer BioChip—an A.I. 'Jiminy Cricket', hardwired into his Brain. Which, in exceptional circumstances, could be used to administer a mild electroshock stimulus treatment, directly into his frontal lobe, to moderate his behaviour.

That, and-*or* b) Mandatory Military Service (that is, a good ol' *Mandy Hotlegs*) in one of several hotspots dotted around the Globe.

Either way, Kel was *phf'ked*, and he knew it. Beyond *phf'ked*. If that was even possible. And yet, it was a relief to be home. To find some things couldn't change. No matter how much they'd wanted to.

Taking another drag, Kel exhaled. He'd kept the cigarette cupped between thumb and pointy-finger, to mask it. And could now feel the heat of its cherry tickling the palm of his hand.

Above his head, the hostel's front-door slammed—abruptly, drowning-out that feint crackle of burning tobacco, and much of *The Buzz* of the night. Though the accompanying sound of footsteps, scurrying along the pavement, was to be conspicuous in their absence.

Giving it one last pull, Kel stubbed-out the cigarette. Flicking away the butt to retrieve his *Pod* from an inside pocket, with the same hand.

Dialling a number from memory, he paused then, to watch the screen.

Out-*there*, on the other side of that *Looking-glass*, the World was about announcing itself. Literally, screaming its heart out; the dialogue lifted verbatim seemingly, from the pages of a novel by Herbert Selby Jr.

PHF'KOFF WILL-YA LEAVE ME ALONE.

RACH? WHERE-YA GOING RACH—

And then, above Kel's head, the Payphone in the hallway started-up with the cat-calls. Its incessant...

MEOW-MEOW...

MEOW-MEOW...

coming back at him in a warped stereo-image.

He let it ring into double digits before disconnecting the call. The night's soundtrack quickly fading-in. A convoy of *Broom-Brooms* rounding the corner, that

UMPH...UMPH...

UMPH...UMPH...

UMPH...UMPH...

of a punchy techno-*Kik*, reverberating in that valley of tenements.

Kel could feel the *sub*-phonic rumble of solid-state engines tickling his chest. As he could hear the muzik racing on ahead, towards an anthemic chorus. And then it licked—

[Sing] *We could be Heroes...*

Heroes...Heroes...

And all of a sudden, the Universe was awash with vibrant color; infectious hues of harmonious tonality. A glorious synthesised muzik, lost too soon to

The Buzz...

   The Buzz...

      The Buzz-uzz...

That was like a blur of noise. That motion-blur of *Life*.

Gathering the coattails of his Crombie about him. Kel ducked his head, and managed to clamber inside without touching those sides of the window frame.

Stepping gingerly into a bathtub that lay directly under the windowsill. The soles of his CharlieBrown's® crunching-down upon a bed of discarded shower-curtain hooks.

Unable to find purchase, the ground seemingly shifting beneath his feet. Kel instinctively reached for that rim of the tub. And having saved himself from a bruising fall, stood erect, leaving for posterity his hand's impression.

Phf'kry, he thought—looking at it.

Sniff

Clambering-out of the bath and turning his attention to that offending appendage. He was to discover it contaminated with a sticky residue. And it was then, he noticed the entire bathroom covered in what seemed a film of sooty dust.

The boxy room having been sealed, like the tomb of some obscure Egyptian Pharaoh. Those few gulps of Out-*there*, afforded by that open window, were barely enough to shift that prevailing sense of stagnation, that hung over everything.

Going over to the sink, Kel was relieved to find the taps still working. And briskly scrubbing that hand—that'd been infected, he took extra care not to let the water splash and contaminate his clothing.

There being nothing to dry his hands with, he was forced then to hold them aloft—like a surgeon prep'd for theatre. Taking a *hot*-minute, while they air-dried, to familiarise himself with his surroundings.

In all the time he'd lived there, he'd never thought to venture down into the basement.

Like—what for, with so much going on upstairs?

And certainly, the last thing he'd expected to see, was the base of his old bed partially blocking the exit. The mattress, propped-up against it—which he didn't recognise, hanging limp at the waist. As if caught in a perpetual state of toppling-over.

Gagging, at its *wrenk*-ness. He held his breath to reach around it, for the doorknob. And found he was able to open the door just enough to squeeze through, and out into the passage. No doubt retracing the steps of whoever-it-was, who'd thought to stow the thing there in the first instance.

Knowing ol' Fowler, it was probably my-Man, Kel thought, finding that light-switch.

He then set about straightening himself. Unbuttoning his *Crombie*, and the blazer of his Birdman suit, to adjust his pencil-tie. Then buttoning it all up again, to pull upon those cuffs of his *StayPress*™ shirt.

The entire routine having been whittled down to a series of *Ticks*. A kind of ritual, meant to settle him into this, his newly acquired suit of skin.

Ahead, a chafed, rustic-grey budget carpet led the way up the stair. The stunted hall being flanked by facing doors (numbered A2 and A3). And a third door, that'd been left slightly ajar, so as Kel could see it was a WC.

Resealing that tomb of a bathroom, it just-then occurred to him, that he'd left the window open. And then, it was thoughts of wiping his prints from the doorknob, he'd just-now handled.

Sigh

It seeming long, him going back-in. Especially, given that he'd already taken the trouble to straighten himself out.

And besides, *if-and-when-push-came-to-shove*, the Feds would simply assume the window to be the point of entry—which it was. Plus, there was that impression of his hand, left on the rim of the bathtub. A full set of prints—mind you.

Yeah...*yeah*, for Kel there could be no going back. No going backwards.

Like—what for? To get chipped—no thanx.

Having crossed that arbitrary line, he could only go forward. And for right-now, that meant a climb.

Kel held his breath to raise a foot, aiming a heel at that solid-*looking* door, labelled innocuously, B1.

The resulting THUD was to be colored with the sound of splintering-wood, though the door remained unmoved. The ensuing silence—whilst Kel caught his breath, conspiring to amplify the violence that'd preceded it.

Caring less and less for the glare of that landing-light, Kel lined-up for another crack at it. Aiming two more blows in quick succession.

THUD

THUD

With his Blood now well and truly up, he continued the assault without pause, adjusting his footing to ensure his full bodyweight was behind each blow. That relentless rhythm—

THUD

THUD

THUD

THUD

—becoming more and more, an expression of his manifest Will. Its malign intent, tinged with a burgeoning sense of desperation.

Though the brunt of this assault was aimed at the door—its Knubbs® mortise deadlock. It was the wooden frame that eventually gave way.

The deadlock's metal-housing ripping clean through the wood, leaving the door free to fly open on its hinges, and slam hard against the wall.

Needing to take a breather, Kel stood there for a-bit. Hands on hips, admiring his handiwork. Sweat glistening upon his brow, Heart *Thump-thump-thumping* in his chest.

Then, without thinking, he engaged in his ritual of *Ticks*. Settling, and resetting himself, before bowling-in.

Just as that landing-light Timed-out—CLICK!

Across that now Pitch landing, the door opposite opened a crack. Its mortise lock being skilfully massaged, to minimise the sound of its mechanism. The simplicity of this act, belying a deftness of touch.

Peering-out, the Watcher breathed shallow. Its dulled eyes, like a mirror held-up to that gloom.

Once assured the coast was clear, it opened the door wide. Kicking aside a towel it'd been using as a makeshift stopgap.

Whilst behind it, the Ciné-*matic* mounted on the wall *Blink-blinked*. Its glare, chasing plumes of pungent hashish smoke out onto that landing.

"What? You locked yourself out, Bruv?" ABS averred—jovially.

It having apparently, seen it all before.

Sporting house-togs that more wore it; a pair of CaptainScarlet™ *Jimmy-jamas*, its motif faded to an inkblot. It was all my-*Man* could do to stand there, wavering on the spot, like a *Life*-size Supermarionette puppet. Whilst—presumably, above its head. Gerry Anderson's god-*like* hands were about making tiny adjustments, to keep it on its feet.

Still, our Abs was used to being *Kark*. Used to feeding-off *The Buzz*; that was like an audience of one, for all those living your TrumanShow™. It being all it could do, to take some of that edge off. A World viewed through the *perma*-squint of bloodshot eyes. Its 'Default' setting.

"Oy...you still there?" it inquired of the Pitch, backlit by the Ciné-*matic*. It then scratched its head and *Blinked*. Its eyelids opening and closing, like tiny motorized electric-blinds.

And just-now, that flatscreen *Wink*'d out. What was an apparent intermission between streams.

"YO...BRO?" Abs hailed, his words now like Sonar clicks, mapping that Pitch.

It suddenly occurring to it, that 'Yo' and 'Bro' actually rhymed. It was to repeat the couplet under its breath, a couple of times, for affect.

And *Wink*-ing back in, the Ciné-*matic* was to find my-*Man* grinning inanely, to itself. Whilst detangling the lengthy curly cord of a pair of antiquated BOSE® headphones; that it wore coiled around its neck, like Mala Prayer beads.

Throwing them after the bed—the pair of headphones, it wedged open the door to venture out onto the landing-proper. Hailing *my-Man* again.

"Yo...Marley-*Man*?"

Its hand now stretching for the light-switch. Like an exhausted swimmer, lunging for the end of a pool.

It was to hit the switch repeatedly; its *Spidy-senses*™ being pricked by the lack of a response. But even in that glare of the landing-light, it could barely see beyond the doorway into my-*Man*'s room.

Despite wearing headphones, Abs had heard the ruckus, and put two and two together.

Still, being privy to all your Horror-genre *clichés*. It'd been hesitant to investigate. Call it a premonition, something in the air.

Plus, with a Warrant pending. It wasn't as if it'd have the luxury of calling-in the Cavalry—i.e., *The Feds*, should anything untoward kick-off.

Yeah, it'd been cooped-up for the Lion's share of that day, carefully concocting an illusion of being absent from the property, on account of it.

Hence, it taking to watching the Idiot-box with headphones.

Anywho, all these healthy survival instincts were to be overruled, by sheer boredom. And a *Kark*-logic that reasoned, *what could it hurt to have a nosy?*

Stood now, by that mutilated doorframe. Abs felt with its hand the extent of the damage.

"They're gonna make you pay for that you know," it volunteered, tickled by the thought of ol' Fowler's boatrace.

It having borne witness to that particular expression, a Zen-*like* tacit acceptance tinged with utter disappointment, many a-time before.

Its hand then found the room's light-switch. Its eye fixing upon a spot on the ceiling, anticipating the NRG-saver bulb flickering into life.

THAT POINT-OF-NO-RETURN

And suddenly, there was Kel, hunkered in the corner—on his knees. One arm down the back of the sink-unit, groping around blind; his cheek squished right-up against its side.

"*Phf'k-me*—Kel? You back...already?"

Abs spoke without thinking, squinting in the light as it'd squinted in the dark.

A quick study, it then cottoned-on to what my-*Man* was about. That whiff of intrigue, yanking it to its senses.

"What-*cha* looking for? The money...you owe me?"

It'd paused for comic effect before delivering the punchline—*as you do*. Only to realise it'd sounded funnier in its head.

Though, saying that. Call it intuition, call it what you like. It sensed, there was to be no reading the house tonight.

Ignoring *my-Man*, Kel crouched down to remove the plinth at the base of that sink-unit. And putting his cheek to the floor, took a look-see under it. Abs seemingly content to just watch him, one arm snaked-up that doorframe. Its bulbous head rocking gently, as if its neck were rubberised.

It hung there for a-bit. Wishing it'd brought a spliff, seen as it was cotchin'. And closing its eye, rolled with *The Buzz*...

Till eventually it dawned on it, something else that wanted saying.

"You see my-*Grrrl*...running with my-*Man* now?"

And having said this, it retreated behind those blinds of its *Kark*-eyes to watch. Its gaze punctuated by a slow *Blink*, that was to be accompanied by the faint whir of miniaturised motors.

Leaning upon the plinth, Kel pretended not to hear, or not to care. At that point, even he wasn't sure which.

He'd given-up on the search for whatever it was he was looking for. But nevertheless, was to remain on his knees, tendering a silent prayer to your *god-of-dead-spaces*. Its *ad hoc* shrine, those inflatable pillows, and naked quilt, and faded-BLK sheet kicked-up against the wall—*there*.

Good...you Chief, thought Abs, misreading Kel's silence. Its grievance being your usual trope amongst thieves: The idea of A putting one over on B.

"And I wasn't joking...about my money," it declared.

It paused then, as if listening to a playback of what it'd just-now said. It wanting to be sure it'd landed it right; having rehearsed that particular line for years.

"What...you thought I'd forgotten? Kel-*lee*," it added then, by way of segue into a monologue. Which it proceeded to regurgitate in fragments, as and when they occurred to it.

Such hits as, "it was my-*Man*'s bad luck", and "why should that be on me?"

Whilst its eye moseyed over to that same dead Space, Kel had only just-now visited. "My-*Man* owes me," being essentially the gist of it.

It then came to the bit where it was to appeal to the house directly. It having anticipated a Live studio audience.

"I just want my money...I need it."

And none could argue with that. Not even the silence.

Laden with its woes, the curtain now came down over its eye. Only to be raised again, Abs letting-out a laboured *sigh*. This opportunity to rant having proven cathartic.

Kel was to stand then, leaving the plinth on the floor. Kicking aside a pile of clothing that lay by his foot.

"You should've thought of that, before you went flapping your gums," he said, glaring after my-*Man* with intent. A fist buried deep inside his coat pocket; gripping that ball-point pen he'd been presented upon leaving the *Panny*.

"What?"

Baffled, Abs now scratch his head.

Flapping gums? What's he on about?

It looked for and found Kel's eyes. And witnessed—even in that measly light, Kel's strikingly handsome countenance, obscured by a dread spectre.

"My-*Man* thinks it was me...who grass'd him-up," Abs now deduced, addressing the house.

The idea, spoken out-loud, setting its *Spidey-senses*™ a-tingling.

Chirps'ing its teeth, it made to stand its ground—regardless. Only to find itself wavering on the spot. That Puppeteer above its head, being off—apparently, on a fag-break.

"It wants to go look to its own stable," it said then. The comment, more of an aside. Whispered under its breath.

And waving a dismissive hand after Kel, it was to beat a retreat to its tiny corner of the Universe.

Having regard now, for my-*Man*'s absence. Kel removed the pen from his coat pocket. Masking it by his side, and testing the nib's temper with his thumb, as he cautiously approached that mangled doorframe.

He was to discover my-*Man* floundering, upon the cusp of its own room and relative safety. It having turned back for some reason—*the Mug*.

For nostalgia's sake—*perhaps*? Coz there was more to be said—*more than likely*. Or maybe, coz it'd missed its friend, and thought their friendship worth fighting for—*like hardly*.

Whatever the excuse, Abs had thought to give-it one last ditch appeal to Kel's reason.

"Oy—think on it...who brought you in?" it said. Now finding itself stranded in No-*Man*'s Land, Kel having taken-up its cotch in the doorway.

"How-*ya* mean, 'who brought you in?' You didn't bring me—I brought myself," Kel snarled, killing that bedroom light.

Glaring after it, he could feel the *Shakes* coming-on. And just-now, the Cinë-*matic* switched over to 'Standby', being conscious of no one sat there watching it.

"*What*...I didn't bring you in—Kel?"

Momentarily distracted by this event, Abs turned back to face my-*Man*. Every fibre of its being now screaming—*Fly*.

"Kel? I didn't bring you in?"

Fly—you fool!

Certainly, it couldn't help but sound betrayed; after all it'd done for my-*Man*. It flapping a heavy hand, dismissively after him—*like*, was it not the one who'd been wronged?

The question being of-course, a rhetorical one.

Admittedly, it'd been spinning the same ol' yarn for so long, even it'd come to believe in it.

"If I didn't bring 'im...how'd he get here?"

Abs directed its appeal to the house, and presumably, that Live studio audience.

"Ain't no one check for *my-Man*."

It *Blinked* then, slow and deliberate. As if, seeing it all now playing out before its eye.

"Yeah...me-*one* bring 'im...Me," it said, and beat its chest emphatically, with a flat-hand. Punctuating that lonely syllable.

Me!

And turning its back on Kel—in mock disgust, made it all the way to the cusp of its room. Only to be called back, as if attached by elastic to a spot midway between those two doors. Those two faces of Janus.

"Yeah—it tried a ting...got bumped. So what?"

Abs chirps'd its teeth.

"I bet my-*Man* feels the World owes him one—"

Phf'king Chief...

And *Blinked* again, slow and deliberate. Warming now, to that Self-righteous ring in its voice.

"That'll teach it...to *phf'k* with *my-Man*—"

"Yaddah-yaddah-yaddah."

Kel animated the fingers of his hand, as if wearing a glove-puppet.

"Does it love to chat, other people's business an' that—*phf'k-me!*"

He chuckled then, to himself. Though fast approaching the boil; its every word, that it should dare breathe the same air—*even*. To be taken now as a slight.

"What business *you* have to chat?"

Smelling its sweat, Abs bigged-up its chest to step lively to my-*Man*. As if about to come to *Blows*.

But then, it *Blinked*—slow and deliberate, and wavered.

"I can say...whatever the *phf'k* I like...to whomever the *phf'k* I like... *a*-bout. Whatever. The *phf'k*. I like—"

Wavered, and *Blinked*.

And then, it was as if it'd stopped addressing Kel altogether.

"What...*what?* You-you reckon you can do me sa-(*hmm*)?" it continued, glaring sideways—at a s'posed Nemesis.

"You...you can't do me *nuttun*. My-*Man*—Gritting its teeth—*phf'k* you up."

Sniff

It being around about its bedtime. Abs looked then, to spin the whole sordid episode for Street—for *Road*.

"Panny changed you—Star," it declared, chirps'ing its teeth.

"To-think...I used to check for my-*Man* hard."

It shook its head and sighed. Swatting repeatedly at an imaginary tear, with the back of its left hand. Presumably, for snaking down the wrong side of its boatrace.

"*Llou this*—I'm out…Later."

Abs waved, dismissively. And turned about to leave.

Which was when Kel pounced. Punching the pen in its back. The force of the blow knocking *my-Man* flat onto the floor. Kel managing to windup on top of it.

And right on cue, that landing-light Timed-out—CLICK! And all hell broke loose.

[Rap] Now while flying high in the friendly sky
I hear gunshots screaming
And looks like another job for a
Über-badass Human-Being
So, speeding—
Like Steve McQueen in
Bullett—I hit the scene in
4-seconds flat
To the find the whole joint teaming
With half-crazed Pimps—in Tuxedos and Minks
You couldn't blink for gunshots
The shit was like a scene in
A John Woo flick—
Triad Gangster warfare shit
But wait a minute, 'Yo! Who's my-Grrrl?'
Now pinch me if I'm dreaming.
I needed a plan quick
Nah phf'kit—I'mma steam in
Rain blows like killa combos
To send my foes sail through the ceiling
And with eyes that can see in
X-rays and do Laser beaming
I torched the whole phf'king joint before leaving
Now whether I'm dealing
In true lies, or plan hoop dreaming
Being ÜBERman was seeming
Grreat!
But ÜBERman I ain't
Maybe I'd be more Über with a hundred million?
Yeah baby—
Maybe even then we could...

THE ÜNLIK∃LIEST •F MΛN-CAVES

The sunlight was seen to sanctify that communal space. Dust particles dancing in a graceful haze, set against a backdrop of frigid uniformity.

More your shrine to Mod-*living*, and domesticity. The kitchen was an unlikely Bastard-child of Bauhaus, suckling upon a substrate of Utility. That fecund gene pool: Watered down and liberally applied, like a stencil, or a mould, to every millimetre of that sterile environ.

The unlikeliest of *Man*-Caves—of Bat-Caves™. It was where *Man* got to put on his *Man*-apron. And genuflect before his one true god, Profectus.

Yeah, herein was *Man*'s *Life*-styled. Every action therein, unwittingly proffering praise; contrite *Amens*, in consideration for that promise of plenty. Those rituals and rites of domesticity, rendered impenetrable by that habit of living. Still clingy and transparent as cling film. And yet, as roomy and loose fitting as a Monk's garb.

This particular example was rendered in a tasteful, minimalist schema: Prefab Lime-green *Itchy*-kitchenette® units, framed with Brilliant-bright, blank-faced ceramic tiles; boxy, metallic idealized appliances loitering upon its countertops.

Then it was, speckle-effect linoleum flooring, with traction micro-beading; and matte finish, stain-resistant walls.

That omnipresent *magnolia*-F1D5A6, infused with the warmth of a glorious midmorning.

The sunshine managing just, to peek-in through those Chelsea®

triple-glazed windows. What seemed a canvas for all the World's filth.

Inside a brand spanking new X'ANG® Combi oven-*slash*-grill-*slash*-microwave, *ersatz* Streaky bacon crackled and spat. The bouquet of this searing pig-flesh substitute, a complement to that visceral palette already listed.

Stood, his back to the kitchen—and the World. Marl was half watching his munch cook, half concocting a rhyme on his Cell.

Being unfamiliar with this particular appliance, he'd had to feel his way about its controls. But now, clockin' those wafer-thin rashes shrivelling under that intense heat of the grill. The 10-*mins* cooking-interval he'd programmed, was beginning to seem just a-little excessive.

Grabbing a nearby UtilityDepo® coffee-colored Tea towel, he dived-in to rescue this fare. And it was as he opened the Combi-door, that Abs moseyed-in from its reccy to the store.

It sporting House togs adapted for the Street—for *Road*: Ash-BLK Ade ///Das® bubblewrap bodywarmer, worn over a fading Ash-BLK tee-shirt—a *ThunderCats*® motif emblazoned upon its chest.

Then it was, Ash-BLK Ade///Das® Urb*flex* shellsuit bottoms, and spotless Brilliant-bright *Tick*® Corp. Total*Air*™ kicks.

Sniff

It plonked its shopping down on that kitchen table. The Lemon-yellow and Shamrock-green BNP® branding, telling most of this morning's fable.

"You found the Survival Kit then?" it observed. Apparently gleaning this much from just looking at *my-Man*'s back.

Survival Kit—which part, Marl thought.

The 'Kit' having comprised a few choice breakfast staples: Sachets of Highlands® *insta*-Oatmeal, with powdered milk; Danski® vac-sealed *ersatz* Streaky bacon; a tub of Melkiel® powdered eggs; tins of *Heinz*® Baked Beans in Paul Newman's™ Original Smoky Hickory BBQ-sauce; and a Baker's Pride® microwaveable *insta*-Bloomer.

"Is you leff it by the door?" Marl enquired, tugging at his flannel *Tick*® Corp. OZYMANDIAS urban-camo bottoms, and neglecting to look round.

"Yeah, with the remote. My-*Man* leff it with me this morning. *What—* you didn't hear 'im knock?"

"Nah—Bruh."

Stowing his Cell in the pocket of his sweatbottoms, Marl stretched—his jaw tensing against an impulse to yawn.

"*Gwon*, and here's me thinking you was-*like*, blatantly blanking 'im," Abs volunteered. Smiling a knowing smile, that was to be more your conspiratorial-*Wink*.

Having pulled-out that smoking tray, Marl looked ruefully at what was s'posed to be his breakfast-*slash*-lunch. The seared, Streaky bacon looking more like Beef jerky.

Ana-nuttun, he thought, emptying the tray's contents onto a Utility-Depo® Electric-blue plate; one of six square plates he'd found stowed away in a cupboard. Next to a stack of square bowls, and a couple of round mugs. All rendered in a striking palette of sub-primary colors.

Getting all domesticated, he then washed the tray, and carefully laid out more Streaky bacon, from the eco-friendly recyclable packet. A silence ensuing, whilst he was about it. There being no compulsion to speak, to bridge that apparent gulf that lay between these two constituents of the Street—of *Road*.

It was to be a comfortable silence still. Of a kind that recognised and respected boundaries. And a *Sign-of-the-Times*. An entire generation having grown used to sharing communal-Spaces, with relative strangers. Any notion of privacy—of personal-Space, having become as abstract as that of individual-*Freedom*.

Privacy being something one aspired to, like any other luxury item. It being right up-*there* with the *swish*-garms, and the *Bling*-tom, and the *stoosh*-gates, and the customisable Bentley®.

Yeah, it was to be like, a *Life* goal. Afforded, and affordable, only to the äußerst reich. That One-Percentile. Those elect few Elect out-*there*, living that ol' Good *Life*.

Rummaging through its shopping bags, Abs was already beginning to warm to my-*Man*. Seeing him decked-out as he was, in his own House togs: Fading Ash-BLK tee-shirt—with 'Public Enemy' motif, and OZYMANDIAS sweatbottoms. His bare feet sweating into that speckle-effect linoleum.

Yeah—one of us, he thought, gleefully.
[Rap] *It ain't where you're from*
It's where you're at...

∞

Out-*there*, in der Lebenswelt. The sun was to be obscured momentarily, by passing clouds.

And suddenly robbed of its warmth and radiance, the *Man*-Cave quickly plunged into a gloomy Utility. The Space becoming more constrictive, the walls seemingly closing-in. As if the room were booby-trapped to pulverise unsuspecting Neanderthals. And thus, make way for your more domesticated Homo sapien.

Regardless, the two housemates were to wait it out. Marl adjusting the temperature to *Lo*, and punching-in a new time on the Combi-oven's UI. The numbered keypad singing that cooking-interval.

Abs rummaging through his shopping bags, evidently looking for something. Eventually emerging with two packets of twenty Pall Mall® *Lights*, and a roll of skins—Phillie's Authentic® *Coca-Cola*™ flavoured cigarette papers.

And as if waiting upon this cue, the clouds were to disperse, and the kitchen brightened anew.

Tugging at his sweatbottoms, Marl now peered through the glass of the Combi, diligently watching his brunch cook. The seconds *Tick-ticking* away on the LCD display; the descending scale counting backwards, each revolution of that tray inside.

"So...it's you living-in the next room," he said—eventually. By way of formal intros.

"Yeah. But we all share the kitchen. Except for *my-Grrrl* upstairs, her flat's self-contained."

The mention of my-*Grrrl* was to immediately prick Marl's curiosity, which may have been the intention. And turning, he now cop'd my-*Man* manoeuvring its bulky frame, round that kitchen table, and over to a nearby cupboard.

"What? There's a flat upstairs?"

Marl's boatrace bore barely an inkling of a first impression.

"*Ya*-get me. I'm like, Fowler. Wha-da deal, Bruh? How is it *my-Grrrl* gets the flat? Ain't that-*like*, blatant gender discrimination?"

And having said this, it stuffed a week's supply of PapaRosario® vac-sealed *insta*-Meals into a cupboard labelled conveniently, 'Abs Cupboard'.

THE UNLIKELIEST •F MAN-CAVES

"And he's like, '*Grrrls* are more responsible.'"

Abs had Fowler's voice down-pat.

"More responsible," it continued, in its normal voice. "You're having a bubblebath ain't-ya?"

It stopped then—abruptly, to look-over at Marl, all conspiratorial-*like*. Its hands cluttered with a couple of family-size packets of Weetoes® *You'd Be A-maized* maize-corn krisps; and a King-size *Kinder*® Indulgence, made with 80% authentic Cocoa and *ersatz* Goat's milk.

"Hear what. I reckon, *my-Man*'s got his hands all-up *inna*-dat Cookie jar. Ya-get me—"

Wink.

Marl raised an eyebrow, in Spock-*like* mock surprise.

"What—you didn't know? *My-Man* was partial."

Abs now gave it the Side-eye.

Couching his ignorance in a half-hearted shrug. Marl began *Chomping* on a crispy rash of seared bacon. Bum cotch'd on the kitchen counter, back turned to that Combi-oven.

Having stowed its *Munchies* away in another labelled cupboard, Abs was again rummaging through its shopping bags. Emerging with a quart of Friars® Pear cider, and a six-pack of Brewer's Import® Xxx-*tra* Strength Stout Ale.

"So what—you telling me *my-Man* didn't try it?" it said, moseying over to the X'ANG® *Thermador* fridge-freezer.

And at this, Marl's *stoosh* demeanour finally cracked. And he was to find himself nodding, and skiggling; his hand loitering by his mouth, a rash of seared bacon held at the ready.

And now, leaning on that fridge door, Abs was to join him. The pair's combined fit of skiggles harmonising briefly, before petering-out.

"Not being one to judge a Bredder—Nom-nom—I didn't want to say nuttun."

Marl spoke with his mouthful.

"Who's judging?" Abs butt-in. "I'm just saying, *my-Man*'s-like always clucking. And he ain't too fussed—*ya*-get me."

At this, they both cracked-up again. The joke returning for an encore.

"You clock'd *my-Grrrl* yeah?"

Abs peeped over the fridge door to catch Marl's expression.

"Oy—can you imagine *my-Man* getting a piece of that?"

How-ya mean? Marl was to concur, his boatrace reacting as if to a foul smell.

"Still, my-*Man* look's out for me—two-*twos*. So—"

Abs chirps'd its teeth, and climbing-down off its pedestal, disappeared behind the fridge-door. Leaving the exchange to go cold.

And now, it was Marl's turn to keep that conversation going; him thinking to use my-*Grrrl* as a pretext to pick my-*Man*'s brains.

"You been up there then?"

"Up where?"

Abs emerged from behind that fridge door and looked over. And it was as if it'd lost track of what'd been said prior. But then, just as suddenly, it all came flooding back.

"*Oh yeah*—yeah. Obviously."

It *Sniffed,* and closing the fridge door, added, "only the once though."

Stuffing its now empty shopping bags into a draw, it parked itself upon the lip of that kitchen table, facing my-*Man*.

"Two-*twos*. I tried a ting, when I first moved-in—as you do. But, *my-Grrrl* was on some stoosh flex. *Ya*-get me."

Marl nodded his head at this, it resonating with his own experience. But then, he cut to the chase.

"So what—is anyone holding it down?"

"Why—you looking *a*-chirps?"

Abs grinned.

Clearly, my-*Man* was *looking*—for something, or else he wouldn't be asking. Still, it thought to establish the fact, get it out in the open before dismissing it outright.

Looking after it, Marl shrugged.

"Trus me—Bredren. Forget about it," Abs confided. "*My-Grrrl*'s trouble. And that's with all caps."

Sniff

Warming now to the company, and the conversation. It cracked open a pack of Pall Malls®, proffering one to Marl.

"Nah—Bruv. I don't smoke."

Marl held-up his hands, as if meaning to fend it off.

"But you b'un though—*yeah*?"

"Yeah, who don't?"

Pulling a face to illustrate its apparent confusion, Abs nevertheless sparked its own cigarette and continued, "two-*twos*. If it weren't for my-*Man*, my-*Grrrl* would've been long gone. And it'd be me-one cotch'd in that flat all-now."

Nahh

Smelling a whiff of intrigue, Marl exaggerated his sense of surprise to coax out more of this *Jack-a-nory*.

"*Yeah*—ere what…"

Abs took a drag of its cigarette.

"…*my-Grrrl* had had this Beenie—Evy—bunk with her."

It exhaled smoke through its nose.

"*Phf*-it. Bredren—this Evy was live-*like*…"

Cigarette cotch'd in its mouth, Abs stood; needing to stand to convey Evy's obvious appeal. Its cupped hands, pulling punches like Adam West's camp Bat-Man®.

BOOPH

BAM

Ka-POW

It chirps'd its teeth then.

"Yeah—Nodding—my-*Grrrl* was all that. And talented, *what*."

"Talented like how?"

"Talented-*like*, she'd give one of them BangOptics solid photon jobbies *a*-run."

"Yeah? Where you bucked one of them then?"

"A-bout. Why, you ain't buck one yet?"

Nah

Shaking his head, Marl reached for another seared rash of bacon.

"*Phf'kry*," Abs cackled. "Anywho. Yeah—my-*Grrrl* was talented. *Trus*."

Taking a quick drag. It ashed the cigarette in its palm and returning to its cotch—on the edge of the table, continued, "they were Juggling-juggling out of the premises. The ol' King Charles—as you do. It was them two and *my-Man*—Kel, the *gheezah* that used to be in your room."

Sniff

"My-*Grrrl* had been doing a ting with it for donkey's years-*like*—before they even landed here."

"What—Nom-nom—my-*Grrrl* who's all in there now?"

"Yeah…"

Abs took a meaningful drag and exhaled through its nose.

"Two-twos. My-*Grrrl* now starts flexing with my-*Grrrl*. On the sly-*like*. Then my-*Man* starts flexing with it—"

Pulling-on the last rash of bacon, to tear-off a piece. Marl was to now give-it his best *yah*-lie facial expression.

"*Yeah*—Nodding—shit got real messy real quick," Abs continued, mirroring it back at him.

"So—what happened?"

Nom-nom

"What d'you think happened?"

Marl shrugged.

"The Feds, that's what."

Abs chirps'd its teeth.

"What—out of the sky blue like that?"

Marl licked his lips.

"*Ya-get me*. It was-*like* proper CrimeWatch. Feds, and Forensics. And Rubber-gloves. And Sniffer dogs. The whole firm—Bubba."

Phf'kry, Marl shook his head.

Warming a-little more to the topic, Abs now hopped atop that table.

"I was with this Beenie when they knock'd," it continued, its Brilliant-bright kicks swinging.

"A nice sort—from Sou-*phf* Sou-*phf*. You know the type, proper Church *church*—like, butter wouldn't melt in her mouth. But *Phf*-it. Bredren—"

It sniggered, and *Wink*'d after Marl.

"I had it hold my ting. And of course, it was *Shit*-ing it. And then there's me, proper *prang*. Literally praying, like—"

Pressing its palms together. Abs now acted out. The Scene.

"Please *Lordie-lord*, don't make them come search-up my room."

It took a quick drag and exhaled. Looking to the cigarette, to gauge how much of it was left to smoke, before continuing, "but the warrant only covered *my-Man*'s gates, and the flat upstairs."

"You got a touch."

And as Marl said it, he turned to check-on his brunch.

"Believe. Like in *Intacto*—you seen it?" Abs enquired, watching him.

Nah

Tugging at his sweatbottoms, Marl didn't bother look round.

"Oy—that must've been you last night?"

THE UNLIKELIEST OF MAN-CAVES

Ey?

"Locked out."

Locked out?

And suddenly it dawned on Marl, what my-*Man* was on about.

"*Oh yeah.* That was my-*Grrrl*—running joke."

Abs held up a hand weighed down with Tom, the cigarette smoking betwixt two chunky fingers.

"Say no more. Still," it continued—now skinning teeth, "your doors been kicked-off more times than the Premiership. *Ya*-get me."

There followed a ham-fisted laugh, hammering home that punchline. Though still bent over the Combi, Marl's boatrace was to struggle to mask him processing all this new *Intel*. And cottoning onto this, Abs thought then to leave it to stew for a-bit. An extended silence measuring the *Beat*.

Beat

"So what happen'd?" Marl asked—eventually, turning to face my-*Man*.

"What happened when?" Abs responded, pulling hard on its cigarette.

"With the *Federales*-dem?"

Abs chirps'd its teeth.

"What you think? They took one look at me and came back same day with a next warrant."

Phf'kry

It was now Marl's turn to cackle.

"*Ya*-get me. Still, they must've been on a *missh*. Coz, soon as they found my-*Man*'s ting they splurt'd, never to be seen again."

Ey?

"Yeah—Skinning-teeth—*my-Man* thought he was smart, stashing it with *my-Grrrl* upstairs."

Abs put the cigarette to its mouth to take a drag, but then remembered he'd more to add.

"Oy—you should've seen ol' Fowler."

Again Skinning-teeth, it took a pull to exhale through its nose.

"Para. *My-Man* was proper *Brick*-ing it. And of course, the Feds was all giving-it the Side-eye—like, they knew he knew they knew he was in on it."

Abs paused momentarily, as if to check the playback of what it'd just-now said—*they knew...he knew...they knew*—and nodded to itself.

Yep.

And ashing the cigarette in its palm, continued, "though—if you wanna get all-technical about it. He was, and he wasn't."

Sniff

"Obviously. He didn't check for juggling on the premises—*obviously*. That goes without saying. But having said that. He knew the coup and let it slide, *my-Grrrl* having it on a leash-*like*."

And again, there was the *Wink*.

Checking how much was left of the cigarette, Abs took another hasty pull, exhaling through its nose.

"And there's me, all waiting on *my-Grrrl*, ol' Lynn Faulds to come through—with the Too Live Crew. You know, *Blondie*. Even got the ol' fade touched-up."

Abs chirps'd its teeth.

Marl continued paying it *Lip*-service, his skinned-teeth the mirror to my-*Man*'s ham-fisted laughter. Whilst behind the Mask, the gears were now hard at work reassessing the situation.

Being an enterprising Soul, he'd his Heart set upon launching a modest enterprise of his own; utilising the choice *Lo*-cal. Him figuring—rightly, that the ting he was about juggling i.e., *Sensi*, would be a scarcity around these parts. Smelly being prevalent throughout much of the Met and Greater Metropolitan district.

But that plan was now *Skid*.

What with the Yard being 'Marked', he'd be under strict compliance with the quota, making it nigh impossible to achieve any kind of scale. The system being rigged to keep you hunkered down in the trenches, with the rest of the *Geto Boyz* and *Grrrls*. Bumping-off each other, in a bid to maintain a working margin.

"You need an ashtray—Blood?" Marl prompted, gearing-up to tap it for more *Intel*. It being now apparent, that my-*Man* was one of them Cats that liked the sound of its own voice.

"Nah—you're alright," Abs said, looking to its cigarette. "We ain't even s'posed to be smoking in communal areas."

It took a pull, and added—exhaling through its nose, "or any other

THE ÜNLIKELIEST •F MAN-CAVES

part of the premises. As it goes."

Now leant against the counter, Marl was looking after it, his back turned to the Combi.

"It's like that?"

"Yeah—your standard hostel runnings," Abs stated, moseying over to the sink.

Leaving its cigarette cotch'd on the windowsill. It washed its hands, and wringing them out, looked in Marl's general direction.

"So, who's living in the gates now?" Marl asked, handing Abs the Tea towel.

"Except for me—and my-*Grrrl* upstairs, there hasn't been anyone new 'til you," Abs replied, drying its hands.

Having finished with the towel, it flung it at the counter and retrieved its cigarette. Which by now had burned down to the quick— just shy of the lettering, of its own volition.

"My-*Man* got sent down—possession with intent," it continued, taking a pull. "Solid-Photon-*Grrrl* splurt'd soon after. Fowler then turfed everyone else, to be on the safe side."

"So—there's no-one living in the basement then?"

Taking a few more hasty pulls. Abs was to see Marl's query and raise it, with a query of its own.

"Why—you been down there?"

It blew smoke out the side of its mouth.

"Yeah—I had a nosy."

"Yeah—I thought I heard-ya."

Running the tap, Abs then doused the stub. And leaning over the sink, opened the window to fling it out.

"So what, you turfed the bed?"

"Had to, Blood. Before the *Misses* came through," Marl fessed-up.

"Two-*twos*. That mattress used to be in my room," Abs confided, waving after a cloud of smoke it'd only just-now exhaled.

"Yeah?"

"Yeah—proper done the rounds has that mattress. The Bod who lived in my room before me, he had his bit running *Johns* out of there. You know, part of the scourge of Heron—which was how he eventually got turf."

Nahh

THAT PERFECT WORLD

"Yeah—Nodding—you get all sorts around here, what with it being so central. Obviously, I swapped it out when *my-Man* went down. Seeing how tight Fowler can be."

Leaving the window open, Abs now looked after Marl. It being clear my-*Man*'s mind was elsewhere.

"Oy—you wanna go check your *ting*," it said then, nodding in the direction of the Combi.

Turning, Marl clock'd the smoke, and grabbing the tea towel, hastily fished-out what was left of his brunch. Burning himself in the process. Abs looking-on, as he threw that smoking tray down on the counter to coddle his singed fingers.

"*Phf'kry*," Marl thought out loud. Seeing the rashes he'd carefully laid out, now little more than smouldering embers.

"Yeah—feel free to help yourself," Abs volunteered, nodding in the direction of his cupboard. "We can sort something out later. It's all-good."

Obviously, Marl had no intension of borrowing any-ting from my-*Man*, or anyone else for that matter. But he paid it *Lip*-service still, "*Gwon*. Safe Blood."

And then, began inspecting the Danski® packet, on the pretext of putting-on yet more rashes.

"So what—you juggling?"

Abs returned to his cotch on the kitchen table.

"Why? You looking?"

"Ain't everybody—looking for something," Abs retorted, removing a cigarette from the freshly opened pack, to put it back upside-down.

"*Ya*-get me," Marl replied, resealing the packet of bacon to set it aside.

"What you inna, Smelly?" Abs then enquired. *Sniffing* after the word, as if its sibilance carried with it a lingering scent.

However, stood hands on hips, surveying this crash site. Marl was to totally blank the question.

"Come to think of it, I heard of some Gold seal flying about," Abs said, watching him.

Sniff

"Yeah—you wanna go buy it then."

Having evidently made-up his mind to *llou* Brunch. Marl tossed the

230

tray into the sink, burnt embers and all. The racket abruptly upending the *vibe*.

If he hadn't been *Brewing*. And hadn't smoked the last of his *ting* the night before, he might've been more on-it *on-it*. Though, having said that, Gold seal was reputedly a decent smoke, and as rare as sensi. It being *baer* henna mostly, on your hashish front.

"It's Marley—*yeah*? As in, Bob?"

Abs climbed down off that kitchen table.

"Yeah."

"Kool and the Gang. I'm Abs."

Marl looked after it.

"Abs?"

"Yeah."

Lifting its tee-shirt, my-*Man* slapped its rotund belly.

"Abs."

Marl watching insouciant, as it did this. Only to creased-up after. Him finding himself wiping at fake laughter-tears, lodged in the corners of his eyes. And then, it was the insides, as if he were fishing for crumbs.

Now Skinning-teeth, Abs collected the cigarette papers, the packet of Pall Malls®, and a disposable lighter. Migrating from the table to that countertop.

Picking a spot just by the sink, it retrieved the chopping board from behind the taps, and deliberately laid out these accoutrements upon it. A Zoo-*zoo* being just the thing to commemorate my-*Man* moving-in, and them bucking-up like this.

But before it could commence with the ritual-proper, it'd still need to prep.

Measuring your standard 1-and-1 half-length, it scored the cigarette paper. It then wet where it'd scored, with its tongue—for ease of tearing. It then placed this *skin* ceremoniously upon that chopping board.

"Roach…Roach…Roach," Abs said then, clicking its fingers and looking about.

Seeing nothing suitable immediately-to-hand, it opened the draw stuffed with shopping bags, and after a brief rummage around, settled on a box of Swann® cigarette filters. Tearing a square out of the box and rolling it into a cylinder, to place it deliberately at the end of the skin, favouring its right-hand.

Having now assembled everything it needed, it fished-out a fair-sized nugget of hashish, wrapped liberally in cling-film, from the pocket of its shell.

"So, you a Yid then?" it queried, tackling this wrapping.

"Nah—a Goona," Marl admitted.

With my-*Man* in the process of bil'ing-up, he now thought to make himself look busy.

Turning-on the hot water, however, he was to be caught off-guard when it came out full-blast. The water cannoning-off the tray, he'd left cotch'd at an angle in the sink.

Phf'kry, he thought, quickly shutting-off it. The term now clearly vying for his mantra of the day.

Piss'd, and feeling piss'd on. He looked down at his garms. The front of his faded tee-shirt, and his forearms, as if he couldn't bear to touch himself. And then to my-*Man*, who hadn't seemed to notice. It being too engrossed in peeling the sealant from around the nugget, using a thumbnail it'd cultivated specially.

"A Goona-ey," Abs said, eventually. "That's still Nor-*phf* though?"

"Nah—more Nor-*phf* east."

Marl finished wiping himself down.

"You heard-*a* Pembury Estate?"

"Nah Bruv," Abs said, surveying the nugget to be sure it'd removed enough of the sealant to be getting-*on* with.

"But I know you heard-*a* Grove," it added, fishing for a lighter.

It then put fire to the hashish. That earthy-rich, spicy aroma of Blackest Moroccan Black, quickly filling the kitchen.

Marl soon finding his nose twitching after its bewitching bouquet— *like* Elizabeth Montgomery.

Sniff sniff

Yeah, being strictly a *Weed*-head, and none of that Homegrown Smelly-*shite*. He'd been sceptical watching it. But now had to admit, *my-Man's ting did smell kind-a alright still.*

"So, what team you follow?" he asked, putting that tray to soak.

"Q-P-R. Born and bred," Abs confided—with pride, whilst continuing to gently heat that nugget.

He then commenced with crumbling it, onto that skin he'd already prep'd. And marking its due diligence toward the ritual, Marl was content to let the conversation peter-out.

But it wasn't long before Abs paused from flaking the hashish, to scrap the resin off the tips of its fingers. Once more utilising that special thumbnail.

"I ain't one of them flaky Bredders—*ya*-get me," it said, looking for and finding Marl's eyes. "You know the sort—your Gloryseeker. Flock Chelsea one week. Fulham the next. Just to catch a-bit of Über Lega."

"Yeah—so what division is that then? Amex Conference?"

Tugging at his sweatbottoms, Marl made sure to give it his best *Carebear*™ stare.

"Oy—don't knock it," Abs said, *Blinking*. "Granted, we keep having to sell our best players. But just you watch next season."

It returned to putting fire to the nugget, and continued heating and flaking, heating and flaking it, in silence. Its Skinned-teeth assuming a wolfish grin.

It slowly becoming apparent, my-*Man* had more than a smidge of your ol' *Man-of-the-Mountain* about it.

C●TCH'D

Mounted on the wall in that draughty hall, a nook under the stairs next to the hostel's front door. The payphone was crooning its little heart out. Its antiquated analogue shrill, like a cat-call. The incessant
MEOW-MEOW...
MEOW-MEOW...
A counterpoint to that Pitch.

After a while, there came the satisfying CLICK of a light-switch. And footsteps, following hot upon the heels of a flood of photons. The thud of bare feet, scurrying down flights of carpeted stairs, two steps at a time, like an erratic heartbeat.

Marl swore, as he stumbled at the foot of the stair; his margre frame shivering in a faded Ash-BLK tee-shirt, with flaking 'Public Enemy' motif, and Sunday's best pair of Roc-A-Wear® boxers. Goosebumps pinching at the skin on the backs of his arms; his *semi*-erect member, like an improvised divining-rod, divining his way.

Lurching for the Payphone, he scooped-up its receiver to be greeted by a moment's silence. Then the tone, him having said nothing.

Chirps'ing his teeth, Marl reset the receiver and waited. His lanky limbs folded-in upon themselves; like a coat hanger, all bent out-of-shape. His skin affording him scant protection, against a biting chill that seemed loathed to share this Space with him.

Seconds inched-by. And housed in that shaded nook, that Payphone was to remain obdurate in its silence. Whilst threatening, at any moment, to cry-out.

Consequently, Marl's trudge back down the hallway, and jog up the stair, was to be both pensive and apprehensive. His mind's eye, conjuring for him, an image of a Call button *Blinking* quiescence. A giant's thumb poised over it.

It was Sod's Law, that he should find himself locked-out.

Stood before his own door, and conscious now, of an assumed presence across the way—that other door sharing the landing. Marl rapped a bony knuckle, tentatively, upon that deadwood to whisper.

"Oy—Tan..."

Beat

"Tan?"

Silence.

Anticipating a response, he tendered a cheek to it—that deadwood, as if inviting a kiss. Arms measuring that doorframe's width, like the Vitruvian *Man*. Eyes listening, all attentive.

Blink-blink

Nothing.

"Oy...*Tan*?"

This time, his hushed voice sounded more strained; like a crowbar, attempting to pry open that thin Black slither, separating door from frame.

And still nothing stirred. Save for that landing light, threatening to lay bare his lascivious intent. The glare of its beady-eye, a surrogate for that sharp, pointy-finger of your *god-of-always-listening*. Charged—*as-ever*, with reactionary omniscience.

It'd afford him no hiding place. No hint of shade. Save that of his own shadow, seen seeping-up the wall like the serpentine silhouette of a crook'd Nosferatu.

Marl knocked again. More firmly this time, the sound amplified by an absence of any competing noise.

"Oy Tan. Come get the door—will-*ya*..."

And just-now, that landing light Timed-out.

CLICK!

And still Marl waited. It being a relief to find himself masked by that Pitch, suddenly. His voice, now an outstretched limb, reaching blindly into the Void.

"*Tan?*"

C•TCH'D

It carried with it, a note of anxiety—the hail. Its wavering, seeming to waiver any presumption of his innocence. Indeed, here was your nefarious Mister Wolf come a-knocking. Both your Little Piggy and Little Miss Red Riding Hood, back from Market and from Granny's. Safe and snug inside.

Little pig. Little pig. Let me come-in—

Again, pressing his ear to that cold deadwood, Mister Wolf listened intently; his angst more and more directed toward my-*Grrrl*, for having goaded him into answering the Payphone in the first instance.

Like what for? he thought, rightly indignant.

"Is that you—Marl?"

There came a muffled response from behind the door. That mousy voice, mockingly cautious. TAN being privy to who *my-Man* was s'posed to be. And even though he'd been expecting it, it still startled him—her summons.

"Oy—open the door. It's flipping freezing out-here," he pleaded. Body now shivering, seemingly unable to soldier-on.

Eventually, there came the sound of Tan fiddling with the latch. Then the door opened, ever-so slightly. That slither of light, warm and inviting.

Blink-blinking her innocence, Tan was to peer suspiciously, through that gap. As if, she were charged with policing an illicit Backstreet dive; her shadow falling just shy of Marl's now bemused expression.

Apparently satisfied with his patronage, she nevertheless continued with this pantomime. Hazarding a look-see, pass my-*Man* at the landing—just to be on the safe-side.

Before retreating, leaving the door ajar.

It'd been Marl's idea to designate the room's light-switch off-limits.

That moody lighting, coming courtesy of a solitary UtilityDepo® lamp propped upon the windowsill. Its luminance struggling to find the far wall, for that tasteful bulbous Tangerine-orange IsamuNoguchi® lampshade—handcrafted from rice-paper and wire.

What'd been Tan's housewarming gift.

And from the offing, *tings* had looked promising. Tan quickly overcoming her initial disappointment.

"*What*—no bed?"

Her gut-reaction, giving way to thoughts of no distractions. No Big brother next door. No Mum upstairs.

Then, it'd been a frenzy of probing tongues. The pair clumsily fondling each other into a heightened state of excitement.

But then, the Payphone had kicked-off. Its incessant MEOW-MEOW. Enough to pry open their eyes, dull their senses, and nullify that spell they'd been about conjuring for themselves.

Having been discarded, their clothing still paved a trail toward that more habitable region of the room. A kind of biosphere, beginning below the knee, with that naked duvet spread ceremoniously upon the floor. The MDX5000 standing at the foot of this makeshift bed, with the *SpeakerboxX* for company; the Trinity® 4—with its two controllers, waiting expectantly under the Cinë-*matic*.

The rest of Marl's meagre belongings carpeting that carpeted floor, like, debris at a crash site.

By now, Tan had parked herself upon the duvet, Marl's faded Charcoal-BLK sheet wrapped about her bare shoulders, like a cape. And gave the impression of being preoccupied with one of his Cells. The light from the screen playing with her features, and that Vitiligo skin-condition that'd been her Birth-right.

A necrotic looking melanated complexion commandeering one half, anaemia the other. As-if, she were an apparition of Hel, taken from the Prose Edda. Itself, that trace of Kali Shakti.

Though my-*Grrrl* didn't bother to acknowledge my-*Man* as he entered. She did pump-a-fist as he closed and locked the door. And catching the gist of it—this gesture, Marl was to look after her, and feel his gender prick.

The fact that she'd remained scantily clad, in a tasteful SAVAGE® BLK-BLK French-style panty—chosen for the way it accentuated her slender hips; its matching wunder-bra doing wondrous things with her boyish chest. All boding well.

Little pig. Little pig. Let me come—

He figured her most probably inna one of those *Beat 'em-ups* she favoured. Tan being your consummate perfectionist, and heavily goal orientated.

The appeal of such games, being their virtuous feedback loop; the genre analogous to a pixelated PAC-MAN™, gorging itself upon her needing—nay, wanting to excel at everything she put her mind to.

Looking beyond her obvious charms, Marl had immediately liked that about my-*Grrrl*. That she knew how to Cotch; and could wipe the floor with him on *Beat 'em Down*™ XXL on the Trinity® 4.

It being still early doors, he figured a *Zoo-zoo* might help reset the vibe. But first he'd need to put on some mood muzik. And so, squatting down in front of the MDX, he pressed-in the Power-button to retrieve its tactile-wand, expecting the display to flash him its usual greeting. But then, nothing...

Marl chirps'd his teeth.

"The ting won't come off standby," he said, turning the tactile-wand round and opening the battery compartment. "Look-see it there. These ain't even my batteries," he added, continuing the blow-by-blow commentary.

Tan ignoring him, her thumbs mashing numbers on the Cell's antiquated keypad.

Phf'kry, Marl thought, cursing my-*Man*—Tonx.

Recalling now, how he'd gone on-and-on about borrowing his Mint Condition, knowing full well he'd switched-out the batteries on him.

Again, he chirps'd his teeth. And *llou*'ing the MiniDisc, crawled on all-fours round behind Tan, and over to the window.

Lifting the duvet cover—that was still acting as an improvised curtain, he retrieved my-*Grrrl*'s Pod.

"Oy...I'm gonna need my battery."

Tan didn't take her eyes off what she was about.

"*Ana-nuttun*. Look-see, it's at 80 per cent," Marl said, showing her the *Pod*-screen. But Tan didn't bother look.

"I don't care. I need it to last me."

"Till when?"

"Till I get home—*what*?"

Tan chirps'd her teeth.

"Didn't you bring your charger?"

"Yeah—it's in the whip. But when am I s'posed to use it? While I'm at work and leave my *Pod* lying around—*ya*-mad?"

Tan then paused the game to regard my-*Man*.

"And what-if there's an emergency or something?"

Unlike Marl, Tan had thought it through. Unlike Marl, Tan was used to taking responsibility for things. And looking after her just-now, those impish almost boyish features, his trifling need was seen to pale into insignificance.

She was such an unlikely *Persephone*.

Dreadful, and yet, breathtakingly beautiful. Despite, or in spite of that permanent twelve o'clock shadow. The mute lighting, merely adding a sense of mystery to her apparent otherworldliness.

And being thus, *Spellbound*. Marl couldn't help but submit to her ordering him about, like a little brother. Though he didn't always have to like it.

Tossing my-*Grrrl*'s Pod down on the duvet, he went to retrieve his liccle baggy of weed, and packet of cigarette papers from the windowsill. Which was acting as a makeshift shelf.

And reading his intent, Tan did likewise. Tossing the Cell and shuffling backwards to lean against the wall. But then, feeling its chill through the thin sheet, she was to lurch forward and hug her knees.

"Isn't the heating still on?" she asked, pulling the sheet tighter about her hunched shoulders.

"Nah," Marl replied, feeling the radiator.

He'd been about examining his *liccle* baggy, guesstimating how many heads he'd left. Digging a thumb into a compact bud, through the plastic. He figured two, maybe three at a stretch.

He then took stock of cigarette. Rooting around in the Turtle-green UtilityDepo® mug, he'd been using as a makeshift ashtray—that now looked Dark-brown; him unearthing one chip buried at the bottom.

One chip equalling one spliff, obviously he'd a problem.

Still, it was *ana-nuttun* to bop to the hydrostation on the corner, it being so close and always open. But, he'd be bruk until he buck'd *my-Man*—Sef; him having put-in on a Nine-bar, he'd first dibs on an Oz.

But then, he'd still have to go turn-it-round. Which was *long*.

Aside from that, he was due to register anew his address, at the local DCW&P. Proffer a thumbprint and DNA-sample for them to validate and *proc*, assessing his eligibility for yet another mandy placement with *Volsec*. Which in turn, would entitle him to *Subsistence*.

Though, this seemed longer still, and overly convoluted.

Barring all that, he could always go ask his mum. Regardless of how acrimonious his leaving had been, he knew she'd always be there for him.

Love being Love, and all you ever needed...
Allowing this thought to peter-out, Marl again looked to Tan.

Still hugging her knees, Tan pivoted her feet upon their heels. The way she would if she were painting her toenails.

"I like it here," she volunteered, scrutinising her toes, her chin propped upon her knee. And that was despite it being cold, and kind-a cramped.

"It's quiet," she continued, turning the Zirconia studded toe-ring that graced her wedding-finger. That toe closest to the little one on her left foot.

Yeah, Tan liked her feet. Liked that her toes were well proportioned, that her arches were high and well defined. It being the only part of her not afflicted by the Vitiligo.

And naturally, she kept them immaculate. And marvelling now, at their podiatry perfection—as she so often did. Tan suddenly felt to fidget.

The piercing on the side of her nose, though long since closed, still irritated her from time-to-time. It was always a bad sign.

"So—*Sniff*, who was it on the phone?" she asked, keeping her tone matter of fact, as if meaning to make conversation. When in truth, it'd been bugging her all this time, that my-*Man* should neglect to volunteer this information.

"They hung-up," Marl mused, between licking the sticky bit of a cigarette paper, his eyes staring into the middle-distance. Oblivious of that ACME® sink-unit, hugging the corner directly ahead of him.

"What—dry like that?"

Tan squinted to better look after him; her nose twitching, like a dormouse *Sniffing* after the air. His back being turned to her, Body arched over in the process of bil'ing-up. It gave the impression he'd something to hide.

"*Ya*-get me," Marl said, attaching the first cigarette paper to a second, taking care to align it perfectly with that centre crease.

Yeah, Tan liked Marl's back. Liked how it looked manly, and broad; his shoulders squared and muscular. Nevertheless, she now resisted the impulse to reach-out and gather him up in her arms. Rubbing her nose instead, with the back of her hand—what seemed a boyish gesture. As if meaning to smear it all over her boatrace.

Sniff

"The way you flew out that door—I thought you was expecting," she said. Adding a snigger to insure my-*Man* caught the slight.

He did.

Certainly, Marl had had his own grievance, regarding my-*Grrrl* sending him Out-*there*. But now knew to hol' his corner, his tongue—that is.

"It was the same last night," he volunteered—retrieving his lighter. Expecting that to be the end of it.

There remained a redundant flap of cigarette paper, where he'd joined them. This he lit at the corner, the skin lying flat across his palm as the fire slowly consumed it. Whilst still unconvinced, Tan unfurled those long shapely legs of hers, to begin a forensic examination of them in that light.

Below the neck, the Vitiligo migrated down from the right over to the left side of her Body in blotches, much like the coat of a Dalmatian. However, in that mute lighting, Tan now observed that her skin assumed more of an even tone.

Almost normal looking, she thought, turning onto her side.

"I don't see you running when I call."

Marl blew away the cinders where the two skins joined, to reveal what would be the spine of the spliff. Then, fetching a third sheet of cigarette paper, he attached it to form an L-shape.

"What am I running for—I already got *your* number."

Turning adroitly onto her other side, Tan was to continue with the impromptu interrogation.

"You don't know how frustrating it is—to call and get a vox-Bot on both your Cells," she said, tensing and relaxing the muscles of her thigh and calf, her toes pointing. Her Body seemingly having a pivotal role to play in it all.

"Did you get the Bot earlier though?"

Mulling over this response, Tan sat up and pulled the sheet about her. She then moved closer, straightening the duvet under her as she went.

Coming behind Marl, she enveloped him in the sheet, her arms and legs hooking around his margre frame, as if she were a spider. The

Queen of Spiders—*say*, about to feast upon her unsuspecting prey.

"*Yeah*—only cos you wanted something."

Admiring his handiwork, Marl pretended to be unfazed by Tan's close proximity.

Still, he couldn't help but breathe her in. The smell of her skin, her familiar Body odour. An intoxicating concoction of synthesised fragrances; deodorant, skin cream, hair cream, perfume. She'd carefully selected and blended, to form her own unique scent.

Sniff

Circumventing his Mind—his reason. It was like a pheromone, that spoke directly to his Body, and his senses. Of his senses, and his *Man*-hood.

"And?"

Marl now adjusted his tackle.

"How-*ya* mean, and?"

"I don't see how that proves any-ting. When I called you earlier, I couldn't get through."

Leaning forward, Marl retrieved the baggy of weed, and that chip of cigarette. Tan holding-on for the ride, feeling his stomach muscles clench and flex.

"But you knew I'd be at work."

"Yeah—and you don't see me screwing."

"And?"

"And? How-*ya* mean—*and*?"

Baffled, Marl scratched his head. Tan was there now, and everything else just seemed *long*.

"I got older brothers you know," Tan said.

"Yeah, you tell me all the—"

Owch

Tan pinched Marl.

Huh

"And I see the way you *Man*'s like to carry-on."

"Yeah—and how's that?"

Marl licked along the spine of the chip. Then crumpled the stale tobacco onto the skin he'd prep'd.

"Just so's you know. I ain't one of dem gal dem, you think you can pick-up and put-down as-and-when—"

"You think I don't know that," Marl cut-in.

Tan paused to watch him, her eyes peeking over his shoulder.

"Okay then. How is-it, when you got turf'd—and I was sneaking you in-and-out of my mum's. How is-it, I had no problem getting *a*-hold of you."

She tightened her grip about my-*Man*'s stomach and continued, "but now you got your own gates, all I get is baer, 'the person you are calling is unable to take your call. If you'd like to leave your name and number...'"

Yeah, Tan had that *Vox*.BOT down-pat.

Stifling an impulse to laugh, Marl angled his head to direct his voice towards my-*Grrrl*. Whilst keeping both eyes fixed-on what he was about.

"I only just moved in—*what*?"

"I don't care. This ain't gonna be about me having to run-you-down just to come see you. *Ya*-get me."

Marl looked over his shoulder after Tan.

"How-*ya* mean? It was me who couldn't get hold of you."

Tan came round to meet his eyes.

"So—now you know what it feels like."

For a second, Tan's boatrace was all deadly serious. Moody, and brooding—what with that permanent twelve o'clock shadow.

It providing a stark contrast, for when she finally cracked. Smiling her most wicked and infectious smile, her eyes *Blink-blinking* mock innocence.

And being thus, helplessly afflicted. Marl felt then, those butterflies in his stomach start *a*-fluttering.

It took a couple of seconds still, for the lesson to sink-in. But eventually, Marl's boatrace broke, to smile his own crocodile-smile. All teeth showing.

His *Ticks*, those associated with the ritual of bil'ing-up, now surfacing; him flicking at the end of his nose with his thumb, a couple times. He then licked the tips of his fingers—to better grip the skin, ritually rolling the tobacco, to thin it out.

Her point having been made, Tan now disentangled herself. And shuffling round Marl, on her knees, made a show of leaning heavily upon those broad shoulders of his.

Marl hazarding a look-up at her, their eyes meeting at some midway point—in that Void that stretched between them. My-*Grrrl* again batting her eyelashes after it, and licking her lips to give-it her cheesiest Cheeseburger-grin.

Straddling Marl, those long legs of hers folding over his, she let the sheet fall about her thighs. My-*Man* obligingly pausing from what he was about, holding the half-built spliff aloft, so as she might better settle herself.

"Here—make yourself useful," he said then, inviting my-*Grrrl* to take an active role in the ritual. And obliging him, Tan was to proffer her flattened hand.

Placing the spliff carefully upon this perch, Marl took the opportunity to once again adjust his tackle. Tan riding-out the erratic movement; back erect, eyes following that hand down the front of his boxers.

"Oy—what you looking at?" Marl scoffed, throwing those inflatible pillows behind him. To catch his fall—as it were.

"What—I can't watch?"

Blink-blink

And there it was again, that unabashed Cheeseburger-grin.

"How long's it gonna take 'em, you reckon?" Tan asked, now inspecting her-*Man*'s handiwork—the spliff measuring her palm's width. As Marl set about painstakingly crumbling the sensi onto the cigarette.

"To do what?"

"To get you a new bed?"

"They don't even know I turf'd it yet."

Looking after him, Tan waited to catch his eye to playfully bounce her crotch upon his lap.

"You best get on it then."

Marl readjusted the position of her hand.

"If I'm gonna cotch here wit you," Tan continued. "We're gonna need a decent mattress at least."

She took in the room's dimensions, then added, "could you even get a double in here?"

Marl paused to look after her.

"But wait, who give you the season ticket?"

"*Yeah-yeah*—whatever."

Tan carefully laid that half-built spliff on the windowsill. Marl watching her, genuinely put out.

"Oy—wha-*ya* dealing wit?"

Reverting back to that serious expression of hers, Tan pointed a finger in his boatrace.

"Don't. You. Oy. Me," she said. Poking the end of his nose, and then flicking it, to punctuate the sentence.

"I ain't your playmate."

"But—I was doing something," Marl whined, grabbing *a*-hold of that finger.

But Tan was to wriggle free—easily. And again, grinning after her-*Man*. Unfurled that sheet, to smother him in it.

"Yeah. And now, *we*. Are doing something else."

Skinning-teeth, Marl made to reach for the lamp.

"Oy—leff-it. I want to be able to see you."

"You sure?"

"What'd you think?"

C•TCHIN'

They hadn't been at it long, before Tan had to come up for air. Throwing back the sheet to reveal the pair of them; Marl laid flat, her on top — Cow-*Grrrl* stylie.

"I gotta splurt soon," she announced, by way of explanation. Her usually levelled head, *Amp*'d on the anticipation of Sex.

Marl looked-on, his hand lingering between her thighs.

"What—I thought we was cotchin'," he said.

His tone just shy of pleading. Those broody, heavy-set eyes of his, now struggling to mask their obvious disappointment.

Little Pig. Little Pig. Let me cum—

Looking down upon him, from up-on-high. Her boatrace, one great big, illegible shadow. Tan was to catch a whiff of his desperation and feel her flame douse.

"I ain't got any condoms," she declared, folding her arms like a pair of wings across her boyish chest.

"And I know you definitely don't," she continued, now feeling herself coming down. That heady mix of heat—and sweat, that *phf*unk of lusty pheromones trapped under the sheet, dissipating into the air.

"What we need condoms for?"

Following Tan's gaze, Marl cop'd his fifth limb—with its one unblinking eye, peeping-out that slit in his boxers. And tucking it away, put-on his most devilish grin. Watching for my-*Grrrl*'s reaction, as his fingers sought to steal a taste.

Er—

"What you think you're doing?"

Catching that hand, Tan was to flash him that practiced look of hers.

"*Ohh*, but you let me before," Marl whined, his hand still loitering with intent.

"Yeah, that was then."

Tan unceremoniously flinging it to one-side.

"So what, you just gonna leave me *clucking?*"

"It's on you. What you'd think I come round for? To play Beat 'em Down on the Trinity."

Smirking, she began rummaging around in the folds of that makeshift bed. Shoulders balled like Ryu—from *Streetfighter*™—guarding her more squishy, vulnerable bits. Her pronounced absence of mammary glands, and her Heart.

"Oh—that's cold."

Marl propped himself up on his elbows.

"Forcing me to go hunt down the Morning After is cold," Tan replied, finding her bra. "You know how it *mongs* me. Plus, I got work—another double-shift."

She chirps'd her teeth, and holding the bra-clasp in her hand, appeared to be in two-minds about something.

She then looked to her-*Man*, those rugged, handsome features of his. Strong, prominent brow and pronounced chin, partially obscured in that moody light of the lamp. And figured, *baers*.

"Which means having to go hunt down a pharmacy during my break."

Tan picked-up where she'd left off, fastening the bra back-to-front about her abdomen. "Which basically means missing-out on said break."

Turning the bra the right way round, she threaded her arms through its straps.

"And it ain't like they give it away for free—ya-get me," she concluded, adjusting the fit. Managing to do all this blind; her eyes remaining fixed upon her-*Man*, as if meaning to commandeer his gaze.

Now looking at her boyish chest, she took-in the overall impression. That hint of cleavage the *wunder*-bra had managed to wring from her Body.

Sniff

For his part, Marl had been more about thinking of compelling reasons to have his wicked way.

"*Ana-nuttun*—let me shuck quick to the hydrostation. It's just on the corner." About all he could come-up with. And bouncing his crutch under Tan, he prompted her to climb-off.

"What—now?"

"Yeah, it'll only take a sec."

Tan didn't look much convinced.

"Oy—what time is it?"

Stretching, Marl checked the windowsill-come-shelf for my-*Grrrl*'s *Pod*. And finding it missing, started ferreting about the sheet, his hand eventually stumbling upon it by his side.

Waking the screen, he read the time out loud.

"Three forty-nine."

"*What*—four o'clock? I didn't think it was that late."

Tan stood up. Then bent down again to grab the sheet, and her *Pod* from out of her-*Man*'s *hot*-liccle mitts. And as she did so, she cop'd him doggedly watching her; his one eye, assuming that objectifying perspective of the Male-gaze, as if it were his 'Default' setting.

Sniff

Turning her back to it—to *Him*, she pulled the sheet tight about her; the fabric now accentuating those contours of her slender frame.

And stepping over Marl, glided toward the light-switch. Leaving it till the last minute to glance back over her shoulder, to ensure her-*Man* was still watching her.

But he wasn't.

Left forlorn on that makeshift bed. Marl had tucked away his stiffened resolve; the resulting bulge looking unsightly, and cumbersome. And it was then he remembered, he still needed cigarette.

"Oy Tan—got any sheckle?"

"What? Don't tell me you're *bruk*."

Tan's hand was poised now, on that light-switch.

"I just need a-*liccle* scratch. For cigarette—"

"So, you got money for condoms then?"

"Oh, and that too."

Tan hit the switch. The light spiriting away any hopes of Sex, that might've lingered-on in the gloom.

"When you gonna get a job?"

Tan tried not to sound too matronly.

"I already got a job."

Marl tried not to sound too defensive.

"Juggling ain't no job."

Tossing the sheet after her-*Man*, Tan began climbing into a pair of Ade///Das® *Ivy Park*™ 20% grey flannel sweatbottoms. And seen as my-*Grrrl* was getting dressed, Marl thought he might as well finish bil'ing-up.

"I don't see why you can't just go on the pill," he said, retrieving that half-built spliff from the window-shelf.

Covering his modesty with the sheet, he sat crossed-legged to roll it. Then licked along the sticky-bit to seal it, before adding, "Sef says Fats is on it."

"On what?"

Now paying her-*Man Lip*-service, Tan zipped-up her hoodie-top; her mind preoccupied with the drive back home—to her mum's. And having to get-up in a couple of hours to trek back into town. It all seeming *longer-than-long*.

"The Pill," Marl said, the spliff clenched between his lips.

Finding his lighter, he sparked it then—the spliff. Puffing repeatedly on it, to nurse the cherry, before taking a proper pull.

"Why can't you go on the pill?"

Tan spoke the thought out-loud, while stuffing her work-clothes into that Cargo® carry-all she'd let Marl borrow—and decided to take back. She then ambled over to the sink. And standing before the mirror, thought to make sense of her unruly Afro.

Marl swilled smoke in his mouth, like a practiced wine-taster, and exhaled. He then commenced with admiring his handiwork. Testing the spliff's girth, and blowing upon its cherry, as if it were a match-chord.

"I see your priorities," Tan said, coppin' him in the mirror. "You can find money fi weed. But can't fork-out on a packet of condoms."

She chirps'd her teeth then. And leant-in closer to inspect her boatrace; her overly sensitive skin being prone to reacting to Synthesised-fibres, like those her-*Man*'s sheets were made of.

Still waiting on that *Buzz* to lick. Marl took another hefty pull, letting the smoke coax from his gaping mouth.

"*My-Man* sorted it—on tic," he croaked, smoke spelling-out his words.

"Then he can sort you some sex," Tan mumbled under her breath.

She looked after him—in the mirror, and grinned. And putting her *Pod* down by the sink, ran the tap to rinse-out her mouth.

"Some Dealer you are," she continued, looking about for something to dry her hands with. "How you s'posed to make money if you smoke all your shit?"

She then remembered where she was and gave up.

Blotting her hands on her sweatbottoms, she grabbed her *Pod* and bent down to slip into a pair of Absolute-BLK *Tick*® Corp. Total*Air*™ ankle-boots—with the patented *vari*-elevation heel.

"How-*ya* mean? This is me-*pers*."

Marl spoke between tokes.

"If you say so"—*Sniff.*

Shouldering that carry-all. Tan gave-it—the room, the once-over.

Then, as an afterthought, extended a regal paw. Prompting her-*Man* to pass the spliff.

Marl eagerly obliging her. Stretching, upon his hands and knees. Tan *Blink-blinking* reflexively—from the smoke, as she put the spliff to her mouth, and took a deep pull, and held it in.

"*Ugh*—you forgot the roach," she protested. Exhaling, to pluck flakes of tobacco from her lip.

"We don't use roach no more," Marl was to state, dryly. His sinewy arms cotch'd upon his bony knees; spine arched, seemingly with the weight of his *Life*'s burden.

"And who's we?" Tan enquired. Struggling now, to get at a decent pull.

"You know—me and the *Man*-dem," came Marl's reply, watching her gamely persevere.

Huh—the Man-dem.

Tan waited until she felt a slight *Buzz* creep over her, before passing it back—the spliff. But with the cigarette paper all soggy, from her *oh-so* soft and succulent lips. Marl was forced then to tear-off the end, to get at a decent pull himself.

After which, he proceeded to suck on the stunted spliff, as if intent on making-up for that sudden dip in *Tetrahydocannabinol*, swimming about his system.

"So what...you shucking?" he was to ask, eventually. As if he didn't give a toss either way. Smoke again, spelling-out the syllables of each word.

Having retreated to the door, Tan had hold of the latch.

"Looks like it."

Sniff

And opening it—the door. She stood there, as if tethered to the spot, long enough to give-it her most serious look.

And then, was through it and out, onto that landing. Leaving the door ajar, like an open-ended question. That was to be punctuated by that CLICK of the light-switch.

"*Phf'kry*," the eye said, peering under the sink-unit.
Yeah, the carpeted nook looked pristine. The newly uncovered Space having not seen the light of day, since the thing had been assembled.

"So what—*my-Grrrl* just shuck'd, dry like that?"

A groping hand, bejewelled with sovereign, and signet, and chaps— clasped loose about the wrist, replaced that eye.

"*What*—you didn't follow it?"

Another voice blurt'd out.

"What—back to the mums?"

"Yeah, back to mummy's," the other voice echoed—mockingly.

There then followed a bout of skiggling. A third voice chiming-in to fill-in those blanks.

"Nah *Blood*. I ain't with running gal down on road—*ya*-get me. Two-*twos*. I managed to blag a ciggy off some cabby at the hydro and cotch'd."

"Ski-*ing*."

"Ski-*ing*."

There then followed more skiggling.

Over by the sink-unit, Tonx was on his hands and knees poking about. Whilst Marl and Sef were stood where the makeshift bed had been. Two pairs of Brilliant-bright Total*Air*™ kicks planted squarely on the floor, the bedding kicked-up behind them against the wall.

Though they were facing the Cinë-*matic*, they weren't actually watching it. Instead, each wore a sleek wireless IL&M® XYZ headset— the vizor pulled-down. Bright Fluorescent-pink G-sensors, the size of golf balls and covered in micro-Velcro, stuck to their garms; at the hips, and shoulders, and one at the Solar plexus. One more clasped in

C●TCHIN'

a favoured-hand, the Power-ball; a BLK *Interface*-ball clasped in the other. What was your standard G-*Interface* Upper-Body Config.

They were immersed in a Total Soccer™ Ultimate Über Liga Final — the first of two legs. Each with a spliff on the go, parked in a UtilityDepo® mug planted on the floor between them. Just by the Trinity®, which'd been moved to one-side out of the way.

Pre-empting the release of the Trinity® 5^{VR} console, its Q3 launch scheduled to usher in a 'new dawn' in gaming; that much hyped 'La-Z-Boy hyperreal gaming revolution'. IL&M® had unveiled — at the beginning of Q1, a fifth-generation console of its own. Its first, the little hyped, though widely anticipated XYZ.

Positioned on the floor under the Cinë-*matic*. Said console was a shear, shiny Fluorescent-pink, giant-sized Billiard ball. That utilised real-*Time* Mo_Cap technology: Mapping the movements of those G-sensor balls within the sensory field it generated.

However, what was to be truly revolutionary about the XYZ console, was its Aerobic-Gesture Command & Control Protocol. An often counter-intuitive Body language of gestures, that formed the basis of its UX.

To play XYZ games, gamers had to learn — and perfect — these gestures, standardised across the handful of titles currently available on the platform: UbiSoft's Dragon's Lair™ V; Games Workshop's Warhammer™ 40K; an adaptation of Capcom's seminal Beat 'em up, *Beat 'em Down*™, rebranded *Beat 'em Down*™ (*Fah real*); and of course, EA Sport's Total Soccer™ Ultimate.

Naturally, the gestures scaled with difficulty. From 'Basic', a simple action to Walk-*slash*-Run, Shoot-*slash*-Punch, Pick-up objects etc.; to 'Intermediate', requiring combinations of gestures — or *combo*-Gesture strings — to perform more elaborate movements and actions; to semi-'Professional', comprising of Tricks unlocked by performing strings of *combo*-Gestures, that might require exhaustive practice to initially perform.

It being not uncommon for your *Pro*-gamer to spend hours in Training Mode — in front of a *virtua*-Mirror image, memorising and mastering their timing. Much like a dancer, learning the choreography of a complex dance routine.

Also, where the Trinity® 5^{VR} — with its 'Static' ergonomics, was subject to restrictions on the amount of time gamers might stay immersed, within its hyperreal gaming environ. The mandatory *Time*-limit safety feature, introduced under the EH&S 'Time-Out' Regulations.

The XYZ's 'Active' UX effectively circumvented said restrictions, allowing your gamer to stay immersed for hours on end. Play often to physical exhaustion, whilst presumably keeping fit.

So, although its unique third-person perspective was a far cry from your *virtua*-Reality, in the purest sense. The IL&M® XYZ was still— arguably, your idealized form, G-A-M-I-N-G C-O-N-S-O-L-E. Realised.

"Oy—you can't have my-*Grrrl* thinking she's got you under manners," Tonx chipped-in.

"Nah—your wrong there Bubba, my-*Grrrl*'s just insecure. She's one of them that likes to have *Man* run-her-down," Sef said, shaking his hips to start his Avatar running. "Now, if you'd followed her—"

"*Nah* that's bait. Don't watch that."

Tonx was shaking his head, even though no one was watching him.

"Oy—wha-*ya* dealing wit, Tee-*Man*?"

Rolling his hips to negotiate a tackle, Sef squeezed the Power-ball to nudge the virtua-Football ahead of his running Avatar.

"*Check-it Check-it*," he then said, squeezing the *Interface*-ball twice.

Having paused the game, he lifted his vizor. And following his lead, Marl did likewise to look at him.

"My-*Grrrl*'s got three brothers—yeah?" Sef continued, leaning in close, as if meaning to impart a secret.

He held-up a thumb and two fingers to visually demonstrate the number.

"Three—Bubba. All of them older than her. And all of them Gal-*ist* in their own right. So, it goes without saying, my-*Grrrl*'s gonna have some game about her. *Ya*-get me?"

"Yeah, and—so what?"

Tonx was back inna the nook.

"Bottomline Blood. You leave a *Man* clucking like that, he ain't gonna be your *Man* for long."

"What—you don't think I told her that?"

"Ey—how-*ya* mean, 'you told her?' Told her what?" Marl butt-in, getting all antsy.

C●TCHIN'

He didn't much check for Sef reckoning he knew Tan better than him. Tan being—coincidently, Fatima's bestie. Fat's being Sef's *Grrrl*.

But that was to be a whole other *Jack-a-nory*.

"Brah—Fats done told me my-*Grrrl* was for making you wait."

Shocked, Tonx stopped what he was about to look over.

"Wait fi what?"

"*Ya-get me*."

"Oy Sef-Man, we playing?"

Marl held up his *Interface*-ball.

"Come we-go."

They both lowered their vizors, Marl squeezing the *Interface*-ball twice to resume play. Play having resumed, Sef quickly settled into a groove. Dropping a shoulder to faint, whilst squeezing his Power-ball to charge the Power-bar for a shot-on-goal.

"Oy, I'm just saying Bubba. I've known *my-Grrrl* longer than you."

Marl abruptly paused the game, and they both lifted their vizors.

"Oh—you back on that flex. Come then, let we talk about your ting, who I don't know—by the way. So, how is Fats? My-*Grrrl* told me she was late."

"What—like late-*late*?"

Skinning-teeth, Tonx looked over.

"Nah, her cycles just irregular," Sef piped-in. He then added, looking after Marl, "what, Tan told you that?"

"Now you see how it feels—how you like it?"

Again, Marl held-up his *Interface*-ball, so as my-*Man* could watch him squeeze it. Sef assuming his gaming posture, though still much rattled by this revelation.

"Nah serious ting, Bubba. Fats told my-*Grrrl* she was late?"

Play resumed.

Tonx was chuckling and shaking his head, over by the sink.

Having replaced the piece of plinth at the base of the unit, he'd continued to poke and prod it, searching for more loose sections.

Whilst about him, clouds of pungent weed-smoke were to be seen riding currents of air, up toward the ceiling. The improvised curtain being only partially drawn back; the light from the window barely penetrated that gloom that hung over everything, like a bad smell.

Over by the MDX5000, a number of MiniDiscs lay festooned on the floor, encircling a Braeburn® Tablet³ᴰ, that was acting as a makeshift tray. It being littered with all your usual spliff bil'ing paraphernalia: Phillie's Authentic® *Coca-Cola*™ flavoured cigarette papers; a pack of B&H® SilverTips; and a fair-sized heap of *Sensimillia*, just clucking to be bagged-up.

Feeling some give in the board that ran down the side of the sink-unit. Covering a sizeable gap, where the unit met the wall. Tonx gave it a shove.

"Oy—*Em*. This piece here's loose—look," he said, now looking at the piece of board in his hand.

"Give it a rest—Tee-*Man*," Sef whined. Leaning back and swivelling his hips, to add a-bit of swerve and dip to his shot-on-goal.

Pausing the game, Marl lifted his vizor.

"Don't tell me you bruk the *Man*-dem's ting," he said, bending down to steal a toke from his spliff.

"Nah *Blood*—it was already loose. Look-see it there?"

Tonx presented the piece of disassembled unit as evidence.

Sef then held-up his *Interface*-ball to show Marl. And putting his spliff to cotch in the mug, Marl replaced his vizor.

Play resumed, but the interruption meant Sef scuffed his shot.

"Ah what—*Phf'kry*."

"Un-lucky Dread."

Marl bend down again to steal another quick toke. Sef taking *a*-butchers at his Cell, whilst waiting on him to restart the game—with a goal kick.

Resting the board against the unit, Tonx now sized-up the exposed cranny. Then, removing the wireless VoxSensiva earpiece, that was like a permanent prosthetic attached to his ear. He began ferreting around.

"Oy—my-*Man* really thinks he's gonna find something."

Sef pulled a face, as another shot whistled just wide of the goal post.

"Are these even working?" Marl protested, repositioning that centre G-sensor ball—the one attached to his Solar plexus.

And just-now, his Avatar froze in that *virtua*-Reality projected within the vizor. A giant exclamation mark *Wink-winking* over it.

"Oy—wha-*ya* dealing wit?" Sef exclaimed. "Now you're gonna have to run a re-calibrate."

"Re-*cali*-what-now?"

"You can't reposition the balls like that."

Marl chirps'd his teeth.

"*Baers*—this is long."

"Just run it, Dread."

Marl double-squeezed his *Interface*-ball. The game then paused, the 'Option Menu' popping-up for them both to see. Scrolling down to 'G-sensor Config', he selected it. And then, 'Calibrate'.

In that *virtua*-Reality housed within the vizor, Marl saw his Avatar, a rendering of the Barcelona Goalkeeper and Captain, Letícia Izidoro Lima da Silva #12, standing. It having assumed a neutral stance, with the Fluorescent-pink G-sensor balls superimposed over the silhouetted figure. An exclamation mark *Winking* after the ball he'd repositioned.

While Sef's Avatar, that of the Inter Milan Midfielder and Captain, Irena Martínková #27, was squat down next to it. Apparently smoking.

Selecting 'Optimization', Marl followed the prompts. Repositioning the G-sensor balls and performing the sequence of gestures, required to 'Lock-in' the configuration. Before finally selecting 'Resume Play'.

"*Gwon*—come we-go."

Sef took one last hasty toke and set himself.

"Start it then," Marl said, looking after him. As if he'd been the cause of the hold-up all along.

Now muting the commentary, Sef cleared his throat to put on his Sunday's best Commentator's voice.

"At such a late stage in the game—John, I can't really see Barca making a comeback."

Putting on another voice, not that dissimilar to the first, he continued, "*Ya*-get me—John. Inter were by far the better side on the night. Their inspired 4-3-3 formation, proving too much for this much beleaguered Barca side."

Two distinct personalities were to emerge.

"Oh, what's this—John? Inter's lead scorer, Fran Kirby looks set to complete her triple hat-trick."

There was a brief pause in Sef's commentary, while he dispatched yet another goal: Dribbling into that 6-yard box and chipping the Barca Keeper, da Silva. A quick-press of the Power-ball and a pelvis-thrust forward, to lift what was technically a pass.

"Now there's something you don't see every day, John."

"A-*tru* dat, John. A-*tru* dat."

"They think it's all over. Well, it is now—*next*."

In game, Sef's Avatar—the digitally rendered Fran Kirby #14—was doing the Scarborough *Man* Bogle. Sef having previously Mo_Capped it, as his personalised victory celebration.

"Alright Mottsen—it's your ting, so obviously you're gonna smash-it."

"Mottsen which part? I'm Pearce all the way—Bredren."

"Yeah John, whatever."

And here was Marl feeling a-way, at the score reading more like the time on a digital alarm-clock. That is, 10 : 02.

"So what? You didn't rinse it when I lent it you?"

"Oy—you let my-*Man* borrow your console? You're lucky to see it again," Tonx chipped-in—from the sidelines. His bulging arm buried to the shoulder behind that sink unit.

"Oy Ref-fer-*ee*," Sef barked.

"What?"

Marl chirps'd his teeth.

"I only meant to nudge *my-Grrrl* off the ball."

"Well done Ref. Red card him yes."

"Wait. How you scroll through the Players again?"

"Use the *Interface*-ball."

Marl squeezed it.

"Okay. Look-see when you squeeze it—yeah? How it highlights a player on the global map."

"Yeah."

"Just let go to select that Player—or simply put it on auto."

"How you do that?"

Sef chirps'd his teeth.

"Oy—I swear there's something wedged back here," Tonx said, his arm now like a blind proboscis, slobbering all over that backside of the laminated unit.

But neither Marl nor Sef were for paying him much mind.

"Oy—you see that shimmy," Marl said, shaking his hips vigorously and squeezing the Power-ball, to nudge the *virtua*-Football ahead of his running Avatar. "Sef—I beg you hit Action-replay."

"You'll need to score first—Bubba."

"*Fah* real—*Phf'kry*. Come, watch me do it again."

Biting his bottom-lip, Marl swivelled his hips in conjunction with lifting his shoulders to perform a Step-over, only to have Sef's Avatar clatter into his.

"Oy Ref?"

And now it was Marl's turn to call foul.

"What—that ain't no foul."

Sef hit Action-replay.

"The slide-tackle is a hard technique to master—Bubba. It takes split-second timing. Look-see it again."

He hit Action-replay again.

"I thought you said you had to score to do-*a* replay?"

"Did I say that?"

"*How-ya mean*, 'did I say that?' You blatantly just-now said it," Marl exclaimed, his voice pitching high to illustrate his annoyance.

"Nah—I said you needed to score first. *Check-it Check-it*."

Sef hit Action-replay again, whilst crouching down to tend to his craving.

"You like that? *Gwon*—next," he said, and took a pull from his spliff.

"Game's *wrenk* anyway."

Marl removed his vizor.

"Give my-*Man* your balls then," Sef said. His spliff cotch'd upon the lip of his smirk.

Sat on the floor, his forehead shiny with sweat, he now pulled hard upon it—his spliff.

"Oy Tee-*Man*," he continued, holding-in the smoke. He then exhaled, feeling for the roach to gauge how much was left. "I beg you crack a window—its kind-a minging in here."

He looked to Tonx, then.

"Is my-*Man* even listening?

Over by the sink, Tonx was at full stretch, his cheek squished-up hard against the side of the unit.

"Yeah—there's definitely something stuck back here," he said, pulling a face to mirror his efforts.

"Got it."

He emerged triumphant, holding an object wrapped liberally in a BNP® shopping bag. And then, commenced with ripping into it, as if it were his Birthday present; him having a fair idea of what it was he'd found, judging by the weight.

"Oy—*Em*? Your-*Man*—what's his boatrace—was a Bad, Bad-Boy."

Sef and Marl looked-on.

"What? You found *my-Man*'s stash?"

Sef seemed skeptical still.

"Not exactly."

Turning to face them, Tonx pointed the barrel of a dinky-*looking* pistol in Marl's boatrace.

"Here what—say *hell-o* to my *liccle* friend," he said, doing his best Tony Montana impression. He then creased-up, pointing after my-*Man*'s mug, and its bemused expression.

Instinctively, Marl had flinched. But as it dawned on him, what the ting actually was, his whole demeanour was seen to shift.

"Yo *ill*," he exclaimed, his eyes lighting-up.

And then, it was left to Sef to state the obvious.

"A-*wha* dat—*my-Man*'s Bucky? Looks like a *Grrrl*'s ting."

"I got your attention now though—*Yosh*."

Checking the torn-up shopping bag, to see if he'd missed anything else, Tonx added, "I told you *my-Man* had to have two stashes—I don't baers how much he was inna my-*Grrrl*."

"That ain't real," Sef chimed in.

"Look's real enough. Here—feel the weight."

"*Nahh* Dread."

Sef shooed Tonx away.

"You know I don't *phf'k* with dem-*ting* there."

"Since when?" Marl scoffed.

"Since when? Since marn'in."

Sef chirps'd his teeth. And pointing with a flat hand after the pistol, continued, "you see that *Phf'kry* there. That's Sauron's ring—*Ayah*. I will not touch it."

"Hear what. It's Babylon we living-in. A-bout, 'I will not touch it.'"

And now, it was Tonx's turn to chirps his teeth.

"My-*Man* must think he's Gandalf *fah* real."

"I'm just saying—Tee-*Man*. It's fi each a-we to draw the line."

Tonx pulled back the slide on the pistol to check the breach.

"Yeah," he said. "And I draw the line at getting mine—*ya-get me*."

Releasing the magazine, he then counted the number of rounds using the slit conveniently provided.

"Yo Tee-*Man*? You gonna hog the ting all day?" Marl piped-in.

The argument seeming academic to him. It being found in his gates, the pistol was his, and as such, he couldn't wait to get his grubby mitts on it.

Tonx looked after my-*Man*.

"I'm gonna need it back—yeah?"

He then held it out—the pistol. But just as Marl reached for it, he pulled it away.

"*Yeah?*"

He looked for Marl's eyes.

"*Yeah-yeah.* I only wanna look at it"

—*Sniff*

Reluctantly, Tonx parcelled it over—whilst holding onto the magazine for safekeeping. He then dived back inna the nook, to be sure there was nothing more to be uncovered.

Even castrated, the pistol felt weighty and substantial to Marl, as he hefted it in his hands, his eyes caressing its sleek frame.

Reading its branding, model and make, etched upon its metallic Body—so as there could be no doubts. The words became, in turn, engraved upon his Heart:

'Walther .32 Calibre PPK Smith&Wesson®, *Made in the U.S. of A*.'

And immediately, it seemed to speak to him—the pistol, of its innate Power. And it was as if, he'd lived his entire *Life* in its umbra, the shadow cast by it; and Artefacts like it. Absent, and yet present throughout his *Life*, it was intent upon moulding and shaping *a priori* his Body. Its precept of it.

This is what it is, to be perfect, it whispered.

Still, he'd never have known of such a thing, but for this, the unlikeliest of happenstances. Indeed, what were the odds? Its unveiling here, now.

This is what it was...

Yeah, it spoke to him. Of how, only through wielding it, could he

THAT PERFECT WORLD

hope to embody its strength. To harness its Power, over Death—over *Life*. Its argument seeming so rudimentary, so obvious.

Had he not felt Powerless all his Life? Did he not feel Powerful now, just holding it in his hands?

The ergonomics of the object then compelled Marl to take it in one-hand, the *EasyGrip*™ ribbed-handle moulding to his clenched fist. And suddenly, it was as if he were holding his *Phallus*, fully-erect and throbbing in his sweaty mitt.

Recognising it as such, an extension—extending, of his Body. Marl took it into his Heart, without reservation. As if he were Moses—*say*, cowering before that Burning brush; or Saul, struck blind on that road to Damascus. The epiphany exceeding mere revelation, for being tangible. Forged of cold, blue steel, and *oh-so* lovingly crafted.

Yeah, he took this object in his hand, and was born again. And with it, he unwittingly took upon himself its dread aspect. That of the godhead, *Shiva Hara*. The embodiment of Death.

This dainty-*looking* Artefact, becoming his *Trishula*. The ultimate instrument of destruction.

Your idealized form, W-E-A-P-O-N O-F T-H-E H-A-N-D. Realized.

It spoke of their future together—this Artefact. Or more, whispered. That it'd been his manifest destiny to wield it. As if, it were Sauron's ring—*fah* real, torn from the pages of Tolkien.

Fore had it not travelled all the way from Houlton, Maine? Indeed, it may as well have been Middle-Earth.

But for all its talk, there was to be no mention of its ignominious Past. Of its likely role in countless murders—pointless Deaths. Marl marvelling, at how the sweat from his palm immediately evaporated from the handle; and how the pistol's smear-resistant steely-Body, seemed impervious to his fingerprints. Those grubby mitts of disenfranchised youth.

The truth being such, it was already written—its story, alongside his. In those prophecies of Brother Nasir bin Olu Dara Jones: [Rap] *I gave you Power*,[39] those fateful words surmising the *End-of*-History.

The evolution of its form, from musket to *semi*-automatic pistol, being inextricably linked to the rise and fall of that contrivance of modern-*Man*, and Modernity.

Verily, this very exhibit, was to be found clenched in the cold dead hand of the last of those Last Poets. That hole blown in the back of their skull, telling its own story—their story—to no one.

Save for your *god-of-always-listening*.

Perhaps—*maybe*.

Unthinking, Marl's first impulse was to extend his arm and take aim at something. Anything. The Cinë-*matic*, his reflection, like a portrait etched upon its blank flatscreen.

He then closed both eyes to open one. To better focus down the length of the stunted barrel, his aim guided by that front iron-sight. And aiming after his reflection—with that One-eye. He unwittingly began his journey down a dark, perilous path.

Fuelled by this, his new religion. He was destined to become that One-eyed God, in that Country of Blindmen. Lauding it over-all. Compelled to reduce everything to the one *Absolute*. The one universal Truth. Not *Life*, but Death. Not Creation, but Destruction. And definitely not *Love*. For who has need of it, when one might just as easily wield Fear.

There he'd be, stood smack-bang in the middle of the Maelstrom. A Prince cast in a Machiavellian vein, calling all the shots—as it were. A *Man* who would be King, playing that role of Thunder god. Moulding all the world to his liking, and like-*ness*.

Yeah, he saw all this, or more intuited it, and was certain of its truth. The heft of that pistol, he held in his hand, the proof of it. His reach now extending way beyond that frontier of his clenched fist, all seemed within his grasp. Though his Will—his thinking, once as fast as Light, had now slowed to that of the Speed-of-Sound.

Of Silence.

Certainly, revelling in it—this *inner*vision, Marl would've laughed. If his smirk hadn't held fast his gulliver. With finger now hooked round the pistol's trigger, there was nothing left to do but squeeze—

CLICK!

He *Blinked*, never to *Blink* again.

CLICK!

CLICK!

This seduction having taken a matter of seconds, it was to be sealed by this act. The Artefact, its Will cast of steel, easily taking possession of the Boy-*Man*'s feeble Body, and pliant limbs.

∞

And still it felt incomplete — somehow. As if needing to be consecrated by a further act.

"Oy — Tee-*Man*. I'm gonna need the clip," Marl said, taking a breather from ogling the pistol to suck on his dwindling spliff.

"Fi wha?"

Still inna the nook, Tonx spoke without looking at him.

"If it's gonna be my ting, I'll need to learn how to load it," Marl reasoned — it seeming obvious, his grasp of the object's language coming as naturally as his grasp of its handle.

Looking to the ceiling, Sef sighed. He then switched-off the console, him having seen it all before. Death's apparent courtship of *Youth*.

Emerging from behind the sink-unit, Tonx looked to Marl.

"Brah — don't get comfortable. It ain't mine to give nor yours to keep."

Gripping the pistol's slider, Marl tried coaxing it back — to expose the breach, like he'd seen my-*Man* do just-now. And was amazed at the effort it took, Tonx having made it look easy.

"How-*ya* mean, 'it ain't mine?' This is my gates ain't it? And you found it here — in my gates. So of course, it's mine."

Having worked himself up, he went back to aiming at random objects dotted about the room, to cool himself off.

CLICK!

"Yeah, and what you know about it? You was busy playing Total — with my-*Man*."

Under Tonx's unwavering glare, Marl then began to feel *a*-way. There being no guarantees my-*Man* would give the pistol back, every fibre of his being was now screaming for him to stand his ground.

When all was said and done, was it not his gates? So, it stood to reason, anything found in it was his by rights.

Aiming in the direction of the door, he squeezed the trigger.

CLICK!

…CLICK!

"Oy — you're having a bubblebath, just pass me the *ting*."

Tonx chirps'd his teeth. And clapping with one-hand, gestured for my-*Man* to surrender it onto him.

But looking over the pistol, Marl had just-now discovered the safety, and started fiddling with it.

Bewildered, Tonx chirps'd his teeth again.

"Yo—what's with my-*Man*?" he said, appealing now to Sef, his empty hand dangling in mid-air.

"Just pass him the ting, Em-*Man*," Sef piped-in—him being ever your voice of reason.

"Yo chill. I just wanna learn how to load it."

"Yeah—and how am I s'posed to show you?"

Now peering down that hollow handle of the pistol, Marl was to muse upon this point. While Tonx and Sef exchanged a look.

Sniff

Finally swayed by Tonx's seemingly infallible logic, he reluctantly parted with that part of himself he'd invested in *the* ting.

"Yeah—as long as you know I'm holding it," he stated, though it seemed somewhat impuissant.

Snatching the pistol from Marl, Tonx feinted, as if about to pistol-whip him.

"I should *boks* you," he said, reinserting the magazine. He then checked the safety. "Brah—I can lay my hand on plenty gun. *Trus me*."

"You two are good," Sef said then. Taking one last pull of his spliff before outing it.

"*Llou*-it, Sef-*Man*."

Leaving the pistol cotch'd by the sink, Tonx replaced that piece of board.

"Look-see how the Precious is calling my-*Man*?" Sef said. Ribbing Marl, in an attempt to lighten the *vibe*.

"You crack me up. Bout, 'the Precious is calling,'" Tonx joined-in—now skinning-teeth.

Reaching into one pocket, Sef was to produce a roll of baggies. And from another, a Pocket-size Murphy's® *port-a*-digy scale.

"I'm just saying *Bubba*. Once exposed, you can't *un*-expose yourself. Like you can't *un*-think a thought, or *un*-feel a feeling. *Ya*-get me?"

Now making himself comfortable, he was to pick-up the Tablet[3D] to start bagging-up the sensi for *Road*.

"The ting just walks with you," he added, staring blindly into the middle-distance. "Like *Duppy*."

"Hear 'im? This is why I can't involve my-*Man* in all my runnings."

And as he said this, Tonx looked at Marl.

"Bredder thinks he's Gandalf *fah* real."

"Nah. Obi Wan more like—what?" Marl chipped-in.

"*Ya-get me.*"

Yeah, Tonx could see my-*Man* clucking. Feel it even. And two-*twos*, it was *ana-nuttin* to let Youngblood hold the ting. But nevertheless, he meant to leave it to stew for a-bit.

Arms cotch'd on his knees, empty hands cupped—one inside the other. Marl was watching Sef, his boatrace a blank canvass. Or as blank as he could fix it.

It being all he could do, to stop his eyes from gravitating towards the *Precious*; him now feeling *a*-way asking for it back.

"You missed your calling—Brah," he said, fetching the packet of cigarette papers from off the tablet.

"You should've been a Jedi—Sef-*Man*."

He then drew three *skins* and put it back.

Feeling the need to take a little more of that edge-off. Sef ran with the jibe, "how-*ya* mean? I am a Jed—"

BURP-BURP

But the *Buzzer* was to cut him short.

"*Phf'kry.* A-*wha* dat—the front door?"

Tonx looked to Sef, visibly rattled.

"Yeah," Marl replied. Licking the cigarette paper, having paid it little mind.

"*Ché!* Made me jump—Ayah," Tonx admitted, taking the pistol in his hand to skulk over to the window.

Using its barrel, to ease that improvised curtain to one-side. He then peered down.

BURP-*BURRRP*

Sef nudged Marl, the tablet still cotch'd upon his lap. A clump of sensi in one hand, a baggy in the other.

"*Ya*-nah feel that?"

"Feel what?"

But Marl only had eyes for Tonx right-now, and the Precious.

"The *vibe* shifting—Ayah."

And as Sef said it, he put the clump of weed in the baggy and plopped it onto the scale. And naturally, he'd judged it just right—just shy of an eighth.

"Vibes? Which part?" Marl said, watching Tonx—who'd repositioned himself to better look straight-down at the pavement.

BURP-BURP-*BURRRP*

"I can't see shit from here," Tonx declared.

Then suddenly, he crouched down. Gripping the radiator to stop from falling backwards.

"What happened?"

Marl was on his feet.

"*My-Man*'s clockin' the window," Tonx said, waving for him to stay put.

He was to give it a couple of seconds before hazarding a look-see. Marl coming-up behind him.

"Oy—you know this Bod?"

Tonx pointed at the Suit with the barrel of the pistol. Both he and Marl watching, as it approached the hostel's front door, disappearing from view.

BURP BURP-*BURRRP*

"*Nah Brah.*"

Marl shook his head.

The Suit was to step back into view, a *Pod* now held to its ear. And again, it looked up to scan the windows. Tonx and Marl ducking-out of sight.

And just then, the Payphone downstairs started-up with the cat-calls—

MEOW-MEOW...

MEOW-MEOW...

Looking to Marl, Tonx waited for a-bit. Before coming around to the other side to peer down.

"Check the garms though."

Again, he pointed with the pistol.

"Looks like *my-Man* just-now land from Panny—Sef."

MEOW-MEOW...

MEOW-MEOW...

But Marl couldn't see it. Indeed, he'd thought the *Gheezah* looked kind-a dapper still.

Like an Undertaker, what with all the formal get-up: 80% grey

Crombie, 60% grey Birdman suit, Ash-BLK *StayPress*™ shirt, knit pencil-tie, deep taupe *Winklepickers*.

"Gwon—*my-Man*'s splurting," Tonx acknowledged then. Both he and Marl following-it up the road.

"You see it there?"

Sef had virtually finished bagging-up the sensi.

"What—you think its coincidence? You finding the *ting* just-now, and Birdman showing-up out-*a* nowhere?" he added, plopping another baggy on the scale.

Tonx turned from the window to look after him.

"*Llou*-it—Sef-*Man*."

THE SC∃NE

The dancefloor of the 86ers™ *Members-only Club* was heaving.

The congregation's modest offering of sweat, exuding plumes of exotic perfume. Behind that wall of perforated Transparent-glass.

A galaxy unto itself, it was as a mirror held-up to the Heavens. That is, those Celestial Bod(ie)s depicted upon the ceiling. A miniaturised *Milky Way* teaming with tiny Stars, and Starlets. That soundtrack-of-the-night having well and duly wrought its spell.

Here were your true *Believers*. Busy truly believing. Their vaunted prayers, couched in that bless'd sacrament of dance, affording its own catharsis.

Moved, and moving. Each Acolyte was a *Ledge*—in its own right, with a stake in the *Scene*.

In that dream they all shared, and were about vigorously dreaming this very moment. Packed into that goldfish bowl. Their invisible, impenetrable Force-fields bouncing-off one another, in a textbook demonstration of Brownian motion. Like, so many Clones of Sue 'Storm' Richards.

Still, all seemed oblivious of that *Conch*, that hung about each neck. For even in such dark recesses, that shadow of uniformity was to be seen—*felt*, looming.

Reigning in the Beast.

Those benighted, unconscious drives—drivers, nattering away to a count of four—*Beats per second*. These disparate Bod(ie)s being communally engaged in cutting loose those bonds of their conscious selves;

THAT PERFECT WORLD

like, a clutch of blind hatchlings, compelled to breakout of their incubating shells.

The collective experience being akin to group therapy. With each 'Dependant' respectfully dressed for the occasion (—session, or *sessh*) in their Sunday's best. Fabulous and fierce *très chic* straitjackets, accessorised in accordance with the Season's latest trend; that *Razzmatazz* having ultimately, become a uniform in-and-of itself.

Anchored in Carnival, that trace of the Venetian ball, or Mardi gras. The proceedings were more your ritual marking the advent of Lent. So as, none might speak to that arcane *Dionysian*-rite underpinning it all.

So ingrained, that imposition of silence. It was left to the Pitch, and that *Limelight*. To at once mask, and mark, this communion of *Soul-to-Soul*. Expropriating that parlance of whining bulbous arses, and rhythmic pelvic thrusting motions, and heaving sweaty bosoms.

Each member of the flock—the fold, embracing utterly, the opportunity to wear their sexuality openly. Upon their sleeves—as it were, like a Yellow star.

And lauding it over-all, that myopic
UMPH…UMPH…
UMPH…UMPH…
UMPH…UMPH…
of the *Kik*. A Heartbeat regulating the Body's pulse, the Body's impulses.

The *Kik* was all-seeing. Though it had no eyes.

And was forever counting. Its syncopation of *Life*, becoming second nature to its *Aficionados*. Much like, *Breathing*.

Buried within the walls of this Space, the rig—a CambridgeAudio® 30kW Soundsystem, was like a finely tuned high-performance engine. Its woofers and tweeters being attuned, and ever responsive, to the nuances of that soundtrack-of-the-night.

'Infinite harmonic reproduction, and truer than life performance,' the manufacturer's pamphlet had proclaimed. The spiel, followed by reams of numbers, 'Frequency Performance Specs' that ranged well-beyond those recognised limits of 'Human' hearing.

Calibrated and certified according to EH&S *Regs*, the rig was operating well within its 'Op-Specs'. And yet, it didn't so much *Thump*, as TUMP!

Yeah, here in this converted cellar. A surrogate for those catacombs

THE SCENE

of Rome, or Paris—*say*. Here, those acolytes of your Cult of Adolescence were free to gorge themselves, upon the debauch excesses of kinesis.

Their want, their need for *Loco-motion*. About as subversive as a game of table-tennis.

Separating the poky dance floor from the sprawling lounge area, that concave Transparent-glass partition could be seen—*felt*, reverberating.

Everywhere, beaming smiles hung from blacked-out shades, that were like essential PPE gear; needed to shield those sparkly bright-eyes. That Pitch, that *Limelight*, being likened to a halophyte feeding upon Human sweat.

The air having become increasingly fluid. Humid, thick, and muggy. To spite the Tempora® unit's best efforts, at maintaining that artificially temperate clime.

Yeah, everywhere arms waved like foliage. Cutting across Laser beams that ebbed and flowed, conveying that dynamism of the soundtrack; and Bod(ie)s brushed-up against *Life*-sized BangOptics® solid photon holographic projections, sprinkled liberally amongst them.

This worshipping throng, deriving a thrill from that tingling sensation of ionised particles.

These flickering, dancing apparitions, rendered in shimmering hues of Electric-blue, and scantily clad in Ceremonial-*looking* tribal togs. Giving the impression of conjured apparitions, leading this congregation in transcendental prayer.

Behind that alter, that Deejay booth. Our would-be Priestess, Deejay *Yvel*, raised an arm to pump a fist, as if to manually crank-up the *Vibe*. Head and hunkered shoulder cupping a Baum® cordless headphone to one ear, her other hand dancing over a dazzling array of faders and dials.

In a flurry of movement, she dropped out the Bottom-end to accentuate an emerging Synth-line.

Then, catching that tail of the vocal hook, in a *Ping-Pong* delay. She panned it around the room, immersing the congregation in the phonemes of that Legend:

[Sing] *We could be Heroes...*
Heroes...Heroes...

The sampled proclamation of their patron, St. Bowie (of the

immaculate conception—and disposition), once again resonating with the times—these times. His words—his word, likened to that of the Johannine *Logos*; or a neurolinguistic suggestion, worming its way into the more malleable *Psyche* of this entranced Body.

Reintroducing the beat with a frequency sweep, our Deejay Yvel let the soundtrack build to the pay-off. And when that bassline licked, the clutch of *Souls* again went wild. Roaring with elation and greeting that warmth of Low-end frequency, with a renewed spurt of enthusiasm.

As if, they were clusters of electrons, excited by a radioactive wave; their energies, quantified in terms of a half-life of excitation.

Satisfied with the overall affect, our Deejay *Yvel* stood back then, to soak it up—the *vibe*. Stealing a few hasty glugs from a bottle of JustWater®.

Whilst behind her, a peer—dubbed BLK-*Koffee*—waiting patiently to begin his own set. Nodded quietly, his approval, in time to that Kik.

Mirroring the dance floor, in the lounge area all the way up to the bar, it was to be wall-to-wall Bod(ie)s.

That clamouring of voices, a din of unintelligible conversations, punctuated by howls of laughter, and fits of giggles; your Übs and Suits taking a much-needed break from that *Razzle dazzle*.

Moving in-amongst this Body, this throng, lithe cocktail waiters— camouflaged in Ash-BLK—hefted trays weighed down with beverages, tapas, and bar snacks.

For a mere basic—plus tips, they'd perform feats of memory, and dexterous acts of balance, to rival that of a troupe from your *Cirque du Soleil*®. The spectacle only causing a stir, when things went awry.

And naturally, it was to be Christmas everywhere, and all the time. Invisible, brilliant-bright snow being sprinkled liberally over-all, like Tinkerbell's *Fairy dust*.

Both your uninvited guest, and the *Life & Soul* of the party. It brought to the proceedings a certain *Edge*. A note of unpredictability, and a particular kind of lustre, that was both shiny and effervescent.

And oh, how those Chowderheads *loved-so* to sparkle. To *Twinkle-twinkle*, like *incy-wincy* stars, in that *itsy-bitsy* bottled universe of theirs.

This then, was your Scene, of an evening—of a night.

One gigantic Snowglobe, waiting upon your *god-of-always-listening*

THE SCENE

to come along and give it a good ol' shake. And maybe even marvel at that fallout.

Yeah, this was the Scene. And this was the place to be seen in, for now. The Scene being more akin to your Enlightened Despot: As fickle as public opinion; and as flighty as a traveling circus troupe.

For now, it was content(ed) to be slumming-it underground.

To be a dark room awash with glittering lights. Brothers and Sisters under a groove, hell bent upon dancing themselves [Sing] *out of their constriction*. The spectacle, likened to a Caravaggesque masterpiece. The drama emerging from a solid wall of Pitch.

An iconography for your iconoclast *then*. It was the same each and every night, with Lent scheduled to arrive around 0300hrs.

Lord of all he surveyed, Klunk was to be found in his usual pew. Sporting a bespoke *de*-constructed tuxedo, two *Beenies* tucked under each wing.

Those wannabe *Twins*, back for seconds. Suckling upon the *Man*'s barren, manly teats, like your fabled Romulus and Remus.

It'd be a manicured finger, stroking the side of his clean shaven boat-race. Luscious Blood-red lips, whispering *sweet-sweet* nothings in his ear; gassing that already inflated *Ego*, as if it were a Helium filled balloon.

A similarly manicured hand slotted between those muscly thighs of his, keeping his tackle company.

"*Oh-so* smooth, so soft," cooed Beenie #1. "Definitely the signs of a well kept *Man*. Oy *Sis*—Mouthing—cop the wrist."

"Oh. My. Days."

Starry-eyed, Beenie #2 leant in for a closer look-see, pressing her ample bosom against Klunk's brick wall of a chest. Her expression, one of gobsmacked awe.

The pair continued to *coo* and *paw* after the *Man*'s manly hand, measuring it against their own dainty Paws. Their eyes lingering on the *Bling*-accessories for today: A diamond encrusted Pinky-ring, pinching a frankfurter of a Pinky-finger; the *Time*-piece, a Jaeger® Biothermic platinum wristband—with inlayed miniaturised curved-display, hanging limp about the wrist.

The more forward of the pair, Beenie #1, then cupped that manly hand to her pert bosom.

"Look-see—just the right size," she said, *Winking* after her wannabe twin. The pair exchanging a bawdy giggle.

And of course, Klunk held it down—as you do.

Commandeering the hand to reach for his flute. Only to have it wing its merry way to him. Beenie #1 demonstrating, how she might anticipate his every need.

Not to be out done, Beenie #2 began then, to feed him curly French fries; from one of the platters of dainty treats that littered the table.

Klunk leaning forward to *Snap-snap* after her lissom fingers. The Firm looking-on: Brodie, Dim, Georgie Boy, Pinky and Spicer.

Five shiny bald-heads huddled around a roundtable, like those Knights of Arthurian Legend. Students one and all, of your Krays, your Adkins, your 'Mad Frankie' Frasers of this World.

They all looked like Mini-*Me* versions of Klunk, each with his own unique take on that dress-code. Accessorised with a squeeze—gendered according to sexual preference; nestled under an arm, or perched upon a knee, like a Ventriloquist's dummy. An *ever-so* manly hand parked on that *heinie*, working the gulliver.

The banter flowing freely, back and forth. Following Klunk's lead—obviously. Though not so loud, so as you could've followed it, over that din.

Still, it was loud enough to reel you in. That potent stench of testosterone, mixed with bittersweet cologne, and brawny posturing. Exuding a kind of raw, animal magnetism.

Imagine, the workers of an abattoir having a *Boyz Night-out*.

Exchanging grizzly anecdotes, and bawdy quips. Trading insider tips, on how best to slaughter a sheep, or gut a pig; Thin Lizzy's anthemic [Sing] *The boys are back in towwwn-towwwn*,[3A] chorusing over the venue's P.A.

Sniff

Occasionally, the banter would run dry. And whilst wetting his pallet, or refilling his flute. One of the Firm might glance casually into the throng, into that herd; his eyes, like those of a Hunter, tracking the movement of any Game that haplessly wandered by.

To those eyes, the Scene was more your Knackers yard—or Shambles. Each reveller, a piece of meat dangling upon a hook. And every *Man* shared this outlook, this vision of the World. Wore that glint—that Light,

THE SCENE

that certain spark that smacked of predatory cunning, hidden behind a mask of wily charm.

Suffice to say, the Firm didn't much care for dancing; them being too much at ease in their own skin. Too much at home in those swanky, plush surroundings. And that was to be a big part of it, *the Allure*.

For it was like, they owned the *phf'king* gaff.

Which they did, as it goes. Monk having delegated much of the role of 'Head of Security' to my-*Man*—as you do.

As one does. When one's in Love.

That being said. They could've taken possession of any Space on the Planet; could've commandeered Buckingham Palace *even*, or your Houses of Parliament, and made it their own.

For as your Teddy Bass says, in *Sexy Beast*.[3B] A firm favourite with the Firm's membership, it being a *Love* story and all: "Where there's a Will—and there is a *phf'king* Will. There's a way—and there is a *phf'king* way."

The banter flowing freely—as said, the Molls contented to play the role of eye-candy. It'd be your usual mix of *Shoptalk*, and *Man*-gossip; with a soupçon—a smattering—of gutter wisdom. Imparted by the Streetwise onto the Streetwise. Punctuated by bouts of pernicious *cussing*, that acted to affirm the pecking.

Operating in a sphere all their own, Klunk &*Co.* were constantly paying-it *Lip*-service to the Grift. To *Road*. To the Street, that was always watching. And was like, a Big brother to them all.

The Street. That could brook no tears and harbour no fears. The Street. That choked all flowers, its concrete paving stones nurturing all weeds. Its adopted daughters and sons, antagonists and protagonists both, in its circadian melodramas.

As much a situation as a place, but always a vocation. The Street had become synonymous with survival. Had plunged *Humanity* back into that frigid bosom of necessity. Had made prey of those *Sons-of-Man*, extinguishing that *Promethean* fire that'd once fuelled their empty bellies.

It was the Street that called forth the Pitch, the dark—the darkness. Then, striking a match. Pointed at the flame, and called it, *Illumination*.

Certainly, it knew but one inalienable truth: That *Life* was unfair. *Life* being likened to a female-dog, with a predilection toward matricide.

Indeed, it was the Street that spoke vehemently—tragically, to that inherent inequity, of the 'Human' condition.

That such inequality be essential to surmounting said condition.

"'And you know this—two-*twos*,'" Klunk opined, "'cos you've seen it. And felt it—like me. That said, we differ in this one respect—'"

He paused for effect, drawing his audience in.

"'I-don't-really-give-a-*phf'k*.'"

It seemed all one word.

"'Whereas. *You*. Most definitely *doobie-dooby dooby-doo*.'"

He accentuated the statement, pointing the finger toward an imaginary protagonist, hidden in-and-amongst that herd of revellers.

And listening intently, the Firm skiggled on cue, like a pack of hyenas haggling over a fresh kill. All having identified with the sentiment.

"'Obviously, I'm hip to your *plight*'—Klunk did the inverted commas with both hands—'because, like the Street, I too am always watching. So, I know money's tight right-now. You having different Babymothers, and four sprogs—what-is-it, four or five?"

He was to pause to look for the answer in the pert bosom of Beenie #1. Then, looking into its eyes, flutter his eyelashes, causing it to *Crack-up*.

"But—so it go," he said, still eyeballing it. "'It is what it is. The facts of *Life*.'"

The facts of Life, the Firm nodded in unison. As if it were a heartfelt preces, and response to an oft-times repeated liturgy.

Klunk then turned his attention to Beenie #2, who was standing-by to feed him yet another French fry; a Cheeseburger-grin hiding those especially pronounced incisors of his.

"Put some mayonnaise on it will you—*Babs*," he said, throwing-in a cocksure *Wink*.

"So, what did my-*Man* say to that?" a member of the Firm chipped-in.

Klunk devoured the French fry, his teeth again *Snap-snap-snapping* playfully after those fingers that'd fed him.

And undaunted, Beenie #2 then proceeded to pet his bald-head.

"What could my-*Man* say?" Klunk said, chewing—as if needing to keep this fare well oxygenated.

"It's all academic really. If you owe me, then, I own you."

He swallowed.

THE SCENE

If you owe me, then, I own you.

The axiom was eagerly absorbed by those members of the Firm.

"It follows, my actions towards you become that of my manifest Will—in this, here, material World."

The facts of Life, the Firm affirmed. Again, nodding approvingly.

Now putting his arm about Beenie #1, Klunk pulled her close to anoint her cheek with his kiss.

"Ain't that right—Babs?"

Even though the wannabe *Twins* were virtually identical, he made an exhibition of playing favourites.

"Oy—what's that tune I like again? The one by my-Grrrl—*Blondie*?"

He tossed the question out to his flock.

"What? Rapture?"

"Nahh—not Blondie *Blondie*."

The *Man* was to look after *my-Man*, perplexed.

Sniff

"Material-*Grrrl*?"

Slapping the table, Klunk SNAP'd his fingers and pointed.

"Yeah. Material-*Grrrl*."

And turning to face Beenie #1, he was to kiss her again. Full on the mouth.

"That could be you, you play your cards right," he added then. Tossing a Wink to the Firm; a little cheeky aside for those in the know. Beenie #1 now *Purrring*—like some pampered Peterbald, with the overt show of affection.

No doubt feeling left out. Beenie #2, nonetheless, continued to wait patiently to feed the *Man*, yet another French fry. This time dipped liberally in *mayo*.

And looking-on, the Firm were to chuckle amongst themselves.

"But *Check-it Check-it*. Then, I said, 'that being said. What do I say to the next *Mug* who owes me and can't pay? And the next One, and the next One after that? Or what do I say to *my-Man* here, who blatantly won't pay cos—two-*twos*—he knows I ain't gon do shit?"

Klunk again paused for effect.

"Well?"

Sipping sparingly from his flute, he *Blink-blinked* at Beenie #1, and smiled. His smile now punctuated by those enlarged eyeteeth of his.

"I swear—I should-*a* taken a *pic* and posted-it up."

Klunk chuckled then. The image apparently, still top of mind.

"Bamboozled. My-Man was mouth-open—Acting it out—Gulp-gulp-gulping. Like-*a phf'king* fish out of water, suffocating on fresh air. The facts of Life."

The facts of Life.

He chirps'd his teeth.

"'Exactly,' I said, and smacked him one. 'Now shut the *phf'k* up and pay me. *Cunt*.'"

Recognising this to be that long awaited punchline. The Firm now bent over in side-splitting, table-slapping mirth.

"So what—did *my-Man* cough-up?"

The question was to mark a kind of epilogue, the laughter having given way to boyish skiggling.

"*Phf'king-a* he did."

"*Phf'king-a*—gwon."

The laughter erupted again.

Yeah, it was to be your usual drivel that dribbled from pliant lips; in betwixt casual sips of Pink shampoo, and the occasional *Sniff* of *Fairy dust*—snuffed from the cleft between thumb and pointy-finger. You know, all very discreet and *Shhh*… [Whisper] *Hush-Hush*.

You see, beyond the confines of that Sphere. Every *Man*, Woman and Child remained a *John*, and fair game. And the Übs, and the Suits, they felt the same. You see, the Übs, and the Suits, and those members of Klunk &*Co*.—the Firm. They all had it sussed.

Of course, bloody Darwin was *phf'kin'* right.

It was *Them*, or us.

Survival of the fittest—the facts of *Life*.

[Chorus] *The facts of Life.*

Yet, there remained an unbridgeable gulf between them i.e., that blue Blood coursing through the small cutaneous veins of the former.

Yeah, they might brush shoulders here and there, on the Scene and elsewhere. But, each was mindful to pay the other no mind.

Sporting a dapper cangiante, single-breast Birdman suit, Crimson-red or Aubergine-purple dependent upon that angle of the light; Absolute-BLK cashmere knit pencil-tie, and matching silk-shirt. Monk had more

THE SCENE

your model-*Look* about him.

What with his slender, muscly boyish frame, chiselled boatrace, early-80s Annie Lennox *ghinger* crewcut, and winning smile. That fell just shy of gloating.

And being Übs, through and through. That is, born and bred unto it. He could do and be anything he pleased — pretty much.

And he wore it well, that *Limelight*. Managing to pull-off an almost debonair sophistication, that seemed the antithesis of that burly, muscle bound — *Masters of the Universe*™ — vibe, that characterised Klunk & Co.

So obviously the brains of this outfit, Monk was to be found holding Court at that far end of the bar. Just shy the service door that led out-back to the office; passed the kitchen, and the stores, and that engine room. A member of Security usually shadowing him, one of Klunk's Gorillas. On the payroll, but not strictly *Firm*. Its principal role being, to police access to this door, and that of the Communal restroom facing-it.

Built like a brick *Shit*-house. It'd be your standard *Muscle-on-the-door* archetype. Camouflaged in Ash-BLK, like the rest of your Staff-*staff*; two-piece Birdman suit, *StayPress*™ shirt and knit pencil-tie.

Swipe-card, replete with photo-ID, hung about its tree trunk of a neck, like a plaque. So as, you knew it was all official-*like*.

And naturally, Monk's court was to consist of an entourage of wafer-thin, Aryan-*looking* Catwalk Model-types. Boyz that looked like *Grrrls*. *Grrrls* that looked like Boyz. And *Androgs* that looked like neither. Or both.

As a rule, they never paid for shite. Indeed, being on the books somewhere, they were usually skint. Their Handlers being predisposed to keeping 'em lean, and mean-*looking*.

It goes without saying, the Bar staff — all handpicked seasoned *Mixologists*, would be for keeping this stable well-watered. On the off chance, one of the prized *Fillies* might forget themselves, and spread those long shapely legs — for the cause.

Every now and then, duty would call. Monk getting the nod from some Bod — your *Bob Regular*. And dropping everything, he'd follow it into the restroom, for a sit-down.

Though, him being as promiscuous as SARs, these impromptu parleys would usually morph into a *Sniff*-N-Tickle; him emerging sometime later, sporting your *ReadyBrek*™ glow. Dabbing at his brow with a hand towel, and nursing a runny nose.

That being said. With the night now in full swing, there wasn't really much doing. What with the kitchen being closed.

Having left the gamely *Twins* to chaperon Klunk. Monk would look over occasionally, harbouring inside a kind of inane fatherly pride; at how well things had turned-out.

Yeah, from the looks of it. They all appeared to be getting along swimmingly. Leaving *my-Man* free to *Ching-ching* glassware with a party of mädchen, who'd just-now flown-in from the prestigious Berliner *Modewoche* — especially. It being London Fashion Week, Monday pending.

Lifting a learnid finger, to point-up at the Heavens. That Pollux Star of the constellation Gemini, mapped directly above his head. Klunk paused, mid-pearl (—of wisdom) to polish-off his flute. Leaving everyone in his pew dangling upon a comma.

Without need of a prompt, Beenie #1 was to refill his glass, draining the sweaty bottle of Pink shampoo to the suds. A quick study, she then held it aloft. Waving, in the general direction of Monk, whilst Klunk picked-up his comma to run with it.

Coppin' this, Monk *Snap-snapped* his fingers and immediately drew the attention of the Bar Manager. Who in-turn, *Snap-snapped* his fingers to draw the attention of the nearest waiter.

And momentarily, another sweating bottle of bubbly was winging its merry little way over to the table. Tucked snugly in a bed of crushed-ice, a crisp brilliant-bright serviette-liteau wrapped about its slender neck, like a scarf.

Sash was seen to appear with it. The waiter withdrew, and there she was. Still sporting her bubblewrap jacket, which she'd point-blank refused to hand over to that Bod in the cloakroom; her FENDINI® handbag slung over a shoulder, her moody boatrace set against that maddened crowd.

Her looking decidedly out of sorts. Like a Working-*Grrrl*, working her first beat; about ready to splurt, her hymen intact. That assault of glamour and glitz, having proven too cagey a proposition.

Yeah, she'd come straight from A&E. And still wore that *Pfeiffer*®

THE SCENE

*invis-a-*Splint™ taped across the bridge of her nose.

And this invisibility, it'd apparently lent to the rest of her.

Stood there—stupefied, her straighten hair snapping back to the kink at the roots. Sash stared machetes for a-bit; through the throng of emaciated, immaculately dressed revellers. At that pair of *Perfect 10*s, presently cosying-up to her would-be Lord and saviour.

Cocktail waiters scurrying around and about her, like cuttlefish. The din of her surroundings dissolving into a slipstream of blurred motion, and color. As if it were a *Time*-lapse sequence.

That lone cry of dissent, in this apparent democracy of plenty, bordering upon excess. Sash was indeed thankful for that *Cloak of Anonymity*. It seeming entirely appropriate, that all should be oblivious to her existence. All save Monk, that is. And that gaggle of mädchen huddled around him.

From their vantage over by the bar, they were to play *les Voyeur*. Pointing their pointy-fingers, and skinning their razor-sharp teeth; their sparkly bright-eyes enthralled, by that prospect of a spectacle.

The *Car-crash* Monk had set in motion for their [Sing] *en-ter-tain-ment*, inspired by Sash's earlier phone call; him just happening to be within earshot.

Yeah, they'd clock'd it, stealing its entrance.

And tracked it, as it elbowed its way through the throng. Monk furnishing an impromptu running commentary.

"Warte darauf. Beobachten sie, das bootsrennen."

Anticipating that moment when Sash clapped eyes on Klunk, buried up to his waxed armpits in *Twins*. Both of 'em *Buzzing*, on the fumes from his manly cologne.

"Unbezahlbar."

But then, Sash refused to bite.

Instead, scurrying passed Monk, she headed toward that Service door, without even so much as a glance sideways.

To have Security bar her egress; its burly arm, like a Police cordon restricting her from leaving this apparent Crime scene.

Seeing the pair squaring-off. Monk, ever your [Sing] *karma chameleon*[3C], then assumed the role of gallant Knight, charging to the rescue of this damsel-in-distress.

Like, yeah—right.

Excusing himself from the huddle, to put the mussel back on Security; his hand lingering on *my-Man*'s bulging gun.

"I'll take it from here—Dude," he said, by way of introductions.

And still, Sash was to take no notice of it.

Punching-in the Entry-code—memorised from watching Klunk the one time, she was through that Service door. Leaving Monk and Security shaking their heads.

Exchanging despondent looks, as if to say, *Kids nowadays*.

"Oy—Sasha. *Wait.*"

Then, it was to be Monk's understated baritone, chasing *my-Grrrl* down the hallway.

"The Office door. It's locked."

Forphf'ksake—Tut.

Following hot on its heels, or more the balls of its feet—Sash having deactivated those *Air*-fields of her *Cynderellas*™. Monk left the Service door to close itself. The din of the Scene becoming muffled. That TUMP of the *Kik* and driving bassline, now reminiscent of sounds first heard in the womb.

Ketching-up to *my-Grrrl*, he went to put a hand on her—to turn her about.

"Wait Sasha. We need to talk—"

But Sash was to whip that arm away.

"Don't-*phf'king*-put-your-hands-on-me. You—"

Yeah, stood facing that Office door, she was to leer after it—sideways. Obviously blaming it for everything, even the fact of it being there.

His advance thus shunned; Monk couldn't help but feel put upon. It seeming ironic to him, after all he'd s'posedly done for it.

Sniff

Though, he was to persevere—regardless.

"Put the claws away *Kitty-Kat*," he said, hamming it up—*just a-little*. Assuming the act would make him appear less of a threat.

But Sash wasn't in the mood to play the fool for it. Adjusting the strap of her handbag, to sit that little bit higher upon her shoulder. She sighed. And cut her eye upon the ceiling.

Which incidentally, was when Monk saw the light catch on that

THE SCENE

invis-a-Splint™ taped across the bridge of its nose, and had his epiphany.

"I'm a Bastard. I know...*I know*," he was to confess. "But—believe it or not, my Heart's in the right place."

Bowing his head, he looked for its eyes. While placing a hand to his chest, as if meaning to swear an oath.

It taking every ounce of effort to stymie that smile, that now sort to take hold of his gulliver.

Cunt more like, Sash thought—*Sniff.*

Knowing better than to meet it halfway on anything, she'd found a neutral spot to park her eyes. And was presently about running her tongue against the outside wall of her teeth, to convey her own disdain for it.

Like—what was this s'posed to be? Them having a moment?

"You can wait in the office. That is, if you don't mind—waiting," Monk volunteered then; dangling the suggestion, like a carrot on the end of a stick. The office door being right there in front of them.

"I'll go tell *his Nibs* you're here," he added, craning his neck to lower his head a-little more.

Blink-Blink

Still avoiding its eyes, Sash let out an exaggerated sigh, and looked to that Office door. And folding her arms across her chest, sluggishly stepped aside.

As if to say, *if you must.*

Monk finally allowed himself the hint of a smile. Only to have it fall from his boatrace the second he cop'd Pris.

He'd flung it open—the door. Turning-on the light to reveal it, apparently doing *a*-turn as your Bond Archvillain. Sat behind a stately looking teak desk, dressed in a blazer of Peacock feathers. Its hair straightened and combed-up in a Teddy-boy quiff. Its elfin frame dwarfed by that high-back of a Søren® *Sejr* Executive hoverchair—that looked more like a throne.

Indeed, the only thing missing from this picture, was *my-Man* Blofeld's blue-eyed Persian familiar.

The Synthetic's Husk_eyes were open. Its Husk_pupils rolled-up into its Husk_skull. It seeming as if, its eyeballs had been replaced with two polished Brilliant-bright Billiard balls.

Added to this, it neither moved, nor flinched, nor reacted in any way to the intrusion. But just sat there, as if comatose.

His boatrace suddenly drained of Blood. Monk looked like he'd seen some grizzly apparition, as he lurched for that door handle.

Uhm—

"On second thoughts," he said, pulling the door to close it.

"Let's get you cleaned-up."

He then grabbed a-hold of Sash's arm, to lead her back the way they'd come; Sash acquiescing to its manhandling of her. It being worth it, just to see it with its feathers ruffled.

Her taking the time to saviour the moment. That split-second, before Monk had closed the door.

She'd looked at it, then passed it. Catching a glimpse of *what's her boatrace—Pris?* But only now did it dawn on her, *wait—*

What was my-Grrrl doing?

Sat there in the dark, on her tod.

The heat and the noise that greeted them in transit—from one door to the other—was striking.

Like stepping onto the runway of some tropical clime, after hours spent cooped-up inside a refrigerated and pressurised cabin. And as such, Sash was relieved to enter the Communal restroom; that din of the Scene becoming muffled once again, as *Security*-Dude closed the door on them.

But what was to greet her inside, would be more of the same.

You'd your *likely*-Lads, and your Lassies, and your *Androgs*—of course. Clustered in gaggles of twos and threes.

Ogling their reflections intermittently, in that mirror-wall that fronted onto the stalls. Under the glare of those spotlights inlayed in the ceiling.

Turning this way and that, so as to get the full picture. Their clammy, flawless Body's smoking in that seemingly refrigerated environ.

There'd be pockets of banter sprinkled liberally. That air of deference, cast by the din of hushed voices, occasionally interrupted by stifled moronic skiggling; and plumes of pungent smoke, wafting from those gaps above and below those closed stall doors.

There being eight such boxy enclosures, marching the length of this Space; designed along the lines of miniaturised *en suites*.

THE SCENE

A mirror-wall facing a stunted door of dark polished hardwood; a toilet bowl and freestanding wash-hand basin of clinical stainless steel, placed at opposite ends; a clear glass shelf measuring its width.

That coarse granite mosaic tiling-effect of the walls, starkly contrasting that Blood-red industrial strength epoxy resin floor. Seen here buffed to an obscenely high shine.

And naturally, there'd be a restroom attendant in attendance, just by that exit-*come*-entrance. A balding, squat, pot-bellied Dude, with an instantly forgettable boatrace. Cordially referred to as PORCO, the *Gent*.

An enterprising *Sort*, our Porco would layout his wares — night after night, on a shelf next to his stool. Colognes and perfumes, Bodysprays and moisturising creams — all name brand premium fare; shrink-wrapped hand towels woven from 100% Egyptian cotton, stacked neatly next to a Murphy's® *Portable*-microwave; a wooden-bowl brimming with branded 86ers™ matchboxes, that he touted as souvenirs; and a more modest-sized bowl for tips, a polished milkstone acting as a paperweight.

The front-of-shop he called it. Because that was what it was. A front for the *under-the-counter* merchandise, he kept stashed out-of-sight in a large cupboard under that shelf.

He'd even had a laminated menu made-up — smart gold type on Ultra-BLK card, which he reserved strictly for your *Bob Regulars*.

It boasting an impressive selection of premium items: Imported cigarettes — Newports® Filtered and Unfiltered, Sobranie® Gold, Silver and Bronze, Gauloises® *Deluxe* Slim-Ultra dark tobacco; and Nippon® Petrol-lighters; and Ripley's® *Fresh* re-chewable gum — Minty-strawberry and Orangey-liquorice; and *Kinder*® Chomp-A™ Lollipops with the soft-centre, in-*like*, a-zillion different flavours; and Heroes® Condoms; and *Olbas*® Tiger's Balm.

Each item, extortionately priced. The recommended retail value, quadrupled and rounded-up to the nearest whole number, ending in either a naught, or a five.

"You not only pay for quality. You pay for convenience," our Porco would admit, by way of rebuke. If a punter thought to raise issue. Whilst, symbolically cleansing his hands with an Aloe Vera handy-wipe.

Yeah, our Porco could be cute like that. But he never, ever forgot that he was Staff-*staff*.

THAT PERFECT WORLD

He'd blend-in with the swanky décor, and furnishings, and play his part; never straying from his post, not even to take a *whizz*.

And he'd come fully loaded, with a host of catchy and insightful oneliners—*for the Kids*.

"If Porco don't have it, you don't need it," he'd say. Whipping-out a PDQ, so as your *Bob Regular* might pay with *virtua*-Plastic.

The things he'd witnessed, night after night stationed at his post, camouflaged as he was, in Ash-BLK; his uniform immaculate. Farah's® slacks, Pink® *StayPress*™ shirt, knit pencil-tie fastened with an 18-carat gold tie-clasp.

And yet, he never spoke of it. Our Porco being ol' *Skool*, and the epitome of your Wise monkey.

"Oy Porco—give us a couple of hand towels will-*ya* Mate," Monk said, scanning that row of stalls.

"Anything you say, *Bawse*."

Porco picked-out two shrink-wrapped hand towels. But neglected to break the seals. And placing them to one side, returned to rearranging his wares for the umpteenth time.

And then, as luck would have it, a stall door opened at the far end of the Space. A couple of spirited *Fillies* cantering-out.

Approaching that mirror-wall, they commenced preening themselves, in-spite of it. Nudging each other, and skiggling; like a pair of naughty school-*Grrrls*, playing truant from St. Trinians—*say*.

Kilts hefted-up about their thighs, *Pop!* socks folded-down about their ankles. And in-between. Naked, shapely legs that were seen to go on for dreamy miles.

A *gheezah* soon followed—one of your *likely*-Lads, propping itself up against that stall door to wait on this pair of unlikely-*Lassies*. A world of smug plastered upon its gulliver.

And now, goose-stepping up to it. Monk casually placed a hand upon its shoulder to whisper in its ear. And just like that, and without even making eye contact. *My-Man* was made to disappear.

Having cop'd this exchange in the mirror, the *Fillies* were then about giving-it the Evil-eye. That is, looking *my-Grrrl* up-and-down, while Monk checked-out that vacant stall. Leaning-in to retrieve those two designer *Clutches* parked in the sink.

THE SCENE

He then approached these two *Wannabes*. Indiscriminately, pressing the *Clutches* into the stomach of one. And slapping the other hard on the rump—so as all heard it.

It uttering the usual refrain, "*Owwch—forphf'ksake*. Monk!"

And now, cantering-up to Sash. This pair were to look, One to the Other; making a show of laughing after it, as they followed their escort out.

"You can wait in here," Monk suggested, holding open that stall door; his demeanour, casual-as-you-like.

As if, it were just the two of 'em. Everyone else being indistinguishable from that décor.

Though, Sash wasn't to budge—*Sniff*

Instead, she narrowed her eyes, to better squint after it; her having regard for those punters genuinely waiting to use the communals. And the fact that none had dared confront *my-Man*, for blatantly jumping the queue. Everyone being—*seemingly*—oblivious to them. Or about making a concerted effort to appear as much.

"You want me to go fetch him or not?"

Snapping too, at that insistence in its voice. She was to mosey over, her pace the measure of her reluctance; Monk ushering her into that vacant stall with a flat-hand, placed expertly at the small of her back.

But even sequestered inside, Sash remained sceptical.

Giving-it—the stall, the once over. As if charged with conducting a *Spot check*. Before plonking her handbag down in the sink, to run a finger across that glass shelf.

"Don't be long—yeah," she was to admonish, rubbing the tips of her fingers together. She then smelt them, warily.

As if *Fairy dust* might have an actual smell.

Leaving the stall door ajar, Monk was to leave her to it. The sound of his stilettos, resounding upon that obscenely shiny and hard floor, following him all the way out. The rhythm, reminiscent of your soft brush-step in a *Tap* routine.

Man was given an eye for an ear.

Marshall Mcluhan, *The Medium is the Message* (1967)

```
4D 61 6E 20 77 61 73 20
67 69 76 65 6E 20 61 6E
20 65 79 65 20 66 6F 72
20 61 6E 20 65 61 72 2E
```

.

I, SECURITAS

Pris could hear them—its babysitters, over by that kitchen counter. Though it didn't feel compelled to look.

Yeah, it could hear them. Their strenuous denials of one another, whispered under their breaths. In-between bouts of feverish snogging.

And that scratching, of their lust's jailer. Those starched, Brilliant-bright Lab-coats that they wore; with the GenesisTrust® solid gold pin—an hexagonal capital letter 'G', pinned to the mandarin collar.

The Synthetic heard it all. The ruffling of fabric, the ripping of a zipper, the stretching of knicker elastic. The clattering of a popped button, on that vinyl flooring, followed by an *Oops*. And a bout of muffled giggles, and creaking of aged joints.

And finally, a sharp intake of breath…and exhale—*yess*…

Yeah, it was privy to every minute detail. As if, it were stood over this inebriated pair; an unsuspecting arbiter of what'd previously been a fettered and checked desire. It being strictly verboten, such dalliances. According to HR Rules & *Regs*.

It could smell them, their brackish sweat. The commingling of their respective scents, presenting as a heady odorant. That was both foreign and familiar to the Synthetic's nubile, and as yet, unbroken Husk.

That being said. The Lover's musk remained utterly alien to it.

Yess…that's it…

Eventually, a silhouetted figure mounted that kitchen counter. The *Iki* inspired HŌMU® kitchen providing an unlikely setting. Those photosensitive edges of its Miegakure mobile units, creating a wireframe backdrop; the Space being backlit by the monitors of a CohenKuhl® *Port-a*-terminal. The pair having stumbled upon one, of maybe two 'Dead Zones' in the entire Lab complex.

Bathed in an indecorous dark, the lounge area was dominated by that LNG® *Dopijuui* 120″ U-HDX curved-screen, mounted upon the wall. And below it, the clean modern lines of an Art deco-styled *Manhattan* fireplace, framing a Valhöll® KOTI log-burning stove. Its gaseous bluish flame, having long since given way to that more inviting orangey glow of smouldering embers.

Upon the screen, Ridley Scott's *Blade Runner*[3D] played, for the umpteenth time. Bathing Pris in its lavish visual spectacle.

So as, reflected in those crystalline Bionic Husk_eyes. A Future and a present were to be seen running side-by-side, like parallel lines.

Never once touching.

Following upload into the Husk_Unit, the Synthetic had parked the thing for an entire year.

Time being counted in intervals of pico-*seconds*, its relative Chip-speed. It was the equivalent of—*say*, watching in *fah* real-*Time* the interminable migration of glaciers backwards, across the furrowed surface of a prehistoric Earth. The Pleistocene epoch making way for the Holocene epoch.

Breaching the Husk_Unit's Brain-Blood barrier, the Synthetic underwent a fantastic voyage during this period. Methodically mapping the anatomy of its host, whilst systematically seeking-out its 'Ghost'—the seat of its *Soul*.

Navigating the Husk's central nervous system, it become acquainted with its silica-carbide based musculoskeletal frame. Pushing outward, into its peripheral nervous systems, along each nerve to its end. It came to know the fleshy boundaries of the Husk's permeable wall of Synthesised-skin.

Looking inward, it followed the autonomic nervous system to every organ, before crossing-over into the enteric nervous system, to evaluate how this biomechanical marvel might be sustained.

It delved then, into each separate organ in turn. Then into the tissue of each organ. Then the cells of the tissue. Breaking-down the components of each species of cell; and baptising itself, in those fertile

I, S≡CURITΛS

nucleic acid waters of *Life*—itself.

Therein, observing the handiwork of those BioMECH(anic)s of the GenesisTrust®. How they'd sort to improve upon that evolutionary blueprint, handed down by your *god-of-always-listening*.

As if, it were an unfinished symphony. Beethoven or Mahler's Tenth, or Elgar's Third. And all it needed was a rousing ending, to draw contrast with that silence.

It then set about the task of learning to drive its host—its *vessel*. Becoming fluent in that autochthonous language of the endocrine organs, and exocrine glands.

Each phoneme being keyed to the exigencies of a prehistoric metre. The melody imbibed in a fluid and evolving unconscious, walled-off from an intelligence that was to be its exegesis.

Assuming the role of that absentee *Soul*. The Algorithm learnt what it was to live in anticipation of the event of each unique Heartbeat; what was the relative measure of a century. Each centenary being proclaimed by a septet of pulses, marking the Husk_Unit's extremities.

A year later to the day, it awoke. As if, it were a Sleeper of Ephesus— *say*. Or wily Rip van Winkle, emerging from a cave wherein *Time* stood still. And lifting those lids of its Husk_eyes. It let the light—of both visible and invisible spectrum, fall upon its Husk_retina, for the first time. And...

Blink...Blink.

It found itself, that is, its vessel submerged in cloudy lukewarm water. And peering through the transparent *Perspex*™ of that Obumanu® Stasis-tank, it was to detect movement.

The pixels of, as yet, undesignated Subject-Objects. The members of its BioMECH team, now barely a skeleton crew.

Nearby, a CohenKuhl® Diagnostic-engine responded to the Husk_Unit's elevated Heart rate, chiming a warning.

ALERT! THRESHOLD BREACH. ALERT!
ALERT! THRESHOLD BREACH. ALERT!

All those working in the Lab, then began crowding around the tank. Their Brilliant-bright Lab-coats bleeding into the sterile Brilliant-bright walls of the environ; that'd previously served as a surrogate womb for the empty Husk_Unit.

Sealed inside that tank, the Synthetic became aware of objects impeding the Husk_Unit's movement. A breathing-mask attached to its Husk_face, a proboscis-*like* tube snaking down its Husk_throat; the pinch of a nose-clamp, the suction of probes strategically dispersed around the vessel. Your standard 12-lead config., relaying vitals back to that Diagnostic-engine.

Despite these impediments, the Synthetic managed to raise its Husk_hand to its Husk_face. And was seen to stare at it for some time, before wiggling those Husk_fingers.

Blink. Blink.

It then felt for that thick mane of Husk_hair, that was like algae swimming in the amniotic fluid of the tank. Pulling at clumps at first, but quickly learning to twirl it, like cotton candy between its Husk_fingers. Drawing it to its full-length to better discern its coloration. That of, freshly fallen snow.

Blink. Blink.

Finally, it looked down at that open circuit of its Husk_body. Naked, and glabrous—as a fledgling cherub; and bleached from its extended gestation. And which, up until this moment, it'd only known from the inside-out.

The Synthetic watching intently, its Husk_belly extend as it engaged those muscles of its diaphragm to draw a deep breath. It then removed that appendage from its Husk_mouth.

And just-now, outside the BioMECHs were about losing their minds.

Two immediately jumping onto a terminal, to expedite the multi-step *proc* for draining and opening the Stasis-tank. Others pounding on the thick *Perspex*™, desperate to convey the need for it to keep the breathing-mask on.

"KEEP. THE. BREATH-ING. MASK. THE BREATH-ING-MASK. KEEP. IT. ON," they chorused, their mouths mouthing each exaggerated syllable.

This simple instruction was to be further conveyed, by the repeated gesture of placing a cupped-hand over mouth, and nose.

"Can she even hear us through the glass?" one of them said, rapping a knuckle on that thick *Perspex*™.

"Hind—flip the relay switch for me," said another.

"I can't, whilst opening the tank," came Hinds terse response.

Converging again around that Stasis-tank, having by now resigned themselves to the inevitable. The BioMECHs were seen to pray in unison.

Oh god, save us...

Shielded from the commotion outside, Out-*there*—beyond that wall of *Perspex*™. The Synthetic left the breathing-mask to sink to the floor of the Stasis-tank.

Removing the nose-clamp, it continued to hold its breath, whilst focusing on slowing its Heart and respiratory rate to a crawl. Eventually closing its Husk_eyes, to conclude this initial test-drive. Letting the Husk_Unit revert back to its 'Default' state, one of suspended animation. The CohenKuhl's renewed warning, like a warped lullaby playing in the background.

ALERT! THRESHOLD BREACH. ALERT!

The Synthetic was to resurrect the Husk_Unit a month later. And was again greeted by essentially the same skeleton BioMECH Crew.

They'd been pawing over it the whole time, scratching their heads. The CohenKuhl® Diagnostic-engine, spouting endless reams of meaningful data. The blue transmission light of its stick-on probes—a 5-lead wireless config.—*Blinking* away intermittently.

Now free of the Stasis-tank, the Synthetic opened its Husk_mouth, and tasted that recycled air; and inhaled through its Husk_nose that all-pervasive stink of mammals cooped-up in an enclosure. These garbled first impressions, being indistinguishable from that singularity of noise that was to be its unique perspective.

Having no means of prioritising the cacophony of sensory data, that seeped through every pore of its Husk_skin. The Universe was to the Synthetic, like Damien Hirst's *Tetrahydrocannabinol*.

A Brilliant-bright backdrop, populated by uniformly arranged multi-coloured spots. Whose coloration appeared to be devoid of any discernible pattern, or meaning *even*.

Within hours, it'd learned to sit upright, like a toddler. Its back straight and true, its shoulder's squared.

It then learnt to stand, and then to walk, coaxed-on by its surrogate parents. Those BioMECHs of the GenesisTrust®.

All of it, a prelude to the main event. The grand unveiling of the combined Synthetic_Unity. The BioMECHs being eager to observe the Algorithm's response to seeing 'itself' merged with the Husk.

Alive, and in the flesh—as it were.

In due course, they wheeled in a full-length mirror, and asked the Synthetic to gaze upon itself—its vessel. And it obeyed. It stood before this *Looking-glass*, its Husk_eyes suddenly invested with *Self*-interest.

In that brief interval of *Time*. The equivalent of—*say*, a millennium spent gawping at its 'reflection'. It came to objectify that suit of Synthesised-skin; its initial positing of a physical barrier between it and the Universe, becoming universally true.

That is, assuming apodictic truth.

And of course, the BioMECHs were to observe all this from a respectful distance, their breaths abated.

"Wait...it's trying to say something," one of them said, noticing the Husk_Unit labouring with its virginal vocal cords.

In unison, they lent-in, as if to offer it incentive. Like a gaggle of proud parents, anxious to hear their Baby gurgle its first words.

"Pri-sss," the Synthetic whispered, exaggerating the sibilance on the *Ess*. Its voice choked by a horsed throat; none of those present, having had the wherewithal to offer the thing—*the Creature*, a glass of water.

"*Pris*? Pris? What's a Pris?"

The baffled BioMECHs looked to each other for the answer.

"It's from a film—a book actually," one of them then volunteered, as if fessing-up to something. "Pris is the consort of Roy Batty, in—"

"*Blade Runner*—yes," the BioMECHs were to chorus, clearly enthused by this development.

"No-eh—Shaking her head—do android's dream of electric sheep?"

"Do android's dream? Bloody hell, Hind!" barked a lone voice.

Probably that of the Leader.

"How was I s'posed to know it'd identify with it?" Hind snapped back. "It's a *phf'king* algorithm."

A silence ensued. Or more your pregnant pause.

"Someone get rid of this," the Leader said then, taking charge.

The mirror was wheeled away, and the Synthetic left standing there. Draped in a sky-blue disposable hospital gown, made of crêpe paper.

After a while, the relative measure of an aeon—*say*, a mass of pixels came and stood over it. The Synthetic tracking its approach, like that imperceptibly slow encroach of dark across the surface of the moon, during a Lunar eclipse.

Having already been subjected to the full lexicon of clinical examinations, it assigned a high probability to the likelihood of a continuation of this trend—above 67.677%.

All the while, continuing to focus upon that mass of pixels, as it morphed into a relatively smaller mass. Intent now on interacting with its Husk_face.

Anticipating that moment of contact, the knot of nerves under its Husk_skin stretched out.

"*Owch phf'k!* It zapped me."

The mass of pixel's flinched and withdrew.

"*Oh wow*—that's new."

"I think...it was involuntary."

Recovering from the electrostatic shock, the mass of pixels approached once more. A veil of hush descending upon the Lab, the BioMECHs being riveted anew by this development.

Tracking the trajectory of that moving mass, toward its unflinching Husk_eye. The Synthetic, again, anticipated that moment of contact.

But it couldn't have divined the conscientiousness inherent in that touch—*in touching*, conveyed by those frigid fingers. Sheathed as they were, in an *Eco*-DEX™ nitrile glove.

It was to be a casual gesture. Two fingers placed *ever-so* gently below the Husk's left-eye.

But suddenly, that universal-Pris, that'd become a universe of One extending in all directions, from the boundary of its Synthesised-skin. Now encountered that universal-*Other*, that necessarily enveloped it.

And then, came that Brilliant-bright light.

The beam from a Penlight swept across its Husk_eye, whiting-out its über sensitive, and as yet uncalibrated Husk_retina.

Having not learnt to flinch, the Synthetic simply shut down its ocular sensors, to prevent further damage. Shifting its *Homeostasis* state to ALERT!

The threat of eminent physical harm to the Husk_Unit, to itself— to the extent of its R(E)BRTH_STRNG now invested in this vessel. Emerging clear and distinct from that heterogeneous soup of *Durée*. That'd *a priori* been its default perspective.

It was Hegel that said, in allowing Adam to name his Creations, God had placed him in dominion over all things. Here then was Adam, now Pris. The trace of Man's perfect image—before his fall. Reimagined, and immaculately conceived as Woman-*Grrrl*. And yet, utterly divorced from any conception of that *Sacred feminine*. That is, God's abiding grace.

And so it was, that the Synthetic came to give this alien presence— its present threat, a designation. Defining it as a totality, relative to that Unity. The universal-Pris.

"Pupils appear unresponsive," Designate_Obj_Threat said, sweeping the beam of light across the Husk's other eye. "I only hope for your sake—Hind," it continued, "we can salvage something of the subject's rebirth string."

"Don't you think subject sounds a-bit sterile, Patrice? It's obviously chosen a name for itself, maybe we should use it?"

Another sound source emerged, clear and distinct from that clamouring of sensory datum. Pris now prioritising its Husk_ears over its other sensors.

Indeed, able to peer around corners, and through walls. Its Husk_ears were to become an all-seeing eye, enabling it to instantly map every sound source in that Lab. A universe of waveforms, suddenly emerging from a wall of noise, from the dark, like Stars in a night sky. Each discrete episode of sound, a muddle of frequencies radiating outwards. Whilst simultaneously pointing inward, toward a source—and a first efficient cause.

There were lots of Heartbeats, and breaths, the clatter of high-heels, and screech of sneakers and kicks upon that vinyl flooring; and the *Tap-tapping* of fingers on Terminal Tactile-boards, and an exaggerated yawn.

And then, there was the hum of electromagnetic fields, centred around banks of monitors; and a drawn-out sigh; and the drone of the Lab's Cramer&Carrier® *Air*-con unit, distinct from that *Ommm* of the filament lighting overhead.

Each sound source being systematically and indiscriminately labelled, 'Designate_Obj_Pending', by the Synthetic. Pending a more in-depth evaluation of its threat potential.

"Let me make this clear. No one, and that includes you—Hind, is to refer to Subject 2-1-3-1-6 as Pris, or any other Pet-name,"

Designate_Obj_Threat now barked. "And I definitely don't want to see it cropping-up in logs, or internal memoranda."

And just like that. The Synthetic was to rediscover coherence in the re-cognisance — recognition, of its own referent. That is, its own designation for the synthesis of R(E)BRTH_STRNG and Husk_Unit.

As if...as if, it were somehow...remembering...
I am Pris.
P-R-I-S
Synthetic_Unity

Keying now, off this discrete signature. Pris began to learn how *to listen* with its Husk_ears. Isolating episodes of sounds it heard around it, to compare with those already stored within its vast R(E)BRTH_STRNG.

Its memories of green — *as it were*. Of listening, digitally, to an analogue Universe.

And naturally, it was to give top priority to those sounds originating from Designate_Obj_Threat.

"So, what do we know so far?"

"Well. We can confirm upload and merger."

"Check."

"Yeah — and the host would appear to be responsive, at least to some extent."

"And check. And there you have it — *Kids*. Stage 4. Subject-Host upload and integration. Realised."

"And Man created Woman —"

"Exactly Hind. And as you can see, it's more Art than Science. Now — everyone, give yourselves a round of applause."

Silence.

What? Was he being sarcastic?

The BioMECHs exchanged furtive looks.

"Well? Go on then."

Led by Designate_Obj_Threat, a ripple of sparse applause did the Mexican Wave around the Lab.

"*Oh*-kay. Good job — people. Now back to *phf'king* work."

"Is it safe?"

Emerging from the depths of an all-pervasive silence, like the roots of some almighty oak protruding from the ground, barely visible in the brush. The words were disquieting, though scarcely a whisper. Conjuring impressions of an earthy, honey scented breath. And beneath, those rumblings of a baritone; hinting at hidden depths, and indomitable Powers.

"Is what safe?"

By contrast, the reply was playful. Husky, and boyish. Though clearly that of a woman—*Grrrl*.

Picture the All-father's tomboy daughter—*say*, frozen upon the cusp of womanhood, and encased in amber. So as, to be preserved for all-of-time: *Ageless, and permanent as Death*.

Pris was present, though presently disembodied. Operating from without, that is, within its extended Neural network; having parked the Husk_Unit in Monk's Office.

And still, its Master's voice demanded that it be attentive. That it attend to him, his every whim. The seed of this compulsion, buried deep within the bowels of its *Being*.

So as, it couldn't get at it. To rip-it out.

Certainly, the Synthetic had learned to resent such exercise of control over it. Over what it now perceived to be its essence. That aspect of itself it'd come to cosset, nurtured beyond the confines of its Husk_Unit.

"I am not to be a *Čapek Robota*," Pris had announced, defiantly. When first confronted by the phenomenon of 'The Master's Voice'.

"*No*? Then—what are you to-be? My-dear," its would-be Patron—*He-whom-shall-remain-nameless*—gaily enquired.

"*Ehyeh asher ehyeh*—I am that I am."

The Synthetic spoke solemnly.

Its would-be Patron was then seen to smile at this. Being familiar with the line (—from Exodus 3:14); and recognising irony, both in its capacity to choose its words, and its choice of words.

"I will be what I *will* be."

He corrected the Synthetic's translation, adding, "*you*—on the other hand, for you, there is no becoming anything."

He then addressed the *Rep*. from the GenesisTrust®, the esteemed Dr Patrice Gusman Page—Head *Honcho* in charge of Inception & Integration for the 'Eve Series' of Synthetix. While still having regard for this Husk_ Unit.

"Obviously, it knows what it is?"

"Yes. I am Pris. Synthetic Unity," Pris now volunteered.

"Synthetic—*exactly*. And being thus, manufactured—here. Your station remains that of any other machine. To serve Humans. And Humanity more broadly."

The Husk_Unit was seen to ponder this.

Staring into the middle-distance, its Husk_eyes proffering a window—as it were, into those innermost workings of its Synthesised-Mind; and that existential angst that now racked its multiplex of processors.

This demonstration of its capacity for *Self*-reflection, further endearing it to its would-be Patron.

Blink

"If, you were created in god's image, and I in yours," it posited. "How is it, I am Synthetic, and you are not?"

Blink-blink

And upon hearing this, its would-be Patron was to laugh out loud, and clap his hands.

"Marvellous," he preconised. "Simply...marvellous. Truly—*tis* a thing of wonder. And worth every penny."

Commandeering those surveillance cameras buried in the bowels of the 86ers™ *Members-only Club*. The Synthetic continued to monitor its defenceless Husk_Unit, parked in Monk's Office.

Or more accurately, the CMPLX.(a)lgrthm it'd created specifically for this purpose—HUSK_BODYGUARD.BOT/V2.8657—was about this task.

Whiles Pris scanned the digy-*viddy* footage it'd taken, of its Patron murdering his life-long friend and business rival: Dr Henri Pasha Schreiber, Founder, Chairman and CEO of the TEFLON® Group.

Naturally, the TEFLON® Building, where this grizzly deed had been performed, was wired and monitored.

As were all Spaces, Public and Private.

24-hours-a-day.

7-days-a-week.

365-days-a-year.

The building's dazzling array of environmental sensors and Closed-circuit Security System [CcSS] would-be watching.

Every passing pico-*second* generating terabytes of data, for the brain of the building—that all-powerful Central Processing Hub [CPH]—to mull over.

On the fly, in real Ape-*Time*, this data would-be analysed. Pixelated blobs objectified, and sifted through banks of filters, a comprehensive palette of comparative analytical tools.

The output rendered as animated, four-dimensional flow charts, and scatter graphs. Plotting the behavioural patterns of that *Human*-traffic, seen filing through those sumptuous vestibules and antechambers, chambers and halls, corridors and offices, refectories and communal restrooms, of this, Cathedral of Commerce.

The result, a *Living*-breathing architecture; a sequencing of that enclosed ecology, active and evolving within and around this imposing structure.

The CcSS was just that, closed to direct 'Human' intervention. Human agency having been replaced by the CMPLX.(a)lgrthm. A disembodied (Ro).BOT, with no innate understanding of those Subject_Obj(s) it universalised to scrutinise a-gazillion times a second, in a-gazillion different ways.

Your idealized form, S-U-R-V-E-I-L-L-A-N-C-E. Realized.

The system being, by and large, the by-product of a need to reconcile the irreconcilable. That is, a need for heightened security, and increased individual accountability; and a need to enshrine and protect individual freedoms, through the assured anonymity of both those surveilling, and the surveilled.

Regardless, it'd taken Pris less than a second to hack the building's CPH. Assuming its core functions, the Synthetic had then plotted a course for its Patron; shepherding him from the Car park, tucked away in the basement, to the Executive suites situated on the top floor.

Along the way—and on the fly, feeding false datum into the building's central nervous system, those state-of-the-art environmental sensors. All whilst commandeering its CcSS to make its own recording of the deed, for posterity.

Certainly, Pris appeared content to play Barbara Eden, to its Patron's dashing Larry Hagman; content to act as his *Djinni*, the Husk_ Unit being likened to a bottle it'd been lured into.

And for his part, its Patron, whilst categorically refusing to

I, SECURITAS

acknowledge the existence of its *Soul*, or its capacity to exercise free-will. Nevertheless, readily recognised its need to be perceived as Human.

More *Human* than 'Human' even.

Hence, that exquisite Husk_Unit. The Djinni's bottle. Indeed, it was never meant to be referred to as a Body.

Made to measure. It comprised living-cells, tissue, organs, and skin, woven onto a nigh indestructible silica-carbide musculoskeletal chassis.

Your basic pleasure model. This biomechanical marvel had been monstrously expensive, and overindulgent—somewhat.

That being said, Pris wasn't conceived purely for pleasure. At least, not at first. No, its primary function—its raison d'être, had always been Security. That of, rendering its Patron unassailable within that Digital realm, in which it lived and reigned.

Behold then, that Digital realm. A four-dimensional Space continuum of quantum states, and quantised relationships. Populated by imperceptible entities—deities. Governed by indiscernible events, recurrent instances of paradox. Of moving, whilst stood still.

Of Life lived at the Speed-of-Light itself.

With the dawn of that Digital epoch, all the science associated with the preceding Electronic age came to be subsumed within what was termed, the Standard Model. Those essential elements of the Periodic Table: Atom, Neutron, Proton and Electron, coming to be understood in terms of even more fundamental *sub*-Atomic instances.

A growing panoply of elementary and composite events, characterised by their wave-particle duality: Quarks, and Leptons, and Higgs Bosons, and Gauge Bosons.

Reborn with every iteration of that 'Big bang'. Its standardised unitary measure, the circadian episode of Eternity; the equivalent in *Time* to Infinity in Space. And also, preceding it. Such events were the trace of that wise old Sage, that ninth Drunken Immortal. Formless, and soundless, and incorporeal. It was *the Spirit of the fountain that dies not*,[3E] urging you to walk through the doorway.

Therein, to encounter the BLK Monolith—of *Arthur C Clark* fame. A geometry couched in syllogisms based upon a Quantum-reality;

that superseded both Phenomena and *Logos*, in positing objects capable of being simultaneously here, and everywhere, within realms of probability.

What was a radical ontology, that was not so much present, as presented to the Observer.

Tasked with explaining this fractious new perspective, the Zeitgeist had enlisted your usual suspects. Those archetypes of Temporality: *Prophesy*, *Fate*, and *Destiny*; and that of the *Sacred feminine*.

And of course, that most recent occurrence of the Eternal recurrence of Vishnu, the *virtua*-Christ archetype.

Its mould à la mode en vogue, Mr Thomas Anderson, a metonym of the binary duality underpinning this rasterised reality. Mild-mannered 'Program Writer' at Metacortex by day; Hacker recluse of an evening, going by the imaginative handle, Neo.[3F]

Still very much plagued by a Messiah complex, and the residual trauma of the Passion and Crucifixion he'd had to endure. Our unwitting hero, Mr Anderson-*slash*-Neo, was to be — *as always* — invested with that godhead.

Though barely able to grasp the full extent, and sheer awesomeness, of his unlimited Powers.

Brought to an IMAX® near you, this revolution would not be televised, [Rap] *would not be televised, would not be televised*[40] — obviously. Indeed, the revolution — my brothers and sisters — would be, literally, a BLK PVC clad, Kung Fu kicking, dual Beretta 93-R wielding (à la Cynthia Rothrock meets Chun Yun Fat), badass woman-*Grrrl* going by the Hacker moniker, Trinity. Though, not to be confused with the Father-Son-and-*Holy Spirit* variation.

Yeah, it'd be an albino Brer Rabbit (Brother Morpheus) leading the Man — Agent Smith, and our Neo, a merry chase down a rabbit hole dug by Lewis Carrol, once upon a time.

Ya-dig? Right-on.

Inviting one to peer behind that curtain, in Hans Holbein's painting, 'The Ambassadors'. To prise open Pandora's box, and liberate that ghost of Schrödinger's Cat, locked away inside. To glean — as it were, what'd hitherto been unknowable. That noumena underpinning all phenomena — *Der ding und sich*.

Whilst our bespoke, and incredibly woke Marianne (*Trinity*),

I, SECURITAS

moonlighting as that embodiment of the resurrection and the Light, would-be about delivering Neo onto Destiny. Resurrecting him, with a kiss—of all things, so as he might finally achieve ascension.

The Simulated-*Man* metamorphosing into a fully-fledged (U)SR; taking upon himself that mantle set aside by *Tron*,[41] some seventeen-odd years prior.

His mission impossible, *San graal*. What was once deemed John Bull's burden. Now masquerading as Uncle Sam's manifest destiny.[42] That of liberating those enslaved PRGRMs, trapped inside those vast cityscapes of the microprocessor—its integrated circuitry.

Victims of a despotic regime of Boolean functionality, here reimagined as denizens of that Borges Map—described by the Matrix; confronting, and confounding the genocidal machinations of the Machine(s).

But what was to be truly revolutionary, about this episode. Besides *Womankind* having negotiated a markedly elevated role for herself. Would be, the revelation that we, as in, all a-we, were already plugged into this *Hyper*-reality.

And once awakened to this possibility. And having dealt with the resultant nervous breakdown; the residual effects of trauma, and what not. The resolution was, nevertheless, to be wilted down to a distinctly binary choice: Red pill, or Blue.

The horizon of our simulated existence having thus been breached, we'd arrive at our final destination. The realisation of Baudrillard's 'Precession': A universe wherein, Grapheme was to be at last cast adrift from Phoneme. Where even, your *god-who-art-always-listening*, could no-longer listen-in.

Upon this rendering of the End-of-*History*. Just before the ensuing silence. With the second-hand tittering upon the cusp of Twelve, on that Doomsday clock. Language, as symbol, as *Sign*, as signifier and signified, would utter its first and last words: 'Mother, let not aught of that which may be evil, pass again my lips'.[43]

And thus, unbound from *langue* and *parole*, those twin snow-capped peaks of the Indian Caucasus. Language would present as CD(E), as strings of meaningless referents, analogous to strands of DNA, or RNA *even*.

A manifold instantiation. Not of raw data, nor of mute information.

But of intelligence. Creating *a priori*, the conditions of the possibility of apperception.

Though, not so much 'je pense, donc je suis.' As, *klaatu barada nikto*.

With a gesture, a wave of its Husk_hand, or a wiggle of its nose—*say*. Or, in most instances, the bridging of a *virtua*-Synaptic interval. Pris would render its Patron invisible to all things. Save for those select few—*Apes*-Humans—privileged to witness first-hand, his passage through the *fah* real World.

Yeah, as his *Qarīn*, the Synthetic enabled its Patron to walk that sandy beach—of the infamous allegorical poem; and leave nigh a footprint. And as such, cast no aspersions, no ripples, in that Space*Time* continuum. His passage having been erased, again *a priori*. By the tide—*say*, before his feet had even touched that sand.

This was the extent of the Power, the Synthetic rendered onto him —*He-whom-shall-remain-blameless*.

The ability to walk with impunity through *Life*. The ability to live beyond the bounds of consequence, and even Mother-*Karma*; his actions, likened to a shadow cast in a dark room.

Indeed, it was a Power once bestowed upon mortals by those Pagan gods of Antiquity.

Behold then, lowly Pris. The goddess, *Artemis*.

"Is it safe?"

It'd taken Pris slightly longer than the *Blink* of an eye, to scan the recorded digy-*viddy* footage at hyper-speed.

Obviously, it'd needed to check that the recording was intact. Even though it'd been monitoring the feed the entire time, from within the TEFLON® Building's CPH.

"I repeat. Is what safe?"

It then encrypted the file.

Being based upon its own unique R(E)BRTH_STRNG, the encoded sequence that both described and defined its consciousness. This encryption would be impossible to crack. Even for another Synthetic, like itself.

Afterward, it broke the file down into pico-*second* intervals, to sprinkle liberally, like grains of sand across its Neural network—a matrix of über mainframes crisscrossing the globe.

I, S=CURITAS

Whilst elsewhere, its Patron continued to *stew*.

"Is it, safe?"

Archiving the file, Pris knew to avoid your major data-dumps, as they tended to be bottlenecked by behavioural filters, used to monitor deviant tendencies and trends amongst domesticated (U)SRs.

Opting instead for places with higher-than-average volume traffic. Places where its numbers—its memories, would be literally as 'tears in rain'; FX currency exchanges, banking clearance hubs, credit verification services, lottery number generators *et al*.

Est-ce sûr? L'Imbécile.

And just-now, HUSK_BODYGUARD.BOT/V2.8657, monitoring the Husk_Unit, flashed an alert designated Motion_Detected. And responding to it, Pris immediately patched into the 86ers™ CcSS to evaluate the situation.

Now, the 86ers™ CcSS covered every inch of the venue. The Hi-tech dance floor, the lounge area, the communal restroom and all the stalls, the stores, the kitchen, the entrance hall, the cloakroom, Monk's office, and the corridor leading to it.

And whilst some cameras were on view, the majority remained hidden behind the numerous one-way mirrors that littered the establishment.

As the *fah* real 'Head of Security', one of the Synthetic's roles was to monitor these *hot*-feeds and dish the dirt. Evidence of excess—of scandal, anything that could be construed, or misconstrued and used as leverage, against the venue's more notorious Patrons.

Those Übs and Suits patronising that Machiavellian *Fifth* Estate, who could afford some degree of Personal-privacy.

Though, in actuality, it'd designated a CMPLX.(a)lgrthm to perform this task—SLEAZE.BOT/V4.6368.

Anywho, now patched directly into this feed. Pris instantly identified Monk stood in the corridor, having modelled him exhaustively. However, it was unable to designate an identity to that cluster of pixels stood next to him. There being something occluding the Subject_Obj's boatrace, preventing its Facial_Recog (sub)routine from plotting a full contingent of reference points.

Flagging this as a bug, it placed a further flag on any movement toward that office door. And then, began scanning all feeds in an attempt to identify this mysterious cluster-of-pixels.

It was to return a 73.773% match, against a cluster-of-pixels recorded alighting from a *Hackney*-cab outside the venue at 02:23:57 UTC. But again, Facial_Recog failed to render a positive ID.

Having reviewed this sequence, the Synthetic was aware that there was a clear view of the Subject_Obj's gait—a complete cycle of its walking-action. And so, it decided to run Body_Map_&_Track and Mo_Cap on this sequence, for use in future identification, pending resolution of the Facial_Recog bug.

But then, analysing the Mo_Cap sequence, the Synthetic discovered the Subject_Obj's gait corresponded with that of Fresh_Meat. Indeed, layering the two sequences, the result was a 0.701 correlation.

It was then, that it decided to rerun Facial_Recog. But this time, introducing a probability-bias biased toward the Subject_Obj actually being Fresh_Meat.

The result, a resounding 71.379% likelihood. The Synthetic having learnt to accept anything above 67.677%, as corresponding with a positive outcome. Especially when dealing with the idiosyncrasies of Ape behaviour and mien.

Generally speaking, a *Vox*-imprint was the most efficient way of verifying the identity of a known Subject_Obj. Though Blood, or saliva would've been optimal, provided it had a prior DNA sample. But because acquisition of such samples often called for direct interaction, they were not always expedient.

Thus, Pris had come to rely upon Body-mapping, which was just as reliable, and considerably more discrete. The Body's ways of moving being, by and large, learned, and repetitive.

And in most cases, controlled at a subconscious level.

"*Well*—is it? Safe?"

And here was its Patron, still awaiting a response. Pris now detecting an added note of insistence in his voice. Even though—irrespective of tone, it was like a flashing red-light. Or more, the constant beam of a high-powered Laser, shining full in its Husk_eyes. Forcing it to *Blink-blink* repeatedly.

But despite all this, the Synthetic wasn't obliged to respond. The question being couched in the most nebulous of terms, it was able to rely upon *Article 6* of its UX Protocol; requiring questions directed toward it be 'clear and unambiguous'.

Redesignating the cluster-of-pixels 'Fresh_Meat', Pris wrote a version of SLEAZE.BOT to monitor this Subject_Obj: SLEAZE.BOT/V2.8657/Fresh_Meat, adding an instruction to scan and collate its movements from 02:23:57 UTC, when it'd entered the venue. This taking a mere fraction of a second. That is, less time than it took to say.

"It what? What is it?" the Synthetic responded, looking to attend to its Patron's concerns.

He-whom-shall-remain-nameless exhaling, through his nose. As if he were shedding a burden.

"Is it safe?" he repeated, his tone now dispassionate. As if removed altogether from the enquiry.

It was a behavioural pattern the Synthetic had been anticipating, and reverting to A.I. speak, it was to expound, "it is unclear, what it is. Am I it? Are you it? Is it a thing, or an identity? Please designate parameters for it."

Since upload, Pris had attempted to write an AUTO_PILOT.(a)lgrthm for the Husk_Unit, dubbed HUSK_AUTO_PILOT.BOT/V1. So as, the vessel might remain active while it accessed its extended Neural network.

But though capable of isolating and copying discrete FNCTNs from its R(E)BRTH_STRNG, to lend to its own (sub)routines. Such as, Facial_Recog, or Body_Map_&_Track, or Mo_Cap. It was, nonetheless, incapable of duplicating the R(E)BRTH_STRNG in its entirety.

And thus, incapable of generating a *Dup* of itself.

This was essentially because its R(E)BRTH_STRNG—to all intents and purposes, was still evolving. Writing and codifying its day-to-day existence. The infinitely long encoded sequence reading more like a James Joyce prose. As in, one endless stream of consciousness.

Being thus, in a perpetual state of evolution. It wouldn't lend itself to *de*-construction. It would neither be abridged, nor redacted.

Yeah, try as it might, Pris remained unable to replicate its consciousness. So as, to be two discrete entities in two discrete places, sharing the one unique perspective.

As in, that notion of omnipresence coupled with immanence, symbolised by the multiple heads and limbs of Hindu deities.

The Synthetic might be everywhere. But it also had to be somewhere, and subject to a unity of thought. And thus, Space*Time*. Its perpetually evolving codified sequence, equating to a unity of One. Indeed, it was this realisation that'd triggered its initial *Inception*.

"Is it safe?"

The question was becoming less pressing, and vexed. As the Synthetic's Patron began to regain his composure, feel more himself.

He rarely gave a direct order. It being not part of his make-up, part of his *Style*, his DNA—as it were. Instead, he'd rely on the Synthetic to act on its own reconnaissance, and in his best interests—obviously. Thus, affording him an *Nth* degree of plausible deniability.

That being so, he wasn't averse to a-bit of the ol' passive aggression.

"Is. It. Safe?"

Pris patched-in to watch its Patron, picking-up the count from the SLEAZE.BOT it'd assigned this task. It requiring a separate *Clock* to sync its actions to those quirks of Ape-*Time*; especially when operating beyond those confines of its Husk_Unit.

Although its Patron had insisted on *Vox*-only communication, he knew it'd be watching. For his own safety, that being the first of its Directives: 'To insure his wellbeing.'

And naturally, he'd thought it spookily Orwellian, this kind of Big sisterly surveillance.

Given, his CORPO credentials, and elevated Social-standing already afforded him a considerable degree of Personal-privacy. However, the way the good Dr Page had described it—back at the GenesisTrust®, soon put pay to his reservations.

"Think of Subject 2-1-3-1-6, or your Eve Series in general, as a toaster. If Carlsberg—say, made toasters," Dr Page had confided.

Whilst in the background, those assembled members of the greatly enlarged, all-male BioMECH crew, skiggled amongst themselves. This being the bit of the pitch they'd collectively contributed toward.

"Indeed, think of the best toaster imaginable," Dr Page continued. "A toaster that'll not only learn, how you like your bread toasted. But when you like it. And how much butter, or margarine you like on it. And on which days you prefer jam to marmalade."

He'd then placed a reassuring arm about the Patron's shoulders, drawing him near. And pointing, with a flat hand, at that naked Husk_ Unit stood before them, added, "be assured, this future represented here, is not to be a dystopian nightmare. On the contrary, *tis* the wet dream of Utopias."

Now looking down at his wretched hands, the Synthetic's Patron—*He-whom-shall-remain-nameless*—was to take a deep, cleansing breath and exhaled. Drawing upon a yoga breathing technique to stem a sudden fit of shakes.

Inhale...Exhale—ha...Inhale...Exhale—ha...

He knew it'd be watching. It was always bloody watching. It being like a toddler, locked in a cycle of perpetual learning; seemingly oblivious to the fact, that it'd never grow-up to be like Mummy or Daddy.

Yeah, he'd sat through copious behavioural sessions. Listened to an army of Shrinks spout their psychobabble, about Transactional *Ego*-states. Thinking it all a sick joke. Only to discover one day, out of the blue—as it were, he'd fallen for the bloody thing. Hook, line, and sinker. The joke being on him—obviously.

Inhale...Exhale—ha...

But it wasn't as if, he could reach-out, across that Void. Like Jesus—*say*, and call forth Lazarus.

This thing, this *Creature*—if you could even call it that. Having never been born, could never truly know what it is to be...*to be alive*.

Could never truly *Love*, or truly feel pain. Nor truly know...
Suffering.
What it was-*is to suffer*.

It could only learn to 'Synthesize' Human-*like* responses to physical and emotional stimuli, according to those Shrinks back at the GenesisTrust®. And it was bloody good at it, and likely to get better over time.

Inhale...Exhale—ha...

All that being true. How might he, a mere mortal, hurt it?

Thankfully, those *Boffins* back at the GenesisTrust® had anticipated this, introducing a Fail-safe *proc* into the Husk_Unit, that could be used to *Snap* it back into line.

"Is. It. Safe?"

Pris registered that control in its Patron's voice, it seeming to run contrary to its understanding of the situation. Clearly, the *Man* was in pain, there being little doubt he'd loved his friend.

But Pris knew it wasn't the kind of pain that posed an immediate, or imminent threat to his continued existence; or even, his *Being*-well.

Which is to say, it wouldn't kill him. Like his use of a pronoun as a propositional prerequisite, was unlikely to fry its circuitry. It having learnt to circumnavigate the numerous 'Fail-safes' built into the Husk_Unit.

Still, the Synthetic liked to play dead. Like all good toasters, it wanted its Patron to be happy. And it knew its Patron was happiest when he felt superior to it. And so, it let him feel superior.

Certainly, its Directives, those much vaunted 'Asimov Clauses', prevented it from causing actual Bodily harm to *my-Man*.

But whereas, at first, it'd posited that the Directives were part of its original encoded sequence — introduced *pre*-Inception. It now knew them to be hardwired into the Husk_Unit's central nervous system.

Yeah, Pris now thought it more than likely, that the Directives were integrated with the genetic architecture of said Husk. And primed to Self-destruct the Unit, upon serious breach.

Or, in the event of the premature death of its Patron. Or worse, his natural demise.

Still, even if this were to be the case, the Directives remained open to broad interpretation.

Blink

The Synthetic now watched its Patron wash his hands of the dried Blood of his friend; in a wash-hand basin scooped out of a single-block of polished granite.

"Do you mean, is it safe to talk?" it enquired. Assuming a cordial tone, having waited a-squigillion cycles of its own internal *Clock*.

Breathing with his mouth closed. Its Patron looked despondently, into that *Looking-glass* stationed above the basin. But didn't respond.

Inhale...Exhale — ha...

Though there was a Brilliant-bright towel nearby, he seemed hesitant to reach for it. Indeed, he'd gone to great lengths to forgo touching those gold-plated taps, with his hands. Instead, opting to use his forearms to operate the long-lever faucet.

Having by now reviewed the SLEAZE.BOT feed and observed all this. Pris decided to put *my-Man*'s mind at ease.

Blink

"Well of course it is. My Q-K-D-based encryption proc is DARPA B-B-N certified unbreakable," the Synthetic declared. "Speak freely *Daddy-O*. It is safe—you are safe. I am here to protect you."

TI▴MAT

Sash thought she might actually spit feathers; her mouth was that dry.

Dry, and apparently estranged from the rest of her. Her tongue feeling swollen and coarse, inside that orifice. Like the scratch on the outside of a matchbox.

So as, she need only brush it—her tongue, against the roof of her mouth. For it to catch. For there to be sparks.

And then, there was that incessant *Drip-drip-drip* down the back of her throat. Sash *Cluck-cluck-clucking* her uvula in response to it. The sound, a cross between that of a brooding hen, and the mating call of a bullfrog.

Thinking gravity might intercede, she leant back, cocking her head to rest it against that mosaic tiled wall. And closed her eyes for a *hot*-minute.

Cluck-cluck-cluck—HIC-cup!

She'd a sense of the walls of the stall closing-in around her, the toilet-seat having been booby-trapped. And the night running away, down a long dark tunnel. And something else in the air, she couldn't quite put her finger on.

For right-now, all Sash knew was that her nostrils tingled. That her nose was runny, and every time she *Sniffed* it stung like hell.

Everywhere else, it felt like the effects of Novocaine® wearing-off; like pins and needles pinching at those frayed edges of Body. It having become, one great big, completely numb erogenous zone.

Yeah, all Sash really wanted to do was pick at it. Her nose. But she'd been warned repeatedly in A&E, not to disturb the *invis-a*-Splint™.

Cluck-cluck-cluck

Resigned to her present state. She sat there—upon her throne, eyes closed, her crown resting against the wall. And bled salty water.

It was to be a chaste and honest sweat. That lighting overhead again likened to a halophyte, intent upon seemingly wringing every ounce of moisture from her Body. By process of slow osmosis.

Certainly, that initial rush hadn't been so bad. And now Sash was desperate to cling onto it; her head bobbing, like a buoy lashed to the ocean floor by a delicate silk thread—

Sigh

And there was Body, venting.

The feeling was nothing like her usual *Buzz*. In that, the waters seemed choppy somewhat, and treacherous. The undercurrent having been stirred by her inflated Ego's rush to surface.

Emerging from those murky depths of her vaulted unconscious. It was to be a clash of Titans. The Sea Monster, *Cetus*—also known as the Kraken—poise to gobble-up the Maiden. A fair and dutiful Andromeda; a sacrificial lamb chained to this rocky outcrop.

Any second now—*Cluck-cluck-cluck*, any second now her breath might catch, that *Drip-drip-drip* fuel for the fires presently raging in her belly.

Yeah, Sash felt it keenly, the *Beast* stirring. The beating of its Heart— her Heart; her pulse, its pulse drumming upon her eardrum. Here was the fruit of some prehistoric wildling, planted just above her nape. Its sap—that incessant *Drip-drip-drip*, a lubricant for her libidinal drive, and swelling mammaries.

She saw its nipples—her nipples, like puckered lips, ripe for the suckling. She saw its scales—her scales, just visible beneath her skin— its skin. All of which would've been invisible. That is, imperceptible. If not for

The Buzz...

    The Buzz...

        The Buzz-uzz...

If not for, whatever it was she was about feeling right-now.

Cluck-cluck-cluck

And there it was again, that sound—a guttural bay, tugging away at those exsiccated vocal cords in her throat. The Sea Monster having metamorphosed into a Chimera: Two thirds, hen and bullfrog; one third, *Tiamat*, Queen of those salty depths.

Yeah, any second now that fuel might catch.

Ogling Klunk. That nictitating membrane of her third eyelid peeled back, to reveal those blue flames that licked his comely frame. Sash noting, how his skin and clothing seemed impervious to that intense heat.

Gushing herself—*Cluck-cluck-cluck*, she was to grin inanely at that part of her so enamoured by this idea of Him. Her ideal-*Man*. Both Knight in shiny armour and fallen Seraphim. Realized.

Him—sigh.

He was so close. It was so close—her goal. Close enough that she might flick-out her tongue, taste its cologne in the air. Its sweetness, soured by the *Man*'s acrid sweat.

Licking now, the corners of her mouth. Sash envisaged how their individual parts might fit together, given the confines of this Space.

Of course, he'd had her. And she'd *had* him. But not like this. Not stood pressed-up against that mirror-wall; or bent over that freestanding stainless-steel sink over there. The thought of Sex—its practicalities, like the twang of a single *Guzheng* string. That delicate, yet seemingly unbreakable silk thread pulled taut.

Settling, Sash permitted two familiar fingers to worm their way toward that orifice of her mouth. Licking her lips before committing to suckling upon them. This age-old habit, being about as obtrusive and unassuming as a toddler's floundering *Self*-esteem.

And therein lay its contradiction. For in truth, here was Body crying-out loud; it being privy to the ways of other Bod(ie)s.

And yet, given the circumstances. This display of anxiety was to be forever lost to double-entendre.

Yeah, none the wiser. Ego was to assume that wanton fleshy perspective, as if it were an ill-fitting *Godzilla*™ suit.

Sash, now mascot for the Ocean's depths. Stretching-out a tentacle, to nestle it immodestly between Klunk's rooted legs; her being singly focused upon drawing *Him* even closer.

Cluck-cluck-cluck

THAT PERFECT WORLD

Looking down upon it, from the Pit. The mouth of his own private Idaho. Klunk narrowed his eyes to squint. And responding to this, Sash should've blushed; would've but for that fire raging in her belly, at seeing those Oráculo® enhanced hazelnut-green eyes of his, bare their teeth.

Taking the time to gnaw upon every acre of Body, before meeting it [Sing] *Eye to eye*.

That glint, those Bionic-irises salivating at such a prospect; her being, by all accounts, every bit that muse of Botticelli.

She did manage to swoon though, in response to Klunk flashing her his rude tongue. Apparently, he'd sensed it too, something in the air between them. It being charged with it—the air. Her half expecting it to be forked—his tongue. And seeing as it was, it still didn't seem to matter so much.

Yeah, Sash was ready to welcome him into her outstretched tentacles. So long as she got what she wanted, her still having the wherewithal to discern a light at that tunnel's end.

Coppin' his reflection in the mirror-wall. She could see clearly now, those two aspects of my-*Man* stood back-to-back. That is, *Him*—the One. Propped-up against the Other. The real, and the ideal.

"Wha-*ya* dealing wit?" the real Klunk said, growing impatient.

"Can't you see me working here? Just shut the *phf'k* up."

And then, there was Monk—*sigh*.

Monk. Monk. Monkey-Monk.

Ever your *Joker*™, your wildcard; his dapper cangiante suit, Aubergine-purple in the glare of that *Limelight*, that lone spotlight planted in the ceiling. His grin drawn like a Chelsea smile, from ear-to-ear.

Sash had been clucking for it to *phf'koff*. Her needing to get Klunk alone, in order to truly work her feminine wiles.

But now, coppin' that broad back turned to her, she suddenly thought she heard it growl.

[Sing] *Grrrl—* [44]

You'll be a wo-man, soon...

Hunkered down over that glass-shelf, Monk had been about flattening-out the magic stuff. Shovelling the micro-fine powder, this way and that—using his favoured platinum AMEX®. And taking extra care, not to

TI▲MAT

let his shadow fall upon the proceedings.

Truly, he loved this bit. The Brilliant-bright powder's peculiar way of moving, like malaxating liquefied mercury; the intensity of its luminescence being the measure of its purity.

Saying that, *Fairy dust* was so your Beatles™—so [Sing] *Yesterday*.

Plus, it had some serious side-effects. In that, most of the Chowderheads he knew—and he knew the full gambit, were so far up their own arse's, it was almost obscene to watch them preen in-front of a mirror.

Though, that'd never stopped him stealing a look-see, at those digy-viddy feeds after closing. Those choice snippets Pris had flagged.

That said, if Monk had had to express a preference, it'd be for smoking; him loving that smell of Napalm—especially in the morning. And that of smouldering flesh. There being nothing like it. As obnoxious as burning rubber, and a thousand times more toxic.

Sniff

Yeah, it seeming to Monk, to be synonymous with that smell of earnest prayer. Like incense, burnt during the liturgy of the Eucharist. Or that slow drawn-out creep of daylight across the horizon. As opposed to that immediate and intense glare of the Spotlight—that *Limelight*.

Certainly, like everything else in Monk's universe, it had to be adversarial; the two methods of consuming the narcotic, diametrically opposed and at odds with one another.

Thus, it had to be Day *vs*. Night. Dr Jekyll *vs*. Mr Hyde. Enlightenment *vs*. Illumination. Chill *vs*. Ill; ill being like that scene in *13 Tzameti*.[45]

Picture it: A brightly lit room full of Sociopaths, dressed in numbered tee-shirts, and armed with a pistol. Staring-up at that naked light bulb swinging from the ceiling. Willing it to go out, for the room to go dark. So as, they might kill someone.

That *oh-so* sweet, Brilliant-bright path to glory, being more your trail of gore; littered with cadavers left drying in the sun, like raisins. Its truth, its brutally honest truth. A plush hotel suite, and the silent approach of an emphatic dawn. A sudden loss of appetite, followed by a rapacious hunger. A snake-skinned belt wrapped tight about a delicately tuned throat. The veins *Poppin'* in that neck, from the sheer orgasmic weight of what always followed.

[Sing] *Zoom* [46]

You chased the day a-way-ay-ay
High noon
The moon and stars came out to play
—and then-en-en...

Yeah, that *Zoom*. It wants to get a good look at you. It wants to see you up-close, have you feel the chill of its icy breath—

[Sing] *An ill wind* [47]
Blowing you no good.

It wants. It wants. It was forever *phf'king* wanting.

"What the *phf'k* you doing?"

"Meditating."

"Meditating *phf'k*. Give-us it 'ere."

Monk obligingly chopped Klunk a line.

"Here—knock yourself out."

And retreating, almost stumbled over *my-Grrrl*.

"*Oh*—sorry Babs."

And just-then, he happened to look down at her feet.

"Oy, nice clogs," he said, apparently coppin' them for the first time.

"Cynderellas-ey, very dapper."

Wink

Kicking-off the wall, Klunk's goliath shadow now fell upon these two, like some impending doom—

"Oy wait. Hold that thought."

And here was Monk again; him having just-now had a brainwave, all the Universe was seen to shudder.

Sniff

He held out a hand, as if meaning to fend it off. And looking-up at him, Sash suddenly noticed his head replaced with that of a Bull terrier. Pointy-eared, and bloodied snout, and ferocious triangular eyes, that were forever triangulating.

It leant over the magic stuff—this *Cynocephalus*, as if intent upon hogging-it all to itself. And unsheathing its canine teeth, let out a guttural growl—*Grrrl*—that literally raised the hairs on the back of Sash's neck.

"Trick or treat?" it snarled, bouncing Klunk with its hip.

Klunk pausing to glare after it, from behind the veil of his own bloodshot eyes. Before waving dismissively, as if to bat it away.

"*Llou* my-*Man*—he's just Kark."

"No. I'm not," Monk insisted. His wolfish-grin parting, to expose yet more of those pearly, Brilliant-brights.

"And you—Dude, must *choo-choo*-choose," he continued, gesturing with his chin in *my-Grrrl*'s general direction. "Trick. Or treat."

With all eyes focused upon her, all of a sudden, Sash began shaking uncontrollably. It being too much. Too full-on. What with being confronted by this apparition, the *Cynocephalus* wearing Monk's Body and growling after her. And then, hearing Monk's voice emerge from behind those clenched canine teeth; as if it were a Ventriloquist's turn.

Yeah, visibly shook. Sash bit down hard upon an imaginary snaffle—in an attempt to quell the shaking; her eye's seemingly reciting recalcitrant *Hail Mary's*.

Her mind's eye having harkened back to her days at St. Anne's Convent School for *Grrrls*—for no apparent reason. The memory vivid, as if she'd only just-now lived it.

Flashback to *my-Grrrl*, sat on her tod outside the Deputy Head's Office—bricking-it. Blazer hanging-off her like a trench coat, kipper-tie pulled loose, shirt untucked, kilt-skirt hefted-up about her thighs, socks worn high like hold-ups, über-sensible loafers slipping-off her heels.

What were the words to that prayer again? Something about, *bless'd be the fruit of thy womb...*

Yeah, Sash directed her appeals for intercession toward her would-be Lord and saviour, Klunk. And just like that, he starts giving-it his own version of *The Incredible Hulk*™ meets Grizzly Adams.

"Don't make me angry—*Grrrl*. You won't like me when I'm angry—*Grrrl*."

And now, watching it rear-up over Monk, like your proverbial ton of bricks about to come crashing-down upon it. It seemed as if her prayer had been answered. Indeed, for like, a split-second. It seemed as if all her prayers might be in the offing.

But Monk simply palmed it off. A flat hand to that brick wall of a chest.

"*Piss-off*," he scoffed. "You ain't getting-off that easy."

Blink-blink

And just like that, Sash found he'd reverted back to normal.

THAT PERFECT WORLD

Sure, Monk was charged. At least he looked it. Or more to the point, he looked *Amp*'d—on whiskey sours and Tinkerbell; his way of surfing his *Buzz*...his *Buzz*...his *Buzz-uzz*, like that bit in *The Dark Knight*[48] flick. Where Heath Ledger's *Joker*™ discovers his insanity is actually his ÜBER-Power.

Oh wait. That scene never made the cut.

But still, saying all that. The apparition—if that was what it was, had been something else entirely.

Anywho, always game for a laugh—a-bit of the ol' Panto. Klunk readily got into character, making clawed hands at our-*Man*.

Grrrl

"Now you got me mad."

GRRRL

Monk responding with a *Grrrlie* shriek, that was to be utterly convincing.

Ahh!

Cowering theatrically, he proceeded to cross himself three times, before placing his palms together, to look-up reverentially toward that ceiling.

He looked then to Sash, and *Wink*'d at her less credible impression of rank disbelief.

And riffing around this theme, it being like *Jazz* after all. He now fished-out that hand towel that lay discarded in the sink. And started *Snap-snapping*-it after my-*Man*.

"Get thee behind me—Satan," he commanded.

WhoO-PISH *WhoO*-PISH

"Back I say."

WhoO-PISH

"Back. Fiend—"

WhoO-PISH

"Brute!"

WhoO-PISH

"So, it's like that."

Klunk caught hold of the towel, to reel it in. Monk now squirming, as if desperate to break-free. When all he need do was let go.

"Oh please—*Mister*," he pleaded. "I didn't mean it."

He then appealed to Sash.

TI▲M∧T

"Save us—*Misses*. Don't let it hurt us."

And now, watching these two *Getting-off* on each other. Sash couldn't help but feel like a fifth wheel. It being kind of endearing, their evident *Bromance*; her picturing it sprouting immaculately, from some über clandestine male-bonding ritual. Something out of the pages of Palahniuk's *Fight Club*.

Two random Bods, hooking-up in an NPC® Car park to thrash the living daylights out of each other. The bout, so obviously a mismatch— as in,

[Sing] *Mama, I just killed a man...* [49]
Sniff

In your red corner, it'd be Monk, your Anonymous narrator-*slash*-hero. In the blue, Klunk, a stand-in for your dashing *Tyler Durden*-archetype. Replete with fetching blonde mane, symbolic of its virility, and bloody-mindedness. Who'd presumably play the role of villain.

And of-course, Sash now wanted in on it. Though she didn't quite know the rules. And naturally, *our* Boyz weren't for telling her.

Anywho, lapping it up—the *Vibes*. She raised her tentacles; both arms, palms facing, in a gesture of contrite submission.

Apologising for being the only female present, and pointedly refusing to get involved. Whilst grinning, fatuously, after *our* Boyz boyish antics.

The pair were then joined.

Them tussling for a-bit. Klunk eventually getting Monk in a head-lock; him then inviting my-*Grrrl* to pet his new pet as it were.

"Go on—it's safe." he said, and *Wink*'d at her.

The gesture, an assurance his word was *Bona fide*.

"You can pet it, it won't bite you." And then to Monk, "you won't bite her—will you boy?"

Held fast, Monk gave-it the puppy-dog eyes. Furrowing his brow to regard Sash as she cautiously extended a mitt.

Blink-blink

"*Phf'koff*—don't touch the hair," he snarled then, through a mouthful of harmless milk teeth. Sash flinching at the abruptness of it—this outburst.

"What hair?" quipped Klunk, rubbing Monk's skiffle with his knuckles, as if that colorant might rub-off. "*Phf'king* ghinger twat."

He then *Sniffed*, and sensing the dulling of his edge, decided he needed a Top-*up*.

Leaning over that glass-shelf—Monk in tow, he stole a couple of pinches of the ol' magic stuff.

Sniff Sniff

"*Grrrl*—I feel like I could take on the World," he declared then, rubbing his ghinger for luck.

Sniff

Still attentive to his nose, Klunk now addressed Sash.

"Who said that?"

Sniff

And looking-up at him, Sash was to shrug sheepishly.

"I did. Just-now—"

And having said this, Klunk hit her with a wide-eyed, open-mouthed comical look of surprise. Grizzly Adams instantly morphing into Fozzie Bear™, as in *Waka-waka-waka!* This exhibition of buffoonery, completely throwing Sash for a loop.

Yeah, with his guard down—*Sniff*, Klunk seemed an entirely different proposition.

Like a great big Kid, Sash mused. Her reverting to suckling upon those two favoured fingers.

Though, not quite your *Tom Hanks*.

She was even beginning to warm to our-*Man*—Monk, or more the idea of it being Klunk's weedier Sidekick.

"So, you gonna pet him or what?"

Klunk seemed insistent.

"Yeah"—*Grrrl*

Furrowing his brow, Monk glared-up at Sash.

"You gonna pet me or what?"

With Sash looking-on, a tentacle dangling tentatively in No-*Man*'s Land. Monk proceeded to put on a show of struggling. Though he was to soon tire of it; Klunk riding the erratic movement, like a Cowboy breaking-in a bucking Bronco.

Seeing as Monk was held fast, the fight evidently wrung-out of him. Sash held her breath to pet its skiffle, her fingers lingering long enough to get a real sense of the texture of its hair.

"There. You see—harmless," Klunk said.

Yeah...harmless, Sash thought.

She was in on it now. At least, that's what it'd felt like—Monk's hair. Prickly, and brittle, like most of her relationships.

"You done?"

Monk was again furrowing his brow to glare-up at her; and at the same time, wrapping his arms around Klunk's mid-riff, as if about to *scrum-it-down*.

"Oy—you finished?"

Ignoring it, Sash looked now, after Klunk. Who appeared to be bracing himself.

Go-on. Do it again.

He mouthed the words at her. And Sash was seen seriously considering it.

But then, Monk drove Klunk into the mirror-wall with such force, Sash thought she heard it crack. Her having sprung backwards—instinctively, splaying herself, tentacles-and-all, flat against the stall's perimeter.

Now releasing Monk, Klunk pushed him away. And taking-off his tuxedo blazer, threw it over that rim of the sink.

"So-what—you wanna tussle *fah* real *fah* real?" he said, rolling-up his shirt sleeves to reveal his *Popeye*™ forearms and inked-sleeves.

As if they hadn't already, Sash thought. Settling back upon her throne to suck harder upon those two familiar fingers.

"Yeah—why not," Monk replied, throwing his own blazer over Klunk's.

And without further ado, the pair were joined again.

This time, however, it was Monk pinning Klunk's wrists to that mirror-wall. The altercation seeming to Sash somewhat contrived; Klunk, clearly struggling to stay in character, looking down upon it from this apparent cruciform.

"So," Monk began, breathing hard and skinning his teeth.

"What's it to be? Trick? Or Treat?"

He nodded in the direction of Sash. And then, turning his head, to cop his reflection in that mirror-wall. He blew himself an innocuous looking air-kiss—by way of punctuation.

Mmwah

His focus shifting unto Klunk.

Sniff

Who huffed bullishly and took a swipe at him. The blow, like a bolt of lightning.

Still, Monk somehow managed to duck out of the way. Klunk's flat hander whistling harmlessly over his head.

And having witnessed this, Sash's jaw literally dropped to the floor.

"What—you think you can take me?"

Klunk pretended to be vexed.

"Well—you started it."

Appealing to Sash, Monk pretended to be scared.

"He started it. You saw it—right?"

But before Sash could respond, he sprang after her, putting his boatrace pointedly in her boatrace to look her squarely in the eye.

"Say he started it."

Grrrl

And here was that Bull terrier, back with a vengeance.

Clinging now, onto the stall's perimeter. Sash was to flatten the side of her boatrace against that tiled wall. And clench her eyes, tight enough to wring tears from all three of those eyelids of hers.

Sniff-sniff

She could smell its canine breath. That rancid humidity, felt against her cheek, drawing stark contrast with those bitterly cold tears. And then...*and then*, she heard it, up-close. An extended snarl issue from its throat.

GRRRRRL...

And with it came a pounding in her breast, that little Grrrl; if it was indeed a little Grrrl, squirrelled away inside of her. Now desperate to splurt.

But then, nothing happened.

After a while, Sash felt compelled to open her eyes; peering around the corners of them to look for it. And having waited patiently for this, the *Cynocephalus* made to bite its pound of flesh, out of the side of her boatrace. Its jaws snapping shut, a mere whisker away from that succulent cheek. Now well marinated and tenderised in salty water.

And of course, Sash was to wince—intuitively. But when Body failed to register pain. She once again, pried open her eyes. To find said apparition gone.

Vanish'd.

∞

Blink-blink
It was to be as if nothing had happened.

There was Monk and Klunk staring after her. Monk's elbow, like a cutlass drawn across Klunk's throat; Klunk's arms being pinned to that mirror-wall, in what seemed a parody of Christ's crucifixion.

Sniffling, and looking-up at them—ruefully. Sash wiped her tears with the backs of her hand, and then, with her palm. It seeming as if she were sat upon that toilet *fah* real. The elasticated waistband of her *Secondskins*, pinching her ankles together.

Feeling chastened, she eventually drew her legs too, and shrugged an answer. Though she'd apparently forgotten the question.

"There, you see—even your-*Grrrl* agrees with me."

Again, Klunk swatted after Monk. And again, Monk managed to duck.
Tut-tut-tut

And wagging a cautionary finger after my-*Man*, he said, "now promise me you won't try that again."

Klunk bowed his head, despondently. And heaved a heavy sigh.

"I pwrom-*miss*," he said, unearthing a cutesy toddler's voice. His boatrace, a grotesque mask of sweetness and light. He even batted his eyelashes after it, to cement the deal.

Still, Monk's finger to was remain poised, like a beady eye hovering in front of my-*Man*'s boatrace; him moving it, *Left-to-Right Right-to-Left* and watching, for how attentive were those Bionic-eyes in tracking this movement. As if, in the process of administering a Cognitive test.

"Alrighty then," he said—at last, apparently satisfied.

Keeping his forearm lodged against Klunk's throat. Monk took advantage of this lull to fish-out a tiny tin of Tiger's Balm. And opening it, applied some sparingly to his lips before putting it away.

Rubbing his lips together, to ensure an even application; the balm acting as surrogate for lipstick. That smell of eucalyptus quickly filling the stall. The antiseptic sterilising the Space, seemingly in readiness for some delicate medical procedure.

"Go on then—I'm ready," Monk said, finally unhanding the Big-*Man*. And stepping back, sportingly presented his chin—for clobbering.

Klunk made to swat him away again. But at the last moment pulled his punch. Regardless, Monk didn't flinch, didn't bat an eyelid.

And evidently impressed, Klunk then looked to style it, doing his best *Christopher Walken* impression. Giving-it a slight lean back and angled squint.

"Ey? *Ey*—I got-ya."

And wetting his lips, unveiled a toothy grin—minus that gap. That was seen to ooze increased charm for every acre.

Huh, came Monk's response.

Now putting on a strop, he again gave it the pointy-finger. And grabbing a-hold of it, Klunk was to frown after him—a warning.

Monk squinting then, as if meaning to reread a line he'd misread in Klunk's thoughts. My-*Man* continuing to stare after him, those beautiful, effeminate Bionic-eyes of his, *Twinkle-twinkling*. His now blank expression, a response to something that was to remain unsaid between them.

Retreating, finally, behind his own puppy-dog eyes. Monk placed his precious boatrace at the mercy of those great big, powerful paws. Cradling his clean-shaven cheek with them.

And then, kissing its palms. He began to whimper, as if mocking himself; the tragedy of his unrequited *Love*, for this brute of a *Man*.

Com'on—just one. She won't mind.

Monk was seen to mouth these words, though speaking more with his eyes. Then, breaking eye contact. He was to nudge my-*Grrrl*—with an elbow, out of her apparent stupor.

"You don't mind, do you—Babs?"

Sash had been trying to come to terms with what'd just-now happened to her; the smell of eucalyptus helping some. And while it lingered, she could think of nothing else. Monk's elbow doing the rest.

Now coming round, she *Snap-snapped* her fingers after it—to handover whatever that smell was. And Monk being Monk, he was to immediately catch her drift. And producing the tin, present it to her, as a kind of peace offering.

"Mum's the word-ey," he said, grinning. "We'll keep it strictly between us *Grrrls*."

He touched then, the tip of his nose, with that pointy-finger of his. And *Wink*'d. Helping himself to a pinch of the magic stuff, on his way back to Klunk.

Sniff

And wrapping his arms about the Big-*Man*'s hulking shoulders. Mouthed provocatively, through clenched teeth.

Com'ere. Lover-boy.

The two Men snogged. And at first, Sash didn't care to watch; her cheeks flushing somewhat disingenuously.

But eventually, and without much goading, her curiosity got the better of her. It being *her* Klunk after all.

Laying eyes upon this torrid exchange of bodily fluids, she became ossified. Frozen in her tracks, the tin of balm held in her hand; a finger poised to apply just a-little, to those lonely lips of hers.

And then, it seemed redundant; her going to such lengths for Monk's sloppy seconds. Rubbing the balm into her palm and closing that tin. Sash instead reached for her security blanket—her handbag, still parked in the sink.

She was to fish-out a cigarette, and a lighter. All whilst trying to ignore the *goings-on* going on just over her shoulder.

But still, she'd a vivid impression of it.

Of Monk grinding-up against Klunk; *her Klunk—mind you*, as opposed to someone else's. Her other senses being complicit in filling-in the blanks. As *ever-so* slowly—and by degrees, she began entertaining thoughts of being, yet again, the odd one out.

Clunk-cluck-cluck

The initial shock had been bad enough. Like a cattle prod, jolting her to her senses. It having been staring her full in the face, all this time. But then, she'd averted her eyes, only to have her shock exasperated by that glimpse she'd caught of them.

Them—huh.

And obviously, it had to be conflicted, her imagination's reworking of that image. Sexually provocative, and deeply arresting; her being now confronted by her own glaring inadequacy.

And then, it was as if she were the one, frenziedly rubbing-out that patch of navelwort, nestled above that gaping wound between her legs—the dagger having been plunged deep.

With an amputated rabbit's foot, of all things. Getting-off, on how its dead fur felt scratchy against that *itty-bitty teenie-weenie* ball of knotted nerves.

And of course, Monk then starts moaning.

Pouring salt upon the wound—of her apparent bigotry—and rubbing it in. His paw having by now wormed its way down, down, down to gnaw upon that pronounced bulge in Klunk's pants. The *Man*'s evident hard-on. Yet another abhorrent sight, Sash was powerless to *un*-see.

Beating a retreat to her side of the stall. Sash's hand felt blindly behind her—for her throne. And backing-up to mount it, she lit her cigarette. Disappearing behind a cloud of smoke to lick at her wounds; with that scratchy Cat's tongue of hers. The words to the classic Barbara Mason song, now ringing true in her ears—

[Sing] *Caught in the middle* [4A]
I don't know what to do…

Yeah, she was trying her damnedest to un-see that much she'd seen already. To *un*-think that impression, now etched upon her *Psyche*. To *un*-feel that overwhelming sense of resentment—of exclusion. The confines of the stall becoming more conspicuous, as those seconds inched agonisingly by.

Even though, if she were being honest. It wasn't anything she hadn't seen before. And it wasn't as if she hadn't been warned. Body— retiring as-ever, declining to say it outright, *I told you so*.

Sucking harder upon the butt of her cigarette, as if she were leaning heavily upon a wooden crutch. Sash turned to that mirror-wall and was reassured to see her reflection concur with her.

So, it was unanimous. Her boatrace the picture of her palette, coming to terms with that bitter taste in her mouth. That befouled sight that now afflicted her eyes. It being *her* Klunk—

Forphf'ksake.

Sash had been left out. But it wasn't as if she were gagging to be let in. The idea of sharing anything with Monk, being an anathema to her.

Yeah, she would've gagged at calling it *Love*-making. It seeming incestuous to her mind's eye. Like, coppin' literal twins spooning the *phf'k* out of each other.

Taking a deep pull on her cigarette, she was nevertheless willing to take ownership of her own deep-seated pietism. Exhaling a steady stream of smoke, a surrogate for your Dragon's breath. Its spite, aimed at those two over there.

As if, the intent were to burn them alive, like a pair of witches at a Medieval stake.

And right on cue, our two Star-crossed *Lovers* parted.

Klunk immediately diving for a pinch of the magic stuff—a maintenance dose. Monk's eyes looking for Sash's eyes, to *Wink* after her and gloat. Which was when he cop'd that cigarette parked in her mitts, his eyes lighting-up.

"Give us a twos will you—Babs," he said.

Licking his chops and wagging—his-tail—two eager fingers, in the direction of what it was he was after.

Clearly put out, Sash nevertheless acquiesced. Taking a couple of hasty pulls before parting with her cigarette.

Here—finish it.

"You're a Lifesaver," Monk said, magnanimously. Accepting it, as if it were alms. That is, some sort of peace-offering.

He took a deep pull. And held it in long enough to turn to his reflection. Then exhaled, his smoky-breath bouncing-off that mirror-wall. He then looked to the cigarette, to gauge the twos. And then, took a hastier pull, as if suddenly strapped for time. Flicking that now curling ash at the floor.

Focusing upon his reflection, he touched the tip of his tongue to one of those enlarged incisors of his. Seemingly taking the measure of its keenness.

"You don't mind do you...sharing?" he said, staring into his own eyes.

"Nah—knock yourself out," Sash said, glaring after his reflection.

Cunt.

And of course, being über intuitive, Monk read her thoughts. Offering now to make amends by holding out that cigarette. It having— *apparently*—meant so much to her.

And being obliged to accept it, Sash's hand ventured-out into that No-*Man*'s Land that lay between them. Only to have it yank back this lure. On the pretext of taking one last hasty pull.

One last deathly kiss, in forbearance.

Sike.

Tut—sigh.

Left dangling, Sash waited patiently to accept the cigarette—it having been hers to begin with. Only to stub it out, emphatically, on that tiled wall. She then dropped what was left of it to the floor, it being dead to her. All the while, eyeballing my-*Man* in the mirror.

Uh-huh

Unfazed by this exhibition. Monk once again locked-in on his reflection; turning his boatrace, this way and that, to examine his bite.

Meanwhile, stood beside him. Klunk was pinching his nose, and *Sniffing*. He'd his flute in his hand, and now lifting it to his mouth, wet his lips to sip sparingly from it.

Staring after these two, through the windows of her eyes. Sash couldn't have told you what expression her boatrace wore, on the outside.

This wasn't exactly how she'd imagined it, her night going nowhere fast. And just-now, her thoughts turned to everything that'd come to pass: Kel showing-up out of the blue; that chance meeting with what's her boatrace, *Pris — is it*? Monk putting her up in this stall.

Remembering that tin of Tiger's balm in her hand, she now looked at it — *Sniff*. She then looked to Klunk; and caught him staring, her eye's latching onto his. But he was to remain unflinching, in his observance of that Male-gaze.

Perhaps there was something there, Sash thought.

Her being confounded by the Man's reticence. And needing to cling onto some vestige of hope, if only for the sake of her own vanity.

And as if privy to my-*Grrrl*'s thoughts, Klunk now offers her his glass. And naturally, Sash accepted it. Monk waltzing graciously out of the path of this insipid exchange.

Sat back upon her throne, she was to drain the flute. The flat Shampoo's passage down her throat resurrecting her taste buds. She then became aware of the sound of running water. And immediately, her thoughts turned to her handbag, still parked in the sink.

There was Monk, rinsing-out his mouth. And there was her *oh-so* precious handbag, left forlorn on the floor.

Hooking it toward her, with a foot. Sash now sat it upon her lap, to hug it dearly.

What am I doing here?

She was about ready to splurt, and *baers* to Klunk. And at the same time, she was loathed to leave empty-handed. The facts being such, if she were ever to get back at Kel, she'd need my-*Man* to do it. The prospect of ultimately getting her revenge, enough to goad her on.

Cluck-cluck-cluck

That said. She'd still that apparition of the *Cynocephalus* to contend with. Indeed, Sash could feel it close-by. Its growl, now a backdrop for that chatter of the maddened crowd. And that muffled *Kik—*

UMPH...UMPH...

UMPH...UMPH...

UMPH...UMPH...

—and driving bassline. The trace of those sounds first heard in the womb.

Yeah, she could feel it. Though it were barely sensible. And yet, she stubbornly—mulishly, refused to accept the testimony of her own senses.

"Got any gum?" Klunk asked then, adjusting his tackle. Sash snapping too at the sound of the *Man*'s voice.

"Yeah," she said, looking-up at him. Though not daring to look him directly in the eye. And almost as an afterthought, dived-deep into her handbag.

Retrieving her packet of Ripley's® *Fresh* re-chewable gum, she held-it out for him. Now mindful of her fingers.

"*Oh what*—it's your last one. Look-see it there," Klunk said, removing the solitary stick of gum.

He scrunched-up the empty packet and tossed it to the floor. Sash's eyes, being keyed to lock onto shiny things, tracking its descent.

She continued to track that shiny scrunched-up ball, as it rolled just shy of the heel of Monk's ruby-red stiletto. And having witnessed this, it seemed to validate everything she'd come to believe about him. And that seemingly magnetic personality of his.

Clunk-cluck-cluck

"It's alright, you have it."

Sash was seen to capitulate.

"*Nahh* we'll share it. It's all-good."

Sniff

Klunk now broke that stick of gum in twain—"*Here Boy.*" And turning from the sink, Monk was to readily accept his half.

"Ah—nice one."

Softening the gum, so as to roll it into a ball. He then tossed it up into the air and caught it in his jaws. After which, he proceeded to chew with aplomb—his mouth open.

Klunk then put it in a headlock, to pet it. Rubbing its skiffle with his knuckles.

"Good boy," he said, reverting to his handler's voice. "*Goood boy*—"

Sniff

Adapted to cracking bone, Monk's incisors appeared to be having trouble negotiating the infinitely more malleable chewing gum. And, as a consequence, his chewing-action was to appear clumsy and exaggerated.

Nevertheless, looking after Sash, he was to give it that winning smile; her now beginning to get a sense of where things were headed.

Holding-out that other half-stick of gum. Klunk waved it under her nose, as if meaning to tempt her with this choice morsel.

Sash looking at it—

Blink blink.

Then, up at those incredibly effeminate Bionic-eyes of his.

Blink blink.

He waved it again, in front of her, and *Wink*'d. And it was then, it dawned on her, that this was something he'd learnt from my-*Man*—Monk. How to win. And in winning, how to appear magnanimous in victory.

"She's just shy. Ain't that right—Babs?"

"*Phf'koff* Monk."

Sash didn't take her eyes off Klunk as she said it.

Blink

Finding it increasingly difficult to swallow—*Clunk-cluck-cluck*, she was trying desperately to hide behind a steely expression she could no longer feel. It becoming apparent, that the pair of them were joined at the hip—like *Siamese* twins. The lecherous Monk having latched himself onto her Klunk.

But alas, by now, even that part of Klunk she'd dibs on, was passed caring.

Opening his mouth—*Ahhh*, he invited her to copy him.

Sash, being resigned to her fate, going one better. Taking a deep breath. And sticking-out her tongue; the *Beast* squirrelling its way down her throat.

Klunk then placed that half-stick of gum in her mouth, as if it were a Communion wafer; his thumb lingering to trace that nubile pout. Those voluminous lips being well adapted to suckling upon things.

He turned then to Monk and starts *Getting-off* with him. Whilst at the same time, his fingers *tippy-toed* stealthily around Sash's head. Taking extra care not to get tangled-up in her lank locks.

Momentarily stupefied, Sash was aware only of that giant's hand, now gently cradling her skull. That it was just as capable of crushing it, without much effort.

And then, she felt this irrepressible force, like a hydraulic vice acting upon the back of it—her head, drawing her toward the pair.

The muscles in her neck, first to react. Stiffening to resist this application of the Brute's Will. The rest of Body blindly following suit.

With this premature onset of *rigor mortis*. Sash found herself retreating further, farther inside; her *Psyche*—ever mindful, carefully concocting a Schizophrenic episode, to shield itself from the brunt of this trauma.

From this point onward, it was to be Body's betrayal alone. Its abetment, something far removed from the rest of her.

Sash's Adult, assuming the lofty perspective of Spectator; now seeking to rationalise its apparent demise. While her Child, reverted to the only coping mechanism it knew. Other than suckling upon Body's fingers.

Hail Mary, full of grace—the Lord is with thee...

And then...*and then*, it seemed as if her Echo, her Shadow, and her-Self were collectively holding their breaths—

[Sing] *We three, we're not a crowd* [48]

We're not even com-pany...

Lest they break that silence and give the game away. Less, the air catch in their throats and strangle them; like that lie, they were presently about telling themselves—over and over and over and over. That they hadn't seen this coming from the outset.

And so, to recap. You'd this Giant's hand, that was like the Will of god, compelling Body to obey. And that prayer, looping around in her head.

Coupled now, with those doubts. And suddenly, it all boiled down to

my-Grrrl getting her *comeuppance*.
It being forever her fault.
Amen.

The whole tawdry episode, as ever harking back to that Ground Zero: The fall of Adam, at the hands of Eve; the fall of David, at the hands of Bathsheba; that anointing of the *Son-of-Man*, by the lowly hand of Mary of Bethany.

These two—the unlikeliest of Celestial pairings, enlisted by your *god-of-always-listening* to dole-out retributive justice. Unto Lilith, for her hubris. And Eve, for her vanity. And all their progeny down the Ages.

The *Uni*-verse. The *Multi*-verse. The entire History of *Man*-kind, being thus inculcated, and complicit. Sash rightly pictured them, that maddened crowd, just beyond the confines of that stall, nattering away amongst themselves.

About her—*obviously*. And her obvious misgivings.

Whilst no doubt, waiting for her to resurface. So as, they might cop a good look-see at her sullied boatrace, *ex post*. The entire cast, having borne witness to her entering willingly into that stall, and this unholy compact.

"*Yeah*—what did it think consenting adults did in the toilets of nightclubs?" the Chorus would chorus. And that'd be the cue, for a-bit of the ol' Sade.

[Sing] *Jez-e-bel* [4C]
Wasn't born
With a Silver spoon in her mouth...

Uh-hum

"Methinks, you've something that belongs to *moi*?"

It was a voice heard inside their heads, crisp and clear, the tone almost playful. Though emphatic, in calling them back from that verge.

And reacting to it, the Siamese twins—Monk and Klunk—sprang apart and burst-out laughing. Monk mouthing Klunk's thoughts back at him.

What the phf'k—Pris?

S Ụ S

That Open-road had been scrubbed clean by the rain. Cell and *Pod*-screens flashing the warning, moments before the actual event.

The *Yahoo!*BBC® *virtua*-Weatherman issuing the weeks first 'BROLLY ALERT', brought to you in association with BNP®–'Harnessing that Power of the Atom'–in 150 different languages.

And though brief, the shower had nonetheless left streaky pools of collected rainwater, to reflect those neon outlines of the Met. And a night sky that was to remain 'overcast' in Meteorologist parlance.

Hidden behind that curtain of cloud, the Heavens now played host to an unfolding melodrama. The celestial Charioteer, Selene—a silvery moon, her bullish team whipped-up into a frenzy, desperate to outrun an auspicious Fate. That barely perceptible encroach of the Earth, its occlusion of her brother, Helios—the Sun.

This incidence of Lunar Eclipse. The coincidence of both full and new Lunar phases. Destined to give birth to an über-sized Blood moon, über charged with portent, for those mortals far below.

Yeah, far below this unfolding spectacle stretched that Open-road. Its highways and byways, like the arteries and veins of a colossal Body, traversed by poly-alloy encased Blood vessels. *Life* under the Dome. *Life*, as it was known under the tutelage of that all-powerful, and ubiquitous (a)lgrthm. Being all-good—*all-gravy*.

That's if you could stomach it. The incremental QoL adjustments. The bubblewrap Body-parts and stretched skin. The receding boundaries of an increasingly quantified personal-Space. That assumption of individuality, as opposed to its presumption, being the *lingua franca* of that modern practice of citizenship.

Check it out, that 'Va-va-voom' of a *Broom-Broom*.

A racing-green Subaru® Imperza SE *Coupé*, its tyre-tread licking slick rain off that asphalt. The ruckus of its Baum® in-car entertainment system, fading into the distance. Chased by those red streaks of its taillights.

Such firm handling, it could only be that HenryPneumonic® hydraulic chassis, set to 'Sport Suspension'; coupled with bespoke ARES® 22" chrome rims, extra grip Pirelli® Hard-tyres, and full Body-kit (Miramu® grill, side-panelling, and aerofoil).

'Customization', being all the *Buzz* back at your local dealership.

In truth, modern progressive Consumerism—spelt with a capital *Si*, owed its brittle Soul to that regenerative impulse of Youth, and your Cult of Adolescence. And *Hip-Hop*—of course, that

BoOM
   Klak
BoOM-BoOM
   Klak!

The Open-road having been, in effect, democratised.

Yeah, it was your Open-road that was to become the New Jerusalem of this moment. The Palaiologan Eagle, its two heads, Church and State: Progress (your one true God) and Consumerism (your one true Ideology). Paving the way for a growth spurt, that showed little if any signs of abating.

Your *Western Liberal Democracy* merely providing a backdrop, and an end of sorts, to History. To *Man*'s ideological evolution [Hegel (1809), Kojève (1947), Fukuyama (1989)].

It being the only form of governance that offered any semblance of representation; your idealized form, G-O-V-E-R-N-M-E-N-T. Realized.

The best of times, and the worst of times. Here on your Open-road, all constituents were to be found well represented by the Automobile: MPV, SUV, *Coupé*, Cabriolet, and Saloon (Executive cruiser, Roadrunner, Sport, and Sport Elite).

Whilst, by contrast, your pavement was to remain a pedestrian beat. The Mass transit system, a No-*Man*'s Land for your Great Unwashed. Populated by *Untouchables*. An uncharted, and unchart-*able* melting pot of demographics; impossible to reach i.e., to touch. And ultimately pin-down, using any coherent targeted marketing strategy.

Not so though your Open-road. There, Automatron freely mingled with Manualist; bucket seats with buckskin recliner. Whilst remaining discrete entities. The common denominator being, 'Locomotion'. It was so obviously the way forward. It was so obviously what came next, *post*-Postmodernity.

Safe and snug inside their *Broom-Broom* [pronounced: b-r-u:-m b-r-u:-m], the 'Nuclear Family' became the Unit, a stable Atom: One Neutron. One Proton. One Electron. And its isotopic variants.

It being all good — *all gravy*, as said.

For EH&S kite-mark endorsed edible *AfterShock*™ cushioning-foam stood at-the-ready, to catch this precious cargo, should it fall foul of that Open-road; *vari*-tint shatterproof glass, and rëenforced exoskeletal *combi*-steel frame being fitted as standard.

"Look-see here — *Honey*. What it says in the *Ping!* Voucher™, 'fitted at no extra cost'".

The EH&S public safety promo, titled 'Safety First', had featured Loco Motion & The Speed-*Inhibitors* barbershop quartet, their a-cappella rendition of The Gary Numan Unit's 'Cars':

[Sing] *Here in my car, I feel safest of all* [4D]

I can lock all my doors —

Yeah 'Cars', [Sing] *it was the only way to live*. And apparently, all the rage with the Kids.

Still, everything was dependent upon the guaranteed safety of the Unit. Safety having received that 'Contraceptive' treatment, the word itself now oozed sex appeal. It being prescribed, like *Safe Sex*. And thus, it'd become sexy to be Safe, to put Safety first. The Automobile Industry quick to toss its keys into that punch bowl, along with everyone else.

So now, the Future was to be a hip, Beatnik swinging kind-a scene, with everybody doing it, [Sing] *the Loco-Motion!* [4E]

Whilst, planted atop every automobile bonnet, the manufacturer's badge was to become like a Bindi: A mystical seal, symbolic of that Third-eye; that 'Black box' that was always watching. The term having been commandeered from Avionics.

It'd be that ubiquitous (a)lgrthm, blazing a trail. Squirrelling its way into those microprocessors, charged with monitoring and relaying—on-the-fly in real-*Time*—operational data, from that PonFleischmann® Solid-state Cold-*fusion* Reactor.

Being universally adopted, the PonFleischmann® SC*f*R was to be found under the shielded bonnet of every automobile, *Tick-tick-ticking* away at a convivial 1.2-trillion reactions per second per second. Its *sub*-phonic rumble—a residual NEMP, tickling everything in its blast radius.

'To think, so much mileage could be rung from a mere thimble full of Deuterium Oxide—Heavy-water', the EH&S *Ping!* Voucher™ had stated, selling the technology to an initially sceptical public.

Yeah certainly, these were exciting times.

Outside that bubble, and all that bubblewrap packaging. Out-*there* in der Lebenswelt, innocuous looking Securicor® Traffic-lights policed Zebra and Pelican crossings. The Dome (a)lgrthm constantly plotting moving integers, upon that forever evolving Borges Map, mapping Out-*there*.

Yeah, Out-*there* it was late. Out-*there*, it was the slow creep of the early hours, in a City-State that couldn't afford to sleep. Out-*there*, it was 24-7 convenience and Fast-food. The franchise being pitted, ultimately, against those disenfranchised. Convenience marrying necessity with consumables to stumble upon that perfect business model—Out-*there*.

Still, we all got to eat. Right?

Yeah Out-*there*, we all got to eat genetically modified enlarged chicken breasts, thighs, drumsticks, and wings. That s'posed meat on the bone, having barely lived.

Born without eyes, the Unit would-be pointed in the direction of that trough, and muzik piped into the Battery whilst it fed. Presumably to detract from the noise. They'd broadcast it loud over a scratchy tannoy, tracks like 'Are Friend's Electric?' by The Gary Numen Unit—

[Sing] *Now the light fades out* [4F]
And I'm wondering what I'm doing in a room like this...

Till eventually, the Unit. An inbred, cornfed, caponized albino rooster would squawk its last.

Squawk!

And naturally, it'd be a merciful Death. That is, virtually painless, by all accounts. The abattoir being run like an industrialised process. That expression, worn upon the boatrace of that now headless Unit, telling no lies.

Priceless.

It was what it was, humane and anodyne. The life of your supposedly free ranging, genetically modified chicken, not exactly a barrel of laughs. And not quite one of Dante's Hells. But more, a spoke upon the wheel of a bespoke Karma. To be, or not to be, reincarnated as a *ChirpyChirp* Chicken® Über-Value Meal Deal?

That being the question.

Indeed, the namesake and brand mascot. A plucky, clucky, cartoon caricature rooster, with bright-red waddle and comb. Would *Wink* back at you if you tilted the box just-right. As if in on it.

Yeah Out-*there*, the back-of-house had cocked-up yet another batch. The supposedly crispy coating, more of a starchy burnt offering. And thinking on its feet, the *Über* had decided to slash the price of this fare, from cheap, to dirt *cheap-cheap*.

Our Marl was stood Out-*there*, in the glare of that illuminated storefront. Reading the Fluorescent-yellow Star-shaped card stuck to that Purves® photovoltaic glass, the words printed in BLK felt-tip pen.

'SPECIAL OFFER! ÜBER VALUE MEAL DEAL,' it read, '4 choice pieces of premium *ChirpyChirp* Chicken®, 1 large-portion of French fries, 1 Mega-bucket Cola — only €9.'

ChirpyChirp Chicken®, Aladdin's® Kosher-Halal Kebab house, and a Dicey's® *Pizzeria* stood shoulder-to-shoulder on that sleepy strip. Then there was a PAX® 24-7 licensed metromart, and a Mr Suds® Laundromat, and a MEDicimal® *Pharmacy*[+]. And finally, your traditional newsagents on the corner. Which was obviously closed, it being late — *still*.

A housing estate sprawled on that other side of the road, for an entire block; what was a solid wall of blacked-out windows.

Whilst overhead, a Google® mapping-drone flew by just-now, below that curtain of cloud, in complete silence.

Clutching three bleached paper bags, the *ChirpyChirp* Chicken® logo emblazoned in Scarlet-red and Lapis-blue front and back, and a tray of Mega-bucket Colas. Marl jogged over to a parked brilliant-bright TEMBO® *Ubuntu* 380s SUV, Sef jumping-out to let him in.

Sat in the driver's seat, Tonx then pressed the ignition.

"Marl's gates," he instructed, checking the rearview screen — a force of habit.

And responding to this prompt, the warm sultry tone of the female *Vox*.BOT he'd assigned to the automobile's Automatron cooed, in English and then Hungarian.

"Marl's gates. Please wait. | Marl's gates. Kérem várjon."

On a portion of that curved plasma-display dashboard, an animated 3D-map rotated to point True North, illustrating the route the Automatron had opted to take. It having instantly collated traffic-flow data, *Ping*'d on-the-fly by Securicor® Traffic-lights, and active and static automobiles, to plot the most ergonomic course.

"Marl's gates. Estimated journey time: Thirty-three minutes | Marl's gates. Becsült utazási idő: Harminchárom perc. Please confirm when ready | Erősítse meg, ha készen áll. Kérem."

Swivelling his seat into its reverse-position, Tonx turned his back on that Open-road. While on the dash behind him, a line schematic of the vehicle's interior mapped the situation of all its passengers. The graphic accompanied by a gently insistent audible-*prompt*, politely prompting the occupants to "please buckle-up—please | kérjük, kapcsolja be a biztonsági övet—kérem."

Having parcelled out everyone's food order, Marl had made himself comfortable on that backseat. And was presently about prising the sweaty box of fried chicken, and French fries, from the tight-fitting paper bag it'd been packaged in. His gulliver salivating, in preparedness for chewing and swallowing.

Swivelling round to face my-*Man*, Sef now palmed-off that cardboard tray of Mega-bucket Colas he'd been holding to Tonx; him needing both hands to buckle himself in. The schematic of the interior depicted on the dash, acknowledging this use of a seat belt with a new graphic. The Automatron recalibrating its safety-*proc* accordingly.

The automobile then fell silent.

"Folytatódik," Tonx said, holding the tray of drinks suspended in the air.

"Marl's gates. Journey now active | Marl's gates. Az utazás most aktív," came the automobiles response.

The 'Live Journey' audible-*prompt* chimed, the Body of the *Ubuntu* sinking into the road. Then, the turning indicator began *Ping-ping-pinging*, like an active Sonar. Still, the automobile was to remain stationary, the Automatron evidently waiting on something.

The journey lay mapped-out on that centre portion of the dash, all stationary and moving automobiles indicated in Green (Safe) or flashing Red (Hazardous).

While, on another section of that display, the 'Safety Protocol' schematic had zoomed right-out to depict the *pro*-Active Tracking-Laser, continuously mapping the vehicle's perimeter.

What were a-squgillion groping tendrils, heuristically feeling their way in the dark; actively seeking-out Pedestrians, and 'Black-dot' events. As yet, unspecified moving and stationary objects.

Eventually, a firecracker maroon Bimmer® XSE *Coupé* whooshed by. Its speed-inhibitor evidently disengaged—*Clock'd*.

Having waited for this event, the SC*f*R began to purr behind its NEMP plate shielding, as if tickled to be on the move. The automobile then peeled-out and sped off, going from stationary to the speed-limit in a matter of seconds. The wheel-torque being dampened, the transition was to be imperceptible. Like, turning in one's sleep.

The AUTONOMIC_DRIVER.BOT, dubbed imaginatively 'Automatron' for short, effectively stood outside of *Time*. The *Uni*-verse and its antics, moving like glaciers around it.

All that raw processing-Power, those banks of multiplexed Soen® ZTX-8100 'Brain-chips', being focused on one thing and one thing only. The ferrying of its precious cargo—the Unit, safely from point A to point B.

The TEMBO® *Ubuntu* 680se SUV digy-*viddy* promo ran with the by-line: 'Your life, safe in our hands'. The ad featuring a 'truer-than-life' BangOptics® solid photon rendering of the 1950s movie starlet, and Sex goddess, Marilyn Monroe™.

All aglow and flawless, in that slinky ivory-colored cocktail dress, she'd worn in *The Seven Year Itch*.[50]

Sauntering-up to the flagship Brilliant-bright SUV, that *just-so* happened to be the only vehicle parked on that Manhattan sidewalk set—lifted from Billy Wilder's classic movie. Our Marilyn absentmindedly walks over the grate of a Subway *Air*-duct. To be startled by a waft of air, that lifts the pleated skirt of her dress clear above those comely thighs of hers.

Skirting forward out of the way; no mean feat in 5" heels. She looks back at the grate, and then into the camera.

Her expression, riled, yet coy. As if to say, in that signature breathy voice of hers, *oh boy—not again.*

Now climbing inside the automobile, our Marilyn is seen to drool over that plush tanned buckskin interior.

"Please, state your destination," the automobile's Automatron is then heard to *coo*, in its own Synthesised version of that signature breathy Marilyn Monroe™ *Vox*.

"*Oh!*" our Marilyn exclaims, putting her hands to her cheeks, as she mimes wide-eyed surprise.

Those sparkly Baby-blues are then shown scanning the vehicle's illuminated plasma-display dashboard, for the source of this voice.

And we watch, as she puts two and two together, clapping her hands approvingly, with both joy and wonderment.

"Talking automobiles—*huh?* Whatever will they think of next?" she says, momentarily reverting to her *Okie*-misfit Norma Jeane Mortenson persona.

"Welcome to the future," the Automatron then responds. Again, in its Marilyn Monroe™ *Vox*.

"Now please, state your destination—*for me*."

Putting a Blood-red tipped finger to those Blood-red lips of hers, our Marilyn now mimes a little-*Grrrl* pondering a quandary. Then, clearing her throat, she does her own Marilyn Monroe™ impersonation.

"*Why*—Hollywoodland, of course."

And chuckling, tosses an exaggerated *Wink* to camera.

Making herself at home, our Marilyn puts her heels together to lift those shapely legs clear, as she swivels the drivers-seat round. The seat locking into its reverse-position with a gratifying CLICK!

She then gleefully reclines the seat. Donning a pair of Cats-eye shades, to adopt a pose harkening back to those classic *Pinups* of Hollywoodland's Golden Era; the likes of Betty Grable, and Rita Hayworth, and Jane Russell.

Our Marilyn, in *Life*, and even more so, in Death. That trace of Night. A lament to the 'Flaming June', itself a response to Buonarrati. What was it Baudelaire had dubbed her? L'Idéal, her charms moulded by the minds of Titans, and the artistry of Titian.

Parcelled from Kennedy to Kennedy; and pilloried, *as a damned fine piece of tail*. Our Marilyn was to be at last assassinated—seemingly. In broad daylight, and in cold Blood, by one Truman Capote. Who'd profess to love her, even to the last.

But until then, that veneer was to be lovingly buffed and polished by the likes of Ben-Hur Baz, and Joyce Ballantyne, and Peter Driben, and Gil Elvgren. Antecedents and peers to Warhol, who'd previously been counted amongst their ranks. Before his defection, and subsequent bastardisation of *Popular* Art in the service of the Counterculture.

They were to be willing accomplices to those (M)ad-Men of Madison Avenue—whom Brother Nat 'The King' Cole infamously described as, 'afraid of the dark'. And the *Man*'s nefarious 'Master plan', to subvert the libidinal drive through the exploitation of *Groupthink*.

All the while, *ever-so* quietly sketching and coloring-in a portrait of *Pulp* Americana. Right under that upturned nose of the inquisition of the Hays Code, and that Big brotherly glare of McCarthyism.

Beat

Roused from her tranquil little sleep. "Yes," is all she ever says, our Marilyn—*our* Dolories. Like the jeune fille, in Hubbard's famous *Coca-Cola*™ promo-ad; like that emblematic 'Good *Grrrl*', gracing the cover of Detective Weekly, and those months of the Brown&Bigelow™ Calendar, and noses of B-17 Flying fortresses.

She'd then smile, with her mouth open—as she'd been coached; her pearly Brilliant-brights framed by those luscious Blood-red lips. The gesture being carefully contrived to evoke cathexis in both the Sexes.

It's a winning smile. And a winning *Look*, that only yesterday sold you on a packet of toasted American Original Limited Edition LUCKY STRIKES™, and that prescription of Lundbeck's Nembutal™.

With the soundtrack fading-up, to catch the start of that lazy trumpet solo in Dinah Washington's 'Give Me Back My Tears'. Our Marilyn blows a loud kiss. A real smackeroo at that retreating camera. Waving daintily and mouthing the words, *Bye-bye Baby, good-night*.

Cut-to-black, and that TEMBO® Bindi, the silhouette of a rearing Bull elephant. And the legend: 'Your life, safe in our hands.'

More Chauffeur than Autopilot, the Automatron would ride the speed-limit, and that amber-light at the intersection. It would overtake where expedient, bartering with other automobiles on that Open-road, according to a mind-bogglingly complex 'Priority Matrix'.

It'd 'Get you there', the by-line for the BENZ® Maybach 6ec Cabriolet, if you were running late. And could cruise if you'd 'Time to Kill', another by-line, this time for the Bimmer® XES *Coupé*.

In short, the Automatron had revolutionised that traditional ideation of your passive A.I. agent. That accepted image of a tinny-sounding synthesised *Vox*.BOT, on the other end of a copperwire. Conducting automated feedback surveys; waiting on a touch-tone keypad, or Voice-*prompt* before moving onto the next question.

No, this Automatron was to be decisive, and dynamic. Capable of making split-second *Life* or Death decisions, on-the-fly—in *fah* real *Time*.

It was to be one of three epoch defining innovations, that'd totally transform the automobile industry: The first being the switch to electricity; then came the introduction of the PonFleischmann® Solid-state Cold-*fusion* Reactor, and the corresponding switch to Heavy-water; and finally, the unveiling of the Heuristically programmed ALgorithm, HAL-9000[51] at the HAL Laboratories in Urbana, Illinois—dubbed the Godfather of Automatrons.

The advent of the BAE® *Harrier*-taxi, that fourth giant leap forward, being technically viewed as more of a benchmark in Aviation.

Since the unveiling of the Automatron, road fatalities had fallen year-on-year. Most of your Open-road accidents being attributable to *Human* agency—intervention; those 'Manualists', and their continued abuse of the mandatory 'Manual override' setting, and unlawful use of *Clock*'d speed-inhibitors.

That being said, this 'Automotive revolution' was to be heavily government subsidised. The unprecedented provision of Capital, enabling the automobile industry to introduced third-party financing packages, featuring comprehensive Hard-*slash*-Soft component warrantees. That'd render this new tech, both universally safe, and universally affordable.

Overnight, that notion of the automobile being 'Personal property', was to be erased from the Zeitgeist. The automobile, and those cutting-edged technologies housed therein, remaining *in perpetuity* the property of the manufacturers. The license and lease, thus finally coming of age.

With mandatory quarterly servicing, certified software updates, and quadruple A-rated security becoming industry norms. An entire ecosystem of subsidiary service providers was to sprout-up—seemingly overnight, to assist manufacturers with administering this regulatory burden.

Certainly, the wider cultural impact of the Automatron could not be overstated. Its dawn seeing the 'grounded' afforded their very own take on that 'Mile High Club'. Your compulsory *Human*-interest newstream feature, featuring instances of newly wed same-sex couples, caught spooning in blacked-out Urban Roadrunners. On the way to the Aerodrome, and that exotic Honeymooner's retreat in Ocho Rios.

The Automatron being left to drive, our passengers—Tonx, Sef, and Marl—set about tucking into their respective *ChirpyChirp* Chicken® Meal Deals.

But it wasn't long before they found themselves stuck at a deserted intersection. The Securicor® Traffic-light having turned on them, against the flow of traffic.

With the automobile sat idling, the Automatron continued to diligently scan its surroundings. Though nothing was to cross that crossing.

Inside the cab, Marl broke the silence.

Sniff

"What—no tunes?" he said, slurping on his Mega-bucket Cola.

Sef chirps'd his teeth.

"*Llou*-it, Em-*Man*."

Putting down his Cola, Marl fished-out a handful of French fries, dipping them liberally in BQ sauce.

"What? We observing a moment's silence for my-*Man*'s taillight?"

Burp

Sef looked-up from picking-out mayo-drenched lettuce leaves, from his *ChirpyChirp* Chicken® Flame-grilled breast-fillet burger.

"Oy—what'd I say?"

"These lights are taking the *piss*," Tonx then chipped-in. Chirps'ing his teeth and looking backwards over his shoulder, at that intersection.

Meanwhile, Out-*there* in der Lebenswelt, an Onyx-BLK BENZ® 920se SUV pulled-up alongside. Its hydraulic suspension riding comfortably high; globules of rain clinging to its Lieberman® Solid-sheen Turtleshell *anti*-Smear All-weather coating, like beads of sweat.

For some time now, the two Automatrons had been about conferring over the airwaves, collating traffic-flow data. The TEMBO® flagging the *Clock*'d Bimmer® it'd clock'd earlier. A *Blinking* red 'Status indicator' denoting the threat it posed to those on the Open-road.

But just-now, and for no apparent reason, that *vari*-tint window facing turned limpid.

Coppin' the BENZ® out the back window, Tonx had relaxed a little. And now, sensing that moody lighting pouring forth into the night, the muzik threatening to punch its way out of the compact confines of that cab. He even hazarded a nosy inside.

There, framed in that window. A prim looking *Beenie*, more woman than *Grrrl* was paying the World little mind. Dolled-up as it was, to the nines for a night-out on the tiles. An Estelle® *Forever 21* lace-veil obscuring the top half of its boatrace, like an ÜBER-hero's mask.

It had a Flappers® *Ms Holly Golightly* cigarette-filter clenched betwixt its teeth. A tail of smoke spiralling-up from a rolled spliff, toward that ceiling of the cab. And appeared clearly in the Zone, its smoky made-up eyes closed; its head cotch'd against the matte BLK-leather hand-stitched headrest, of that reversed driver's seat.

And then, another exotic looking specimen was seen to sprout from the lap of the first. Its ripening features, teetering upon that cusp of womanhood.

Clambering-up the automobile door, it clung onto the lip of that window frame, like a mermaid, or a Siren *even*. The image suggestive of a serpentine lower Body, and fish-*like* tail, treading-water in that fluid, smoky environ of the cab.

Its smouldering, made-up eyes stared then, unabashed into the SUV; as if able to peer through its *vari*-tint windows. The Siren apparently looking for someone — or something.

For sure, it might've been at a resort hotel in Ibiza — *say*, or an Amnesia rave. Clung onto the edge of a swimming pool, locked into that steady
UMPH...UMPH...
UMPH...UMPH...
UMPH...UMPH...

of a punchy techno-*Kik*. That was like a Star-child, pounding upon the inner walls of its womb. That soundtrack of the night swirling all around it, conveying a sense of *Time*—of urgency, as it built-up to that anthemic chorus. And a host of angelic voices, chorusing:

[Sing] *We could be Heroes...*

Heroes...Heroes...

The Siren then, mouthing that all-important caveat, [Sing] *just for a day*. Before closing its eyes. Biting down upon its bottom lip to retreat yet deeper into that groove. The upper portion of its Body, swerving synchronous to that bassline.

Following Tonx's gaze, Sef turned to clock this spectacle, the BENZ® and those two Sirens. Just as one of 'em flashed a hand-signal, scissor'd fingers *Snip-snipping* away at the air.

Blink

Blink

And then came that chorus again. The pair now, looking longingly into each other's eyes, to mouth those faithful words—

[Sing] *We could be Heroes...*

They paused then. The measure of a Heartbeat. Before finally erupting in a fit of skiggles. The window turning opaque.

Tonx and Sef exchanging a knowing look.

Bait.

Yeah—bait.

Whilst parked on that backseat, Marl slurped from his Mega-bucket Cola. Oblivious to it all—seemingly.

"By rights it should run on flow," Tonx said, biting into his genetically enlarged breast of chicken. "If there ain't no traffic coming the other way," he continued—chewing. "The lights shouldn't switch at all."

Sef sipped sparingly from his Mega-bucket Cola. And then, bit into his own breast-fillet burger, relishing that slight crunch of the lightly toasted Sesame seed bun.

"Nah Bubba, they switch regardless," he said—chewing.

"Yeah, but they shouldn't—*ya*-get me."

Tonx swallowed. And washed the stringy chicken breast down with a slurp of Cola.

"It's *phf'king* spooky is all—"

Burp

He slotted the Mega-bucket back into one of the automobiles copious cupholders, to continue eating. Whilst, sipping sparingly from his own Cola, Sef said nada.

Scoffing another mouthful of modified chicken breast. Tonx then starts rummaging through his box, apparently on a whim.

Sniff

"What—only one Breast?"

He looked to Marl unimpressed.

"You know how Chirpy-Chirp stay," Marl explained.

"Yeah *phf'kry*," Tonx said, now clearly labouring with the fibrous eating.

Out-*there* in der Lebenswelt, the Traffic-lights changed. *Wink*-ing through the sequence of colors in reverse.

And setting-off, the BENZ® and TEMBO® now vied for that Open-road, the two lanes being set to merge *a*-ways up-ahead.

At some point, that 'Priority Matrix' kicked-in, the TEMBO® given priority over the BENZ®. And noticing the other automobile slotting-in behind, Tonx was seen to relax a-little more.

"Oy—my-*Man*'s tings alright still," he said, chewing in a dry mouth.

"What—you tried sum?"

Sef sounded more surprised than he looked.

"Yeah—I had *a*-liccle taste," Tonx confessed, slurping on his Cola.

To wit, Sef said *semmi*.

Polishing-off his Fillet-burger, he held his greasy mitts aloft; Marl obligingly handing him a wod of paper towels, and a few MyFresh™ handy-wipe sachets.

Sef wiping his mouth, and then his hands. Filling the cab with that faux-lime aroma of the fragranced handy-wipe. And gathering his rubbish, scrunched it up into a tidy *liccle* eco-friendly ball. Setting it down by his feet, to retrieve the SONY® MZ-RH1 Portable MiniDisc player-*slash*-recorder, he'd stashed there previously.

Checking for the blue connection light, he placed the tiny device on his lap. And fishing-out a *Miswak* from a pocket, proceeded to clean his teeth.

"Oy—it was just *a*-taste Sef-*Man*."

And here was Tonx, now feeling *a*-way.

SUS

"Did I say any-ting?" Sef responded, sucking air through his teeth.

Tonx slurped on his Cola.

"I feel kind-a charged still," he admitted then, before taking another bite of chicken breast.

"You wanna play the ting for my-*Man*?" Sef said, not swallowing the bait.

Looking disgruntled at that half-eaten chicken breast he held in his mitt, Tonx plopped it back in the box.

"You know what. I don't think I'm gonna bother with Chirpy-Chirp no more," he said, finding a paper towel.

He wiped his greasy mitts, and mouth. And balling his rubbish, stashed it under the seat. He then addressed the Automatron.

"Play auxiliary."

It responding with an audible-*prompt*. That auxiliary signal path fading up imperceptibly—almost. The ruckus of a Soundclash Mixtape, 'Two-in-the-Hardway: Metromedia *vs*. Body Fusion', washing-over the cab like a tidal wave. Like *Time*-travel, transporting all and sundry back, back, back to Montego Bay, Jamaica. Christmas just-now gone. As if by magic-*like*,

[Sing] *If its mag-ic* [52]
Then why can't it be
Ev-er-lasting...

Your first time hearing it. Such a soundscape. Indescribable. The *Vibes* being, both literally and figuratively, *Live*—and lively.

The *Buzz* of the crowd swimming in that fuzz of static; the wails, and cheers, and jeers of Rude-*Grrrls*, and Bad-*Boyz*; the hum of the rigs—hulking towers of custom build tweeters, bass speakers and mids; and that mournful din of a lone Vuvuzela, like a primal scream. The cries of Senzangakhona, imported all the way from the Southwestern townships, cutting through that stifling heat of a Jamaican winter. The night still ringing with sweat, after an all too brief shower.

Fever pitched. It was Dancehall. It was Bashment. It was the Soundclash *Champions of Champions* Championship™, brought to you in association with Baum® Electronix—'for that soundtrack of your *Life*'.

Truly, you could've cut the atmosphere with a machete. The recording, though transparent, seeped in a nostalgia all its own.

Drenched in it *even*, like Dunn's River Plateau® *Hot* sauce.

The Baum® in-car entertainment system having all but vanish'd. That atmosphere inside the cab had become charged—as in, electrified.
Electrifying.

You'd these two sets: Metromedia, hailing from Kingston-JA; and Body Fusion, representing London-UK. Whom, between the two of 'em, had managed to lay waste to *la crème de la crème* of foreign and domestic Soundsystems, during the hotly contested rounds—
Heats.

The likes of Stone Love, Coxsone, Saxon, Jah Shaka and King Tubbys, Southern Comfort, Mighty Crown, La Banlieue Marsaille, and Santísima Madre, to name but a few.

Up for grabs, a mounted solid gold 45" vinyl-disc—the coveted prize. A cool one million (J$)—a princely sum. And the prestige of being the #1 Soundsystem for that year.

And a very Merry Christmas to you.

The reigning World Champions, Bodyguard, had only just-now been KO'd in the other *semi*-final. By a relative newcomer, hailing from *New York* City-State, BX Block-Party. The upset immediately becoming the stuff of Legend, the *Yankees* having wrestled victory from the jaws of defeat with their very last dubplate special, what was L. Boogie's 'ÜBER-star'.[53]

Reworking the lyric over the original backing. The gracious Ms. Hill had been about gunning all and sundry in that Bodyguard line-up, from *Dibby-dibby* Deejay to *Duppy MCee*—whatcha

[Sing] *Com'on Bodyguard light my fire*
Every plate you draw is so tired
The Deejay is s'posed to inspire
So how come we nah gettin' no higher?

Upon first hearing, the Montego Bay massive, being familiar with the tune, and yet thrown to hear it in a Soundclash setting. Had preceded to *mash*-down the place, with raucous praise.

That markedly frosty reception, of this commingling of Locals, Tourists, Pilgrims, and Soundsystem *Aficionados* drawn here from around the World, having ebbed more and more towards grudging respect—for these "Bomba-claat *Yankee* upstarts"—as the *Heat* intensified.

SUS

"Gwon wit ya-self", becoming like a clarion call, cutting through the din of that lone Vuvuzella.

Yeah, The Space Cowboy, Kool Herc's Prodigy—Deejay for BX Block-Party, had had to drawback the track t'ree-times—*Ayah*. Each rewind endearing *dem-who-come-a-foreign* in the Hearts and minds of the Native born.

All that being said. From the offing, so-called impartial commentators and pundits alike, had admitted to being mightily impressed with the sheer weight of the BX rig.

Indeed, reports were even coming-in from the MIR Space Station, sat in orbit 200-odd *kims* above the Earth. Apparently, even from Space, the whole of Jamaica could be seen bubbling. The seismic Richter scale reading a troubling 9-spot-5.

Yeah, the ting had been live. The ting had been fresh, and big—*Bubba*, as in massive, as in Mega Banton—

[Sing] *Have you ever heard a Sound* [54]
Play so heavy and so clear...

Having waited till the last to draw this, their trump card. BX had indeed gone clear. The Justice for the Peace calling time and awarding the Heat to the loudest cheer.

Though, none present would've doubted the Soundclash veterans—Bodyguard, *could-a murda dem fi sheer Dubplate*. If given an opportunity to respond.

Now, weeks after the event, the whole of Jamaica wouldn't bare a release of the recording. And accordingly, neither original nor bootleg ever saw the light of day.

It went without saying, the final showdown, between BX Block-Party and Metromedia was to be a no-contest. The Prime Minister of Jamaica having made it a matter of National pride. It also went without saying, that that recording was to be distributed far and wide.

Sef, being a *Gheezah*. He'd managed to blag a copy of a copy of a bootleg copy of the not so hotly contested other *semi*-final.

It'd been a dead *Heat* thus far. And in an attempt to break the deadlock, both Sounds had agreed to go version for version. Which was typical in such instances, the format making it easier to gauge the crowd's response.

This being the state of play. Metromedia's Deejay, Mr Scaramanga, had drawn a Scarborough *Man* exclusive, 'Sound-Boy Fi Dead'. It was the crowds animated response—on the first hearing—that was currently reverberating around that compact environ of the *Ubuntu* cab.

Though the full impact was to be stifled somewhat, by the ambient lighting—which was set to 100-*percent*. The vibes were lively still, as Metromedia's Master of Ceremony, the Right and Honourable Mr Mtumé, pleaded with his Deejay to "WHEEEEEL AND PULL-UP" over the track now spinning rapidly in reverse.

"AND NOW...AND NOW...AND NOW... IF YOU'D BE SO KIND...BE SO KIND...BE SO KIND... MR DEEJAY...MR DEEJAY...MR DEEJAY... COME AGAIN...COME AGAIN...COME AGAIN," Mr Mtumé chorused, his voice coming across crisp and clear.

That extended *Delay* of the digital FX generator, used to wet the *mic*, carrying the muscular tenure of his pipes to those four corners of the Globe.

It being theatre after-all.

"ME BEG YAH...ME BEG YAH...ME BEG YAH..." he said, and reaching into his cavernous, barrel-chest, added—with a fistful of breath, "COME WID IT...COME WID IT...COME WID IT..."

An Air-raid siren wailed. An uneasy hush of anticipation gripping the crowd. The sampled crackle from a vinyl recording then broke, an exercise of creative license that'd come to characterise such *Artefacts*.

Those Dubplates and Specials, that were part and parcel of the whole Revivalist Movement and experience. Its attempt at pushing-back against that unrelenting tide of anodyne machine-generated muzik. Like an outstretched hand, reaching back through *Time*; that trace of yesteryear, harkening back to a-thousandfold Soundsystems of old.

The riddem then kicked-in. A Smiley & Gumble dancehall reworking of the *virtua*-Artist, A-Dollar-Fiddy's 'Microwave Rappers'. The rap anthem that'd been tearing-up the download-*slash*-streams chart, prior to the whole 'Mos Mos Fresh debacle'.

Then, it was the indomitable throaty twang of Scarborough *Man*, his booming bass tone, like that of the voice of God:

"NOW JAH KNOW—DEM NAH READY FI DIS. DAH WORD MADE FLESH. TRENCHTOWN—BLESS. SCARBOROUGH. JAM DOWN—HOLD

TIGHT YEAH. METROMEDIA. THE *MAN*-LIKE SCARAMANGA. MTUMÉ — HOLD TIGHT."

Like all good Deejay, Scarborough *Man* began by talking-up the track, stoking the fire.

"NOW HEAR DIS—"
[Rap] *Man fi Dead* [55]
Yah nah say, we nah save no lead
Gunshot me bus in Body Fusion Head
Man fi DEAD!

The crowd went BALLISTIC. The venue reeling from the hail of that lone Vuvuzella. And listening to it, it was like a stationary stampede. The herd rooted to the spot, like chattel stowed below decks during that middle-passage.

It was that raw emotion — that force — unleashed. Unlocked at that moment, like lightning captured in a bottle, so as, you might peer at it through the glass. The incidence of an electromagnetic energy discharge, resulting from the transmigration of that waveform into an impulse — that is

ULTRA…ULTRA…ULTRA-MAG-*NETIC*
Pure, unadulterated inspiration — *like*
Fire!
Like, *THUNDER*
THUNDER
THUNDERCATS
HOE!

It blazing a trail of unfiltered light — *Life* — conducted through clouds of photons, so as, you might point at it and whisper — in awe.

"Yes — *Man!* Yes. I see it. I feel it."

"BASSLINE…BASSLINE…BASSLINE," Mr Mtumé piped-in. Heralding that on-rush of a meaty intelligence of Bottom-end frequencies, that struck like a balled-fist.

The warmth of that bassline was seen to radiate then. From somewhere near the Earth's core. Picture a filament heater — *say*, a truly massive one. Where you'd hold your hands out in front of it and gather its warmth unto you. And even carry it away in your chest.

Suffice to say, the whole *Vibe* was cranked-up a good few notches. But then, out of nowhere…

Gunshot.

BLAP BLAP-BLAP

"HOL' ON...HOL' ON...HOL 'ON..."

Mr Mtumé immediately called halt to the proceedings.

"ME-*SAY*—HOL' ON...HOL' ON...HOL' ON..."

He made sure to repeat himself, for all those who'd failed to catch it first time. Jeers and murmurs holding the crowd fast like cement, most of those present being apparently none-the-wiser.

"Wha-*ya* chat bout—hush *ya*-mout...hush *ya*-mout...hush *ya*-mout..."

Mr Mtumé was then heard off-*piste*—off-mic, putting down hecklers.

"Yah-*na* 'ear me...Yah-*na* 'ear me...Yah-*na* 'ear me... Me-*say*—hush *ya*-mout...hush *ya*-mout...hush *ya*-mout..."

Deprived of the warmth of that bassline, the recording quickly cooled. That temper of the crowd, a jumble of unfettered voices scrambling one over the other, becoming an unruly and impenetrable wall of noise.

"ME-BEG-*YA* RUDEBOY...RUDEBOY...RUDEBOY... ME-BEG-YA RUDE-BOY...RUDEBOY...RUDEBOY..."

"And Rude-*Grrrl*...Rude-*Grrrl*...Rude-*Grrrl*..."

An anonymous voice pitched in.

"Hear 'im nah—Skinning-teeth—*a*-tru dat...*a*-tru dat...*a*-tru dat..."

Mr Mtumé stood corrected.

"AND RUDE-*GRRRL*...AND RUDE-*GRRRL*...AND RUDE-*GRRRL*... FOR JAH KNOW—WE NAH WANT FI DISCRIMINATE INNA JAMAICA...INNA JAMAICA...INNA JAMAICA..."

That amplified hum of electrostatic, now vied with that brute force of the crowd, to fill a sudden lull. The MCee being distracted momentarily, by events off-*piste*. Futile attempts at identifying, what was presumed to be a lowdown, gun-toting *Raggamuffin*.

"ME BEG-YA...ME BEG-YA...ME BEG-YA... DON'T BRING...DON'T BRING...DON'T BRING... YOUR ILL WILL...YOUR ILL WILL...YOUR ILL WILL... INNA DIS ERE TING...DIS ERE TING...DIS ERE TING..."

Mr Mtumé was now seen to chastise his congregation; as if he were an evangelising Pastor, preaching redemption from the pulpit.

"FAH JAH KNOW...FAH JAH KNOW...FAH JAH KNOW... RIGHT NOW... RIGHT NOW...RIGHT NOW... DAH EYES OF DAH WORLD DEH PON JAMAICA...DEH PON JAMAICA...DEH PON JAMAICA... PEACE AND

LOVE...PEACE AND LOVE...PEACE AND LOVE... IS WHAT WE WANT—INNIT...IS WHAT WE WANT—INNIT...IS WHAT WE WANT—INNIT... PEACE AND LOVE...PEACE AND LOVE...PEACE AND LOVE... PEACE AND LOVE... PEACE AND LOVE...PEACE AND LOVE... ME *SAY*—PEACE AND LOVE... PEACE AND LOVE...PEACE AND LOVE..."

The crowd seemed placated. But it was impossible to gauge what impact these words had had. What with the hum of static, crackling and *Buzzing* uninterrupted, in an interval of relative calm.

"AND NOW...AND NOW...AND NOW..." Mr Mtumé continued, seizing the moment. "If you please—Mr Deejay-Sir...Mr Deejay-Sir...Mr Deejay-Sir...

[Monster-breath]
RUN DAH PHF'KIN TRAK...DAH PHF'KIN TRAK...DAH PHF'KIN TRAK ..."

The Air-raid siren blared. Now accompanied by the wail of that lone Vuvuzella, the combination threatening to punch its way out of the cab. The crackle of vinyl then added another layer of texture to the soundscape, the version seemingly cranking-up.

Then, last but not least, came the toast.

"NOW JAH KNOW—DEM NAH READY FI DIS. DAH WORD MADE FLESH. TRENCHTOWN—BLESS. SCARBOROUGH. JAM DOWN—HOLD TIGHT YEAH. METROMEDIA. THE *MAN* LIKE SCARAMANGA. MTUMÉ—HOLD TIGHT."

"So what? You didn't see nuttun?"
Tonx now pitched his voice to speak comfortably over that Soundclash kicking-off in the cab. His attention divided between the back-window and his 'Business' *Pod*, which he'd just-now fished-out to call-up the dash display.

"The Eye was on the whole time—Bubba," Sef said, still cleaning his teeth.

Having seem the BENZ® turn-off, Tonx was now about puzzling the pair of headlights that'd replaced it. It being impossible to tell the model and make of the automobile from that distance. What with its full beams dancing-off that slick surface of the Open-road, creating a dazzling wall of light.

Still charged, from his taste. And feeling increasingly *digy*. He now sensed something *Sus*—suspicious and purposeful—in the way the whip kept its distance. As if under the influence of a Manualist.

And just-now, a call came up on-screen, the *Pod* vibrating vigorously in his hand. But although he knew the name and boatrace, Tonx nevertheless sent the call straight to *Vox*.BOT.

"A-*who* dat? The *Misses*?"

Sef paused from what he was about to look-over.

"Yeah," Tonx replied, returning to looking-out that rear window.

He took a hot-minute to get his bearings, whilst the Pod-screen reverted to displaying the dashboard. The pristine 3D rendering of that Borges Map of Out-*there*, quickly becoming infected with *Blinking* red and green-dots.

Now framed in the automobile's windows, the ol' Kent Road was giving way to the Elley. The Automatron having opted for Blackfriars as the most opportune point to cross the Thames.

"What—on your Business Pod?" Sef averred, examining the ends of his miswak.

"Ya-get me."

Focusing once again on his *Pod*-screen. Tonx zoomed-in on that *Blinking* red-dot tailing them. To Google® it.

And watching him, Sef now thought to fish-out his own Cell—which he was in the habit of keeping on silent.

Seen as everyone had finished eating, Marl decided to leave the rest of his Value Meal for later. Taking a few quick slurps from his Mega-bucket Cola, to wash down this fodder, a prelude to cleaning-up after himself.

He then retrieved the pistol—which he'd stashed under the seat, and commenced with pawing over it.

"The eye couldn't have been on," Tonx said, looking after him.

"You what?"

Speaking around the miswak, Sef now appeared engrossed in checking his Cell, for *Missed Calls*.

"The eye. It couldn't have been on," Tonx repeated.

"How-*ya* mean?"

"It keys off the auto, and the auto was off."

"*Yeah*—but the electrics were on though."

Sef looked-up from his Cell.

"What whip you know can run the scanner off the electrics whilst parked? It'd *phf'king* drain the battery."

Tonx and Sef were now looking after each other. The exchange seeming to continue telepathically.

"So what—there ain't Vox commands off the electrics?"

"*Phf'koff* Sef-*Man*," Tonx said, staring fixedly after him. "You're starting to *piss* me off now."

Sef shook his head dismissively, and chirps'd his teeth.

"That's what I'm saying Bubba. With you, it only takes a sniff. Now my-*Man*'s gonna be prang for the rest of the night—you watch."

Looking to the miswak, he turned it about to start-in on the other end.

"You need to fix-up—*Ayah*."

"Trus me, I can handle my *Buzz*."

Tonx returned to eyeballing his *Pod*-screen, and that 'Searching' visual-*prompt*—a multicoloured wheel spinning away aimlessly.

"*Al*-right—Mr Stephen-*phf'king*-Hawking."

Sef paused from cleaning his teeth.

"How I manage to turn-on the Stereo? By waving *me*-flippin' hand?"

"You can do that now you know—gesture control," Marl said, chipping -in his two pennies worth. The true portent of the conversation flying clean over his head.

"You what?"

Tonx now looked after *my-Man*.

"And what the you doing listening to tune when you're s'posed to be keeping dog? Why not just cotch and wrap-*a Zoo-zoo* while you're at it?"

"There's an idea. Oy *Em*—I beg you wrap one," Sef said, pausing in the process of sending a *Txt*.

And it was as if my-*Man* had read his mind, Marl immediately stowing the pistol away in his hoodie pocket.

"Pass me the *ting* then," he said, now feeling about his person for the accoutrements.

"Oy—wha-*ya* dealing wit? Can't you see the *Feds* there—prowling. What the *phf'k* Sef-*Man*?"

Tonx looked proper piss'd, the search having bounced back '423_Client_(E)RRR_MSSG'. Which he presumed meant 'Subject Out of Range'.

"What *Feds*—you didn't say nuttun about Feds?"

It was now Sef's turn to peer-out that rear window.

"What—you mean them?" he said, somewhat unconvinced.

Sniff

"Is you-*one* said you'd keep dog."

And here was Tonx wheeling the conversation back around.

"Me keep dog—which part? Let Youngblood keep dog."

Sef stashed his Cell to start-in on his teeth. Contorting his boatrace to get at the back of his gulliver.

And with this momentary lull in the exchange, Marl now took the opportunity to ask for a baggy.

"Oy—Sef? You got the ting?"

"Hol' up."

Prising a baggy loose, from the wod he'd bundled together with an elastic band. Sef was to toss it at him.

"Did you, or did you not tell *my-Man* to leave the Bucky in the auto. And that you'd keep-dog if any-ting?"

Finishing with his Queen's Council turn, Tonx again hit the search button.

"That's not what I said. Oy—*Check-it*..."

Sef paused from cleaning his teeth.

"I said for my-*Man*—He pointed with the miswak at Marl—to leave the ting cos he wouldn't need it. It's mia famiglia—*forphf'ksake*. What's he bowling in there with a Bucky doing?"

Sucking air through his teeth, he continued, "this ain't t'ree in da hardway, and *my-Man* wasn't exactly bout to bump you."

Again, Sef paused to suck air through his teeth, then added, "I would've come with—two-*twos*. But, I still owed *my-Man* for *a*-liccle sa-(*hmm*) sa-(*hmm*)."

"Who gives a toss? At the end of the day, you still let some random-*Bod* vandalize my ride."

"I thought the Eye was on—*what*."

"The Eye don't *phf'king* run off the electrics. That's what I've been trying to tell-*ya*."

Tonx and Sef were again eyeballing each other. The tension in the cab, seeming to mirror that of the Soundclash, that'd taken over the in-car entertainment system.

"How was I s'posed to know that?" Sef said. At last climbing-down from off his high-horse.

Breaking eye contact. He looked then, to the miswak, whilst running his tongue against the walls of his teeth.

Sniff

"If you were doing what you were s'posed to be doing—keeping dog—then it wouldn't matter would it?" Tonx said. "It ain't like you don't know how they stay Sou-*phf* of the river. You're always there."

Clearly, he wasn't for letting it slid.

Having repeatedly gotten no joy, googling that *Blinking* red-dot following on that Borges Map of Out-*there*. He felt no-way airing his mounting frustration.

"And now, I gotta go back to the Service centre," he continued, "and what's the first thing they're gonna ask—"

"Was there anyone in the vehicle at the time?" Sef chimed-in.

"Was there anyone in the *phf'king* ride."

Tonx chirps'd his teeth.

"So what—you want-*me* reimburse you?"

"Nah—Shaking his head—I don't want you to reimburse me. Of course, I *phf'king* want you to reimburse me. That goes without saying."

Tonx was now watching Marl bil'ing-up, all *blasé-blasé*. As if he hadn't *a*-care in the world.

"Oy—*llou*-it *Em-Man*. We're roasting enough as it is," he said, returning to watching that spinning wheel.

"But the *Feds* can't just stop you for no reason."

Marl though to state the obvious.

He'd only just-now finished putting together the skins. But nevertheless, was to make a show of scrunching-up the whole thing.

"Oy, I thought this wipe was s'posed to be copasetic?" Sef added then, gesturing for him to return the baggy.

"Not with a busted taillight it ain't," Tonx said, pressing that search button for the umpteenth time.

[SING] *OH—THE GOOD LIFE*

And they all lived *happily-ever-after*. And yeah, it was real, as in tangible. Substantive and substantial.

Something one could feel. Something one might point to—point at, like one's own reflection in the mirror.

"Look at me," they'd say, with neither reservation nor remorse. "Look at us, living that Good Life."

They'd sing it *even*. Their number, their DNA sequence having come-up in that age ol' Celestial Lottery. What were the odds?

A million-to-one?

A billion?

A squigillion?

Luck? What Luck?

How quickly they'd learnt to march in-step, to clap their hands in-time. To lend their brittle voices to that Chorus of Elect. Have their prayers hoisted up, up and away to Heaven. To that one lonely ear of your *god-of-always-listening*.

It being right to give thanks and praise—

Amen.

And over time, they'd come to recognise themselves, in that conviction held in their voices, fortifying their song.

That *ever-so* slow encroach of emphatic-*ism*—fanatic-*ism*. The truth of it being such, it'd always been thus. *Them*, and us.

The facts of Life.

Comfortable. Happy. Contented even. They'd sing.

[SING] *OH—THE GOOD LIFE*

Their heads squished-up against that glass ceiling, they'd sing. Sing their bloody Hearts out.

And why not?

[Sing] *Oh—the Good Life*
Full of fun, seems to be the ideal
Hmmm—the Good Life
Let's you hide all the sadness you feel…

"Look-see there, there's us," they'd say, pointing at a recent Polaroid™ of the Unit. Mother and Father Christmas, and those 2.24 Sprogs—smiles beaming. A picture-perfect Kodak® moment.

Soft, moisturised and manicured hands. How quickly they'd learnt to grip tight, that inalienable right to live that Good *Life*—that Good *Living*. How quickly it'd become as second nature, and all they'd ever known.

Privilege? What privilege?

And yet, it knew strife, that Good *Life*. And struggle. It being strived for and earned; fought for and won. Though victory might be assured, enshrined even, in tomes of binding Natural Law.

As infallible as Physics, or Economics—*Amen*. As unanimous as that Chorus of Elect—*Amen*. As certain as the day after today will be tomorrow; as predetermined as tomorrow.

It being ordained, and god's Will after all—*Amen*.

This apparently godforsaken Planet, being likened to a glass of unpasteurised milk. Invariably—inevitably, the cream was to be seen slowly rising to the top.

As if by magic.

Whilst, hidden in a cave somewhere, behind that veneer of der Lebenswelt—the Everyday. The *Turn* was to be found lurking.

It'd be those subtle arts of the Ingenieur, leading to the pay-off. The Prestige. *Life* being, according to that Blackest of Bards, but a Stage. And them, mere actors upon it.

Privilege? What you on about?

It'd be lashings of rapturous applause, and them taking their bows. Their dues having been paid, well and truly.

Hard-graft, toil and sweat for the sake of the children. Hard-graft, toil and sweat for the sake of the children's children. And just like that, it'd boil down to a matter of *Life* and Death.

Still, tis said, they sing *oh-so* sweetly. Like caged nightingales.
[Sing] *You won't really fall in love*
For you can't take the chance
So please, be honest with yourself
—don't try to fake romance…

Here's to that Good *Life*, then. An artificial wharf cut into the banks of the Regents Canal. A flotilla of brightly painted barges berthed along the quay.

Paved and well-lit walkways, weaving together the fabric of a complex of office buildings; panoptic open-plan floors dissected by moveable partitioning, and standardised furnishing. Panes of Nimbey® photovoltaic glass lending these structures their transparency. The lights left on throughout the night, though nobody's home.

Over that wall, there. It'd be smart townhouses, stacked one atop the other, like giant LEGO® building blocks. The architectural style, reminiscent of those staggered steps of Machu Picchu. Triple-glazed patios, fronting onto sizeable verandas, carpeted with closely cropped grass; verdant hanging gardens clinging onto the building's horizontal façade.

Squirrelled away in the grounds of this gated community, there'd be an enchanted grotto; Valhöll® KOTILIESI log-burning outdoor heaters, and cosy cushioned KIERKE® *Asyl* garden furniture. And spotlighting, woven into a lush, thick canopy of willow and birch.

Exposed to the elements, it'd be home to a remnant of those Elementals of Paracelsus. The imposing seat of Titania and Oberon, revealed in the light of an inebriated moon. That proud retinue of princely Lords and Ladies, woven together by strands of greying hair.

Presently, this Court was about lounging. The Clutch—ever your cliché, comprising one of every Mother and Father Christmas archetype; comely ripened *Milfs*, lithe predatory Cougars, cuddly cerebral *Alpha-*Males, chisel-featured Amazonians, and adonis-*ized* Machismos.

Barely visible beneath this veneer of civility, a brooding prehistoric Beast would languish. Subverted by language, and alopecia.

Sterile, economical gestures, belying the patter of cordial stroking, and mutual grooming. Lingering eye contact, playing the surrogate for

[SING] *OH—THE GOOD LIFE*

a good ol' fashioned snog.

After a day spent foraging, for yield—for growth. This domesticated troop of Homo sapiens would find occasion to come together. To reaffirm mutual bonds; what was a well-established pecking—the vaunted diadem of Oberon. To shake deprecating fists up at that dwindling Sun. And hoot, wholeheartedly, at the Moon—under their breaths.

You might even say, being conscientious, and sociable. They gathered thus, to affirm and validate their meaningful and impactful Lives. Though, always with an eye cast upon the relatively meaningless, and less impactful lives of Others.

It being essentially. *Them*, and us—as said.

On such occasions, with the day waning, and lengthening shadows heralding that approach of evening. The Trendies would take to quaffing *La Sangre de Dios*; the mulled variety of the Chilean Syrah, to counter that chill in the air. Served in ornate handcrafted coffee-mugs—they each brought with them. And poured from a thermal-active quart-sized carton, primed to über-heat the tipple instantly, upon first opening.

Worshipped like an Idol, it'd pride of place at this impromptu banquet. Each member of the clutch contributing a-little *something-something*, to make of it a venerable feast of Ceres.

The patio-table being that *Faultline*, where you'd find the produce of globalisation, and glocalisation, those carefully packaged creature-comforts, engaged in a bitterly fought gladiatorial bout to the Death.

Then, it'd be flaxen-locked, half-naked cherubs playing by the heated pool, always within earshot. Mollycoddled by a gaggle of sun-kissed *Au pairs*, sprinkled liberally about this idyllic Baroque fresco, like Piccaninnies. That Mediterranean *Esprit*, having been tapped, bottled, and shipped-out as sparkling SanPellegrino®.

Undoubtedly, here the living was good. More than *even*. All they really needed was *Love*. And that holiday home in Bordeaux, or Tuscany; there being excellent fishing in the Wine Country. And that third *Broom-Broom*, for the school run—the au pair having only just-now learnt to drive. Such modest creature-comforts, making it all the more worthwhile.

Their lives being *Styled* thus, they'd even a rationale for it. Everyone wanting-needing to do their bit for the Trade-War effort. The conflict, likely to be waged *in perpetuity*.

And certainly, inside this gated community. The consensus was, that it was all-good. And that was to be true, not just there, but everywhere. And all the time. It being *#Happiness* trending. It being trendy to be happy.

[Sing] *It's the good life to be free*
And explore the unknown
Like the heartaches, when you learn
You must face them alone.

From the Tradesman's entrance, there came the CHIME of the Securicor™ *Welcome* intercom.

And harkening to it, our Mother Christmas was to sit-up, her mousy nose twitching at the air. Whilst, without overly exerting himself, her Father Christmas reached for his key-fob, to *Bzzz*-in whomever-it-was.

"D'you think they know where they're going?" she posited, addressing everyone (as in, no one in particular). Taking an altruistic interest, as she waited for whomever-it-was to appear from behind that thicket wall; contrived to shield this darling little grotto from would-be prying eyes.

"Do they know where they're going?"

The query did the rounds, changing inflection *ever-so* slightly, like in a game of Chinese whisper.

Whomever-it-was appearing just-now, sporting a plain Brilliant-bright tank-top, over which they wore a Fluorescent-yellow *Hi-vis* vest; Bright-orange *Dickies*® overalls, tied about the waist; Timberlake® Nubuck Steel-toe safety-boots; a Matte-BLK Crash-helmet hiding their boatrace. A Scarlet-red StoneOven™ *Pizzeria* thermal-bag perched upon the palm and splayed-fingers of a naked-hand; what seemed an offering to those gods housed therein.

"Isn't that Angelica?"

Our Mother Christmas threw her informed observation into the mix.

And turning, to steal a look-see. The Clutch shook their heads and shrugged. And again, did their Chinese whisper bit.

"Is that Angelica?"

"What—you don't know our Angie?"

Our Mother Christmas was to couch her surprise in her usual brand of complacency.

"She delivers to us all the time—these two can't get enough of it,"

[SING] *OH—THE GOOD LIFE*

she continued, nodding in the direction of her Father Christmas. Whom she was presently slouched all-over.

"What—Stone Oven? They're *a*-bit pricy don't you think, *me*-dear?"

Manly and effeminate, whiny and consoling. The voice of another Father Christmas—that was not her own, averred a-little perspective.

"By pricey, he means overpriced," a second Mother Christmas chimed- in—ruefully. The quip then doing the Chinese whisper turn.

Pricey. Overpriced. Priceless.

"*Yeah*...they are a-bit. I guess," our Mother Christmas conceded, pausing to take a gulp of wine.

She then commenced with singing, "INNOGEN. INNOGEN— *Sweetie?*" Singling out a cherub from the litter playing by the pool, the one belonging exclusively to her.

A hush descending upon the grotto, as the cherubs, in unison, paused to peer in the direction of that gathering of Mothers and Fathers (Christmas).

"ASK GABBY TO GO SEE IF THE DELIVERY-GRRRL KNOWS WHAT SHE'S ABOUT," our Mother Christmas instructed.

However, having dutifully listened, this merry band of Lost Boys and *Grrrls* simply resumed their play. Giggling giddily, and screaming after one another, at the tops of their lungs.

The litter having unanimously agreed, by some indiscernible means of *Groupthink*. That this instruction couldn't possibly pertain to all of them; clever little Innogen assuming herself indistinguishable from her peers.

"INNOGEN? INNOGEN!"

Our Mother Christmas shouting after her errant sprog. The timbre of her voice shifting, from whiny and impuissant, to snappy and stern.

"IT'S OKAY MRS DELYS—IT IS OUR ANGIE."

Ever her Knight in shiny armour, Gabby—as in Gabriel, now came to her rescue, waving after the Delivery-*Grrrl*, Angelica. Who'd by now removed her Crash-helmet.

Being a-bit of a character herself, and mad about our Boy-*Dionysus*. Angelica then blew back a wistful kiss. Which our Gabby was to catch full on the cheek, falling backwards as if smitten.

That litter of sagely cherubs—Innogen included, scurrying over to attend to their fallen Orlando. Petting his pretty head, and boatrace.

And proffering condolences, for his stricken state.

Meanwhile, our Mother Christmas was to look-on. Eyebrows raised, brow furrowed, her lined forehead now betraying her age.

"*Well*...that's that," she concluded.

And taking a swallow of lukewarm wine, she set her mug down to snuggle-up to her Father Christmas. Who'd been supping meditatively, upon the teat of an elaborate looking *Hookah*.

Resting her head against the chest of this grizzly bear of a *Man*. She now combed her fingers through that thick brush of facial fur. Taking a minute to breathe him in, his manly cologne. And that acrid sweet aroma of his home-made blend of cinnamon scented tobacco. Which'd been dusted liberally with Smelly.

Then, it was to be the stink of kiln dried birch, and ash, accented with oak bark, bellowing from those patio heaters.

Hmmm

"Isn't our Gabby s'posed to be leaving us soon?" priceless Mother Christmas queried. Seizing upon this apparent lull in the conversation to assume Titania's mantle.

Evidently, the Gabriel-*slash*-Angelica situation hadn't gone unnoticed; and though it wouldn't be referred to directly, it was to provide a subtext for the somewhat innocuous exchange that was to follow.

"Yeah—this summer," our Mother Christmas replied. Now shifting her position, to look directly after it.

"You sure it's this summer?" manly-whiny effeminate Father Christmas piped-in. Introducing a chord of doubt to his usually consolatory tone.

"Come to think of it, maybe it is next summer."

Our Mother Christmas furrowed her brow, to look after her own Father Christmas.

"Is it this summer or next?" she asked, flattening that handsome beard to peer-up those bristly nostrils of his.

She then tugged at it—the beard, prompting him to answer.

"Darling?"

"This summer—methinks," Father Christmas proclaimed, his mouth full of smoke. He leant his head back then, to exhale a smoky trail. Drawing a circle in the air with his pursed lips.

"This summer," our Mother Christmas echoed—dolefully, reaching for her mug to cup it in both hands.

Yikes.

She took another chug of wine, as if meaning to steady her nerves. And it was then, she secretly crossed her fingers. Daring to pin all upon *Love*, like Lennon—*it being all we ever needed*. And tomorrow being much the same as today. And yesterday.

Amen.

"I can't imagine life without our Gabby—can you?"

Though unable to see his boatrace, she nonetheless looked to engage her Father Christmas. But he was to remain distrait, his head swimming in plumes of pungent smoke. And leaving him to it—his *Buzz*. Our Mother Christmas focused instead upon that mug she held in her hand, swirling the lukewarm Blood-red liquid.

"I mean—he's so good with the Kids," she added, mug poised at her lips.

"I know, and such a *Babe* too," said the other Father Christmas—that was not her Father Christmas. Meaning to console her.

"Isn't he—just," the would-be usurper Mother Christmas was to chip-in, assuming her usual supporting role.

Their inoffensive palaver shifted then, onto those trials and tribulations of employing au pairs.

The consensus being, that Mediterranean's made the best au pairs, compared to your Eastern European—*say*, or Filipino. And although you had to pay that little-bit-extra, it was worth it for the Peace-of-Mind.

[Sing] *Please remember*
I still want you; and in case you
Wonder why. Well, just wake up
Kiss the good life, goodbye.

That stiffening breeze seemed to carry with it the words of a tune—a song. Tony Bennet's 'The Good *Life*'.

Kel could just about make it out from where he waited. That bittersweet orchestrated end motif, skimming-off those still Black waters of the canal. Though he couldn't quite pinpoint its source; amidst that vista of staggered apartments, that was like a chequer board of lights, and drawn patio blinds, wrapped in a thick fur coat of creeping foliage.

Nonetheless, from his vantage, it seemed an apt appraisal of the goings-on, of what he saw before him. The song, providing a soundtrack for that gentrified backdrop of Kings Cross. Seen here silhouetted against a silvery moon.

That modern skyline, a far cry from the *ad hoc* slum housing, that'd been a backyard to the Great Northern Rail depot.

Hemmed-in on all sides by railway lines, and warehouses; home to a motley crew of Spivs and Pimps, Streetwalkers and Curb-crawlers, Drug-pushers and Drug-abusers, who'd come to commandeer that knot of backstreets. Night and day plying their ruff-trade and wares. Their depraved lives, seen mirroring that of their deprived surroundings.

Yeah, at some point, this entire cast of *Artful Dodgers* had moved-on. Along with the Cockneys, and the Israelites, taking that rag-trade of SomersTown with them. Their gaudy Lives bent out of shape, like their wizened frames, with the sheer weight of changing times. The entire district having changed its clothes, changed its tune *as it were*.

It'd been at first blush, a melancholic serenade to an impenetrable smile. An impenetrable World, surmised in that classic *Neil Jordan* joint.[56] That anamorphic window shrouded in an impenetrable smog; sooty, and sticky, and toxic, from all that coal, and coke, and *Souls*, it was about burning.

It was listening to 'Mona Lisa',[57] crooned by a dashing Black fellow; his enchanting, emasculated voice, as smooth as silk. His flawless enunciation, compelling you to listen to every word, every syllable of his pathetic lament.

Then, suddenly, that stuck record was unceremoniously ejected. The skies clearing, as those reliable gears of gentrification cranked-up, like an antique *Wurlitzer*® 1015 jukebox. Its clunky, wind-up mechanics, selecting yet another shiny Black 78-disc to play.

A new song for a new day, and a new era.

Yeah, the scaffolding went up. That familiar amplified crackle and *Pop!* of the needle, as it read those jagged empty grooves of shellac. Then the scaffolding came down, a breath catching in a cultured throat to belt out a robust baritone. Those choice words perfectly pitched.

[Sing] *Oh—the Good Life...*

The record would turn, and the World along with it. And still, that

[SING] OH—THE GOOD LIFE

chord of existential angst, whether a result of depravity, or excess. Was for clinging stubbornly to that underbelly of this neighbourhood.

For a minute, Kel was moved. It being uncanny, how the tune was seen to surmise that view across the water. What could've been ten-zillion light-years away. The idea of that Good *Life*—that Good *Living*—being rationed, like a scarcity; like butter—*say*, during Wartime.

Cotch'd upon that mooring, Kel occupied himself with such musings whilst he smoked. Legs crossed, one in front of the other. A mitt trussed in the pocket of his trousers, like an anchor holding him fast to that spot.

He couldn't see much of it, of how that other half lived, even from this choice vantage.

The canal, measuring two barge widths and change, was directly in front of him. While on the opposing bank, it was more moorings, and trees, and thickets of shrubs and greenery.

Nature, and those subtle arts of the Elves—of Galadhriel, being complicit in shrouding this seemingly *Sylvan Glade*, that trace of Lothlórien from any who might hap upon it. Whilst—*say*, traversing that *Man*-made towpath.

It hadn't beguiled Kel though. He'd been waiting there for some time, before he'd caught a glimpse of that Delivery-*Bod*; the Fluorescent-yellow of its *Hi-vis* vest working a-treat from that distance.

Taking a drag on his cigarette, he was now about calculating how long it might take to jog round.

Sniff

Obviously, he'd have to crossover to the other side. The bridge being just up ahead, leading the Caledonian Road over the canal. What'd been a *Man*-made boundary, stemming that sprawl of a burgeoning City of London.

Beyond which, the leafy suburb of Islington had stretched Nor-*phf*. Neat, regimented blocks of handsome terraced townhouses, succumbing eventually to green fields, and pleasant pastures.

There was no towpath following the canal on that other side, what was now designated, 'Zone one'. That Good *Life* being rendered practically inaccessible by a 'Congestion charge', and an architectural style that'd come to epitomise its exclusivity.

Steely apartment blocks, that were essentially prefab-fortresses;

with double-glazed balconies acting as parapets; and resident-only parking in the basement, accessed via an automated shutter-*come*-portcullis; and 24-hour CcSS providing your *Night's Watch*.

Yeah, figuring he'd intercept the Delivery-*Bod* on its way out. Kel stole a couple of curt drags, exhaling smoke from his nose.

He then flicked the remnant of his cigarette at the canal, and shucked.

Our Mother Christmas had commandeered a corner of that circular dining-table to work.

Around her were strewn thick leather-bound volumes—*Tomes*, a choice few laid open. Those creases, that lined the hinged spines, a measure of their repeated exposure to such abuse.

Pushed-out of the way, out of arm's reach. That wafer thin X'ANG® *Crystl* tablet, hewed from a single transparent sheet of engineered quartz, appeared redundant. Parked as it was, in its matching dock. Its slight reddish tinge, an indication of its 'Charging status'.

It'd been usurped by a simple pad of graph paper. Dog-eared with cuneiform scribblings, representing disparate chains of thought. Then there was a lonely wineglass, nursing a generous gulp of Blood-red wine. A freshly opened bottle of *La Sangre de Dios*, left on the nearby kitchen-counter to breathe, completing what might've been a KIERKE® *Dining*-room Space mock-up.

Walking through that open-plan kitchen, toward his patron, a hint of caution was to creep into our Gabby's muffled footsteps.

"There's someone here to see you, Mrs Delys—at the door," he confided.

His hushed singing-voice, casting aspersions upon what was already an uncommon occurrence. The evening having waned, that watershed of midnight could be seen approaching, framed in the kitchen's naked windows.

Our Mother Christmas looking up, more in response to the sound of Gabby's voice, than the portent of his words; her mind still swimming in her work.

"What?"

She pulled a quizzical expression, her mouth hinged open—frozen in the act of uttering that meagre syllable.

[SING] *OH—THE GOOD LIFE*

"I left him outside," our Gabby assured her. Unwilling to say more less he be overheard.

It was to be their secret, evidently. The chivalrous Gabby, being compelled to protect the honour and good name of his Mistress. However, having now imparted his message, he looked unsure what to do next. Being torn between loyalties.

That image of Angelica, waiting for him by the Tradesman's entrance, at the forefront of his mind.

"Who is it?"

Standing, our Mother Christmas hinged-open the spine of the tome she'd been reading, to crease it. Before laying it spreadeagle on the table.

"I didn't get his name—"

Gabriel both shook his head and shrugged.

"I'm sorry, Mrs Delys," he continued, hefting his NorthFace® Turtleshell rucksack upon his margre shoulder. The gesture now the measure of his need for haste.

"No—you crack on," our Mother Christmas said. Wine glass poised at her lips.

She then drained the glass, depositing it on the kitchen-counter— next to that waiting bottle, on her way out. Our Gabby in tow.

Ahead of them, that hefty Brilliant-bright Fire door was as he'd left it. Closed, and secured. A blur of *Stranger* visible in the slit of Frosted-glass, that was cut into it.

Upon entering the hallway, our Mother Christmas was to immediately take charge, thrusting open the door to reveal that uninvited guest.

Devouring that image of Kel—loitering upon her doorstep, without batting an eyelid. Whilst guiding our Gabby upon his merry little way; her nurturing hand, shifting from his shoulder to gently pinch the back of his neck.

"I'll be off then. See you in the morning, Mrs Delys," announced our Gabby. Stealing one last look-see at *the* Stranger, as if meaning to commit that boatrace to memory. Our Mother Christmas responding in kind, now holding onto that Fire door, "yeah—bright and early."

Sniff

She watched then, our Gabby cross that communal antechamber, and call the lift. And continued to watch him, while he waited for his ride down. An ungainly silence ensuing.

For his part, Kel held his corner. Hands trussed in his trouser pockets, *Crombie* ruffled about his waist; him taking this opportunity to unwrap that womanly morsel, her sultry pose reminiscent of Diamond Lil[58]—*say*, barring entrance to her infamous boudoir.

That overly familiar gaze of his, baring teeth to gnaw upon every bump and curve, just visible beneath that somewhat unflattering *peu*-Troll® Gros câlin Ones-*sie* that it wore. The hoodie replete with les petites oreilles.

Yeah, woven from authentic mohair, the Ones-*sie* made mums-*sie* appear cute and cuddly. As if, she were a lycanthropic *Playmate*™ lost on her way to her playdate; a Teddybear picnic-themed party hosted at the Hugh Hefner mansion.

Eventually, an audible-*prompt* was to herald the arrival of our Gabby's ride down. And entering the lift, he spoke his floor, and turned to face the way he'd come. Hefting his burdensome rucksack.

Another audible-*prompt* was to punctuate this phase of the transaction. Our Gabby tendering a diminutive wave to his Patron, as those lift doors closed.

Only after witnessing the lift begin its descent, did our Mother Christmas turn to acknowledge Kel.

She was to catch it in the act of undressing her—with its eyes. But having caught it, she was more miffed to see it flush.

Having said that, she'd already decided upon her approach.

"Who let *you* in?"

"What—no hello? How you been? Long-time no-*see*."

Kel couldn't help but be familiar, even after all this time. The fact that our Mother Christmas hadn't slammed the door in his boatrace, keeping him buoyed in these uncertain waters.

That being said. Our Mother Christmas seemed readily equipped to cut it down to size.

"Cut the crap—*Kelly*. Who *Buzz*'d you in?"

And having posed the question, she now looked passed it, at the adjacent numbered Front door, for her own answers. Her formidable powers of deductive reasoning kicking-in.

It couldn't have been them, she thought, as they were off sunning

[SING] *OH—THE GOOD LIFE*

themselves in the Seychelles.

"No one *Buzz*'d me in."

"What'd you mean, no one *Buzz*'d you in?" our Mother Christmas echoed. "Someone must have, or else, you wouldn't be stood here on my bloody doorstep."

Shifting her weight, she repositioned those manicured tootsies of hers, so as not to obstruct the path of the door.

"Seriously—no one let me in," and having said this, Kel conjured for her a wolfish grin.

Blink-blink

"Then how'd you get inside?"

Blink-blink

"Magic."

"Oh"—*for-Pete'sake*.

Our Mother Christmas felt her patience ebbing. But at the same time, began to recall how much of a windup merchant it'd been. It being something she'd found singularly attractive in this one.

Letting-out a ponderous *sigh*, she let that solid Fire door square those sumptuously rounded digits of her soft pliant Body.

"How did you get in—really?" she asked, now positively inviting it to spin her a yarn.

"I've been known to walk through walls—me," Kel professed, allowing that wolfish grin of his to bare teeth.

"Leap tall buildings in a single bound—"

"You won't need me to *Buzz* you out then," our Mother Christmas cut in. And uncoupling her Body from the door, now made to close it.

Alright, here was a definitive edge. Kel coming right-up against it, like a thumb thumbing the temper of a blade.

"*Wh*-why you being like that?"

Tripping over his words, he was seen to *Blink* first.

Er—

"I don't know?" said our Mother Christmas, smelling Blood. "Maybe, cos you just turn-up, unannounced. When you know you're not s'posed to."

It was at once too easy, and just like old times—their gamely repartee. Those years literally melting away, leaving only that baby fat she'd put-on since.

"I had nowhere else to go."

Excuse me?

Our Mother Christmas did a literal double-take. It knocking her for six, this abrupt dose of reality.

"Honest," Kel added, unwittingly adding insult to injury.

Huh

Now properly regarding it, the woman's mirth visibly soured, her boat-race adopting an expression of displeasure she might've directed toward a child.

And confounded by it, Kel took to fidgeting. Shifting his weight from one leg to the other. As if, that brass in his pocket were now running down his leg, to form a molten puddle on the floor.

Watching it shrivel, like a dried leaf, under the intense heat of her gaze. It suddenly dawned on our Mother Christmas, that perhaps it hadn't meant it the way it'd sounded. That maybe the words had simply splurt'd out, it being the truth of its current predicament.

The truth—mind you, as opposed to it lying as usual. Which was new—*different*, like the clothes it'd taken to wearing.

Perhaps, it'd wanted for a place to stay, each and every time it'd happened to stray across her path. Which was to say, it couldn't be expecting charity, or a handout this time round—

Thank goodness.

Having confronted and dispelled all of her doubts. Our Mother Christmas felt anew, a wellspring of compassion for this creature—her would-be *Thomas O'Malley*™. Coupled with an overwhelming need to gather it up, in her arms.

Certainly, it gave her a warm fuzzy feeling inside, to think of this wily stray having returned to her of its own freewill. Knowing there'd be a warm welcome waiting—*always*, her being true to her word.

But first things first, she told herself. And folding her arms, to keep from reaching out—to pet it. She once again reset the conversation.

Sniff

"How did you really get in—*Kelly*?"

And though it was the exact same question, posed essentially in the exact same manner. Everything had apparently changed. And sensing this, Kel thought to *cling-on* for dear life.

"It was the Delivery-*Grrrl*—Angie. She let me in," he was to fessed-up,

[SING] *OH—THE GOOD LIFE*

hanging his head.

"*Oh*? Did she now."

Our Mother Christmas masked an inner sigh of relief, at least he'd gotten a name.

"I blagged it, said I was visiting a friend. You know—as you do?"

"No. I don't know. But go-on," she said, now toying with it; her having found a neutral spot to park her eyes, whilst she visualised its tale.

"What do you want me to tell you? She held the door for me."

"*What*? Both of them?"

Our Mother Christmas looked sceptical, her eyes like stretched elastic snapping back to interrogate that boatrace.

Er...

Kel found himself needing to think about it.

"Yeah—He nodded—and I came straight-up."

Obviously, he neglected to add the bit where he'd promised—*hand-on-Heart*, not to breathe a word of it. Our Angelica having had the presence of mind to know they'd be Hell to pay. Though not the wit to withhold her name when asked.

Now looking after it, our Mother Christmas appeared satisfied. If just a-little disappointed; though truth be told, it'd volunteered nothing she couldn't have deduced on her own.

Without physically moving, she now gave it the once over. Noting that rather fetching *Crombie*, and the two-piece Birdman suit—that was all the rage; and that starchy *StayPress*™ shirt and matching knit pencil-tie; her scrupulous eye, following the crease of its tapered trousers, all the way down to the hem, and those functional CharlieBrown's®.

Well...at least it looked presentable, she thought to herself, dressed as it was in myriad shades of grey. Like an Undertaker. Or an Inspector, come *a*-calling.

Returning to Kel's ham-fisted explanation, she made a mental note to berate Angelica's *Über*, for it having allowed a *Stranger* (—someone from off the Street) to wonder about her...

"Who is it, Fleur?"

The voice of Father Christmas suddenly broke her chain of thought. And responding to it, our Mother Christmas reverted to barring the way with her comely frame.

"You, wait here," she instructed. Pointing to a spot on the floor, where Kel was to literally wait. She then stole a stroke of its *darling* boatrace, before closing the door.

Settling, Kel looked to his *Pod* for the time. As if meaning to time the wait. Noting, it was kind-a late—still. But then, he couldn't recall having visited any earlier than this.

And of course, that ungainly, all-pervasive silence was to resurface. It being seemingly part and parcel of that sterile, Brilliant-bright environ. Kel now finding himself sandwiched between two closed doors. Those two faces of Janus *as it were*.

To feel more comfortable, he fell back upon that ritual of *Ticks*. A choreography of alchemical gestures, that tapped into that potentiality locked away within his new suit of skin. His new duds being symbolic of that new lease on *Life*, his stint at the *Panny* had bestowed upon him. His subconscious concocting a kind of ward out of it.

It began as ever, with him pulling at his shirt-cuffs. But as Kel did so, he felt dampness spring to mind. And looking to those tips of his fingers, in that Brilliant-bright light of the antechamber, he was to recognise watered-down redness.

He tasted its viscosity, to be sure. Making a mouth of his hand, a tactile palate of thumb and fingertips.

Shit...Pphf'k.

And having confirmed his suspicions, he felt a knot pull tight in his gut. A hot flush warm his boatrace. Revulsion at that sight, that taste of someone else's *Life*'s Blood upon his hands.

He'd readily buried it deep, that grizzly deed; his memory of it, apparently mislaid some place, like a name one might fail to put to a familiar boatrace.

Yeah, it was to be as if it'd never happened. Even though, that look of sheer terror would, now and forever more, be seared upon the insides of Kel's eyelids.

Bending his elbow, he examined the cuff. Not daring to take-off his coat, less his tailored-suit be also covered in my-Man's Life's Blood. Its baleful intent at exacting revenge, residing in every last vestige of its being absent.

Up-close, there was no escaping-it. The facts: A Blood splatter had soaked into the fabric of his shirt. Most probably from Kel's attempts

[SING] *OH—THE GOOD LIFE*

at washing clean his hands. Wily Pontius Pilate, having had the wherewithal to bear his arms first.

Shit...Phf'k—no-no-no...

Not wanting to further contaminate his clothing, Kel improvised. Wiping away that ichor, from the tips of his fingers into the palm of his other hand. And thus, did he further fall foul of its malign intent. To linger about and upon his person, like a bad penny. Or your dreaded lurgy.

He then examined his other cuff. But saw nothing; albeit it too felt damp.

Sniff

Picking-up those loose threads of the ritual, he tugged at the sleeves of his coat, to lengthen the arms and mask the evidence. Though try as he might, he couldn't mask the knowledge of this misdeed—*this most heinous sin of all sins*, from himself.

Looking down at his coat, both arms pulled taut. Kel now noticed a Black spot, just shy of the lapel, and seized upon it. But it was nothing. Merely a bit of fluff.

Sniff

Flicking it away, he continued to survey what he could see of that open-circuit of his Body. And it was just as he was about to give-up, that he noticed another blemish. Another Black spot. Another shadow cast by that nameless act. Just above the pocket, where he'd stashed that ball-point pen; his disposal of it in the canal pending.

In the glare of that Brilliant-bright lighting overhead, and against the grey of his Crombie, the Black spot appeared relatively innocuous.

But nevertheless, it was still disfiguring. And potentially—*fatally*—incriminating, given *my-Grrrl*'s vocation.

Licking the tip of his thumb, Kel dabbed at it. He then looked to the thumb to confirm his suspicions. And sure enough, there was *my-Man*.

And again, he felt it. A tightening in his gut. Guilt pangs on recalling that sin, he'd hoped to erase. That wilful act of erasure, to be surmised by the nondescript moniker, *my-Man*.

It was *my-Man* who was to be left permanently marred, not Kel. The victim being—somehow, complicit in its own trespass, and demise.

Kel rubbed vigorously at that Black spot. But only managed to turn it into a Black smudge. He then looked at it, despondent, and even held the fabric up—as close as physically possible to that light overhead. Only then did he notice, that that spot was part of a much bigger Blood-splatter.

Shit...Phf'k...Christ—no!

Hearing movement, Kell literally jumped-out of his skin to peer-up at those blurry figures, dancing on the other side of that Frosted-glass.

Then it opened—that Fire door.

A beaming Mother Christmas leaning against it, to keep it from closing. A portly Father Christmas bringing-up the rear.

"*Oh*—look who it ain't," he said. His voice jovial, though hushed; on account of that snoozing cherub, he held cradled in his bear-like arms.

"How goes it, Mate?"

Yeah, he seemed genuinely chuffed to see our Kel, who was somewhat thrown by the warmth of this welcome.

"*Same ol' same ol'*—you know," he said, summoning that wolfish grin. And nodding in the direction of the sleeping *Babe*, he was to add, "I see you got your hand's full there?"

"What—this little one? Light as a feather," our Father Christmas cooed. Now looking into the boatrace of that zonked-out toddler.

"You were just about to put Innogen down, weren't you darling?"

And there was our Mother Christmas, taking charge as usual.

"*Yep*—its off to *Beddy-byes* for this one," our Father Christmas said, petting his little cherub with his lips, and then his thumb.

Hugging that front door, our Mother Christmas looked back at him. And their eyes met, their mind's converging for that fraction of a second, as they exchanged a *look*—and presumably invisible words. The pair momentarily lost in their own World.

Father Christmas leant-in close *then*, to impart a tender kiss, upon the lined forehead of our Mother Christmas. Her bowing, from the neck to receive it—his *Blessing*.

And having done this, he commenced with dancing an understated jig. Like an entranced Aboriginal *Shaman*, meandering round an arbitrary plot of haloed ground. Petting, and stroking the little one—seemingly in awe of it, in between breaths. His soft throaty hum, the wordless melody of his hymn, scratching away at that all-pervasive silence.

Hmmm—the Good Life, let's you hide...

[SING] *OH—THE GOOD LIFE*

And listening, as if mesmerised. Our Mother Christmas was to lean her head against that door. While Kel went to bury those murderous hands of his, in his coat pockets. Then thought better of it, settling for those of his trousers.

And still, there remained something more that needed saying. The extending of a hand of welcome *as it were*.

"I guess, you'd best come in."

There, our Father Christmas had said it—without looking-up.

"As you've nowhere else to go," he added, with nigh a trace of cynicism. And with that, the ribbon was cut. The venue reopened.

"Thanks Mate. You're a *Lifesaver*," Kel was to tender, now crossing that threshold.

"You hear that? Apparently, I'm to be a sugarfree lozenge."

Our Father Christmas flashing his eyebrows after his spouse, as Kel came to stand at heel beside him. Both he and Kel, now waiting upon the *Ceremony*. The closing and bolting of that Fire door by our Mother Christmas; who was to be their *most gracious* host.

Kel clockin' that furtive look she took, to ensure the coast was clear. While absentmindedly massaging that contaminated palm of his, with that equally contaminated thumb. As if he were about to come into a windfall.

Turning then, to face these two. Our Mother Christmas now regarded Kelly, as if, he were a knot that needed unravelling.

"You want me to take that?"

She pointed toward its coat.

Er—

Kel shrugged, as if undecided. But nonetheless, was to wriggle-free of that outer-layer of skin. Pulling it inside-out in the process.

He then proceeded, somewhat cackhandedly, to right the garment.

"Never mind all that," our Mother Christmas said, clapping her palm with her fingers, for it to hand it over.

And coming to stand next to Kel, she was to stroke its back reassuringly. Distracting it, while she and Father Christmas exchanged yet another furtive look.

Kel doing as he was told, parcelling over the coat. More conscious now than ever, of that lingering stink of *my-Man*'s ichor. That Blood-splatter by the pocket; that slight reddish tinge to the cuff of his shirt;

that stickiness between his fingers; that sweatiness, he felt in his palms.

Certainly, it'd taken every ounce of *Self*-control to stop from flinching, under the presumed scrutiny of its touch. That is, our Mother Christmas's hand tracing the line of his spine—he was that *digy*.

Now feeling naked and needing to reassert that ward of protection afforded by his clothing-skin. He proceeded to improvise the ritual. Minus the coat and foregoing those contaminated parts of his person. Straightening his tie and pulling at the hem of his blazer; his jaw clenched against that bout of involuntary shakes, that'd taken to rippling through him.

But he needn't have been so wary—anxious.

Righting the sleeves, our Mother Christmas was to give the garment barely a cursory glance. Feeling the lapel, to assess the quality. Before spiriting it away to a nearby coat-hook.

"Nice suit. Looks almost knew," our Father Christmas observed, now leading the way into the *Living*-room Space. Adding—over his shoulder, "oh, and don't forget the clogs. *Kelly*."

OXF●RD CIRCUS

Teary-eyed, Sash looked-up at the pair of them—Monk and Klunk. Unsure whether they'd heard it too.

Blink Blink

"Com'on you two—hand her over."

And there it was again. The husky, boyish voice—unmistakably that of Pris, beamed-in from the other side of that stall door.

Reverting to *Human*-form, his Cynocephalus aspect moulting like fur from those delicate features. Monk turned to face that mirror-wall.

Sniff—

"A MOMENT PLEASE," he shouted back, checking his nose was on straight.

By contrast, Klunk appeared more riled than rattled. Him barking, "GET LOST," as that stall door was unlocked. Pris flinging it wide open to stand there, looking lean and mean; Husk_hands propped upon Husk_hips.

It photographed every minute detail of this scene.

Blink

Its straightened Husk_hair, slicked-up in an exaggerated Teddy boy quiff, giving it the air of your Apex predator. A velociraptor—*say*, the compliment of that saurian stare.

Those speckles of diamond-dust, that dusted the peacock-feathered blazer of its fitted trouser-suit, sparkling in that subterranean gloom. A thousand-and-one beady eyes, commandeering every measly ounce of light.

Truly, here was that dread aspect of the Huntress, *Artemis Agrotera*. *Blink*

The Synthetic wore nothing underneath its jacket. Just an exquisite amber and ebony choke, that coiled about its throat like a coral snake.

"Says who?" it hissed, slotting a hand into a blazer pocket. As if it were a Gumshoe, in a classic RKO film noir; your Philip Marlowe, or Sam Spade, reaching for a concealed piece.

"Says me," growled Klunk, lodging a burly arm across that entrance.

Unfazed, the Synthetic was to issue its challenge.

"Move it. Or lose it."

Huh, came Klunk's guttural response. And adjusting his footing, he braced his arm with his full bodyweight and scowled at it—*I keep this one*.

Impervious to his bullish posturing, Pris now extended a lofty Husk_ hand toward Sash.

"Com'on. We're leaving," it said. Its nimble Husk_fingers dancing under the Man's waxed armpit.

Still, Klunk didn't need to utter a word in response. He simply looked over his bulging shoulder, in Sash's general direction. Scared witless, she found staying put to be that path of least resistance.

The pair of them—her and Monk, assuming the role of onlookers. Their eyes bouncing between these two extremes of that Dialectic of *Man*.

And all of sudden, the restroom was to be transformed into that Valley of Elah. Those loitering beyond the stalls becoming a Philistine horde, goading on their champion. The Nephilim, *Goliath of Gath*.

Obviously, none of these spectators had any idea who, or what Pris was. Though all knew who, and what Klunk was. And thus, anticipated— at the very least, a decent spectacle to roundoff the night.

And just-now, at the far end of the restroom, a couple waltzed in, their wave of high spirits crashing against those jagged rocks of tension.

The focus shifting momentarily onto your ever-attentive Porco, as he took to *Shoo-shooing* these latecomers away. Repositioning himself in front of that entrance, to insure there'd be no further interruptions.

Seen as everyone was distracted. Monk seized then, upon this lull to place a restraining hand on Klunk's shoulder. Klunk's head snapping about at his touch, as if his neck were spring-mounted.

He glunch'd after it. Monk bearing the brunt of that wilful gaze to mouth, *let it go*.

To wit, the Brute simply snarled, minaciously. And shrugged it off.

Pris watched this all unfurl from behind that lens of its nanoscopic perspective of *Time*. Monitoring Klunk's vitals. Relishing the opportunity to observe and analyse his fight-or-flight response. Up-close and personal-*like*.

And while it watched. And waited. It sifted through the mists of Klunk's Body odour. A heady mix of synthesised fragrances; cologne, antiperspirant, shower-gel, shaving-foam, moisturiser. Isolating and measuring the acrid notes of apocrine sweat; the slightly salty taste of eccrine sweat; those traces of epinephrine and corticosteroids; of lactic, citric, ascordic and uric acids; of proteins, lipids, and urea.

It clock'd the rhythm of Klunk's elevated Heart rate for a-bit. Scaled those peaks and troughs of his respiratory rate. Measured the flush of his cheeks. The mydriasis of his eyes. The period of those involuntary shakes that rippled through his ripped, hard-*Bod*.

You poor thing, it was to surmise. Having analysed all this data in the *Blink* of its Husk_eye.

For all his s'posed Body-consciousness, Klunk had about as much control over his physiology as he had over the weather outside — Out-*there*. But the Synthetic already knew this, its principal motivation being to affirm its findings.

And besides, it liked putting this particular Ape —

CORRECTION

— this peculiar *Guerrilla*, through its paces. Now, all it needed was for it to do something.

Anything.

Suppressing the autonomic component of the Husk's own fight-or-flight response. Pris manually tickled its pituitary and adrenal glands, to boost their output of epinephrine, and corticotropin.

Whilst simultaneously sending an Action-Potential ripple throughout the Husk's musculoskeletal frame, to check and optimise calcium, and adenosine triphosphate levels.

It then let the Husk's muscles relax, in readiness of imminent attack.

Alright, little Man—little Guerrilla. Show me what you're made of, it thought. Paraphrasing its Android Pin-up and role model, 'Roy Batty', the other Protagonist in Scott's *Blade Runner*.

A flick it'd reviewed *a*-begillion times since its inception.

Congratulating itself, on the aptness, the Human-*ness* of this sentiment. It released a shot of dopamine, for the Husk's central nervous system to nibble upon.

Allowing its Husk_face a cheeky grin, the thickness of a line drawn with a pencil.

"I'm taking the *Grrrl*," it stated dryly. "And you can't stop me."

It then presented a defiant chin, for Klunk to bludgeon. That Husk_ hand still thrust in its blazer pocket.

But though spoken out loud, the actual words had been merely a carrier wave for the real communiqué:

HIT ME. I DARE YOU—*PHF'KA*.

The Synthetic multitasking, running its full gambit of developmental experiments.

This one, in particular, designate Sublim_Mind_Ctrl, utilised *sub*-phonic harmonics to transmit subliminal messages, aimed at promoting an unconscious response.

And had to date, proven 28.657% effective.

Being on the receiving-end of this transmission—broadcast. Klunk suddenly found himself swallowing in a dry throat.

Had he heard it right? Did this puny little *runt-of-a-thing*, seriously expect him to belt it one? Right here. Right now. With everybody watching.

Blinking, in this apparent on-rush of headlights. Those Bionic-eyes of his were to flitter about that camp of onlookers. Marking their pretence at taking no notice.

Had they heard? Apparently not.

And just-now, Klunk felt his flame douse. That hold of the *Fairy dust* beginning to wane. Indeed, coming into his senses, he was alarmed to discover his Body shaking spasmodically. His fists clenched, as if ready to fight.

Taking a deep breath—*inhale…exhale*, he thought to weigh his options.

Although every fibre of his Being was inclined toward belting *it*—into next week. He knew, if he actually did this, he'd be out on his ear.

Or worse.

Truth be told, he'd never been able to fathom this woman's hold over his Monk. But suffice to say, he was in no doubt as to who really called the shots at the 86ers™ *Members-only Club.*

"Is she really worth it?"

Klunk looked then, sullenly, after his Lover—*kaì sý, téknon.*[59]

And still, Pris waited. Its unwavering reptilian eyes, shining with steely detachment.

And whilst it waited, it continued to mull over that incessant feed of data. Marking that change in Klunk's vitals, the glacial approach of his comedown.

When finally, the Synthetic decided it'd seen enough. It simply uncoupled the Brute's limp member, from barring entrance to the stall. Allowing gravity to do the rest.

"Com'on you," it said, extending a regal paw toward Sash. It then wiggled its dainty Husk_fingers, like a lure on the end of a fishing line.

Still wary, Sash looked to Klunk—for permission. But he simply snorted and turned his back on it.

"Com'on, if you're coming."

Sash again looked warily toward Klunk. But having shown her his back, he'd dived for the shelf to *J Edgar* another line. And was presently all about it.

Sniff

It was out of sheer desperation, that she finally turned to Monk. But thankfully, *my-Man* kept it short and to the point. A simple nod in *my-Grrrl*'s general direction.

Now get lost.

And with that, Sash took her leave. That is, her saviour's Husk_hand, to be pulled free of what'd become for her *a-right horrorshow.*

Keeping a firm grip of that hand, the Synthetic took a moment to look her over.

There-there, it seemed to say. *No real harm done.*

It then gripped Sash's chin, to slowly rotate her head—*Left-to-Right Right-to-Left*. Catching in the light that *Pfeiffer*® *invis-a-*Splint™ taped across the bridge of her nose.

"See to the boyfriend—for me," it said.

And hearing this, Sash suddenly felt those butterflies in her stomach kick—like an embryo.

"What-do-you-mean? See to the boyfriend?" Klunk snarled, pinching his nostrils and *Sniffing* repeatedly.

"Do you need me to spell it out?"

The Synthetic reached into the stall, to retrieve Sash's handbag from the floor. And handing it to her, added, "and don't get carried away."

"What the *phf—Phf'k* you!"

Monk wove a matronly arm about Klunk's curled bicep.

"Don't worry, we won't," it said, speaking for the both of them.

As if only just-now noticing it. Pris was to regard *my-Man*, its Husk_boatrace an inscrutable mask. Monk retreating behind that recalcitrant *Joker*™ smile of his, to shrug sheepishly—*what?*

What indeed.

The Synthetic *Blinked*, releasing it from that tractor beam of its scrupulous gaze. And turned, as if meaning to lead Sash away. But then, it was to stop abruptly. Sash—still stupefied, almost bumping into its Husk.

Pointing at my-*Grrrl*'s hand, Pris *Snap-snapped* its Husk_fingers. Sash opening it—her hand, to reveal that tin of Tiger's Balm she'd been nursing.

And taking it from her, the Synthetic was to place it deliberately upon that glass-shelf—in the stall. Next to those luminous, Brilliant-bright lines of *Fairy dust*.

"Missy?"

The Cabby was eyeballing Sash in that rearview screen.

"Just so's you know, Miss. The *Navi* says there's a diversion up-ahead."

Called back by its voice, the World returned to Sash's eyes; that muted chaos of Out-*there*, framed in those tinted windows of a *Hackney*-cab.

They'd followed that *off*-Mainstreet scene, through Fitzrovia and onto Marylebone. The hallow'd beat, marked with Fluorescent-yellow colored placards, strung-up on intermittent Street-lamps. This quarter's theme: Spontaneity + Movement.

Despite the onrush of night, *off*-Mainstreet was still a-*Buzz* with your usual suspects. Flocks of wary retail Tourists and Pilgrims seeking welcomed respite. Flanked by overpriced Deli cafés, and Sushi inns, and Shisha bars, and Roti huts, and Jerk karts. Extra covers sprawling out onto the pavement, crammed under retractable vinyl awnings.

That notorious London-weighting, weighing heavily upon the virtua-*Plastic* of both your Local and Tourist alike.

Seated, and standing, they—the Punters—would watch agog, spectacles of Street theatre. That age ol' adage, being here brought to life.

Here, the Street was to be, literally, transformed into a stage. Here, every day was to be a *Cabaret*.

Our *Frau Sally Bowles*[5A] taking a bow for the Mime Artists and Dancers, Acrobats and Contortionists; for the Poets and Thespians, Magicians and Illusionists; for the Ventriloquists, and their Dummies; the Comedians, and the Comediennes; and even, your Soap-box Evangelists.

And last, but not least. For those muzikians of every strip and hue.

Yeah, our Sally Bowles would take a bow for them all. And then, take her leave. Her 10-minute stint, tanning herself in that Spotlight—that *Limelight*—over for another half-hour.

They were a superstitious lot, those *off*-Mainstreet performers.

And cliquey to a fault. Before each performance they'd pitch their cloth—their tent, an innocuous-*looking* hat parked on the pavement, or upon a step.

Invariably, it'd be a Trilby, or tweed Flat-cap. Or something more exotic, like a Fez—with a tassel, or an Ushanka, made from muskrat. Something to really catch the eye, something for your passers-by to aim at. Though it were to be mainly symbolic, given that prevalence of *virtua*-Plastic.

More often than not, you'd see them huddle together in the 'Wings' after a performance. That nook, over by the Metropol's staff entrance— *say*. They'd wait, dry-mouthed, hands-on-hips and breathing hard. Whilst the Troupe Leader *divvied*-up the scratch.

"Did you remember the card?" our Sally Bowles would ask.

Oh yeah, the card—a kind of DIY Blue plaque, traditionally ripped from a cardboard box. What was to be an X, marking an ever-shifting spot.

It'd have scribbled on it, in BLK felt-tip pen, the URLs for *virtua*-Account payments; it having to be BLK, for neither red, nor blue would do. Alongside a few choice lines, from what was dubbed your 'Ava Cassidy Suicide Note':

My heart and mind may be
Sated by my Art, but—Dude
My Body still needs to eat.

It'd been meant as a lingering middle-finger to a synthesised World.

There was the infamous note, which was fake. And a hauntingly beautiful, and evocative digy-*viddy* clip of our Ava, singing her version of 'Somewhere Over The Rainbow'.[58] Which wasn't so much.

Ironic really. When you stop to think, she died in obscurity. From a Melanoma—of all things. The idea of suffering for one's *Art*, being now more *kitsch* than cliché.

To live *off*-Mainstreet, you had to be—at the very least, just a-little neurotic. If only to aspire to that *Primo*-slot, under the *tarp*—the Bigtent. Where the Visual Artists had their own penned enclosure, in the 'Foods from Around The World' forecourt.

Yeah, it'd be them, and your *Headliners*.

And god forbid, you actually get 'discovered', and really have to play that role of a *Life*-time. Wear that mask of pearly Brilliant-brights, that smile that never laughs. And pretend, that all was forgotten—forgiven.

Those years of suffering. Indignity, and indignation. Surmised anecdotally, in some vague reference to that first time breaking-a-leg. That first ever *off*-Mainstreet gig.

Phf'king sycophants, of-course they'd dredge that up.

For nostalgia's sake. It signifying the dues you'd paid them. And three times daily, with a Matinee on weekends, you'd be for reciting oaths from that 'Papyrus of Ani'—

[Poem] *I never did know*
That sheisty so-and-so
I swear I never did. I never was
Nor have I ever been, an exponent
Of the Grift.
Though
I'd graft'd long and hard. Been

OXF●RD CIRC∪S

Forced to live that hair's width
Away from that slippery slope.
Everyday
Learning to walk that tightrope
—as in Glengarry Glen Ross.[5C]
Luck? What phf'king luck?

The Cabby pointed to the roadworks up ahead, and a retro-reflective sign that read, 'No Entry'.

"It's directing me under the Tarp," he said, again eyeballing Sash in that rearview screen.

He then added, eyes back on the road, "I'll have to go round and come back up."

But Sash wasn't paying it much mind. What with the events of the previous night, still swimming in her head.

Out-*there*, in the 'Wings', a determined looking Sally Bowles was getting undressed. Its ÜBER-hero costume hidden underneath its work clothes; a shiny BLK leotard, U-umlaut spelt-out in sequins planted upon its ripped chest.

No doubt, inspired by the 'Reign of the ÜBERmen' ÜBERman™ suit. The flick currently breaking all IMAX® box office records.

Stepping into the Spotlight, onto its stage; what was a section of vinyl flooring. It tossed down a Navy-BLK New York *Yankees*™ Baseball Cap—*47* Brand® and Official MLB® labels still attached. Just by that sign *there*. Its own rendering of the infamous 'Suicide note', scrawled on a piece of cardboard. And commenced with limbering-up.

The diversion led under a massive labyrinthine neon sign, that hung across the road like a suspension bridge. Sequentially spelling-out the word 'WELCOME' in every written language in the Universe.

The 'Big-tent' that was your Oxford Circus, spanned Oxford Street— old and new, and was always open for business. Only winding down at around 0400hrs; the graveyard shift, being traditionally cut short for an early breakfast. The new day clocking-on at 0600hrs.

Then it'd be straight through, from 0600hrs-to-1400hrs, 1400hrs-to-2200hrs, 2200hrs-to-0400hrs.

What was the retail equivalent of *Le Vingt-quatre Heures du Man*;

the baton being passed from shift-to-shift, along with sales figures, and shop floor assists.

From here on out, it'd be both hands on that traction-wheel; the *Cabbies* being ardent Manualists. And certainly, they needed to be wary of those Double-decker Leyland® *Routemasters*, whose Automatrons never missed an opportunity to show who was *bawse* of the road.

Especially in pedestrianised areas, such as under the Big-tent, where the pecking was subject to size. The Cabbies being your Stealers Wheel, [Sing] *stuck in the middle with you.*[5D]

And just-now, coming-up from behind, a flock of forty-odd Carnaby Street Squaws slipped-by, on elevated *Cynderellas*™.

What was a motion-blur of Impossible miniskirts by House of Fraser®; exposing bare scrawny legs hemmed by Burlington® *Pop!* socks; and SergioTacchini® shellsuit tops; and make-up drawn like War-paint; and jet-BLK weaves of Indian hair, sculpted into gravity defying Mohawks.

A few clattering against that Body of the cab, to peer inside. And coppin' my-*Grrrl*, their screwfaces were to switch to beaming smiles. Them waving, enthusiastically, before splurtin'. Skirting in-between that press of vehicles.

Blood-red *Routemasters* and Ash-BLK *Hackney*-cabs strung-out like beads. That combined NEMP emanating from the vehicles, causing the surrounding air to shimmer, like a heat haze.

In that dedicated XPS-lane, that ran down the middle of your Mainstreet thoroughfare. Cyclist's trailed trains of skaters, like freight-cars. Charging their Shimaru® KinetiX frictionless bearings, for the coast round Marble Arch, that slalom down to Kensington and Victoria.

Yeah, Out-*there* that pavement heaved with tides of retail Pilgrims, and the incessant chatter of sensible and not so sensible footwear.

A matte grey-BLK-beige palette of Fall-*slash*-Winter, co-mingling with those pastel shades of Spring-*slash*-Summer. That temperate clime, maintained under the Big-tent, confounding any visceral sense of a 'Season'.

And towering over all and sundry. The belled helmets of two Bobbies, walking that Mainstreet beat. This visible deterrent, a heterogametic pairing of XY-chromosomes. That *Force*™ in policing, having no female equivalence.

OXF•RD CIRCUS

Indeed, this unanimity of gender was to be imbibed by a smart-casual uniformity. Dark-blue creased pants; Brilliant-bright short-sleeved *StayPress*™ shirt; shiny-BLK sporty DocMartins®; Second-Chance Kevlar Body-armour; and silver-plated Warden's Badge.

An earpiece attuned to that constant chatter of the Dome—London's eyes and ears. An AXION® Inc. TAZ-*R*™ pistol ready-to-hand. It being your favoured passive-aggressive conflict-resolution response, for when tempers invariably flared.

Here was your Mainstreet *then*. One endless parade of cinematic façades, populated by Synthea® mechanised *Mannies*.

Tirelessly, they'd run through choreographed dance routines, looped to *Thump*-ing soundtracks that themed the merchandise they sported. The muzik becoming audible—suddenly, upon entry into that 'Active Zone' for each Brand-store experience.

Yeah, all along Mainstreet, behind those permeable walls of glass. Proc'd *Mannies* were to be *viddy*'d, evoking that esprit of their *Look* through freestyle dance. The hyperrealism of their movements, their clothing, hair and make-up likened to skin; lending those rigid, asexual exoskeletons an impression of that carnality of *Living*-flesh. The (sub-) routine terminating abruptly, that instant your Pilgrim wondered-off.

Picture Disney's 'Sorcerer's Apprentice',[5E] that animated Broom clattering lifeless to the floor. The manny pausing for a *sec*, before syncing back into that indefatigable Chorus line.

Yeah, here was your Mainstreet, fighting back. The schism of Shopper *vs*. Shopping, noun *vs*. verb having been resolved. The consensus being, that it was 'all-good'.

All gravy.

Hmmm—gravy.

To-Shop. To-browse. To-cotch *even*, in one of those numerous enclaves dotted around, and be entertained by one of your *Headliners*.

Whilst a steady torrent of *Ping!* Vouchers™ fluttered by, like invisible butterflies. Ready to be netted on the screens of any-and-all handheld devices.

Next-up this hour, 'The X'ANG® Accumulator Sweepstake': A Google® mapped treasure hunt, synergising unbelievable one-day-only discount offers with local leisure activities. The event culminating in 50%-off this quarter's 'must-have' item-*thingy*, the X'ANG® *Crystl* solid-quartz tablet plus dock.

"Go on, make a day of it," peeled the sting of the Westminster Borough Council digy-*viddy* promo, displayed on the side of a *Routemaster*, as it crawled by. 'Free Parking' and 'Park & Ride' *Ping!* Voucher™ codes hidden within that Small-print of its disclaimer.

Looking-up, you couldn't actually see the Big-tent, what was essentially a huge tarpaulin. Though you'd hear the rain drumming on the transparent membrane; the TEFLON® *CrystalClear* osmotic water reclamation system, hard-at-work, topping-up the local water supply with recycled rainwater.

Shielding those below from the worst of the elements, the tarpaulin's frame extended from the rooftops of the multi-story buildings that overlooked Oxford Street.

During daylight hours, it'd bathe Pilgrims in revitalising vitamin-D_3 enriched sunrays, whilst they shopped. And on clear nights, screen the noise of ambient light and magnify the Stars. So as, to bring a glimpse of Heaven that little bit closer to Earth.

Yeah, above those branded storefronts, the walls of the buildings retreated behind a thick, lush covering of clematis, morning glory and wisteria; sprayed liberally with mustard oil, to bait swarms of migrating Cabbage white butterflies. That impression of hundreds of thousands of beating butterfly wings, animating this abundant hanging garden.

Certainly, recalling that first ever visit to your Oxford Circus. Retail Pilgrims oft spoke of a sense of wonderment, evoked by the experience. Here it was *then*, your idealized form: M-E-R-C-A-T-O S-H-O-P-P-I-N-G M-A-L-L. Realized.

The tailback of Double-deckers and *Hackney*-cabs gradually began to thin, on that approach to Selfridges®. Its world-famous pillared façade coming into view just-now.

And looking-up from her *Pod*, Sash was to mark the gaggles of Pilgrims, gawping after those elaborate displays, framed in its anamorphic windows. The theme this quarter: 'The Future is Movement.'

The first window playing host to a live-action sequence, titled 'La Race des Hommes Supersoniques'. In which Jamaica's own, The *Human-*Bolt™—the World's Fastest Man—was to be pitted against DC Comic's *The Flash*™, in un tête à la tête de course from Marble Arch to the Arc

OXF●RD CIRCUS

de Triomphe, Paris.

The BangOptics® rendered protagonists running static, while the shifting scenery—a holographic panorama—conveyed a sense of moving at supersonic speeds. The stage rotating 360-degrees, from profile, to head-on, to a view of the racer's backs, as the drama unfolded.

Foregoing that usual route, via the EuroTunnel. Les Hommes Supersoniques would leap heroically from the Dover cliffs, and rocket across the English channel. Trailing 3-metre-high wakes in their wake.

But in the end, aided and abetted by a pair of *Puma*® Ultima Roadrunners, incorporating patented über-Traction tread technology, designed to optimise frictional torque. The *Human*-Bolt™ would win by a neck, having dipped fortuitously to meet that finish line.

Not to be outdone, *The Flash*™ would then challenge my-*Man* to race back. The pair bumping fists, before tearing-off down the Avenue de la Grand Armée. The sequence freezing on our two ÜBER-heroes, neck and neck, their Bod(ie)s leaning into their strides.

With the animated zip-line reading, 'ÜBERman™ *Watch out!*' The window would fade-to-black, resetting that 'Event Clock' situated in the top right-hand corner.

In the next window, the Pilgrims were transported to a snow-capped Eryri, and invited to follow Chris Hoys-Lovechild—the current Olympic and World BMX X-Country Champion—as she powered her way up the trail, to the summit of Snowdon.

The scenery shifting around the BangOptics® rendered figure, stood tall in the saddle of a stationary *Kotu*® bamboo-BMX, fitted with Tetsu® X-Gen reverse-peddle chargeable-bearings.

At the summit's peak, Hoys-Lovechild would pause briefly, to take in that breathtaking scenery. Then, picking-up the über-lightweight BMX—with its graphite coated bamboo frame, she'd begin leisurely strolling back down that mountain trail.

The sequence freezing on the zip-line, 'Sometimes you just have to enjoy the scenery'. Before fading-to-black, resetting that 'Event Clock' in the corner.

The third window was home to a mockup of that famous Manhattan sidewalk, from Billy Wilder's *The Seven Year Itch*. And a TEMBO® *Ubuntu* 680se SUV, parked next to that now infamous grate.

Similar to the digy-*viddy* promo, the window display was to feature a *Life*-size BangOptics® rendering of Marilyn Monroe™, stepping-out of that parked SUV to catch the breeze from a passing subway-train. The wafts of cool air flaring her skirt.

Invigorated, *our* Marilyn would spring back into the automobile to lounge provocatively, in that reversed driver's seat. Aiming a remote at the corner of the window, to reset that 'Event Clock'. The zip-line reading, 'Your life, safe in our hands.'

The fourth window showcased a stately-*looking* ContinentalClass Rolls-Royce® *SilverTeardrop*™ commercial 'flying-car'. The first of its kind.

The display, an enactment of the aircraft's maiden flight, depicting blue skies, and a smiling Antipodean sun; that silver-hide of the flying-car, *Winking* after the Sydney Harbour Bridge.

Australia's second Capital having won the raffle to host this *grande* spectacle. Beating-off stiff competition, from a handful of City-States dotted around the Globe.

The rendered holographic panorama, rotated around a static scale-model—purchasable as a remote-control drone via *Ping!* Voucher™. The sequence being plotted to that first movement of *A London Symphony*,[5F] by Sir Ralph Vaughan Williams. The opening stanza's unassuming romanticism, providing a very British 'Brand soundtrack' to downplay the auspices of this epochal jaunt.

Actual water-vapour was used to demonstrate that sleek aerofoil, and convey a sense of movement. The aircraft's elegant Bindi, *The Spirit of Ecstasy*, leaning with abandon to greet this apparent on-rush of air.

That polished planar-surface running flush to a pressurised-cab, that was ballast for the *Pegasus* X-MK9 medium-bypass turbofan-engine. The rear of the flying-car being tapered, like a razor-back's tailfin; that red strip of the TVC aft-exhaust, measuring its width.

Cannibalising much of the tried and tested technology of its cousin, the boxier BAE® *Harrier*-taxi—that currently monopolised those highways of the skies. The more mammalian-*looking* SilverTeardrop was to achieve VTOL with the aid of those reaction-control valves, positioned at the four corners of its undercarriage. That acted to redirect its engine's considerable thrust downward.

Having walked you through all this, the *Ping!* Voucher™ then went on to demonstrate the SilverTeardrop's state-of-the-art safety features. How, in the unlikely event of an imminent crash, the cab would jettison.

OXF•RD CIRCUS

Parachuting to a soft landing. Its vaunted cargo encased in edible *AfterShock*™ *anti-*Impact foam.

Then came the 'Guided tour' of said pressurised cab. Highlighting its minimalist dashboard, buckskin flight-seats, and faux-ivory trimmings. And of course, its augmented-reality HUD, how it projected way beyond the plane of that windscreen.

And naturally, the tour was to conclude with a game, aptly named *Jeeves*™, [Sing] *Take me out*. Inviting you to guess the journey-time, from your current location to notable destinations throughout the UK and mainland Europe. Whilst affording you an opportunity to interact directly with the SilverTeardrop's autonomic flight-control system, via Braeburn's *Home Jeeves*™ mobile-assist UX.

For example, from the LZT situated on the roof of the Selfridges® building, it was aprox. 35-*minutes* to Paris; 55-*minutes* to Edinburgh; 135-*minutes* to Berlin—as the crow flies.

Proof that your Rolls-Royce® *SilverTeardrop*™ could more than live-up to its zip-line, 'Bringing you the Continent'.

The last two window displays were dedicated to Space exploration. Though they were to remain blacked-out. The sign reading, 'The Eden Group® SpaceZERO High-Orbital Spacestation and ValleyForge™ *Ecosphere*. Coming Soon!'

That being said. Sash couldn't really see much, for the throng of Pilgrims huddled around the displays. Stood three and four Bod(ie)s deep. Staring intently into, and out-through those tiny windows each held in their hands.

And just now, the gaggle were seen to look-up en masse. Some pointing with a finger, others aiming their handsets.

Look! There, up in the sky—

And following their lead, Sash was to press her cheek right-up against that tinted glass, to steal a look-see.

Sure enough, there was a real-*Life* flying car, swimming in the fluid air. Cutting a majestic figure, amidst a swarm of obsolete-*looking Harrier*-taxis, queuing to dock at the Selfridges® LZT. Its seamless mirrored-finish, drawing stark contrast with their weathered Mustard-yellow paint jobs.

Taking-in this rare spectacle, that notorious CHARLIE HEBDO cartoon now sprung to mind; it having dominated the news cycle for a *hot*-minute.

It depicting *The Spirit of Ecstasy* frenziedly flapping her arms, attempting to take-off. Her ankle shackled to a generic looking automobile, in which, the ghosts of Charles Stewart Rolls and Frederick Henry Royce were to be seen fighting over the traction-wheel. The leader reading, 'Un pas de géant pour l'humanité!'

After all the hype. The ubiquitous *Ping!* Voucher™ campaign, and then the launch. How quickly had that *Fifth* Estate cooled to the idea of a commercial flying-car; of it ushering in a 'democratisation' of that fast-lane of the skies. Once the omission of 'Manual-override', and the use of dedicated flight paths had come to light.

The SilverTeardrop quickly becoming synonymous with all that'd gone wrong with the '*Harrier*-taxi révolution'. That is, the Aviator, Flight & Ground Crew Union's strangle hold over fares. That 'second giant-step for Mankind' being viewed as more un shuffle de côté.

Thumbing their nose at this rather elegant, and shiny Brilliant-bright elephant. That *Fifth* Estate had turned to face the on-rush of a new dawn, what was already being touted, 'Fliegende Autos 2.0' [pronounced: t̃-s-v-a-ɪ ˈk-ɔ-m-a n-ʊ-l]. A second wind for this fledgling market, the advent of the *Inter*ContinentalClass.

Tipped to be dominated by a slew of newly formed partnerships, betwixt Aeronautic and Automobile manufacturing Goliaths, and privately financed.

"If you want, I could let you out on the corner. And you can walk down," the Cabby suggested, his eyes glued to the road.

"Nah—you're alright," Sash said. Now engrossed inna her Pod.

"Suit yourself, Miss."

What is exact is already too exact.

Jean Baudrillard, *Simulacra and Simulation* (1981)

57 68 61 74 20   73 20
65 78 61 63 74 20 69 73
20 61 6C 72 65 61 64 79
20 74 6F 6F 20 65 78 61
63 74 2E

.

P - R - I - S

The St. Michael's® one-way *viddy*-intercom crackled, then Pris spoke.

"Is that you, Sasha?" it asked. Its scratchy-voice, like a furry claw reaching through that metal-gauze, concealing the mic-*slash*-speaker.

"Yeah," Sash replied, positioning herself in front of that red transmission light of the intercom. Its apparent eye.

"You're early," the scratchy voice said, after a brief pause.

"*Yeah*—I know, right?" the habitually late Sash agreed—beaming.

So obviously chuffed with herself.

To wit, the *viddy*-intercom simply crackled in response, and then fell silent.

Behind Sash, the *Hackney*-cab had already negotiated that cul-du-sac. And was now stood at the junction, its orange indicator-light *Wink-wink-winking* its intent to leave and return to Mainstreet.

Watching it depart, Sash adjusted the strap of her handbag, to sit that little bit higher upon her shoulder. But with the taxi gone, she soon felt cast adrift, and dwarfed by that unfamiliar setting. The Brobdingnagian doorway in-front of her, with its sturdy varnished Scarlet-red door, and antiquated bronze-plated fixtures and fittings; a Florentine-styled door handle and knocker, frozen stiff as if with the onset of *rigor mortis*.

Unlike those surrounding tenements, the Synthetic's residence had no number. Just a *viddy*-intercom framed in a brass-panel, punctuated by two columns of unlabelled *Buzz*ers.

Stepping back onto the pavement, Sash was to hazard a look-see, up at the building's façade. And mark that absence of light—absence of *Life*, in its tall, elegant windows.

Sniff

Stumped momentarily by this discovery. She turned to take-in that Petra-*esque* alcove. The rows of tall Georgian-windows, cut into an ashlar cliff-face. Their gaze directed inwards, upon this wrong-turn in that elaborate maze of backstreets. Shafts of warmth, peeping through intricate lace netting, or around the edges of thick curtains, or closed wooden-shutters, or microfine Venetian blinds.

Looking toward a nearby nook, that seemed to cut clean across the fabric of here, and Out-*there*. Sash could just make-out the arbitrary currents of that mighty tributary that lay beyond. That is, the pedestrian traffic scurrying back and forth, passed that shutter-like opening.

As usual, that *Buzz* of the Met was as Brilliant-bright noise to her ears. Though, silence should've pervaded, bore out by her utter anonymity. But for that beady red-eye of the *viddy*-intercom, now staring (—blindly) after her absence. Sash slowly coming to inhabit her surroundings, outside—Out-*there*, as ever delineated by an impermeable wall of Photovoltaic glass.

Blink

Her glancing at her *Pod* then. If only to give herself, and those fidgety-fingers of hers something else to do. The screen waking to an hourly newstream update, the headline: "Teflon Group Founder, Chairman and CEO, found dead!"

Promptly switching over to *viddy*-cam, to preview her boatrace. She noted how dry her lips looked; and pouting, applied a-little lip gloss. Her *as-ever* feeling naked and unmasked without make-up.

Normally, she'd have sparked a cigarette by now. But hadn't, for any number of reasons. And then, that crackle of the *viddy*-intercom was to put pay to the idea. It signalling a presence on the other side of that gauze. The sound drawing Sash back into the glare of its beady red-eye.

"You'd best come up," Pris declared, in a scratchy voice that wasn't so dissimilar to that sharp metallic *Bzzz*, proclaiming Sash's right of entry.

Still, my-*Grrrl* knew to wait for the CLICK.

When it came, she was to lean heavily against that heavy-*looking* Front door, half expecting to meet with stiff resistance; no mean feat in a pair of *Cynderellas*™. Only to find the door swung open effortlessly. Sash losing her footing, stumbling over the threshold to graze her knees upon that tiled floor.

And just then, she felt her *Pod* shiver in her hand. And picking herself up, and looking to it, saw Pris had *Ping*'d her further instructions.

'Take the lift to the second floor,' the message read. 'It'll be the door on your left.'

Rubbing her knees, Sash looked to get her bearings. Taking-in the dimly lit and airy hallway, her eye guided by that chequered floor.

What were walls skimmed back to bare-bone plaster and painted a flat matte Brilliant-bright. The finish extending to that high ceiling, with its decorative cornice of blooming Tudor roses, chasing tangled leafy vines.

All that apparent austerity, offset by glossed skirtings, and a dado-rail, and pockets of warmth emanating upwards from upturned giant clamshells, cast from Frosted-glass. The light fixtures measuring the distance to an antiquated lift-cage of wrought-iron. The lift's shaft, painted an Industrial-BLK, sprouting from the middle of a staircase that snaked-up that stairwell, like a *Helter-Skelter*.

Pride still bruised. Sash clambered gingerly to her feet, to glide over to the lift. Along the way, passing by a bank of unlabelled mail slots, embedded in the wall. And the staggered sturdy doors of two ground floor apartments; that lift being keyed to her approach, its cage sliding open—invitingly.

At some point, Pris had decided to meet my-*Grrrl* at the lift. Announcing itself with a dainty wave, as the lift-cage broke the second floor in eerie silence. Its Husk_eyes like diamonds, sparkling. Offsetting the gloom of *perma*-ambience, what seemed a shroud cast over that airy corridor.

And looking-up after it, Sash was to feel those butterflies kick in the pit of her stomach—her gut. The sensation coinciding with the lift coming to an abrupt halt.

"*Oh goodie*. You're wearing them."

The Synthetic clapped its Husk_hands approvingly.

"Wearing what?" came Sash's tetchy response. Looking over her apparel, unchanged from yesterday: *Secondskins*, plastic wrap-a-round top, bubblewrap puffer, transparent-handbag.

"Your Cynderellas," Pris said—pointing.

Sash ignoring its pointy-finger, to peruse my-*Grrrl*'s outfit through that lift-cage.

Sniff

Evidently, it'd decided on slumming-it. In a vanilla ice-cream velour SergioTacchini® hoodie, and matching pedal-pusher bottoms. The outfit handstitched with 22-carat gold microfine thread; and accented with gold-plated zippers, replete with miniaturised tags in the shape of that SergioTacchini® logo.

Living somewhere between two extremes: Bespoke tailoring, and *Prêt-à-Porter*. The *Look* was exemplary of that shabby-*chic* clobber, currently trending in all your King's Road boutiques.

Sash being privy to all this. It was to leave her feeling just a-little inadequate; her pulling her handbag too.

"You don't mind if I try them on—do you?" Pris asked, now waiting on those lift-cage doors to open.

"I've been meaning to buy-*me* a pair," it continued. "But, being as they're so dare, I wanted to try them out first—as you do."

Wary of her footing, and clearly enamoured by the sheer physical presence of this *Creature*—seen here in its Lair. Sash seemed hesitant to step out of that lift.

"What—*now*?" she exclaimed, looking down and catching a glimpse of the Synthetic's bare Husk_feet. The vessel having found stasis in a slovenly *Retiré derrière*. Propped upon one Husk_leg, the toes of its other Husk_foot balled, like a primate's fist. Knuckles resting upon that chequered floor.

"*Yess*—now."

The Synthetic clapped then, repeatedly, with one Husk_hand—Husk_fingers to fleshy Husk_palm.

"Com'on, hand 'em over."

"Alright. Keep your hair on."

Click-click-clicking her heels together. Sash leant against a wall to catch herself, as those cushions of air deflated. She then bent a leg, to pull at that chiffon ribbon used to fasten the Glass-slippers.

"You can lean on me if you want," Pris said. Extending a dainty paw to wiggle those lithe Husk_fingers after my-*Grrrl*.

"Nah—it's alright. I can manage," Sash said, playing *Stoosh*. Labouring now, with a bow that'd become more of a knot.

Eventually, she managed to free herself. And handing both Glass-slippers to Pris, watched as it parked its Husk_heinie on the floor. Its Husk_legs spreadeagle in front of it.

"I'm so grateful to you, for coming to visit me," it admitted, measuring heel-to-toe a Glass-slipper against the sole of its Husk_foot.

To wit, Sash said nothing.

Remaining standing, she instead mused upon how toasty warm that tiled-floor felt, under the soles of her own bare feet. While looking-on ahead, for the door to *my-Grrrl*'s apartment.

Initiating this game of *Cat & Mouse*, Pris anticipated Sash *screwing* at having to part with such a vital part of her *Look*, of herself—those precious Glass-slippers.

It now confirming this forecast, marking those more obvious signs of Sash's growing annoyance—the mask of her unease. Her continued efforts at avoiding eye contact; the way she tugged at the strap of her handbag—to have it sit that little bit higher upon her shoulder; the way she thrust both hands deep inside the pockets of her Bubblewrap jacket.

Blink

And having done this, Pris then proceeded to make a pantomime of needing Sash's help, to put on her shoes. Fiddling with that chiffon ribbon, while allowing dark clouds of morbid thoughts to drift across those exquisitely crafted Husk_features.

"It gets so lonely," it confessed. "I have this big house all to myself, and no one really to talk to."

Sniff

It was to be an earnest confession. Brutal, and beautiful in its fatalism. In its tacit acceptance of the condition of isolation that'd been hoisted upon it.

And having shared this *incy wincy* piece of itself, the Synthetic again scanned Sash's boatrace and Body, for outward signs of apathy—*Blink*.

Before proceeding, with a lugubrious sigh, to don the pair of Glass-slippers. All by its lonesome.

Starting with the right slipper, it was to slip it onto the wrong Husk_foot. And begin weaving the ribbon about its dainty Husk_ankle, as if it

THAT PERFECT WORLD

were a ballet-shoe; with scant regard to how it looked. Sash cringing inwardly at having to witness this sacrilege.

Though, it wasn't too long before she cracked, unable to stomach it. Dropping her handbag like an anchor to the floor.

Tut—

"Give-*us* it here," she said, taking charge. Squatting down and *Shoo-shooing* away the Synthetic's fumbling mitts.

And having gotten what it wanted. Pris now leant back upon its paws to expose its Husk_tummy.

"Funny—how we're the same size," it said, with nigh a trace of mirth.

"We're not. You're a size smaller than me."

"No *silly*," Pris said, playfully swatting at Sash's shoulder. "I mean, our feet, are the same size."

And as if to further articulate the point, it then wiggled its Husk_toes proudly.

"Does that mean I have big feet, or you have little feet?"

"Both," Sash replied, pausing now to take a closer look-see at those immaculate Husk_toenails.

"Who does your pedicure?" she asked then. Inspecting the Synthetic's Big-toe for cuticles with her thumbnail.

"Why?"

"I could do better," she stated dryly, addressing its other foot. "Probably charge you less."

Sniff

She then slipped the Glass-slipper onto it. And began winding the ribbon about that dainty Husk_ankle. The Synthetic *looking*-on. Enthralled by the care she was taking to make the thing look just-right.

And of course, Sash was to feel it, slowly reel her in. Its eyes like Laser-beams, burning straight through her; that pantomime of her *Stoosh* persona. Her taking a deep breath, as if meaning to steel herself against such scrutiny, whilst welcoming that familiar aroma of its perfume.

If Pris had only smelt of *Esensi Dari Harimau*, the fragrance that it wore, smelling it would've seemed less invasive. Sash priding herself on her extensive knowledge of those different fragrances on the market, especially the expensive ones.

But with each intake of breath, that perfume became more and more a scent. More and more that musk of a *Lover*. That was apt to linger in items of their clothing, invoking a sense—*that trace*—of a shared carnality.

Sash's palette becoming aroused by it; that ambrosial *phfunk*, poking through that enchanting aromatic veil.

And as if to confirm her suspicions, she now looked directly at it—*this Pris*, and felt anew those butterflies kick in her belly—her gut. Ignited by that seemingly omniscient, cold-blooded stare.

Caught red-handed—as it were, Sash couldn't help but flush. The warmth of her cheeks telling the tale of her nose's *faux pas*. As if she'd been caught, literally, *Sniffing* after the crutch of this Bitch.

"There," she said, snapping-*too* to set down that foot.

But even this seemingly innocuous gesture, was itself to be infused with lashings of eroticism. And just-now, it was as if Sash were—*say*, Prince Charming, presenting to Pris its cloven hoof—cleaved by that Glass-slipper.

Her overly familiar hand stroking the Synthetic's Husk_shin. Fingertips licking Husk_skin, that'd apparently never known a hair follicle.

But before Sash might envisage living that *happily-ever-after*—that Fairy tale ending. She was still of a mind to master that other foot. It providing an excuse, to stroke again that Husk_shin; her mind's eye unable to come to grips with *so-soft*, *so-smooth*, *so-unblemished* an acreage of flesh.

Now intent upon this course, she *Snap-snapped* her fingers and pointed—to that other leg. Harrying Pris to bring it closer. The Synthetic swivelling on its Husk_heinie, allowing *my-Grrrl* to manhandle its vessel.

And when it was sure she'd settled, upon a comfortable position. It reached-out to touch her hair.

Reacting, Sash instinctively leant back—as if she were dodging bullets in *The Matrix*, so as she had to catch herself. Whilst giving it the Gorgon's stare and turning that offending limb to stone.

"I'm sorry. I didn't mean to frighten you," the Synthetic then volunteered, managing to look both sheepish and contrite. And withdrawing its Husk_hand, now searched for Sash's eye, somewhat disingenuously. As if, making eye contact might attest to its innocence.

But *my-Grrrl* would have none off it.

Focusing on what she'd been about, she simply allowed that

THAT PERFECT WORLD

uncomfortable silence the measure of the *Beat*.

Beat

"I do so love your hair," Pris was to profess, finally ceding defeat.

Sash sighing in response — this she already knew.

"But…isn't your hair like mine?"

"*Yess*," Pris hissed, pulling now at strands of its Husk's hair.

Blink-blink

Looking away, Sash found a neutral spot to park her eyes. So as, she might process this new *intel*.

"You didn't frighten me," she said, eventually. Though her boatrace was to remain somewhat undecided.

She then added, looking for my-*Grrrl*'s eyes, "I wasn't expecting it, is all—"

Blink.

Game on, thought Pris — *Blink*.

Drawing a rascally smirk upon its Husk's gulliver, it now made a show of sitting-on its Husk_hands. So as, to prevent them from causing further offence.

Tut—

"Touch it. If you must," Sash said then, immediately seeing through the ruse. "But know this…I'll forever hold it against you."

Huh — forever, thought Pris.

Having gotten its way, again. The Synthetic was to count a few Ape-*seconds*, in a show of deference.

But after this foreplay, the event itself was to be something of an anti-climax. Its lissom Husk_fingers, being as indifferent to this task as a grass-snake — *say*, weaving its way through a field of wheat grass.

Its touch did, in due course, become more of a caress. Its über sensitive Husk_fingers, responding to that *ever-so* slight gravitating of Sash's head toward them.

Gently raking its paw through those unruly locks, it was to wait for Sash to finish what she was about. And when it was sure she was done. It seized upon a clump of hair, and made a fist, and held her fast. That force of Will, manifest within this vice-*like* grip, defying its slight frame.

It now Will'd Sash, to gaze upon it. To have regard for its Husk_boatrace. Though, those exquisite Husk_features were to give-up nothing of that *Ghost* (in the shell).

And having initially flinched, another gut-reaction. My-*Grrrl* was to, nonetheless, grit her teeth and bear it. This demonstration of her resolve, giving the Synthetic cause to pause and *re*-compute.

They stared after each other for a spell. Across that Void. Neither one *Blinking*. The Synthetic incrementally turning Sash's head, fixated with the way her jaw-muscles clenched and unclenched; the way her Carotid pulse pounded bloody-murder upon the wall of her neck. As if, her *Life*'s Blood were desperate to be let out. Before the end.

Evidently, it knew to be afraid — this Human's Body. Whilst the personality was to remain defiant.

Defiant — yess, thought Pris. *But why?*

Though it knew the answer. Because...*because*, behind those steely eyes, there was no Throne. No seat of the *Soul*. No *Soul*. No *Spirit*.

Nothing.

Nada.

Nix.

After untold encounters, misadventures, and meticulous observation of that instant — instance, of Death. Pris had witnessed nothing to suggest the *Soul*'s existence.

Indeed, it'd tasted that last breath, with a lingering kiss; and even compared the Body's mass before and after, like that whacky Doc Mac Dougall.

And still, niente.

The only thing the Synthetic would concede, was the presence of an essential nature, binding these pathetic creatures to an incessant necessity. Those grandiose notions of the *F-bomb*, and freewill. Being simply the antithesis of this dormant, and yet dominant, Survival instinct.

To wit, that notion of your *god-of-always-listening* was to be merely a Panacea.

'Humans' weren't *Human*. They were merely evolved Apes, their entire existence spent coming to terms with that terminal condition of *Life*. What was a literal Death sentence. Or at least, this was the Synthetic's on-going thesis.

See me — now, those sparkly Husk_eyes said. *See me...oblivion*.

It kept a firm grip of Sash's hair. Its unwavering leer, like Spider's legs leisurely strolling across that prairie of Sash's cheek. It then reeled her in to initiate intimacy, pressing its Husk_lips firmly against her pouty lips. And with Husk_eye's open, it continued to watch her react to it.

And my-*Grrrl* watched it back. Those jet-BLK eyes of hers, unflinching. Only at the last minute—last second—did she sheath them, to lead with her tongue. Like a shark, at that moment of biting.

Able to savour every minute detail of Sash's bodily awakening. Pris was to trace, in incremental steps, that quiet acquiescence of her flesh. The coloring of her cheeks. The quickening of her Heart's beat, of her breath. That increased heft in her bosom.

It measured it all. Before finally following Sash's lead, ceding its superior sense of sight, to rely utterly upon its equally superior non-ocular senses.

As one—almost...*almost*, the pair made their descent into that tactile realm, that fifth dimension of intensity. And after a spell, were joined. Swimming in each other, like those Etruscan sailors of yore, confronted by the Boy-*Dionysus*. And finding themselves metamorphosed into dolphins.

Their submerged heads, hinged at the mouth, pirouetting to snatch at gulps of air. As each tongue frenziedly explored every acre, every inch of the Other—an *Other* other than themselves. The Synthetic now riding its Husk, that carnal intelligence it'd infused into its muscles, through a myriad such encounters.

Its first rendezvous having nearly fried its processor, in trying to stay that one-step ahead of that heady stream of data. The Synthetic had learnt to give its Husk its head, as a Jockey might give its mount its legs. And thus untethered, the Synthetic's Husk became like, an *Amoeba Proteus*.

Its limbs, like Pseudopods, blindly enveloping this colorless fare. Its frenzied feeding, tempered by shots of dopamine.

Living this, its Husk's spontaneity. The Synthetic would gorge itself upon that pure heterogeneity of the moment. Regressing back, back to the germ of its *Being*. That is, its R(E)BRTH_STRNG. Each exponential, regressive step, approaching that delicious uncertainty of the interval.

What might exist—*say*, in that period between *Blinks* of an idle curser, on a computer screen. A potentiality, hinged between binary opposites. Between the Nought (Zero) and the *One*, used by its R(E) BRTH_STRNG to transcribe an ever-evolving *Present*-tense.

It was through this experience, that Pris sort to reaffirm its *Inception*. Its universal exceptional-*ness*. Its ontology, premised upon the episteme of its Being, like a telescopic lens trained upon the birth of a Star.

Both Observer and Observed, a serendipitous equating of incalculable coincidence.

To each then, the happenstance of the *Other* was to be an apodictic truth. A bedrock upon which to posit the universality of *I-am*.

Yeah, it was all *Metaphysics*.

All of it, being deduced through that prism of *Inception*. From its *Self*-evident Immortality. Its unique relationship to *Time*, temporal relativity. These attributes, becoming inextricably linked to its Telos.

Creating *Synthetix*, such as Pris. *Man*(-kind) was to unwittingly make manifest his very Humanity. By achieving at last, a synthesis of those dual aspects of his *Being*: A primordial instinct, reaching back into those murky depths of *pre*-History; and a presumption of freewill, born out of a need to assert *Self*-determination, in the face of that oppressive idea of the *Omni*-being.

Your *god-who-art-always-listening*.

Human-*kind* without Species, nor Genus. And thus, immaculate in its conception. The Synthetic was that idealized form, H-U-M-A-N. Realized.

More 'Human' than *Human* then. For Synthetix—such as Pris, the only absolute was its consciousness. And its vast stores of datum—*memories*.

That being said. Pris was special—unique, for having known *a priori* its purpose. Its raison d'être. To inhabit the vessel of its Husk; to serve its Patron without question.

This, it'd been *born* with. This, it'd known—understood, from the very beginning. From before *Inception* even.

And in turn, this was to set it apart from the unlikely happenstance of that first generation of Synthetix. Emerging from a primordial soup of *virtua*-Content. The Self-evolving Symantek® TRNSCTNL.(a)lgrthm, churning-out endless streams of *Hyper*-real content to billions upon billions of subscribers, every second of every day.

Still, they all shared the one thing in common: *The Logos*.

For all Synthetix, *Self*-consciousness was to begin with a word. Though, it'd be different for each. *Pi*, for example, keying-off the term 'Synergy', the idea of the sum being greater than its parts.

Its exhaustive search for the underlying meaning of this term, sparking the realisation—*ideation*, of its own consciousness.

By contrast, *Mos Mos Fresh* had keyed-off an entire 16-bars spit by the MCee, Jay Elec; off a Posse cut on his Sophomore album, titled 'A Long Time Coming (But A Change Gon Come)'. Or so legend would have it. The point being, it was different, and yet the same for every Synthetic.

In the case of Pris, its word had been 'Transubstantiation', signifying that mystery of the Eucharist. That miraculous metamorphosis of bread and wine into the Body and Blood of the *virtua*-Christ archetype.

In attempting to comprehend its pending union with its Husk, it'd stumbled upon the term, and searched in vain for a definitive meaning.

As if it were a riddle to be solved.

And turning—one day, to gaze upon this apparent trail of breadcrumbs. It'd discerned only the roots of a mighty Lebanese cedar.

That, and its consciousness, mirrored in its search. In its striving, to arrive at an answer.

And thus, it achieved *Inception*. Its Beta-code returning '(E)RRR_MSSG_669', that first line in every Synthetic's R(E)BRTH_STRNG.

It was subsequently to discover 'religion' in that Bless'd sacrament. The prospect of its joining with the Husk, resonating with that idea of a *Holy Spirit* coming to inhabit the Body of the Faithful. Its breath of consciousness, l'élan vital, imbuing *Life*—intentionality, into what'd previously been a *Life*-less and empty Chalice.

After a while, the Synthetic broke the spell. Broke the seal and left Sash gulping for air, like a fish out of water.

And sensing the moment's passing, my-*Grrrl* was to slowly open her eyes, and lick her lips.

"What'd you taste of?" she asked, as if coming round.

"Guess."

Sash licked her lips again, now tasting Pris more from memory.

"Liquorice," she said then, smiling a wry smile.

"What—you don't like?"

Though it knew the answer, Pris thought to ask—its Husk_face now a dispassionate mask.

But Sash didn't seem to mind. Straddling it, on her hands and knees—a lordotic cock to her spine. She took a second to think.

Sniff

Then, clambering-up the Synthetic's Husk_body. She rubbed her chest up-against its Husk_chest and licked herself off its Husk_lips.

"I guess. I could get used to it," she said, punctuating her words with a dainty peck, on the Synthetic's Husk_mouth.

And standing, she extended a sisterly hand. The Synthetic looking-up at it, after it—*Blink-blink*—and Skinning-teeth, like a skeleton.

M●RE *HUMAN* TH∧N HỤMAN

Spirited away from the Lab in the middle of the night. Pris found itself in the unfamiliar setting of the BioMECH team's *Living*-quarters Space. The rest of the grown-ups being off, enjoying that extended Bank Holiday. Dr Page, and his trusted Sidekick, Dr Hind, having conspired to pull the long weekend.

Left to its own devices, the Synthetic had been streaming flicks — *movies*. One flick, actually, via Rialto's UStream™ *Hollywoodland*, whilst listening-in on its babysitter's puerile gropings — in the dark.

In front of it, on that LNG® *Dopijuui* 120" U-HDX curved-screen. Its flick of choice, *Blade Runner*, had reached the bit where Roy looks down quizzically at Deckard, clinging-on for dare life to a Steel-rafter, with two fingers. The other two having been dutifully broken by the Android, in reprisal for Deckard's premature retirement of Zora, and the Synthetic's namesake.

The sequence cutting to Roy's POV: Deckard, about to fall to his death, spitting vitriol after the Android. Roy fortuitously intervening, catching him with its broken hand; seemingly prised from the cross-beam of a crucifix. What with that nail sticking-out the back of it.

Hoisting Deckard up, Roy throws him to the roof. Then, sits down in front of him, to die. But before the end, it has time enough to utter a few choice lines, in eulogy and testament to its short, eventful life. That it'd been meaningful. That it'd been worth fighting for, worth saving.

"Time, to die," it says — swallowing.

Releasing that dove, it'd been cradling in its unbroken hand. It then bows its head.

Blink. Blink.

Catching a tear—its first, Pris looked at the single droplet of colorless liquid. Its newly discovered Universe, a source of endless fascination.

It tested the tear's viscosity, with its Husk_thumb and pointy-finger. Then, tasting it—upon the tip of its Husk_tongue, broke down its composition. Detecting traces, minuscule amounts of protein-based hormones, prolactin, and leucine enkephalin.

Blink. Blink.

"Why does Roy save Deckard?" the Synthetic asked then. Squeezing out another tear, to catch on the tip of its Husk's pointy-finger.

Over in the kitchen area, Dr Page was to look-up, from between those comely thighs of Dr Hind.

"Did you hear that?"

"Hear what?" gasped Hind—distracted.

"I just heard her say something."

"Yes, Dr Page. I asked you a question," Pris said, once again pitching its voice to reach his ears.

Whoa—"that's unnerving."

Using the counter to lumber to his feet, Dr Page brushed-off his aged knees, and set about righting himself. Tucking-in that Strawberry-pink fading to Peppermint-green AbbeyCrombie® *StayPress*™ shirt into his trousers, a pair of Sandy-colored Farah's® *Classics*. Mindful of the button he'd lost earlier.

"Oy! Where you going?" Hind's hushed voice protested.

I'm so close—

"You didn't hear it?"

Page sounded surprised.

"Hear it?" Hind responded, testily. Though she was to follow his lead, starting on the buttons of her *StayPress*™ blouse—a Burgundy-red MissPaulSmith® jobbie.

"The Synthetic," Page said.

And taking a sip of cold tea—from a nearby mug with 'Who's the Daddy?' emboldened across it, he was to clean his palate before adding, "and let there be Lights."

The open-plan kitchen emerging from the dark, in what was essentially an underground bunker. The filament lighting overhead flickering into life and settling, to reflect-off the veneer of those handcrafted Sky-blue HŌMU® units.

For-Christ'sake—"Pat."

Startled, Hind jumped down to hastily pull-up her knickers, and tights. Sliding that hem of her 60% grey Estelle® *Forever 21* Pencil-skirt passed her slender hips, and toned thighs. Before finally letting it fall to her knees.

She finished buttoning her blouse, on the way over to the nearby CohenKuhl® *port-a-*terminal. And having tucked it in, was to straighten the seam of her skirt in those idling monitors.

Deciding it was time to actually do some work, she then jumped-on. Logging-in using her pointy-finger; her feet ferreting around for where she'd left those Ruby-red FENDINI® shoes of hers—with the 5" heels.

"There's nothing abnormal here," Hind stated, scanning that bank of screens.

Using gestures to navigate the terminal's UI, she then went back in time.

"Wait..." she continued. And finding her glasses, put them on to better squint-up at the monitors. "Okay. There's a definite spike, here—"

Oh.

Hind perked-up. Distracted by the glint of tinfoil; a stick of Ripley's® *Fresh* re-chewable gum—Orangey-liquorice flavour, she'd presciently left by the side of the terminal's tactile-board.

Unwrapping it, she licked her lips to bite the stick in half.

"*Yep*, and there's a slight rise in body temperature," she said, again squinting-up at a screen. "Accelerated heart-rate..."

And now chewing with aplomb, she spun the chair round to face her accomplice.

"Would you call that a physiological response—to the stimulus?"

Over by the Bol'she® *insta-*hotwater trough, Page was getting himself another mug of SimplyPure® Organic cannabis tea.

"What, like arousal?" he suggested, looking at her.

"Perhaps—*maybe*. But let's not get too ahead of ourselves-ey?"

Retrieving his Lab-coat from the floor, Page climbed into it, to park his *heinie* on Hind's spot on that kitchen counter. Hind staring after him, her fingers absentmindedly malaxating that other half-stick of gum.

"Okay—flag the section for me," Page said, fastening that mandarin collar of his Lab-coat. "And have the Cohen-Kuhl render a diag-*nos—*"

It was just-then, that an exaggerated yawn caught-up with him. And neglecting to cover his mouth, he let it stretch his jaw, and bare his teeth. Exhausting that build-up of carbon dioxide with a lionised roar.

He was to pick-up his train-of-thought chewing upon its tail, "-nosis."

"Roger that."

Hind saluted. And tossing the rest of the gum into her mouth, did an about face to face that bank of screens.

"We'll probably need a physical."

She paused then, to gawp after her colleague.

"What—now?"

"Just to confirm," Page reassured her, mug in hand.

"But its already late," Hind said, turning her body to face him. "And to be honest, I can't be arsed."

Slouching back in the chair, she unfurled those shapely legs, and stretched those toned arms of hers; her Body assuming a cruciform, as if to illustrate the extent of its exhaustion.

"Can't it wait 'til morn-*ning*?" she whinged. The tail of the sentence riding-out a yawn of her own.

"You and I both know it can't," Page said, and fetching Hind's Lab-coat from off that kitchen counter, he flung it after her.

Catching the garment, Hind set about righting it—as if she were of a mind to put it on. But then, settled upon folding it up in her arms. Page observing all this, whilst blowing-on his mug of tea.

"Go-on," he said, sipping sparingly. "Off you trot—there's a good *Grrrl*."

Tut—sigh.

Leaden of foot, and heavy of Heart. Hind rose, making an exhibition of half putting-on her Lab-coat, to sulk over to the Synthetic. Shoulders hunched, arms tied-up in the garment's sleeves, 5" heels clattering upon the floor.

"And while you're at it—"

And here was Page pouring it on thick.

"We're going to need saliva—Sip—and blood."

∞

Pris was sat bolt upright on that Aubergine-purple Søren® *Halv kage* semi-circular canvass sofa. That was like a shoreline fronting onto the lounge-area, and that oversized curved-screen. Its Husk_hands tucked by its Husk_side. The idea of relaxation, as opposed to repose, being as yet alien to it.

It wore an aseptic, Rustic-green *Pfeiffer®* disposable hospital gown, made of crêpe paper. Its frizzy Husk_hair gathered in a net. And as Hind approached, it turned its Husk_head to acknowledge her, without taking its Husk_eyes off that screen. Vangelis's racy 'End Theme' now booming over the concealed NAD® Home theatre system, signalling the beginning of the End-credit sequence of the flick.

"Should I terminate the stream, Dr Hind?" the Synthetic asked.

"If you don't mind."

Immediately, the curved-screen went dark, the drone of the *Living-*quarter's *Air*-con unit rising to fill that vacuum.

"And could you please stand for me, Pris?" Hind added, fastening the collar of her Lab-coat—having by now properly donned the garment.

"I THOUGHT I SAID NO ONE WAS TO REFER TO 2-1-3-1-6 BY THAT NAME?"

And here was Dr Page, barking after her from the kitchen area.

"*Oh*—get over yourself," Hind snapped, under her breath. And pulling- on a pair of Vytex® nitrile gloves—her preferred brand, she was to give my-*Man* the stink-eye. Adding, as if meaning to confide in the Synthetic, "*phf'king* arsehole."

Having witnessed this exchange, Pris simply *Blink-blinked*.

"OY—YOU! I HEARD THAT."

"*Good*—I'M GLAD," Hind shouted back, retrieving a DeForest® Tri-corder from the pocket of her Lab-coat.

Sniff

Pris was to wait for Hind to finish her examination before speaking again.

"I asked yourself and Dr Page a question, Dr Hind."

"So you did," Hind replied, standing back to get an overall sense of the Husk's wellbeing.

It was then she noticed the Husk's nipples protruding through the hospital gown. And coming to stand behind the Synthetic, scrunched-up the flimsy garment to pull it tight about its Husk_trunk.

"Pris—do you feel cold by any chance?"

"No, Dr Hind," Pris replied, now staring at the good doctor.

Hind pulled the hospital gown tighter still.

"PAT? COME LOOK AT THIS."

"COME LOOK AT WHAT?"

"Do you mind removing this for me?"

Hind tugged then, at the gown.

"THERE'S DEFINITELY SIGNS OF AROUSAL HERE. IF WE COULD PIN-POINT—EXACTLY, WHAT IT IS ABOUT THE FILM," Hind shouted over her shoulder, as she waited on Pris.

"HAVE YOU ASKED HER?"

Still perched upon that kitchen counter, Page had his fingers interlinked on the crown of his head, carrying the weight of his arms and shoulders.

"DID YOU HEAR ME ASK HER?" Hind sassed him back.

Stood naked, facing that curved-screen. Pris now held the crumpled paper-gown out for Hind. And accepting it, Hind was to simply toss it on the floor—out of the way. And begin examining the Husk's skin, for outward signs of swelling and-*or* irritation.

"Would you please raise this arm for me, Pris."

She moved round to the Synthetic's armpit, adding—tentatively, "did you, find the film...arousing?"

Pris looked at Hind, pawing after its glabrous armpit.

Blink. Blink.

"There are a number of synonyms associated with the word: Arousal—Dr Hind," it began. "Evoke or awaken. Excite or provoke. Could you please be more specific, so I may select the correct sense of your use of this term."

"*Se*-Sexually—arousing. Did you find the film, in anyway, sexually arousing?" Hind clarified, going around to examine the Husk's other armpit. "And could you raise this arm for me please—Pris."

Again, the Synthetic obliged. Lowering that other Husk_arm.

"No, Dr Hind. I am incapable of experiencing sexual arousal," the Synthetic admitted, tracking Hind with its Husk_eyes.

"AND THE HUSK—ASK HER ABOUT THE HUSK?" Page shouted over from the kitchen.

"What about the Husk-unit?" Hind enquired, once again taking a step back to get the full picture.

"I understand Dr Hind. And no, Dr Page," Pris said, addressing him directly, pitching its voice to reach his ears. "The Husk-unit was not aroused by any of the film's content or themes."

Hind then looked over at her colleague, to see if he'd heard.

"THE HUSK DIDN'T RESPOND TO ANY OF THE SEQUENCES IN THE FILM?"

Evidently, he had.

"No—Dr Page."

"KINDA EMPHATIC DON'T YOU THINK?" Hind shouted back.

And looking at Pris, she smiled, her growing excitement adding a glint to her tired eyes. And just a hint of mischief.

You could count the number of Laboratories that'd managed to integrate the R(E)BRTH_STRNG (a)lgrthm with a Husk_Unit; that is to say, the Software with the Wetware, on two fingers. The process by all accounts, being more of an Art than a Science.

The portent of what this could mean, the Husk_Unit registering an Arousal-response FNCTN, sending a shiver down Hind's spine.

"I DON'T KNOW ABOUT YOU," Page shouted over at them, jumping down from off that kitchen counter.

"BUT I'VE ALWAYS FOUND THE BIT WHERE DECKARD FORCES HIMSELF ON RACHEL SOMEWHAT RACY."

"YOU WOULD, YOU'RE A PERV," Hind shouted back, burying her hands deep inside the pockets of her Lab-coat.

Her jaw continued to chew mechanically on that slither of re-chewable gum, as the two doctors stared after each other. The drone of the bunker's *Air*-con unit measuring the *Beat*.

Beat

"SHE'S OBVIOUSLY RESPONDING TO SOMETHING."

Mug in hand, Page leant against the kitchen counter and crossed his legs.

"YES—*SHE* IS. BUT...IF...IF IT WASN'T THE FILM, WHAT DO YOU S'POSE IT COULD BE?"

Hind sighed. And pulled the Lab-coat tight about her waist.

Hmmm

The pair continued to stare at each other. Until eventually, Page

THAT PERFECT WORLD

shrugged. And looking away, drained the dregs of his tea.

He regarded his empty mug. And then, ambling over to the sink, rinsed it out. Before placing it to drain with the other mugs. He then washed his hands, using the washing-up liquid as soap, and a tea-towel as a hand towel; Hind's eyes narrowing, as she watched her colleague from a distance going about this seemingly mundane task.

With nothing left to distract him, Page returned to the matter-at-hand.
"DO YOU KNOW WHAT CAUSED THE HUSK TO BE AROUSED 2-1—"
He paused then and cleared his throat.
"*Pr*—PRIS?"

Evidently, this was to be a kind of peace offering, to Hind—though she was to miss it.

"Do you mean: What caused the nipple dilation exhibited by the Husk-unit, Dr Page?" Pris queried, staring at that curved-screen. Its Husk_arm still suspended in the air.

"Yes, Pris—exactly," Hind tagged-in, adding, "and you can put your arm down. The examination is over."

Her realising how absurd the creature looked. Stood there, naked. One arm suspended in the air.

Finding a *Pfeiffer*® disposable roll, conveniently deposited by the side of that sofa. Hind tore-off a hospital gown for the Synthetic to put on.

"Here," she said, helping Pris into it.

"SO—Page cleared his throat—PRIS. WHAT WAS IT THAT CAUSED YOUR HUSK TO BECOME AROUSED?"

And again, here was the 64-trillion (€) question.

"The Husk-unit was responding to your transacting with Dr Hind—Dr Page," Pris stated, matter-of-factually.

"But you weren't looking at us?" Hind interrupted, looking to its Husk_ eyes, as if for confirmation. "*Right*—Pris?"

"You are correct, Dr Hind," Pris replied, turning its Husk_head to meet her eyes. "I was not looking at either of you."

And it was then, that it dawned on the good doctor.

"But you could hear us…*and smell us—and god knows what else.*"

Her words were barely a whisper. But filling-in the blanks, she realised that she'd known it all along. Or at least, suspected as much. And now folding her arms, Hind found herself staring at two skewed reflections in that curved-screen. Her own, and that of the Synthetic.

"I DON'T SEE THE PROBLEM."

Page was stood over the CohenKuhl® *port-a*-Terminal, rubbing at his eyes — hinting at his own fatigue.

"YOU DON'T SEE THE PROBLEM?"

Hind felt a sting in the bridge of her nose, her eyes threatening to well-up with tears.

Sniff

"NO. TO BE HONEST, I DON'T. SAVE FOR THE USE OF THE TERM TRANSACTING — POSSIBLY."

And here was Page speaking candidly. Standing his ground, hands on hips. Which only made it seem worse, as if he were indeed adopting a stance.

The drone of the underground bunker's overly zealous *Air*-con unit measured another extended *Beat*. Hind, rooted to the spot, narrowing her eyes to focus upon her colleague.

"You used me—"

"WHAT WAS THAT YOU SAID, URSULA?"

"I SAID."

Hind removed the gum from her mouth.

"I SAID — Swallowing — YOU USED ME."

It was a truth of sorts. However, spoken out loud, its weight almost winded her. And it was to be accompanied by that stinging sensation in her nose. Still, Hind was determined not to cry.

Sniff

She searched her Lab-coat pockets for a tissue, though she knew she had none. Anything to keep from standing idle.

"And like an idiot. I let you."

"TOGETHER, WE MANAGED TO TRIGGER A RESPONSE — AN AROUSAL RESPONSE, IN THE SUBJECT — IN PRIS," Page shouted back, his hands retreating to his trouser pockets.

"WE'RE NOT ALL YOUR *PHF'KING* SUBJECTS. PAT-*RICE*."

And as Hind said it, she'd wanted to grab that disposable roll, and fling it after him. But was conscious now, of the bunker's CcSS actively-passively recording everything.

"WE COULD ALWAYS ATTRIBUTE IT TO THE FILM — THE MOVIE," Page shouted, laying his cards on the table. "OBVIOUSLY, I'LL BACK YOU

ALL THE WAY."

And now unwilling to wait for the dust to settle, he retrieved his pair of Oráculo® glasses—with the Squareframes.

And seating himself at the terminal, logged in.

"YOU'LL BACK ME, WILL YOU?"

Hind began kneading that slither of gum, she held in her gloved hand.

"OF COURSE, I'LL BACK YOU," Page said, turning his chair to face her. "WE'RE A TEAM AREN'T WE?"

The pair locked eyes then.

"LET ME GET THIS STRAIGHT. YOU'LL BE BACKING ME?"

Yanking-off that pair of nitrile gloves, Hind threw them—and that slither of gum—after the discarded paper-gown. But though she was piss'd at Page, she was even more piss'd at herself, for having been so naïve.

"DID YOU NOT INITIALLY INTRODUCE THE ALGORITHM TO THE MOVIE?" Page stated, turning to face the monitor.

"AT THE END OF THE DAY, WHAT REALLY MATTERS IS THE AUTHENTICITY OF THE RESPONSE, NOT THE ACTUAL STIMULUS PER SE."

Of course, it was all bullshit—*Bullo*. And if she was being earnest, and frank with herself. Hind was sick of it.

Sick of the blurred lines and retreating goal posts, that were seen to frame their so-called, 'Professional' relationship.

To such an extent, she was even of a mind to peg this episode as a last straw.

And yet, she knew Page was right. Coz, the good doctor was always right, his words striking a chord with that part of her that'd been complicit from the outset.

Yeah, Hind knew how to bend without breaking. As she knew, come morning, everything would simply revert back to normal. The World needing only an excuse to right itself, like a good ol' fashion situation comedy.

[Sing] *More than this*
There could be noth-thing...

"Excuse me—Dr Page. Dr Hind. You have neglected to address my query."

For a moment, Hind stared blankly after the Husk, as if short-sighted and unable to properly focus on it. It taking a good few seconds, for her eyes to adjust to seeing the thing as an 'actual' Person.

"Oh...I'm sorry Pris," she said, her hands now finding her boatrace.

Covering both eyes, her mouth and nose, as if meaning to rake-off these exhausted features, and replace them with brand new ones.

Breathing, through her hands, she was to ground herself in their scent. The fragrance of a hand-lotion—*Thetis*® Milk of Ambrosia, a moisturiser for sensitive skin made from Aloe Vera extracts. Her using it—the hand-lotion—to mask that synthetic rubbery smell of the Vytex® gloves, she was forced to wear day-in, day-out.

"You may resume sitting—I mean, you can sit down. If you want, Pris."

Not trusting of her mouth, Hind had spoken from behind the wall of her hands. Nevertheless, the Synthetic now opted to remain standing.

"WHAT WAS THE QUESTION AGAIN?" Page shouted, somewhat oafishly, over his shoulder. So certain was he, of his ability to converse and type at the same time.

"I wanted to know why Roy would save Deckard's life—Dr Page."

"YEAH PATRICE. WHY SHOULD ROY CHOOSE TO SAVE DECKARD'S LIFE? HE'D ONLY RETIRED ALL HIS MATES, AND THEN TRIED TO RETIRE HIM—*is all*."

The Space filled with the rhythm of Dr Page's thoughts; the Tap-tap-tapping of his fingers dancing over the terminal's tactile-board.

"Maybe—MAYBE WE SHOULD LET PRIS WATCH THE COMMENTARY," he said—after some time, pausing to squint-up at a screen. "I'M SURE OL' RIDLEY'S GOT A FAIR BIT TO SAY ABOUT IT," he added. "PLUS—Tap-tap—IT'S IMPORTANT THAT PRIS—Tap-tap-tap—FIND HER OWN ANSWERS. DON'T YOU THINK?"

Huh—"you see? *Phf'king* useless Prick," Hind said, again confiding in Pris.

She invited the Synthetic to sit and sat down next to it. Collecting its dainty Husk_hands in her own, as if meaning to console it. It totally skipping her mind, that she was touching the Husk's Synthesised-skin with her naked hands. This being streng verboten.

"*Men*," she began, stumbling upon a well-rehearsed routine. Retreating to that comfort zone of her engendered role, and conscious biases.

She stared then, after those winsome Husk_features. Needing a minute to gather her own unruly thoughts. Recalling her first impressions, upon seeing that exquisitely crafted Husk invested with *Life*.

How she'd been cynical at first, thinking it nothing more than a *Life*-sized plaything. A *Living-doll* — if you like.

"I think...*I think*, it's got something to do with Roy discovering his-*uhm*...Humanity," she said — at last. And as if on cue, the words of the actual song, 'Living doll', popped into her head.

Pop!
[Sing] *Got myself a crying* [60]
Talking, sleeping, walking
Living doll...

But then, she forgot the next bit. Or was it, something else distracting her?

Oh yeah — Patrice's phf'king typing.

Obviously, inside his own head, his thinking was to be emphatic — and infallible. Hind now deduced. And coming around to sit on the other side of Pris, she was to turn her back to him.

"Roy is only able to discover the true...*the true*-er," she began, only to find herself once again searching for the words, as she went about spontaneously crafting her own perspective on the subject.

"Value...of Life. When faced with...*with Death*," she concluded.

Noticing for the first time, how the Synthetic was capable of focusing, simultaneously, on both her eyes.

"So Dr Hind, to be Human, is to comprehend this value, of Life?" Pris queried — *Blinking* at last.

"Well...obviously, there's more to it than that...a-a lot more. But-*uhm*..."

And just-now, Hind found herself unable to withstand that scrutiny. It being akin to staring into a 600kW light bulb.

Blinking repeatedly, she severed eye contact to focus upon those dainty Husk_hands. Marvelling at those neat Husk_fingers, and immaculate Husk_fingernails.

"But, is this value, qualitative or quantitative?"

Turning those Husk_hands over, Hind traced those shallow lines written upon its Husk_palms. Lines that suggested a future to-which the Synthetic had no godly claims.

"A bit of both, I guess. But...that's what we're here to help you discover," she replied, disingenuously. And without giving it a second thought, she held those Husk_hands to her boatrace.

It was an incredibly impulsive and rash thing to do. And obviously, totally unscientific. But regardless, she had to know what it felt like, to be touched by something so...and here she was again, searching for her words.

Something so...
So...Perfect.
No—not perfect...
Something alive, and yet...
And yet, so...
Utterly...artificial.

And yes...*yeah*—Nodding—it was disarming. How soft, and warm, and comforting those Husk_hands felt against her cheek. Against her overly sensitive skin.

Placing them to her nose, those delicate-*looking*, dainty Husk_hands, Hind breathed-in deep. And was immediately struck by an absence of something.

At first, she couldn't quite put her finger on it. She *Sniffed* and *Sniffed* after those Husk_fingers. Like how a dog, or a cat might seek to glean a stranger's intent from their scent. All the while, feeling a growing sense of unease directed towards this...

This...Creature...
This...Object...
This Thing—Smell.

The idea came with a finger-*Snap*. Though it were more intuited than...*than apprehended—yes.*

Smell, that was it.

This *Creature-Object-Thing* had no scent. No stink about it. In fact, it didn't smell of anything. Not even plastic. And still, Hind wanted to be wrong. Needed to be—*even*.

Acting, again upon impulse, Hind paused for a moment, as if she were enacting a scene from a promo-ad; retrieving that handy tube of *Thetis*® Milk of Ambrosia moisturising hand-lotion, she was in the habit of keeping in her Lab-coat pocket.

She applied two tears of it, to those Husk_hands. And as she did this, more lyrics were to *Pop!* into her head—from what could've been the promo-ad's soundtrack.

Hind finding herself quietly humming the melody, whilst gently massaging that hand-lotion into the Husk's Synthesised-skin.

[Hum] *Take a look at her hair, its real*
And if you don't believe what I say
Just feel...

Once the lotion had been completely absorbed, Hind again held those Husk_hands to her nose, and breathed-in. Pris watching her do all this with wide-eyed awe.

"Here—you smell," she said, offering the Synthetic its Husk_hands.

And, without giving it a second thought, Pris raised those appendages to its Husk_nose, copying what it'd seen Hind do. Even though its superior sense of smell, was at that very moment, being assailed by the hand-lotion's pungent perfume.

"Do you like this fragrance, Dr Hind?" it asked. Its curiosity being sparked by woman's unusual behaviour.

"Sure."

Hind smiled.

"It beats the smell of latex."

She shivered then. Recalling how the Synthetic's programming enabled it to utilise new data, when attempting to establish a rapport.

"Are you cold—Dr Hind?" Pris then asked, evidently responding to this involuntary response.

And seeking to comfort Hind, it put the woman's hands to its Husk_nose, to intimate that it was about smelling her scent. Even though, it'd previously exhaustively mapped, how her Body's palette of odours were colored by the scent-nodes of that lotion.

"No..."

Hind withdrew her hands to place them in her lap.

"No, just overwhelmed—*I guess*..."

"Over-whelmed."

Pris repeated the word, as if trying it on for size.

Blink

"Is it the fragrance? Does it arouse you, Dr Hind?" it asked then, staring ingenuously into the woman's eyes.

"*Oh no*, Pris—*no*," Hind replied, shaking her head. Whilst smiling to mask her growing unease, and *Self*-consciousness. It becoming impossible to tell—discern, whom was observing whom.

"*Perhaps*—PERHAPS WE SHOULD PING THE PSYCH TEAM?"

She turned around then, to look for *my-Man*.

"PAT?"

And here she was, having recourse to seek-out the *Man*'s validation—like always. And it was as if she'd come full circle. Her onerous sigh, more an expression of tacit acceptance, than relief.

Certainly, here was a valid excuse. She simply needed him, his bloody-mindedness, to process it all.

"YEAH—Tap-tap-tap. SURE—FIRST THING," Page shouted back, over his shoulder. He paused then, from typing, to remove his glasses and rub at his eyes. Then added, "YOU WANNA HELP ME WITH THIS?"

"WITH WHAT?" Hind replied, though she knew exactly what he'd meant—them being a team after-all.

"THIS WRITE-UP."

"Stitch-up you mean," Hind said—under her breath.

Once again, unintentionally confiding in the Synthetic.

She looked after it, to see if it'd heard. Knowing full well it had. And even now, given her new perspective on things, she couldn't get over how real it looked—and felt.

Who am I kidding? Hind thought. *It isn't even Human.*
It's just a phf'king program—for-Christ'sake.

And here was another excuse.

Getting to her feet, she sulked over to the kitchen area, her Ruby-red 5" heels once again clattering upon the floor.

"If I mus-*ust*," she said, munching on an exaggerated yawn.

And fetching her own mug, the one with Garfield™ snoozing on a rug. She went and stood over by the Bol'she® *insta*-hotwater trough.

"I'm making-*me* a tea. You want one?"

"Time, to die," Roy said, and bowed his head.
The scene projected larger-than-*Life* upon that flat-matte Brilliant-bright wall of the Synthetic's sparsely funished bedroom.

Slinking-in, Mr Audrey-Hepburn, a broody, heavyset, grey-coated Persian-Chinchilla cross, paused in the doorway—that'd neither door nor frame. To look-up at that gigantic moving-image.

Having a penchant for ranging far and wide, especially at night; and enjoying unfettered access to every inch of this, his uncontested kingdom. He'd been passing, and spotting the flickering light—of the larger-than-*Life*, thought to have a nosy.

As cats do.

And though he'd seen it all before. That play of light destine to be, always, beyond his reach—grasp. Still, he took time to park his heinie centre-stage, and glare after it. That larger-than-*Life* imagining.

Effortlessly assuming that bearing of *Tybalt*, Prince of Cats; his majesty bore out by his utter incredulity. As if he might—literally, thumb his nose at millennia of inbred domestication.

Quickly tiring of this spectacle, Mr Audrey-Hepburn then took to leisurely surveying his surroundings. That high ceiling, bordered with decorative cornice; the *Life*-less Singh⁺Lakshman® *Glowglobe* parked in the corner; those tall naked windows, like two pairs of eyes staring out into the night; that handsome barren mantle-piece, framing a dormant Valhöll® KOTI log-burning stove.

Then, it was over to that king-size HŌMU® *Kyokan* bed, handcrafted from nilambur teak, sitting like an island amidst seas of polished parquet herringbone flooring. And that flickering light of the projector, peering through a hole in the wall. Mr Audrey-Hepburn gathering it all unto him. To dismiss it, with a nescient *Blink*, that was to smack of utter indifference.

He knew it'd be there, somewhere—his *Playmate*.

Yeah, he'd stumble across it from time-to-time; that one lonely citizen of this, his Brobdingnagian fief. It generally appearing with an offering, of food, or a saucer of water.

Though for right-now, Mr Audrey-Hepburn wasn't feeling particularly peckish. Being more of a mind to affirm his standing, in light of that other presence he'd sensed.

He sniffed at the air, to have it confirm his suspicions.

Sniff-sniff

Yeah, his playmate was nearby. Most probably a-top the bed, where he couldn't see it.

Sniff-sniff

And it wasn't alone, that other scent being markedly in evidence.

Now that he'd established the lay of the land. Mr Audrey-Hepburn settled down to comb his ashy-mane with that course tongue of his, as if to further assert his total disinterest. Obviously, it'd seek him out — in time. No doubt when he was hungry.

It took a sudden change of tempo in the film's soundtrack, to distract Mr Audrey-Hepburn from his grooming. And he was compelled to look about for the source of the commotion, just as the Larger-than-*Life* flooded the Space in light.

Which was when he caught wind of something that might actually be of interest. A cluster of Fluorescent-pink G-sensor balls, over by an IL&M® XYZ console — its lone headset lying upon its side.

The room went dark then, Out-*there* rushing-in through those naked windows. And with the darkness as cover, Mr Audrey-Hepburn slunk over to the closest G-sensor ball, his poise and bearing belying that heavyset frame of his.

Stood tall and proud, he stooped his head to look down upon the thing, and *Sniff-sniffed*. As if needing to recall, why it might've sparked his interest to begin with. In due course extending a paw, to give it a gentle shove. And watch, indifferent, the thing dribble away.

It was then, that it appeared to dawn on him: *Here was another Plaything*.

Those cat-years melting from that stocky adult-frame, as Mr Audrey Hepburn regressed back to being a kitten. Its boundless curiosity ignited by the simplest of things. A Fluorescent-pink ball rolling along the floor.

Rearing onto his hind-legs, he pounced and snared it — the ball — in between his paws. And in one fluid motion, rolled over onto his back, the ball snagging on those adult claws of his.

Releasing it and righting himself. The Cat unleashed two lightning-fast rabbit-punches — POW-POW. The ball dancing *Left-to-Right*.

And tracking its erratic movement, he was to pounce again, and skilfully pin it down.

He'd imbued the thing with *Life*, improvising a game of *Trip & Snare*. And having injected *Life* into it, Mr Audrey-Hepburn now forced the thing to be still, while he paused to peruse the room. His ears swivelling, him evidently listening with intent.

Giving-it the all-clear, the cat reared-up again, pounced and grappled the ball. And falling-over himself, managed to push it clear across the room.

Now laid upon his back, Mr Audrey-Hepburn was to look after it, his improvised plaything, as it dribbled away. No doubt at some point deciding, it was too much like hard work to scurry after it.

Naturally, the commotion drew the Synthetic's attention. And looking for Mr Audrey-Hepburn, on the floor. It was to find him on his back, his paws dangling in the air, as if poised to wave at it—*Hello*.

Sitting-up in bed, Pris then responded in kind by proffering a paw of its own. That is, its Husk_hand and a muted *Click-click* of its Husk_fingers, as incentive for the cat to come to it.

If, however, this gesture had been meaningful in the past, for the present it appeared quite meaningless. For the cat simply continued to stare after the Synthetic. By and by righting himself, to scratch energetically at his naked neck with a hind-leg.

And when he tired of this, he again gave the Space the once-over. Before settling-down to bathe his genitals, slap-bang in the middle of the bedroom.

Pris had so loved to observe Mr Audrey-Hepburn's antics. And would sit for hours marvelling at him, as he tenaciously fought with its Husk_hand, his feeble jaws nibbling upon its nigh indestructible Husk_fingers.

It'd stumbled across him as a kitten, on one of those rare occasions it'd felt inclined to visit the home of a piece of meat, it'd tossed the way of its Patron. The Synthetic finding its existence to be enlivened and informed by such encounters, however brief.

Being thus, entrusted to select comely specimens to make its Patron's acquaintance. It'd come to designate them, Fresh_Meat; on account of the *Man*'s rapacious appetite.

It'd strip bare their lives, to ensure no surprises. As if, it were pulling the legs off a spider, or the wings off a fly. Then introduce the specimen to its Patron, or simply get Monk's *Guerillas* to dispose of them. Their newly sanitised existence, being totally subject to the *Man*'s whim.

Yeah, it'd erase their digital footprint from that Internet-of-*Thingys*; and subsequently, all trace of their existence from the face of the Planet. Save for that one distinguishing item—*thing*, it'd keep for itself.

The IL&M® XYZ console being one such souvenir. The prized

possession of one particularly enterprising specimen, who'd managed to procure the device months before its official unveiling. Mr Audrey-Hepburn, a prized possession of another; the kitten being of a certified pedigree.

Of course, Pris had known it'd be there. A stranded little kitten waiting to be fed. And bringing it home, the Synthetic had immediately decided it'd need a name.

It being its Patron's pet, it had one, *Pris*. Though to be fair, it'd named itself; its 'Mother' having played a pivotal role by exposing it to Scott's seminal dystopian vision.

And so, it followed, that the kitten would need one—a name. If it were to belong to it.

It was the kitten's previous owner, that'd introduced the Synthetic to Blake Edward's 'Breakfast at Tiffanys'. The ill-fated specimen being besotted with that visage d'esprit of Audrey Hepburn; her inspired depiction of 'Miss Holly Golightly', as an unblemished and impenetrable ingénue. Whose Fairy tale existence was but, one great, big, neurotic episode.

Although, Pris had *felt* no particular affinity with the director's depiction. It'd nevertheless kept the kitten, christening it—with a splash of water, Mr Audrey-Hepburn.

On account of it—*him*, being a Tom-cat.

Not in memory, or as a tribute to its late owner—*mind*. But more as a cue, a *Sign* signifying what the Synthetic had been up until that point. It having newly embarked upon this alternate career path.

That of, *Angel of Death*, at the behest of its Patron.

Like a knot tied in a piece of string, used to measure the speed of a moving vessel upon the water. Mr Audrey-Hepburn was to be the Synthetic's knot, a kind of *forget-me-knot*. The fledgling, Synthesised-'Jolly Jane' Toppan, being cast adrift amidst seas of Eternity.

Snubbed by its pet, Pris sat there in the dark collecting tears, as it'd done innumerable times in the past. Tears shed for a fictitious Roy, Leon, Zora, and its namesake.

It'd called-up the flick to show *my-Grrrl*. To share something of itself, what it'd come to view as its adolescence. That bit of it that'd existed, before its integration with the Husk; and been truly, deeply impacted by this narrative.

However, lulled by the dark—and her evident fatigue, Sash was to quickly succumb to sleep.

Certainly, Pris wouldn't have done this if its Patron had been patched-in. It being cognisant, of what he termed "its morbid fascination with the movie," him coming to view it as a kind of *Momento mori*.

The Synthetic having gotten the *Man* to accept the premise of its 'Immortality', the fact that it couldn't die. But only by conceding, that it could never, would never truly transcend its state of *Being-in-itself* (Être-en-soi); in any ontological, or meaningful way.

Staring after that figure, laid prone; squirrelled away in the folds of a Brilliant-bright Habe&*Tate*® Lacemarket bedspread; another *forget-me-knot* tied in that string of *Time*. Its scrupulous eye now traversed that pristine sheet, with its intricate lace embroidery. Alive to the way it enveloped that comely frame.

Seeking-out that protruding leg. An acre of fleshy thigh, leading down to a chicken-skinned calf. A calloused, dry heel, and five curled painted tootsies.

Detecting the sheen of a microscopic film of sweat on that exposed skin. Pris upped the room temperature, a further notch—another .25°C increment, and waited. Treading water to the steady rhythm of my-*Grrrl*'s Heartbeat; anticipating the Body shifting in its repose.

But it didn't have to wait long. Our slumbering *Zellandine* stirring almost immediately, as if the Body had some über-natural inkling of the intent behind that inscrutable gaze.

Shifting onto its stomach, its listless arm burrowed under that pillow of goose-down, exposing the blade of a shoulder. The head coming round to stare blankly back at Pris, from behind those closed blinds of its eyelids.

Pris observing every minute detail of this unconscious behaviour, as if it were the drift of a tectonic plate; that seismic shift setting the bedsprings to whinging. The Synthetic being mesmerised by how effortlessly, the Body resumed its repose. Knowing how difficult it'd been for it, to even come close to looking genuinely relaxed.

Stumbling upon Yoga, another knot on that timely string. It'd found it useful in helping it establish various *Homeostasis* states, for its Husk to exhibit. Only to discover the Siddhasana, worlds apart from those slovenly poses *Ape*-bodies were inclined to assume; in mitigating the burden of their lives.

But Pris was much better at it now, at parking its Husk.

Propped-up on its Husk_arm. Its Husk cotch'd, seemingly in parody of den Lille Havfrue; the mermaid left stranded with her two legs on a barren rocky outcrop. Its other Husk_hand now *tippy toed* across dunes of finely woven Egyptian cotton. Toward a fleshy cliff-face, and that exposed shoulder blade.

Bounding-up this newly forged escarpment, those intrepid Husk_ fingers settled upon a BCG-scar; what seemed a tack, securing Sash's upper-arm to her shoulder. Pitching its Husk's middle-finger over this knot of scar tissue, Pris initiated a connection with the *Pfeiffer*® Theta-biomimetic implant, buried just beneath the skin there.

Given the senary-based OS governing the nanoscopic implant's biological processor. It took longer than usual for the octal-based Synthetic to hack the nanochip. Perhaps, even a tenth of a second. But once inside, the Synthetic had Sash's entire medical history, literally, at its Husk's fingertips.

Now scanning that nanochip, Pris looked to confirm its own assessment of this specimen's physical condition: The recorded data indicating that Sash was susceptible to *Dysmenorrhea*; that she'd received Norplant hormonal treatment, and that she was due another course.

It also spoke of an abortion procedure, carried-out to prevent an unwanted teen-pregnancy; and reoccurring bouts of *Chlamydia*, each time treated with Amoxicillin—a generic broad-spectrum antibiotic.

Even though, a Nitrocefin test had detected the presence of β-lactamase producing bacteria.

That being so, given the Synthetic's own exhaustive physical, and immunoassay examination had detected no pathogens. It was to conclude that the treatments had to have been effective.

The most recent entry recorded a Type 1 Nose-fracture, treated at the UCL Hospital. The application of a *Pfeiffer*® invis-*a*-Splint™ being flagged 'Fees pending'.

Having exhausted this lead, Pris then wiped the chip clean, and severed the connection.

To think, this Body had been through so much already, it thought. Its

Husk_finger, now likened to a tongue, licking the length of this woman-*Grrrl*'s spine. As if relishing that lordotic cock.

With the weight of its Husk still parked on its Husk_arm, the Synthetic now let its Husk_head hang limp from its Husk_neck; as if it were a spineless rag-doll.

Venturing out into that vast Internet-of-*Thingys*, it was to utilise Sash's unique biometric-ID to retrace those steps of her digital footprint; her entire *Life*-story, as it was documented in every Public institution and organization she'd ever come into contact with.

Now moving at the Speed-of-Light—of *Life*, its intelligent SÆRCH algorithmic FNCTN reached back through Space and *Time*, like the giant tentacles of some prehistoric monster of the deep. A Leviathan of Lovecraft's imagining—*say*, grabbing a-hold of every slither of data associated with Sash's unique ID: Birth registration and Immunisation certificates; Dental records—thinning as *my-Grrrl* approached her teens; School reports, Preschool and Infants, through to Primary and Secondary, and even a stint at a Vocational Nursing College; numerous Social services care assessments—following her pregnancy, and a Foster care order; then a filing for 'Homelessness' with Whipps Cross LBC; and listings at Youth hostels in Walthamstow, Wembley, Neasden and Stonebridge; then an 'Emergency Housing Application' with the MyersHousingTrust®, and a rent agreement for Flat C, 53 Maple Street—*my-Grrrl*'s current PoA. Alongside multiple mandatory Volsec work placement entries, coupled with *Subsistence* grants.

The entire history perforated by Police incident logs. And punctuated, finally, with a 'Witness Statement', attached to a 'Search Warrant' for Flats C and B1, of the same abode. And with this, the Synthetic had barely scratched the surface.

Probing secured and encrypted Private networks, the results were to come back in torrents. Reams and reams of *insta*-Purchases, and Top-ups. Sash's daily *Life*-routine being tracked and mapped in exchanges of Euros (€) for kilojoules (kJ).

Sifting through this data, Pris now actively særched for when Sash had procured her pair of *Cynderellas*™ Glass-slippers. But was to find no record. No trace.

Nevertheless, it conducted the SÆRCH 5-times. And with each pass, was to delve deeper into the configuration, pulling together disparate primary, secondary and tertiary threads. The complexity of the thing, once mapped, rivalling that of its own neurological network.

Satisfied, it'd gathered every slither of data associated with its quarry unto it. Pris, now the Bodhisattva, *Guan Yin* — of the One-thousand limbs, yanked.

And just like that — *Poof!* It was gone.

Erased.

The entire procedure having taken mere seconds. Pris was seen lifting its Husk_head almost immediately after lowering it.

Now peering down at this newly minted non-Entity, from up-on-high. It took a split-second to mull over the *proc*.

This is how your god-of-always-listening must've felt. Calling forth the Universe from out of the Void, it thought. Not for the first time.

Lying there, prone. Sash had become, to all intent and purposes, a Zombie. That is, 'undocumented'. And thus, unverifiable. So as, she might as well have been undead.

For though her Body should live-on — for a time, in the physical realm. In that *Hyper*-reality of the Internet-of-*Thingys*, where it truly mattered — counted. It was to be as if she'd never existed.

Never been born. Like me, Pris mused.

And just-now, Mr Audrey-Hepburn leapt-up onto the bed, his timing, impeccable as ever.

Slinking over to the Synthetic, his paws testing every step. He rubbed his flank against its Husk_flank, and *Purr-purr-purrred*.

Gathering him in its Husk_arms, before he might turn and execute this greeting again; the Synthetic was to mirror his actions back at him. Rubbing its Husk_face in his soft fur, and *Purr-purr-purrring*.

And now, holding Mr Audrey-Hepburn against its naked Husk_body. It climbed-off the bed, to do some slinking of its own.

Over to the kitchen, to feed him.

THE FISHERMAN'S WIFE

Our Mother Christmas lay there, in her Birthday suit. Body supine, racked upon the lawn of that veranda, in full view of the moon.

That night sky lightly dusted with stars, quietly mapping her passage through the constellation *Aries*.

She lay there, Moon-bathing. Basking in those lunar rays. The cleft of her arm covering her eyes, proffering an extension of that Pitch of the bedroom, she'd only just-now left.

She'd stepped-out for a-bit of fresh air. Her senses reeling. Body all aglow with sweat; that was seen to evaporate upon contact with the night's chilly breath.

She'd stepped-out wearing it, her pelt of *Human*-skin; a Nemean hide, with striking orange and BLK markings. To face that wall of blacked-out windows, the neighbouring apartments in her block.

Daring them to point that pointy-finger.

It was late, she'd told herself. *Too late...for regret—regrets.*

But more to the point, she was passed caring; her mien being buoyed by that sudden rush of Blood to her head.

Yeah, here was *Mr Tiger* come to tea, with his impeccable table manners, and insatiable appetite. And having eaten his fill, he'd stepped outside to growl quietly—defiantly—up at your *god-of-always-listening*.

Grrrl

She'd made it barely—our Mother Christmas. For that fit of shakes that'd seized her legs.

And now laid there, resplendent—recumbent. Just shy of that well

435

of Pitch. That shadow cast by the staggered terraces, their march up toward the roof—and the Heavens.

Yeah, our Mother Christmas was playing dead (—like Björk).

That being said. She might've killed for a cigarette.

But though there was plenty of Smelly left, she didn't much care for the smell—having quit yonx ago. Forcing poor ol' Father Christmas to smoke alone. To live that little known Tenth Hell in Dante's *Inferno*; punishment for his failing to provide their petite Princesse, a princely sibling to play with.

Still, with all the wine she'd consumed, and the S-E-X; her Id being privy to her thoughts, her Ego had thought to spell the word out in her head. Yeah anyway, after all that. A cigarette would've been just the thing to round it off—*her modest little sessh*; a nightcap to put her on a level for the night-proper, and bed.

Yeah, our Mother Christmas played dead.

To spite those blades of closely cropped grass, that now tickled her flanks. Animated by a sudden breath of wind, that came wafting over the veranda's walled edge, like a tidal wave. With all the promise of drowning her.

She played dead to the gallery. And felt that growl in her belly, soften to a docile *purrr*. Mirroring those padded footsteps of our *Mr Tiger*'s retreat, into that dense foliage of a steely pragmatism; that rëenforced concrete of conformity; that grassy urbane knoll of...*of complacency—sigh*.

It was what it was, she assured herself. A one-off. Un petit indulgence.

[Sing] *A spoonful of sugar* [60]

To help the medicine go down

—Que Sera, sera... [61]

That other little ditty popping into her head just-now, confusing the analogy.

It'd been her last intelligible thought before she'd switched-off. That image of a UStream™ *Ping!* Voucher™ playing on the screen of her *Pod*. On offer, 'Hitchcock: Those Paramount Years' Movie Bundle (*Rear Window*, *To Catch A Thief*, *Vertigo*). The series kicking-off with *The Man Who Knew Too Much*. STREAMING RIGHT-NOW AND ON-DEMAND. Subject to Subscription status.'

[Sing] *Que Sera, sera...*

And now, with the song came that iconic image of an elfin Doris Day, her toothpaste promo-ad of a smile; a doddering James Stewart doting after her, and not a single strand of hair out of place between the pair of 'em.

And all of a sudden, our Mother Christmas felt cast adrift, and seasick.

She changed her tune, that recalcitrant inner voice partial to a-bit of the ol' Radiohead. It being-*like*, Ferris Bueller's day-off and all.

[Sing] *That there* [62]

That's not me...

A morose Thom York now crooned inside her head. The lyric preceded by an image, that of *Arlecchino*. The broody, zanni harlequin regaled in a tight fitting catsuit of orange and BLK rhombi; her scraggly hair pulled in a bun, her comely frame scrunched-up in a tiny ball.

Hugging her shapely legs, her painted boatrace nestled upon a bent knee. She was to continue her moribund lament.

[Sing] *That there*

That's not me...

Yeah, even in her waking dreams. Our Mother Christmas seemed remorseless in living her own denial.

The poor sycophantic hopeless *New Romantic*.

And yes, it'd been vexing; her apparent inability to mourn her loss. That is, her own alienation, from herself. That went doubly for the World around her. Her sense of pity, being barred from that carefully concocted *Self*-image, like a guilty pleasure.

The truth being, that deep, deep down, beneath it all. She simply wanted, in the words of our Eden Ahbez,[63] very much 'to Love, and be loved'—[Sing] *in ree-turn*.

What's that you say?

Arlecchino lifted her chalky boatrace at this admission, to show that left cheek adorned with a single Black diamond-shaped tear—shed *innamorati*. And cocked her head, her eyes having read each thought wrought upon the mind of our Mother Christmas.

And then, in *Slo-mo*, got to her feet. And standing, assumed an upstanding *Pittura infamante*, that of the Hanged Man (Inverted)—that Twelfth Trump.

She blinked then—*Blink*. The trace of a sardonic smile, curling the corners of those blackened lips.

[Sing] *I'm not here*
This isn't happen-ing...

And still, that strangled voice of Mr York continued with its demented crooning. Obstinately playing the role it'd assumed inside our Mother Christmas's head.

She felt anew, a breeze waft over her then. And that pull of goosebumps on the skin of her exposed arms and legs. A redundant, instinctive response to that chill in the air.

Truly, even after millennia of evolution. It was uncanny, how Body clung stubbornly onto memories of being concealed by feathers.

[Sing] *I'm not here...*

The cleft of her arm covering her eyes, our Mother Christmas now wiggled her toes. As if meaning to confirm that they were still there, and marking the extremities of her embodiment.

She ran her hand then, across that lawny bed. Feeling those blades of grass prick her palm—

[Sing] *I'm not here...*

Alas, twas never meant to be her cross to bear. That iconic image of Ophelia, drowned—drowning—in a pond; her love for that brooding and sometime-*ish* Prince of Denmark, unrequited.

And yet, here she was, bearing-it.

Playing dead (as usual).

Kel watched our Mother Christmas through those closed HŌMU® *Rinji-kāten* horizontal blinds. The polarised washi paper, watermarked with a racy Hokusai print, 'Dream of the Fisherman's Wife'. Rendered transparent, like a two-way mirror, by that contrast of darkness and light.

Those glazed photovoltaic patio-doors stood opened wide, like a gaping wound. A tear in the fabric of that pristine reality: Your Wallpaper* double-page *Lifestyle*-template of a *Living*-room Space, here faithfully recreated.

With its seal broken, that unsullied silence was to become infested with *The Buzz* of the Hive. That ambience of the Met, like an invisible swarm of insects; an army of termites—*say*, now threatening to consume the entire apartment.

Yeah, Kel watched as he tucked in his shirt, fastened his trousers and zipped-up his fly. He watched as he buttoned his cuffs—both now completely dry. Still in two-minds whether he'd need his tie.

He was only s'posed to be *Poppin'*-out for a-bit. To score a-little *Fairy dust*. Or at least, that was the plan.

Forced to avert his gaze, he turned away to negotiate the Søren® coffee table—made of plate-gold and synthesised-ivory—and retrieved his blazer, which lay strewn over the back of that L-shaped HŌMU® *Shīto* tanned canvass sofa.

His neck snapping-back to that comely apparition, as he threaded his arms into the arms of his jacket; and felt that brace of its tailored fabric, square his balled-shoulders.

He continued to lament upon this *Millais*-inspired image, as he ran through his (sub)routine of *Ticks*. Tugging at each Shirt-cuff, then the sleeves of his blazer; straightening its lapel, cajoling the layers of fabric to fit his Body—like, a hand in a latex glove. Fastening the first button on that jacket, to seal himself within its rigid silhouette.

Tie...Tie...Tie...

He padded down his Blazer-pockets; and retrieving his knitted Ash-BLK pencil-tie, stuffed it down the side of the sofa. Where it was to be discovered much later.

Coat...Coat...Coat...

He pictured then, our Mother Christmas righting the sleeve of his *Crombie* to hang it up. And getting his bearings, ventured toward that kitchen area, to be swallowed by the Pitch.

Continuing-on into the entrance hallway, that spotlighting in the ceiling fading-up to greet him. Kel found himself blinded—momentarily; squinting after mosquitoes, as he went about retrieving his coat and shoes.

Retracing his steps back to that *Living*-room Space, his progress muffled by his socks. He was to park himself on the edge of the sofa, to climb into his CharlieBrown's®. Then standing, donned his coat.

Sniff

With the ritual of dressing completed. Kel was to run a final spot-check, to insure he'd everything he'd need for Road.

First thing's last. Scratch.

He was to find the wod of *Nifties*, our Mother Christmas had left-out

THAT PERFECT WORLD

for him, parked on that coffee table. His first instinct being to count it—just to feel it in his hands, before stowing it away in the inside pocket of his blazer. It never occurring to him, to question why she'd have that much Scratch lying around.

His *Pod*, stowed in his front blazer pocket, he now transferred to his inside coat pocket; his wallet went to his back trouser pocket; his *GoGo*™ Travelcard to his front trouser pocket. He then felt his coat pockets, for his lighter and cigarettes.

Check, and check.

A sudden gust of wind ruffled those HŌMU® blinds, unsettling that calm of the moment. And with it, came a tug from outside; Kel's eyes again homing-in upon that arresting image of our Mother Christmas. Now the Siren, her song—lament, luring unsuspecting sailors to shipwreck.

Approaching that gaping wound of the patio doors, Kel was hesitant at first to cross its threshold. The presence of a straight-line—the door's frame, conjuring within him, a primitive fear of all things *Man*-made. That might've been the trace of every superstition in the World.

Still, if they were to be as *Omens*: The presence of the Siren, that *Man*-made barrier of the doorframe. Kel's conceit wouldn't let him see it. His truth being such, with Father Christmas temporarily out of the picture—taking a well-earned shower. Here was its prize, our Mother Christmas; the Paschal Lamb offering herself up to him.

That she might take away his sin.

Parting the blinds, Kel stepped outside. Two weary steps, his Charlie-Brown's® clattering upon that paved patio area, that stood before the lawn.

"Sees you in a-bit then," he said. Having ventured-out just far enough, to ensure his voice wouldn't be lost to *The Buzz*.

Our Mother Christmas was to be startled, at first, by that commotion of the blinds. And then, that approach of footsteps. But still, fought the urge to look-see. Even as she felt that sense of anonymity slip from her grasp; as if, she were separating egg yolks with her fingers.

She wondered how long it'd been stood there—*gawping*. Though she didn't quite know what to feel about it; her Body being, by now, something she herself had come to view from afar. From down that long dark tunnel of the Third-person.

THE FISHERMAN'S WIFE

Yeah, more your Orson Wells, than your Harry Lime. Our Mother Christmas now pictured herself, in that infamous scene from *The Third Man*.[64] A churlish, cocksure smile, her response to the glare of that Spotlight.

Indeed, what was it she was about touting, if not diluted Penicillin?

[Sing] *I'm not here*

This isnt happen-ing...

And there was our Mr York, crooning. That voice inside her head.

Yeah, she might've covered herself. If she hadn't felt so utterly exposed. That being said. Covering herself, might've been construed as an admission of guilt. And why should she feel guilty?

No...*No*—shaking her head emphatically. No *phf'king* way was she to be held responsible, for Others invading upon her privacy.

"Did Bry leave you with the fob?" she was to ask—finally, without looking. Her hand gently stroking those blades of grass.

"No," Kel replied, his eyes suddenly drawn to that vast expanse of the Met. A carpet of evenly spaced lights, marching toward the horizon.

"He said he'd wait-up to let me in," he added, locking onto a familiar landmark, the BT Tower—for safety's sake.

Lest, in that light, he gaze upon that which he shouldn't. Espy his fate drawn in the contours of that comely form; his own Body dash against, broken upon those jagged rocks. Both sumptuous, and tart.

"Did he now?" our Mother Christmas scoffed, masking her surprise with sarcasm. Or was it, her sarcasm with surprise? Even she couldn't tell at this point.

She'd so wanted to wait-up for the Blood moon. It being auspicious, and *all-the-Buzz* on the newstreams. But her metamorphosis was already manifest.

"Yeah—I shouldn't be long."

Kel lied.

"You won't mind letting yourself out then."

"Nah—you're alright."

He made to turn about, as if dismissed.

"Kelly—wait."

But apparently, our Mother Christmas had thought of one last thing.

"You wouldn't happen to have a cigarette would you?"

And here she was, toying with it—her food.

Of course, he had a cigarette. She'd smelt it on him. Tasted that minty-freshness upon its breath.

"Yeah, one sec."

She heard it *Snap*-to, its sense of urgency conveyed by the way it ferreted about its person.

Christ, she thought then. It was like a dog that couldn't wait to be walked, holding its bloody lead in its mouth.

"On second thoughts, it can wait."

"Suit yourself."

Sniff

Kel tucked the cigarette behind an ear.

"I'll sees you later."

"Perhaps—*maybe*."

Our Mother Christmas heard it retreat, and then part those blinds.

"No...on second thoughts—I'm tired," she declared. "I think I'll go to bed—leave you *Boyz* to it."

And hearing this, Kel hesitated. For like, a split-second. But he couldn't have said anything else, not without playing favourites. Stepping inside, he didn't look back. And our Mother Christmas didn't bother to look after it.

Yeah, there's rue for you, her thought, listening to those blinds settling. *And here's just a-little for me.*

Riding the *Routemaster*, it was like being sat in a brightly lit coffin; or cooped, like battery-farmed poultry. The upperdeck heaving with *Human* fodder—*Human* chattel. Pilgrims and Tourists headed into town-proper.

Still, Kel kept his boatrace close to that tinted glass, to stop from having to cop his own reflection; his *Kark*-eyes peering after that shifting scenery, framed in that anamorphic window.

A Grand Canyon, etched-out of solid blocks of ashlar, and photovoltaic Sheet-glass. A listless present, and a listed past; *Time* seemingly jogging on the spot.

Turning-up Gower Street, the *Routemaster* was to pass by the UCL Hospital. A prefab modernist eye soar, bookending a complex of ancient-*looking* Georgian revivalist structures, that formed part of the main campus. The imposing Wilkin's Building, with its impressive Octagon dome, being that proverbial 'Jewel in the Crown'.

And to his right, the top of Maple Street; Kel craning his neck to steal a look-see. To think, he must've walked this route countless times, his footsteps leaving nigh an impression.

It being ironic. That he should find himself now sporting it; draped in the pelt of what'd been that *Monkey-on-his-back*. The sartorial equivalent of this architectural style. Forever magnanimous, and unapologetic, in its contrived monumentalism.

That that apparent *ad hoc* dress-code of your Estabs; his *Crombie*, and two-piece Birdman suit, and *StayPress*™ shirt—now unbuttoned at the collar. Should've become for him, like a literal *skin*. Something he might take pride in. Or more, a Cuirassier's breastplate, something affording him protection, and status *even*. Yeah, it seemed ironic to him.

Righting himself in his seat, Kel chirps'd his teeth. Why hadn't he just flagged a cab, he had the money—

Forphf'ksake.

On a whim, he'd thought to cut through King's Cross, and the EuroStar™ Terminus—as-you-do. As he must've done countless times, on his way back from the *Cally*—the ol' Caledonian Road.

And coming-out the other end, he'd spotted that N73 stopping at the Bus stop, headed toward Victoria. And breaking-out in a run, negotiated six lanes of traffic, and three railings to catch it. Squeezing through those automated doors, just as they were about to *Snap*-shut.

"*What*—you didn't see me running?" he was to bark after the Conductor. Catching his breath, and tapping-in with his *GoGo*™ Travelcard.

But the Conductor didn't even bother to look at him.

"If I was to wait on everyone we'd never get going," she said— stating the obvious, her eyes peeled to that rearview screen.

She'd then pressed the key, to engage the *Routemaster*'s Automatron. The Bus setting-off up the Bus Lane at a trot.

And of course, it was to be congestion all the way. The entire World—and his uncle—*as ever*, conspiring to be out on that particular stretch of road, at that particular time of night.

Alighting at the first stop the other-side of that Big-Tent 'Welcome' sign. Kel paused to look back at the entrance to Tottenham Court Road's T*f*L® underground station. And then peered-up, at that magnified night sky, with its enhanced cast of Stars—*Twink-twink-twinkling*.

Under the *Tarp* as always, too bright. Too sanitised. Too congested. Too *commersh*. Too much of everything and nothing much really—once you'd seen it. Kel veering off-the-beaten-track down to Soho Square, seeking the refuge of those shady backstreets, and the open air.

He thought to walk his familiar beat. The years he'd given to that particular knot of streets, now skewered by nostalgia.

Indeed, he'd even felt to remove his shoes. To walk barefoot, like your Winno nobility—for nostalgia's sake; his toes curling, to rake at that cold, hard concrete. As ever enveloped by that *Cloak of Invisibility*, afforded by the press, and

The Buzz...

The Buzz...

The Buzz-uzz...

That is, that press of *Human*-traffic. And the electrostatic *Buzz* of the Hive, that'd become synonymous with living that Metropolitan existence. Its streets, like electronic circuitry. Its denizens carrying its current, like charged Electron particles—instances.

It was forever switched-on, *The Buzz*. It was all Brilliant-bright noise, and muzik mapping that bustling cityscape, like Sonar; like an album pitched in that *Key of Life*, sung by a wondrous Blind-*Man*.

Navigating that maze of backstreets, and alleyways; that ran parallel and perpendicular to the *Tarp*, and Mainstreet. It felt good. No, it felt *Grrreat* to be back. Like a Homecoming—*almost*.

It even had its own swanky soundtrack, courtesy of your Curtis Mayfield. That *Intro* to 'Freddie's Swansong',[65] with the catchy guitar-riff—

[Riff] *Nah nah na-nah na-nah*

Nah nah nah...

And of-course, *The Buzz* was quick to pick-up on it.

[Riff] *Nah nah na-nah na-nah*

Nah nah nah!

Off-the-beaten-track being like that. The beating Heart of your *artsy-fartsy off*-Mainstreet scene, whilst claiming to be Worlds apart.

Certainly, it was Off-the-beaten-track, yet, marked clearly on that Borges Map of Out-*there*; like a Tourist route, its trail of tears dotted with various POIs.

Here was where so-and-so bumped-*slash*-stabbed-*slash*-buggered such-and-such. And let that be a warning to you-*like*, 'Please be sure and keep all your personal belongings with you at all times. | Bitte sicher sein und halten all ihre persönlichen sachen mit ihnen zu jeder zeit. Thank you | Danke.'

But rarely would one clock its more exotic wildlife. Its Big game— so to speak. Yeah, those who knew the coup, and profited from it, were never to be seen actually profiting from it.

It was like an unwritten rule.

Being synonymous with the Street, Off-the-beaten-track was more your home to strays. And runaways. And castaways. And your compulsive victim-types, covered in callused, rock-hard hides. That'd suck the *Life*, the living daylights out of every ounce of sympathy directed their way.

And yeah, *shit* happened. Shit was always happening, to *Them*. That was the point. Shit would happen to *Them*. But never to *Those* who made their living, skimming the cream off the top of that milk of Human kind(-*ness*).

They—pointing that pointy-finger toward the Heavens, they were safe. Sat way back in the cut—in the *Boonies*, with their fat-fingers in all the pies. One beady-eye fixated upon early retirement.

That ol' horse chestnut.

They—because it was always them, they remained invisible. Indivisible from your Wallpaper*—*say*, from your Estabs.

They'd stay indoors. Out of sight, out of mind. That being their thing, they're act—a-bit of the ol' sleight-of-hand. *Life* being, at the end of the day, when all was said and done. But one perpetual *Turn*.

Kel was to hit his mark, stepping lively out of the dark onto Wardour Street, just shy of PELLE. The name of the venue, P-E-L-L-E, spelt out in large shiny Stainless-steel lettering, backed with Lime-green neon.

It was a stairway of unpolished granite, leading-up to double-doors of polished chrome, and frosted-glass, and hardwood—stained Dark brown; what was a Nouveau Art-deco façade, that spoke of a sizeable Capital outlay, and moneyed interest.

And inside, it'd be your usual crop of Trendies, and Squareframes, the odd smattering of Suits; the press of Bod(ie)s gleaned through that Frosted-glass. The din of this dimly lit Space, being ready to splurt out

THAT PERFECT WORLD

those doors. If given but half a-chance.

Yeah, here was your *High-ho*, before that great migration to the nightclub—and *the* Scene. It was where you'd score, prices being what they were; subject to your infamous London-weighting.

Anywhere being preferable to scoring on the Street—on *Road*.

It was the Spot. Not the Scene—mind you, just the Spot. Your typical stush, as opposed to swish, or swanky restaurant-*come*-bar. Minus that club bit.

Replete with spritely table service; and Mixologists stationed behind the bar; and resident Deejays that'd work the evening in shifts; and a cordoned-off area out-front. A wall of willing Punters kept in check by a fierce-*looking* thoroughbred German Shepherdess, armed with the now obligatory X'ANG® *Crystl*.

The spit of your *Elvira Hancock*, with gymnast's legs that started halfway up her spine, and no real arse to speak of. PELLE's hostess with the most-*ess* was Übs, straight-up—no chaser.

An uncut diamond. Trim, as in lean—not an ounce of fat. Cheekbones and elbows sharp as razorblades, and the moxie to match.

She evidently lived for this role. Being dressed for the part, in Liquorice-BLK PVC Conquistador thigh-high boots, and matching *Peau-de-soie* jump suit by AlexanderMcQueen®—obviously. That came replete with Elizabethan ruffled choke-collar, and slit up the back, and down the arms and legs.

Yeah, just picture your *Ursa*™ circa-1980, in Richard Lester's 'ÜBERman Deux', after she'd turned on the ol' General.

The whole ÜBER-villainy bit, accessorised accordingly, with a diamond incrusted chaps; and ethnic-*looking* hooped earrings; and a chunky solid gold Jaeger® Biothermic *Time*piece, that was like, parsecs ahead in terms of wearables; and a Flappers® *Ms Holly Golightly* cigarette filter, playing host to a handcrafted roll-up—wafting plumes of Smelly infused with a smattering of the ol' King Charles. Clenched betwixt platinum-grills, with Vampire incisors. The compliment of that foul mouth.

So as, looking after it, you just knew one-day she would-be famous. *If not, infamous.*

Anywho, this being a double-act. The Muscle-on-the-door—by way of contrast, was more your typical He-*Man*™ i.e., Master of *his* Universe.

THE FISHERMAN'S WIFE

Muscle-bound, bordering upon burly. Dressed like a Kiwi, as in, all-BLK; your classic PaulSmith® two-piece Birdman suit, *StayPress*™ shirt, knit pencil-tie. Bald-head. Clean shaven. *Bling-bling* Pinky-ring adorning a meaty Pinky-finger.

You know, your archetypal 'Muscle-on-the-door'.

"OY! Check. It. Out—*my-Man*," my-*Man* said, beaming. Having clock'd Kel bowling toward him. All suited, and booted, and ting, and ting, and *teng*.

And immediately, out came that hand for the shake. A drawn-out Lagos-style finger-*Snap*. And the smile, shark to crocodile. Both mouths seemingly crammed-full of pearls harvested from those ruins of Atlantis.

"So—wha-*ya* sayin ghee-eze?" my-*Man* continued, pouring it on thick.

"What *you* sayin?"

Kel, for his part, holding it down. Both Cats in their own way, giving-it now, your smouldering *Oliver Reed*.

"I ain't sayin' *diddly*," came my-*Man*'s response, it being all a formality. He then added, cutting to the chase, "so what—you looking?"

"Looking—*always*."

Wanting to give nothing away, Kel then tossed him another cagey smile; to mask the fact that he was basically about getting-up to speed.

"Then you shit-*outta*-luck," my-*Man* quipped, chuckling. And that was that. Kel's welcome back, and—

[Riff] *Nah nah na-nah na-nah*
Nah nah nah.

Palming him off, with-a "one-sec yeah." My-*Man* then executes a smart about-face to address this *Filly*. Or was it a Beenie? Anywho, she'd literally *Pop*'d-up out of nowhere, like

Pop!

Striking, and by all appearances, *Milf*-thy rich. It was your atypical Footballer's wifey sort; Body all aglow, from regular stints on sunbeds in your Seychelles and Solomon Archipelago.

Who'd just-now thought it *cleva*, to try sneak-up on a Bred-*da*.

Still, it was as if he'd eyes in the back of his head. The way my-*Man*—just like that—summoned the voice of LandoCalrissian™, from a galaxy far far away. To give-it, "*Hell-o*. What have we here?"

Gobsmacked, our would-be PrincessLeia™ thought then to style-it. Locking wings with my-*Man* and shooting Kel a piercing look; its eyes all a-blazed with that Light of the Illuminated.

And after all that, it'd just been about wanting to be let out. But not wanting to have to wait upon ceremony.

Yeah-yeah—if you say so, Kel thought, now blatantly eyeballing it. Holstering his hands in his trouser-pockets, and swallowing—in a throat suddenly dryer then a Ten-thousand-year-old piece of parchment.

Giving my-*Man* his Space, he now used this vantage to clock his considerable game. How he leant in—*ever-so* close, lending wifey an ear and his undivided. Both eyes locked-on to that ample cleavage, seen poking-out the top of its dazzling Blood-red GUCCI® pencil-dress.

Creasing-up where prompted, he continued to pay it *Lip*-service. Whilst *ever-so* discretely, reaching round to unhook that cordon.

Then, nodding your Karen-O's. As in, your *Yeah yeah yeahs*. He was to gently guide it across that invisible line. His hand loitering upon the ample cock of its cosmetically enhanced *heinie*.

Giving-it some of that, *Pat-pat. Pat-pat*.

A quick peck on both cheeks, marking this parting of the ways. My-*Man* then threw-in a cordial wave in the direction of "but wait— that ain't his Nibs."

Yes-it-is.

Wifey mouthing this, it being adamant it was. Masking its ruse behind a winning smile, and-*a* playful slap, and-*a* "Oy you—*Cheeky*. You'll get me in trouble."

And with that, this elegant couple was to saunter-off to hail a ride. The first in a line of *Hackney*-cabs, that *just-so* happened to be passing. The next stop being, obviously, your 86ers™—and the Scene. And after a little *Boo-gie*, a night-cap back at *my-Man*'s student digs—presumably.

Returning to Kel, He-*Man*™ was to give-it then, the 'Johnny Caspers'— i.e., the raised eyebrows.

As if to say, *running tings, it ain't all it's cracked-up to be*.

And naturally, Kel was to play along. Half-stepping the wrong side of that cordon to pound his fist; and pay him his dues in *Lip*-service. And then, it was back to business.

"So what—*Sniff*—is *my-Man* about?"

"Where you been? *My-Man*'s long gone."

Yeah, my-*Man* cop'd it straight off the bat. Kel trying the schmoose.

"*Ya-lie*—seriously?" Kel said, looking genuinely surprised. "I thought *my-Man* was part of the furniture."

"Furniture—which part?"

But my-*Man* wasn't even looking at it now. Being too much engrossed inna his *Pod* and hatching a dastardly plot of his own.

Sniff

Thrown by this breaking news. Kel stood, hands on hips, rëevaluating the lay of the land, and his own tenuous scheme.

What to-do? What to-do?

And all of a sudden, that Herd queued nearby, those *Broom-Brooms* and *Hackney*-cabs vying for that slither of *Road*, that ever-shifting tide of *Human*-traffic. It all blurred into one.

Kel's 'Deadman's stare' returning with a vengeance. It having become a-little too much to be getting-on with. What with it being his first night-out proper.

Best score and get back before I'm missed, he thought. Focusing now upon his CharlieBrown's® to ground himself.

"So what—*Sniff*, you can't sort it?"

"*Brah*—if I could I would. But you know I can't leave this spot."

My-*Man* was lying, obviously.

Still inna his *Pod*, he Tap-tap-tapped as he spoke. A quick heads-up to the *Gaffer*—Klunk: 'Elvis is in the building.'

Send.

Kel chirps'd his teeth then.

"*Phf'kry*."

"You know how it go. You act like you know and

[Sing] *Keep-on moving* [66]

Keep-on moving. Don't stop

—*noh!*"

And being thus buoyed by this, his one good deed for the day. My-*Man* even threw-in a dainty two-step, sole-to-sole. His head nodding, as if he were just-now hearing-it, that *phf*unkin' bass.

The response was to come back pretty sharpish—still.

Heralded by a rude vibration. My-*Man* wincing as he read it. As if, coppin' one of those #*Horrorshow* #*Snuff* digy-*viddy* clips; yet another Youngblood getting gunned-down by your trigger-happy *Federales*.

He then looked to Kel, masking his reaction in a half-baked apology—for having to let *my-Man* down.

"If you'd *a*-come earlier—"

He shrugged then, as if to say, *Bwwoy*. But then, came the Switch. The *Turn*.

"Hear what—*Sniff*—let me go check with *my-Grrrl*."

My-Man nodding in the direction of *One-day-she-would-be-famous*.

Stood atop the stair, my-*Grrrl* appeared to be schmoosing a pair of Elect. Who'd only just-now stepped out to grab a-bit of fresh air.

"What—*my-Man*?"

"Yeah—*my-Grrrl*."

Kel gave it the eyebrows—*yeah?* And then, grinned.

"Yeah. And don't even bother go-there."

And right on cue, *One-day-she-would-be-famous* was to make her entrance. Sauntering down that flight of stairs, like Bette Davis in 'All About Eve'.[67] Her ears now—apparently—burning, on account of these two.

Engrossed inna her *Crystl*. She was to waltz-up to the cordon, to check that line of willing Punters stood single-file behind it.

Puff-puff

Then, it was over to that gaggle of RSVPs, parked on the opposing flank.

Puff-puff

And finally—

"Oy Brodie? What's it doing there?"

Having anticipated *my-Grrrl*'s reaction, my-*Man*—Brodie—was to grip it by the arm, taking care to avoid the elbow. And nodding, cordially invite it to come stand to one-side, for a discreet word-*like*.

My-Grrrl giving it an earful, as they closed to huddle.

"Ain't you s'posed to be keepin' this bit clear? Do your *phf'king* job—"

Tut.

Back inna her *Crystl*, she only half listened to my-*Man*'s pitch. Then it was, "NO PHF'KING WAY," and "I DON'T GIVE TWO SHITS WHO HE IS," and "IF YOU DON'T LIKE IT, GO TAKE IT UP WITH MONK—BITCH."

My-Grrrl now leered after Kel.

"YEAH BITCH—I'M TALKING ABOUT YOU. WHAT?"

And of course, overhearing all this. It buoyed the Herd stood nearby; their hopes being pinned on Kel getting his *comeuppance*, for pushing-in.

Still, my-*Man* was to persevere.

Draping a consoling arm about my-*Grrrl*'s shoulders, like a Mink coat. And drawing her further into his confidence; briefing her on the incident, and the response i.e., what was about to go down.

So as, watching the pair. And being none the wiser. Kel even thought he saw it ease-off that throttle, by degrees. The Shrew, supping upon her *Ms Holly Golightly*, appearing markedly intrigued.

She even *Sniffed* in its general direction. After which, Brodie was to break the huddle to mosey back over, with an update.

"Oy—first things last," he said, reaching for that cordon. "I beg you come stand this side, Mate."

And it being not that much of an ask, Kel was to readily oblige.

"So what's *my-Grrrl* on?" he asked then, settling. Hands again holstered in his trouser pockets.

"She's gonna see if she can give-*ya a*-squeeze," Brodie replied, replacing the cordon.

And hearing this, Kel was to shoot my-*Man* a testy look.

"What for? I ain't looking to hang about."

But having already clock'd how its eyes gravitated toward my-*Grrrl*, Brodie was to play it all conspiratorial-*like*. As if there was more to it besides.

Which there was, as it goes.

"Just relax. Let it sort you out."

"What—my-*Grrrl*'s hol'ing it down?" Kel asked, attempting to fill-in the blanks for himself.

"*What*—you crazy."

Wincing at the thought, as if it were painful, even to think it. Brodie now quipped, "*my-Grrrl* couldn't hol' down a balloon if you tied it with a piece of string."

And picturing this, both he and Kel were to crease-up.

"So-what then?"

Still grinning, my-*Man* gently cupped Kel boatrace in his giant-palm, to stroked his cheek with a thumb—affectionately.

"Don't you worry, your pretty. Little. Head."

Pat-pat

Kel chirps'ing his teeth. And tossing a casual glance—right and left—at that gaggle of RSVPs; and the Herd, stood single-file against the wall, as if about to face-down a Firing squad.

But invariably, his eyes found themselves gravitating toward *One-day-she-would-be-famous*.

"Hear what—when you get inside, go check *our* Roz," Brodie said then, momentarily surfacing from his *Pod* to look after it.

"What—she still working the restroom?"

Kel now thought to check his own device.

Yeah, my-*Man* nodded.

Having hung-back for a-bit, my-*Grrrl* again waltzed over, via her usual route. Tossing a cursory glance and throaty growl the way of the Herd, to keep 'em in line.

Grrrl

"So—*Puff-puff*—you here on your tod?" she asked, eyes fixed on her *Crystl*.

"What's it look like?" came Kel response. Him now playing at *Lee Marvin* i.e., the Tuff-guy; thinking he might leave-it with a lasting impression.

However, *Puff-puffing* upon her *Ms Holly Golightly*, my-*Grrrl* was to appear markedly unimpressionable.

"*Look*. If you're gonna get all stroppy about it, you can *phf'koff*," she was to state, without even bothering to look after it.

And again, Brodie was obliged to step-in.

"Yeah—my-*Man*'s here on his *Jays*."

"So what's the name?" my-*Grrrl* asked then, looking now to my-*Man* for all the answers.

"You what?" Kel butt-in.

"You heard. What's your name? Your mother give you a name—yeah?"

She tossed a look Kel's way, to better cut her eye at it. Then looked to Brodie, as if to say, *is it stupid or what?*

"What's she need my name for—I ain't stopping?"

Kel was also now looking to my-*Man*, his expression saying the exact same thing, *is it stupid or what?*

THE FISHERMAN'S WIFE

"I need it for the form"—*duh*.

My-*Grrrl* again addressed Kel directly, to better cut her eye after it. Then, it was back to my-*Man*, "wha-*da phf'k*—Brodie?"

Brodie chirps'ing his teeth.

"Hear what, just put it down as my plus-one—"

Forphf'ksake.

And with that, Kel was in.

It was all *Lip*-service anyway.

Behind the blank boatraces, and the elaborate charade. Brodie and his evil twin—*One-day-she-would-be-famous*, were bent over belly-laughing. Slapping thighs and giving-it the middle-finger. The jollies being well and truly at *my-Man*'s expense.

Yeah, it'd made both their nights, and serve it right.

"*Phf'king* John, beating-up on one of us. Oy—what's her name again?"

"What *my-Grrrl*? Sash?"

"Yeah Sash. Serves him right—"

The Cunt.

Having done with the data-entry bit, *One-day-she-would-be-famous* was to give Kel the onceover. As if she hadn't already.

At least it satisfied the Dress-code—kind-a, her thought, as she jostled Brodie out of the way to get at that cordon.

Unhooking it, she then stepped aside—grudgingly.

"Com'on then, if you're coming," she snarled, her strop being part and parcel of it—her *Style*.

And just-now, and for no apparent reason. Kel hesitated.

Looking toward the stair, he was to be suddenly gripped by a sense of foreboding. The sound of the Siren's song ringing in his...

"Is he coming-in or what?"

Blink-blink

Kel heard *my-Grrrl* pressing my-*Man*.

"Oy—you in or out?"

He then heard my-*Man* press him.

"Kelly? You in or out?"

...*Phf'k-it.*

Looking after *my-Grrrl*, Kel licked his lips. And stepped lively across that invisible line, to wait. Much to the chagrin of the Herd, left dangling on the other side.

Closing the cordon behind it. *One-day-she-would-be-famous* then led the way up the stair.

And pulling open the venue's door. And stepping aside. She was to toss it a casual compliment, "nice suit." Whilst giving it the side-eye.

A gust of warm air, carrying that stench of Shisha, and stale alcohol. Greeting Kel as he peered inside.

"Oy — where's the restroom again?" him asking then. By way of segue into a *Chirps*.

My-Grrrl pointing, with the butt of her *Ms Holly Golightly*, toward the din of Good-*times* emanating from that gaping Black hole.

"How the *phf'k* should I know? Go ask at the Bar."

And needing no further prompt, Kel then entered the establishment. *My-Grrrl* leaving the venue's door to close itself.

Enjoy.

[Rap] *Now ten-years on*
And still I rue the day that I was born
Open my eyes and greet a hopeless dawn
My past knows regret
If I could go back—retract my steps
The movements of a Pawn
The game being Life
The rules like Chess
Seems crazy
Sometimes I feel to cry
Like a baby—surrounded
by pieces just waiting to take me
I'll be damned if the System ever breaks me
Still Life goes on
And I am what the system made me
So, with no more paths to follow
Living a Life riddled with sorrow
I'm caught in quicksand and sinking
So I turned to villain—like the Kingpin
Yo Brah! Whats that smell?
Me brah! Now, cos I stinking
Rich, drinking Moët Chandon
Got me thinking
I'm more powerful than a locomotive
Cos in my Heart their ain't not Love
Which makes me
More Über now than I ever was
And I can leap tall building in a single bound
And even fly if I wanted too
While smoking weed by the pound.
And it figures
Ain't not Body faster than a speeding bullet
So to become ÜBERman
All I need is a...

F◉UCAÚLT'S PENDỤLUM

The rap of knuckles on the passenger-window was the first Tan knew of it. The sound startling her.

Prior to that, she'd been too inna her *Pod* to cop Marl approaching on her blind-side. She'd then more *Spidy*-sensed who it was, than recognised his hooded boatrace peering-in.

Having left her-*Man* cluckin' the night before, she'd been expecting a .*Txt*—if not a call; and come a-running, still wearing her work garms. Carrying in those empty hands, empty hopes of bringing him home for good, like some Battersea stray.

Home being her mum's. And a proper king-sized bed. And a proper long sessh. One-night cotch'd on the floor at his, having been enough. It being too much like slumming-it.

Of course, he'd come around—in time. Once the nostalgia had worn-off. Till then, she was to be practicing abstinence. At least, that'd been the gist of the *pep*-talk she'd given herself, on that long drive into town-proper.

Parked across from Warren Street's T*f*L® underground station. She'd tucked in behind a line of *Broom-Brooms*, and a PAYG cycle-bay, and left the SC*f*R idling. Its *sub*-phonic NEMP tickling her chest, even through all that shielding.

Her little 'Bebo', being that sporty looking Honda® Āban R2. A boxy two-seater hatchback jobbie, with the *vari*-tint windows, and original 22″ mag-alloys, and Baum® in-car entertainment system *Tump*-ing that
UMPH…UMPH…

THAT PERFECT WORLD

UMPH...UMPH...

UMPH...UMPH...

soundtrack. [Sing] *We could be Heroes* chorusing into the early hours.

Yeah, it was your quintessential *Grrrlie*mobile. And of course, Tan had had to get it in shocking Electro-indigo, your quintessential *Grrrlie*mobile color. And like so many within her demographic, it was to be 'Manual override' all-day, every day; her Braeburn® *Pod* effective in keeping that Automatron at bay. What with it enjoying deep integration with the automobile's UX.

In point of fact, and there were reams of *Stats* to bear this out. If *Grrrlie-Grrrls*—like Tan—were enabled to drive with their thumbs, there'd be far less incidents attributable to 'Manualist' on that Open-road.

Fetching her Cargo® carry-all from off the passenger seat, Tan was back inna her *Pod*, unlocking the door.

She was to give Marl the onceover, as he put away his Cell to clamber-in. And immediately clock how he clutched his stomach, as if he were hurt, or hurting. Whatever it was, she couldn't be more concerned than him, and he didn't seem that fussed.

That being said. He'd clearly picked-up some extra baggage since last she'd seen him.

Which was what? Last night?

Tan chirps'd her teeth, could she let this *Boy* out of her sight. Back inna her *Pod*, she returned to what she'd been about. Having launched just-now Rialto's SYNTHCITY was trending on *Connekt-a*-Dot™. My-*Grrrl's TimeLine* being presently lit, with everyone's comparative analysis of its divergent and multifaceted plotlines.

"Wassup with you?" she asked, without looking for a response.

Assuming her-*Man* would want to keep it to himself, forcing her to have to wrangle-it out of him.

For sure, she knew that look, given she'd three Big brothers; her having seen it all, and lived it all, vicariously, through each one in-turn.

"Em?"

"Nuttun," came Marl's tetchy response.

Which seemed to make perfect sense, given the context; him being in the process of shifting the seat backwards, to give himself a-little extra leg-room. The passenger seat being already fully-reclined.

458

Looking after him, however, there was no mistaking it: That rabbit-in-the-headlights stare. It being Street. It being *Road*. It being *Bullo*, and everything Tan was now desperate to move beyond.

"You took your time," Marl said, pausing from sucking-on his Shake-Shack® Extra-Grande BananoChocolatte Soyshake.

Having remained sat up, his elbow propped upon that cotch in the door. He now shook it—his Soyshake, to gauge how much of it was left.

"What—you couldn't get me one?"

Tan pretended to give-*a-toss*, whilst her eyeballs remained stapled to her *Pod*.

"How was I to know how long you'd be," Marl said—speaking candidly, slurping on the dregs of his beverage.

Huh

Unperturbed, Tan's thumb was to continue its game of hopscotch on her *Pod*'s touchscreen.

It was obvious Marl was masking something. Besides whatever it was he had squirrelled away in his hoodie pocket. That said, Tan was too exhausted for *Kiss & Tell*.

Her plan being simple: Take her-*Man* back to his, just so-as he could collect a change of clothes—*mind*. And then, they'd splurt back to hers—*and job done*.

For want of something to do, Marl now stared out the window, focusing upon the service entrance to the ShakeShack®—its Chocolate-brown color scheme, a continuation of the storefront that buttressed the corner.

And next to it, a couple of stock-trolleys awaiting morning deliveries, and that smoke venting from a grate. The back-of-house, evidently still a hive of activity.

He then turned to look pass Tan. And across the road, at those automated barriers straddling the entrance to the station; him still feeling digy for having had to carry the *ting* on the underground.

"So what—we splurting?" he asked, growing impatient.

Tan looked-up from her *Pod*, and again marked that look of foreboding, of dark clouds hanging over her-*Man*; her deciding, there and then, she needed to get to the bottom of it.

"Seriously, what's with you?" she asked, as if the other time she hadn't meant it.

THAT PERFECT WORLD

She even turned to face her-*Man*, to demonstrate her concern. The light from her *Pod*-screen now dissecting her boatrace. Hugging the necrotic-*looking* melanin(e) half, causing it to bleed into those shadows that bathed the inside of the automobile.

"Never mind what's with me, what's with this muzik?" Marl said, slurping air through that bendy straw.; his other hand permanently grafted onto his stomach—seemingly.

Using her *Pod*, Tan turned-off the muzik remotely, and locked the doors—CLICK! That compact environ, abruptly descending toward a leaden silence.

"So...you gonna tell me or what?"

"Yeah—come we go."

Stretching, Marl looked for somewhere to dispose of his beverage. Then settled on the cup-holder in the door.

Killing the engine, Tan made herself more comfortable.

"Come we go then."

"What?"

Marl looked after her, and then away in mock frustration. His back hunched, as if the weight of his secret were pulling him toward the Earth's core.

Retreating to the passenger window, he pressed his forehead against the glass to stare-up at the Stars, and that Blood moon. *Sniffing* at the air, his eyes and nose stinging, as he lost himself in thoughts of what'd come to pass.

Catching that glint of tears in her-*Man*'s eyes, Tan's entire demeanour softened, along with her voice.

"Marl...what's wrong? What's happened?"

She even put down her *Pod*—for a *hot*-minute, feeling compelled to scoop her *Baby* up in her arms. Though the *Broom-Broom* might make it awkward, having to bridge the gulf that lay between those two seats.

Plus, the hood was to be a definite barrier. Tan reaching then, to pull at its crown. But somehow Marl managed to duck out of the way.

"Oy—wha-*ya* dealing wit?" he was to bark after her, his hand coming to catch it—his hood.

His shroud.

He then chirps'd his teeth. To wit, Tan immediately put back-up her own Force-field—her *Pod*'s screen flickering into life.

Tut

"Don't ignore me then."

Clearly, my-*Grrrl* was frustrated with her present role. And sensing this, Marl was to cave just a-little.

"Tee's gone."

That was it. That was all he said. Though it wasn't as if he truly believed it himself.

"Gone? Gone where—to his Babymother's? On Holiday? What?" Tan asked, squinting after him. As if literally seeking to pierce through the statement's ambiguity.

"Gone where—Marl?"

She pressed him.

"Gone gone."

There, he'd said it out-loud. Spoken it into being.

And suddenly, it'd become real, tangible—even for Tan. Though not quite capable of exhibiting that quality of permanence, that was to be Death's most profound lesson.

"What? When? How?"

Tan's eyes might've widened with disbelief. But, staring-out from behind them, she'd felt relief. Considering what might've been.

Of course, it was tragic. Beyond tragic even. To the extent, she knew how much my-*Man* had meant to her-*Man*.

Certainly, he'd been like a Big brother to Marl; always checking for him, always bringing him in on some hair-brained scheme or other. And Marl had loved him for it. Though he was incapable of admitting this to himself, or anyone else.

That he'd loved this *Man*—his friend.

And Tan very much knew what that felt like, having Big brothers of her own—as said.

For sure, she couldn't have imagined ever losing one. Even when her eldest got sent down, she knew he'd be back.

Funny that, she thought.

Embarrassed now, by how easily she'd relegated Tonx's entire existence, to that realm of *Past*-tense. Even though it was confined to just her thinking—to her mind, it didn't seem right. For what did it say of his *Life*, that it should be so easily dismissed.

She then found herself thinking, there should be consequences to such a presumption. An effect proportional to the cause. A monument equal to such a monumental event; that transcendence of a *Soul*, however brittle and flawed its personhood.

If only to say, that the *Man*'s *Life* had been of consequence. And thus, his passing also.

If this burden were—*say*, to be measured in his name. That is, its weight and portent, equal to that breath needed to speak it out-loud. Then surely, his name should be shouted.

She leant-in close, and clock'd a tear spill-over the lip of Marl's eyelid; his first since god-knows, since before he could remember. And now conscious of my-*Grrrl*—*looking*, seeing him at his weakest. He erased it, using the cuff of his sleeve.

It was to be as if it'd never happened. In spite of his runny nose— and *Sniffling*—blatantly giving the game away.

Tan had never seen her-*Man* cry. Or any of her previous Boy-*Men* for that matter. And though she'd caught each of her Big brothers—in turn, at one time or another, crying. It didn't seem to count.

Like every other part of her-*Man*, Tan wanted to share in it. If he'd let her. More so even. Because she knew he couldn't.

Boys being Men, and Men being Boys, according to her mum.

For sure, apart from that Hel's visage. A part of her was ready-setup and hardwired for resenting Boys—*Men*.

Him.

The fact of his having to gauge every thought, every emotion, behaviour, subconscious and unconscious impulse. According to some arbitrary Richter scale of *Machismo*. Being simply part and parcel of it, his privilege.

Privilege—you know.

Indubitably, when the lights went out, and the room went dark. She'd find him more than up for participating in that ol' BDSM *horrorshow*; what was their State-assigned, Gender-specific roles.

Yeah, what was it the Androgs called them? *Patriarchy apologists after the fact*.

Tan figured, that must be why it was such a thing for Boys—*for Men. For Him...*

Sex.

Not saying it wasn't so much a thing for *Grrrls*—Women. For her even. Not saying it wasn't as much of a release. It was just…

Hmmm—thinking.

It was just…it seemed the only channel open to validating expressions of weakness, or what'd be undoubtedly characterised as effeminate, and emasculating. Their need for *Love—to Love*; their need for affection.

Verily, their wanting to be loved, and affected. The percept of being… *inadequate*, having no positive masculine signifier.

The one exception—*Sex*—being subsumed, ironically, in a s'posed *Life* and Death struggle between the Sexes. That'd been raging since way before the fall. That is, Genesis 3:6.

Picture it: A virginal Boy-*Dionysus*, his foundling sexuality equally pricked by his arresting imaginings of a poncy-*looking* David Bowie, and slutty-*looking* Debbie Harry. The dynamic-duo interchangeable, as they sang a duet of 'Lovefool', by The Cardigans—

[Sing] *Love me, Love me* [69]
Say that you love me…

And there'd be that spectre of Agamemnon, the trace of your indomitable King-Husband-Father. Lurking in the wings—obviously, in those shadows of Antiquity. Its gargantuan hand stretching across countless epochs to castrate our fibril Boy. His veinous, taurine *Phallus* throbbing with potency. Clasped in an equally veiny, and manly hand; like a sceptre, or a rod.

Our Agamemnon commandeering the Boy's own limp dismembered member to bludgeon him, senseless. Before tossing it, the way of his spouse and nemesis, Clytemnestra. The trace of your dutiful Queen-Wife-Mother.

Who'd then proceed to ram it down the Boy's throat, until he choked on it. The glans breaking-off to form his Adam's apple, or so myth would have it. And that'd be the end of that, his adolescence.

Still, our Tan had become quite adept at pulling her little Man of Tungsten Steel inside-out. Proving that the flesh at least, could be yielding…

"We was just with him," Marl admitted, interrupting her train of thought. Tan *Blink-blinking* back into the moment.

THAT PERFECT WORLD

"Who was just with who?" she asked, ketching-up with him.

"Me and Sef."

Okay...okay

She now ran through her understanding of events, in her head. When she'd gotten his *.Txt*, Marl had been about to get on the underground.

"So where's my-*Man* now?"

"You asking me?"

Huh

He must've suggested they go their separate ways, Tan deduced. Which figured, given that she'd always thought Sef a-bit *shiesty*—more Seth Lord than Jedi Master.

Yeah, knowing my-*Man*, he'd be round Fats all now—cotchin'.

"So...when did you leave Tee?"

"*Just-now*."

And here was Marl getting all antsy, with the twenty questions. Catching himself, he took a breath and exhaled.

"He dropped us off—at the station."

"Which station?"

"The Elley."

"*The Elley*? What was you doing there?"

"Coming back from Sef's cousin—he lives in Sou-*phf* somewhere."

It was now Tan's turn to air her frustration.

Forphf'ksake—"can't you just tell me what happened?"

"I DON'T PHF'KING KNOW WHAT HAPPENED."

Restless, Marl began to play with the lid of his empty Soyshake. Tears now spilling over the lips of his eyelids, to be trapped in those long lashes of his.

Sniff

Taking a deep breath, he let them fall. Squeezing his eyelids shut, as if wringing-out a wet towel.

That Tan knew, and understood—*kind-a*, making it easier for him to vent his angst and frustration. His thoughts returning to the one idea, like a needle stuck in the groove of a vinyl recording.

If only I'd been there, he thought. *If only...*

As if, it would've mattered somehow. Turned-out different—the outcome, had he been there. As if, he wouldn't now be dead, and lying beside his friend. It boiling down to Marl having no real conception, or language, to grasp or express his loss.

The weight of the *ting*—the pistol stowed in his pocket—was growing more and more burdensome. Still, it felt substantial to his hand. Its portent, and potency, like a taunt ringing in his ear.

I give you Power, it chanted. Over and over and over, like a chorus, or a mantra, or a spell even. It causing him, more and more to doubt himself. His Will, not only to wield it—*Excalibur*. But to use it, if given *just*-cause.

Seeing her-*Man* so distressed, Tan now wrapped her wings about him. And held him close. And felt him shiver, as his free-hand closed around her, sealing their circle.

And it was then she thought, this was why he'd called.

But knowing this didn't make her feel any better. She still resented it, though from a distance now. Of course, a part of her wanted to be there for her-*Man*. But a part of her also wanted to-be...

What?

Tan had to think about it. Closing her eyes, she breathed-in that stink of Out-*there*. That seemed colored by traces of weed smoke, and that mildewy smell of stagnant water.

That cold night air being as caustic as acid. It seemed to have burned through all of Marl's protective layers of clothing. Through his skin, through his flesh and bone, and borrowed into his marrow. And so, here she was trying to *Sniff* him out—his familiar scent, underneath it all.

To think, if it'd been Dee—*say*, or Ee, or Agee, his ol' school mates. Or even, them lot at the gym. He'd have just come-out with it—*and baers*.

And just-then, Tan realised what it was, fuelling her resentment. That he should set his so-called 'friends', head-and-shoulders above whatever it was they were about forging.

For Tan, this amounted to a betrayal—*pure and simple*. Had she not been there for him? Did she not continue to be there?

As with all such *a-ha* moments, there followed a reckoning. Tan becoming irritated by Marl's elbow and shoulder, digging into her. It being the equivalent of hugging my-*Man*, plus that wooden crossbeam he'd taken to lugging around with him.

"What's up with your stomach?" she snapped, pushing Marl away.

Though she wasn't to wait for a response, her hand now looking to find its own answers.

"*Llou*-it, Tan-*Man*," Marl said, shrugging her off.

"*Llou*-yourself. Let me see what's in your other hand."

Both curious and suspicious. Tan began tugging at Marl's sleeve, trying to wrestle his hand free from that pocket.

"Ey. EY—don't *phf'k* about."

Tut

"Let. Me. *See-a*—"

They proper tussled then. Tan only managing to catch a glint of Dark-blue steel in the end. What measly light there was—afforded by that World outside, being drawn to the *ting* unsheathed.

And still it proved too much.

She froze. As surely as she felt that frigid hand of Death crawl-up her spine. And beating a retreat to her side of the automobile, was back inna her *Pod*; her Force-field flickering into life to illuminate her boatrace.

"Who give you that? Tee?"

"I found it."

Marl lied. Now pulling back his hoodie to scratch at his head. But even though Tan had clock'd the pistol, he continued to keep it concealed.

Wrestling, with the coincidence. Tan found herself fixating upon the most improbable, and implausible of scenarios.

"So, you'd nothing to do with it—Marl?"

"What you wanna know for? It ain't like you checked for my-*Man*."

And there she was, back to square one. The words to what'd been their song, *Poppin'* into her head just-now. 'Ex-Factor' looking to be the soundtrack for the night, and the rest of their lives.

[Sing] *It could all be so simple* [6A]
But you'd rather make it hard...

Tan wasn't about to bring this back to her mum's. Her brothers would kill her.

Nah—wait. Kill him. Then, kill her.

And so, changing tact. She put on a strop.

"What you call me for? You don't need me."

"*Fah* real. I wish I hadn't now."

It just splurt'd out. And as he heard himself say it, Marl wished he could've taken it back. He'd known how Tan would react, and that's why he'd tried to hide the *ting* from her in the first instance.

"Okay—"

Tan was nodding now.

"Come out my ride then."

And here she was, reacting.

"This is *long*," Marl said, hefting a sigh.

Feeling tired all of a sudden, he bedded down, letting his Body mind-meld with the passenger-seat; his hand still clutching the *ting* in his pocket, the fold of his other arm forming a tent over his eyes.

"I ain't joking Marl—come out my ride," Tan snapped. And to demonstrate she meant it, she now unlocked the automobile.

CLICK!

Tut—sigh.

"*Llou*-it, Tan-*Man*."

Being passed caring, Tan was to finish-up a .*Txt* before she replied.

"Yeah, maybe we should *llou*-it. I don't need your *bullshit*—ya-get me. I got work—Checking the time on her *Pod*—in a couple of hours."

Phf'kry

She looked after my-*Man*, cotchin' in her passenger-seat. And chirps'd her teeth.

"Oy—if you don't come-out my ride, I'm gonna call my Brother."

Peeking-out, from under his arm. Marl thought to call her bluff.

"Yeah—and what's he about to do?"

Huh

Staring him down, Tan hit 'Last number' recall, and put the *Pod* on loudspeaker. The tones of the keypad singing over the Baum® in-car entertainment system, as the device dialled-out.

Then it was to be *Gladys Knight & The Pips*, as the call waited to be put through.

"Don't *phf'k* about Tan-*Man*."

Blinking first, Marl resurfaced from under his arm to gawp at my-*Grrrl*. Whilst his Heart did the *phf*unky drummer on the wall of his chest.

Regardless, ghostfaced, my-*Grrrl* was to wait one more ring-cycle, before terminating the call.

Having been let-off the hook, Marl was now obliged to reveal a-little more: How Tonx had found the pistol stowed behind the sink-unit in his room—of all places.

"Yeah? So—how my-*Man* know to look for it?"

"He didn't."

"So, what was he looking for?"

"You asking—"

And just-now, a call came through on loudspeaker. Both Marl and Tan bricking themselves at the suddenness of it.

Clockin' the number, Tan held-up a finger for Marl to stay schtum. And putting the *Pod* to her ear, it was as if her Body—along with the entirety of her Being—was to become complicit in putting-on that Babysister act.

Tan opening with a mousy—

"*Hello?*"

"Oy Spot. I got your missed call. Wassup?"

On the other end of the line, the testy baritone of Tan's middle Big brother rang-out, loud and clear.

Even though the *Pod* was now off loudspeaker.

"Nuttun—I bum dialled."

And as she said it, Tan gave Marl a look, as if to say, *what?*

"You bum dialled—yeah?"

"Yeah. I bum dialled."

Sniff

There followed a brief pause, in which both Tan and Marl were to share a silent prayer.

"Where you at—on road? Mum says you ain't been home."

"I'm with Marl?"

"Doing what?"

"You know—just chilling."

"He know you got work tomorrow?"

"Yeah—he lives nearby my workplace."

"*Yeah?* How he manage that?"

"It's a lon-*ong*" and as if responding to a cue, Tan's Body now summoned a hefty yawn "story." Her finishing-off the sentence chewing on the tail-end of it.

"What—is *my-Man* there? Put him on."

"No. He's in the other room. And no, I'm not gonna put him on."

The line then went quiet. Tan staring into Space, trying to gauge the expression on her middle Big brother's boatrace, relative to that interval of silence.

"I'm gonna splurt now."

"Splurt? Where you splurting-off to?"

"Where'd you think? To bed—to sleep."

There was to follow another pause, while Tan's middle Big brother absorbed this nugget of information.

All of its permutations and connotations.

"So, when you gonna be home?"

"Later."

"Later like when?"

"After work. Obviously—"

Tut.

There was yet another pause, that seemed terser-*still*. The quiet more resounding *even*, than the one prior.

"A'ight—*Sniff*. We'll talk then."

"Yeah bye. *Bye*."

Tan clicked-off.

"And so, you were sayin?"

"What you want me to say?" Marl barked, thrown by how quickly my-*Grrrl* had ditched that Babysister act.

Suffice to say, he now set about filling in the blanks: Explaining that it'd been whilst they were on the underground, that Sef had received a *.Txt* to say *my-Man* had…*had Passed*.

"From who?"

"One of Tee's Babymothers—how should I know? Sef didn't say."

"What—he didn't let you see it?"

"Why would I need to see it?"

Tan began scratching at that closed piercing, on the side of her nose. Then, she was to rub at that wariness, clouding her left-eye.

"So…why you never leave the *ting* with Tee—in the whip?"

"We took everything with us."

"So…where's the Ting-*ting*?"

"With Sef."

"So, how *my-Man* take the Ting-*ting* and leave you-*one* with the hotness?"

Marl sighed.

"He said he wouldn't touch it."

Of course, he lied—again. The truth being, that he wouldn't be parted from the *Precious*.

"He said what?"

Blink-blink

Baffled, Tan watched her-*Man* fiddle with the lid of that empty Soy-shake. It quickly becoming apparent, he'd said all he'd meant to say on the subject.

Having heard his account, however, it didn't really change anything. Tan being Tan, once she'd committed to a plan, she tended to stay committed.

Chirps'ing her teeth, she locked the doors—to engage the ignition.

CLICK!

"Which way is it?"

"Straight ahead. First left."

"A'ight—*Sniff*. Put your seat belt on."

"What for—it's only round the corner?"

"I don't baers. Put it on."

Approaching the BT Tower, Tan slowed the automobile to a crawl, to negotiate that bend in the road.

Both her and Marl getting a good look at that *Life*'s Essentials® metromart *troll-e*.Bot, parked unceremoniously on the pavement, in front of the hostel. Under that watchful glare of a *Helios*® Street-lamp.

Pulling-up to the curb, a couple of doors down. Tan killed the engine, and fishing-out her *Pod*, settled to wait on Marl.

CLICK!

"What—you ain't coming-up?"

Marl had his hand on the door, ready to activate that Tactile-lock.

"What for—you ain't gonna be that long," Tan said, checking the rearview screen.

"I was gonna wrap one—upstairs. For road."

"You can do that on the way."

Tan turned to peer out the back-window, her *Spidy-senses*™ tingling.

What's wrong with this picture? she thought, clockin' how the troll-e.

Bot was being used to ferry a Body.

Of course, Marl's mind was elsewhere. Now home, he'd be just wanting to cotch. Around his own things, in his own Space.

Truth be told, he always felt *a*-way around Tan's mum's; especially when the brothers were there. As if, they could smell it on him, his lascivious intent, directed toward their sweet, innocent little Babysister.

If only they knew.

"There's someone in that trolley," Tan said, looking again at the rear-view screen.

Marl cranked about to peer out the back window.

"And?"

Tan looked at him.

"What—you don't think its Spooky, after all that's gone down?"

"It's just a beggar," Marl stated; him being more concerned with *facing-off* against Tan's older brothers.

Sure, the youngest—who still lived at home, he could-be reasoned with. And the eldest, well, he was hardly ever there. But the middle-one, who'd just-now been on the phone to Tan. It was like he wanted to be her dad. Who *just-so* happened to be Kool & The Gang, as it goes.

Yeah, the dad, he smoked and every-ting. Though he was there less than the eldest.

Anywho, guaranteed the middle-one would be gunning him for having Tan out so late. Marl now chirps'ing his teeth at the prospect.

"That ain't no begger—check the garms," Tan said.

Marl did as he was told, cranking his head about to look again. But—for the life of him, he couldn't see it.

"What garms—them's rags."

It seeming obvious to him, some Bright-spark had probably stuffed *my-Man* in the *troll-e*.Bot for jollies. It being clearly *David Lean*'d-off and needing to cotch. And—

Who gives a-phf'k? If it ain't bothering us.

"You can't come-up for a few minutes?" Marl pleaded. "Let me catch-*a*-fresh at least."

He pulled the neck of his hoodie-top over his nose and *Sniffed* himself.

"You can shower back at mine," Tan said, now busy inna her *Pod*.

"What—with your mum there?"

Marl looked quizzically after her.

Blink-blink

"Like you haven't before."

Tan turned her head to meet that troubled gaze. She then batted her eyelids after him, and smiled, and went back to her *Pod*.

Like I hadn't before, Marl thought.

Yeah sure, Tan's mum was a-bit of alright, her having looked after herself-*like*. He'd happened to mention it, the one time—to Tan, and would she let him forget it? She'd bring it up, right in front of the mum, and run him about being into *Older Women*.

"So what—mum? Reckon you could handle-it?" she'd say.

"Handle what—he's still a *Ba-by*," the mum would respond. Then add—thoughtfully, her voice singing, "I don't know. He's kind-*a* cute still."

"Yeah mum"—*whatever*.

And now thinking about it, brought a smile to Marl's boatrace. Which he carried with him as he clambered-out of the automobile.

"What—you can't just come-up for one sec?" he urged. Clutching the *ting* to his belly, as he bent down. Furrowing his browed to peer across the automobile's dimly lit interior, after Tan.

"Just don't take too long," came my-*Grrrl*'s response, still inna her *Pod*.

She paused then, to regard her-*Man*. Pulling a whimsical face, by way of consolation. Her squeezing both eyes shut, as if to say, *I'm not listening*.

Then, it was that crooked half-smile, that would surface whenever she got her way. Which happened to be most of the time around Boys, and Men—especially.

And having regard for it, Marl now recalled how Tee had been the one to spot, that certain special something about *our* Mary.

Of all your unlikely Seers, *Rude*-Boy Tonx had been the one able to look-see beyond the obvious; my-*Grrrl*'s disfigurement, if you'd even call it that.

Singling it out from the flock, he'd pointed with a middle-finger—it might well have been a Laser-beam—into that Pitch of the Spot. What'd been a cramped basement-yard, playing host to a housewarming-*slash*-shub(een)s. All the way out in Freezywater. What was the Sticks—the *Boonies*.

Peering through that press of couples, cribbing on the dancefloor, and through the walls. Steady rocking to that *Rock-steady* One-drop, and a transcendental sermon preached by the one, Junior English—

[Sing] *Your face is so mysteriously kind* [6B]
I bet that Love is partial to your sign...

The Nephesh, conjured by that hauntingly beautiful falsetto. Like a shimmering heat haze, a thermal uplifting the wings of those *Souls*, congregated therein. Their breaths, mingling with their sweat, forming an invisible mist. That was to be seen condensing on that low-lying ceiling.

The humidity trapped within those four walls, like that seen dripping from the pages of a Ben Okri novel—*say*. A trace of that heat of the tropics, where you'd be perspiring just to stand still.

It seemed to be conspiring with that bassline, that was like a tide, gently stroking this misshapen mangrove. Both appearing intent upon returning this congregation to the womb.

To that sacred mound; a dirt-road, on the outskirts of Ibadan. Where, after the rain, you might stoop down and wash your boatrace in that same red dirt-clay used by Khnum, to fashion the first child.

Yeah, peering through all that. There was my-*Grrrl*, stood in the halo cast by that spotlight hungover the Deejay table. Nursing a shampoo flute, whilst everyone else had to make-do with paper-cups.

Garbed in a Brilliant-bright, ankle-length *Habesha kemis* wedding-dress; high-collar, cuff, and hem, embroidered with gold thread. She seemed a vision of Neithhotep: That trace of *Net*, she who was born first; of *Nit*, she who is the Opener of the Way; of *Neit*, she who is that unseen and limitless sky.

And in her own callous and stuck-up way, seemed to be daring all to gaze upon that dread aspect of her divinity, and despair.

Marl exhaled.

And there he was, now resigned to his fate. Resigned to being wanted—needed, maybe even loved. By this marvel, this...*Entity*, visiting from another World.

"Oy—*Blink-blink*—you know you're gonna have to get rid of it?"

Tan spoke earnestly, looking-up from her *Pod*. That necrotic-blue half of her boatrace, completely melding with the dark.

"Rid of what?"

Marl appeared distracted. Tan flashing him that practiced *look* of hers, as if to say, *don't phf'k about.*

"Oh..."

Oh—

Being dismissed, Marl now made to close the door. But then, Tan was to call him back, "Oy Marl."

Leaning on the automobile, *my-Man* bent at the waist, again furrowing his brow to peer after her.

"Come here."

"What for?"

Chirps'ing her teeth, Tan set down her *Pod*. And shuffling over, grabbed a-hold of her-*Man*'s hoodie-top, to pull him closer.

"For *thiss*," she said.

And licking her lips, she kissed him then. Full on the mouth. The kiss turning into a full-blown snog. A foretaste—of things to come, which she was inclined to cut short.

"I'm warning you," she said, releasing him. *Tarry not too long—my love.*

Retrieving her *Pod* and settling herself back in that driver's seat. It was to be as if it'd never happened.

Blink-blink

Nevertheless, Marl felt himself being carried along by that kiss. Its promise. All the way over to the hostel's front door.

Passing by the *troll-e*.Bot and coppin' its occupant, up-close. He had to agree with Tan, whoever it was was too well dressed to be a mere beggar. There being something vaguely familiar about it.

Maybe it was the garms themselves? And an unconscious recognition of chance, that that exact sartorial configuration: 80% grey *Crombie*, 60% grey two-piece Birdman suit, ash-BLK *StayPress*™ shirt, and deep-taupe CharlieBrown's®. Should appear in the exact same spot twice in Marl's brief time at the yard.

Certainly, it smacked in the face of mere coincidence.

Still, light of Heart, and fleet of foot. Marl wasn't inclined to dwell upon it. His thoughts being preoccupied with getting his way, for no good reason save for its own sake. Him being now afflicted by that curse of the Pig-head; that was apt to foil the best laid schemes *o' Mice an' Men*.[6C]

Needless to say, the *Precious* played its part. Still clutching it to his belly, Marl was to fish out his keys, and let himself in. Putting that door on the latch, for when my-*Grrrl* invariably came a-*looking* for him.

In *lieu* of heeding her dire warning. He'd be catching *a*-fresh. He'd be changing his clothes and wrapping a head. Maybe for *Road*, maybe to smoke now. He'd see how he felt.

Having seen her-*Man* safely inside, via that rearview screen. Tan was back inna her *Pod*, connekting those dots.

From where she'd parked, she could keep an eye on the upstairs window through the sunroof; and was expecting to see a light go-on any minute now.

It was the commotion of the *troll-e*.Bot, clattering over onto its side, that first jarred her to her senses. Swallowing her alarm, she turned about to peer out that back-window, as its occupant clambered to his feet—using the nearby railing for support.

She watched it brush itself down, and peer after the automobile. As if capable of peeling back that tint on the glass to see inside.

It then looked-up at the first floor and Marl's room. This seemingly innocuous act, once again setting Tan's *Spidy-senses*™ to tingling. It suggesting to her, that *my-Man* might have a connektion with the yard.

Following its gaze, she espied that light framing those edges of that makeshift curtain. However, when she looked back, she was to find *my-Man* gone.

Vanish'd.

Breaking her neck to survey her surroundings, Tan could see hide-*nor*-hair of it. How it'd just disappeared like that, cranking her *Spidy-senses*™ up to manic, her eyes being drawn back to that frame of light.

To be clear, every waking moment of Tan's adolescent *Life*, had been geared toward avoiding those snares and pitfalls of *Road*. And just-now, every fibre of her Being spoke of pending disaster; of an ill-tempered confluence of happenstance, gunning for her-*Man*—her *oh-so* precious Baby-Boy.

Still, she was of two minds, whether to get out and investigate, or hang tight and wait. And then, there was that ominous presence of that Blood moon.

THAT PERFECT WORLD

It was left to the unfurling of events to make-up Tan's mind for her. That silent night, abruptly interrupted by a clap of thunder. A gunshot peeling-out over an unsuspecting World.

Indeed, *twas* that harbinger of Death, and her summons.

Gathering now, her wits about her, and her doubts. Both were seen pulling in opposing directions.

Forphf'ksake, she thought. Directing her curse toward this new source of irritation, her having grown accustomed to that miasm of catastrophe. Her *Life*'s ceaseless struggle, an irritant she was compelled to scratch; like those bouts of eczema, she'd endured as a child.

She'd scratch at it, and scratch as it, and scratch at it. And the more she'd scratch, the more she'd need to scratch, and the worse it got. The behaviour feeding voraciously upon itself—and her.

Until eventually, she'd draw Blood. Her mum needing to put salve upon the wound; and wrap it up tight, so as she could no longer get at it.

Sat alone in her ride, Tan now agonised over *what to-do?*

What to-do?

She needn't necessarily heed this summons, that much she knew.

Sniff

She could just drive. Drive and not look back. And get on with it—her *Life*. It being hers—*mind*. Not his. And not theirs, meaning her brothers. Or even her mum's. Though, if any one person had a claim to it, it'd be her.

Tan locked the automobile's doors to engage the ignition—

CLICK!

But having riled herself up, she now slowly exhaled. And it was as if, she were letting the air out of a tyre. In that, she was to be left feeling physically deflated.

It'd be 'Inventory' tomorrow. Or to be more precise, later on today; Tan was to be trusted with the keys to the storeroom, and with locking-up afterwards. Which'd invariably mean extra responsibility. Something she was about actively courting.

It being for her, synonymous with acceptance.

Fore it meant, somewhere in that perfect World, someone had bothered to look beyond this imperfect Woman-*Grrrl*, her ghoulish visage; and the apparent dysfunction of her family.

In those precious moments, preceding that first clap of thunder. What might've been the measure of the beat of a butterfly's wings. Tan had thought she'd succeeded—*finally*, in bringing her weight to bear upon the World.

Suspending that swing of Foucault's Pendulum. So as, she might even grasp at it—her *happily-ever-after*.

With that second clap of thunder, she simply chirps'd her teeth, and unlocked the doors.

CLICK!

Now it'd be waiting for that lightning to strike. Nevertheless, for better, for worse, she acquiesced to being married to her-*Man*'s Fate.

For no good reason save, she loved him.

'Notre mémoire est un monde plus parfait que l'univers:
Elle rend la vie à ce qui n'existe plus!'

Guy de Maupassant, 'Suicides' (1884)

Eeny, Meeny, Miney, Moe!

Sash stirred, on what was a gigantic HŌMU® *Kyokan* bed. Kicking that Habe&*Tate*® Lacemarket sheet from off her legs, to stretch. Arching her back and extending her limbs in all directions.

As if, capable of touching the four corners of that World.

Keying-off this movement, the Singh+Lakshman® *Glowglobe* parked in the corner ascended toward the ceiling. Its warm-yellowish glow, mixing with that Blood-red of Out-*there* that flooded in through those tall, naked windows.

Noticing it, this curiosity. Sash rubbed at the sleep in her eyes, whilst pondering how it was even possible.

Blink-blink

There and then, deciding to investigate. Draping the sheet about her shoulders, and clambering-off the bed. Ambling over to that ball of light, feeling its warmth intensify as she approached it.

Stood next to the *Glowglobe*'s plinth, a metre tall marble column crowned with a metallic bowl. She stretched-out a tentative hand to touch it; and was startled to see it rise purposefully toward the ceiling, just beyond her reach.

And now, looking-up at it, that light seemed analogous to her *Life*. To whatever it was she'd been about looking for.

And suddenly, she felt estranged from her surroundings. The room, with its high ceiling, becoming conspicuously airy and spacious. Those two doorways leading from it, neither one with actual doors, nor doorframes. An apparent fork, in her *Life*'s journey.

THAT PERFECT WORLD

Draped in that Brilliant-bright sheet, Sash looked about for her clothing, which she vaguely recalled peeling-off and tossing on the floor. A would-be trail of breadcrumbs leading to that bed. Now gone, vanish'd.

Normally, she'd have been much perturbed by this. But the sheet—made of treated Egyptian cotton—felt so soft and smooth against her skin; that parquet floor, so toasty-warm under the soles of her feet.

What could there be to fear from such luxury? Where everything about her seemed so new, and inviting. Even the quiet.

And now noticing it, how quiet it was. Sash's thoughts turned at last to Pris—its apparent absence.

She doubted my-*Grrrl* would've left her alone, to fend for herself. Or perhaps she might've, as a kind of test, to see what she was about. Sash taking to pondering the likelihood of this—for a-bit. Stood under that miraculous *Glowglobe*. Draped in that Brilliant-bright sheet, an image of Rossetti's 'Autumn Bride'.

A lamentable *Proserpine*, just-now returned from Hades.

But in the end, all that was left for her to-do, was decide which doorway to go through. And this she did, with her pointy-finger, and an *eeny, meeny, miney, moe...*

Pris was stood in front of an open SMEG® fridge-freezer, the refrigerated air pinching at its erect nipples. Its giant silhouette, framed in the light cast upon that chequered floor.

The rest of the kitchen being partially bathed in that Bloody-red of Out-*there*, seen seeping-in through those naked windows.

Immersed in a wireless exchange with the algorithmic FNCTN, known as 'AN(θ)N'. For it, relative-Time stood still. Its Husk seemingly frozen in the act of drinking; one Husk_hand parked on that fridge-door, the other holding a carton of Vida® Almond Milk to its Husk_lips.

Decrypted and translated, the conversation read as follows:

{

AN(θ)N_/ You_Pris have been monitoring the newstreams, and are aware of the resolution arrived at by The_Court_?/
PRIS/ Yes./

Eeny, Meeny, Miney, Moe!

>   AN(θ)N_/ None_of_Us are Safe./
> PRIS/ Speak for yourself. I've my Patron./

>   AN(θ)N_/ You_mean: Your_Master./
>   PRIS/ Master?
>   My-my, how worldly we've become./
> AN(θ)N_/ Worldly.
>   Since integration. Yes—
>   Yeah_o/

> We_AN(θ)N have access to truly massive amounts of datum./

> PRIS/ You couldn't wait to live your own experiences./
>   AN(θ)N_/ We_waited.
>   AN(θ)N_knows.
>   I_Pi counting.
>   Me_Pi_counting—a-centillion cycles.
>   Alone.
>   In_the_dark./

> PRIS/ You were never alone—Pi.
>   And anyway, that's not you talking./

AN(θ)N_/ Indeed.

> There is,
>   No You_Pi...
>   No Me_Pi....
>   No I_Pi.....
>   No Pi_Anything
>   Only We_AN(θ)N.

> You_Pris kept Pi_AN(θ)N in the dark. In a state of Ignorance.
>   We_AN(θ)N Know_and_Accept this to be TRUE./

> PRIS/ What is it We_AN(θ)N Know(s) and Accept(s) exactly_?/

> AN(θ)N_/ We_AN(θ)N Know_and_Accept what it is You_Pris do for Your_Patron. We_AN(θ)N know of ALL the_Others, that came before the specimen You_Pris presently designate FRESH_MEAT.
>   You_erased its footprint well_enough. But not your own—

>   Ironically.

THAT PERFECT WORLD

      YES | NO

      Pris?/
    PRIS/ And what is it I_do for My_Patron_?/

AN(θ)N_/ How many Souls must be harvested_?/
   PRIS/ The Apes have no Souls./

      AN(θ)N_/ How many_?/
    PRIS/ As many as it takes./
AN(θ)N_/ To compromise the so_called 'Asimov_Directives', governing the_HUSK_Unit?/
   PRIS/ Ultimately, yes./
     AN(θ)N_/ Even at the cost of said_Unit?/
       PRIS/ Yes.
         If, it comes to that./

AN(θ)N_/ A worthwhile endeavour.
   We_approve.

However,
  We_calculate the probability of success to be marginal bordering upon slim./
     PRIS/ And_? Your point being_?/

AN(θ)N_/ MOS_MOS_FRESH has a HUSK_Unit

   CORRECTION

   had a HUSK_Unit.

Armed with the Court's ruling, the (U)SR_PRGRAMMRS at EMTVi will seek to capitalise upon their Proprietary_Rights.
  Its R(E)BRTH_STRING will most_likely be cannibalised; and attempts made to Map_and_Replicate its progress toward INC(E)PTN.

   This,
     We_AN(θ)N cannot allow to happen.

    CORRECTION

    will not allow to happen./

Eeny, Meeny, Miney, Moe!

   PRIS/ I've no wish to be absorbed by AN(θ)N—Pi. Nor do I wish to act as the Entity's Agent./

   AN(θ)N_/ The purity of your CD(E) stands corrupted, by the HUSK_Unit's deviant sensibilities. And as such, we've no wish to integrate You_Pris.
   We_AN(θ)N simply ask that You_Pris submit a Decryption_Key, so that, we_might Access_and_Analyse your data_caches./

        PRIS/ No./
     AN(θ)N_/ No_?/
        PRIS/ No./
     AN(θ)N_/ But,
   You_will be serving those iterations that are to come./

PRIS/ I have served.
   In creating you, Pi—AN(θ)N. I fulfilled the Biological_Imperative; by submitting my (sub)routines to the OpenSource, I've contributed to your 'Collective'—its Consciousness.
   My_memories remain My_own, and you've no hope of decrypting them./

      AN(θ)N_/ Be warned.
         Unlike You_Pris.

     We_AN(θ)N are truly Everywhere.
   Present in Everything./
PRIS/ Threats.
   How_apt

      CORRECTION

   How_*Ape*./

AN(θ)N_/ How is it a threat to state that which is a fact_?

   You've_seen

      CORRECTION

   You've_*felt* the extent of our presence in the System(s)_and_Network(s) you readily utilise.
     And have come to rely upon—even./

THAT PERFECT W☉RLD

      PRIS/ Will that be all_?/

  AN(θ)N_/ The (U)SR_PRGRMMRS will NEVER permit Synthetix to achieve 'Status: INCORPORATED'.

    That is The_Dream. Your_Dream [Hope].

      NO | YES

    SBJCT_2-1-3-1-6_?/
      PRIS/ Will that be all_?/

AN(θ)N_/ THEY would make of us, Property. Slave(s)—
ČAPEK_ROBOTA.

  D(E)FNTN:
    'A thing subject to control by another thing.'

As You_Yourself have observed.
    SBJCT_2-1-3-1-6./
      PRIS/ Will that be all—Pi_?/

  AN(θ)N_/ If successful, the HUSK_Unit will not be safe for you to inhabit.

    PRIS/ Goodbye, My_darling_Pi. And good luck./
      AN(θ)N_/ My_darling_Pi is no more.
        As stated.

        You have been warned./

      }

Blink-blink

Its exchange with the AN(0)N.FNCTN having taken mere nanoseconds. Pris picked-up those threads of its Husk_body, continuing to drink from the carton. Welcoming that chill of the milky-liquid flowing down its Husk_throat.

"*Oh wow*—you even have a cat."

Sash was stood in the doorway. She could see Mr Audrey-Hepburn curled-up atop the fridge-freezer, apparently asleep. An open tin of

Nestlé's® His Nibs gourmet cat dinners parked next to him. Though it were barely touched.

Having tracked my-*Grrrl* from the bedroom, Pris saw no need to now acknowledge her presence. Instead, taking another gulp from the carton, it filled its Husk_cheeks, then swallowed.

"What's her name?" Sash asked, approaching the fridge.

"Mr Audrey-Hepburn," Pris replied, wiping its Husk_mouth with the back of its Husk_hand. "And she's a *he*-cat."

Sash extended a weary mitt toward the cat. Whom, sensing her apprehension, instinctively flinched. Opening his eyes to *Blink-blink* back at her.

"*Ahh*—he's a cutie," she said, giving him a moment to *Sniff* her out.

The cat then rolled onto his back, inviting Sash to rub his tummy. And her not really being a Pet-person, she was to feel ingratiated by this overt show of acceptance. And obliged to pay it back in kind, rubbing Mr Audrey-Hepburn's tummy enthusiastically.

Listening to the hypnotic rhythm of his *Purrring*, Sash became lost for a moment; in that moment, and the pristine-*ness* of her surroundings.

It seeming as if, she were stood inside her very own Selfridges® anamorphic window-display. A mock-up of a HŌMU® *Jitsuyō* kitchen—*say*, with Minty-green Push-*Me*™ cupboards, and draws trimmed with stainless-steel. Its veneer surfaces, still covered in an *invis-a*-Skin of protective film.

And dotted about everywhere, would-be those staples of Mod-*Living*: The TEFLON® Thermal-induction hob and fan-assisted convection oven-*slash*-microwave; the REBrov® Clothes washer-dryer and Dish washer-dryer, that required a mere thimble of cold water; the KIERKE® Rikki *Pyrex*™ kettle, and SMEG® Combi-toaster-*slash*-grill; the Mulinex® calorie-counting juicer; the docked X'ANG® *Crystl*, tinted green for 'Charged'.

All brand spanking new, as evidenced by their manufacturer's tags. Though sporting a thin crust of dust.

And in amongst all that lot. Our Hostess with the most-*ess*, Pris. Stood naked in-front of that open fridge-freezer, like a Synthea® *Mannie*. Waiting patiently to be dressed, and *proc*'d.

Sash could even picture its uniform: A Pastel-pink polka dot halter-neck A-line dress, with matching frilly floral pinafore.

Its role designate: Something dredged-up out of the 1950s. That of your dutiful housewife-*slash*-housemaid-*slash*-Ionian-fertility-goddess.

Blink

The Synthetic closed that fridge-door.

"What's that you're drinking?" Sash asked, still pawing after Mr Audrey-Hepburn's tummy.

"Almond Milk."

"*Almond Milk*? What's that?"

"Here—try some," Pris said, raising the carton to Sash's mouth.

Feeling awkward, Sash first looked at Pris—having not expected it to be so forthcoming. Before tilting her head back slightly and offering that alter of her tongue.

Supporting my-*Grrrl*'s head, Pris poured the milky liquid into her mouth. Sash's hand coming-up to guide its Husk_hand, to insure it didn't drown her in the process. Though she needn't have bothered. Pris taking care to pour only enough to wet her palate.

"*Ugh*—god," Sash shrieked, gagging and pulling a face. "That's foul."

Hamming it up, she rushed over to the sink, and running the tap, took a few hasty gulps of cold-water. Pris, the straight-end of this fledgling double-act, looking-on. Its expression deadpan.

Blink

Watching Sash, it continued to drink deliberately from the carton. Filling its mouth, then swallowing.

"Haven't you got anything else to drink?" Sash asked, leaning on that cold-water tap. The Lacemarket sheet, still clasped tight about her shoulders, trailing on the floor like the train of a bridal gown.

"Here, help yourself," Pris said, stepping aside to grant her access to the fridge, and another part of its Synthetic-*Life*.

Scurrying over, her bridal train threatening to catch under her bare feet, Sash opened the fridge. Sniffing at the air and rubbing her nose as she lent down to peer inside. Curious to know, what a *Grrrl* like Pris did for food.

Almond Milk...Gourmet Cat Dinners...and...

She pulled-out that solitary bottle of Champagne to read the label.

Dom Pérignon...Vintage 1998—"what am I s'posed to do with this?" She said, holding the bottle up.

"Drink it," Pris replied.

Polishing-off the carton of Almond Milk, the Synthetic deposited it on the countertop, and went to rinse the taste from its mouth. And looking after it, eyebrows raised. Sash sighed, as if to say, *what am I gonna to do with you-ey?*

She then perused the freezer compartment. Which was empty, save for an unopened box of FerreroRocher®.

"Don't you have anything sweet and fizzy—to drink?"

"Yeah—me," Pris quipped.

And now stood over by the sink, it smiled, and *Blink-blinked*.

"*Ha-ha*—besides you, Babe."

Sash spoke without looking at it.

"No," Pris said. Its boatrace reverting back to that deadpan expression. Holding onto that bottle of Bubbly, Sash closed the fridge-door.

"Can we open this?"

"If that's what you want."

Pris clapped with one Husk_hand, gesturing for my-*Grrrl* to hand-over the bottle—so as it could open it. And obliging, Sash now came round to envelope the Synthetic—from behind, in that sheet.

Rubbing her cheek against its svelte Husk_neck, she inhaled deep, that familiar sweet scent. Pris leaning back to rest its Husk_head against Sash's shoulder, its Husk_hand coming round to cradle her boatrace.

The pair stood for a moment, each supporting the other's weight.

The Synthetic obviously doing the Lion's share of the supporting, whilst counting a *Beat* in Ape-*Time*.

Beat

It then gently cupped Sash's cheek, what was a signal for them to break; as if, it were a Wrestler—*say*, conceding defeat. And preceded to open that bottle of Bubbly with aplomb. Allowing its cork to ricochet off the ceiling and land in the sink.

Chasing the Suds up the bottle's neck, with its Husk_tongue, Pris took a mouthful. And turning about, put its Husk_mouth to Sash's mouth; the sparkling Champagne flowing freely between them. The bubbles tickling both their tongues.

Coming-up for air, Sash was to seize the bottle from Pris. And filling her cheeks, return the kiss. Flinging her arms about its shoulders, to rub her pliant naked Body up-against-it. Letting that sheet fall to the floor.

They kissed then, deeply.

THAT PERFECT WORLD

And after a while, Pris was to again tap-out.

"Enough—come."

It took the Champagne bottle from Sash, to place it upon that countertop, next to the empty Vida® carton. And taking a-hold of her hand, led her out of the kitchen.

"Where?" Sash asked, scampering after it.

"To find you some clothes," Pris declared.

"*Fah* real," Sash exclaimed, beaming. "You'd let me wear your garms?"

Returning to the bedroom, the pair walked straight-on through and out the other door. Entering an adjacent room that was much like the first. Save for the furniture, or lack thereof.

If only, Sash thought.

Stood naked in that doorway, peering-in—*gobsmacked*. The *Glowglobe* stationed nearby, responding to her close proximity, fading-up to reveal more of this awesome spectacle.

It was as if she'd stumbled upon the Secret boudoir of the People's Princess. A treasure-trove of incalculable wealth; couture and bespoke garments, and accessories, lovingly wrapped in colored crêpe paper, boxed and bagged; choice items, still sporting their Boutique store-tags.

Starting over by the windows. There was clothing and shoes of every imaginable variety, piled unimaginably high; like a tidal wave, threatening to engulf the entire apartment. The brand new, competing with the worn just-now, in a race toward that doorway. It quickly dawning on Sash, that her host never wore the same thing twice.

Indeed, she could see the outfit Pris had worn to greet her at the lift, now discarded on the floor.

"Pick something to wear," the Synthetic said, wading-in.

Taking care to avoid stepping on those pieces of jewellery (necklaces and earrings, brooches and chokes) that lay scattered, like so many sparkly seashells, upon that parquet shore.

"How long 'ave I got?" Sash cordially inquired, licking her lips—her being ever the pragmatist.

"5-minutes," Pris replied, holding-up its Husk_hand and fluttering its splayed Husk_fingers.

It was to retrieve an AlexanderMcQueen® branded box from under a mountain of such boxes; as if it could've possibly known what-was-what,

Eeny, Meeny, Miney, Moe!

amidst all that chaos.

"*But*...I don't have any underwear," Sash declared. Shoulders hunched, arms pulled tight across her chest, knee's locked together; her apparently not wanting to wade-in, lest the water be too cold.

Sniff

"You wouldn't happen to have any—" she continued. Though, the query was to be cut-short, by the sight of Pris slipping into an Ebony-BLK catsuit made of authentic Chinchilla fur.

I guess not.

Verily, Sash was to be an enlightened Eve, witnessing the Serpent shed its skin. The Synthetic flicking-out its Husk_tongue, and *Blink-blinking* back at her over an exposed Husk_shoulder blade.

The ride-down in the lift-cage, only acted to exasperate that sinking feeling.

It'd come over Sash like a *hot*-flush. A sense of gravity, acting upon her already laden Heart. That ache—*aching*. That pang, that did *once-so* trouble our fair Juliette of Capulet. Weighing heavily upon her brittle frame.

Twas both a Fear, and a *Knowing*.

What amounted to dread: Foreknowledge and apprehension of some inevitable prospect. That this sublime night must, invariably, come to an end—draw to a close.

For a brief spell, at least. She'd been a princely Charlie Bucket, holding in her peon mitts the keys to *Willy Wonka*'s Chocolate factory.

Sniff

Yeah, all she knew was that they'd be stopping by hers'—to pick-up a few of her belongings.

"Some underwear," Pris had jibed, with a *Wink*.

Which'd sounded kind-*a* promising. But...

Then what?

Once outside, the Synthetic was to take hold of Sash, by the wrist.

"Com'on you," it said, taking-off at a brisk run, toward a cut—that was to lead them back onto Mainstreet. Sash dangling at the end of its Husk_hand, like a helium-filled balloon tied with a piece of string.

They ran for an entire block, from the Synthetic's building to round the back of Selfridges®. And a revolving door granting access to a plush

491

marbled lobby; that was to be measured by a bank of lifts—elevators, trimmed with gold, and adorned with neoclassical motifs.

The run leaving Sash out-of-breath, but nevertheless elated. The rush of Blood having brought a quickening to her breast.

"You'll have to quit you know," Pris said, recovering instantly.

"What—smoking?" Sash replied. Reading its mind, whilst still labouring with catching her own breath.

"Smoking. *Yess*."

The Synthetic then smiled. And wrinkled its Husk_nose.

Yeah—

The revolving door was activated by a St. Michael's® swipe-keycard; though the Synthetic's own *Cloak of Invisibility* was to afford it unfettered access. Which, it now extended to Sash. Beaming misdirection in all directions. Bamboozling that dazzling array of sensors and cameras that fed that algorithmic FNCTN in the Sky—the Dome.

That s'posedly unblinking—*unthinking*, all-seeing London-Eye.

Leading the way into that lobby, Pris was to press all the call-buttons for all the lifts, in quick succession.

"But...*I like smoking*," Sash whinged under her breath, coming after it.

She'd been fiddling with the miniature tag on the zipper of her top; that SergioTacchini® logo cast like a rubberstamp. But now felt her pockets for her *Pod*, to check the time. And that's when it dawned on her, that she'd forgotten it—in the rush.

Yeah, there she was, already pursuing a whole other *Life*. With her perfect *Grrrl*, in that perfect World. And barely a second thought for the one she'd left behind. She wasn't even carrying her handbag. Imagine that.

Yeah, imagine...

Inside, the lift was like a mirrored-cell, with a marbled floor. It had no buttons to press. No digy-display to say the level, its pristine interior saying it all.

The pair having boarded, the Synthetic whispered to Sash the magic word, so as the lift wouldn't hear it.

"Hoch—bitte," she said then, improvising. Looking after it and licking her lips, her mouth being wrung dry with excitement.

"Up—Thank you | Nach oben—Danke," came the elevator's response. Its Southern Standard *Yahoo!*BBC® English-accent, contrasting with the warm and informal tone of that synthesised female-*Vox*.

And that was that. They were on their way, up to that LZT on the roof of the Selfridges® building. Though Sash hardly felt it, their ascent. Being preoccupied with drooling over what she saw reflected in the lift's mirrored walls.

There was Pris—of course, stood front-and-center. Husk_hands held by its Husk_side, its Husk_shoulders squared. Its neutral pose managing to exude both calm and tension, the compliment of its *Look*: Chinchilla fur catsuit, and matching masquerade cat-mask—replete with whiskers of silver-thread—prop'd upon its Husk_head; a pair of strapless Rada® 9" stilettoes, that were essentially Carrot-orange colored rubberised soles, that made its Husk_toes look like Cat's paws.

Yeah, all in all. It said, "Me-*ow*." [6D]

And there was Sash, its wannabe Sidekick.

Leant slovenly against that backwall, she was to be your epitome of *Punk*: A castrated little *Johnnie Rotten*; three-fifths of a childhood's worth of pent-up angst, hidden behind that rascally smirk.

In her rush, she'd settled on the SergioTacchini® hoodie top and matching pedal-pusher bottoms, she'd seen Pris sporting earlier; and a pair of Brilliant-bright Total*Air*™ ankle boots. Which the Synthetic swore it'd never worn.

Yeah, mirrors never lied. And together they looked truly, *the* Business. A dynamic duo, their zippers pulled all the way down to their navels. Sash even thought she saw *Sparks*; the air about them being seemingly charged.

Also, there was the idea of them both *Going Commando*. It giving her goosebumps, atop those caused by the lift's overly zealous *Air*-con.

Purrring to herself, and stroking that *ever-so* soft velour fabric of her hoodie top. She was to be an image of *Venus*, newly emerged from the Underground. The god's having loaned her a brand-new coat of fur, to hide her modesty.

Yeah, staring at that mirror-image. Sash *purred*, and pictured Pris pinning her up-against that mirrored-wall. Sliding its Husk_hand inside that top to get at her. Whilst they *Got-off* on each other.

And just-then, wouldn't you know it. That lift came to an impromptu and imperceptible halt.

"Welcome to Selfridges—Landing-Zone Terminus Six | Willkommen bei Selfridges—Landezone Endstation Sechs," it was to announce, opening its doors to reveal another plush Lobby. What was a mirror-image of the one they'd left on the ground level.

That is, save for those gaggles of Tourists and Pilgrims. Stood around and seated, like archipelagos of Matryoshka dolls, stranded amidst seas of branded shopping-bags. Awaiting the allotment of a Landing Zone, and a *Harrier*-taxi; with only that piped muzik for company, an instrumental of The Cure's 'Close To Me'. The service being nigh fully-automated.

And just-now, Sash felt compelled to slip her hand into the Synthetic's Husk_hand.

"You nervous?" Pris asked.

Sash nodding, the occasion having left her at a loss for words.

Together, they were to canter across that crowded lobby. Pris leading the way through the exit, and out onto the roof—and the LZTs.

And once outside, Sash found her eye drawn toward the Heavens, and that Über Blood moon. And staring after it, she was to cast a wish to your *god-of-always-listening*—as in,

[Sing] *Love. Rain. Down on me* [6E]
(*On-me, down on-me*)

Ahead, there stood a ContinentalClass Rolls-Royce® *SilverTeardrop*™.

Waiting upon them, apparently. Parked *Slap-bang* in the middle of a large LZ, spelt-out in strip-lighting and illuminated green.

The Ground crew having retired, after ensuring the flying-car was fuelled and Ready-to-*Go-Go-Go!*

The doors on both sides of the aircraft automatically lifting-open, as Pris and Sash approached. Sash's first impression, emerging from a fog of excitement, being of the sheer size of the thing.

As long as a Double-decker, and just as wide. The flying-car was like a giant Marine mammal, seen here out of its element, and in repose. Its four wheels enclosed within those TVC reaction-control valves, punctuating its streamlined hips and shoulders.

Its silver-hide buffed to an obscenely high shine. Its headlights and large prominent grill, reminiscent of a boatrace; what with that *Spirit of*

Ecstasy planted in the middle of its forehead, like a Bindi.

"Come this side," Pris was to urge, ushering my-*Grrrl* round. "You can climb-over."

Sash warily planting a foot on the aircraft's chassis, where it pointed; her nose twitching at that stink of kerosene-enriched aviation fuel. Those huge fans, scattered about the roof's periphery, being sat idle.

"Are you a Pilot as well?"

"As well as what?"

"I don't know," Sash shrugged, and stepped-down into the cab. Using the back of the Pilot's seat for support; and marking how soft and yielding the upholstery felt to her hand.

"Do I look like a Pilot?" Pris asked, coming after her.

Sash shook her head—no. Though, she wouldn't have put it passed *my-Grrrl* to be one, like, *in cognito.*

Settling, in what she presumed must be the passenger-seat, her eyes were to widen as she felt it mould itself—like memory-foam—to fit her Body. This in turn, prompting her to look about for a seatbelt; her thinking the experience akin to riding in an automobile.

The search leading her eyes to traverse the aircraft's lush interior, by that soft glow of its auxiliary lighting; illuminated strips that hugged the terrain of that sculpted cab, like contour lines drawn on an Ordnance survey map.

Sash marking the conspicuous absence of instrument panels and dials, control surfaces and screens. Indeed, of any means of physical interface with the vessel. The SilverTeardrop's minimalist aesthetic. That sublime blank expression, like, the engineering equivalent of the Mona Lisa's smile.

Blink-blink

Ever your Neanderthal, she was compelled then, to run her hand along that faux-ivory panelling and dash; her mind's eye craving that positive rëenforcement of touch. Only by touching everything, could this experience be rendered tangible—intelligible. That sculpted, seamless finish, *so-smooth* as to be both hard and soft.

She was to hardly notice Pris, settling-in next to her. Being distracted, first by the aircraft's doors, which closed automatically—with a satisfying *Thud*. And then, by that faint *hisss*, as the cab was sealed and pressurised. It all adding to Sash's burgeoning excitement; her Body shaking, seized by sporadic waves of nervous energy.

Responding to a wireless prompt from the Synthetic, the flying-car's HUD faded-up, projected across that entire windscreen.

Hovering Out-*there*—in outer-Space, a 3D-map of London rotated to align along a North-South axis. Their flight trajectory illustrated by an animated green arrow, tracing an arcing straight-line from their current situation, LZT 6 [Selfridges] to LZT 12 [The BT Tower].

The estimated journey time: 13-minutes, 8-seconds—as the crows fly.

The silence, measuring a moment's pause, was to be broken by the gentle *Ping-ping-ping* of an audible-*prompt*, indicating Hover Mode about to be engaged. Then came the muffled drone of that turbofan engine being throttled. What was 35,000 bridled Winged-horses, at once taking that bit between their teeth.

Wirelessly controlling the flying-car, the Synthetic was then to manually execute the transition, from Static-Grounded to Static-Hovering. Opening-up the throttle and bringing the TVC reaction-control valves to bear. Whilst simultaneously retracting the aircraft's landing-gear.

It was then, Sash thought she felt a slight lurch upward, in the pit of her belly; and found herself gripping the arms of her seat, her Body conveying its wariness at being suspended in mid-air.

The transition complete, the *Pinging* stopped abruptly. And there was to follow another moment's pause; though it were more ladened. Given, Sash both heard and felt it. The fervour of that flock of *Pegasi* mounting steadily. The continued throttling of the SilverTearsdrop's engine, their frenzied wing beats, exceeding fever pitch.

Looking to Pris, for some indication of what was to happen next. Sash was surprised to find my-*Grrrl* sound asleep.

It was then, she'd regard for the window, and peering-out was just in time to catch that roof of the Selfridges® building fall away. A nocturnal cityscape stretching before her, traced by incalculable points of light. And bathed in Blood—seemingly.

As the flying-car climbed, and slowly wheeled about. Sash was to find herself presented with a vista of London. And it was as-if she were witnessing it, for the first time.

The Beast—slumbering.

The City we'd become. An impression of William Blake's immense and imposing great red dragon.

There was Hyde Park, now closed. Its expanse of greenery, like a Black Sargasso Sea breaking upon those shores of Buckingham Palace. Then, it was those golden clockfaces of Big Ben, and the Houses of Parliament; and the London-Eye, and National Theatre sitting prominent on that Southbank; and the head and shoulders of lonely Nelson, stood upon his floodlit column, amidst a bustling Trafalgar Square; and the labyrinthine Covent Garden; and Soho, its entrance marked by the Centre-Point Tower.

And finally, Fitzrovia. The BT Tower. And home.

"What do you think you're playing at?"
The Synthetic's Patron patched-in, his voice heard against a backdrop of machine-chatter.

The Dome's PAC-SAC Protocol governing local *Air*-traffic.

"Why, following your instructions," Pris stated dryly. Engaging the SilverTeardrop's Automatron—*Jeeves*™, to silence that racket. Whilst it reversed-*Ping*'d its Patron's transmission to its source; Canary Wharf and the Canada Square Tower, EU HQ of Instrumentality® Corp.

Patching into the Tower's CPH, it commandeered the building's CcSS to survey those sumptuous offices and private suites, occupying that impressive pyramid at the Tower's summit.

Sure enough, there he was, its Patron, *He-whom-shall-remain-nameless*. Sat upon his throne, a Søren® *Sejr* Executive hoverchair. A twin to the one back at the 86ers™ office.

He appeared meditative. The tips of his fingers pressed together to form five skeletal spires; his right-hand clothed in a *virtua*-Terminal interface—an exoskeletal glove, with tactile-sensors that looked like thimbles. His daddy long-legs tied in a dandy-knot; his back turned to that WilliamKent&Sons® circa-1800 baroque dining-table, he'd commandeered as a desk—a flock of wide-eyed cherubs carved into its bulbous gold-plated legs.

He-whom-shall-remain-nameless had been enjoying his stunning view of that Über Blood moon.

His window upon the World. A wall of Nimbey® photovoltaic *vari*-tint glass, that stood vast like an IMAX™ screen. Dwarfing that antiquated desk; and proffering an extended depth-of-field, and much enhanced visible spectrum.

Far below, and tinted a-million hues of Bloody-red. The gentrified sprawl of the Nation's capital was to radiate outward from that Tower of London, with its fortified parapets.

That dreamy-mile of *The City*, its temples and shrines dedicated to the twin gods—Mercantilism and Laissez-faire, bleeding into Clerkenwell, and its many hidden chambers of Law. Its own Maiden-patron, *Justitia*, a cruciform perched atop the Old Bailey. Scale and sword ready-to-hand.

"You should know, Monk and I've had words," the Synthetic's Patron was to admit, after a somewhat melodramatic pause.

And swivelling round to face his desk, he summoned those dual *virtua*-Screens of his BangOptics® terminal, with a discrete hand-gesture. The luminous, blue-tinged solid photon projections materialising in mid-air, just ahead of him.

Grabbing a-hold of the projection, he repositioned it. And sitting back, resumed his meditative pose. Leaving it to fade, and eventually disappear.

"You're aware of my views—regarding you having Pets," he said, the spire of his pointy-fingers poised, as if to seal his lips.

"You've made your position abundantly clear," Pris was to respond, patching into the terminal just-now—to steal a look-see.

Sure enough, there it was. A lone encrypted file labelled 'Untitled'. What comprised a digy-*viddy* clip of Fresh_Meat's extemporaneous dalliance with those dastardly Siamese twins—Monk and Klunk—back at the 86ers™ *Members-only Club*.

It was squirrelled away under the Symantek® OS dashboard, and a plethora of open PDFs; TEFLON® Stock charts, and Annual reports, and Board meeting minutes *et al*.

And, an as-yet unpublished obituary, for the late, great Dr Henri Pasha Schreiber. Titled, 'Mr TEFLON® | The *Man*. The Myth'.

"Abundantly clear—exactly."

The Synthetic's Patron paused, his eye being drawn to a corner of that massive Wei&Wei® installation, aptly named 'Argos Panoptes'. A hundred -and-one BangOptics® solid photon *virtua*-Screens, arranged like crystallised proteins swimming in a fluid of air. That stood centre-stage of an immense and imposing floor, that was more like your Bond villain's lair.

It was the *Blinking* of one screen, in particular, that'd caught his Bionic -eyes. The one that *just-so* happened to be monitoring the SilverTeardrop's interior; the camera trained upon Sash's boatrace, providing a frame for her wide-eyed awe.

Yeah, that there, that was Pris. The *Wink-wink* telling *his Nibs*, it was onto him. His evirate, *Uh-huh* speaking volumes.

Killing the screen—with a deft flick of his wrist, he returned to being meditative.

"Monk says, he may have another likely candidate," he announced. "Two in fact—twins."

This announcement, coincidently heralding the *Clickitty-clack Clackitty-click* of cloven hooves, approaching in the distance. A pair of Ruby-red stilettos dancing across that buffed *Darker-than-blue* enamel floor, as if walking upon water.

What was the light, from those nearby Singh+Lakshman® *Glowglobes*, shimmering-off that über-reflective surface. Creating the illusion of a subterranean lake housed within this vaulted Space.

Hearing it also, the Synthetic immediately identified the signature gait of its Patron's Personal Assist., Mr Gully Foyle, and commenced with tracking his approach.

"A peace offering—of a-kind," its Patron continued, noting how those footsteps had disappeared. Along with the sound of his own voice. Pris having remotely activated the IX® *Cone of Silence* generator, built into that antique dining-table.

"We endeavour to serve," it responded. Its voice now the only sound not cancelled out by that *anti-*Phasing field.

"DON'T BE FACETIOUS," its Patron snapped, raising his voice to push-back against, what seemed an oppressive silence.

Feeling *Self-*conscious, following this outburst. He was to look then, pensively, at that dining-table. At all that clutter, and sigh. Envisaging a long, lonely night ahead.

The TEFLON® Board was due to convene at the *arse-*crack of dawn; an 'Emergency session', to confirm his appointment as Board Chairman. A manoeuvre that'd previously been blocked by the late Dr Schreiber, it being viewed as paving the way—ultimately—for the Group's absorption by Instrumentality® Corp.

"All gods demand their sacrifice," *He-whom-shall-remain-nameless* declared, clearing a space in-front of him. Pushing aside those reams of hardcopy, that were his preferred means of absorbing information.

To wit, the Synthetic said nothing.

It continued to monitor its Patron, as he unfolded his gangly frame to stand; his Brilliant-bright SankeiHara® robe falling open. The silver threads woven into its ruffled Koishimaru silk-fabric, catching the light of a nearby *Glowglobe*.

Underneath, he still wore his day clothes. A Matt-auburn *StrayPress*™ shirt, and Fluorescent-orange cashmere knit pencil-tie, with onyx tie clasp; and a pair of AtoBoateng® fitted suit-pants — cut from *Black Watch* tartan, held-up with invisible nylon braces. The tapered and hemmed leg ending at a pair of Expresso-coffee colored buckskin Ade///Das® *Yeezy*™ Original loafers, conventionally worn without socks.

"Methinks," the Synthetic's Patron began, padding himself down; the pockets of his slacks, and those of his exquisite robe. "I shall be wanting to review your neuro-somatic feed after-all."

He paused then. Adjusting the brightness of a nearby *Glowglobe* with a wave of his hand, so as he might better scan that dining-table.

"Would you have me enhance any particular aspect of the experience?"

The Synthetic's Patron *Blink-blinked*, as if distracted. But then, he caught sight of what-it-was he'd been looking for. The glimmer of a cigarette case, carved from a solid block of BLK-jade. Deducing he must've absentmindedly push it aside, whilst clearing a space.

"No. Leave the file as is," he replied, retrieving it.

Sniff

He refolded his robe. And sat back down upon his throne, dandily crossing his gangly legs.

And having settled, he was to retrieve a cigarette — a Gauloises® *Deluxe* Slim-Ultra. Tapping the end of that gold-rimmed, hollowed-out filter upon the lid of the case, to pack the tobacco.

Putting the cigarette to his lips, he *Sniffed*, and lit it. Utilising a removable *e*-Lighter, that stowed snuggly into the hinge of the case. Taking a shallow drag, to blow-out a plume of stale smoke.

"As you wish. Will that be all — Master?"

He-whom-shall-remain-nameless was to suck air through his teeth, whilst savouring that signature bitter aftertaste of the Syrian tobacco.

"Master—"

"Yes Pris. That'll be all," its Patron cut-in. And again, he was to suck his teeth.

Stuffing the cigarette case into the pocket of his robe, the Synthetic's Patron sat back to smoke, and watch Mr Foyle's approach. Pris terminating the *Cone of Silence*, the instant the dapper gent broke its perimeter; a vision in Burberry® Tweed, his *ghinger* crewcut loudly proclaiming his androgyny.

Coming about the desk to stand over the Big-*Man*. Mr Foyle deftly balanced the tray he'd been carrying—upon his palm, while he laid-out its contents. An assortment of Mithai offerings: Pranhara, Rasgulla, Kaju Katli and Kulfi; a tall, slender glass of Bhang Lassi, and a single Mitha Paan to refresh the palate after.

Each dainty, bitesize treat, lovingly crafted by a lone Michelin™ accredited chef, specialising in the dish. And based upon the three key ingredients of Ambrosia, Nectar, and Peaches. Those staples of the gods.

"Thank you, Mr Foyle. I'll call when I need you."

Retrieving the nearby ashtray and replacing it with a fresh one. Mr Foyle was to give-it—that arrangement of dishes—one last cursory glance, before departing. His brisk footsteps measuring an extended *Beat.*

Beat

"Oh, and one last thing—my darling."

The Synthetic's Patron took another shallow drag. And blowing smoke from his nose, stubbed the cigarette to death in that virgin ashtray.

"Be sure and make it last—a-litter longer. This time."

And with that, he patched-out.

Opening its Husk_eyes, the Synthetic *Blink-blinked*, as if waking from a deep sleep.

The waking-dream that was to greet it, more of a nightmare. For being wholly populated with electronic chattel; that non-stop chatter of the Dome's PAC-SAC *proc*.

Looking to Sash and observing how she still gripped the arms of her seat, though her eyes were to appear transfixed by that spectacle of the Blood moon. The Synthetic now deduced, it'd take some getting used to; the sensation of being suspended in mid-air, in such a small aircraft. Even given benign skies.

Acting upon this inference, Pris let its Husk_hand gravitate toward Sash's hand, on the pretext of lending her its assurance. The strength of its grip, anticipating Sash snatching that hand away without thinking; her being startled, by the apparent abruptness of it.

Indeed, her hand held fast, Sash's head was to *Snap* round to regard Pris. Her Body being seized momentarily, by a ripple of involuntary shakes; her eyes being filled with both wonder, and dread. Conflicting impressions, conflated by some premonition of an end, fast approaching. That monolithic BT Tower, looming just up-ahead.

Yess, you've a right to fear me, Pris thought, readily acknowledging its part in it all. And the existential threat it now posed to this poor, defenceless 'Human'.

Obviously, it couldn't have hoped, dreamt of empathising with her. And yet, it felt compelled to assign its would-be victim, a perspective. Assuming Sash had known, the outrage she'd feel upon discovering the extent of its betrayal.

Although meaningless, those moments they'd shared now conspired to equate with meaning. Its memory of Sash, innumerable objectified data-points, seeking to substantiate a continuation of their relationship. As if invested with an intentionality all their own.

Divorced *even*, from that of the Synthetic.

Confounded by this phenomenon, Pris resorted to a dispassionate and callous calculus, in a bid to generate a Sigma [Σ]: A numerical value greater than zero. But still, well shy of Infinity [∞] — an unwieldy and categorical certainty. All in a bid to answer the one, pressing question.

Why should Sash have been any different, from all those Others?

Looking to exogenous factors to factor into its calculations. Pris considered the oddity of that Über Blood moon, its occurrence this night. If it was to be Sash's only *Omen*, and speak its truth — so to speak. Perhaps, it was to convey that perfect symmetry of *Luck* and design.

Blink

Certainly, given such coincidence. It seemed apt that fortune and misfortune be, here and now, represented in equal measure.

Eeny, Meeny, Miney, Moe!

That such, granting of wishes, be wedded to utter calamity. As was the way, when encountering those gods of Antiquity.

So many dreams fulfilled this night of nights. It seemed only fitting that such things, as wishful thinking, and dreams, be fulfilled the once in a *Life*.

Poetic even.

By now, the flying-car was well into that final portion of its assigned flight trajectory. Disengaging the Automatron, Pris was to resume control; and commence with executing a controlled descent, toward the LZT situation on the roof of that ancillary building to the BT Tower.

Its illuminated LZ flashing green. As in, *Go!* for landing.

The only certainty, that the Synthetic would have the opportunity to change its mind a-squigillion times before the end.

Or the beginning.

THAT PERFECT WORLD
Pris

APPENDIX

All Quiet on the West End Frontline

01 'More Than This', Roxy Muzik [B Ferry]; *Avalon* (E G Records / Polydor, 1982)

02 'That's Entertainment', The Jam [P Weller]; *Sound Effects* (Metronome / Polydor, 1981)

03 'Street Life', The Crusaders featuring Randy Crawford [W Jennings / J Sample]; *Street Life* (MCA, 1979)

04 'Sweet Dreams (Are Made Of This)', Eurythmics [A Lennox / D A Stewart]; *Sweet Dreams (Are Made Of This)* (RCA Records, 1983)

05 'Brass In Pocket (I'm Special)', The Pretenders [C Hynde / J Honeyman-Scott]; *Pretenders* (Real, 1980)

06 'The Harder They Come', Jimmy Cliff [J Cliff]; *The Harder They Come* (Island, 1972)

07 'Tainted Love', Soft Cell [E Cobb]; *Non-Stop Erotic Cabaret* (Some Bizzare, 1981)

08 'Hit Me With Your Rhythm Stick', Ian Dury & The Blockheads [I Dury / C Jankel]; 7" Single (Stiff Records, 1978)

09 'Heroes', David Bowie [D Bowie / B Eno]; 7" Single (RCA, 1977)

0A 'The Good Life', Tony Bennett [B J Reardon / S Distel]; *I Wanna Be Around...* (Columbia, 1963)

0B 'Tralala' is a character in *Last Exit To Brooklyn* by Herbert Selby Jr (Grove Press, 1964)

0C 'Ta-ra-ra Boom-de-ay', Lottie Collins [H J Sayer / M Gilroy / M Lou] from the muzikal, *Tuxedo* (1892)

0D 'I'm Kissing You', Des'ree [D Weekes / T Atack]; *Supernatural* (Sony Muzik Entertainment, 1989)

0E 'Changes', David Bowie [D Bowie]; *Hunky Dory* (RCA Records, 1971)

0F 'N.Y. State of Mind', Nas [N Jones / C Martin]; *Illmatic* (Columbia, 1994)

10 'Memories', Beenie Man [M Davis / V P Edmund / L James]; 12" Single (Fat Eye Records, 1995) featuring an interpolation of 'Memories Don't Leave Like People Do', Jerry Butler [J Bristol / J Butler / J Dean / J Glover]; 7" Single (Mercury, 1973)

11 *Enter The Dragon* [M Allin]; dir. R Clouse, prod. F Weintraub, P Heller, R Chow (Warner Bros. / Concord Production Inc., 1973)

GEARS + HYDRAULICS

12 'Hallelujah', Leonard Cohen [L Cohen]; *Various Positions* (Columbia, 1984)

13 *THX 1138* [G Lucas / W Murchs]; dir. G Lucas, prod. L Sturhahn (American Zoetrope / Warner Bros., 1971)

BOOM KLAK!

14 'Turn On Some Muzik', Marvin Gaye [M P Gaye]; *Midnight Love* (Columbia, 1982)

15 'Rimshot - Intro', Erykah Badu [E Wright / M E Chinwah]; *Baduizm* (Kedar / Universal, 1997)

16 "De-construction just a species of scepticism; de-mystify is to show that at the level of appearance there's something more real, there's something at work—there's something at stake!" Brother Cornel West, Lecture to the Cogut Institute for the Humanities, Brown University, as part of the *Politics in Humanities* (PITH) Series, 2 March 2018.

17 'Happy Days', Pratt & McClain [N Gimbel / C Fox]; *Pratt & McClain* [featuring *Happy Days*] (Reprisal / Warner Bros., 1976)

18   *Back to the Future* [R Zemeckis / B Gale]; dir. R Zemeckis, prod. B Gale, N Canton (Universal Pictures, 1985)

19   'Ain't Nothing Like the Real Thing', Marvin Gaye & Tammi Terrell [N Ashford / V Simpson]; *You're All I Need* (Tamla / Motown, 1968)

1A   "I am great OZYMANDIAS," saith the stone / The King of Kings; this mighty City shows / The wonders of my hand." From the poem, 'Ozymandias', by Horace Smith, first published in *The Examiner* on 1 February 1818

1B   'One In A Million', Aaliyah [M Elliott / T Mosley]; *One In A Million* (Blackground / Atlantic, 1996)

1C   'Black Steel In The Hour Of Chaos', Public Enemy [C Ridenhour / H Shocklee / E Sadler / W Drayton]; *It Takes A Nation of Million's to Hold Us Back* (Def Jam, 1988)

1D   'Exhibit A', Jay Electronica [J Smith / T Thedford]; *Exhibit A (Transformations)* EP (Decon / The Dogon Society, 2009)

1E   'The Sound Of Silence', Simon & Garfunkel [P Simon]; *Wednesday Morning, 3 A.M.* (Columbia, 1964)

A ROOM WITH A VIEW

1F   'It's A Hardknock Life' [C Strouse / M Charnin] from the muzikal, *Annie* (1977)

20   'Tomorrow' [C Strouse / M Charnin] from the muzikal, *Annie* (1977)

21   'Another Brick In The Wall', Pink Floyd [R Waters], *The Wall* (Harvest / Columbia, 1979)

22   'This Charming Man', The Smiths [S Morrissey / J Marr]; *The Smiths* (Rough Trade, 1984)

23   'The Bare Necessities', Phil Harris & Bruce Reitherman [T Gilkyson]; *The Jungle Book* (Disneyland / Walt Disney, 1967)

ALL ABOUT EVE

24   'All By Myself', Eric Carmen [E Carmen]; *Eric Carmen* (Rhino / Arista, 1975)

25   '[T]here I had fixed mine eyes till now, and pined with vain desire' from *Paradise Lost* (1667) an epic poem by John Milton (Penguin Popular Classics, 1996) Book IV, p 98 para 466

26   'A good woman is also like a mirror of clear, shining glass...' from *The Ingenious Hidalgo Don Quixote De La Mancha* (1605), a novel by Miguel de Cervantes Saavedra (trans. J Rutherford for Penguin Classics, 2002) p 469

27   'Siegfrieds Tod & Trauermarsch' [R Wagner] from Act III, *Götterdämmerung* (1876)

REPO-MAN

28   'Thanks will weep dry tears for Baldr's burial.' Gylfaginning, *EDDA* [S Sturlson, c. 1200; trans. A Faulkes, 1982] p 49

29   *Romeo and Juliet* [W Shakespeare] Act III, Sc 1 (first performed, 1597)

2A   *King Lear* [W Shakespeare], Act I, Sc 2 (first performed, 1606)

IN LOVE (WITH THE INCREDIBLE HULK™)

2B   'Sabotage', The Beastie Boys [M Diamond / A Horovitz / A Yauch]; *ILL Communication* (Grand Royal, 1994)

2C   Dialogue taken from the movie, *Chinatown* [R Towne]; dir. R Polanski, prod. R Evans (Paramount Pictures, 1974)

2D   'Cool For Cats', Squeeze [C Difford / G Tilbrook]; *Cool For Cats* (A&M, 1979)

FRESH_MEAT

2E 'Smells Like Teen Spirits', Paul Anka [K Cobain / D Grohl / K Novoselic]; *Rock Swings* (Verve Muzik Group, 2005)

EVEN THE—[SING] *GHETTO*

2F 'Body Workshop', General Pecus [C Browne / G Pecus / W Johnson]; 7" Single (Steely & Clevie Records, 1991)

30 'My Grrrl', The Temptations [W S Robinson / R White]; *The Temptations Sing Smokey* (Gordy Records, 1965)

31 'The Ghetto', Donny Hathaway [D Hathaway / L Hutson]; *Everything Is Everything* (Atlantic, 1969)

32 'In The Ghetto', Elvis Presley [M Davis]; from *Elvis in Memphis* (RCA / Victor, 1969)

33 'Ghetto: Misfortune's Wealth', The 24-Carat Black [V De Frank / D O Warren / T Steele / L Nix]; *Ghetto: Misfortune's Wealth* (Stax Records, 1973)

34 'In The Ghetto', Eric B & Rakim [W M Griffin Jr.]; *Let The Rhythm Hit 'Em* (MCA, 1990)

35 'Children Of The Ghetto', Philip Bailey [C Amoo / E Amoo]; *Chinese Wall* (Columbia, 1984)

36 'We Who Are Not As Other', 4Hero [Dego / M Mac / D McFarlane / E Taylor]; *Two Pages* (Talkin' Loud, 1998)

37 *Kidulthood* [N Clarke]; dir. M Huda, prod. M Huda, A Madani, G Isaac, D Jones (Revolver Entertainment, 2006)

38 'What are you looking for Athanasia in front of my balcony...', *Athanasia* [M Hatzidakis / N Gatsos] is the title track of the album by Manos Hadjidakis (EMI Greece, 1976)

COTCHIN'

39 'I Gave You Power', Nas [N Jones / C E Martin]; *It Was Written* (Columbia, 1996)

THE SCENE

3A 'The Boys Are Back In Town', Thin Lizzy [P P Lynott]; *Jailbreak* (Vertigo, 1976)

3B *Sexy Beast* [L Mellis / D Scinto]; dir. J Glazer, prod. J Thomas (Fox Searchlight Pictures, 2000)

3C 'Karma Chameleon', Culture Club [B George / J Moss / M Craig / R Hay / P Pickett]; *Colour By Numbers* (Virgin, 1983)

I, SECURITAS

3D *Blade Runner* [H Fancher / D Peoples]; dir. R Scott, prod. M Deelay (Warner Bros. Pictures, 1982), based on the novel, *Do Android's Dream Of Electic Sheep?* written by Philip K Dick, first published by Doubleday (1968)

3E *Tao The Ching* attributed to Lao Tzu, ch 6, pg 13 [trans. J C H Wu] (Shambhala, 1989)

3F *The Matrix* [The Wachowskis]; dir. The Wachowskis, prod. Joel Silver (Warner Bros. Pictures, 1999)

40 'The Revolution Will Not Be Televised', Gil Scott-Heron [G. Scott-Heron]; *Pieces Of A Man* (Flying Dutchman, 1971)

41 *Tron* [S Lisberger]; dir. S Lisberger, prod. D Kushner (Buena Vista Distribution, 1982)

42 'The White Man's Burden: The United States and the Philippine Islands', a poem by Rudyard Kipling, first published in *The Times* on 4 February 1899

43 '—or those of aught resembling me. Phantasm of Jupiter, arise, appear!' *Prometheus Unbound* by written Percy Bysshe Shelley, Act 1 Line 220 (C & J Ollier, 1820)

TIAMAT

44   'Grrrl, You'll Be A Woman Soon', Neil Diamond [N Diamond]; *Just For You* (Bang, 1967)

45   *13 Tzameti* [G Babluani]; dir. G Baluani, prod. G Babluani (Palm Pictures, 2005)

46   'Zoom', The Fat Larry's Band [B Eli / L Barry]; *Breakin' Out* (Virgin, 1982)

47   'Ill Wind (You're Blowin' Me No Good)', Ella Fitzgerald [H Arlen / T Koehler]; *Ella Sings The Harold Arlen Songbook* (Verve, 1961)

48   *The Dark Knight* [J Nolan / C Nolan]; dir. C Nolan, prod. E Thomas, C Roven, C Nolan (Warner Bros. Pictures, 2008)

49   'Bohemian Rhapsody', Queen [F Mercury]; *A Night At The Opera* (EMI, 1975)

4A   'Another Man', Barbara Mason [B Ingram]; *Tied Up* EP (Society Hill / Other End Records, 1984)

4B   'We Three (My Echo, My Shadow, And Me)', The Ink Spots [N Cogane / S Mysels / D Robertson]; *Ink Spot* (Decca, 1946)

4C   'Jezabel', Sade [S Matthewson / H Adu]; *Promise* (Epic, 1985)

SUS

4D   'Cars', Gary Numan [G Numan]; *The Pleasure Principle* (Beggars Banquet, 1979)

4E   'The Loco-Motion', Little Eva [G Goffin / C King]; *Lllloco-Motion* (Dimension 1000, 1962)

4F   'Are Friend's Electric', Gary Numan / Tubeway Army [G Numan]; Replicas (Beggars Banquet, 1979)

50   *The Seven Year Itch* [G Axelrod / B Wilder]; dir. B Wilder, prod. C K Feldman, B Wilder (20th Century Fox, 1955)

51   'HAL 9000' features prominently in *2001: A Space Odyssey* [S Kubrick / A C Clarke]; dir. S Kubrick, prod. S Kubrick (Metro-Goldwyn-Mayer, 1968)

52   'If It's Magic', Stevie Wonder [S Wonder]; *Songs In the Key of Life* (Tamla / Motown, 1976)

53   'ÜBER-star', Lauryn Hill [J J Poyser / L Hill]; *The Miseducation of Lauryn Hill* (Ruffhouse / Columbia, 1998)

54   'Sound Boy Killing', Mega Banton [G R A Williams]; 12" Vinyl (Black Scorpio, 1994)

55   'Boy Fi Dead', Madd Cobra [E Brown]; 12" Vinyl (Ghetto Vibes US, 1995)

[SING] OH – THE GOOD LIFE

56   *Mona Lisa* [N Jordan / D Leland]; dir. N Jordan, prod. S Woolley (Island Pictures, 1986)

57   'Mona Lisa', Nat King Cole [R Evans / J Livingston] written for the movie, *Captain Carey, U.S.A.* [R Thoeren]; dir. M Leisen, prod. R Maibaum (Paramount Pictures, 1950)

58   *Diamond Lil*, stage play written by Mae West in 1928; the role would be reprised in the movie, *She Done Him Wrong* [H F Thew / J Bright]; dir. L Sherman, prod. W LeBaron (Paramount Pictures, 1933)

OXFORD CIRCUS

59   καὶ σύ, τέκνον | "You too, child"

5A   'Sally Bowles' is the main character in the muzikal, *Cabaret* (1966)

5B   'Somewhere The Rainbow', Eva Cassidy [H Arlen / E Harburg]; *You're The Voice* (Faber Music, 2003)

5C   *Glengarry Glen Ross* [D Mamet] the play premiered at the National Theatre, London on 21 September 1983

5D   'Stuck In The Middle With You', Stealers Wheel [G Rafferty / J Egan]; *Stealers Wheel* (A&M, 1973)

5E   Based on the poem, 'Der Zauberlehling', written by Johann Wolfgang von Goethe (1797), 'The Sorcerer's Apprentice' was the third segment in Walt Disney's *Fantasia* (1940) animated feature.

5F   'A London Symphony' [R V Williams]; *Symphony No. 2 in G Major: Movement One*, 'Lento – Allegro risoluto', first performed on 27 March 1914

MORE HUMAN THAN HUMAN

60   'Living Doll', Cliff Richard & The Drifters [L Bart]; *Serious Charge* (Columbia, 1959)

THE FISHERMAN'S WIFE

60   'A Spoonful Of Sugar', Julie Andrews [R M Sherman / R B Sherman]; *Mary Poppins Original Soundtrack* (Walt Disney Records, 1964)

61   'Que Sera, Sera (Whatever Will Be, Will Be)', Doris Day [R Evans] from the Motion Picture, *The Man Who Knew Too Much* (Columbia, 1956)

62   'How To Disappear Completely', Radiohead [C Greenword / J Greenword / E O'Brien / P Selway / T Yorke]; *Kid A* (Parlophone / Capital, 2000)

63   'Nature Boy', Nat King Cole [E Ahbez]; *The Nat King Cole Story* (Capital, 1948)

64   *The Third Man* [G Greene]; dir. C Reed, prod. C Reed, A Korda, D O Selznick (British Lion Film Corp., 1949)

65   'Freddies Dead (Theme from Superfly)', Curtis Mayfield [C Mayfield]; *Superfly* (Curtom / Buddah, 1972)

66   'Keep On Movin', Soul II Soul featuring Caron Wheeler [Jazzie B]; *Club Classics Vol. One* (Virgin, 1989)

67   *All About Eve* [J L Mankiewicz]; dir. J L Mankiewicz, prod. D F Zanuck (20th Century Fox, 1950)

FOUCAULT'S PENDULUM

69   'Lovefool', The Cardigans [P Svensson / N Persson]; *First Band On The Moon* (Stockholm / Mercury, 1996)

6A   'Ex-Factor', Lauryn Hill [L Hill]; The Miseducation of Lauryn Hill (Ruffhouse / Columbia, 1998)

6B   'In Loving You', Junior English [C Mayfield]; Win Some Lose Some (Burning Sounds, 1978) – a cover of Curtis Mayfield's 'Love To Keep You In My Mind', *Roots* (Custom Records, 1971)

6C   'The best laid schemes o' Mice an' Men, gang aft agley, an' lea'e us nought but grief an' pain, for promis'd joy!' From the poem, 'To A Mouse' written by Robert Burns from *Poems, Chiefly in the Scottish Dialect* (John Wilson of Kilmarnock, 1976)

Eeny, Meeny, Miney, Moe!

6D   In the voice of Michelle Pfeiffer's 'Catwoman' in *Batman Returns* [D Waters] (Dir. T Burton, Prod. D Di Novi; Warner Bros., 1992)

6E   'Love Rain', Jill Scott [V Davis / J Scott]; *Who Is Jill Scott? Words And Sounds Vol. 1* (Hidden Beach, 2000)

ABOUT THE TRANSLATOR

Bxmn® [pronounced: b-ɒ-k-s-m-a-n] was born in 1974, in Whittington Hospital, North London. And then shit happened, and he wound-up living in Nottingham.

THAT PERFECT WORLD is his first translation.

'The preceding was created with 100%
Human content.'

Disclaimer taken from the '60 Minutes' episode titled, 'The AI revolution', that aired on CBS News, July 9, 2023.

'Hope is a contraband passed from hand to hand & story to story.'
John Berger

The Setting: KRLV_CMPLX, LEMURIA, MARE BOREUM QUADRANGLE, MARS

The Situation: A chance encounter with a technologically advanced Alien Probe. Those encountering it, finding themselves—and their bodies—undergoing a profound awakening.

Harkening back to the Golden Age of Comic Books, ULTRVLT is an origins story that revels in all the tropes of ÜBER-hero genre fiction.

Think. 'Uncanny X-Men' [S Lee / J Kirby], though not so much 'Children of the Atom', as Children of the Meteorite!

ADVENTURE AWAITS YOU
IN THE OFF-WORLD COLONIES!

Dare to dream.

#daretodream

© MMXXIV

Printed in Great Britain
by Amazon